Praise for *The Armor of Light*

"Ken Follett is a master storyteller.... His works of historical fiction have made him a legend.... Follett's latest marks the end of a storytelling journey that spans a thousand years. *The Armor of Light* is also the final entry in his Kingsbridge series."
—Jeff Glor, CBS

"We can't stop turning the pages.... It is Follett's generosity and adeptness with historical detail and nimble depictions of technical matters that set this book, like its predecessors, above mere historical melodrama."
—*The Washington Post*

"A treat for fans of historical fiction."
—*Kirkus Reviews* (starred review)

"This epic canvas holds a mélange of relationships, which all work out exactly as they should while Follett brings Kingsbridge up to the Regency era."
—*Booklist*

"An impressive and immersive epic."
—*Publishers Weekly*

PENGUIN BOOKS
THE ARMOR OF LIGHT

Ken Follett is one of the world's best-loved authors, selling more than 188 million copies of his thirty-six books. Follett's first bestseller was *Eye of the Needle*, a spy story set in the Second World War. In 1989, *The Pillars of the Earth* was published and has since become Follett's most popular novel. It reached number one on bestseller lists around the world and was an Oprah's Book Club pick. Its sequels, *World Without End* and *A Column of Fire*, and prequel, *The Evening and the Morning*, proved equally popular, and the Kingsbridge series has sold more than fifty million copies worldwide. Follett lives in Hertfordshire, England, with his wife, Barbara. Between them they have five children, six grandchildren, and three Labradors.

THE KINGSBRIDGE NOVELS
(in historical order)

The Evening and the Morning
The Pillars of the Earth
World Without End
A Column of Fire

THE CENTURY TRILOGY
(in historical order)

Fall of Giants
Winter of the World
Edge of Eternity

WORLD WAR II THRILLERS

Eye of the Needle
The Key to Rebecca
Night over Water
Jackdaws
Hornet Flight

OTHER NOVELS

Never
Triple
The Man from St. Petersburg
Lie Down with Lions
A Dangerous Fortune
A Place Called Freedom
The Third Twin
The Hammer of Eden
Code to Zero
Whiteout

EARLY NOVELS

The Modigliani Scandal
Paper Money

NONFICTION

On Wings of Eagles
Notre-Dame

KEN FOLLETT

The Armor of Light

PENGUIN BOOKS

PENGUIN BOOKS
An imprint of Penguin Random House LLC
penguinrandomhouse.com

First published in Great Britain by Macmillan,
an imprint of Pan Macmillan, 2023
First published in the United States of America by Viking,
an imprint of Penguin Random House LLC, 2023
Published in Penguin Books 2024

Copyright © 2023 by Ken Follett
Penguin Random House supports copyright. Copyright fuels creativity, encourages diverse voices, promotes free speech, and creates a vibrant culture. Thank you for buying an authorized edition of this book and for complying with copyright laws by not reproducing, scanning, or distributing any part of it in any form without permission. You are supporting writers and allowing Penguin Random House to continue to publish books for every reader.

Map by Daren Cook

ISBN 9780593512685 (international mass market edition)

THE LIBRARY OF CONGRESS HAS CATALOGED THE
HARDCOVER EDITION AS FOLLOWS:
Names: Follett, Ken, author.
Title: The armor of light / Ken Follett.
Description: First edition. | [New York] : Viking, [2023] | Series: Kingsbridge ; book 5
Identifiers: LCCN 2023005900 (print) | LCCN 2023005901 (ebook) | ISBN 9780525954996 (hardcover) | ISBN 9780593655320 (ebook)
Subjects: LCGFT: Historical fiction. | Novels.
Classification: LCC PR6056.O45 A76 2023 (print) |
LCC PR6056.O45 (ebook) | DDC 823/.914—dc23/eng/20230223
LC record available at https://lccn.loc.gov/2023005900
LC ebook record available at https://lccn.loc.gov/2023005901

Printed in the United States of America
1 3 5 7 9 10 8 6 4 2

DESIGNED BY MEIGHAN CAVANAUGH

This is a work of fiction. Names, characters, places, and incidents either are the product of the author's imagination or are used fictitiously, and any resemblance to actual persons, living or dead, businesses, companies, events, or locales is entirely coincidental.

This book is dedicated to the historians.
There are many thousands of them all over the world. Some sit in libraries, hunched over ancient manuscripts, trying to understand dead languages in mysterious hieroglyphs. Others kneel on the ground sifting earth on the sites of ruined buildings, seeking fragments from lost civilizations. Yet more read through interminably dull government papers dealing with long-forgotten political crises. They are relentless in their search for the truth.

Without them we would not understand where we come from. And that would make it even more difficult to figure out where we're going.

Cast off the works of
darkness, and let us put
on the armor of light.
> *Romans 13:12*

Edinburgh

GREAT
BRITAIN
Badford   Oxford
KINGSBRIDGE   London
Combe   Antwerp
Charleroi   Brussels
Waterloo
1815

Paris

FRENCH
EMPIRE

KING
OF
ITA

Grenoble

Toulouse
Cannes
Vitoria
Valladolid   KINGDOM
Ciudad Rodrigo   Madrid   OF
SPAIN

Trafalgar
1805

EUROPE IN 1815

*AUSTRIAN
EMPIRE*

PART I

The Spinning Engine

1792–1793

CHAPTER 1

Until that day, Sal Clitheroe had never heard her husband scream. After that day she never heard it again, except in dreams.

It was noon when she got to Brook Field. She knew the time by the quality of the light gleaming weakly through the pearl-gray cloud that sheeted the sky. The field was four flat acres of mud with a quick stream along one side and a low hill at the south end. The day was cold and dry, but it had rained for a week and, as she splashed through the puddles, the sticky sludge tried to pull off her homemade shoes. It was hard going but she was a big, strong woman, and she did not tire easily.

Four men were harvesting a winter crop of turnips, bending and lifting and stacking the knobbly brown roots on broad shallow baskets called corves. When a corf was loaded the men would carry it to the foot of the hill and tumble the turnips into a stout oak four-wheeled cart. Their task was almost done, Sal saw, for this end of the field was bare of turnips and the men were working close to the hill.

They were all dressed alike. They wore collarless shirts and homespun knee-breeches made by their wives, and waistcoats bought secondhand or discarded by rich men. Waistcoats never wore out. Sal's father had had a fancy one, double-breasted with red and brown stripes and braided hems, cast off by some city dandy. She had never seen him in anything else, and he had been buried in it.

On their feet the laborers had hand-me-down boots, endlessly repaired. Each man had a hat and all were different: a cap of rabbit fur, a straw cartwheel with a wide brim, a tall felt hat, and a tricorne that might have belonged to a naval officer.

Sal recognized the fur cap. It belonged to her husband, Harry. She had made it herself, after she had caught the rabbit and killed it with a stone and skinned it and cooked it in a pot with an onion. But she would have known Harry without the hat, even at a distance, by his ginger beard.

Harry's figure was slender but wiry, and he was deceptively strong: he loaded his corf with just as many turnips as the bigger men. Just looking at that lean, hard body at the far end of a muddy field gave Sal a little glow of desire inside, half pleasure and half anticipation, like coming in from the cold to the warm smell of a wood fire.

As she crossed the field she began to hear their voices. Every few minutes one would call to another, and there would be a short exchange ending in laughter. She could not make out the words but she could guess what they were saying. It would be the mock-aggressive banter of workingmen, jovial insults and cheerful vulgarity, pleasantries that relieved the monotony of repetitive hard work.

A fifth man was watching them, standing by the cart, holding a short horsewhip. He was better dressed, with a blue tailcoat and polished black knee boots. His name was Will Riddick, he was thirty years old, and he was the eldest son of the squire of Badford. The field was his father's, as were the horse and cart. Will had thick black hair cut to chin length, and he looked discontented. She could guess why. Supervising the turnip harvest was not his job, and he felt it was beneath him; but the squire's factor had fallen ill, and Sal guessed that Will had been drafted in to replace him, unwillingly.

At Sal's side her child stumbled barefoot across the boggy ground, struggling to keep pace with her, until she turned and stooped and picked him up effortlessly, then walked on with him in one arm, his head on her shoulder. She held his thin, warm body a little tighter than she needed to, just because she loved him so much.

She would have welcomed more children, but she had

suffered two miscarriages and a stillbirth. She had stopped hoping and had begun to tell herself that, poor as they were, one child was enough. She was devoted to her child, probably too much so, for children were often taken away by illness or accident, and she knew that that would break her heart.

She had named him Christopher, but when he was learning to talk he had mangled his name to Kit, and that was what he was called now. He was six years old, and small for his age. Sal hoped that he would grow up to be like Harry, slim but strong. He had certainly inherited his father's red hair.

It was time for the midday meal, and Sal was carrying a basket with cheese, bread, and three wrinkled apples. Some way behind her was another village wife, Annie Mann, a vigorous woman the same age as Sal; two more on the same errand were approaching from the opposite direction, down the hill, baskets on their arms, children in tow. The men stopped work gratefully, wiping their muddy hands on their breeches and moving toward the stream, where they could sit on a bed of grass.

Sal reached the path and let Kit down gently.

Will Riddick took a watch on a chain from his waistcoat pocket and consulted it with a scowl. "It's not noon yet," he called out. He was lying, Sal felt sure, but no one else had a watch. "Keep working, you men," he ordered. Sal was not surprised. Will had a mean streak. His father, the squire, could be hard-hearted, but Will was worse. "Finish the job, then have your dinners," he said. There was a note of disdain in the way he said *your dinners*, as if there was something contemptible about laborers' meals. Will himself would be going back to the manor house for roast beef and potatoes, she thought, and probably a jug of strong beer to go with it.

Three of the men bent to their work again, but the fourth did not. He was Ike Clitheroe, Harry's uncle, a gray-bearded man of about fifty. In a mild tone he said: "Better not overload the cart, Mr. Riddick."

"You leave it to me to be the judge of that."

"Begging your pardon," Ike persisted, "but that brake is about worn through."

"There's nothing wrong with the damned cart," Will said. "You just want to stop work early. You always do."

Sal's husband spoke up. Harry was never slow to join in an argument. "You should listen to Uncle Ike," he said to Will. "Otherwise you could lose your cart and your horse and all your bloody turnips, too."

The other men laughed. But it was never wise to have a joke at the expense of the gentry, and Will frowned blackly and said: "You shut your insolent mouth, Harry Clitheroe."

Sal felt Kit's little hand creep into her own. His father was getting into a conflict, and young Kit sensed the danger.

Insolence was Harry's weakness. He was an honest man and a hard worker, but he did not believe the gentry were better than him. Sal loved him for his pride and his independent thinking, but the masters resented it, and he was often in trouble for insubordination. However, he had made his point now, and he said no more, but went back to work.

The women put down their baskets on the bank of the stream. Sal and Annie went to help their men gather turnips, while the other two wives, who were older, sat with the dinners.

The work was finished quickly.

At that point it became obvious that Will had made a mistake in leaving the cart at the foot of the hill. He should have stationed it fifty yards farther down the track, to give the horse room to pick up speed before tackling the slope. He thought for a moment, then said: "You men, push the back of the cart, to give the horse a start." Then he jumped up on the seat, deployed the whip, and said: "Hup!" The gray mare took the strain.

The four laborers got behind the cart and pushed. Their feet slipped on the wet path. The muscles of

Harry's shoulders rippled. Sal, who was as strong as any of them, joined in. So did little Kit, which made the men smile.

The wheels shifted, the mare lowered her head and leaned into the traces, the whip cracked, and the cart moved. The helpers fell back and watched as it headed up the slope. But the mare slowed, and Will yelled back: "Keep pushing!"

They all ran forward, put their hands on the tail end of the cart, and resumed. Once again the cart picked up speed. For a few yards the mare ran well, powerful shoulders straining against the leather harness, but she could not keep up the pace. She slowed, then stumbled in the slippery mud. She seemed to regain her footing, but she had lost momentum, and the cart jerked to a halt. Will lashed the beast, and Sal and the men heaved with all their might, but they could not hold the cart, and the high wooden wheels began to turn slowly backward.

Will hauled on the brake handle, then they all heard a loud crack, and Sal saw the two halves of a snapped wooden brake pad fly off the left rear wheel. She heard Ike say: "I *told* the bugger, I *told* him."

They pushed as hard as they could, but they were forced backward, and Sal had a sick feeling of imminent danger. The cart picked up speed in reverse. Will yelled: "Push, you lazy dogs!"

Ike lifted his hands from the tail and said: "It won't hold!" The horse slipped again, and this time she fell. Parts of the leather harness broke, and the beast hit the ground and was dragged along.

Will jumped down from the seat. The cart, out of control now, started to roll faster. Without even thinking, Sal picked up Kit with one arm and jumped aside, out of the path of the wheels. Ike shouted: "Everyone out of the way!"

The men scattered just as the cart swerved, then turned over sideways. Sal saw Harry crash into Ike and they both fell. Ike tumbled to the side of the track, but Harry fell in the path of the cart, and it landed on him with the edge of the heavy oak flatbed on his leg.

That was when he screamed.

Sal froze, cold fear gripping her heart. He was hurt, badly hurt. A moment went by when everyone stared, horrified. The turnips from the cart rolled across the ground, and some of them splashed into the stream. Harry cried hoarsely: "Sal! Sal!"

She shouted: "Get the cart off him, come on!"

They all got their hands to the cart. They lifted it off Harry's leg, but its rise was made difficult by the big wheels, and she realized they had to raise it onto the wheel rims before they could roll it upright. "Let's get our shoulders under it!" she yelled, and they all saw the sense of that. But the wood was heavy, and they were pushing against the upward slope of the hill. There was a terrible moment when she thought they were in danger of dropping the cart, and it would fall back down and crush Harry a second time. "Come on, heave!" she shouted. "All together!" and they all said: "Heave," and suddenly the cart tipped over and came upright, its far wheels landing with a crash.

Then Sal saw Harry's leg, and she gasped in horror. It was flattened from thigh to shin. Fragments of bone stuck out of his skin, and his breeches were soaked with blood. His eyes were closed and a terrible moaning sound came from his half-opened lips. She heard Uncle Ike say: "Oh, dear God, spare him."

Kit began to cry.

Sal wanted to cry, too, but she controlled herself: she had to get help. Who could run fast? She looked around the group and her eye lit on Annie. "Go to the village, Annie, as fast as you can, and fetch Alec." Alec Pollock was the barber-surgeon. "Tell him to meet us at my house. Alec will know what to do."

"Keep an eye on my children," said Annie, and she set off at a run.

Sal knelt at Harry's side, her knees in the mud. He opened his eyes. "Help me, Sal," he said. "Help me."

"I'm going to carry you home, my dear love," she said. She got her hands under him, but when she tried to take the weight and lift his body, he screamed again. Sal pulled back her hands, saying: "Jesus, help me."

She heard Will say: "You men, start putting the turnips back in this cart. Come on, look lively."

She said quietly: "Someone shut his mouth before I shut it for him."

Ike said: "What about your horse, Mr. Riddick? Can she get up?" He went around the cart to look at the mare, distracting Will's attention from Harry. Sal thought: Thank you, clever Uncle Ike.

She turned to Annie's husband, Jimmy Mann, the owner of the three-cornered hat. "Go to the timber yard, Jimmy," she said. "Ask them to quickly knock up a stretcher with two or three wide boards that we can carry Harry on."

"On my way," said Jimmy.

Will called: "Help me get this horse up on its legs."

But Ike said: "She's never going to stand again, Mr. Riddick."

There was a pause, then Will said: "I think that might be right."

"Why don't you fetch a gun?" said Ike. "Put the beast out of its misery."

"Yes," said Will, but he did not sound decisive, and Sal realized that underneath his bluster he was shocked.

Ike said: "Have a mouthful of brandy, if you've got your flask about you."

"Good idea."

While he was drinking, Ike said: "That poor lad with his leg crushed could use a drink. It might ease the pain."

Will did not reply, but a few moments later Ike came back around the cart with a silver flask in his hand. At the same time, Will was walking briskly away in the opposite direction.

Sal murmured: "Well done, Ike."

He handed her Will's flask and she held it to Harry's lips, letting a trickle flow into his mouth. He coughed, swallowed, and opened his eyes. She gave him more and he drank it eagerly.

Ike said: "Get as much as possible into him. We don't know what Alec will need to do."

For a moment Sal wondered what Ike could mean, then she realized he thought Harry's leg might have to be cut off. "Oh, no," she said. "Please, God."

"Just give him more brandy."

The liquor brought a little color back into Harry's face. In a barely audible whisper he said: "It hurts, Sal, it hurts so much."

"The surgeon is coming." It was all she could think of to say. She felt maddened by her own helplessness.

While they waited the women fed the children. Sal gave Kit the apples from her basket. The men started picking up the scattered turnips and putting them back in the cart. It would have to be done sooner or later.

Jimmy Mann came back with a wooden door balanced precariously on his shoulder. He lowered it to the ground with difficulty, panting with the effort of carrying the heavy object half a mile. "It's for that new house going up over by the mill," he said. "They said not to damage it." He put the door down alongside Harry.

Now Harry had to be moved onto the improvised stretcher, and it was going to hurt. She knelt beside his head. Uncle Ike stepped forward to help, but she waved him away. No one else would try as hard as she would to be gentle. She grasped Harry's arms close to the shoulders and slowly swiveled his upper half over the door. He did not react. She pulled him, an inch at a time, until his torso was resting on the door. But in the end she had to move his legs. She stood over him, straddling him, then she bent down, grasped his hips, and moved his legs onto the door in one swift movement.

He screamed for the third time.

The scream tailed off and turned to sobbing.

"Let's lift him," she said. She knelt at one corner of the door, and three of the men took the other corners. "Slowly does it," she said. "Keep it level." They grasped the wood and gradually lifted, swinging themselves under it as soon as possible, then balanced it on their shoulders. "Ready?" she said. "Try to keep in step. One, two, three, go."

They headed across the field. Sal glanced back and saw Kit, dazed and upset, but following her close and carrying her basket. Annie's two small children were trailing behind their father, Jimmy, who was carrying the back left-hand corner of the stretcher.

Badford was a big village, a thousand residents or more, and Sal's home was a mile distant. It was going to be a long, slow walk, but she knew the way so well she could probably have done it with her eyes closed. She had lived here all her life, and her parents were in the graveyard alongside St. Matthew's Church. The only other place she knew was Kingsbridge, and the last time she had been there was ten years ago. But Badford had changed in her lifetime, and today it was not so easy to go from one end of the village to the other. New ideas had transformed farming, and there were fences and hedges in the way. The party carrying Harry had to negotiate gates and winding pathways between private kingdoms.

They were joined by men working in other fields, and then women who came out of their houses to see what was going on, and small children, and dogs, all of whom followed them, chattering among themselves, discussing poor Harry and his terrible injury.

As Sal walked, her shoulder hurting now under the weight of Harry and the door, she recalled how her five-year-old self—called Sally then—had thought of the land outside the village as a vague but narrow periphery, much like the garden around the house where she lived. In her imagination, the whole world had been only slightly larger than Badford. The first time she had been taken to Kingsbridge she had found it bewildering: thousands of people, crowded streets, the market stalls crammed with food and clothes and things she had never heard of—a parrot, a globe, a book to write in, a silver dish. And then the cathedral, impossibly tall, strangely beautiful, cold and quiet inside, obviously the place where God lived.

Kit was now only a little older than she had been on that first astonishing trip. She tried to imagine what he was thinking right now. She guessed he had always seen his father as invulnerable—boys usually did—and now he was trying to get used to the idea of Harry lying injured and helpless. Kit must be scared and confused, she thought. He would need a lot of reassurance.

At last they came within sight of her home. It was one of the meaner houses in the village, built of peat and the interwoven branches and twigs called wattle. The windows had shutters but no glass. Sal said: "Kit, run ahead and open the door." He obeyed, and they carried Harry straight in. The crowd stayed outside, peering in.

The house had only one room. There were two beds, one narrow and one broad, both simple platforms of unvarnished planks nailed together by Harry. Each was covered by a canvas mattress stuffed with straw. Sal said: "Let's put him down on the big bed." They carefully lowered Harry, still lying on the door, onto the bed.

The three men and Sal stood upright, rubbing sore hands and stretching aching backs. Sal stared down at Harry, who was pale and motionless, hardly breathing. She murmured: "Lord, please don't take him from me."

Kit stood in front of her and hugged her, his face pressed into her belly, which had been soft ever since his birth. She stroked his head. She wanted to speak comforting words but none came to mind. Anything true would be frightening.

She noticed the men looking around her house. It was quite poor, but theirs would not be much different, for they were all farm laborers. Sal's spinning wheel was in the middle of the room. It was beautifully made, precision carved and polished. She had inherited it from her mother. Beside it stood a small stack of bobbins wound with finished yarn, waiting to be picked up by the clothier. The wheel paid for luxuries: tea with sugar, milk for Kit, meat twice a week.

"A Bible!" said Jimmy Mann, spotting the only other costly object in the house. The bulky book stood in the center of the table, its brass clasp green with age, its leather binding stained by many grubby hands.

Sal said: "It belonged to my father."

"But can you read it?"

"He taught me."

They were impressed. She guessed that none of them could read more than a few words: their names, probably, and perhaps the prices chalked up in markets and taverns.

Jimmy said: "Should we slide Harry off the door and onto the mattress?"

"He'd be more comfortable," Sal said.

"And I'll be happier when I've returned that door safely to the timber yard."

Sal went to the other side of the bed and knelt on the earth floor. She put out her arms to receive Harry when he slid off the door. The three men took hold of the other side. "Slowly, gently," Sal said. They lifted their edge, the door tilted, and Harry slid an inch and groaned. "Tilt a bit more," she said. This time he slid to the edge of the wood. She got her hands under his body. "More," she said, "and pull the door away an inch or two." As Harry slid, she eased her hands and then her forearms under him. Her aim was to keep him as near to still as possible. It seemed to be working, for he made no noise. The thought crossed her mind that silence was ominous.

At the very end they pulled the door away a little too sharply, and Harry's smashed leg landed on the mattress with a slight thump. He screamed again. This time Sal took it as a welcome sign that he was still alive.

Annie Mann arrived with Alec, the surgeon. The first thing she did was check that her children were all right. Next she looked at Harry. She said nothing, but Sal could tell that she was shocked by how bad he looked.

Alec Pollock was a neat man, dressed in a tailcoat and breeches that were old but well-preserved. He had had no medical training other than what he had learned from his father, who had done the job before him and bequeathed him the sharp knives and other tools that were all the qualifications a surgeon needed.

He carried a small wooden chest with a handle, and now he set it on the floor near the fireplace. Then he looked at Harry.

Sal studied Alec's face, looking for some sign, but his expression gave nothing away.

He said: "Harry, can you hear me? How do you feel?"

Harry made no response.

Alec looked at the crushed leg. The mattress under it was now soaked in blood. Alec touched the bones sticking out through the skin. Harry gave a cry of pain, but it was not as terrible as his screams. Alec probed the wound with a finger, and Harry cried out again. Then Alec grasped Harry's ankle and lifted the leg, and Harry screamed.

Sal said: "It's bad, isn't it?"

Alec looked at her, hesitated, then said simply: "Yes."

"What can you do?"

"I can't set the broken bones," he said. "Sometimes it's possible: if just one bone is broken, and it's not too far out of place, I can sometimes ease it back into the right position, strap it up with a splint, and give it a chance to heal itself. But the knee is too complex and the damage done to Harry's bones is too severe."

"So . . . ?"

"The worst danger is that contamination will enter the wound and cause corruption of the flesh. That can be fatal. The solution is to amputate the leg."

"No," she said, her voice shaking with desperation.

"No, you can't saw his leg off, he's suffered too much agony already."

"It may save his life."

"There must be something else."

"I can try to seal the wound," he said dubiously. "But if that doesn't work, then amputation will be the only way."

"Try, please."

"Very well." Alec bent and opened the wooden chest. He said: "Sal, can you put some wood on the fire? I need it really hot." She hurried to build up the fire under the smoke hood.

Alec took from his chest an earthenware bowl and a stoppered jug. He said to Sal: "I don't suppose you have any brandy."

"No," said Sal, then she remembered Will's flask. She had tucked it into her dress. "Yes, I do," she said, and she drew it out.

Alec raised his eyebrows.

"It's Will Riddick's," she explained. "The accident was his fault, the damn fool. I wish it was his knee that got smashed."

Alec pretended not to hear the insult to the son of the squire. "Make Harry drink as much as possible. If he passes out, so much the better."

She sat on the bed beside Harry, lifting his head and trickling brandy into his mouth, while Alec heated oil in the bowl. By the time the flask was empty, the oil was bubbling in the bowl, a sight that made Sal feel ill.

Alec slid a wide, shallow dish under Harry's knee. A horrified audience watched with Sal: the three laborers, Annie and her two children, and a white-faced Kit.

When the moment came, Alec acted with swift precision. Using tongs, he lifted the bowl from the fire and poured the boiling liquid over Harry's knee.

Harry gave the worst scream of all, then fell unconscious.

All the children cried.

There was a sickening smell of scorched human flesh.

The oil collected in the shallow dish under Harry's leg, and Alec rocked the dish, making sure some of the hot oil seared the underside of the knee to make the seal complete. Then he removed the dish, poured the oil back into the jug, and stoppered it.

"I'll send my bill to the squire," he said to Sal.

"I hope he pays you," Sal said. "I can't."

"He ought to pay me. A squire has a duty to his workers. But there's no law that says he must. Anyway, that's between me and him. Don't you worry about it. Harry won't want to eat anything, but try to get him to drink if you can. Tea is best. Ale is all right, or fresh water. And keep him warm." He began to pack his things into the chest.

Sal said: "Is there anything else I can do?"

Alec shrugged. "Pray for him," he said.

CHAPTER 2

Amos Barrowfield realized something was wrong as soon as he came within sight of Badford.

There were men working in the fields, but not as many as he expected. The road into the village was deserted but for an empty cart. He did not even see any dogs.

Amos was a clothier, or "putter-out." To be exact, his father was the clothier; but Obadiah was fifty and often breathless, and it was Amos who traveled the countryside, leading a string of packhorses, visiting cottages. The horses carried sacks of raw wool, the sheared fleece of sheep.

The work of transforming fleece into cloth was done mainly by villagers working in their homes. First the fleece had to be untangled and cleaned, and this was called scribbling or carding. Then it was spun into long strings of yarn and wound onto bobbins. Finally the strings were woven on a loom and became strips of cloth a yard wide. Cloth was the main industry in the west of England, and Kingsbridge was at its center.

Amos imagined that Adam and Eve, after they ate the fruit of the tree of knowledge, must have done these different jobs themselves, in order to make clothes and cover their nakedness; although the Bible did not say much about scribbling and spinning, nor about how Adam might have built his loom.

Reaching the houses, Amos saw that not everyone had vanished. Something had distracted the farm laborers, but his cloth workers were in their homes. They were paid according to how much they produced, and they were not easily diverted from their work.

He went first to the home of a scribbler called Mick Seabrook. In his right hand Mick held a large brush with iron teeth; in his left a block of plain wood the same size; between the two was stretched a pad of raw wool, which he was brushing with firm, tireless strokes. When the thicket of dirty curls mixed with mud and vegetation had been transformed into a hank of clean, straight fibers, he would twist them into a loose rope called a roving.

Mick's first words to Amos were: "Did you hear about Harry Clitheroe?"

"No," said Amos. "I've only just got here. You're my first visit. What about Harry?"

"Got his leg crushed by a runaway cart. They're saying he'll never work again."

"That's terrible. How did it happen?"

"People tell different stories. Will Riddick says Harry was showing off, trying to prove he could push a loaded cart all on his own. But Ike Clitheroe says it was Will's fault for overloading the cart."

"Sal will be heartbroken." Amos knew the Clitheroes. Their marriage was a love match, he thought. Harry was a tough guy but he would have done anything for Sal. She bossed him around but she adored him. "I'll go and see them now."

He paid Mick, gave him a fresh supply of fleece, and took away a sack of new rovings.

He soon found out where the missing villagers had gone. There was a crowd around the Clitheroe cottage.

Sal was a spinner. Unlike Mick, she could not work at it twelve hours a day, for she had a host of other duties: making clothes for Harry and Kit, growing vegetables in their garden, buying and preparing food, doing laundry and cleaning and every other kind of housework. Amos wished she had more time for spinning, because there was a shortage of yarn.

The crowd parted for him. He was known here and provided many villagers with an alternative occupation to low-paid agricultural labor. Several men greeted him warmly, and one said: "The surgeon's just left, Mr. Barrowfield."

Amos went inside. Harry lay on the bed, white and still, eyes closed, breathing shallowly. There were several people standing around the bed. When Amos's eyes became more accustomed to the dim interior he recognized most of them.

He addressed Sal. "What happened?"

Her face was twisted in a grimace of bitterness and loss. "Will Riddick overloaded a cart and it ran away. The men tried to stop it and it crushed Harry's leg."

"What did Alec Pollock say?"

"He wanted to saw Harry's leg off, but I made him try boiling oil." She looked at the unconscious man on the bed and said sadly: "I don't really think he could be helped by either treatment."

"Poor Harry," said Amos.

"I think he may be getting ready to cross that river Jordan." Her voice cracked then, and she began to sob.

Amos heard a child's voice and recognized Kit, who said in a panicky voice: "Don't cry, Ma!"

Sal's sobs died away and she put her hand on the boy's shoulder and squeezed. "All right, Kit, I won't cry."

Amos did not know what to say. His imagination was defeated by this scene of terrible domestic grief in a poor family's dismal house.

Instead he said something mundane. "I won't trouble you to spin yarn this week."

"Oh, please do," she said. "I want the work now more than ever. With Harry out of action, I'll really need the money from spinning."

One of the men spoke, and Amos recognized Ike Clitheroe. "The squire should take care of you."

Jimmy Mann said: "He should. But that doesn't mean he will."

Many squires felt responsible for widows and orphans, but there was no guarantee, and Squire Riddick was mean.

Sal pointed to the stack of bobbins beside her spinning wheel. "I've nearly finished last week's. I expect you're staying in Badford tonight?"

"Yes."

"I'll do the rest overnight and get everything to you before you leave."

Amos knew she would work all night if she needed to. "If you're sure."

"As the gospel."

"All right." Amos stepped outside and untied a sack from the back of the lead horse. A spinner could process a pound of wool a day, in theory, but few of them spent all day at the wheel: most were like Sal, combining spinning with other duties.

He carried the sack into the house and put it on the floor beside the wheel. Then he took another look at Harry. The injured man had not moved. He looked like death, but Amos had never seen a man die, so he did not really know. He told himself not to be fanciful.

He took his leave.

He went to a building not far from Sal's house, a stable that had been repurposed as a workshop by Roger Riddick, the third and youngest son of the squire. Amos and Roger were the same age, nineteen, and had been pupils together at Kingsbridge Grammar School. Roger was a keen student, uninterested in sports or drinking or girls, and he had been bullied until Amos had stepped in to defend him, after which they had become friends.

Amos tapped on the door and went in. Roger had improved the building with large windows: a workbench stood against one of them for light. Tools hung on wall hooks and there were boxes and pots containing coiled wire, small ingots of different metals, nails and screws and glue. Roger loved to make ingenious toys: a mouse that squeaked and waved its tail, a coffin whose lid opened as the corpse sat upright. He had also invented a machine that would unclog pipes when the blockage was yards away and even around bends.

Roger greeted Amos with a broad smile and put down the chisel he was using. "Good timing!" he said. "I was about to go home for dinner. I trust you'll join us?"

"I was hoping you'd say that. Thank you."

Roger had fair hair and pink skin, unlike his black-haired father and brothers, and Amos guessed he must take after his late mother, who had died some years ago.

They left the workshop and Roger locked the door. Walking to the manor house, Amos leading his string of horses, they talked about Harry Clitheroe. "My brother Will's pigheadedness caused that accident," Roger said frankly.

Roger was now at Kingsbridge College, which had been founded at Oxford by the monks of Kingsbridge in the Middle Ages. He had started a few weeks ago and this was his first return home. Amos would have loved to go to university, but his father had insisted he work in the business. Perhaps things will change with the generations, he thought; I might have a son who goes to Oxford. "What's it like at the university?" he asked.

"Great fun," Roger said. "Tremendous larks. I've lost a bit of money at cards, unfortunately."

Amos smiled. "I meant the studying, really."

"Oh! Well, that's all right. Nothing difficult yet. I'm not keen on theology and rhetoric. I like maths, but the maths professors are obsessed with astronomy. I should have gone to Cambridge—apparently the maths is better there."

"I'll bear that in mind when it's my son's turn."

"Are you thinking of marrying?"

"Thinking about it all the time, but there's no chance of it happening soon. I haven't a penny and my father won't give me anything until my apprenticeship is over."

"Never mind, you've got time to play the field."

Playing the field was not Amos's way. He changed the subject. "I'll impose on you for a bed tonight, if that's all right."

"Of course. Father will be glad to see you. He gets

bored with his sons and he likes you, despite what he sees as your radical views. He enjoys arguing with you."

"I'm not a radical."

"Indeed not. Father should meet some of the men I know at Oxford. Their opinions would scorch his ears."

Amos laughed. "I can imagine." When he thought of Roger's life, studying books and arguing about ideas with a group of bright young men, he felt envious.

The manor house was a fine red Jacobean building having windows with many small leaded panes of glass. They took Amos's horses to the stable block to be watered, then went into the hall.

It was an all-male household and the place was none too clean. There was a whiff of the farmyard, and Amos glimpsed the tail of a rat as it wriggled under a door. They were the first to enter the dining room. Over the fireplace was a portrait of the squire's late wife. It was darkened with age and dusty, as if no one cared much to look at it.

The squire came in, a big, red-faced man, overweight but still vigorous in his middle fifties. "There's a prize-fight meeting in Kingsbridge on Saturday," he said with enthusiasm. "The Bristol Beast is taking on all comers, offering a guinea to any opponent who can stay upright for fifteen minutes."

Roger said: "You'll have a wonderful time." His family loved sports, most of all prizefighting and horse-racing, especially if they could bet on the result. "I prefer to gamble with cards," he said. "I like to calculate the chances."

George Riddick, the middle brother, came in. He was bigger than average, with black hair and dark eyes, and looked like his father, except that his hair was parted in the center.

Finally Will arrived, closely followed by a butler with a steaming cauldron of soup. The fragrance made Amos's mouth water.

On the sideboard was a ham, a cheese, and a loaf of

bread. They helped themselves, and the butler poured port wine into their glasses.

Amos always greeted servants, and now he said to the butler: "Hello, Platts, how are you?"

"Well enough, Mr. Barrowfield," Platts said grumpily. Not all servants reciprocated Amos's friendliness.

Will took a thick slice of ham and said: "The lord lieutenant has called out the Shiring Militia."

The militia was the home defense force. Conscripts were chosen by lottery, and so far Amos had escaped being selected. For as long as he could remember, the militia had been inactive except for six weeks a year of training, which involved camping in the hills north of Kingsbridge, marching and forming squares, and learning to load and fire a musket. Now, it seemed, that was to change.

The squire said: "I heard the same thing. But it's not just Shiring. Ten counties have been mobilized."

It was startling news. What kind of crisis was the government expecting?

Will said: "I'm a lieutenant, so I'll be helping to organize the muster. I'll probably have to live in Kingsbridge for a while."

Although Amos had avoided conscription so far, he might be called up if there was a new levy. He was not sure how he felt about that. He had no wish to be a soldier, but it might be better than being his father's slave.

The squire said: "Who's the commanding officer? I forget."

Will said: "Colonel Henry Northwood."

Henry, Viscount Northwood, was the son of the earl of Shiring. Leading the militia was a traditional duty of the heir to the earldom.

The squire said: "Prime Minister Pitt clearly thinks the situation is serious."

They ate and drank in reflective silence for a while, then Roger pushed his plate away and said thoughtfully: "The militia has two duties: to defend the country from invasion, and to suppress riots. We may go to war with France—I wouldn't be surprised—but even if we do it would take the French months to prepare an invasion, giving us plenty of time to call out the militia. So I don't think that's the reason. Which means the government must be expecting riots. I wonder why."

"You know why," said Will. "It's barely a decade since the Americans overthrew the king to create a republic, and three years since the Paris mob stormed the Bastille. And that French fiend Brissot said: 'We cannot be calm until all Europe is in flames.' Revolution is spreading like the pox."

"I don't think panic is necessary," Roger said. "What have the revolutionaries actually done? Given equality to Protestants, for example. George, you as a Protestant clergyman must surely allow them credit for that?"

George was the rector of Badford. "We'll see how long it lasts," he said sullenly.

Roger went on: "They've abolished feudalism, they've done away with the king's right to throw people into the Bastille without trial, and they've instituted a constitutional monarchy—which is what Britain has."

Everything Roger said was true, but all the same Amos thought he had got it wrong. As Amos understood it, there was no real liberty in revolutionary France: no free speech, no freedom of religion. In truth, England was more open.

Will spoke angrily, making a prodding gesture with his forefinger. "What about the September massacres in France? Revolutionaries killed thousands of people. No evidence, no jury, no trial. 'I think you're a counter-revolutionary. So are you.' Bang, bang, both dead. Some of the victims were children!"

"A tragedy, I grant you," said Roger, "and a stain on the reputation of France. But do we really think the same will happen here? Our revolutionaries don't storm prisons, they write pamphlets, and letters to the newspapers."

"That's how it starts!" Will took a draft of wine.

George said: "I blame the Methodists."

Roger laughed. "Where do they hide their guillotine?"

George ignored that. "Their Sunday schools teach poor children to read, then they grow up and read Thomas Paine's book and become indignant, so they join some club for malcontents. Riot is the logical next step."

The squire turned to Amos. "You're quiet this evening. You normally speak up for new ideas."

"I don't know about new ideas," Amos said. "I've found it pays to listen to people, even those who are uneducated and narrow-minded. You get better work out of the hands if they know that you care what they think. So if Englishmen believe that Parliament ought to be changed, I think we should hear what they have to say."

"Very well put," said Roger.

"But I have work to do." Amos stood up. "Once again, Squire, I thank you for your kind hospitality. I must now get on with my calls, but if you permit I'll return this evening."

"Of course, of course," said the squire.

Amos went out.

He spent the rest of the day visiting his cottage craftspeople, collecting their finished work, paying them, and giving them fresh materials to process. Then, as the sun went down, he returned to the Clitheroe home.

He heard the music from a distance, forty or fifty people singing at the tops of their voices. The Clitheroes were Methodists, as was Amos, and Methodists did not use musical instruments in their services; so to compensate they worked harder to keep time, and often sang in four-part harmony. The hymn was "Love Divine, All Loves Excelling," a popular composition by Charles Wesley, brother of the founder of Methodism. Amos quickened his pace. He loved the sound of unaccompanied singing, and he was eager to join in.

Badford had an active Methodist group, as did Kingsbridge. As yet Methodism was a reform movement within the Church of England, led mainly by Anglican clergy. There was talk of a breakaway, but most Methodists still took Communion in the Anglican church.

As he drew nearer he saw a crowd of people around Sal and Harry's cottage. Several were holding blazing torches for light, and the flames sent flickering shadows dancing around like malign spirits. The Methodists' unofficial leader was Brian Pikestaff, an independent farmer with thirty acres. Because he owned his land, the squire could not prevent him holding Methodist meetings in his barn. If he had been a tenant he would probably have been evicted.

The hymn came to an end and Pikestaff spoke of the love between Harry and Sal and Kit. He said it was true love, as near as mere humans could get to the divine love the group had been singing about. People began to cry.

When Brian had finished, Jimmy Mann took off his three-cornered hat and began to pray extempore, holding the hat in his hand. This was the normal way in Methodism. People prayed, or suggested a hymn, whenever the spirit moved them. In theory they were all equal under God, though in practice it was rare for a woman to speak.

Jimmy asked the Lord to make Harry well so that he could continue to look after his family. But the prayer was rudely interrupted. George Riddick appeared, with a lantern in his hand and a cross on his chest. He wore full clerical garb: cassock, gown with balloon sleeves, and a Canterbury cap, square with sharp corners. "This is outrageous!" he shouted.

Jimmy paused, opened his eyes, closed them again, and continued: "O God our father, hear our prayer this evening, we ask—"

"Enough of that!" George bellowed, and Jimmy was forced to stop.

Brian Pikestaff spoke in a friendly tone. "Good evening, Rector Riddick. Will you join us in prayer? We're asking God to heal our brother Harry Clitheroe."

George said angrily: "The clergy summon the congregation to prayer—not the other way around!"

Brian said: "You didn't, though, did you, Rector?"

For a moment George looked baffled.

Brian said: "You didn't summon us to pray for Harry, who stands now, as we speak, on the bank of that great dark river, waiting to know whether it is God's will that he should cross tonight into the divine presence. If you had called us, Rector, we would gladly have come to St. Matthew's Church to pray with you. But you didn't, so here we are."

"You're ignorant villagers," George raved. "That's why God sets a clergyman over you."

"Ignorant?" It was a woman's voice, and Amos identified Annie Mann, one of his spinners. "We're not so ignorant as to overload a turnip cart," she said.

There were cries of agreement and even a scatter of laughter.

George said: "God has made you subordinate to those who know better, and it's your duty to obey authority, not defy it."

There was a brief silence, then everyone heard a loud, agonized groan from inside the house.

Amos moved to the door and stepped inside.

Sal and Kit were kneeling on the far side of the bed, their hands folded in prayer. The surgeon, Alec Pollock, stood at the head of the bed, holding Harry's wrist.

Harry groaned again, and Alec said: "He's going, Sal. He's leaving us."

"Oh, God," Sal moaned, and Kit cried.

Amos stood silent and still at the door, watching.

After a minute, Alec said: "He's gone, Sal."

Sal put her arm around Kit, and they cried together.

Alec said: "His suffering is over, at last. He's with the Lord Jesus now."

Amos said: "Amen."

CHAPTER 3

On the grounds of the bishop's palace, where once—according to Kingsbridge legend—the monks had cultivated their beans and cabbages, Arabella Latimer had created a rose garden.

Her family had been surprised. She had never shown any interest in cultivating anything. Her duties were all geared toward her husband, the bishop: managing his household, giving dinners for senior clergy and other county bigwigs, and appearing at his side in costly but respectable clothing. Then one day she had announced that she was going to grow roses.

It was a new idea that had caught the imagination of a few fashionable ladies. It was not exactly a craze, but it had become a fad, and Arabella had read about it in *The Lady's Magazine* and had been taken with the notion.

Her only child, Elsie, had not expected the enthusiasm to last. She anticipated that her mother would quickly grow tired of the bending and the hoeing, the watering and the manuring, and the way the earth got under the fingernails and could never be completely cleaned out.

The bishop, Stephen Latimer, had grunted: "Nine days' wonder, you mark my words," and had gone back to reading *The Critical Review*.

They had both been wrong.

When Elsie went out at half past eight in the morning, looking for her mother, she found her in the garden, with a groundsman at her side, piling muck from the stable around the bases of the plants as a fall of wet sleet came down on their heads. Catching sight of Elsie, Arabella said over her shoulder: "I'm protecting them from frost," and continued her work.

Elsie was amused. She wondered whether her mother had ever held a shovel before today.

She looked around. The rose plants were all bare sticks now, in winter, but the shape of the garden was visible. It was entered through a basketwork arch that supported a riot of climbing rosebushes in summer. That led to a square of low rose trees that would burst into flaming color. Beyond that, a trellis fixed to a stretch of ruined wall—built by those monks to shelter some long-forgotten kitchen garden, perhaps—gave support to climbing plants that grew like weeds in hot weather, and bloomed with bright splashes, as if the angels above had been careless with their paints.

Elsie had long felt that her mother's life was dismally empty, but would have wished her a pursuit more meaningful than gardening. However, Elsie was an idealist and an intellectual, whereas Arabella was neither. To every thing there is a season, Father would say, quoting Ecclesiastes, and a time to every purpose under heaven. The roses brought joy into Arabella's life.

It was cold, and Elsie had something important to say. "Will you be long?" she said.

"Nearly finished."

Arabella was thirty-eight, much younger than her husband, and still glamorous. She was tall and shapely, with a head of light-brown hair that had a touch of auburn. Her nose was freckled, which people considered a blemish, though somehow it looked charming on her. Elsie was different from her mother in looks as well as character—with dark hair and hazel eyes—but people said she had a lovely smile.

Arabella handed the shovel to the groundsman and the two women hurried inside. Arabella took off her boots and cloak while Elsie patted her damp hair with a towel. Elsie said: "This morning I'm going to ask Father about the Sunday school."

It was her big project. She was horrified by the way

children were treated in her hometown. They often started work at seven years of age, and they worked fourteen hours a day Monday to Friday, and twelve hours on Saturday. Most never learned to read or write more than a few words. They needed a Sunday school.

Her father knew all that and did not seem to care. However, she had a plan for winning him around.

Her mother said: "I hope he's in a good mood."

"You'll support me, won't you?"

"Of course. I think it's a grand scheme."

Elsie wanted more than a vague expression of goodwill. "I know you have misgivings, but—please don't mind me saying this—could you keep them to yourself, just for today?"

"Of course, dear. I'm not tactless, you know that."

Elsie knew nothing of the kind, but she did not say so. "He'll raise objections, but I'll deal with them. I just want you to murmur encouragement now and again, saying 'Quite right,' and 'Good idea,' and things like that."

Arabella seemed amused and only slightly irritated by her daughter's persistence. "Darling, I get the message, don't worry. You're like an actor, you don't want thoughtful criticism, you want an applauding audience."

She was being ironic, but Elsie pretended not to notice. "Thank you," she said.

They went into the dining room. The staff were lined up along one side of the room in order of precedence: first the men—butler, groom, footman, boot boy—then the women—housekeeper, cook, two maids, and the kitchen skivvy. The table was laid with china in the fashionable flowered style that was called chinoiserie.

Beside the bishop's place was a copy of *The Times* two days old. It took a day to travel from London to Bristol on the turnpike road and another day to reach Kingsbridge via country lanes that were muddy in the wet and rutted otherwise. Such speed seemed miraculous to people as old as the bishop, who could remember when the journey had taken a week.

The bishop came in. Elsie and Arabella drew back their chairs and knelt on the carpet with their elbows on the seats, hands folded. The tea urn hissed as he went through prayers reverently but briskly, impatient for his bacon. After the last amen the servants returned to their work and the food was quickly brought from the kitchen.

Elsie ate some bread and butter, sipped her tea, and waited for the right moment. She felt tense. She wanted this Sunday school very badly. It broke her heart that so many Kingsbridge children were completely ignorant. She discreetly studied her father as he ate, judging his mood. He was fifty-five, his hair gray and thinning. He had once been an imposing figure, tall and broad shouldered—Elsie could just remember—but he was too fond of his food, and now he was heavy, with a round face and a huge waist, and he stooped.

When the bishop was pleasantly full of toast and tea, and before he opened *The Times*, the maid, Mason, came in with a jug of fresh milk, and Elsie made her move. She gave Mason a discreet nod. This was a prearranged signal, and Mason knew what to do.

"Something I want to ask you about, Father," Elsie said. It was always best to frame anything she had to say as a plea for enlightenment: the bishop enjoyed explaining, but he did not like to be told what to do.

He smiled benignly. "Go on."

"Our town has a reputation in the world of education. The library of your cathedral draws scholars from all over western Europe. Kingsbridge Grammar School is nationally famous. And of course there is Kingsbridge College, Oxford, where you yourself studied."

"Very true, my dear, but I know all this."

"And yet we fail."

"Surely not."

Elsie hesitated, but she was committed now. With a thudding heart she called out: "Come in, Mason, please."

Mason came in leading a dirty little boy about ten or eleven years old. An unpleasant smell entered the room with him. Surprisingly, he did not seem intimidated by the surroundings.

Elsie said to her father: "I want you to meet Jimmy Passfield."

The boy spoke with the arrogance of a duke, though not the grammar. "I was promised sausages with mustard, but I ain't seen none yet."

The bishop said: "What on earth is this?"

She prayed that he would not explode. "Please, Father, listen for a minute or two." Without waiting for his consent, she turned to the child and said: "Can you read, Jimmy?" She held her breath, not being sure what he would say.

"I don't need to read," he said defiantly. "I know everything. I can tell you the times of the stagecoach every day of the week without ever looking at the bit of paper nailed up at the Bell Inn."

The bishop harrumphed, but Elsie ignored him and asked the key question. "Do you know Jesus Christ?"

"I know everyone, and there's nobody of that name in Kingsbridge. My oath on it." He clapped his hands once and spat into the fire.

The bishop was shocked into silence—as Elsie had hoped.

Jimmy added: "There's a bargee from Combe comes upriver now and again called Jason Cryer." He wagged an admonitory finger at Elsie. "Pound to a penny you're getting his name wrong."

Elsie pressed on. "Do you go to church?"

"I went once, but they wouldn't give me none of the wine, so I walked out."

"Don't you want to have your sins forgiven?"

Jimmy was indignant. "I never committed no sins, ever, and that piglet that was stole off Mrs. Andrews in Well Street was nothing to do with me, I wasn't even there."

The bishop said: "All right, all right, Elsie, you've made your point. Mason, take the child away."

Elsie added: "And give him sausages."

"With mustard," said Jimmy.

"With mustard," Elsie echoed.

Mason and Jimmy left.

Arabella clapped her hands and laughed. "What a splendid little tyke! He fears no one!"

Elsie said seriously: "He's not unusual, Father. Half the children in Kingsbridge are the same. They never see the inside of a school, and if their parents don't make them go to church they never learn about the Christian religion."

The bishop was clearly shocked. He said: "But do you imagine there is something I can do about it?"

This was the moment she had been leading up to. "Some of the townspeople are talking about starting a Sunday school." This was not the exact truth. The school was Elsie's idea, and although several people were in favor, it probably would not happen without her. But she did not want him to know how easy it would be for him to prevent it.

He said: "But we already have schools for little children in the town. I believe Mrs. Baines in Fish Street teaches sound Christian principles, although I'm doubtful about that place in Loversfield where the Methodists send their sons."

"Those schools charge fees, of course."

"How else should they function?"

"I'm talking about a free school for poor children on Sunday afternoons."

"I see." He was thinking up objections, she could tell. "Where would it take place?"

"The wool exchange, perhaps. It's never used on Sundays."

"Do you think the mayor would permit the floor of the wool exchange to be used by the children of the poor? Half of them aren't properly house-trained. Why, even in the cathedral I've seen . . . But never mind that."

"I'm sure the children can be kept under control. But

if we can't use the wool exchange there are other possibilities."

"And who would do the teaching?"

"Several people have volunteered, including Amos Barrowfield, who went to the grammar school."

Arabella murmured: "I thought Amos would come into it somehow."

Elsie blushed and pretended not to have heard.

The bishop ignored Arabella's aside and failed to notice Elsie's embarrassment. He said: "Young Barrowfield is a Methodist, I believe."

"Canon Midwinter will be the patron."

"Another Methodist, despite being a canon of the cathedral."

"They have asked me to be in charge, and I'm no Methodist."

"In charge! You're very young for that."

"I'm twenty, and sufficiently well-educated to teach children to read."

"I don't like it," the bishop said decisively.

Elsie was not surprised, though his definite tone dismayed her. She had expected him to disapprove, and she had a plan for winning him around. But now she said: "Why on earth don't you like it?"

"You see, my dear, it's not good for the laboring classes to learn to read and write," he said, shifting into paternal mode, the older man dispensing wisdom to utopian youth. "Books and newspapers fill their heads with half-understood ideas. It makes them discontented with the station in life that God has ordained for them. They get foolish notions about equality and democracy."

"But they ought to read the Bible."

"Even worse! They misunderstand the scriptures and accuse the established church of false doctrine. They turn into dissenters and nonconformists, and then they want to set up their own churches, like the Presbyterians and the Congregationalists. And the Methodists."

"Methodists don't have their own churches."

"Give them time."

Her father was good at the cut and thrust of argument: he had learned at Oxford. Elsie enjoyed the challenge normally, but this project was too important to be defeated by debating points. However, she had arranged a second visitor, one who might be able to talk her father around, and she had to continue the discussion until he showed up. She said: "Don't you think reading the Bible would help laboring people to resist false prophets?"

"Much better that they should listen to the clergy."

"But they don't, so that's a counsel of perfection."

Arabella laughed. "You two," she said. "You argue like a Whig and a Tory. We're not talking about the French revolution! It's a Sunday school, children sitting on the floor scratching their names on slates and singing 'We're Marching to Zion.'"

The maid put her head around the door and said: "Mr. Shoveller is here, my lord bishop."

"Shoveller?"

Elsie said: "The weaver. They call him Spade. He's brought a length of cloth for me and Mother to look at." She turned to the maid. "Show him in, Mason, and give him a cup of tea."

A weaver was several steps down the social ladder from the bishop's family, but Spade was charming and well-mannered: he had taught himself drawing room etiquette in order to sell to the upper crust. He came in carrying a bolt of cloth. Attractive in a craggy sort of way, with unruly hair and an appealing grin, he was always well-dressed in clothes made from his own fabrics.

He bowed and said: "I didn't intend to interrupt you at breakfast, my lord bishop."

Father was not very pleased, Elsie could tell, but he pretended not to mind. "Come in, Mr. Shoveller, do."

"You're very kind, sir." Spade stood where they could all see him and unwound a length of cloth. "This is what Miss Latimer was keen to look at."

Elsie was not very interested in clothes—like Mother's

roses, they were too frivolous to hold her attention—but even she was struck by the gorgeous colors of the cloth, earthy red and a dark mustard yellow in a subtle check pattern. Spade walked around the table and held it in front of Arabella, being careful not to touch her. "Not everyone can wear these colors, but they're perfect for you, Mrs. Latimer," he said.

She stood up and looked at herself in the glass over the fireplace. "Oh, yes," she said. "They seem to suit me."

"The fabric is a mixture of silk and merino wool," Spade said. "Very soft—feel it." Arabella obediently stroked the cloth. "It's warm, but light," Spade added. "Perfect for a spring coat or cape."

It would be expensive, too, Elsie thought; but the bishop was rich and he never seemed to mind Arabella spending his money.

Spade stood behind Arabella and draped the cloth around her shoulders. She gathered the material at her neck and half-turned right, then left, to see herself from different angles.

Mason handed Spade a cup of tea. He put the bolt of cloth on a chair so that Arabella could continue to pose in it, then sat at the table to drink his tea. Elsie said: "We were discussing the idea of a free Sunday school for the children of the poor."

"I'm sorry I interrupted you."

"Not at all. I'd be interested in your opinion."

"I think it's a splendid notion."

"My father fears it will indoctrinate the children with Methodism. Canon Charles is to be the patron, and Amos Barrowfield will help with the teaching."

"My lord bishop is wise," said Spade.

He was supposed to support Elsie, not the bishop.

Spade went on: "I'm a Methodist myself, but I believe that children should be taught the basic truths, and not be troubled by doctrinal subtleties."

It was a good plain argument, but Elsie could see that her father was unmoved.

Spade went on: "But if everyone involved in your school is Methodist, Elsie, the Anglican church would have to start its own Sunday school, to provide an alternative."

The bishop grunted in surprise. He had not seen this coming.

Spade said: "And I'm sure many townspeople would love the idea of their children being told Bible stories by the bishop himself."

Elsie almost laughed. Her father's face was a picture of horror. He hated the idea of telling Bible stories to the unwashed children of Kingsbridge's poor.

She said: "But, Spade, I will be in charge of the school, so I can make sure the children are taught only those elements of our faith which the Anglican church and the Methodist reformers have in common."

"Oh! In that case I withdraw everything I said. And by the way, I think you'll be a wonderful teacher."

The bishop looked relieved. "Well, have your Sunday school if you must," he said. "I must go about my duties. Good day to you, Mr. Shoveller." He left the room.

Arabella said: "Elsie, did you plan that?"

"I certainly did. And thank you, Spade—you were brilliant."

"A pleasure." He turned to Arabella. "Mrs. Latimer, if you would like a garment of this lovely cloth, my sister will be delighted to make it."

Spade's sister, Kate Shoveller, was a skilled seamstress and had a shop on the High Street that she ran with another woman, Rebecca Liddle. Their clothes were fashionable and the shop did well.

Elsie wanted to reward Spade for the good turn he had done her, and she said to her mother: "You should order a coat, it will look wonderful."

"I think I will," said Arabella. "Please tell Miss Shoveller that I'll call in at the shop."

Spade bowed. "A pleasure, of course," he said.

CHAPTER 4

he night before the funeral Sal lay awake, alternately grieving for Harry and worrying about how she would manage without his wage.

His body lay in the cold church, wrapped in a shroud, and she had the bed to herself. It felt empty, and she kept shivering. The last time she had slept alone had been the night before she married him, eight years ago.

Kit was in the small bed, and she could tell by his breathing that he was asleep. He at least was able to forget his sorrow in slumber.

Buffeted by bittersweet memories and anxiety for the future, she drifted in and out of a doze until she saw light around the edges of the shutters, then she got up and lit the fire. She sat at her spinning wheel until Kit woke, then made their breakfast of bread-and-dripping with tea. Soon she would be too poor to buy tea.

The funeral was scheduled for the afternoon. Kit's shirt was worn thin and unmendably torn. She did not want him to look bad today. She had an old one of Harry's that could be remade to fit the boy, and she sat down to cut and sew.

As she was finishing she heard gunfire. That would be Will Riddick, shooting partridges in Mill Field. He was responsible for her sudden poverty. He ought to do something about it. Anger rose in her throat and she decided to confront him. "Stay here," she said to Kit. "Sweep the floor." She went out into the cold morning.

Will was in the field with his black-and-white setter. As she approached him from behind, a flurry of birds rose out of the adjacent woods, and Will followed their flight with his shotgun and fired twice. He was a good shot, and two birds fluttered to the ground, gray with striped wings, about the size of pigeons. A man emerged from the trees, and Sal recognized the lank hair and bony frame of Platts, the butler at the manor house. Evidently he was scaring up the birds for Will.

The dog raced to where they had fallen. It brought one bird back, then the second. Will shouted to Platts: "Again!"

By that time Sal had reached the spot where Will stood.

She reminded herself that there was nothing to be gained by abusing those in power. They could sometimes be persuaded, or cajoled, or even shamed into doing the right thing, but they could not be browbeaten. Any attempt to force the issue only made them obstinate.

"What do you want?" Will said rudely.

"I need to know what you're going to do for me . . ." She added: "Sir," a bit too late.

He reloaded his gun. "Why should I do anything for you?"

"Because Harry was working under you. Because you overloaded the cart. Because you didn't listen to Uncle Ike's warning. Because you killed my husband."

Will reddened. "It was entirely his own fault."

She forced herself to adopt a mild, reasonable tone of voice. "Some people may believe what you've told them, but you know the truth. You were there. And so was I."

He stood casually, holding the gun loosely, but letting it point at her. She had no doubt that the threat was intentional, but she did not believe he would pull the trigger. It would be hard to pretend it was an accident only two days after he had killed her husband.

He said: "I suppose you want a handout."

"I want what you've taken from me—my husband's wage, eight shillings a week."

He pretended to be amused. "You can't force me to pay you eight shillings a week. Why don't you find another husband?" He looked her up and down, scorning her drab dress and homemade shoes. "There must be someone that would have you."

She was not insulted. She knew she was attractive to men. Will himself had gazed at her lasciviously, more than once. However, she could not imagine marrying again.

But that was not the argument to use now. Instead she said: "If that happens, you can stop paying me."

"I'm not going to start."

There was a clapping of wings as the birds rose again, and he swung around and shot. Another two partridges fell to earth. The dog brought one and went to fetch the other.

Will picked up the bird by its feet. "Here you are," he said to Sal. "Have a partridge."

There was blood on its light-gray breast, but it was still alive. Sal was tempted to take it. She could make a fine dinner for Kit and herself with a partridge.

Will said: "As compensation for your husband, it's about the right level."

She gasped as if he had punched her. She could not catch her breath to speak. How dare he say her husband was worth a partridge. Strangled with rage, she turned and strode away, leaving him holding the bird.

She was seething, and if she had stayed longer she would have said something foolish.

She stomped across the field, heading for home, then changed her mind and decided to go to the squire. He was no Prince Charming but he was not as bad as Will. And something had to be done for her.

The front door of the manor house was forbidden to villagers. She was tempted to break the rule, but hesitated. She did not want to use the back door and meet the staff, for they would insist she wait while they asked the squire if he would see her, and the answer might be no. But there was a side door used by villagers when they came to pay their rents. She knew that it led via a short corridor to the main hall and the squire's study.

She went around the house to the side and tried the door. It was not locked.

She went in.

The study door was open and there was a haze of tobacco fumes. She looked in and saw the squire at his desk, smoking a pipe while writing in a ledger. She tapped the door and said: "Begging your pardon, Squire."

He looked up and took the pipe out of his mouth. "What are you doing here?" he said with irritation. "It's not rent day."

"The side entrance was unlocked and I need to speak to you urgently." She stepped in and closed the study door behind her.

"You should have used the servants' entrance. Who do you think you are?"

"Sir, I have to know what you will do for me now that I've lost my husband. I have a child to feed and clothe."

He hesitated. Sal thought that Squire Riddick might slide out of his responsibility if he could. But she guessed he had a guilty conscience. Publicly, he would probably deny that Will was to blame for Harry's death. But he was not as evil as his son. She saw indecision and shame cross his ruddy face. Then he seemed to harden his heart, and said: "That's why we have Poor Relief."

Householders in the village paid an amount every year toward helping the poor of the parish. The fund was administered by the church.

"See the rector," said the squire. "He's the overseer of the poor."

"Sir, Rector Riddick hates Methodists."

With the air of one who plays a trump card, the squire said: "Then you shouldn't be a Methodist, should you?"

"Poor Relief is not supposed to be just for people who agree with the rector."

"The Church of England gives out the money."

"But it's not the church's money, is it? It comes from the householders. Are they wrong to trust the church to be fair?"

The squire became exasperated. "You're one of these

folk who think you should correct your betters, aren't you?"

Hope drained out of Sal. An argument with one of those who ruled always ended like this. The gentry were right because they were the gentry, regardless of laws, promises, or logic. Only the poor had to obey the rules.

She had no energy left. She would have to beg from Rector Riddick, and he would do his best to avoid giving her any help.

She left the room without speaking again. She went out by the side door and walked home. She felt hopeless and depressed.

She finished Kit's shirt and they had a dinner of bread and cheese, then the bell began to toll, and they walked to St. Matthew's Church. A lot of people were there already, and the nave was crowded. The church was a small medieval building and should have been extended to accommodate the growing village, but the Riddicks were not willing to spend the money.

Some of the mourners had not known Harry well, and Sal wondered why they had taken time off work to come; then she realized that his death was special. It had not been brought about by disease or old age or an unavoidable accident, none of the normal causes. Harry had died because of the foolishness and brutality of Will Riddick. By coming to the funeral the villagers were making it clear that Harry's life mattered, and his death could not be brushed aside.

Rector Riddick seemed to understand that. He walked in wearing his robes, stared in surprise at the large crowd, and looked angry. He moved quickly to the altar and began the service. Sal was quite sure he would have preferred not to conduct the funeral, but he was the only clergyman in the village. And the fees for all the christenings, weddings, and funerals in a large village added up to a significant bonus on top of his salary.

He raced through the liturgy so quickly that the congregation began to murmur their dissatisfaction. He ignored them and hurried to the end. Sal hardly cared. She kept thinking that she would never see Harry again, and all she could do was weep.

Uncle Ike had organized the pallbearers, and the congregation followed them out into the graveyard. Brian Pikestaff stood beside Sal and put a comforting arm around her trembling shoulders.

The rector said the last prayer as the body was lowered.

The service being over, he approached Sal. She wondered if he would speak words of insincere consolation, but he said: "My father told me of your visit. I'll come to see you later this afternoon." Then he hurried away.

When he had gone, Brian Pikestaff gave a short eulogy. He spoke about Harry with affection and respect, and his words were greeted with nods and murmurs of "Amen" from around the grave. He said a prayer, then they sang "Love's Redeeming Work Is Done."

Sal shook hands with a few close friends, thanking them for attending, then took Kit's hand and quickly walked away.

Shortly after she arrived home, Brian turned up, bringing a quill pen and a small vial of ink. "I thought you would want to write Harry's name in your Bible," he said. "I won't stay—just give me back the quill and the bottle when it suits you."

She was better at reading than writing, but she could write dates and copy anything. Harry's name was in the book, with the date of their wedding, and as she sat at the table with the book in front of her and the quill in her hand she recalled that day, eight years ago. She remembered how happy she had felt to be marrying him. She had worn a new dress, and she was wearing it today. She had said the words *till death us do part* but had never imagined that would be so short a time. For a few moments she allowed herself to feel the full weight of grief.

Then she dried her tears and wrote, slowly and carefully:

Harold Clitheroe, died December the 4th, 1792.

She would have liked to put something about how he died, but she did not know how to write words such as *run over by a cart* or *by the foolishness of the squire's son*, and anyway it was probably wiser not to set such things down in ink.

Life had to return to normal, and she sat at her spinning wheel and worked by the light from the open door. Kit sat beside her, as he often did, passing the loose ropes of unspun wool from his hands to hers while she fed them into the orifice and at the same time turned the wheel that spun the flyer and twisted the wool into a tight thread of yarn. He looked thoughtful, and after a while he asked her: "Why do we have to die before we go to heaven?"

She herself had asked questions like this, although she thought she had done so at a later age, more like twelve than six. She had soon realized that there was rarely a helpful explanation of the puzzling aspects of religion, and she had stopped asking. She had a feeling Kit was going to be more persistent.

"I don't know why, I'm sorry," she said. "Nobody knows. It's a mystery."

"Does anyone ever go to heaven without dying?"

She was about to say no when something tugged at her memory, and after a few moments' thought it came back to her. "Yes, there was one man, called Elijah."

"So he wasn't buried in a graveyard next to a church?"

"No." Sal was fairly sure there had been no churches in the time of the Old Testament prophets, but she decided not to correct Kit's error.

"How did he get to heaven?"

"He was taken up in a whirlwind." To avoid the inevitable question she added: "I don't know why."

He went quiet, and she guessed he was thinking about his father being up there in heaven with God and the angels.

Kit had another question. "Why do you need the big wheel?"

She could answer that one. "The wheel is much larger than the flyer it turns—you can see that, can't you?"

"Yes."

"So when the wheel goes around once, the flyer spins five times. That means the flyer goes much faster."

"But you could just turn the flyer instead."

"And that's what they did before the big wheel was invented. But it's hard to turn the flyer fast. You'd get tired quickly. Whereas you can turn the wheel slowly all day." He stared at the device, deep in thought as he watched it turn. He was a special child. Sal knew that every mother thought this, especially mothers who had only one; but still she thought Kit was different from the rest. When he grew up he would be capable of more than just laboring, and she did not want him to live as she did, in a peat house with no chimney.

She had had aspirations once. She had hero-worshipped her aunt Sarah, her mother's elder sister. Sarah had left the village, moved to Kingsbridge, and started selling ballads on the street, singing them as a sales aid. She had married the man who printed the ballads and had learned arithmetic in order to become his bookkeeper. For a while she would visit the village once or twice a year, well-dressed, poised, confident, bearing generous gifts—silk for a dress, a live chicken, a glass bowl. She talked about things she had read in the newspapers: the American Revolution, Captain Cook in Australia, the appointment of twenty-four-year-old William Pitt as prime minister. Sal had wanted to be just like Aunt Sarah. Then she had fallen in love with Harry, and her life had gone in a different direction.

She could not quite imagine the course Kit's life might take, but she knew the beginning of it, which was learning. She had taught him letters and numbers, and he could already scratch the three letters of his name in the earth with a stick. But she herself had not had much schooling, and soon she would have taught him everything she knew.

There was a school in the village run by the rector—the Riddick family controlled just about everything here. The school charged a penny a day. Sal sent Kit there whenever she had a penny to spare, but that was not often, and now that Harry was gone it might be never. She was as determined as ever that Kit would prosper, but she did not know how.

Kit said: "Shall we read?"

"Good idea. Fetch the book."

He crossed the room and picked up the Bible. He put it on the floor so that they both could see it while they worked. "What shall we read?"

"Let's read the story of the boy who killed the giant." She picked up the heavy volume and found chapter 17 of the First Book of Samuel.

They resumed their work as Kit tried to read. She had to help him with all the names and many of the words. As a child she had asked for an explanation of "six cubits and a span," so now she was able to tell Kit that Goliath was more than nine feet tall.

While they were both struggling with the word *countenance*, the rector came in without knocking.

Kit stopped reading and Sal stood up.

"What's this?" the rector said. "Reading?"

Sal said: "The story of David and Goliath, Rector."

"Hmm. You Methodists always want to read the Bible for yourselves. You'd do better to listen to your rector."

This was not the moment to engage him in debate. "It's the only book in the house, sir, and I didn't think the child would come to any harm from God's holy word. I'm sorry if I've done wrong."

"Well, that's not what I'm here about." He looked around for somewhere to sit. There were no chairs in the house, so he pulled up a three-legged stool. "You want the church to give you Poor Relief."

Sal did not say that it was not the church's money. She needed to be humble, or he might refuse her altogether. There was really no curb on the overseer of the poor, no one above him to whom Sal might appeal. So she lowered her eyes and said: "Yes, please, Rector."

"How much is your rent for this house?"

"Six pence a week, sir."

"The parish will pay that."

So, Sal thought, your first concern is to make sure the landlord doesn't lose any income. Still, it was a relief to know that she and Kit would still have a roof over their heads.

"But you make good money as a spinner."

"Amos Barrowfield pays a shilling per pound of wool spun, and I can manage three pounds a week, if I stay up most of one night."

"So that's three shillings, which is almost half a laborer's wage."

"Three-eighths, sir," she corrected him. Approximations were dangerous when every penny counted.

"Now, it's about time Kit started work."

Sal was taken aback. "He's six years old!"

"Yes, and he'll soon be seven. That's the usual age for a child to get his first job."

"He won't be seven until March."

"March the twenty-fifth. I looked up the date in the parish records. It's not far away."

It was more than three months, and that was a long time at the age of six. But Sal made a different objection. "What work could he do? It's winter—no one needs to hire help in winter."

"We need a boot boy at the manor house."

So that was the plan. "What work would Kit have to do?"

"He'll learn to polish boots to a shine, of course. And similar tasks: sharpening knives, bringing in firewood, cleaning out chamber pots, all that sort of thing."

Sal looked at Kit, who sat listening, wide-eyed. He

was so small and vulnerable that she wanted to cry. But the rector was right: it was almost time he went to work.

The rector added: "It will be good for him to learn how to behave in the squire's house. Perhaps he will grow up to be a less insolent man than his father."

Sal tried to ignore the slur on Harry. "What would he be paid?"

"A shilling a week, which is very fair for a child."

That was true, Sal knew.

"Of course he'll get his food, and clothes, too." The rector looked at Kit's patched stockings and oversize coat. "He can't be dressed like that."

Kit perked up at the idea of new clothes.

The rector said: "And he'll sleep at the manor house, of course."

The thought dismayed Sal, although it was no surprise: most servants lived on the premises. She was going to be on her own. How lonely life would be.

Kit, too, was distraught, and his eyes overflowed with tears.

The rector said: "Stop blubbering, lad, and be grateful for a warm house and plenty of food. Boys your age work in coal mines."

They did, Sal knew.

Kit sobbed: "I want my mother."

"I want mine, but she's dead," said the rector. "You'll still have yours, and you'll have a half-day holiday every Sunday afternoon, so you can see her then."

That made Kit cry even more.

Sal lowered her voice. "He's only just lost his father, and now he feels he's losing his mother."

"Well, he's not, and he'll find that out next Sunday, when he comes to see you."

That shocked Sal. "You want to take him today?"

"There's no point in waiting. The sooner he starts, the sooner he'll get used to it. But if your need isn't as urgent as you pretend . . ."

"Very well."

"So I'll take him now."

Kit spoke in a high-pitched defiant voice. "I'll run away!"

The rector shrugged. "Then you'll be chased and brought back and flogged."

"I'll run away again!"

"If you do, you'll be brought back again; but I think the first flogging will be enough."

Sal said: "Now, Kit, stop crying." She spoke firmly, but she herself was close to tears. "Your father's gone and you must be a man sooner than expected. If you behave you will have dinner and supper and nice clothes."

The rector said: "The squire will deduct three pence a week from his wages for food and drink, and six pence a week for the first forty weeks for his clothes."

"But that means he'll only get three pence a week!"

"And that's all he'll be worth, at the start."

"And how much will you give me out of the Poor Relief?"

The rector pretended to be indignant. "Nothing, of course."

"But how shall I live?"

"You can spin every day, now that you don't have a husband and son to care for. I should think you could double your earnings. You'll have six shillings a week and only yourself to spend it on."

Sal knew she would have to spin twelve hours a day, six days a week, to achieve that. Her vegetable garden would be weed-grown, her clothes would become threadbare, she would live on bread and cheese, but she would survive. And so would Kit.

The rector stood up. "Come with me, lad."

Sal said: "I'll see you on Sunday, Kit, and you can tell me all about it. Give me a goodbye kiss."

He did not stop crying, but he hugged her and she kissed him, then she detached herself from his embrace and said: "Say your prayers, and Jesus will take care of you."

The rector took Kit's hand firmly and they walked out of the house.

"Mind you be good, Kit!" she called.

Then she sat down and cried.

Rector Riddick held Kit's hand as they walked through the village. It was not a friendly, reassuring grasp, but much stronger than that, tight enough to stop Kit running away. But he had no intention of running away. The rector's talk of flogging had scared him out of that.

He was scared of everything right now: scared because he had no father, scared because he had left his mother, scared of the rector and of the spiteful Will and of the all-powerful squire.

As he hurried along at the rector's side, running every now and again to keep up, villagers gazed at him in curiosity, especially his friends and their parents; but no one said anything or dared to question the rector.

He was scared all over again as they approached the manor. It was the biggest building in the village, bigger than the church, and made of the same yellowish stone. He knew its exterior well, but now he looked at it with fresh eyes. The front had a door in the middle with steps up and a porch, and he counted eleven windows, two either side of the door, five upstairs, and two more in the roof. As he got closer he saw that there was a basement, too.

He had no idea what could be inside such a huge structure. He remembered Margaret Pikestaff telling him that everything there was gold, even the chairs, but he suspected she was getting it mixed up with heaven.

The church was big because everyone in the village had to get inside for services, but the manor was for only four people, the squire and his three sons, plus a few servants. What did they do with all that space? Kit's home was one room for three people. The manor was mysterious, which made it sinister.

The rector led him up the steps and through the big door, saying: "You never come in this way unless you're with the squire or one of us three sons. There's a back door for you and the other servants."

So I'm one of the servants, Kit thought. I'm the one that polishes the boots. I wish I knew how to polish boots. I wonder what all the other servants do. I wonder if they run away and get brought back and flogged.

The front door closed behind them and the rector let go of Kit's hand.

They were in a hall that was bigger than the inside of Kit's house. There was dark wood on the walls, four doors, and a wide staircase leading up. The head of a stag over the fireplace stared balefully at Kit, but it seemed unable to move, and he was almost certain it was not alive. The hall was quite dark, and there was a faint unpleasant smell Kit did not recognize.

One of the four doors opened, and Will Riddick stepped into the hall.

Kit tried to hide behind the rector, but Will saw him, and scowled. "That's not Clitheroe's little whelp, is it, George?"

"Yes," said the rector.

"What the devil did you bring him here for?"

"Calm down, Will. We need a boot boy."

"Why him?"

"Because he's available, and his mother needs the money."

"I don't want that damned puppy in the house."

Kit's mother never used words such as *damned* and *what the devil*, and she frowned on the rare occasions when Pa said them. Kit had never uttered them.

The rector said: "Don't be stupid, there's nothing wrong with the boy."

Will's face got more red. "I know you think it was my fault that Clitheroe died."

"I never said that."

"You brought the child here as a permanent reproach to me."

Kit did not know the word *reproach* but he guessed that Will did not want to be reminded of what he had done. And the accident *was* Will's fault, even a child could see that.

Kit had always wanted a brother to play with, but he had never imagined brothers quarreling like this.

The rector said: "Anyway, it was Father's idea to hire this boy."

"Right. I'll talk to Father. He'll send the boy back to his mother."

The rector shrugged. "You can try. I hardly care."

Kit wanted with all his heart to be sent back to his mother.

Will crossed the hall and went through another door, and Kit wondered how he would ever find his way around such a complicated house.

But he had something more important on his mind. "Am I going to be sent home?" he asked eagerly.

"No," said the rector. "The squire rarely changes his mind, and he won't do so just because Will's feelings are hurt."

Kit slumped back into despair.

"You need to know the names of the rooms," the rector said. He opened a door. "Drawing room. Take a quick look."

Kit nervously stepped inside and looked around. There seemed to be more furniture in this room than in the rest of the village put together. There were rugs, chairs, numerous small tables, curtains and cushions and pictures and ornaments. There was a piano that was much bigger than the only other piano he had ever seen, which was in the Pikestaff house. But there was nowhere in the drawing room for a person to do some drawing.

He was still trying to take it all in when the rector pulled him back and shut the door.

They moved to the next door. "Dining room." This was

simpler, with a table in the middle and chairs all around, plus several sideboards. On the walls were paintings of men and women. Kit was puzzled by a spidery object hanging from the ceiling with dozens of candles stuck into it. Perhaps that was a handy place to keep the candles, so that when it got dark they could just take one out and light it.

They crossed the hall. "Billiards room." Here was a different kind of table, with raised edges and colored balls on a green surface. Kit had never before heard the word *billiards* and was baffled as to what the purpose of the room could be.

At the fourth door the rector said: "Office." This was the door Will had taken, and the rector did not open it. Kit heard raised voices inside. "They're arguing about you," the rector said.

Kit could not make out what they were saying.

At the back of the hall was a green door he had not noticed before. The rector led him through this door into an area of the house that had a different atmosphere: there were no pictures on the walls, the floors were bare of carpets, and the woodwork needed painting. They went down a staircase to the basement and entered a room where two men and two women sat at a table eating an early supper. All four stood up when the rector came in.

"This is our new boot boy," said the rector. "Kit Clitheroe."

They looked at him with interest. The older of the two men swallowed a mouthful of food and said: "The son of the man who . . . ?"

"Exactly." Pointing at the speaker, the rector said: "Kit, this is Platts, the butler. You will call him Mr. Platts and do everything he tells you." Platts had a big nose covered with little red lines.

"Next to him is Cecil, the footman." Cecil was quite young, and had a lump on his neck which, Kit knew, was called a carbuncle.

The rector indicated a middle-aged woman with a round face. "Mrs. Jackson is the cook and Fanny there is the maid."

Fanny was about twelve or thirteen, Kit guessed. She was a skinny girl with spots, and she looked almost as scared as he was.

"I expect you'll have to teach him everything, Platts," said the rector. "His father was insolent and disobedient, so if the boy turns out the same you'll have to give him a good thrashing."

"Yes, sir, I'll do that," said Platts.

Kit tried not to cry, but tears came to his eyes and rolled down his face.

The cook said: "He'll need clothes—he looks like a scarecrow."

Platts said: "There's a trunk of children's clothes somewhere—probably worn by you and your brothers when you were young. With your permission we'll see if there's anything that fits Kit."

"By all means," said the rector. "I'll leave you to it." He went out.

Kit looked at the four servants, wondering what he should do or say, but he could not think of anything, so he stood still and said nothing.

After a moment Cecil said: "Don't upset yourself, little man, we don't do much thrashing here. You'd better have some supper. Go and sit next to Fanny and have a piece of Mrs. Jackson's pork pie."

Kit went to the foot of the table and sat on the bench next to the maid. She got a plate and knife and fork and cut a slice of the big pie in the middle of the table. "Thank you, miss," said Kit. He felt too upset to eat, but they expected him to, so he cut a piece from the slice and forced himself to eat it. He had never had pork pie and he was amazed at how delicious it was.

The meal was interrupted again, this time by Roger, the squire's youngest son. "Is he here?" he said as he walked in.

They all stood up again, and Kit did the same. Platts said: "Good afternoon, Mr. Roger."

"Ah, there you are, young Kit," said Roger. "I see you've got a slice of pie, so things can't be too bad."

Kit was not sure how to respond, so he said: "Thank you, Mr. Roger."

"Now listen here, Kit. I know it's hard to leave home, but you must be brave, you know. Will you try to do that?"

"Yes, Mr. Roger."

Roger turned to Platts and said: "Go easy on him, Platts. You know what he's been through."

"Yes, sir, we know."

He looked at the others. "I'm relying on you all. Just show some compassion, especially at first."

Kit did not know the word *compassion* but he guessed it meant something like pity.

Cecil said: "Don't worry, Mr. Roger."

"Good man. Thank you." Roger went out.

They all sat down again.

Roger was a wonderful person, Kit decided.

When they had finished eating, Mrs. Jackson made tea, and Kit was given a cup, with plenty of milk and a lump of sugar, and that, too, was wonderful.

Finally Platts stood up and said: "Thank you, Mrs. Jackson."

The other three echoed him. "Thank you, Mrs. Jackson."

Kit guessed he was supposed to do the same, so he said it, too.

"Good lad," said Cecil. "Now I'd better show you how to polish a pair of boots."

CHAPTER 5

Amos Barrowfield was working in a cold warehouse at the back of his family's home near Kingsbridge Cathedral. It was late in the afternoon, and he was getting ready for an early start in the morning, preparing the loads for the packhorses which were being fed in the adjacent stable.

He was hurrying, because he hoped to meet a girl later.

He tied the sacks in bundles that could be quickly loaded onto ponies tomorrow in the chilly dawn, then he realized he did not have enough yarn. This was a nuisance. His father should have bought some at the Kingsbridge wool exchange on High Street.

Resenting the delay to his plans for the evening, he left the barn and crossed the yard, smelling snow in the air, and entered the house. It was a grand old residence in poor repair: there were roof tiles missing and a bucket on the upstairs landing to catch the water from the leak. Made of brick, it had a basement kitchen, two main stories, and an attic floor. The Barrowfields were a family of only three, but nearly all the ground floor was taken up by business space, and several servants slept on the premises, too.

Amos walked quickly through the hall, with its black-and-white marble floor, and went into the front office, which had its own door to the street. A big central table bore bolts of some of the cloths the Barrowfields sold: soft flannel, tight-woven gabardine, broadcloth for topcoats, kersey for sailors. Obadiah had an impressive knowledge of traditional types of wool and styles of weave, but he would not branch out. Amos thought there was profit to be made in small runs of luxury fabrics, angora and merino and silk blends, but his father preferred to stick to what he knew.

Obadiah was sitting at a desk, reading a heavy ledger, with a candle lamp beside him. They were opposites in looks, Amos knew: his father was short and bald, he was tall with thick wavy hair. Obadiah had a round face and a pug nose; Amos had a long face with a big chin. Both were dressed in costly fabrics, advertising the goods they sold, but Amos was neat and buttoned up, whereas Obadiah's neckcloth was loose, his waistcoat undone, his stockings wrinkled.

"There's no yarn," Amos said without preamble. "As you must know."

Obadiah looked up, seeming irritated at being disturbed. Amos braced himself for an argument: his father had become tetchy in the last year or so. "I can't help that," Obadiah said. "I haven't been able to buy any at a reasonable cost. At the last auction a clothier from Yorkshire bought it all at a ridiculously high price."

"What do you want me to tell the weavers?"

Obadiah sighed, like someone being pestered, and said: "Tell them to take a week's rest."

"And let their children go hungry?"

"I'm not in business to feed other people's children."

This was the biggest difference between father and son. Amos believed he had a responsibility to the people who depended on him for their living. Obadiah did not. But Amos did not want to get into that argument again, so he changed his line. "If they can get work from someone else, they'll take it."

"So be it."

It was more than just tetchiness, Amos thought. It was almost as if his father no longer cared about the business. What was wrong with him? "They may not come back to us," Amos said. "We'll be short of material to sell."

Obadiah raised his voice. In a tone of angry exasperation he said: "What do you expect me to do?"

"I don't know. You're the master, as you never cease to tell me."

"Just deal with the difficulty, will you?"

"I'm not paid to run the business. In fact I'm not paid at all."

"You're an apprentice! You will be until you're twenty-one. It's the usual way."

"No, it's not," said Amos, getting angry. "Most apprentices get a wage, even if it's small. I get nothing."

Obadiah was panting just from the effort of arguing. "You don't have to pay for your food or clothing or accommodation—what do you need money for?"

He wanted money so that he could ask a girl to walk out with him, but he did not tell his father that. "So that I don't feel like a child."

"Is that the only reason you can think of?"

"I'm nineteen years old and I do most of the work. I'm entitled to a wage."

"You're not a man yet, so I'll make the decisions."

"Yes, you make the decisions. And that's why there's no yarn." Amos stomped out of the room.

He was bewildered as well as angry. His father would not listen to reason. Was he just becoming bad-tempered and tightfisted as he got older? But he was only fifty. Was there something else going on, some other reason for this behavior?

Amos did feel like a child, having no money. A girl might get thirsty and ask him to get her a pot of ale in a tavern. He might want to buy her an orange from a market stall. Walking out was the first step in a courtship, for respectable Kingsbridge girls. Amos was not much interested in the other kind of girl. He knew about Bella Lovegood, real name Betty Larchwood, who was not respectable. Several boys of his age said they had been with her, and one or two might even have been telling the truth. Amos would not have been tempted even if he had the money. He felt sorry for Bella, but not attracted to her.

And what if he became serious about a girl, and wanted to take her to a play at the Kingsbridge Theatre, or a ball at the Assembly Rooms? How would he pay for the tickets?

He returned to the warehouse and quickly finished his packing. It bothered him that his father had so carelessly run out of yarn. Was the old man losing his grip?

He was hungry, but did not have time to sit down to eat with his parents. He went to the kitchen. His mother was there, sitting by the fire in a blue dress made of a soft lambswool cloth that had been made by one of the Badford weavers. She was chatting to the cook, Ellen, who was leaning against the kitchen table. Mother patted his shoulder affectionately and Ellen smiled fondly: both women had indulged him for most of his life.

He cut a few slices off a ham and began to eat them standing up, with a piece of bread and a cup of weak ale from the barrel. While he was eating he asked his mother: "Before you were married, did you walk out with Father?"

She smiled shyly, like a girl, and for a moment it seemed that the gray hair turned dark and lustrous, and the wrinkles disappeared, and she was a beautiful young woman. "Of course," she said.

"Where did you go? What did you do?"

"Not much. We put on our church clothes and just strolled around the town, looking at the shops, chatting to friends of our own age. It sounds quite boring, doesn't it? But I was excited because I really liked your father."

"Did he buy you things?"

"Not often. One day at Kingsbridge market he bought me a blue ribbon for my hair. I've still got it, in my jewelry box."

"He had money, then."

"Certainly. He was twenty-eight, and doing well."

"Were you the first girl he walked out with?"

Ellen said: "Amos! What a question to ask your mother!"

"Sorry," he said. "I wasn't thinking. Forgive me, Mother."

"Never mind."

"I must hurry."

"Are you going to the Methodist meeting?"

"Yes."

She gave him a penny from her purse. The Methodists would let you attend without contributing if you said you could not afford it, and for a while Amos had done that, but when his mother found out she had insisted on giving him the money. Father had objected: he thought Methodists were troublemakers. But for once Mother had defied his authority. "My son isn't a charity case," she had said indignantly. "For shame!" And Father had backed down.

Amos thanked her for the penny and went out into the lamplight. Kingsbridge had oil lights along Main Street and High Street now, paid for by the borough council on the grounds that light reduced crime.

He walked briskly to the Methodist Hall on High Street. It was a plain brick building painted white, with large windows symbolizing enlightenment. People sometimes called it a chapel, but it was not a consecrated church, as the Methodists had emphasized when they were collecting for the building fund, seeking funds from the small clothiers and prosperous craftsmen who made up most of their members. Many Methodists thought they should break away from the Anglican church, but others wanted to stay and reform the church from within.

Amos did not much care about all that. He thought religion was about how you lived your life. That was why he got angry when his father said: "I'm not in business to feed other people's children." Father called him a foolish young idealist. Perhaps I am, he thought. Perhaps Jesus was, too.

He enjoyed the lively Bible study discussions at the Methodist Hall because he could give his opinion and be listened to with courtesy and respect, instead of being told to keep quiet and believe what was said by the clergy, or by older men, or by his father. And there was a bonus. A lot of people his own age went to the meetings, so the Methodist Hall was unintentionally a sort of club for respectable youth. A lot of pretty girls attended.

Tonight he was hoping to see one girl in particular. Her name was Jane Midwinter, and in his opinion she was the prettiest of all. He thought about her a lot when he was riding around the countryside with nothing to look at but fields. She seemed to like him, but he was not sure.

He went into the hall. It was about as different from the cathedral as possible—which was probably deliberate. There were no statues or paintings, no stained glass, no jeweled silverware. Chairs and benches were the only furniture. God's clear light came through the windows and was reflected by pale painted walls. In the cathedral, the holy hush was broken by the ethereal singing of the choir or the drone of a clergyman, but here anyone could speak, pray, or propose a hymn. They sang loudly, with no accompaniment, as Methodists usually did. There was an exuberance about their worship that was quite absent from Anglican services.

He scanned the room and saw, to his delight, that Jane was already here. Her pale skin and black eyebrows made his heart beat faster. She wore a cashmere dress the same delicate shade of gray as her eyes. But unfortunately the seats either side of her were already taken by her girlfriends.

Amos was greeted by her father, the leader of the Kingsbridge Methodists, Canon Charles Midwinter, handsome and charismatic, with thick gray hair he wore long. A canon was a clergyman who served on the chapter, the governing committee of the cathedral. The bishop of Kingsbridge tolerated Canon Midwinter's Methodism, albeit reluctantly. The reluctance was natural, Amos thought: a bishop was bound to feel criticized by a movement that said the church needed to be reformed.

Canon Midwinter shook Amos's hand and said: "How is your father?"

"No better, but no worse," Amos said. "He gets breathless and has to avoid lifting bales of cloth."

"He should probably retire and hand over to you."

"I wish he would."

"But it's hard for someone who has been master for so long to give it up."

Amos was focused on his own discontent, and he had not considered that the situation might be a trial for his father, too. He felt slightly ashamed. Canon Midwinter had a way of showing you yourself in a mirror. It was more telling than a sermon on sin.

He moved nearer to Jane and sat on a bench next to Rupe Underwood, who was a bit older at twenty-five. Rupe was a ribbon maker, a good business when people had money to spend, not so much otherwise. "It's going to snow," said Rupe.

"I hope not. I've got to ride to Lordsborough tomorrow."

"Wear two pairs of stockings."

Amos could not take a day off, regardless of the weather. The whole system depended on his moving the material around. He had to go, and freeze if necessary.

Before Amos could get any closer to Jane, Canon Midwinter opened the discussion by reading the Beatitudes from the Gospel of Matthew. "Blessed are the poor in spirit, for theirs is the kingdom of heaven." To Amos this statement by Jesus seemed mystical, and he had never really made sense of it. He listened attentively and enjoyed the to-and-fro argument, but he felt too baffled to make a contribution of his own. It will give me something to mull over tomorrow, on the road, he thought; a change from thinking about Jane.

Afterward tea was served, with milk and sugar, in plain earthenware cups with saucers. The Methodists loved tea, a drink that never made you violent or stupid or lustful, no matter how many cups you drank.

Amos looked for Jane and saw that she had already been buttonholed by Rupe. Rupe had a long blond forelock, and every now and again he would toss his head to get his hair out of his eyes, a gesture that somehow irritated Amos.

He noticed Jane's shoes, sober black leather but with a ribbon tied in a big bow instead of laces, and a raised heel that made her an inch or two taller. He saw her laugh at something Rupe said, and pat his chest in a mock reprimand. Did she prefer Rupe to Amos? He hoped not.

While waiting for Jane to be free he talked to David Shoveller, known as Spade. He was thirty, a highly skilled weaver of specialty cloths that sold for high prices. He employed several people, including other weavers. Like Amos, he wore clothes that advertised his products, and today he had on a tweed coat in a blue-gray weave with flecks of red and yellow.

Amos liked to ask Spade's advice: the man was smart without being condescending. Amos told him about the yarn problem.

"There's a shortage," Spade said. "Not just in Kingsbridge, but all over." Spade read newspapers and journals, and consequently was well-informed.

Amos was puzzled. "How could something like that happen?"

"I'll tell you," said Spade. He sipped hot tea while he gathered his thoughts. "There's an invention called the flying shuttle. You pull a lever and the shuttle leaps from one side of the loom to the other. It enables the weaver to work about twice as fast."

Amos had heard of it. "I thought it hadn't caught on."

"Not here. I use them, but most weavers in the west of England won't. They think the devil moves the shuttle. However, it's popular in Yorkshire."

"My father said a Yorkshireman bought all the yarn at the last auction."

"Now you know why. Double the cloth requires double the yarn. But we make yarn on a spinning wheel, the way it's been done since I don't know when, probably before Noah built his ark."

"So we need more spinners. Are you short of yarn, too?"

"I saw this problem coming up the road, and I laid in a stock. I'm surprised your father didn't do the same. Obadiah was always farsighted."

"Not anymore," said Amos, and he turned away, for he had seen that Jane was no longer talking to Rupe, and he was eager to catch her before another boy moved in. He crossed the hall in a few strides, carrying his cup and saucer, and said: "Good evening, Jane."

"Hello, Amos. Wasn't that an interesting discussion?"

He did not want to talk about the Beatitudes. "I love that dress."

"Thank you."

"It's the same color as your eyes."

She tilted her head to the side and smiled, a characteristic pose that made his mouth go dry with desire. She said: "Fancy you noticing my eyes."

"Is that unusual?"

"Many men don't know the color of their own wives' eyes."

Amos laughed. "That's hard to imagine. Can I ask you something?"

"Yes, although I may not answer."

"Would you walk out with me?"

She smiled again, but shook her head, and he knew at once that his dreams were doomed. "I like you," she said. "You're sweet."

He did not want to be sweet. He had a feeling that girls did not fall for boys who were sweet.

She went on: "But I don't want to grow fond of a boy who has nothing to offer but hopes."

He did not know what to say. He did not think of himself as one who had nothing but hopes, and he was shocked that she saw him that way.

She said: "We're Methodists, so we must tell the truth. I'm sorry."

They looked at each other a moment longer, then she put her hand on his arm lightly, a gesture of sympathy; and she turned away.

Amos went home.

CHAPTER 6

Kit was awakened at five o'clock by Fanny the thirteen-year-old maid. She was skinny and spotty, with thin mousy hair tucked into a dirty white cap, but she was kind to Kit and showed him how to do everything, and he adored her. He called her Fan.

This morning she had bad news. "Mr. Will is back."

"Oh, no!"

"He arrived late last night."

Kit was dismayed. Will Riddick hated him and was mean to him whenever he got the chance. When Will had gone to Kingsbridge, Kit had thanked God. Will had been away for six blessed weeks, doing something with the militia. Now the reprieve was over.

Will was not an early riser, so Kit was safe for a few hours, probably.

Kit and Fan dressed quickly and moved quietly through the cold dark house, lighting their way with a rush lamp that Fan carried. Kit would have been scared of the shadows in the high rooms, but he felt safe with her.

Her first duty was to clean the downstairs fireplaces, and his to clean the boots; but they liked working together so they shared both tasks. They removed the cold ashes from the fireplaces, rubbed blacklead onto the ironwork with rags and buffed it to a shine, then made up the fires with tinder and wood ready to be lit as soon as the family got up.

They talked in low voices while they worked. Fan's family had all caught a fever six winters ago, and she was the only survivor. She told Kit that she was lucky to have this job. They had food and clothes and somewhere to sleep. She did not know what might have happened to her otherwise.

After hearing her story Kit did not pity himself quite as much. After all, he still had a mother.

When they had finished the fireplaces they went along the bedroom corridor picking up the boots and then took the back stairs down to the boot room. They had to clean off the mud, apply dubbin mixed with lampblack, and shine the leather to a high gloss. Kit's arms quickly ached with the rubbing, but Fan had shown him the easy way to get a shine, by spitting on the boots. However, his arms were much weaker than hers, and she usually finished the job for him.

When the family appeared for breakfast they could go into the bedrooms. Each one had a fireplace and a chamber pot with a lid. First they cleaned the grate and built the fire, just as they had in the ground-floor rooms, then Kit carried the chamber pot downstairs, sluiced it out in the scullery, washed it, and returned it to the bedroom, while Fan made the bed and tidied up. Then they moved to the next bedroom.

Today they did not get through their work.

The trouble occurred in Will's room. He was the last to get up, so they left his room to the end. They worked quickly, now that Kit was used to it, and they were usually finished well before Will came back upstairs.

But not today.

Fan was buffing the ironwork, and Kit had just picked up the chamber pot, when Will walked in. He was dressed for riding, with his crop in his hand, and he had evidently forgotten his hat, for he picked it up from the dresser.

Then he noticed them and made a surprised noise, almost as if he had been frightened.

After a moment he recovered and shouted: "What are you two doing in here?" He knew perfectly well what they were doing, but he was angry because he had been startled.

They were so scared that Fan knocked over the bottle of blacklead, staining the rug, and Kit dropped the chamber pot, spilling its contents. He stared in horror at the mess he had made, a wide puddle with three brown turds in the middle.

"You idiots!" Will roared. When he was angry his eyes bulged so much they looked as if they would burst. He seized Kit by the arm and whacked his rear with the riding crop. Kit yelled in pain and tried to struggle free, but Will was far too strong.

Will hit him again and he sobbed in despair.

Fan screeched: "Leave him alone!" and threw herself at Will.

Will shoved Kit to the floor and grabbed Fan. "Oh, you want some, too, do you?" Will said, and Kit heard the swish of the whip and the thwack as it struck her. He got up and saw Will pull up Fan's dress and start flogging her skinny bottom.

Kit wanted to defend Fan as bravely as she had defended him, but he was too scared, and all he could do was cry.

A new voice said: "What on earth is going on? Will, what do you think you're doing?"

It was Will's brother Roger. Will stopped thrashing Fan and turned to him. "Stay out of this."

Roger said: "Leave the children alone, you stupid great ox."

"If you're not careful I'll lash you, too."

Roger did not seem frightened, even though he was small and slight where Will was big and strong. "You could try," he said with a smile. "At least it would be a fairer fight than this. Do you like whipping little girls' bottoms?"

"Don't be a damned fool."

Although they were arguing, Kit could see that Will was calming down. Kit felt passionately grateful to Roger for saving him and Fan. Will might have killed them both.

Roger said to Will: "I don't understand why you would beat these wretched infants with all your might."

"Children need to be chastised, everyone says so. It makes them obedient. The girls need it most—it turns them into respectable wives who venerate their husbands."

"You know nothing about wives, you idiot. Come and have some breakfast—it might improve your temper."

Will looked at Kit and Fan, and Kit shuddered with fear; but all Will said was: "Clean up this mess or I'll beat you again."

In terrified voices they both said: "Yes, Mr. Riddick."

Will went out and Roger followed.

Kit ran to Fan and buried his face in her dress, shaking. She put her arms around him and hugged him. "Never mind, never mind," she said. "It will stop hurting in a minute."

He tried to be brave. "I think it's getting better already."

She released her embrace. "Come on, then," she said. "Let's clean up."

On Sunday afternoon he saw his mother.

When the Riddick family's dinner had been cleared away the servants were free until bedtime. Ma was waiting for him at the back door of the manor as usual. He threw himself into her arms and hugged her fervently, burying his head in her soft bosom. Then he held her hand as they walked through the village.

When they reached the house they sat at her spinning wheel, as in the old days, just the two of them. He passed her the ropes of scribbled wool and she eased them into the mechanism while turning the wheel. On the floor were spindles of finished yarn, and Kit said: "You've done a lot—Amos will be pleased with you."

She said: "Tell me what you've been doing."

As they worked, he told her everything that had happened in the week: the jobs he had done, the food he had eaten, the times he had been happy and the times he had been scared. She got so cross about Will Riddick that he quickly started talking about Fan and how kind she was. He loved her, he said, and when they were grown up he was going to marry her.

Ma smiled. "We'll see," she said. "You used to say you would marry me."

"That's silly. You can't marry your mother, everyone knows that."

"You didn't know it when you were three years old."

Talking to her on Sundays made him feel better about the rest of the week. He hated Will, but most of the people in the house were neither kind nor cruel, and Roger and Fan were on his side. He worshipped Roger.

He felt quite grown-up already as he told Ma how he cleaned and polished, especially when she said: "Why, you're a proper little worker!"

The afternoon flew by too fast. She usually had a little treat for him: a slice of ham, a mug of fresh milk, an orange. Today she gave him a piece of toast with honey.

The taste stayed in his mouth while they walked back in the evening. As they drew near to the manor house, and he realized he would not see his mother for another week, he began to cry. "Come on, now," she said. "You're nearly seven. You must act like a little man, because that's what you are."

He did his best, but the tears kept coming.

At the back door he clung to her. She hugged him for a long moment, then she detached his arms, pushed him through the door, and closed it behind him.

Kit's job on Monday morning was to clean and polish the saddles and other riding tack. Some of it got dirty in use, and all of it had to be rubbed with dubbin to keep the leather supple and waterproof. Kit did the work in the scullery while Fan swept carpets upstairs. The saddles were heavy and Kit had to carry them one by one across the stable yard.

He did not like horses. They scared him. He had never seen either of his parents on horseback.

The squire and his sons had nine beasts in the stable. Squire Riddick drove about in a cabriolet, a two-wheeled cart with a hood, drawn by a sturdy pony. Both Rector George and Mr. Roger had their own horses, a big mare for the rector and a light-footed gelding for Roger. Will preferred big, fast hunters, and he had two, one a recent acquisition, a dark bay stallion called Steel. There were also four carthorses.

Kit had a bundle of leather straps in his hands when he stepped into the yard and saw Steel standing by the mounting block. An old groom called Nobby was holding the bridle to keep the beast still. It was a difficult task: the horse was restive, tossing its head as if to throw off the bridle. Its eyes were wide, its teeth bared, and its ears pinned back. Its tail swished rapidly, and its front legs were splayed as if it was about to dart forward.

Kit headed across the yard, giving the beast a wide berth.

Will was on the block with one foot in a stirrup and the reins in his hand, about to mount, and Roger was watching. Roger said: "I'd lead him around the meadow at a slow walk for a few minutes, to calm him down. He's in a bad mood."

"Nonsense," said Will. "He's just high-spirited. He wants to be ridden hard for half an hour. That'll calm him." He swung his leg over the back of the horse. "Open the gate, Nobby."

As soon as Nobby let go of the bridle, Steel began to step nervously sideways. Will hauled on the reins, shouting: "Stand still, you devil." The horse ignored orders and stepped backward.

Suddenly the horse was near Kit.

Roger shouted: "Look out, Kit!"

Kit froze in terror.

Will, sawing at the reins, looked back over his shoulder and yelled: "Get out of the damned way, you stupid boy!"

Kit turned, took two steps, and slipped in a pile of horse manure, dropping the straps. He fell to the ground. He saw Roger running to him, but Steel's hind legs were closer. Will was yelling incoherently and deploying his crop, and Nobby was trying to catch hold of the bridle, but the horse kept coming.

With Steel almost on top of him, Kit got to his hands and knees. Then he saw Steel's leg fly out. The iron horseshoe hit Kit on the head.

There was a terrible pain, then he blacked out.

The next thing Kit knew was an agonizing headache. Nothing in his short life had hurt this much. At the same time he heard a man's voice say: "The boy's lucky to be alive."

He began to whimper because of the pain, and the voice said: "He's coming round."

Kit opened his eyes and saw Alec Pollock, the surgeon, in his well-worn black tailcoat. "My head hurts," Kit sobbed.

"Sit up and drink this," Alec said. "It's Godfrey's Cordial. There's laudanum in it to ease the pain."

Another man approached the bed, and Kit recognized the blond hair and pink face of Roger, who put an arm under his shoulders and gently lifted him into a sitting position. The movement made the headache worse.

Alec held a cup to Kit's mouth, saying: "Careful, don't spill any—laudanum is costly."

Kit drank. He did not know what laudanum was but the drink seemed to be warm milk. Perhaps Alec had put something in it, like sugar in tea.

"Lie back, now, and keep as still as you can."

Kit did as he was told. His head still hurt but he felt calmer and stopped crying.

Alec said: "Do you know what happened to you?"

"I dropped all the straps! I didn't mean to. I'm sorry."

"And what happened then?"

"I think Steel kicked me."

"It's good that you remember. How does your head feel now?"

Kit was surprised to realize that the pain was less. "Not as bad as it was."

"That's the effect of the drink I gave you."

"Am I in trouble for dropping the straps?"

Roger said: "No, Kit, you aren't in trouble. It wasn't your fault."

"Oh, good."

Alec said: "Now listen to me while I explain something."

"Yes, sir."

"The bone in your head is called your skull. I think Steel's kick probably caused a small crack in it. It will heal if you can keep really still for the next six weeks."

Six weeks was such a long time that Kit could hardly imagine lying still that long.

"Fan will bring you food, and when you need to shit and piss she'll bring a special bowl that you can use without getting out of bed."

Kit looked around him for the first time. This was not the drab attic bedroom where he normally shared a bed with Platts and Cecil. There the sheets were gray and the walls were painted green. This room had flower-patterned wallpaper, and the sheets were white. "Where am I?" he said.

Roger said: "This is the guest bedroom."

"In the manor house?"

"Yes."

"Why am I in here?"

"Because you've been injured. You have to stay here until you're well again."

Kit felt uneasy. He was being treated like a guest. He wondered what the squire thought of that. He said anxiously: "But I have to clean the boots!"

Roger laughed. "Fanny will do that."

"Fan can't do it, she has too much work already."

"Don't worry, Kit," said Roger. "We'll work things out, and Fanny will be fine."

He seemed to think there was something humorous about Kit's anxiety, so Kit said no more about it. He thought of something else. "Can I go and see my mother?"

Alec answered: "Certainly not. No unnecessary movement."

Roger said: "But your mother will come and see you. I'll make sure of that."

"Yes, please," said Kit. "I really want to see her, please."

CHAPTER 7

Amos dreamed he was having an intense, intimate talk with Jane Midwinter. Their heads were excitingly close, they spoke in low tones, and the subject of their conversation was something deeply personal. He had a warm, happy feeling. Then Rupe Underwood came up behind him and tried to get his attention. Amos did not want to end this special moment with Jane, and at first he ignored Rupe, but Rupe shook his shoulder. Then he knew that he was dreaming, but he so badly wanted the dream to continue that he tried to ignore the shaking. It did not work, and he left the dream with the sadness of a banished angel falling to earth.

His mother's voice said: "Amos, wake up."

It was still dark. Mother did not normally wake him in the morning. He always got up in good time for whatever he had to do, and he usually left the house while she was still in bed. And anyway, he remembered, today was Sunday.

He opened his eyes and sat up. She stood fully dressed by the bed with a candle. He said: "What's the time?"

She began to cry. "Amos, my dear son," she said. "Your father has passed away."

His first reaction was incredulity. "But he was fine last night at supper!"

"I know." She wiped her nose with her sleeve, something she would never do in normal circumstances.

That convinced him. "What happened?"

"I woke up, I don't know why. Perhaps he made a noise . . . or somehow I just knew. I spoke to him but he didn't answer. I lit the bedside candle so that I could see him. He was lying on his back with his eyes open, staring up. He wasn't breathing."

It struck Amos that to wake up next to a corpse must be a dreadful experience. "Poor Mother." He took her hand.

She wanted to tell him the whole story. "I got Ellen up and we washed his body." They must have been quiet about it, Amos thought; but anyway he was a heavy sleeper. "We wrapped him in a shroud and put pennies on his eyelids to close his eyes. Then I washed myself and got dressed. And I came to tell you."

Amos threw back the blankets and got up in his nightshirt. "I want to see him."

She nodded, as if this was what she expected.

They went together across the landing to the parental bedroom.

Father lay on the four-poster bed with his head on a spotless white pillow, his hair combed, his body covered with a blanket tightly tucked in, neater in death than he had been in life. Amos had heard people describe a corpse as looking so well that the person might still have been alive, but this was not the case here. Father was gone, and Amos was seeing a shell, and somehow that was horribly obvious. Amos could not have said what it was about the face that gave him that impression, but there was no room for doubt. Death was unmistakable.

He was seized by a feeling of grief so strong that he burst out crying. He sobbed loudly and shed a waterfall of tears. At the same time a part of his mind asked why he felt this way. His father had been unkind and ungenerous to him, and had treated him like a carthorse, a beast of burden valued only for its usefulness. And yet he was bereft, weeping uncontrollably. He wiped his face repeatedly but the tears kept flowing.

When at last the storm subsided his mother said: "Get dressed now, and come to the kitchen for a cup of tea. There's a lot to do, and doing things will help us bear our loss."

He nodded and let himself be led out of the room. Back in his own bedroom he began to dress. Thoughtlessly, he started putting on his everyday clothes, and he had to take them off and start again. He chose a dark gray coat with a waistcoat and a black neckcloth. The routine of tying and buttoning soothed him, and his self-control had returned by the time he appeared in the kitchen.

He sat at the table. Mother handed him a cup of tea and said: "We must think about the funeral. I'd like the service to be in the cathedral. Your father was an important man in Kingsbridge, he merits it."

"Shall I ask the bishop?"

"If you would."

"Of course."

Ellen set a plate of buttered toast in front of Amos. He had not thought he wanted to eat anything, but the smell made his mouth water. He took a slice and ate it quickly, then said: "What about the wake?"

"Ellen and I can manage that."

Ellen said: "With a bit of extra help, perhaps."

Mother added: "But I'll need some money from the safe."

"I'll see to that," said Amos. "I know where the key is." He ate more toast.

She gave a watery smile. "It's your money, now, I suppose. And the business is yours, too."

"As I'm only nineteen, I imagine it's yours, at least until I turn twenty-one."

She shrugged. "You're the man of the house."

He was—sooner than expected. He had long been impatient to take charge, but now he felt no thrill of satisfaction. Rather, he was daunted by the prospect of running the enterprise without the benefit of his father's knowledge and experience.

He reached for another piece of toast but it was all gone.

Day was breaking outside. Mother said: "Ellen, go

round the house and make sure all the curtains are drawn." That would serve as a sign to passersby that there had been a death in the house. "I'll cover the mirrors," she said. That, too, was customary, although Amos did not know why.

"We need to start telling people," Amos said. He thought of the mayor and the editor of the *Kingsbridge Gazette*. "I should probably see the bishop now, if it's not too early."

"He will consider it a courtesy to be informed first," said Mother. "He's fussy about that sort of thing."

Amos put on an overcoat and stepped out into the cold Sunday morning. His father's house—his house, now—was on the High Street. He walked to the crossroads of High Street and Main Street, the commercial center of the town, its four corners occupied by the wool exchange, the Guild Hall, the Assembly Rooms, and the Kingsbridge Theatre. There he turned into Main Street and walked downhill, past the cathedral. Its graveyard was on the north side. Soon Father's body would lie there, but his soul was already in heaven.

The bishop's palace, opposite the Bell Inn, was a grand house with tall windows and an elaborate porch, all built in stone from the quarry that had supplied the cathedral builders. Amos recognized the middle-aged maid who let him into the hall, Linda Mason. "Hello, Linda, I need to see the bishop."

"He's resting after the early morning service," she said. "Can I tell him what it's about?"

"My father died in the night."

"Oh! Amos, I'm so sorry."

"Thank you."

"I'll let the bishop know you're here. Sit by the fire."

He pulled a chair up to the coal fire and looked around the hall. It was tastefully decorated in light colors, with several bland paintings of landscapes. There were no religious images, probably because they smacked a bit of Catholicism.

A minute later the bishop's daughter, Elsie, appeared. Amos smiled, pleased to see her. She was bright and strong-willed, and they were planning the Sunday school together. He liked her, though she did not have the irresistible allure of Jane Midwinter. Elsie was quite plain, with a wide mouth and a big nose, but—as he was now reminded—she did have an enchanting smile. She said: "Hello, Mr. Barrowfield, what are you doing here?"

"I've come to see the bishop," he said. "My father has died."

She gave a squeeze of sympathy to his upper arm. "How sad for you. And for your mother."

He nodded. "They were married for twenty years."

"The longer you're together, the worse it must be."

"I suppose so. I haven't seen you for a few days. What news of the Sunday school?"

"People seem to think it will just be me in a small room teaching twelve children to read. I want to do more than that—to have more children, maybe a hundred, and to teach them writing and arithmetic, too. And we must give them a treat to attract them—perhaps some cake at the end."

"I agree. When can we start?"

"I'm not sure exactly, but soon. Here comes my father."

The bishop came down the wide staircase in his full Sunday regalia. Elsie said: "Father, Amos Barrowfield is here. His father, Obadiah, has died."

"Mason told me." The bishop shook Amos's hand. "A sad day for you, Mr. Barrowfield," he said in a resonant voice, as if he were preaching. "But we can comfort one another with the knowledge that your father is with Christ, which is far better, as we're told by the apostle Paul."

"Thank you, Your Grace," said Amos. "My mother wanted you to be the first person to know."

"That was thoughtful of her."

"And she told me to ask you whether the funeral might be held in the cathedral."

"I would think so. An alderman and a regular churchgoer is entitled. I must check with my clerical confreres, but I foresee no problem."

"My mother will be much consoled."

"Good. And now I must conduct household prayers. Come, Elsie."

The bishop and his daughter went into the dining room, and Amos let himself out by the front door.

Two days later Amos and five clothiers, all wearing black hats, carried the bier from the house along High Street and down Main Street and into the cathedral, where they laid it on trestles that stood in front of the altar.

Amos was surprised by the crowd in the nave. More than a hundred people had come, maybe two hundred. Jane was among them, which pleased him.

Amos had mixed feelings about the cathedral. Methodists disliked the pomp of the traditional church, the robes and jeweled ornaments; they preferred to worship in a simple room with plain decoration. The focus was what went on in the mind of the believer. Despite that, Amos always felt uplifted by the cathedral's great pillars and soaring vaults. The only thing he really disliked about the Church of England was its dogmatic attitude. The clergy thought he should believe what he was told to believe, whereas the Methodists respected his right to his opinion.

The church had the same attitude as his father, who now lay in the coffin.

He was free of his father's tyranny at last, he thought as the service began, but the freedom brought anxiety. He had to be in Kingsbridge to meet customers and purchase wool, so he needed someone to take over his rounds. He planned to stockpile materials so that he would not be thrown off course by unexpected shortages, but that was not a simple matter, for he would need to buy when prices were low. He wanted to expand the business, but he did not know where he would find more craftspeople, especially spinners. I need help, he thought, now that the old man is gone. I didn't expect this.

He was so absorbed in his worries that the end of the service surprised him, and it took him a moment to realize that he had to help pick up the coffin.

They carried Obadiah down the nave, out through the great west door, and around to the north side of the church where the graveyard was. They continued past the monumental tomb of Prior Philip, the monk responsible for building the cathedral more than six hundred years ago. They came to a halt at the new grave.

The sight of the deep hole and the pile of loose soil beside it struck Amos forcefully. There was nothing unusual or unexpected about the sight; what shocked him was the thought that his father's body would lie in this cold muddy pit until the Day of Judgment.

There was another prayer, and they lowered the coffin into the grave.

Amos took a handful of earth from the pile. He stood at the edge of the grave for a moment, looking down, struck by the grim finality of what he was about to do. Then he trickled the earth from his hand onto the coffin. When it was all gone he turned away.

His mother, sobbing loudly, did the same, picking up a handful of earth and dropping it into the grave, then she walked unsteadily away. As the other mourners lined up for their turn, Mother grabbed Amos's arm and said: "Take me home."

Ellen had transformed the house for a big gathering. There was a barrel of ale in the hall, together with dozens of earthenware tankards, and the dining room table was covered with cakes, tarts, cheesecakes, and treacle bread. Upstairs the drawing room had been prepared for the more important guests, and there was sherry,

Madeira, and claret with more refined snacks: venison pasties, salted fish, rabbit pie, and prawns.

Seeing all this, Mother pulled herself together. She took off her coat and set about making everything just right. Amos prepared to welcome the guests, and it was only a couple of minutes before they began to arrive. He shook hands, thanked people for their condolences, urged the ordinary guests to help themselves to ale, and directed the special ones upstairs, including Canon Midwinter and Jane. He began to feel like a weaver, repeating the same actions again and again until they became almost unconscious.

Everyone was talking about France. The revolutionaries had beheaded King Louis XVI, and then had declared war on England. Spade said that most of the regular British Army was in either India or the Caribbean. The Shiring Militia drilled every day now in the fields on the outskirts of Kingsbridge.

Amos was keen to talk to Jane, and when the guests began to leave he sought her out. He thought she might take him more seriously now that he owned a business. She was practical, which was a good thing in a wife, he told himself, even if it was not very romantic.

He went upstairs and found her on the landing. Her dress was made of a lustrous black flannel that was strikingly glamorous with her black hair. "I dreamed about you," he said, speaking quietly so that others could not hear.

She looked at him with those gray eyes, and as always he felt helpless. "A good dream?" she said. "Or a nightmare?"

"It was very good. I didn't want it to end."

She opened her eyes wide, making a startled face. "I hope you behaved respectably in this dream!"

"Oh, yes. We just talked, as we are now, but it was . . . I don't know. Perfect."

"What did we talk about?"

"I'm not sure, but it seemed to be something we both cared about a lot."

"I can't imagine . . ." She shrugged. "How did it end?"

"I woke up."

"That's the trouble with dreams."

As always with her he wished he did not have to talk so that he could concentrate on looking at her. She did not have to do anything: she bewitched him without trying. He said: "My world has turned upside down since the last time I talked to you."

"I'm very sorry about your father."

"He and I have quarreled a lot in the last year or two, but I'm surprised at how sad I am to lose him."

"That's how it is with families. Even if you hate them, you love them."

That was wise, he thought; like something her father might have said.

He did not know how to ask the question he wanted to put to her. He decided to come right out with it. "Would you walk out with me?"

"You asked me that already," she said. "And I answered you."

That was discouraging, but on the other hand it fell short of outright rejection. "I thought you might have changed your mind," he said.

"Why would I have changed my mind?"

"Because I'm no longer a boy with nothing to offer but hopes."

She frowned. "But you are."

"No." He shook his head. "I own a profitable business. And I have a house. I could get married tomorrow."

"But your business is deep in debt."

He was not expecting that. He took a step back, as if he had been threatened. "Debt? No, it's not."

"My father says it is."

Amos was astonished. Canon Midwinter did not repeat idle gossip. "How come?" he said. "How much? Who to?"

"You didn't know?"

"I still don't know."

"I can't tell you why, and I don't know how much

money was lent, but I do know who it's owed to: Alderman Hornbeam."

Amos was still mystified. He knew Hornbeam, of course; everyone did. He had come to the wake, and Amos had seen him talking to his friend Humphrey Frogmore a minute ago. Hornbeam had come to Kingsbridge fifteen years ago. He had bought the cloth business belonging to Canon Midwinter's father-in-law, Alderman Drinkwater, and had turned it into the biggest enterprise in town. Obadiah had respected him as a hard-nosed businessman without much liking him. "Why would my father have borrowed money from him? From anybody?"

"I don't know."

Amos looked around for a tall, frowning figure in sober but costly clothing, a curly light-brown wig his only concession to vanity.

Jane said: "He was here, but I'm pretty sure he left."

"I'll go after him."

"Amos, wait."

"Why?"

"Because he's not a kind man. When you talk to him about this you should be armed with all the information."

Amos forced himself to stand still and think. "You're absolutely right," he said after a moment. "Thank you."

"Wait until your guests have left. Help your mother put the house straight. Find out the truth about your finances. And then go to see Hornbeam."

"That's exactly what I'll do," said Amos.

Jane left with her father, but some of the guests lingered, keeping Amos from what he urgently needed to do. A downstairs group seemed determined to stay until the barrel was empty. Amos's mother and Ellen began to clear away around them, taking away the used crockery and the remaining food. Finally Amos politely asked the last stragglers to go home.

Then he went to the office.

In the two days since his father died he had been too

busy with funeral arrangements to look at the books. Now he wished he had made time.

The office was as familiar to him as every other part of the house, but he now realized he did not know where to find everything. There were invoices and receipts in drawers and in boxes on the floor. A notebook had names and addresses, in Kingsbridge and elsewhere, with no indication of whether the people were customers, suppliers, or something else. A sideboard bore a dozen or so heavy ledgers, some upright and some lying flat, none titled. Any time he had asked his father a question about money he had been told that he did not need to bother about that until he was twenty-one.

He started with the ledgers, picking one at random. It was not difficult to understand. It showed money received and money paid out day by day, and totaled at the end of every month. Most months, receipts exceeded spending, so a profit was made. Occasionally there would be a loss. Turning to the first page, he saw that it was dated seven years ago.

He found the most recent ledger. Checking the monthly totals, he saw that receipts were usually less than costs. He frowned. How was this possible? He went back over the last two years and saw that losses had been increasing gradually. But there were several large receipts mysteriously labeled: "From H. account." They were round figures—ten pounds, fifteen pounds, twenty—but each roughly balanced the deficit of the previous few months. And there were regular small amounts marked: "Int. 5%."

A picture was forming, and it was very worrying indeed.

On a hunch he turned to the back page of the most recent book and found a short column headed: "H. Account." It began eighteen months ago. Each entry corresponded to an entry in the monthly figures. Most of the numbers on the back page were negative.

Amos was appalled.

Father had been losing money for two years. He had borrowed to make up his losses. Two positive entries on the back page showed that he had paid some of the money back, but had soon been forced to borrow again.

"Int." meant interest, and "H." had to be Hornbeam. Jane had been right.

The balance at the foot of the back page was one hundred and four pounds, thirteen shillings, and eight pence.

Amos was devastated. He had thought he was inheriting a viable business, but he had been landed with a massive debt. A hundred pounds was the purchase price of a fine house in Kingsbridge.

He had to pay it back. To Amos, it was wicked and shameful to owe money and not pay. He could hardly live with himself if he became that kind of person.

If he could turn the losses into a modest profit of a pound a month it would still take him almost nine years to pay off the debt—and that would be without buying food for himself and his mother.

This explained his father's meanness and secrecy in recent years. Obadiah had been keeping his losses hidden—perhaps in the hope of turning the business around, although he seemed to have done little to that purpose. Or maybe the illness that had shown itself in shortness of breath had also affected his mind.

Amos would find out more from Hornbeam. But he could not just ask Hornbeam questions. He needed to reassure Hornbeam that the debt would be paid just as fast as possible. He had to impress Hornbeam with his determination.

And it was not just Hornbeam he had to worry about. Other Kingsbridge businessmen would be watching him. Having known his father, and having seen Amos prove himself a competent assistant, they would look kindly on him, at least at first. But if he began by going bankrupt their friendship would melt away. It was important that everyone should know how hard Amos was working to pay his father's debts.

Would Hornbeam be understanding, despite his stern demeanor? He had tried to help Obadiah cope with business difficulties, which was a good sign—although he had charged interest, of course. And he had known Amos since childhood, which ought to count for something.

Braced by that optimistic thought, Amos left the office by the street door and headed for the Hornbeam residence.

It was north of the High Street, near St. Mark's Church, in a formerly run-down neighborhood where old cheap terraces had been flattened to make room for large new houses with stables. Hornbeam's place had symmetrical windows and a portico with marble columns. Amos recalled his father saying that Hornbeam hired a cheap Bristol architect, gave him a pattern book of Robert Adam's designs, and demanded a low-cost version of a classical palace. To one side and slightly behind the main building was a stable yard where a carriage was being washed by a shivering groom.

A footman opened the door. He had a lugubrious look, and when Amos asked for Alderman Hornbeam the man said: "I'll see if he's in, sir," in a mournful voice.

Stepping inside, Amos immediately felt the atmosphere of the house: dark, formal, strict. A tall clock ticked loudly in the hall, and a couple of straight-backed chairs made of polished oak offered scant comfort. There was no carpet. Above a cold fireplace, in a gilt frame, was a portrait of Hornbeam, looking stern.

While he was waiting Hornbeam's son, Howard, appeared from a basement staircase like a family secret coming to light. He was a big fellow, affable enough when away from his father. Amos and Howard had been together at Kingsbridge Grammar School; Howard was a couple of years younger and something of a dunce. The father's brains and forceful personality had been inherited by his younger child, Deborah, who had not been allowed to attend the grammar school, of course.

Howard greeted Amos and they shook hands. The doleful footman reappeared and said Mr. Hornbeam would see Amos. Howard said: "I'll take him there, Simpson." He led Amos to a door at the back of the hall and showed him into Hornbeam's study, then withdrew.

The room was like a cell: no rugs, no pictures, no draperies, and a mean fire in the small fireplace. Hornbeam sat behind a desk, still wearing his funeral clothes. He was in his late thirties, with a fleshy face and heavy eyebrows. He hastily took off a pair of spectacles, as if embarrassed to need them. He did not ask Amos to sit down.

Amos was not a complete stranger to hostility, and he was not intimidated by Hornbeam's coolness. He had met disgruntled weavers and spinners, and unhappy customers, and he knew they could be mollified. He said: "Thank you for coming to my father's funeral, sir."

Hornbeam was socially awkward, and now he shrugged, an inappropriate response. He said: "We were both aldermen." After a moment he added: "And friends."

He did not offer tea or wine.

Standing in front of the desk like a misbehaving schoolboy, Amos said: "I've come to see you because I've just learned that Father had been borrowing money from you. He never told me."

Hornbeam just said: "A hundred and four pounds."

Amos smiled. "And thirteen shillings and eight pence."

Hornbeam did not smile back. "Yes."

"Thank you for helping him in his hour of need."

Hornbeam did not want to be seen as dispensing largesse. "I'm not a philanthropist. I charged him interest."

"At five percent." For a risky personal loan it was not extortionate.

Hornbeam clearly did not know what to say to that, so he just inclined his head in acknowledgment.

Amos realized that his charm was ineffective against Hornbeam's flinty indifference. He said: "However, it's now my duty to repay the loan."

"Indeed it is."

"I didn't create the problem, but I must solve it."

"Go on."

Amos collected his thoughts. He had a plan, and it was a good one, he thought. Perhaps it was good enough to overcome Hornbeam's irascibility. "First, I have to make the business profitable, so that no more loans will be required. Father had accumulated old stock that had been unpopular with customers: I will drop the price to get rid of it. And I want to concentrate on finer cloths that can be sold for higher prices. That way I believe I can turn a profit in a year. I hope to begin repayments on New Year's Day in 1794."

"Do you."

This was not an encouraging response. Hornbeam should surely have been happier to know he was going to get his money back. But he had always been taciturn.

Amos plowed on. "Then I hope to make the business even more profitable so that I can increase the speed of repayment."

"And how would you do that?"

"By expansion, mainly. I will look for more spinners, so that I have a reliable supply of yarn, and then more weavers."

Hornbeam nodded, almost as if he approved, and Amos felt a little better.

In the hope of getting a clearer endorsement he said: "I hope you feel my plan is practical."

Hornbeam did not answer that, but instead asked a question. "When do you expect to clear the debt?"

"I believe I can do it in four years."

There was a long pause, then Hornbeam said: "You have four days."

Amos did not understand. "What do you mean?"

"What I say. I give you four days to pay me back."

"But . . . I've just explained to you—"

"And now I will explain to you."

Amos had a very bad feeling, but he bit his tongue and just said: "Please do."

"I didn't lend money to you, I lent it to your father. I knew him and trusted him. But now he's dead. I don't know you, I don't trust you, and I don't care about you. I will not lend you money, and I will not allow you to take over your father's loan."

"What does that mean?"

"It means you must repay me in four days."

"But I can't."

"I know. So at the end of four days I will take over your business."

Amos went cold. "You can't do that!"

"But I can. It's what I agreed with your father, and he signed a contract to that effect. You'll find a copy of that document somewhere in your father's papers, and I have one here."

"So he left me nothing!"

"All the stock is mine, and next week my travelers will begin to call on the craftspeople who have been producing for you. The business will continue. But it will be mine."

Amos looked hard at Hornbeam's face. He was tempted to say *Why do you hate me?* But there was no hate, just a sly satisfaction that showed in the merest hint of a triumphant smile, little more than a twitch of one corner of the mouth.

Hornbeam was not malicious. He was just greedy and pitiless.

Amos felt helpless, but he was too proud to admit it. He went to the door. "I will see you in four days, Mr. Hornbeam," he said.

He went out.

CHAPTER 8

Spade was at his loom, winding yarn onto the vertical heddle to form the warp, fixing the threads carefully so that they would remain taut. There was a tap at the door, he looked up, and Amos came in.

Spade was surprised to see him out and about so soon after the funeral. Amos did not look mournful so much as defeated. For him that was unusual: he might look anxious, or angry, but he was sustained by youthful optimism. Now he appeared to have given up hope. Spade felt a pang of compassion. "Hello, Amos," he said. "Would you like a cup of tea?"

"Yes, please," Amos said. "I've been with Hornbeam and he didn't offer me a damn drink of water."

Spade laughed. "He'd claim he couldn't afford it."

"Bastard."

"Come and tell me about it."

Spade had a warehouse and workshop with a small apartment for a single man. He did a lot of weaving himself, but he also used other weavers, including one who was almost as skilled as he was, Sime Jackson. Weaving was well paid, but Spade had ambition, and he wanted more.

Now Spade led Amos to his private room, which had a narrow bed, a round table, and a fireplace. It was a spartan home. Spade put all his creative energy into his weaving: that was what excited him. "Sit down," he said, pointing to a wooden chair. He put a kettle of water on the fire and spooned tea into a pot, then sat on a stool while the kettle heated. "What's the old devil up to now?"

Amos held his hands to the warmth of the fire. He

looked miserable, and Spade felt sorry for him. Amos said: "I've discovered that my father has been losing money for two years."

"Hmm. He did seem to have lost energy."

"But Hornbeam has been keeping him afloat, lending him money."

Spade frowned. "It's not like Hornbeam to lend a hand to a fellow in trouble."

"He charged interest."

"Of course. How much do you owe him?"

"A hundred and four pounds, thirteen shillings, and eight pence."

Spade whistled. "That's a lot."

"I can hardly believe I've got into this position," Amos said, and Spade was touched by his youthful bafflement. "I'm an honest dealer and a hard worker, but I'm bankrupt. I feel such a fool. How can this be happening to me?"

The poor lad was in agony. Spade got up, thinking, and poured boiling water onto the tea leaves. "You'll just have to pay it back. It might take you years, but the ordeal will give you a good reputation."

"Years, yes. But Hornbeam has given me four days."

"What? That's impossible. What is he thinking of?" Spade stirred the tea in the pot and poured it into cups.

"I told Hornbeam it couldn't be done."

"What did he say to that?"

"He said he'll take the business away from me. He's got a contract."

Enlightenment dawned on Spade. "So that's it."

Amos said: "What do you mean, *so that's it*?"

"I was wondering why someone as tightfisted as Hornbeam would lend money to a failing business. Now I know." He handed Amos a cup. "He wasn't being kind. He expected your father to go bankrupt, and all along he planned to take the business into his own."

"Is he really that sly?"

"The man is insatiable. He wants to own the world."

"Perhaps I should just wring his neck, and be hanged for murder."

Spade smiled. "Don't do that just yet. I wouldn't like to see you hanged, and most people in Kingsbridge would feel the same."

"I don't know what else to do."

"How long did you say Hornbeam gave you?"

"Four days. Why?"

"I'm just thinking."

Eagerness gleamed in Amos's face. "What are you thinking?"

"Don't get your hopes up. I'm trying to devise another way out, but it may not work."

"Tell me."

"No, let me mull it over."

Amos controlled his impatience with a visible effort. "All right. I'll try anything."

"It's Tuesday. Four days will take us to Saturday. Come and see me on Friday afternoon."

Amos drained his cup and stood up to go. "You can't give me an inkling?"

"It probably won't work. I'll tell you on Friday."

"Well, thank you for even thinking. You're a true friend, Spade."

When he had gone Spade sat for a while, reflecting. There was something wrong with Hornbeam. The man was rich; he was a leading figure in the town, an alderman and a justice of the peace; he was married to a nice, obedient woman who had borne him two children. What was driving him? He had more money than he could spend, given that he had no interest in throwing lavish parties, owning a string of racehorses, or going to plush London gambling clubs and losing hundreds of pounds on the turn of a card. Yet he was so greedy that he would exploit a dead man's inexperienced son in a bid to grab the business.

But perhaps he could be foiled.

An idea was taking shape in Spade's mind.

He put on his greatcoat, went out into the cold, and walked to Canon Midwinter's home.

The oldest and most elegant houses in Kingsbridge were owned by the church and reserved for the senior clergy. Midwinter had a Jacobean mansion opposite the cathedral, probably the most desirable location in the city. Spade was shown into a comfortable sitting room decorated in the classical style that had been fashionable ever since Spade had been old enough to notice such things: a colorful painted ceiling, chairs with spindly legs, and on the mantelpiece a pair of cream-colored urns decorated with swags and festoons—probably made at Josiah Wedgwood's famous factory. Spade guessed the room had been designed by Midwinter's late wife.

The canon was taking tea with Jane, his daughter. She was rather beautiful, Spade thought, with large gray eyes. Everyone knew that Amos was in love with her, and Spade could see why, though he found her rather cool and perhaps a bit devious. The town's leading gossip, Belinda Goodnight, had told Spade that Jane would never marry Amos.

Midwinter also had two sons, clever boys, older than Jane, both away at the university in Edinburgh. Methodists preferred to send their sons to Scottish universities, which taught less Church of England dogma and more of useful subjects such as medicine and engineering.

Midwinter and Jane greeted Spade warmly. He sat down and accepted a cup of tea. After some polite small talk he told them the story of Amos and Hornbeam.

Jane was outraged on Amos's behalf. "What a thing for Hornbeam to do—on the day of Amos's father's funeral!"

Midwinter commented: "Hornbeam will have made sure the paperwork is in perfect order, and there can be no legal challenge to the contract."

"Undoubtedly," said Spade.

Jane said: "Surely we can stop this happening!"

"There is a possible solution," said Spade. "That's why I've come here."

Midwinter said: "Go on."

Spade formulated the idea he had been incubating. "Amos is a bright lad and a hard worker. Given time, I feel sure he could pay off his debt."

Midwinter said: "But time is just what Hornbeam won't give him."

"What if a few of us clubbed together and lent Amos the money he needs to pay Hornbeam by Saturday?"

Jane said enthusiastically: "What a splendid idea!"

Midwinter nodded slowly. "There's a risk but, as you say, Amos is very likely to repay, eventually."

"I think we could find enough men to support a fellow Methodist in a time of difficulty."

"I feel sure of it."

Spade was pleased that Midwinter liked the idea, but there was one thing he could do that would almost guarantee its success—and that was to contribute to the loan fund himself.

First, Spade said: "I'd be happy to contribute ten pounds."

"Very good."

"If you were to support me, Canon Midwinter, by also subscribing ten pounds, I'd be in a strong position to persuade other Methodists to join in."

There was a pause, and Spade waited on edge for Midwinter's reaction.

At last he said: "Yes, I'd be glad to put in ten pounds."

Spade breathed easier and moved on. "We'd have to set a repayment date in, say, ten years from now."

"I agree."

"And charge Amos interest."

"Of course."

Jane said thoughtfully: "Amos will have to save all his

money to pay back the loan. He's going to be poor for ten years."

"True," said Spade. "And most important of all, I'd like you, Canon Midwinter, to be treasurer of the fund."

Midwinter shrugged. "You could be treasurer. People know you're honest."

Spade smiled. "But you're a canon of the cathedral. You're gilt-edged."

"Very well."

Jane clapped her hands. "So Amos will be rescued . . . eventually."

"I haven't done it yet," Spade said. "I've only started."

Spade liked his sister's shop. Kate and he shared a love of fabrics: the colors, the different weaves, the soft touch of merino, the sturdy heft of tweed. Their father had been a weaver and their mother a seamstress, so they had been born into the clothing industry just as princes and princesses were born into idleness and luxury.

He examined the coat Kate had made for Arabella Latimer, the bishop's wife. It had a three-tier cape collar, tight sleeves, and a high, gathered waist that fell in pleats to the ankles, showing off the rich colors and understated check pattern of the material. "That will look gorgeous on her," Spade said. "I knew it would."

"It had better," Kate said. "She's paying a lot for it."

"Trust me," said Spade, "I know what pleases a woman."

Kate made a scornful noise, and Spade laughed.

Kate herself was wearing a lot of lace: a lace scarf over her shoulders, long lace frills to her sleeves, and a lace overskirt. She had a pretty face, and lace suited her; but the real reason was that she had invested in a large stock and was showing it to the customers.

The shop occupied the ground floor of a house in the

High Street that had been Kate and Spade's childhood home. Kate lived there with her partner, Rebecca. On the floor above were bedrooms that could be used as changing rooms by customers trying on clothes. Above that level were Kate and Rebecca's rooms, and the kitchen was in the basement.

While Spade was admiring Mrs. Latimer's coat, his brother-in-law came down from the upstairs wearing a brand-new militia uniform. Kate did not normally make clothes for men, but Freddie Caines was the young brother of Spade's late wife. Freddie was eighteen, and had just been recruited into the militia, and Kate had made his uniform as a special favor.

"Well," said Kate, "you look quite splendid!"

He did, and the grin on his face said he knew it.

Spade said: "You'll be the only recruit in the entire Shiring Militia wearing a made-to-measure uniform." Officers had their uniforms tailored, but other ranks wore cheap ready-mades.

"Can I keep it on?" Freddie said. "I want to show it off."

"Of course," said Kate.

"I'll come back for my old clothes—they're upstairs."

As Freddie left, Mrs. Latimer came in through the street door, the end of her nose red with cold. Spade bowed and Kate dropped a curtsy: a bishop's wife merited respect.

But Arabella Latimer was always informal and friendly. She immediately saw the new coat on the table. "Is this it?" she said. "It's gorgeous." She stroked and squeezed the fabric with both hands, evidently enjoying the feeling. She's a sensual woman, Spade thought; wasted on that fat bishop.

"Try it on," said Kate. "Take off your cloak."

Mrs. Latimer was still in her funeral clothes. Spade stepped behind her. "Let me help you." He noticed that her hair smelled good. She was using a perfumed pomade on her auburn curls.

She shrugged out of her cloak and Spade hung it on a hook. Underneath the coat she was wearing a stunningly glamorous silk in the black-brown color of scorched wood. Mrs. Latimer knew what suited her.

Kate picked up the new coat and held it for her to put on.

Spade looked hard, concentrating on her rather than the coat. Her hair was a poem in different hues: strong tea, autumn leaf, ginger, and hay blond. The coat set it off perfectly.

She buttoned the coat. "It's a bit tight," she said.

Kate opened the door to the workroom. "Becca, my dear, please come and look."

Her partner, Rebecca, came in from the back room carrying a pincushion and a thimble. She was a contrast to Kate, plain looking and plainly dressed, her hair tightly pinned, her sleeves rolled. She curtsied to Mrs. Latimer, then walked around her in a circle, looking critically at the coat. "Hmm," she said. Then, as if remembering a duty, she said: "It looks wonderful."

Kate said: "It really does."

Becca said: "It's too tight across the bodice." She took a piece of chalk from her sleeve and made a mark on the coat. "By an inch," she added. Moving behind Mrs. Latimer, she ran her hands down the sides of the coat. "Also the waist." She made another chalk mark. "Shoulders are perfect." She stepped back. "The skirt of the coat hangs nicely. Everything else is excellent."

Mrs. Latimer looked at herself in the big cheval glass. "Goodness, my nose is red."

Spade said: "It's the gin."

Kate said: "David!" She used his real name only when reproving him—exactly as their mother had.

"It's this icy wind," said Mrs. Latimer, but she giggled, showing that she did not mind the joke. She studied the coat in the mirror. "I can't wait to wear it."

Becca said: "I can have it ready for you tomorrow."

"Wonderful." Mrs. Latimer unbuttoned the coat and

Kate helped her out of it, then Spade held her cloak. As she tied the ribbon that fastened it at the neck, she said to Becca: "I'll drop in tomorrow."

"Thank you, Mrs. Latimer," said Becca.

Mrs. Latimer went out.

Kate said: "What an attractive woman. Beautiful and charming, and a lovely figure, too."

Becca said sharply: "If you like her so much, make a pass at her, go ahead."

"I would if I didn't have someone better, my darling."

Becca looked mollified.

Kate added: "Besides, she's not inclined our way."

"What makes you so sure?" Becca said.

"She likes my brother too much."

"Rubbish," said Spade with a laugh.

He left the house by the back door. When he and Kate had inherited the place, Spade had built his warehouse at the back, where there had formerly been an orchard, and his sister had taken the house.

Kate and Becca were like husband and wife in every way that mattered. They loved each other and shared a bed. They were very discreet, but Spade was close to his sister and he had known her secret for many years. He was pretty sure no one else did.

He crossed the courtyard. As he reached his warehouse he saw the tall figure of Amos Barrowfield enter by the gate from the back lane.

It was Friday, and Spade was expecting him. Amos was a picture of nervous tension, pale, wide-eyed, agitated. Spade held open the door to the warehouse. "Come in," he said. He led the way to his private quarters. They sat down, and he said: "I have news for you."

Amos looked frightened. "Good or bad?"

Spade reached inside his shirt and took out a piece of paper. "Read that."

Amos took it.

It was a handwritten banknote drawn on Thomson's

Kingsbridge Bank, the oldest of the three banks in town, and it ordered one hundred and four pounds, thirteen shillings, and eight pence to be paid to Joseph Hornbeam.

Amos seemed unable to speak. When he looked up at Spade his eyes filled with tears.

"That's a loan, of course," Spade said.

"I can hardly believe it. I'm saved."

Spade talked details to calm Amos down. "Canon Midwinter is the trustee for a group of your fellow Methodists who have clubbed together to help you out."

"I can't believe how fortunate I am."

"However, I advise you to keep the source of the money to yourself. It's no one else's business."

"Of course."

"You'll have to pay four percent interest and return the capital in ten years' time."

Amos looked at Spade with something akin to worship in his eyes. "You made this happen, didn't you, Spade?"

"Canon Midwinter and I did."

"How can I ever thank you?"

Spade shook his head. "Just work hard, run the business well, and pay everyone back when the time comes. That's all I want from you."

"I will, I swear it. I can hardly believe my good fortune. Thank God, and thank you."

Spade stood up. "It's not over yet. We need to make sure Hornbeam doesn't try any tricks."

"All right."

"First you need to sign an agreement about the loan with Canon Midwinter in front of a justice of the peace. Then you need to give the banknote to Hornbeam, and I strongly suggest you also do that in front of the same justice."

"Which one?" There were several in Kingsbridge, and some were cronies of Hornbeam's, such as Humphrey Frogmore.

Spade said: "I've spoken to Alderman Drinkwater, the chairman of justices. He's father-in-law to Midwinter, as you may be aware."

"Good choice." Drinkwater was known to be honest.

"You'll have to pay him, of course: he'll want five shillings. Justices often charge for such services."

Amos grinned. "I can afford it now."

They left Spade's warehouse. First they went to Amos's house to get the five shillings from his safe. Then they went to Drinkwater's home in Fish Lane. It was a modest house, old and half-timbered.

Drinkwater was expecting them. He was in a room that served as an office, sitting behind a table with all the necessary stationery: quill pens, paper, ink, sand, and sealing wax. His head was bald but today he wore a wig to signify that he was playing a formal role.

He read the loan agreement that Spade produced. "Perfectly normal," he said, and pushed it across the table. Amos picked up a quill, dipped it in the inkwell, and signed his name, then Drinkwater signed as witness.

Spade took the document, sanded it to dry the ink, then rolled it carefully and put it inside his shirt.

Amos said: "Now I have to make sure I pay it back."

"You will," said Drinkwater. "We all have faith in you."

Amos looked daunted but determined.

Drinkwater put on a rather shabby old greatcoat and the three men went out and walked to Hornbeam's place.

Waiting in the hall, looking at the portrait of Hornbeam, Amos said: "Last time I was here I got the worst shock of my life."

Spade said: "Now it's Hornbeam's turn to be shocked."

A footman showed them into the study. Hornbeam was startled to see them. "What's this?" he said, annoyed. "I was expecting young Barrowfield, not a delegation."

Spade said: "It's about young Barrowfield's loan."

"If you've come to beg for mercy, you're wasting your time."

"Oh, no," said Spade. "We don't expect you to show mercy."

Hornbeam's arrogant attitude was disturbed by a worm of doubt. "Well, don't waste my time, what do you want?"

"Nothing," said Spade. "But Barrowfield has something for you."

Amos handed over the banknote.

Drinkwater spoke. "Hornbeam, before you present that note at the bank you'll need to hand over all the documents you have relating to the debts owed you by the late Obadiah Barrowfield. I imagine that's the bundle on the desk, but if you're not able to put your hand on them immediately you must give the note back to young Barrowfield."

Hornbeam's fleshy face turned pale, then pink, and finally red with rage. He ignored Drinkwater and looked at Amos. "Where did you get the money?" he shouted.

Amos looked intimidated but he did not quail. "I don't think you need to know that, Alderman."

Well done, Amos, thought Spade.

"You stole it!" Hornbeam yelled.

Drinkwater intervened. "I can assure you, Hornbeam, the money was come by honestly."

Hornbeam rounded on Drinkwater. "What business do you have interfering here? This is nothing to do with you!"

Drinkwater said mildly: "I'm here as a justice of the peace to witness a legal transaction, the repayment of a debt. For the avoidance of doubt, perhaps you would write a simple note saying that Barrowfield has cleared his debt to you in full. I will witness it and Barrowfield can keep it."

Hornbeam said: "There has been some underhand business here!"

"Calm down, before you say something you may come to regret," Drinkwater said. "You and I are both justices, and it's unseemly for us to yell at each other like costermongers."

Hornbeam seemed on the point of shouting a rejoinder, then he controlled himself. Without speaking, he snatched up a sheet of paper, wrote on it quickly, and handed it to Drinkwater.

Drinkwater studied it. "Hmm," he said. "It's just about legible." He took a quill and signed, then handed the document to Amos.

Hornbeam spoke with a clenched jaw. "If that concludes our business I'll bid you all good evening."

The three stood up and left the room with muttered goodbyes.

When they were out on the street, Spade permitted himself to laugh. "What a scene," he said. "The man was apoplectic!"

Amos said to Drinkwater: "I'm sorry he was so rude to you, Alderman."

Drinkwater nodded. "I've made an enemy of him tonight."

Spade thought about that. "I suspect all three of us have made an enemy of Hornbeam."

Amos said ruefully: "I'm so grateful to you both. He's a bad enemy to have."

"I know," said Spade. "But sometimes a man just has to do what's right."

Spade went to the shop the next morning, hoping to see Mrs. Latimer when she came in for her new coat. He was lucky. She came in like a warm breeze, and he thought again how attractive she was.

When she tried on the coat he gazed at her body, pretending to be checking the fit. She was delightfully rounded, and he could not help imagining the breasts under her clothes.

He thought he was being discreet, but she caught his

eye, to his profound embarrassment. She raised her eyebrows a fraction, and gave him a look of candid interest, as if his gaze had surprised her without really displeasing her.

He felt mortified at having been caught staring, and quickly looked away, feeling his cheeks redden. "A good fit," he muttered.

"Yes," said Kate. "I think Becca has got it exactly right."

Spade said: "Excuse me, ladies, I must get back to work." He left by the back door.

He was cross with himself for having been rude. But he was also intrigued by Mrs. Latimer's reaction. She had not been offended. It was almost as if she was glad he had noticed her breasts.

He thought: What am I doing?

He had been celibate for a decade, ever since his wife, Betsy, had died. He did not lack desire: rather the opposite. He had thought about several other women. Widowers often married again, usually to younger women; but girls could not hold his attention. You had to be young to marry a young person, he thought. Then there had been Cissy Bagshaw, a clothier's widow, a briskly practical woman of his age. She had made it clear that she would be glad to go to bed with him for what she described as a "fitting," as if they might try one another on like new clothes. He liked her, but liking was not enough. His love for Betsy had been a passion, and nothing less was worth thinking about.

But now, rather suddenly, he felt that he might perhaps come to feel passion for Arabella Latimer. Something stirred in his soul when he was with her. It was not just the way she looked, though that moved him, too. It was to do with the way she seemed to see the world, as if it was amusing but ought to be better. He saw it the same way.

When he imagined being married to her he felt that

they would never tire of making love, and they would always have something to talk about.

And she had not minded when he noticed her breasts.

But she was already married.

To the bishop.

So, he thought, I'd better forget her.

CHAPTER 9

hen the jubilation of defeating Hornbeam began to fade, Amos's mind turned to the years ahead. He faced an uphill climb. He was ready to work hard—that was nothing new—but would it be enough? If he could expand the business, he could repay faster and even start to accumulate some cash. But the shortage of yarn stood in his way. How could he get more yarn?

It crossed his mind that he could pay the spinners better. Because they were almost all women, they were paid badly. If the rates were increased, might more women become spinners? He was not sure. Women had other responsibilities and many simply did not have the time. And the industry was conservative: if Amos put up his rates, other clothiers in Kingsbridge would accuse him of ruining the business.

But the thought that he might face years of struggling to make ends meet was depressing.

Late one evening he ran into Roger Riddick on Fish Street. "I say, Amos, old chum," Roger said, dropping into university slang. "Might I stay at your house tonight?"

"Of course, with pleasure," said Amos. "I've enjoyed so much hospitality at Badford Manor. Stay for a month, if you like."

"No, no, I'll go home tomorrow. But I lost all my money at Culliver's place, and I can't get any more until the squire gives me my next installment."

Hugh Culliver, known as Sport, had a house in Fish Street. The ground floor was a tavern and coffeehouse, upstairs was a gambling den, and above that was a brothel. Roger was a habitué of the middle floor.

Amos said: "There's supper waiting at my house."

"Marvelous." They began to walk. "Anyway," Roger said, "how are things with you?"

"Well, the girl I love prefers a yellow-haired ribbon maker."

"There's an answer to that problem, I believe, on the top floor of Culliver's place."

Amos ignored that suggestion. He was not even tempted by prostitutes. He said: "I've got such a lot of ground to make up before I can start repaying my father's debt."

"Will this war affect you? The French are winning everything—Savoy, Nice, the Rhineland, Belgium."

"A lot of West of England cloth is exported to the European continent, and the war will disrupt that. But there should be military contracts to compensate. The army will need a lot of new uniforms. I'm hoping to benefit from some of that business—if I can get the yarn."

They reached the house. Amos's mother had put out a supper of ham and pickled onions with bread and beer. She quickly set a place for Roger, then she went to bed, saying: "I'll leave you boys to talk."

Roger took a long draft of beer. "So there's a shortage of yarn?" he said.

"Yes. Spade thinks it's caused by the flying shuttle. Weavers are working faster, but spinners aren't."

"I was in Combe not long ago and visited a cotton mill owned by the father of a university chum of mine."

Amos nodded. Most cotton manufacture took place in the north of England and the Midlands, but there were a few mills in the south, mostly in port cities such as Combe and Bristol, where the raw cotton was landed.

Roger went on: "You know the cotton people have invented a spinning engine."

"I've heard that. It doesn't work for wool."

"They call it the spinning jenny—it's a marvelous device," Roger said enthusiastically. He loved any kind of machine—the more complicated, the better. "One person can spin eight bobbins at a time. And the thing is so easy to use that a woman can do it."

"I wish I had a machine that could work eight times as fast as the old spinning wheel," Amos said. "But cotton fibers are stronger than wool. Wool breaks too easily."

Roger looked thoughtful. "That's a problem," he said. "But I don't see why it should be insuperable. The tension on the threads might be reduced, and maybe you could use it for thicker, coarser wool, and save the hand spinning for the finer material . . . I need to look at the machine again."

Amos began to see a glimmer of hope. He knew how ingenious Roger was in his workshop at Badford. He said: "Why don't we go to Combe together?"

Roger shrugged. "Why not?"

"There's a stagecoach the day after tomorrow. We could be there by midafternoon."

"All right," said Roger. "I've nothing else to do, now that I've lost all my money."

Amos placed an advertisement in the *Kingsbridge Gazette* and the *Combe Herald* newspapers:

> *For the benefit of esteemed cloth merchants*
> *Mr. Amos Barrowfield wishes to announce*
> *that the long-established business of his father,*
> *the late Mr. Obadiah Barrowfield,*
> <u>***continues without interruption***</u>*.*
> *High-quality fabrics a specialty:*
> *mohair, merino, fancy cassimeres*
> *pure and in blends with silk, cotton, and linen.*

ALL ENQUIRIES ANSWERED
BY RETURN OF POST.
Amos Barrowfield, Esq.
High Street
Kingsbridge

He showed it to Spade in the Methodist Hall. "Very good," said Spade. "Without criticizing your father you hint that recent failings have come to an end, and the enterprise is under new and more dynamic management."

"Exactly," said Amos, pleased.

"I'm a believer in advertising," Spade said. "It doesn't sell your goods all by itself, but it creates opportunities."

That was what Amos thought.

It was Bible study night, and the subject was the story of Cain and Abel but, once the topic of murder had been raised, they started to talk about the execution of the king of France. The bishop of Kingsbridge had preached a sermon saying that the French revolutionaries had committed murder.

That was the view of the British nobility, the clergy, and most of the political class. Prime Minister William Pitt was violently hostile to the French revolutionaries. But the opposition Whigs were divided, most siding with Pitt but a substantial minority seeing much that was positive in the revolution. The people were similarly split: a minority campaigning for democratic reforms along French lines, but the cautious majority declaring loyalty to King George III and opposition to the revolution.

Rupe Underwood sided with Pitt. "It was murder, plain and simple," he said indignantly. "It's iniquitous." His forelock fell over his eyes, and he tossed his head to throw it back.

Then he glanced at Jane.

Rupe was performing for Jane's benefit, Amos realized.

She was the picture of elegance tonight, as usual, in a navy blue dress and a tall-crowned hat like a man's. Would she be attracted by Rupe's high moral stance?

Spade saw things differently, as he so often did. "On the day the French king was guillotined, we here in Kingsbridge hanged Josiah Pond for stealing a sheep. Was that murder?"

Amos would have liked to say something clever to impress Jane and make Rupe look foolish, but he was not sure which side he was on, or what he thought about the French revolution.

Rupe said piously: "God made Louis king."

Spade said: "God made Josiah a poor man."

Amos thought: There, now, why couldn't I have come up with that?

Rupe said: "Josiah Pond was a thief, tried and found guilty by a court."

"And Louis was a traitor, accused of conspiring with his country's enemies," Spade countered. "He was tried and found guilty, just like Josiah. Except that treason is worse than stealing a sheep, if you ask me."

Amos decided he did not need to make Rupe look foolish because Spade was doing it for him.

Rupe became pompous. "The stain of that execution will remain on every Frenchman for hundreds of years."

Spade smiled. "And do you, Rupe, bear a similar stain?"

Rupe frowned, not understanding. "I have never killed a king, obviously."

"But your ancestors and mine executed Charles I, king of England, a hundred and forty-odd years ago. By your reasoning we bear the stain of that."

Rupe was weakening. "No good can come of killing a king," he said desperately.

"I disagree," Spade said mildly. "Since we English killed our king we have enjoyed more than a century of gradually increasing religious freedom, while the French have been forced to be Catholics—until now."

Amos thought Spade was going too far, and now at last he found the words to speak up. "An awful lot of French people have been killed for having the wrong opinions," he said.

Rupe said: "There you are, Spade, what do you say to Amos?"

"I say Amos is right," said Spade surprisingly. "Only I remember what the Lord said: 'First cast the beam out of thine own eye, and then shalt thou see clearly to cast the mote out of thy brother's eye.' Instead of concentrating on what the French are doing wrong, we should be asking what needs reforming here in our own country."

Canon Midwinter intervened. "Friends, I think we've taken the discussion far enough for one evening," he said. "When we leave here tonight, we might all ask ourselves what our Lord would think, remembering that he himself was executed."

That startled Amos. It was easy to forget that the Christian religion was about blood and torture and death—especially here in the plain interior of the Methodist Hall, looking at its whitewashed walls and homely furniture. The Catholics were more realistic, with their statues of the crucifixion and their paintings of martyrs being tortured to death.

Midwinter went on: "Would the Lord condemn the guillotining of the French king? If so, would he approve of the hanging of Josiah Pond? I don't offer you answers to these questions. I simply believe that thinking about them in the light of the teachings of Jesus may clarify our minds, and show us that such matters are not simple. And now, let us close in prayer."

They all bowed their heads.

The prayer was brief. "O Lord, give us the courage to fight for what is right, and the humility to know when we are wrong. Amen."

"Amen," said Spade loudly.

The Bristol-to-Combe stagecoach stopped in Kingsbridge at the Bell tavern in the market square. Amos and Roger got outside seats. Amos could not afford inside seats and Roger had no money. "I'll pay you back!" Roger said, but Amos refused. He was fond of Roger, but it was unwise to lend to gamblers.

The coach left the market square and went down Main Street, where most of the houses were now shops. It crossed the river by the double span that was called Merthin's Bridge after its medieval builder. It went from the north bank to Leper Island, passed Caris's Hospital, then crossed to the south bank. After that it wound through the prosperous suburb called Loversfield. Amos imagined that long ago this had been a place where unmarried couples went to be alone together. There were no fields here now, though some of the gardens had orchards. Then the coach passed through a long straggle of poorer houses and at last emerged into open country.

It was cold, but they both had massive greatcoats and knitted mufflers and hats. Roger smoked a pipe. At the taverns where the coach stopped to change horses they bought warming drinks: tea, soup, or whisky and hot water.

Amos was buoyed by optimism. It was too soon to rejoice, he told himself, but he could not help thinking that his business could be transformed by Roger's idea. A machine that could spin eight reels at a time!

They spent the night at a lodging house, then in the morning went to the home of Roger's friend Percy Frankland. Percy's father was prosperous, and welcomed them to a substantial breakfast with his wife and two adolescent children as well as Percy. Amos did not eat much. He felt quite tense about the visit, fearing that his hopes would be disappointed.

Straight after breakfast they went to the warehouse, which was in the grounds of the Frankland home. The lower floor was dedicated to storage; spinning was done upstairs.

When finally Amos entered the spinning room, it took him a long moment to understand what he was looking at; then he realized it was not one but a whole row of spinning engines.

Each machine was like a small table, waist high, about three feet long and half that wide, standing on four sturdy legs. The device seemed to be operated by two people, a woman and a child. The woman stood at one narrow end, the threads stretching to the spindles at the far end. She turned a large wheel on one side with her right hand. The wheel spun the eight spindles that wound the cotton into a tight thread. When she judged the thread was tight enough, she used her left hand to push forward a beam that brought into play eight fresh lengths of loose roving.

There were eight machines in the room.

Amos asked Mr. Frankland: "What does the child do?"

"He's the piecer, he mends broken threads for his mother," said Mr. Frankland.

They watched a boy of about eleven mending a break. He crawled under the machine to do it, so that his mother would not have to stop work. Cloth workers were paid by how much they produced, never by the hour. The boy took the ends of the two threads and placed them in his left palm so that they overlapped by two or three inches. Then he used his right palm to rub the threads together with short strokes, pressing hard. When he took his right hand away the two threads had interwoven to become one again. The process had taken a few seconds.

Amos noticed that the boy's palms were calloused from the constant rubbing. He took the boy's right hand and touched the thickened part.

The boy said proudly: "I got hard hands. They don't bleed no more."

Amos asked Mr. Frankland: "Threads must break often, to require a piecer on permanent duty."

"I'm afraid they do."

That was bad news. Amos said to Roger: "If cotton breaks often, wool might break all the time. Even hand spinners such as Sal Clitheroe break a thread sometimes."

Roger said to the boy: "Is there a moment, in the process, when the thread is most likely to break? Do you see what I mean?"

"Yes, master," said the boy. "It's when the slack thread is made taut. Especially if the old woman jerks too hard."

Roger said to Amos: "I might be able to do something about that."

Amos was transported. This machine could provide him with the yarn he needed to expand the business. But it would do more than that. It would remove the need to traipse around the countryside calling on village workers. A room full of spinners in his warehouse could provide more yarn than all the women in the villages. And if one was sick, and could not do her work, he would not have to wait a week to find out. The machine would give him more control.

Suppressing his excitement, he tried to be practical. He said to Mr. Frankland: "I don't know whether the spinning jenny could be modified to work with wool, but if I decide it could, where would I go to buy one?"

"There are several places up north where they make them," Mr. Frankland said. He hesitated, then added: "Or I could sell you one of mine. I'm about to start replacing the jennies with a bigger machine called a spinning mule. It spins forty-eight threads at a time."

Amos was flabbergasted. "Forty-eight!"

Roger commented: "Spindles sprouting like rhubarb in May."

Amos concentrated on practicalities. "When do you expect to get your spinning mule?"

"Any day now."

"How much would you ask for a secondhand spinning jenny?"

"They cost me six pounds. And they don't wear out. So I could sell you a used one for four pounds."

And I'd get it in a few days, Amos thought.

He could scrape up four pounds, though he would be left with nothing for emergencies.

But his mind kept coming back to the same question: Would it work for wool?

And the answer never changed: the only way to find out was to try it.

Still he hesitated.

Mr. Frankland said: "I've got a cotton master coming to look at the machines tomorrow."

"I'll give you an answer by this evening," Amos said. "And thank you for this opportunity. I appreciate it."

Mr. Frankland smiled and nodded.

"Meanwhile, I must have a serious discussion with my engineer."

They all shook hands, and Amos and Roger went away.

They went to a tavern and ordered a light dinner. Roger was all enthusiasm, his pink face flushing with excitement. "I know how to reduce the incidence of broken threads," he said. "I can picture it."

"Good," said Amos. He knew he was at a crossroads. If he did this and it went wrong he would have to reconcile himself to spending even more years saving the money to pay his debt. But if it went right he could start to make real money.

"It's a risk," he said to Roger.

"I like risks," said Roger.

"I hate them," said Amos.

But he bought the machine.

Amos decided to be optimistic and bid for a military contract before the spinning jenny arrived.

The colonel of the Kingsbridge Militia was Henry, Viscount Northwood, the son and heir of the earl of Shiring. The job was normally a figurehead role, but the Shiring tradition was that the earl's son was a working colonel. Northwood was also member of Parliament for Kingsbridge: the nobility liked to keep the important jobs in the family, Spade said.

Northwood normally lived with his father at Earlscastle, but after the militia was called out he had rented Willard House, a large building on the market square with room for the colonel and several senior staff officers. Kingsbridge legend said the house had once belonged to Ned Willard, who had been something very important in the court of Queen Elizabeth, though no one knew quite what.

Northwood's arrival had caused a social stir: he was single and twenty-three, and easily the most eligible bachelor in the county.

Amos had never met him, and he did not know anyone who could introduce him, so he decided to go to Willard House and try his luck.

In the spacious hall he was stopped by a fortyish man in sergeant's uniform: white breeches and gaiters, a short red jacket, and a tall shako hat. The red of the jacket was really a dusty rose color, indicating a poor dye job. "What's your business, young sir?" the sergeant said abruptly.

"I'm here to speak to Viscount Northwood, your colonel."

"Is he expecting you?"

"No. Kindly tell him that Amos Barrowfield would like to speak to him about your uniform."

"My uniform?" the man said indignantly.

"Yes. It should be red, not pink." The sergeant looked at his sleeve, frowning. Amos went on: "I'd like to see the Shiring Militia well-dressed, and I expect Viscount Northwood feels the same way."

The sergeant hesitated for a long moment, then said: "Wait here. I'll ask."

Standing in the hall, Amos noticed an air of bustle: men walked quickly from room to room and held brisk conversations as they passed on the stairs. It gave an impression of busy efficiency. Many aristocratic army officers were idle and insouciant, everyone knew; but perhaps Northwood was different.

The sergeant returned and said: "Follow me, please."

He led Amos into a large room at the front of the house with a window that faced the west façade of the cathedral. Northwood sat behind a large desk. A big fire blazed in the hearth.

Sitting close to the desk, wearing a lieutenant's uniform, clutching a sheaf of papers, sat a man Amos knew: Archie Donaldson, a Methodist. Amos nodded to him and bowed to the viscount.

Northwood wore no wig and had short, curly hair. His nose was large and his face had an amiable look, but his eyes appraised Amos with sharp intelligence. I've got about a minute to impress this man, Amos thought, and if I fail I'll be out of here in no time. "Amos Barrowfield, my lord, Kingsbridge clothier."

"What's wrong with Sergeant Beach's uniform, Barrowfield?"

"It's been dyed with rose madder, a vegetable dye which is pink rather than red and fades fast. That's all right for regular soldiers, but the cloth for sergeants and other noncommissioned officers should be colored with lac dye, which comes from a scaly insect and forms a deep red—although it's not as costly as cochineal, which gives the true bright 'British red' and is used for officers' uniforms."

"I like a man who knows his business," said Northwood.

Amos was pleased.

Northwood went on: "I suppose you want to supply the militia with cloth for uniforms."

"I'd be glad to offer you a hard-wearing, weatherproof sixteen-ounce broadcloth for private soldiers and sergeants. For commissioned officers I propose a lighter, superfine broadcloth, equally practical but with a smoother finish, made from specially imported Spanish wool. Fine cloths are my specialty, my lord."

"I see."

Amos was in full flow. "As to prices—"

Northwood held up a hand for silence. "I've heard enough, thank you."

Amos shut up. He guessed he was about to be turned down.

But Northwood did not dismiss him. He turned to Donaldson and said: "Write a note, please." Donaldson picked up a sheet of paper and dipped a quill in the inkwell. "Ask the major to be so good as to speak to Barrowfield about cloth for uniforms." Northwood turned to Amos. "I'd like you to meet Major Will Riddick."

Amos suppressed a startled grunt.

Donaldson sanded the note and handed it to Amos, not troubling to seal or even fold it.

"Riddick is in charge of all purchasing, assisted by the quartermaster. He has an office in this house, just up the stairs. Thank you for coming to see me."

Amos bowed and went out, hiding his dismay. He had impressed Northwood, he thought, but it had probably done him no good.

He found Riddick on the upstairs floor at the back of the house, in a small room foggy with pipe smoke. Will was there in a red coat and white breeches. He greeted Amos warily.

Amos summoned up as much bonhomie as he could. "Good to see you, Will," he said cheerily. "I've been talking to Colonel Northwood. He wrote a note to you." Amos handed over the note.

Will read it, his eyes resting on the paper for longer than seemed necessary for such a short message. Then, making a decision, he said: "I tell you what, let's discuss this over a pot of ale."

"As you wish," said Amos, though he did not feel the need of ale in the morning.

They left the house. Amos assumed they would go to the Bell, which was only a few steps away, but Will led him downhill and turned into Fish Street. To Amos's dismay he stopped at Sport Culliver's establishment.

Amos said: "Do you mind if we go somewhere else? This place has a bad reputation."

"Nonsense," said Will. "We're only going in for a drink. No need to go upstairs." He went inside.

Amos followed, hoping none of the Methodists happened to be watching.

He had never been here before but the ground floor looked reassuringly like any other tavern, with little indication of the wickedness that took place elsewhere on the premises. He tried to take comfort from that, but he still felt uneasy. They sat in a quiet corner and Will called for two tankards of porter, a strong beer.

Amos decided to get straight down to business. "I can offer you plain broadcloth for the uniforms of recruits at a shilling a yard," he said. "You won't get a better price anywhere. The same cloth dyed with lac for sergeants and other noncommissioned officers, three pence more. And superfine, for officers, British red, only three shillings and six pence a yard. If you can do better with another Kingsbridge clothier, I'll eat my hat."

"Where would you get the yarn? I hear there's a shortage."

Amos was surprised that Will was so well-informed. "I have a special source," he said. It was almost the truth: the spinning jenny would be delivered any day now.

"What source?"

"I can't reveal that."

A waiter brought the beer and stood waiting. Will looked at Amos, and Amos realized he was expected to pay. He took some coins from his purse and gave them to the man.

Will took a long draft of the dark beer, sighed with satisfaction, and said: "Suppose the militia needed a hundred sergeants' uniforms."

"You'd need two hundred yards of lac-dyed broadcloth at one shilling and three pence, so that would cost you twelve pounds and ten shillings. If you place the order with me right now you could have it for twelve pounds flat. I'm giving away far too much, but I know you'll be so happy with the cloth that you'll order more." Amos sipped his beer to hide his tension.

"That sounds good," Will said.

"I'm glad." Amos was surprised as well as pleased. He had not expected it to be so easy to sell to Will. And although this was not a huge order, it could be just the beginning. "I'll go home and write an invoice now and bring it to you to sign in a few minutes' time."

"All right."

"Thank you," said Amos. He lifted his tankard and held it for Will to clink, a gesture that symbolized an agreement. They both drank.

"One more thing," said Will. "Make out the invoice for fourteen pounds."

Amos did not understand. "But the price is twelve."

"And twelve is what I'll pay you."

"So how can I invoice you for fourteen?"

"It's the way we do things in the army."

Suddenly Amos understood. "You'll tell the army the price was fourteen pounds, you'll pay me twelve, and you'll keep two for yourself."

Will did not deny it.

Amos said indignantly: "It's a bribe!"

"Keep your voice down!" Will looked around, but there was no one nearby. "Use your discretion, you fool."

"But this is dishonesty!"

"What's the matter with you? It's how business is done. How naïve can you be?"

For a moment Amos wondered whether Will was telling the truth, and all such deals involved bribery. Perhaps this was one of the things his father had not told him. Then he recalled how many Kingsbridge clothiers were Methodists, and he felt sure they would not be guilty of corruption. He said: "I will not issue a false invoice."

"In that case you don't get the order."

"You think you'll find a clothier willing to bribe you?"

"I know I will."

Amos shook his head. "Well, it's not how Methodists do business."

"More fool you," Will said, and he emptied his tankard.

CHAPTER 10

ill Riddick returned to Badford the day before Kit's six-week confinement in bed came to an end.

By a stroke of bad luck Kit's protector, Roger, had gone away a week before. He was staying at Amos Barrowfield's house in Kingsbridge, the servants heard, working on a mystery project, no one knew what.

Kit had been looking forward to getting out of bed.

At first, when his head ached and he still felt shocked, he had not even wanted to move. He had been so tired that he was relieved just to stay in the soft, warm bed. Three times a day Fan helped him to sit upright and fed him oatmeal, broth, or bread soaked in warm milk. The effort of eating had exhausted him, and he lay down again as soon as he had finished.

Things had changed gradually. Sometimes he could watch birds through his window, and he persuaded Fan to put bread crumbs on the sill to attract them. Fan often sat with him after the servants' supper, and when they had nothing to discuss he told her the Bible stories he had heard from his mother: Noah's ark, Jonah and the whale, Joseph and his coat of many colors. Fan did not know many Bible stories. She had been orphaned at the age of seven and had come to work at the manor, where no one thought to tell a child stories. She could not read or even write her name. Kit was surprised to learn that she was not paid wages. "It's as if I'm working for my parents," she said. "That's what the squire says."

When Kit told his mother she said: "I call it slavery," then she regretted saying it and told Kit never to repeat it.

Ma came to see him every Sunday afternoon. She entered by the kitchen door and came up the back stairs, so that she would not meet the squire or his sons, and Fan said they did not even know that she visited.

And Kit became impatient to get back to normal. He wanted to put on clothes and eat with the other servants in the kitchen. He even looked forward to cleaning the fireplaces and polishing the boots with Fan.

But now his eagerness vanished. With Will in the house, Kit was safer shut away.

On the day of his release he had to stay in bed until the surgeon, Alec Pollock, had seen him. Soon after breakfast Alec walked into the room in his threadbare tailcoat, saying: "How is my young patient, after six weeks?"

He told the truth. "I feel well, sir, and I'm sure I could go back to work." He did not mention his fear of Will.

"Well, you seem to be getting better."

Kit added: "I'm grateful for the bed and the food."

"Yes, yes. Now tell me, what is your full name?"

"Christopher Clitheroe." Kit wondered why the surgeon would ask that question.

"And what season of the year is this?"

"End of winter, beginning of spring."

"Do you remember the name of the mother of Jesus?"

"Mary."

"Well, it seems your brain has not been seriously damaged by that damned horse of Will's."

Kit realized why the surgeon had asked him questions with obvious answers: to make sure his mind was normal. He said: "Does that mean I can work?"

"Not quite yet, no. Your mother can take you home, but you should do nothing strenuous for another three weeks."

That was a relief. He would escape from Will a little longer. Then perhaps Will would have to go to Kingsbridge again. Kit's spirits lifted.

Alec went on: "Keep the bandage around your head so that the other boys know you can't play rough games. No football, no running, no fighting, and definitely no work."

"But my mother needs the money."

Alec seemed not to take that very seriously. "You can work when you're fully recovered."

"I'm not lazy."

"No one thinks you're lazy, Kit. They think you've been kicked in the head by a dangerous horse, which you have. Now I'll go and talk to your mother. Just enjoy your last morning in bed."

Sal had missed Kit. She felt almost as bereft as she had when Harry died. She disliked being alone in the house, with no one to speak to. She had not realized just how completely her life was based around Kit. She constantly felt the impulse to check on him: is he hungry, is he cold, is he nearby, is he safe? But during the last six weeks other people had been taking care of him, for the first time since he was born.

She was glad when Alec Pollock walked into her house. She knew that it was six weeks to the day since Will's horse had kicked Kit. She stood up from her spinning wheel. "Is he well enough to get up?"

"Yes. This could have been very nasty, but he's come through, I believe."

"God bless you, Alec."

"He's a bright lad, isn't he? He's six, you said."

"Almost seven, now."

"Advanced for his age."

"That's what I think, although mothers always believe their children are exceptional, don't they?"

"Regardless of the truth, yes." Alec laughed. "I've noticed that."

"So he's well again."

"But I want you to keep him at home now for three weeks. Don't let him play games or do anything energetic. He mustn't fall and hit his head."

"I'll make sure of that."

"But after three weeks let him return to normal."

"I'm so grateful to you. You know I can't pay you."

"I'll send my bill to the squire, and hope for the best."

He left. Sal put on her shoes and her hat, and wrapped a blanket around her shoulders. The weather was still cold, but no longer freezing.

In the fields the men were starting the spring plowing. People greeted her as she wended her way between the houses, and she said the same thing to each: "Going to fetch my Kit home from the manor house at last, praise the Lord." She walked fast. There was no real need to hurry but, now that Kit was about to be liberated, she could hardly wait.

She went in through the kitchen door, as usual, and up the back stairs. When she saw Kit standing in the bedroom, in the ragged clothes he had been wearing when he moved into the manor house, she burst into tears.

Still crying, she knelt on the floor and hugged him gently. "Don't worry, I'm crying for happiness," she said. She was happy because he had not died, but she did not say that.

She pulled herself together and stood up. She noticed that Fanny was in the room, standing by the bed, and Sal hugged her, too. "Thank you for being kind to my little boy," she said.

Fanny said: "It comes natural, he's so lovely."

Kit hugged Fanny, kissed her pimply cheek, and said: "I'll come back soon to help you with the fireplaces and the boots."

"You take your time and get well," she said.

Sal took his hand and they left the bedroom—and there, on the landing, was Will.

Sal let out an involuntary cry of shock, then stood still for a frozen moment. She felt Kit squeeze her hand in fear. Then she curtsied, lowering her gaze so as not to look at him directly, and attempted to pass him without speaking.

He stood in her way.

Kit cringed back and tried to get behind Sal's skirt.

"Don't bring him back," Will said. "The pup is no use."

Sal suppressed her anger. Had Will not done enough? He had killed her husband and injured her child, and yet he still wanted to taunt her. In a voice barely controlled she said: "I shall do as I'm told by the squire, of course."

"The squire will be glad to get rid of the little runt."

"In that case we will leave you now, sir. Good day to you."

Will did not move out of the way.

Sal stepped closer to him and stared in his face. She was almost as tall as him and just as broad. Her voice changed without her intending it. "Let me pass," she said in a low, clear tone, and she could not quite hide her rage.

She saw a flash of fear in his eyes, as if he might be regretting this confrontation. But he would not back down. He seemed determined to cause trouble. "Are you threatening me?" he said. His scorn was not entirely convincing.

"Take it how you will."

Fanny spoke in a high, frightened voice. "Kit has to go home, Mr. Will, the surgeon said."

"I don't know why my father bothered to send for the surgeon. It would have been no great loss if the whelp had died."

That was too much for Sal. Wishing someone dead was a terrible curse, and Will had already nearly killed Kit. Without thinking she swung her right arm and punched the side of Will's head. Her back was broad and her arms were strong, and there was an audible thud as the blow connected.

Will staggered, dazed, and fell to the floor, crying out in pain.

Fanny gasped in shock.

Sal stared at Will. There was blood coming from his

ear. She was horrified by what she had done. "God forgive me," she said.

Will made no effort to get up, but lay there, moaning.

Kit started to cry.

Sal took his hand and led him around Will, who was groaning in pain. She had to get out of the house as fast as possible. She led Kit to the stairs and hurried down. They passed through the kitchen without speaking to the other servants, who stared at them.

They left by the back door and went home.

That afternoon she was summoned by the squire.

She had broken the law, of course. She was guilty of a crime. Worse, she was a common villager who had attacked a gentleman. She was in deep trouble.

Law and order was the responsibility of justices of the peace, also called magistrates. They were appointed by the lord lieutenant, the king's representative in the county. They were not lawyers but local landowners. In a town such as Kingsbridge there were several justices, but in a village there was usually only one, and in Badford it was Squire Riddick.

Major crimes were tried by two or more justices, and charges that carried the death penalty had to be heard by a judge at the assize court, but lesser offenses such as drunkenness, vagrancy, and minor violence could be dealt with by one justice sitting alone, usually in his home.

Squire Riddick was going to be Sal's judge and jury.

She would be found guilty, of course, but how would she be punished? A justice could order an offender to spend a day in the stocks, sitting on the ground with her legs clamped, a punishment that was more humiliation than anything else.

The sentence Sal feared was flogging, commonly ordered by justices and an everyday event in the army and navy. It was usually public. The convicted person was tied to a pole naked or half-naked—any clothing was likely to be shredded during the ordeal anyway. The whip used was usually the dreaded cat-o'-nine-tails, with nine leather thongs studded with stones and nails to quickly break the skin.

Drunkenness might be punished with six lashes, fighting with twelve. For attacking a gentleman she might get twenty-four, a real ordeal. In the military men were often given hundreds of lashes, and sometimes died; civilian punishments were not so savage, though bad enough.

She left immediately for the manor house, taking Kit with her—she could not leave him alone. As they walked side by side she asked herself what she could possibly say in her defense. Will was at least partly responsible for what had happened, but it would be unwise for her to point that out: it would add insult to injury, literally. The gentry were allowed to make excuses for their offenses, but common people were expected to be contrite: any attempt at self-justification would probably bring a harsher punishment.

At the manor Platts, the butler, showed her into the library, where Squire Riddick was sitting behind a desk. Will was beside him, with a bandage over his ear. Rector George sat at a side table with pen and ink and a ledger. Sal was not invited to sit.

The squire said: "Now, Will, you'd better say what happened."

"The woman confronted me on the upstairs landing," said Will.

He was already lying, but Sal said nothing.

"I told her to get out of my way," Will went on. "Then she punched my head."

The squire looked at Sal. "And what have you got to say for yourself?"

"I'm very sorry for what happened," Sal said. "I can only say that I think I have been driven mad by the tragedies my family has suffered in recent months."

The squire said: "But that's no reason to attack Will."

"I got it into my head that Mr. Will was partly responsible for the death of my husband and the terrible injury to my son. He seemed to have no pity for me and to feel that my son was not important."

Will said: "Not important? Look at the puppy dog! He's absolutely worthless—why would I shed tears for him? Of course I feel that he's not important. These villagers have too many children anyway. One less is nothing to cry about."

Sal tried to speak in a humble way. "His mother would cry, sir."

The squire frowned at Will and looked uncomfortable. Squire Riddick was a hard man but not as malicious as his eldest son. Sal could see that Will was doing himself no good with this line of talk. He was displaying contempt for a little boy. Even his family would not respect him for that.

Sal said: "I'm sorry, Squire, but Kit is my only child."

Will said: "And a good thing, too! You can't even look after one—he has to come here for his bed and board."

"Sir, all my life before and after my marriage I never asked for parish relief, not until my husband was killed."

"Oh, so it's all the fault of other people, is it?" said Will.

Sal just looked him directly in the eye and said nothing.

Her silence was eloquent enough to jerk the squire into action. "All right, I think the picture is clear," he said. "Unless either of you has something you feel you have to add."

Will said: "She must be flogged."

The squire nodded. "That is an appropriate punishment for violence against a gentleman."

Sal said: "No, please!"

The squire went on: "However, this woman has suffered a great deal lately, through no fault of her own."

Will said indignantly: "Then what will you do?"

The squire turned on him. "Shut your mouth, boy,"

he said, and Will flinched visibly. "I'm your father—do you think I'm proud of what you've done to a humble village family?"

Will was too shocked to answer.

The squire turned back to Sal. "I have some sympathy for you, Sal Clitheroe, but I cannot overlook the crime you have committed. If you remain in this village you must be flogged. But if you leave the matter will be forgotten."

"Leave!" said Sal.

"I can't let you live here unpunished. You would always be pointed out as the woman who punched the squire's son and got away with it."

"But where would I go?"

"I don't know and I don't care. But if you're not gone by sunrise tomorrow you will receive thirty-six lashes."

"But—"

"Don't say any more. You've got off lightly. Leave this house now, and leave Badford at first light."

She stood up.

Will said: "And think yourself damned lucky."

Sal took Kit's hand and they went out.

Everyone in the village knew that Sal had knocked Will Riddick to the floor. Many of Sal's friends were waiting for her when she came out of the manor house. Annie Mann asked her what had happened. Sal felt it would be painful to recount the story and she wanted to do so only once. She asked Annie to tell people to meet her at Brian Pikestaff's place.

When she got there Brian was cleaning the mud off his plow after a day in the fields. She asked if she could meet everyone in his barn, and as she expected he agreed readily.

Waiting for her friends to gather, Sal tried to collect her thoughts. She found it hard to imagine what her life would be like from tomorrow. Where would she go? What would she do?

When everyone was there she told them the whole story in detail. They muttered imprecations when they heard that Will had wished for Kit's death; cheered when she told how she had knocked him to the floor; and gasped in shock when she revealed her sentence of banishment. "I'll be gone early in the morning," she said. "I just want you all to pray for me."

Brian stood up and gave an extempore prayer, asking God to look down on Sal and Kit and take care of them whatever happened. Then the questions began. They asked her all the things she was asking herself, and she had no answers.

Brian was practical. "You'll have to leave with just what you can carry. We'll store the rest of your possessions here in this barn. When you're settled somewhere else you can come back with a cart to collect everything."

His concern and kindness made Sal want to cry.

The scribbler Mick Seabrook said: "My aunt has a lodging house in Combe—it's cheap, and clean."

"That could be helpful," Sal said, although Combe was two days away, an intimidating distance for someone who had rarely left Badford. "But I have to make a living. I can't apply for Poor Relief—you only get that in the parish where you were born."

Jimmy Mann said: "What about the quarry at Outhenham? They always need labor."

Sal was doubtful. "Do they hire women?" She had never been to Outhenham, but she knew all about men's prejudices.

"I don't know, but you're as strong as most men," Jimmy said.

"That's what bothers them."

People wanted to be helpful, and they had all sorts of suggestions, but the ideas were speculative, and Sal and Kit could starve to death checking them out. After a while she thanked them all and took her leave, holding Kit's hand.

Night had fallen while she was in the barn, but she found her way easily in the dark. Tomorrow evening she would be in a strange place.

Back at home she heated some broth for supper, then put Kit to bed.

She sat by the fire for a while, brooding, then there was a knock at the door. Ike Clitheroe, Harry's uncle, came in with Jimmy Mann. Jimmy was holding his three-cornered hat in his hands. "The friends had a collection," Uncle Ike said. "It's not much." Jimmy showed her that his hat contained a small pile of pennies and a few shillings. Ike was right, it was not much, but it could be a crucial help in the next few desperate days. Homeless people had to buy food in taverns, where it cost more.

Jimmy poured the coins out on the table, a little stream of brown and silver. Sal knew how hard it was for poor people to give money away. "I can't tell you . . ." She choked up and started again. "I can't tell you how grateful I am to have such good friends." And how miserable I am to be leaving them all behind, she thought.

Ike said: "God bless you, Sal."

"You, too, and you, Jimmy."

After they had gone she went to bed, but she did not fall asleep for a long time. People said *God bless you*, but sometimes God did not, and lately she had felt cursed. God had sent her good friends but also powerful enemies.

She thought of her aunt Sarah. She had left the village voluntarily and gone to Kingsbridge to sell ballads on the street. Sal had always admired Sarah. Perhaps Sal, too, could prosper by leaving. Village life had never been what she wanted, before she met Harry.

Aunt Sarah had gone to Kingsbridge. Perhaps that was the place for Sal, too.

The more she thought about it, the better it seemed. She could get there in half a day, though the walk would be hard on Kit's little legs. And she did know one person in the city: Amos Barrowfield. Perhaps she could continue to spin yarn for him. He might even help her to find a room where she and Kit could live.

She felt a little better having glimpsed some possibilities. She was exhausted and drained, and eventually sleep took over. However, she woke before dawn. Unsure what time it was, she moved about the house by the dim glow of the embers in the fireplace. She put together the few things she would take with her.

She had to take her mother's spinning wheel. It was heavy, and she would have to carry it ten miles, but it might be her only means of making a living.

She had no spare clothes. She would wear her only dress, shoes, and hat. She wished she had shoes for Kit, but he had never worn them before he went to work at the manor house. His coat was far too big, which was a blessing, for he would not grow out of it for years.

She would take her cookpot, kitchen knife, and what little food there was in the house. She hesitated over her father's Bible, but decided to leave it. Kit could not eat a book.

She wondered whether she would ever have the money to hire a cart and fetch her furniture. There was not much of it—two beds, a table, two stools, and a bench—but it had been made by Harry, and she loved it.

When the first hint of gray appeared in the sky beyond the fields to the east, she woke Kit and made porridge. Afterward she washed the pot, the bowls, and the spoons, and used an old piece of string to tie them in a bundle. She put the food in a sack and gave it to Kit to carry. Then they went out, and Sal closed the door, feeling sure she would never open it again.

They went first to St. Matthew's Church. There in the graveyard was a simple wooden crucifix with *Harry Clitheroe* written neatly on its crosspiece in white paint. "Let's just kneel down here for a few moments," she said to Kit.

He looked puzzled, but did not question her, and they both knelt at the grave.

Sal thought about Harry: his wiry body, his argumentative disposition, his love for her, and his care for Kit. She felt sure he was in heaven now. She remembered their courtship: first the flirting; then the tentative kissing and holding hands; the secret meetings in the woods after church on Sunday, when they could not keep their hands off each other; and finally the realization that they wanted to spend their lives together. She also remembered how he had died in agony, and she wondered how such cruelty could possibly be God's will.

Then she prayed aloud extempore, as Methodists did in their meetings. She asked Harry to watch over her and their child, and she begged God to help her look after Kit. She asked forgiveness for the sin of punching Will. She could not quite bring herself to pray for Will's ear to get better. She asked that her trials would not go on much longer, and then she said amen, and Kit said amen, too.

They stood up and walked out of the graveyard.

Kit said: "Where are we going now?"

"Kingsbridge," said Sal.

Amos and Roger had spent the last few days adapting the spinning jenny.

They had worked in a back room of Amos's warehouse, behind a locked door. They did not want the news of the new engine to get out before they were ready.

They were testing it with English wool, which was tougher than imported Spanish or Irish, the long fibers making it less liable to break. Roger had tied a loose roving to each of the eight spindles, then threaded it through the clamp that held it taut during spinning. When it was done, Amos operated the machine.

Hand spinning was an art that had to be learned, but

operating the machine was simple. With his right hand Amos turned the big wheel slowly, making the spindles turn, twisting the threads. Then he stopped the wheel and carefully moved the beam forward, up the length of the machine, to feed new lengths of roving to the spindles.

"It works!" he said jubilantly.

Roger said: "At the Frankland place they turned the wheel much faster."

Amos increased the pace, and the threads began to break.

"As we feared," said Roger.

"How can we fix that?"

"I've got some ideas."

Over several days Roger had tried out different ideas. The one that worked involved weighting the threads to keep them taut at every stage of the process. It had taken more trial and error to get the weight exactly right. Today, after a frustrating morning of trial and error, they succeeded; and then Amos's mother called them to dinner.

Sal's memory of Kingsbridge was vivid. Although her last visit was ten years ago, it had been an astonishing experience, and she remembered every detail. And today she could see how much the city had changed.

Approaching from the high ground to the north, she could see the familiar landmarks: the cathedral, the domed wool exchange, and the river with its distinctive double bridge. The place seemed bigger, especially to the southwest, where there were more houses than she remembered. But she also saw something new. On the far side of the river, upstream from the bridge, where previously there had been nothing but fields, she saw half a dozen long, high buildings with rows of large windows, all close to the water. She recalled, vaguely, hearing people talk about constructions like this: they were mills, where cloth was made. They were narrow and had tall windows so that the hands could see their work clearly. The water was needed for fulling, or felting, the cloth, and for dyeing; and where the river ran fast it could also drive machinery. Some of this must have been here ten years ago, she reasoned, for Kingsbridge had been a cloth town since before she was born. But previously the buildings had been small and scattered. They had grown and spread, and now there was a distinct manufacturing district.

"Nearly there, now, Kit," she said. He was exhausted, stumbling. She would have carried him but she had the spinning wheel and the cooking pot.

They entered the town. Sal asked a friendly looking woman where Amos Barrowfield lived, and was given directions to a house near the cathedral.

The door was opened by a maid. "I'm one of Amos Barrowfield's spinners," Sal said. "I would like to speak to him, if I may."

The maid was wary. "What name, please?"

"Sal Clitheroe."

"Oh!" said the maid. "We've heard all about you." She looked down at Kit. "Is this the little boy who got kicked by the horse?"

"Yes, this is Kit."

"I'm sure Amos will want to see you. Come in. My name is Ellen, by the way." She led them through the house. "They're just finishing dinner. Shall I bring the two of you some tea?"

"That would be a godsend," said Sal.

Ellen led them into the dining room. Amos was sitting at the table with Roger Riddick. They were both startled to see Sal and Kit.

Sal curtsied, then said abruptly: "I've been banished from Badford."

Roger said: "What for?"

Sal said shamefacedly: "I'm sorry to say, Mr. Roger,

that I punched your brother Will's head and knocked him to the ground."

There was a second of silence, then Roger burst out laughing, and a moment later Amos joined in. "Good for you!" said Roger. "Someone should have punched his head long ago."

When they quietened down she said: "It's all very well to laugh but I've got no home now. Mr. Barrowfield, if I can find a place to live here in Kingsbridge, I'm hoping I could continue to spin yarn for you, if you still want me."

"Of course I want you!" said Amos.

A weight fell from Sal's shoulders.

Amos went on: "I'll be very happy to buy your yarn." He hesitated for a moment, then said: "But I've got a better idea. I might be able to offer you work that would pay you a bit more than hand spinning."

"What work would that be?"

Amos stood up. "I need to show you," he said. "Come to the warehouse. Roger and I have a new machine."

PART II

The Revolt of the Housewives

1795

CHAPTER 11

Sal and Kit had worked for Amos for more than two years. In that time the location had changed. The enterprise was too large for the warehouse behind Amos's house: he now had six spinning engines and a fulling room. He had rented a small mill by the river, in the northwest of Kingsbridge where the river ran fast enough to drive the fulling hammers that shrank and thickened the cloth.

They toiled from five o'clock in the morning until seven at night, except on Saturday—blessed Saturday—when they worked only until five in the afternoon. All the children were tired all the time. Nevertheless, life was better than before. Kit's mother had money, they lived in a warm house with a real chimney, and—best of all—they had escaped from the Badford bullies who had killed his father. He hoped he would never live in a village again.

However, the war had changed things, slowly and gradually, for the worse. Kit at the age of nine was aware of money, and he understood that war taxes had raised the price of everything, while cloth workers were paid the same. Bread was not taxed but its price went up because of a poor harvest. For a while after learning to operate the spinning jenny, Sal had been able to afford beef, tea with sugar, and cake; but now they ate bacon and drank weak ale. All the same, it was better than life in the village.

Kit's best friend was a girl called Sue, who was about his age and, like him, had lost her father. She worked with her mother, Joanie, on the spinning engine next to Sal's in Barrowfield's Mill.

Today was a special day. All the hands had realized

that as soon as they walked into the mill and saw, on the ground floor near the fulling engine, shrouded in sacking, an object about the size of a four-poster bed or a stagecoach. It must have been delivered last night after they had all gone home.

They had talked about it all through the half-hour dinner break, and Kit's mother had said it must be a new machine, though no one had ever seen a machine that big.

Amos Barrowfield's friend Roger Riddick showed up around midafternoon. Kit would never forget Roger's kindness to him back in Badford. He also remembered that it was Roger who had adapted Amos's first spinning jenny. Now there were six such machines, and Amos had been planning to get more until the war began to affect business.

Amos stopped the work half an hour early, and asked the hands to gather with him and Roger on the ground floor around the mystery object. He ordered the men to stop the fulling machine, for no one could talk over its thumping and clanking. Then he said: "Not long ago, Mr. Shiplap of Combe asked me for five hundred yards of linsey-woolsey."

That was a big order, even Kit knew, and they all cheered.

Amos went on: "I priced the order at fifty-five pounds, and was willing to be beaten down to fifty. But he offered me thirty-five and said he knew another Kingsbridge clothier who was ready to make a deal at that price. Now, I know that the only way a clothier could make that deal would be by reducing what he pays his hands."

There was a discontented murmur. The men and women around Kit looked wary and mutinous. They did not like talk of reducing piece rates.

Amos said: "So I turned him down."

The hands were relieved to hear that.

Amos said: "I didn't like to refuse an order, because

we're not getting as many as we used to, and if things go on the way they are, then some of you will have to be laid off."

Now Kit was worried. He knew that no Kingsbridge clothier was looking for extra hands right now. He had heard his mother say that they were not replacing people who left, because they were uncertain what the future held and how long the war would go on. Amos's dilemma was not unique.

"But I've found a solution. I know how I can fulfill Mr. Shiplap's order without reducing piece rates or dismissing people."

There was a silence. Kit sensed that the hands were suspicious, unsure whether to believe Amos.

Amos and Roger pulled the canvas covers off the mystery object and dropped them on the floor. When the thing was completely visible, Kit still did not know what it was. He had never seen anything like it.

Nor had anyone else, he could tell. They were all muttering in puzzlement.

There were eight cylindrical metal rollers in a black pyramid. It reminded Kit of a stack of water pipes he had once seen on the High Street. These cylinders seemed to be studded with nails. The whole thing was mounted on a stout oak platform with short thick legs.

It was obviously a machine, but what did it do?

Amos answered the unspoken question. "This is the solution to our problem. It's a scribbling engine."

Kit knew what scribbling was. He remembered Mick Seabrook, a hand scribbler in Badford. Mick used brushes with iron teeth, and now Kit saw that each roller was wrapped in a leather cover studded with nails just like the teeth of Mick's brushes.

Amos went on: "Machines like this have been around for a long time, but they've caught on in recent years, and this is the up-to-date version. The fleece is fed through the first pair of rollers, and the nails untangle the wool and straighten the fibers."

Kit said: "But the scribbler has to do it again and again, all day."

The hands laughed, because a little boy had spoken up, but a moment later Joanie said: "He's right, though."

"Yes," said Amos. "And that's why there are so many rollers. One pass is never enough. So the fleece goes through a second pair, with teeth placed closer together; then a third, then a fourth, each combing more finely, removing more dirt, making the fibers straighter."

Roger added: "This machine was made for cotton, and wool is softer, so I've modified the iron teeth, making them less sharp, and enlarged the gaps between upper and lower rollers, so that the process is less brutal."

Amos said: "And we've tested it, and it works."

Sal spoke up. "And who turns the rollers?"

"No one," said Amos. "Like the fulling engine, the scribbling machine is driven by the mighty power of the river, channeled into the millrace and transmitted, via cogs and chains, to the rollers. It just needs one man to mind the mechanism and make small adjustments as it rolls."

Joanie said: "And then what will the hand scribblers do for work?"

That was right, Kit thought; Mick and other scribblers might not be needed if there were scribbling machines driven by the waterwheel.

Amos seemed to be ready for this question. "I won't lie to you," he said. "You all know me—I don't want people to lose their living. But we have a choice. I could send this machine back where it came from, forget about Mr. Shiplap's order, and tell half of you not to come back tomorrow because I've got no work for you. Or I could keep you all working but reduce your piece rates. Third choice: we can hold piece rates at the same level, fulfill Mr. Shiplap's order, and keep you all working—if we use the scribbling engine."

Joanie said defiantly: "You could use your own money to keep things going."

"I haven't got enough," Amos said. "I'm still paying off the debts my father left me three years ago. And do you know how he got into debt?" His tone became a bit emotional. "By running this business at a loss. One thing I can tell you for certain is that I will not do that. Never."

A woman said: "I've heard these machines don't do a proper job." There was a murmur of agreement.

Another said: "It looks devilish to me. All them nails." Kit had heard people speak like this about machinery. People did not understand how the machines worked so they said there must be an imp trapped inside and driving it. Kit understood machines and he knew there were no imps in them.

There was a discontented silence, then Kit's mother spoke up. "I don't like this machine," she said. "I don't want to see hand scribblers lose their living." She looked around at the other hands, mostly women. "But I trust Mr. Barrowfield. If he says we got no choice, I believe him. I'm sorry, Joanie. We have to accept the scribbling machine."

Amos said nothing.

The hands looked at one another. Kit heard a hubbub of comments, mostly in undertones; they were unhappy, but not angry. They just sounded resigned. Gradually they moved away, looking thoughtful, saying good night quietly.

Sal, Kit, Joanie, and Sue left together. The four of them trudged homeward in the twilight. It had rained during the day, while they were inside the mill, and now the setting sun glinted off the puddles. They crossed the market square as a lamplighter went around with his flame. In the center of the square the implements of punishment stood in the half dark: the gallows, the stocks, and the whipping post—actually two posts and a crosspiece, where a wrongdoer would be bound, hands tied above the head, to be flogged. The woodwork was spotted brown with blood. Kit tried not to look: it scared him.

As they passed the cathedral, the bells began to ring. Monday was practice night for the ringers. Kit knew there were seven bells: the highest in pitch, number 1, was called the treble, and the deepest, number 7, was the tenor. As usual they began with a simple row, ringing all seven in descending order, 1-2-3-4-5-6-7. Soon they would change to something more complicated. Kit was interested in the way they altered the tune by varying the order of the bells. There was something satisfyingly logical about it.

Sal and Kit shared a house with Sue and her family in the low-rent neighborhood in the northwest of the city. On the ground floor at the back was the kitchen, where they all cooked and ate. The front room was occupied by Sue's uncle Jarge, five years younger than Joanie at twenty-five, a weaver in one of Hornbeam's mills. Jarge was also one of the bell ringers, and Kit had picked up some of the lore from him.

There were two beds upstairs. Joanie and Sue slept together in the front room, and Sal and Kit had the back. Most poor people shared beds for warmth, saving the cost of firewood or coal.

The low-ceilinged attic room was occupied by Joanie's aunt, Dottie Castle. She was elderly and in poor health, and scraped a living darning socks and patching trousers.

As soon as they got home Kit lay on the bed he shared with his mother—the large one brought from Badford. He felt Sal take off his boots and cover him with a blanket, and then he fell asleep.

She woke him a little later and he stumbled down the stairs for supper. They had bacon with onions and bread spread with dripping. They were all hungry and ate quickly. Joanie wiped the frying pan with another slice of bread and divided it between the children.

As soon as they had eaten, both children went to bed. Kit was asleep within moments.

Sal washed her face, then brushed her hair and tied it with an old red ribbon. She climbed to the attic room and asked Aunt Dottie to keep an eye on the children for an hour or two. "If they wake up, give them some bread," she said. "Have some yourself, if you're hungry."

"No, thank you, dear. I'm quite all right. I don't want much, sitting here all day. You mill hands need it more."

"If you're sure."

She looked in on Kit, fast asleep. A slate and a nail were beside the bed. Every evening Sal spent time practicing her writing, copying passages from the Bible, her only book. She was getting better. On Sundays she taught Kit, but every other day he was too tired.

She kissed his forehead and went to the other bedroom. Joanie was putting on a hat with flowers that she had embroidered herself. She kissed Sue, who was asleep. Then the two women went out.

They walked down Main Street. The city center was busy as people left their homes for the evening in search of pleasure, companionship, and perhaps love. Sal had given up on love. She was pretty sure Joanie's brother, Jarge, would have liked to marry her, but she had discouraged him. She had loved Harry and he had been killed, and she was not willing to risk that kind of pain again, not willing to put her happiness in the hands of gentry who could get away with murder.

They crossed the square. The Bell was a large establishment with a carriage entrance leading to a courtyard and stables. Hanging at the top of the entrance arch was—of course—a bell, which was rung to warn that the stagecoach was about to leave. Not long ago it had been rung to invite people to a play, but nowadays plays were put on in the theater.

The Bell had a large taproom with a row of barrels like a barricade. It was loud with conversation and laughter, and fogged by pipe smoke. The ringers were there already, sitting around their usual table near the fireplace, battered hats on their heads and earthenware tankards in front of them. They got paid a shilling each for ringing, so they always had money for ale on Monday nights.

Sal and Joanie asked the server for a pot of ale each, and learned that the price had gone up from three pence to four pence. "It's the same as bread," said the server. "And for the same reason: wheat is too dear."

When Sal and Joanie sat down, Jarge gave them a grim look and said: "We been talking about Barrowfield's new engine."

Sal took a long draft of ale. She did not like getting drunk, and anyway she could never afford more than one tankard, but she loved the malty taste and the warm glow. "A scribbling machine," she said to Jarge.

"A machine to starve workingmen, I call it," said Jarge. "In past years, when the masters tried to introduce newfangled engines here in the west of England, there were riots, and the masters backed down. That's what should happen now."

Sal shook her head. "Say what you like, but it saved me. Amos Barrowfield was about to send half of us home, because the market price of cloth is so low, but the new machine means he can do business at the lower price, so I'm still working the jenny."

Jarge did not like this line of argument, but he liked her, and he controlled his anger. "So, Sal, what do you say to the hand spinners about the new machine?"

"I don't know, Jarge. But I do know that I was destitute and homeless until I started operating Barrowfield's first spinning jenny, and I might have lost that work today if he hadn't bought a scribbling machine."

Alf Nash spoke up. He was not a bell ringer, but he often joined them, and Sal thought he was sweet on Joanie. He was sitting next to her now. Alf was a dairyman, and because of the milk constantly spilled on his clothes he smelled cheesy. Sal did not think Joanie would fall for him. Alf said: "Sal's got a point there, Jarge."

Sime Jackson, a weaver who worked with Spade, was one of the more thoughtful members of the group. "I can't reason it out, I can't," he said. "Machines help some and take work away from others. How can you tell what's for the best?"

"That's our trouble," said Sal. "We know the questions but we don't know the answers. We need to learn."

"Learning's not for the likes of us," said Alf. "We're not going off to Oxford University."

Spade spoke for the first time. He was Master of the Bells, which meant he was the ringers' conductor. "You're wrong about that, Alf," he said. "All over this country, working people are educating themselves. They join libraries and book-sharing clubs, musical societies and choirs. They go to Bible study groups and political discussion meetings. The London Corresponding Society has hundreds of branches."

Sal was excited by the idea. "We ought to be doing that—studying and learning. What's this Corresponding thing you said?"

"It was founded to discuss reform of Parliament. Votes for workingmen, and so on. It's spread everywhere."

Jarge said: "Not to Kingsbridge, it hasn't."

Sal said: "Well, it should. It's just what we need."

Another bell ringer, Jeremiah Hiscock, a printer with a shop in Main Street, spoke up. "I know about the London Corresponding Society," he said. "My brother in London prints some of their material for them. He likes them. He says they decide everything by majority vote. No difference between master and men in their meetings."

"Shows it can be done!" said Jarge.

"I don't know," said Sime anxiously. "We'll get called revolutionaries."

Spade said: "The London Corresponding Society isn't about revolution, it's about reform."

"Just a minute," said Alf. "Didn't some of the London Corresponding men get tried for treason, just before last Christmas?"

"Thirty of them," said Spade, who read newspapers avidly. "Charged with plotting against the king and Parliament. The evidence was that they had campaigned for parliamentary reform. It seems it's a crime now to say our government isn't perfect."

Alf said: "I don't remember whether they were hanged, or what."

Spade said: "They had the cheek to call Prime Minister William Pitt to court. He had to admit that thirteen years ago he campaigned for reform of Parliament himself. The case collapsed in laughter and the jury threw the charges out."

Sime was not reassured. "Even so, I shouldn't like to be tried for treason. A London jury might do one thing and a Kingsbridge jury the opposite."

Jarge said: "I don't care about juries. I'll take my chances."

Sal said: "You're as brave as a lion, Jarge, but we need to be clever as well as brave."

"I agree with Sal," said Spade. "Start a society, yes, but don't call it an affiliate of the London group—that would be asking for trouble. Call it . . . the Socratic Society, if you like."

"Buggered if I know what that means," said Jarge.

"Socrates was a Greek philosopher who believed you could get at the truth by discussion and argument. Canon Midwinter told me that. He said I was Socratic because I like a debate."

"I knew a Greek sailor once. He drank like a fish but he was no bloody philosopher."

The others laughed.

Spade said: "Call it whatever you like, as long as it doesn't sound subversive. Start with a meeting about something else, like science, the theories of Isaac Newton, say. Don't keep the meeting secret—tell the *Kingsbridge Gazette*. Have a committee to run it. Ask Canon Midwinter to be chairman. Make everything respectable, at least at first."

Sal was thrilled. "We have to do this!"

Jeremiah said: "But who's going to come to talk about science to a few Kingsbridge workingmen?"

They all agreed that that was unlikely. But Sal had an inspiration. "I know someone who went to Oxford," she said.

They all looked at her skeptically, except for Joanie, who smiled and said: "You're talking about Roger Riddick."

"That's right. He's a friend of Amos Barrowfield and he's often at our mill."

Spade said: "Can you ask him?"

"Of course. I was the first to work on his spinning jenny and I'm still operating the same machine. He always stops to ask me how it's going."

"He won't find that too forward of you?"

"I don't think so. He's not like his brother Will."

"So you'll ask him?"

"Soon as I see him."

Shortly after this they broke up. As Sal and Joanie walked home, Joanie said: "Are you sure about this?"

"About what?"

"Getting involved in this society."

"Yes, I can hardly wait."

"Why?"

"Because I work and sleep and take care of my child and I don't want that to be the whole of my life." She thought again of her aunt Sarah, talking about what she read in the newspapers.

"But you'll get into trouble."

"Not for learning about science."

"But it's not going to be just about science. They all want to talk about freedom and democracy and the rights of man. You know that."

"Well, Englishmen are supposed to have a right to their opinions."

"When they say that, they're talking about the gentry. They don't believe people like us should have opinions."

"But those men in London were found not guilty."

"All the same, Sime is right—you can't be sure a Kingsbridge jury will do the same."

Sal began to think Joanie might be right.

Joanie went on: "If mill hands start talking about politics, the aldermen and the justices are going to get scared—and their first instinct will be to punish a few people and frighten the rest. It's all right for Jarge and Spade—they've got no children. If they get transported to Australia, or even hanged, no one suffers but them. But you've got Kit, and I've got Sue, and who's to take care of them if we're not here?"

"Oh, Jesus, you're right." Sal had been so enchanted by the idea of the Socratic Society that she had not paid enough attention to the risks. "But I've said I'll speak to Roger Riddick. I can't let the others down now."

"Be careful, then. Be very careful."

"I will," said Sal. "I swear it."

CHAPTER 12

In a side chapel of Kingsbridge Cathedral was a wall painting of Saint Monica, the patron saint of mothers. The painting was medieval and had been whitewashed over in the Reformation, but the whitewash had thinned over two hundred and fifty years, and the face of the saint was now visible. Her skin was pale, which puzzled Spade, because she had been African.

Spade lit a candle there on the first day of August, exactly twelve years since his wife, Betsy, had died. Outside was a sky of hurrying clouds, and when the sun broke through it lit the arches of the nave, briefly turning gray stones to swoops of bright silver.

Spade stood looking into the candle flame and remembering Betsy. He thought of how exciting it had been for the two of them, both nineteen years old, to set up home together in a little cottage on the outskirts of Kingsbridge. They had felt like children playing at marriage. His loom and her spinning wheel had filled one of the two small rooms, and they had cooked and slept in the kitchen. As he worked, he could always glance up and see her dark head bent over the spindle, and he was never unhappy. They had been even more excited when she became pregnant, and they had talked endlessly about what their child might be like: beautiful, intelligent, tall, mischievous? But Betsy had died giving birth, and their child had never entered the world.

Time passed unnoticed while he remembered, until he became aware of someone standing nearby. He turned to see Arabella Latimer watching him. Without speaking, she held out a red rose—from her garden, he assumed. Guessing her intention, he took the rose from her hand and gently placed it in the center of the altar.

The blossom gleamed like a fresh bloodstain on the pale marble.

Arabella walked silently away.

Spade remained a few moments, thinking. A red rose was for love. She had intended it for Betsy. But she had given it to Spade.

He stepped out of the chapel. She was waiting for him in the nave. "You understand," he said.

"Of course. You come to the same chapel on the first of August every year."

"You noticed."

"You've been doing it for a long time."

"Twelve years."

"Methodists don't usually pray to saints."

"I'm a funny kind of Methodist. I'm not good at following rules." Spade shrugged. "The best thing about Methodists is that they think the heart matters more than the rules."

"And you believe that, too?"

"Yes."

"So do I."

"You'd better join the Methodists."

She smiled. "What a scandal that would be. The bishop's wife!" She turned and picked up a small pile of freshly laundered choir robes that she had put down on the font. "I must stow these in the vestry."

He did not want the conversation to end. "I assume you don't do the laundry yourself, Mrs. Latimer."

Of course she did not. "I supervise," she said.

"Well, you can supervise me if I carry the robes for you." He took the bundle from her and she let it go willingly.

She said: "Sometimes I feel that half my life is about supervision. If it were not for books I don't know what I'd do to fill the time."

He was interested. "What do you like to read?"

"I've got a book about the rights of women, by Mary Wollstonecraft. But I have to keep it hidden."

Spade did not have to ask her why. The bishop would disapprove strongly, he felt sure.

"I like novels, too," she said. *"The History of Tom Jones, a Foundling."* She smiled. "You remind me of Tom Jones."

The two of them walked across the nave. Nothing much was happening, but he felt tension between them like an unspoken secret.

He had not forgotten that moment in his sister's shop, more than two years ago, when she had caught him admiring her figure and had raised her eyebrows as if intrigued rather than offended. That look was vivid in his memory. He had told himself to forget about her, but he had failed.

He followed her through a low door in the south transept. The vestry was a small, bare room containing a bookshelf, a looking glass, and a large oak box called a cope chest. She lifted the heavy lid of the chest and Spade carefully laid the robes inside. Arabella scattered some dried lavender to keep away the moths.

Then she turned to him and said: "Twelve years."

He looked at her. There was a moment of sun outside, and a beam from a small window fell on her hair, picking out the auburn lights, which seemed to gleam.

He said: "I was remembering how much fun everything was when we were naïve youngsters. Innocent delight. It'll never happen again."

"You were in love with Betsy."

"Love is the best thing in the world to have, and the worst to lose." For a moment he felt terrible grief, and he had to fight back tears.

"No, you're wrong," she said. "Even worse is to be trapped and know you will never have it."

Spade was startled, not by what she had said—which he and others might have guessed—but by the fact that she had made such an intimate confession. However, he was curious as well as surprised, and he said: "How did that happen?"

"The boy I wanted married someone else. I thought I was brokenhearted, but wasn't, really, I was just angry. Then Stephen asked me and I said yes because it would be a poke in the eye for the boy."

"Stephen was much older."

"Twice my age."

"It's hard to imagine you being so rash."

"I was foolish when I was young. I'm not very wise now, but I used to be worse." She turned away and lowered the lid of the chest. "You asked me," she said.

"Sorry to be nosy."

"But most men would have told me what I ought to do."

"I have no idea what you ought to do."

"Something few men are willing to admit."

It was true, and Spade laughed.

Arabella walked to the door. Spade put his hand on the doorknob, but before he could open it for her, she kissed him.

It was clumsy. She lunged, and planted her lips inaccurately on his chin.

She hasn't had much practice at this, he thought.

But she quickly adjusted and kissed his mouth. She then drew back, but he sensed that she was not finished, and after a moment she kissed him again. This time she put her lips to his and let them linger. She really means it, he thought. He put his hands on her shoulders and returned the kiss, moving his mouth against hers. She clung to him, pressing her body against him.

Someone might come in, he thought. He was not sure what Kingsbridge would do to a man who kissed the bishop's wife. But he was too deeply sunk in pleasure to stop. She took his hands from her shoulders and moved them down, and he felt her soft breasts. They filled his hands. When he gently pressed them she made a quiet sound deep in her throat.

She came to her senses suddenly. She pulled away, looking intensely into his eyes. "God save me," she said quietly. Then she turned away, opened the door, and hurried out.

Spade stood still, thinking: What was that?

⁂

Alderman Joseph Hornbeam liked to see a good display at breakfast: bacon and kidneys and sausages, eggs, toast and butter, tea and coffee, and milk and cream. He did not eat much of it—coffee with cream and some toast—but it pleased him to know that he could feast like a king if he wanted to.

His daughter, Deborah, was like him, but his wife, Linnie, and their son, Howard, tucked in, and both were plump. So were the servants, who consumed the leftovers.

Hornbeam was reading *The Times*. "Spain has made peace with France," he said. He sipped his creamy coffee.

Deborah said: "The war's not over, though, is it?" She was quick. She took after him.

He said: "Not over for England, no. We haven't made peace with those murderous French revolutionaries, and I hope we never will."

He looked appraisingly at Deborah. She was not very attractive looking, he thought, though it was hard to judge your own children that way. She had abundant dark wavy hair and nice brown eyes, but her chin was too big for beauty. At eighteen she was old enough to be married. Perhaps she could be steered toward a spouse who might do some good to the family business. He said: "I saw you talking to Will Riddick at the theater."

She gave him a level look. She was not scared of him. Her brother was, and so was her mother. Deborah was respectful but not submissive. "Did you?" she said neutrally.

Trying to sound casual, Hornbeam said: "Do you like Riddick?"

She paused thoughtfully. "Yes, I do. He's the type of man who gets what he wants. Why do you ask?"

"He and I do good business together."

"Army contracts."

She did not miss much. "Exactly," he said. "I've invited him here for dinner tonight. I'm glad you like him—that should make for a pleasant evening."

The footman, Simpson, stepped into the room and said: "Alderman Hornbeam, sir, the milkman would like a word with you, if it should be convenient."

"The milkman?" Hornbeam was puzzled. "What the devil does he mean by it?" Hornbeam rarely spoke to the tradesmen who supplied the house. Then he remembered that he had lent money to this man: Alfred Nash was his name. He stood up, dropped his napkin on his chair, and went out.

Nash was standing in the back entrance hall, known as the boot lobby. Rain dripped from his coat and hat. Hornbeam caught a whiff of the dairy.

"Why have you come to see me, Nash?" he said abruptly. He hoped the man was not going to ask for more money.

"To give you some information, Alderman."

That was different. "Go on."

"I happened to hear something that would interest you and I thought I would pass it on, as you have so kindly loaned me the money to extend my dairy."

"Very well. What did you hear?"

"David Shoveller, the one they call Spade, is setting up a Kingsbridge branch of the London Corresponding Society."

That really was interesting information. "Is he, by the devil!"

Hornbeam hated Spade. He had frustrated Hornbeam's long-cherished plan to take over the business owned by Obadiah Barrowfield and inherited by Amos. The loan Spade had organized for Amos had thwarted Hornbeam and his work had been wasted.

Nash went on: "And you being the chairman of the Reeves Society..."

"Yes, of course." The Reeves Society had been set up by the government in opposition to the London Corresponding Society. The Kingsbridge Reeves Society had held a few lackluster meetings and petered out, but Hornbeam still had a useful list of right-thinking men who opposed radicalism. "Who else is involved in this new group?"

"Jarge Box, a weaver. Also Sal Clitheroe, who operates a spinning jenny for Amos Barrowfield. Even though she's only a woman they listen to her."

Such people maddened Hornbeam. "They just want to drag us all down into the gutter with them," he said bitterly. "We'll stamp out these troublemakers like the vermin they are. Spade will be hanged for treason."

Nash looked taken aback by Hornbeam's vehemence. He said: "But they were saying that the London men were found not guilty."

"Weakness, weakness. That's what allows this kind of thing to flourish. But London is London. This is Kingsbridge."

"Yes, sir."

"Keep an eye on this for me, Nash, would you?"

"I could do, sir. They asked me to be on their committee."

"Did you agree?"

"I said I'd think about it."

"Join the committee. That way you'll know everything."

"Very good, sir."

"And you'll report everything to me."

"I'll be happy to oblige you."

"We'll teach them a lesson."

"Yes, sir. May I mention another matter?"

Hornbeam had guessed Nash would want something. There was always a quid pro quo. "Go ahead."

"Business is bad, what with the war taxes and the price of food and so many hands not finding enough work."

"I know. It's bad for me, too." This was not true. Hornbeam was profiting from army contracts. But it was his policy never to admit to doing well.

"If I could miss my next quarterly payment it would be a big help."

"A postponement."

"Yes, sir. I'll pay it all off eventually, of course."

"You certainly will. But you have my permission to skip the next installment."

"Thank you, sir." Nash touched his cap.

Hornbeam went back to his breakfast.

A few days later, Roger Riddick showed up at Barrowfield's Mill.

The more Sal thought about it, the more important it seemed that Roger should give the first lecture to the Socratic Society. No one could object to a talk about science. And Roger was the son of the squire of Badford, which made him a member of the ruling elite. Furthermore, Roger would not ask for payment, which was important because the society could not afford to pay.

She had known Roger since childhood. Children did not pay much attention to the rules of social class, and a squire's child could splash about in a stream with the offspring of farm laborers. She had seen Roger grow up, and in his teens he had shown that he was different from the rest of his family.

But that did not mean he would do anything she asked.

He had lost the boyish look, Sal thought when he came into the spinning room. He was in his early twenties now. He was still good-looking, slender and fair, but he was not the type who appealed to her—she preferred a more manly man. All the same he had charm, especially when he grinned that impish grin. All the women liked him, and he even permitted a little light banter.

He said: "Hello, Sal, how's the old machine? Still going strong?"

"Yes, and the spinning jenny's fine, too, Mr. Riddick."

It was a joke they had shared several times before, and they both laughed.

"It seems so small now," Roger said. "These days they make engines with ninety-six spindles."

"So I hear."

Roger noticed Kit. "Hello, lad," he said. "How's your head?"

"Gives me no trouble, sir," Kit said.

"Good."

The other women had stopped work to listen. At the next machine, Joanie said: "Why aren't you in Oxford, Mr. Riddick?"

"Because I'm no longer a student. I've done my three years."

"I hope you passed your exams."

"Yes. I came top of the class in losing money at cards."

"And now you know everything."

"Oh, no. Only a woman can know everything."

The others cheered at that.

He said: "After Christmas I'm going to another university, the Prussian Academy of Sciences in Berlin."

"Prussia!" said Sal. "You'll have to learn German."

"And French. For some reason the lectures are in French there."

"More studying! Is there no end to it?"

"As a matter of fact I don't think there is."

"Well, the people of Kingsbridge are going to educate themselves, so watch out, we may catch up with you."

He frowned. "How so?"

"We're starting a new group called the Socratic Society."

"You're starting a Socratic society." He was trying to hide how astonished he was, she could see.

"And I've been told to ask if you would give the opening lecture."

"Really." He was still on the back foot in this conversation, which amused Sal. "Lecture," he said, evidently gathering his thoughts. "Yes, well."

"We thought you might speak about Isaac Newton."

"Did you."

"But actually you could pick any scientific subject."

"Well . . . at Oxford I studied the solar system."

She had no idea what the solar system was.

He sensed her perplexity and said: "The sun and the moon and the planets, you know, and how they go round and round."

That did not sound very interesting. But, she thought, what do I know?

He added: "I've made a little model showing the way they all move in relation to one another. I did it just for pleasure, but it could help people understand."

That sounded good. And Roger was coming around to the idea quickly. She might succeed.

"It's called an orrery," he said. "The model. Other people have made them."

"I think you should show it to everyone, Mr. Riddick. It sounds marvelous."

"Perhaps I will."

She tried not to grin with triumph.

Amos Barrowfield appeared. "You've stopped the women working, Roger," he said.

Roger said: "They're starting a Socratic society."

"Not during working hours, I hope." Amos put his arm around Roger's shoulders. "Come and see the scribbling machine working. It's a wonder." They walked away.

Then Roger stopped at the head of the stairs. "Let me know the date," he called to Sal. "Send me a note."

"I will," she replied.

The two men disappeared.

One of the women said: "You can't sent him a note, Sal. You can hardly write."

"You'd be surprised," said Sal.

Arabella spoke to Spade as if nothing had happened. When their paths crossed, in the market square or at his sister's shop or in the cathedral, she smiled at him coolly, spoke a few polite words, then passed on; as if she had never given him a red rose, they had not been alone together in the vestry, and she had never kissed him with hungry lips or pressed his hands to her breasts.

What was he supposed to think? He needed advice, unusual for him, but he could not speak of this to anyone. The little they had done—a kiss, fully clothed, lasting a minute—was dangerous to Arabella and him, but mainly to Arabella, for the woman always got the blame.

Perhaps there would be no repeat. Perhaps she wanted the kiss never to be spoken of, a secret that would be buried with them and be forgotten until the Day of Judgment. If so he would be disappointed, but he would do as she wished. However, his instinct told him she would not stick to such a plan. The kiss had not been casual, flirty, playful, a trifle. It had expressed an emotion, something deeply felt.

He tried to imagine what her life was like. The bishop was not just older: that might have been all right if he had been a lively, energetic old man fervently in love with her. But he was heavy, slow moving, self-important, and humorless. Perhaps there was nothing left of the desire that had given them Elsie. Spade had never been upstairs in the bishop's palace but he felt sure they had separate bedrooms.

And this had probably been going on for a long time, long enough for a normal woman of middle age to feel disillusioned and angry, and to start entertaining fantasies about other men.

Why Spade? He knew, though he would hesitate to say it to anyone else, that women often liked him. He enjoyed chatting to women because they made sense. If he asked a woman a serious question, such as: "What are you hoping for in life?" she would say something like: "Mainly I want to see my children become settled and happy adults, preferably with children of their own." If he asked a man the same question he would get a stupid answer, like: "I want to marry a twenty-year-old virgin with big tits who owns a tavern."

If Spade was right, and Arabella would eventually give in to her desire and try to start a real affair, how would he respond? The question was superfluous, he realized immediately. He would not make a rational decision; it would not be like buying a house. His feeling for her was a dam ready to burst at any moment. She was a smart, passionate woman who seemed to be in love with him, and he would not even try to resist.

But the consequences could be tragic. He recalled the case of Lady Worsley, who had been agonizingly humiliated. He had been eighteen at the time, and in love with Betsy, but he had already developed the habit of reading newspapers, usually out-of-date issues that had been thrown away by wealthier people. Lady Worsley had had a lover. Her husband had sued the lover for twenty thousand pounds, the value he put on his wife's chastity. Twenty thousand was a huge sum, enough to buy one of the best houses in London. The lover, no gentleman, had argued in court that her chastity was worthless because she had committed adultery with twenty other men before him. Every detail of Lady Worsley's romantic life had been revealed in court, reported in the newspapers, and drooled over by the public in many countries. The court had taken the lover's side and awarded Sir Richard damages of one shilling, implying that Lady Worsley's chastity was worth no more, a cruelly contemptuous verdict.

This was the kind of nightmare Spade would be risking if he made love to a bishop's wife.

And Arabella would suffer most.

Spade passed through the grand pillared entrance to the Kingsbridge Assembly Rooms, where the first meeting of the Socratic Society was to begin shortly.

He was anxious that it should go well. Sal and the others had high hopes invested in it. Kingsbridge workers were trying to improve themselves and they deserved success. Spade himself thought it was a big step in the progress of the town. He wanted Kingsbridge to be a place where workers were seen as people, not just "hands." But what if no one could understand the lecture? What if bored people became rowdy? Worst of all, what if no one came?

He entered the building at the same time as Arabella Latimer and her daughter, Elsie. The elite of the town were taking an interest. He shook the rain from his hat and bowed to the two women.

"I hear you've been to London, Mr. Shoveller," said Arabella stiffly. "I hope your visit went well."

It was standard small talk for social occasions, and he was disappointed by her formality, but he played along. "I enjoyed it, and did some good business as well, Mrs. Latimer. How have things been in Kingsbridge?"

"The same," she said, not looking at him. Then she added quietly: "Always the same."

Spade wondered whether Elsie could feel the tension. Women were sensitive to that kind of thing. But Elsie showed no sign. She said: "I want to go to London. I've never been. Is it as exciting as they say?"

"Exciting, yes," said Spade. "Busy, yes. Crowded, noisy, filthy, yes."

They entered the card salon, where the lecture was to be held. It was almost full, which eased one of Spade's worries.

A wooden box stood on a table in the middle of the room, and Spade guessed that Roger Riddick's orrery was inside it. The chairs and benches were arranged in circles around the table.

The audience was a mixture, the well-off in their best clothes and the mill workers in the drab coats and battered hats they wore every day. He noticed that the workers were all sitting on benches at the back, while the well-dressed had chairs near the front. That had not been planned, he knew; people must have instinctively created a social division. He was not sure whether that was amusing or just a bit sad.

Only a handful of women were there. Spade was not surprised: events like this were thought to be for men, although there was no prohibition against women.

Arabella turned away from Spade, pointed across the room to where two or three women sat together, and said to Elsie: "We should sit over there," making it clear that she did not want to sit with Spade. He understood, but he felt rejected.

Elsie turned that way. For a second Spade felt Arabella's hand on his upper arm. She squeezed hard, then instantly took her hand away and stepped across the room. It had been very brief but it was an unmistakable message of intimacy.

Spade felt slightly dizzy. An inexperienced girl might send false signals, but no mature woman would touch a man like that unless she meant it. She was telling him that they had a secret understanding, and he should take no notice of her superficial coldness.

He was thrilled, but he would do nothing about it. She was the one in most danger, so she had to be in control. He would just follow her lead.

Jarge Box came up to him, looking cross. It did not take much to make Jarge cross, so Spade was not worried. "Something wrong?" he said mildly.

"So many masters here!" Jarge said indignantly.

It was true. Spade could see Amos Barrowfield, Viscount Northwood, Alderman Drinkwater, and Will Riddick. "Is that so bad?" he said to Jarge.

"We didn't start the society for them!"

Spade nodded. "You've got a point. On the other hand, with them here we can hardly be accused of treason."

"I don't like it."

"Let's talk about it later. We have a committee meeting afterward."

"All right," said Jarge, pacified for the moment.

They sat down. Canon Midwinter stood up and called for quiet, then he said: "Welcome to the first meeting of the Kingsbridge Socratic Society."

Those at the back applauded.

Midwinter went on: "God has given us the ability to learn, to understand the world around us; night and day, the winds and the tides, the grass that grows and the creatures that feed on it. And he gave that ability to all of us, rich and poor, lowborn and high. For hundreds of years Kingsbridge has been a center of learning, and this new society is the latest manifestation of that hallowed tradition. May God bless the Socratic Society."

Several people said: "Amen."

Midwinter went on: "Our speaker tonight is Mr. Roger Riddick, recently graduated from Oxford University. He will speak about the solar system. Over to you, Mr. Riddick."

Roger got up and stood at the table. He looked relaxed, Spade thought; perhaps he had done this sort of thing at the university. Before speaking he turned a full circle slowly, looking at the audience with a pleasant smile. "If I spin round like this, but faster, it will look to me as if all of you were hurtling around me," he said, continuing to turn. "And when the Earth spins, creating night and day, it looks to us as if the sun is moving, coming up in the morning and going down in the evening. But appearances are deceptive. You're not moving, are you? I am. And the sun is not moving—the Earth is." He stopped, saying: "I'm getting dizzy," and the audience laughed.

"The Earth spins, and it also flies. It goes all the way around the sun once a year. Like a cricket ball, it can spin while it flies through the air. And the Earth is one of seven planets that all do the same. This is getting complicated, isn't it?"

There were chuckles and murmurs of agreement. Spade thought: Roger is good at this—he makes it all sound like everyday common sense.

"So I made a model to show how the planets go around the sun."

People leaned forward in their seats as he opened the box on the table and took out a device that looked like a stack of small metal discs. Sticking up from the center of the stack was a prong with a yellow ball at its end.

"This is called an orrery," Roger said. "The yellow ball is the sun."

Spade was pleased. This was going well. He caught sight of Sal and saw that she was glowing with pleasure.

Each disc in the stack had attached to it an L-shaped rod with a little ball stuck to its end. "The small balls are planets," Roger said. "But there's one thing wrong with this model. Does anyone know?"

There was silence for a few moments, then Elsie said: "It's too small."

There was a murmur of disapproval at a woman speaking up, but Roger said loudly: "Correct!"

Elsie had not been to the grammar school, for girls were not allowed there, but Spade recalled that she had had a tutor for a while.

Roger said: "If this model were to scale, the Earth would be smaller than a teardrop and ten yards away across the room. In reality the sun is ninety-three million miles from Kingsbridge."

They reacted to the impossibly large distance with sounds of amazement.

"And they all move, as we're about to see." He looked around the audience. "Who's the youngest person here?"

Immediately a small voice said: "Me, me."

Spade looked across the room and saw a boy with red hair standing up: Sal's son, Kit, He was about nine years old, Spade guessed. People laughed at his eagerness, but Kit saw nothing funny. He was a rather serious child.

"Come forward," Roger said. He turned to the audience. "This is Kit Clitheroe, born in Badford, like me."

Kit came up to the table and they gave him a clap.

"Just take hold of that handle gently," Roger said. "That's right. Now turn it slowly."

The planets began to move around the sun.

Kit was watching the effect of his turning with fascination. He said: "The planets all move at different speeds!"

"Correct," said Roger.

Kit looked closer. "That's because you've put gears in. It's like clockwork." His tone was admiring.

Spade had guessed that Roger's model used gearing, but he was surprised and impressed that a nine-year-old would figure that out. All mill hands worked with machines, of course, but not all of them understood how they worked.

Roger sent Kit back to his seat, saying: "In a few minutes everyone who wants to can have a go at turning the mechanism." Continuing with his lecture, he named the planets and gave their distances from the sun. He pointed out the moon, attached by a short rod to the Earth, then explained that some of the other planets had one or more moons. He showed how the tilt of the Earth made the difference between summer and winter. The audience was rapt.

At the end he got an enthusiastic round of applause, then people crowded around the table, eager to try making the planets turn around the sun.

Eventually the audience drifted away. Roger put his orrery back in its box and went off with Amos Barrowfield.

When only the committee members were left, they drew some benches into a circle and sat down.

The mood was triumphant. "I congratulate you all," said Canon Midwinter. "You made this happen—you didn't need me."

Jarge was dissatisfied. "This isn't what I wanted!" he said. "The solar system is all very well, but we need to know more about how we can change things so that our children don't go hungry."

Sal said: "Jarge is right. This was a good start, and it's made us look respectable, but it doesn't help us when food prices are sky-high and people can't find work."

Spade agreed with them both.

The printer Jeremiah Hiscock said: "Perhaps we should discuss *Rights of Man*, Thomas Paine's book."

Midwinter said mildly: "I believe it says a revolution is justified when the government fails to protect the people's rights, and therefore the French revolution was a good thing."

Sime Jackson said: "That would get us into trouble."

Spade had read *Rights of Man* and was a passionate believer in Tom Paine's ideas, but he saw the sense in the misgivings expressed by Midwinter and Jackson. "I have a better notion," he said. "Pick a book that criticizes Paine."

Jarge protested: "Why?"

"Take, for example, *Reasons for Contentment: Addressed to the Labouring Part of the British Public*, by Archdeacon Paley."

Jarge was outraged. "We don't want to promote that sort of thing! What are you thinking?"

"Calm down, Jarge, and I'll tell you what I'm thinking. Whether we pick Paine or Paley, the topic is the same, the reform of the British government, so we would have the same discussion. But it would look different to outsiders. And how can they object to us discussing a book that is addressed to us and tells us to be satisfied with our lot?"

Jarge looked angry, then bewildered, and then thoughtful, and at last he smiled and said: "By the deuce, Spade, you're a sly one."

"I'll take that as a compliment," said Spade, and the others chuckled.

Midwinter said: "A very good plan, Spade. The group may find that Archdeacon Paley's arguments are disappointingly weak, of course, but that couldn't possibly be construed as treason."

Jeremiah said: "There's a pamphlet called *A Reply to Archdeacon Paley* published by the London Corresponding Society. I know because my brother printed it for them. I've even got a copy at home. I could print a stack."

Sal said: "That would be very useful, but remember that this is for people who may not be able to read. I think we need a speaker to introduce the subject."

"I know someone," said Midwinter. "A clergyman who teaches at Oxford, Bartholomew Small, something of a maverick among the professors. He's no revolutionary, but he's sympathetic to Paine's ideas."

"Perfect," said Spade. "Please ask him, Canon." He turned to the group in general. "We need to keep this to ourselves for as long as we can, and announce it at the last minute. Believe me, there are plenty of people in this town who want to keep workingmen in ignorance. If we let the news out too soon we give our enemies time to organize. Secrecy is the watchword."

They all agreed.

CHAPTER 13

As a boy growing up in London, Hornbeam had been terrified of justices and the punishments they could impose. Now he was one of them, and he had nothing to fear. All the same, there remained, deep in the back of his mind, a faint tremor, the ghost of a memory, that made him feel momentarily cold when the clerk called the Michaelmas quarter sessions to order, and the trials began; and he had to touch his wig to remind himself that he was one of the masters now.

The council chamber in the Guild Hall was also used as the courtroom for the quarter sessions and for the assizes. Hornbeam liked the grandeur of the old room. The varnished paneling and the ancient beams confirmed his high status. But when it was full of Kingsbridge offenders and their tearful families he wished for better ventilation. He hated the smell of the poor.

With the assistance of a clerk who was legally trained, the justices tried cases of theft, assault, and rape in front of a jury of Kingsbridge property owners. They judged all crimes except those that carried the death penalty, for which they had to convene a grand jury to decide whether to commit the case to the assizes, the superior court.

Today they dealt with a lot of theft. It was September, and the harvest had failed—for the second year running. A four-pound loaf of bread now cost a shilling, almost double the usual price. People stole food, or stole something they could sell quickly for cash to buy food. They were desperate. But that was no excuse, in Hornbeam's view, and he argued for stiff sentences. Thieves had to be punished, or the whole system would collapse, and everyone would end up in the gutter.

At the end of the afternoon the justices gathered in a smaller room for Madeira wine and pound cake. The most important decisions in the life of the town were often made at informal moments such as this. Hornbeam took the opportunity to raise the subject of Spade's Socratic Society with Alderman Drinkwater, the chairman of justices. "I think it's dangerous," said Hornbeam. "He'll get speakers who will cause trouble, telling the hands they're underpaid and exploited and they should rise up and overthrow their rulers as the French did."

"I agree," said Will Riddick, who had become squire of Badford and a justice of the peace when his father died. "That violent woman Sal Clitheroe is part of it. She was banished from Badford for trying to attack me."

Hornbeam had heard a different version of that story, in which Sal had actually knocked Riddick to the floor, but it was understandable that Riddick left out that humiliating detail.

Hornbeam hoped that other justices would appreciate the danger, but he was disappointed. Alderman Drinkwater pushed a finger under his wig to scratch his bald head and said mildly: "I was at the meeting. It was about the solar system. There's no harm in that."

Hornbeam sighed. Drinkwater had never known anything but a comfortable life. He had inherited his father's business, sold it to Hornbeam, bought a dozen large houses, rented them out, and lived in idleness ever since. He did not know that prosperity could be fragile; he had learned nothing from the French revolution. His opposition was not surprising, but all the same Hornbeam had to resist the feeling of panic that rose within him when liberal-minded people turned a blind eye to the threat of insurrection by the lowborn. He took a calming sip of the sweet wine, making an effort to seem relaxed. "Very crafty of them," he said. "But I happen to know that their second meeting will advocate reform of Parliament."

Drinkwater shook his head. "You've got that wrong, Hornbeam, if you'll pardon my saying so. I understand from my son-in-law, Canon Midwinter, that they're studying Archdeacon Paley's book, which argues that laboring people should be content, and not get agitated about reform or revolution."

Riddick pointed a prodding finger at Drinkwater. "Your son-in-law won't be a canon much longer. He's broken with the Church of England and he's going to be the Methodist minister. They're already collecting money to pay him a salary."

"But Paley is still an archdeacon," Drinkwater countered. "And his book is *intended* to be studied by the laboring folk. I really don't see how anyone can object."

Looking around the small group, Hornbeam could see that he had failed to convince them, so he quickly dropped the subject. "Very well," he said grudgingly. He had a fallback plan, anyway.

The justices broke up, and Hornbeam walked away from the Guild Hall with Riddick. It was raining hard, as it had all summer, and they turned up their coat collars and pulled their hats forward. The second year of bad weather was sending the price of grain soaring; Hornbeam had bought a hundred bushels and stashed them in a warehouse. He expected to double his money when he sold.

As they walked, Riddick spoke hesitantly, which was unusual for him. "I must say . . . I admire your daughter, Deborah . . . very much," he said. "She's . . . quite lovely, and also, um, very, um, intelligent, too."

He was half right. Deborah was intelligent, and she looked pleasant enough, with the lithe figure that girls of nineteen had, but she was not really lovely. However, Riddick had fallen for her, or at least had decided she would make a good wife. Hornbeam was pleased: his plan was moving forward. But he tried to give no hint of his satisfaction. "Thank you," he said neutrally.

"I thought I should tell you that."

"I appreciate it."

"You know my position and my means," Riddick said. He was proud to be squire of Badford, though as ruler of a mere thousand or so villagers he belonged only to the minor gentry. "I presume I don't need to prove to you that I can afford to keep her in the style to which she's accustomed."

"Indeed not." Hornbeam was more interested in Riddick's position in the Shiring Militia. Hornbeam was paying him fat bribes—and getting good value for his money. Other suppliers queued up to pay Riddick backhanders and sell to the military at inflated prices. Everyone gained.

Riddick said: "I don't know whether Deborah reciprocates my feeling, but I would like to try and find out—with your permission."

Hornbeam muted his enthusiasm, not wanting to encourage Riddick to ask for a generous marriage settlement. "You have my permission, and my best wishes."

"Thank you."

Deborah was sensible enough to understand that she should make a match that was good for business, and she seemed to like Riddick. But he had a reputation for treating his villagers harshly, and that might put her off. In that case Hornbeam would have a problem.

They reached the Hornbeam house. "Come in for a moment," he said to Riddick. "There's something else I want to discuss with you."

They took off their wet coats and hung them up, dripping onto the tiled floor. Hornbeam caught sight of his son, Howard, crossing the hall, and said: "Get someone to mop up here, Howard."

"Of course," Howard said obediently, and headed down the stairs to the basement.

That reminded Hornbeam that he had also to solve the problem of a bride for his son. Howard would not even try to choose a wife for himself. He would be content with whomever his father selected. But what woman would want to marry Howard? One who wanted ease and plenty but was not able to win such a life with her looks. Or, to be blunt, a girl who was ambitious but plain. Hornbeam would have to keep his eyes open.

He led Riddick into his study, where there was a fire. He noticed his guest looking eagerly at a decanter of sherry on the sideboard, but they had just had Madeira in the Guild Hall, and Hornbeam felt it was not necessary for a man to drink wine every time he sat down.

Riddick said: "I'm sorry you didn't get your way with the other justices. I did my best, but they didn't follow my lead."

"Don't worry. There's more than one road to London, as they say."

"You've got a contingency plan." Riddick smiled and nodded knowingly. "I might have guessed."

"I didn't tell Drinkwater everything I know."

"You kept something up your sleeve."

"Exactly. Jeremiah Hiscock is printing copies of a pamphlet from the London Corresponding Society called *A Reply to Archdeacon Paley*. I understand it contradicts everything Paley says. They're planning to distribute the copies at the meeting."

"Who told you that?"

It was Nash, the dairyman, but Hornbeam did not say so. He touched the side of his nose in the common gesture of secrecy. "I'll keep that to myself, if you'll forgive me."

"As you wish. How can we use the information?"

"I think it's straightforward. I suspect the pamphlet is seditious to the extent of criminality. If so, Hiscock will be charged."

Riddick nodded. "How do we handle it?"

"We go to Hiscock's house with the sheriff and search the place, and if he's guilty we exercise our right, as justices, to give summary judgment."

Riddick smiled. "Good."

"Go and see Phil Doye now. Tell him to meet us here tomorrow at first light. He'd better bring a constable."

"Very good." Riddick stood up.

"Don't tell Sheriff Doye what it's about—we don't want the news to leak out and give Hiscock a chance to burn the evidence before we get there. And anyway Doye doesn't need a reason, it's enough that two justices tell him the search is necessary."

"It certainly is."

"I'll see you at dawn."

"Count on it." Riddick left.

Hornbeam sat looking into the fire. People like Spade and Canon Midwinter thought they were clever, but they were no match for Hornbeam. He would put a stop to their subversive activities.

It occurred to him that he was taking a risk. Alf Nash's information could be wrong. Alternatively, Hiscock might have printed the pamphlets and hidden them, or given them to someone else for safekeeping. These were uncomfortable possibilities. If Hornbeam raided Hiscock's house at dawn with the sheriff and a constable and found nothing incriminating he would look foolish. Humiliation was the one thing he could not bear. He was a man of importance and merited deference. Unfortunately, risks were necessary sometimes. In his forty-odd years he had taken some dangerous chances, he reflected, but he had always come through—usually richer than before.

His wife, Linnie, opened the door and looked in. He had married her twenty-two years ago, and she was no longer suitable as his spouse. If he could have his time over he would make a better choice. She was not beautiful and she spoke like a lowborn Londoner, which she was. She clung stubbornly to habits such as putting a large loaf of bread on the table and cutting slices as needed with a big knife. But getting rid of her would be too much trouble. Divorce was difficult, requiring a private act of Parliament, and it was bad for a man's reputation. Anyway, she ran the house efficiently, and on the infrequent occasions when he wanted sex she was always willing. And the servants liked her, which oiled the domestic wheels.

The servants did not like Hornbeam. They feared him, which he preferred.

She said: "Supper is ready, if you are."

"I'll come right away," he said.

Simpson, the lugubrious footman, woke him early, saying: "A wet morning, sir. I'm sorry."

I'm not sorry, Hornbeam said to himself, thinking of the grain stockpiled in his warehouse, making more money for him with every rainy day.

"Mr. Riddick is here, with the sheriff and Constable Davidson," said Simpson, as if announcing a tragic death. His tone never changed. He sounded disappointed even when saying that dinner was served.

Hornbeam drank the tea Simpson had brought and dressed quickly. Riddick was waiting in the hall. He was talking in a low voice to Sheriff Doye, a pompous small man in a cheap wig. Doye carried a heavy stick with a large knob of polished granite for a handle, an object that could pass for a walking cane and also serve as a formidable weapon.

By the door stood the constable, Reg Davidson, a big-shouldered man who bore the scars of several fights: a broken nose, one half-closed eye, and the mark of a knife wound on the back of his neck. Hornbeam thought that if Davidson had not been a constable he would probably have made his living as a footpad, attacking and robbing incautious men carrying money after dark.

Rain dripped from the coats of all three men.

Hornbeam briefed them. "We're going to Jeremiah Hiscock's house in Main Street."

"The printing works," said Doye.

"Exactly. I believe Hiscock is guilty of printing a

pamphlet that is seditious and treasonable. If I'm right, he'll hang. We're going to arrest him and confiscate the printed matter. I expect him to protest loudly about his freedom of speech but offer no real resistance."

"His employees won't be at work yet," said Davidson. "There'll be no one there to give us a fight." He sounded disappointed.

Hornbeam led the way out of the house. The four men walked quickly along the High Street and down the slope of Main Street. The cathedral gargoyles were gushing rainwater. The print shop was at the bottom end of the street, within sight of the river, which was high and flowing fast.

Like all but the most prosperous Kingsbridge tradesmen, Hiscock lived at his business premises. There was no basement, and the front of the house had not been altered, so Hornbeam guessed the print shop must be at the back.

Hornbeam said: "Knock on the door, Doye."

The sheriff banged four times with the knob of his stick. The family inside would know that this was not a polite call by a friendly neighbor.

The door was opened by Hiscock himself, a tall, thin man of about thirty who had hastily put on a coat over his nightshirt. He knew immediately that he was in trouble, and the sudden fear in his eyes gave Hornbeam a shiver of pleasure.

Doye spoke in a tone of immense self-importance. "The justices have been informed that these premises are being used for the printing of seditious material."

Hiscock found a measure of courage. "This is a free country," he said. "Englishmen are entitled to their opinions. We are not Russian serfs."

Hornbeam said: "Your freedom does not include the right to subvert the government—as any fool knows." He made a gesture urging Doye forward.

"Get out of the way," said Doye to Hiscock, and he barged into the house.

Hiscock stood back to admit them, and Hornbeam followed Doye, with the other two in tow.

Having made a masterful gesture, Doye found himself unsure where to go. After a moment of dithering he said: "Um, Hiscock, you are ordered to escort the justices to your print shop."

Hiscock led them through the house. In the kitchen they were stared at by his frightened wife, a bewildered maid, and a little girl sucking her thumb. Hiscock picked up an oil lamp as he passed through the room. The back door of the house led directly into a workshop that smelled of oiled metal, new paper, and ink.

Hornbeam looked around, suffering a moment of uncertainty, staring at unfamiliar machinery, but he quickly figured out what was what. He identified trays containing metal letters, neatly sorted in columns; a frame in which the letters were arranged to form words and sentences; and a heavy device with a long handle that had to be the press. All around were stacked bundles and boxes of paper, some plain and some already printed.

He looked at the letters in the frame: this must be Hiscock's work in progress. Perhaps it was the incriminating pamphlet, he thought, his heart beating a little faster. But he could not read the words. "More light!" he said, and Hiscock obediently lit several lamps. Still Hornbeam could not read what was in the frame: the words seemed to be spelled backward. "Is this in code?" he said accusingly.

Hiscock looked at him with contempt. "What you're looking at is a mirror image of what will appear on the sheet of paper," he said; then, in a tone of scorn, he added: "As any fool knows."

As soon as this was pointed out, Hornbeam realized it was obvious that the metal letters must be a right-to-left reversal of the printed image, and he felt foolish. "Of course," he said abruptly, smarting from Hiscock's *As any fool knows*.

Looking at the type in this light he saw that it was a calendar for the coming year, 1796.

Hiscock said: "Calendars are my specialty. This one features all the church festivals of the year. It's popular with the clergy."

Hornbeam turned away from the frame impatiently. "This isn't what we're looking for. Open all those boxes and untie the bundles. There's revolutionary propaganda here somewhere."

Hiscock said: "When you realize there's no such material here, will you help me repack the boxes and tie up the bundles?"

Such a stupid question did not merit an answer, and Hornbeam ignored it.

Doye and Davidson began the search, and Hornbeam and Riddick looked on. Hiscock's wife came in, a slim woman with chiseled good looks. She assumed a defiant air that was not quite convincing. "What's going on?"

Hiscock said: "Don't worry, my dear. The sheriff is looking for something that isn't here."

Hornbeam was a bit worried by how confident he sounded.

Mrs. Hiscock looked at Sheriff Doye. "You're making an awful mess."

Doye opened his mouth to speak, but apparently failed to think of what to say, and he just closed his mouth again.

Hiscock said to his wife: "Go back to the kitchen. Give Emmy her breakfast."

Mrs. Hiscock hesitated, evidently not pleased at being dismissed; but after a moment she disappeared.

Hornbeam looked around. The woman was right, the place was beginning to look untidy; but more important, they had not found anything subversive. "Just calendars, mainly," said Doye. "A box of leaflets for the theater, all about their coming shows, and a flyer for a new shop selling fancy tableware."

Hiscock said: "Are you satisfied now, Hornbeam?"

"Alderman Hornbeam, to you." He feared this was going to be mortifying. Stubbornly he said: "It's here somewhere. Search the living quarters."

They went through the ground floor without finding anything. The place was furnished comfortably if cheaply. Hiscock and his wife watched the search attentively. Upstairs were three bedrooms, plus an attic room that was probably for the maid. They went first to what was plainly the marital bedroom, where a large double bed was still unmade, strewn with colorful blankets and rumpled pillows. As Doye searched Mrs. Hiscock's chest of drawers she said sarcastically: "Anything of interest to you among my underclothes, Sheriff?"

Hiscock said: "Don't bother, dear. They've been sent on a wild goose chase." But there was a tremor of fear in his voice, and Hornbeam thought the searchers might be getting close to a discovery.

They found nothing in the wardrobe or blanket press. There was a large Bible beside the bed, bound in brown leather, not old but much thumbed. Hornbeam picked it up and opened it. It was the standard King James translation. He riffled the pages and something fell out. He bent to the floor and picked it up.

It was a sixteen-page pamphlet, and the title on the cover was *A Reply to Archdeacon Paley*.

"Well, well," said Hornbeam with a satisfied sigh.

"There's nothing subversive in that," said Hiscock, but he had gone pale. Sounding desperate, he added: "It's an aid to Bible study."

Hornbeam opened the pamphlet at random. "Page three," he said. "'Benefits of the French revolution.'" He looked up, his lips twitching in a sneer. "Tell me, pray, where in the Bible do we find mention of the French revolution?"

"The Book of Proverbs, chapter twenty-eight," said Hiscock without hesitation, and he quoted: "'As a roaring lion and a raging bear, so is a wicked ruler over the poor people.'"

Hornbeam took no notice, but continued to examine the pamphlet. "Page five," he said. "'Some advantages of the republican form of government.'"

"The author is entitled to his opinion," Hiscock said. "I don't necessarily agree with everything he says."

"Last page: 'France is not our enemy.'" Hornbeam looked up. "If that's not undermining our military forces, I don't know what is." He turned to Riddick. "I think he's been found in possession of seditious and treasonable material. What do you think?"

"I agree."

Hornbeam turned back to Hiscock. "Two justices have found you guilty. Treason is a hanging offense."

Hiscock began to tremble.

"We will go outside to consider the punishment." Hornbeam opened the door and held it for Riddick. They stepped onto the landing and Hornbeam closed the door, leaving the sheriff and the constable with the Hiscocks.

Riddick said: "We can't hang him ourselves, and I don't trust the assize court to find him guilty."

"I agree," said Hornbeam. "Unfortunately, there is no evidence that he printed or otherwise disseminated this poison. It's possible that the pamphlets have already been run off and stashed somewhere secret, but that's no more than a guess."

"So, a flogging?"

"It's the best we can do."

"A dozen lashes, perhaps."

"More," said Hornbeam, remembering how disdainfully Hiscock had said *As any fool knows*.

"Whatever you like."

They went back inside. "Your punishment will be light, considering your offense," he said to Hiscock. "You will be flogged in the town square."

Mrs. Hiscock screamed: "No!"

With satisfaction Hornbeam said: "You will receive fifty lashes."

Hiscock staggered and almost fell.

Mrs. Hiscock began to cry hysterically.

Hornbeam said: "Sheriff, take him to Kingsbridge Jail."

Spade was at his loom when Susan Hiscock burst into his workshop, hatless, her dark hair soaked with rain, her large eyes red with weeping. "They've taken him away!" she said.

"Who?"

"Alderman Hornbeam and Squire Riddick and Sheriff Doye."

"Who did they take away?"

"My Jerry—and he's going to be flogged!"

"Calm yourself. Come with me to my room." He led her through the doorway. "Sit down. I'll make you some tea. Take a deep breath and tell me all about it."

She told him the story while he put a kettle on the fire and assembled tea leaves, a pot, milk, and sugar. He made her tea extra sweet, to give her strength. What she said disturbed him. Hornbeam was moving against the Socratic Society despite Spade's precautions.

When she had finished he said: "Fifty lashes! That's outrageous. This isn't the navy." Fifty lashes was not punishment, it was torture. Hornbeam wanted to terrify people. He was fanatically determined to stop Kingsbridge workers from educating themselves.

"What am I going to do?"

"You must visit Jerry in jail."

"Will they let me?"

"I'll speak to the jailer, George Gilmore, they call him Gil. He'll let you in. Just give him a shilling."

"Oh, thank God, at least I can see Jerry."

"Take him some hot food and a flagon of ale. That will help keep his spirits up."

"All right." Susan was looking a little brighter. Being able to do something for Jeremiah had braced her.

Now he had to make her misery worse. "He will also need an old pair of trousers and a wide leather belt."

She frowned. "Why?"

It had to be said. "The trousers will be shredded by the whip. The belt is to protect his kidneys." Some men pissed blood for weeks. Some never recovered.

"Oh, God." Susan cried again, more softly now, in grief rather than panic.

Spade asked the question that weighed heavily on his mind. "Did they say who informed against your husband?"

"No."

"Any hint?"

"No."

Spade nodded. It had to be someone on the committee. There were two or three possibilities, but he thought the likeliest was Alf Nash. There was something shifty about that dairyman.

I'll find out, he thought grimly.

Susan hardly cared who the traitor was. She was thinking of her husband. "I'll take him a stew of bacon and beans," she said. "His mother used to make that for him." She stood up. "Thank you, Spade."

"Give him my best . . ." Spade did not know how to finish the sentence. Wishes? Regards? Blessings? "Best love," he said.

"I will."

She left, still grief-stricken but calmer now and resolute. Spade returned to his loom and mulled over the news as he operated the machine. If the Socratic Society needed print work in the future he would have to use a different printer, one out of the reach of the Kingsbridge justices, probably in Combe.

He did not get much work done before he was interrupted again, this time by his sister, Kate, wearing a canvas apron with pins stuck in it. "Can you come to the house?" she said. "Someone to see you."

"Who?"

She lowered her voice, though there was no one nearby to hear. "The bishop's wife."

Spade felt a mixture of eagerness and trepidation. Just to see Arabella was a thrill, and now she was asking for him. But their attraction to one another was dangerous. All the same, he was not going to refuse her summons. "Right away," he said, and he hurried across the rain-swept courtyard with Kate.

When they were inside Kate said: "She's upstairs, door on the right. No one else is up there."

"Thanks." Spade climbed the stairs. The three rooms on this floor were bedrooms, but were mainly used as changing rooms for customers. Arabella was in the largest room, standing by the bed, wearing the check coat Kate had made from Spade's cloth three years ago. Spade said formally: "Mrs. Latimer! This is an honor." She was agitated, he saw.

In a low voice she said: "Shut the door."

He closed the door behind him. "What's the matter?"

"Jeremiah Hiscock is to be flogged for possessing a seditious pamphlet."

"I know. His wife just told me. News travels fast. Why are you so concerned?"

She lowered her voice to a frantic whisper. "Because you could be next!"

The fact that she cared so much touched Spade's heart. But was she right to worry? Was he breaking the law? He did not have seditious materials in his possession, but he was certainly involved in organizing a meeting that might criticize the government, question the wisdom of the war against France, and argue for republicanism. Whether that was a crime was not clear, but justices had wide powers to interpret the law as they pleased.

Flogging was a painful and humiliating punishment.

But he could not back out of the Socratic Society now. Hornbeam and Riddick were bullies and crooks and they could not be allowed to rule Kingsbridge as if they were royalty. "I don't think I'm in danger," he said to Arabella, managing to sound more confident than he felt.

"I can't bear the idea!" she said, and she threw herself into his arms. "I've thought about your body so often and so long, and now I can't stop imagining your skin torn and gouged and bloody."

He hugged her. "You really care," he said, bemused by the strength of her passion.

She stepped back and wiped her eyes. "You have to give up the Socratic Society. It's going to cause trouble. The bishop says the justices won't allow it."

"I can't give it up."

"That's just your pride speaking!"

"Perhaps it is."

"But really, does all this revolutionary talk do any good? It just makes people discontented with their lot."

"Is that what the bishop says, too?"

"Well, yes, it is, but isn't he right?"

"He doesn't understand. People like us cherish the right to have our own opinions and express them. You can't imagine how important it is."

"You say *people like you*. Do you think I'm different?"

"Well, yes. You're the bishop's wife. You can do what you like."

"You know that's not true. If I could do as I like I'd be in that bed with you." She gazed at him, and he marveled at the wonderful orange-brown color of her eyes. "Naked," she added.

This was extraordinary. He had never heard any woman speak like this, let alone a bishop's wife. He felt exhilarated beyond measure. He said: "That would be worth getting flogged for."

She stepped closer and unbuttoned her coat. It was an invitation, and he stroked her body, exploring the curves, feeling her warm flesh through the dress. She looked into his eyes as he touched her. He felt sure they were going to make love now, here, on the bed.

Then he heard Kate's voice outside saying: "You can try it on up here, Mrs. Tolliver."

Spade and Arabella froze.

There were footsteps on the stairs, and another voice said: "Oh, thank you."

Spade turned to the door. It was closed, but there was no key in the lock. He saw that Arabella had turned pale. He stood with the toe of his boot against the bottom of the door, to prevent its being opened.

Then he heard the sound of another handle being turned and another door being opened. Mrs. Tolliver had gone into the room across the landing. That door closed, then there was a soft tap and Kate's voice said quietly: "All clear."

Spade opened the door for Arabella. "You go first," he said.

She left without a word.

Kate looked down at the lock and said: "I'd better get a key for that."

He knew she would keep his secret. He had kept hers for years. He remembered walking into her bedroom, when they were adolescents, and seeing her kissing her girlfriend's breasts. He had left hastily, but they had talked later, and she had told him that she loved women, not men, but no one must know. He had promised not to tell, and he never had.

Now she looked hard at him and said: "Be careful, for goodness' sake."

He smiled. "I've said that to you many times. But we take risks for love."

"It's not the same. No one suspects two women. They think you can't have sex without a cock. But you're a single man and she's the bishop's wife: if they find out they'll crucify you."

They would not literally crucify him, of course, but

they could make it impossible for him to do business in Kingsbridge. "We've never done anything!" he said. "Well, one kiss."

"But you're going to do more, aren't you?"

"Well . . ."

She shook her head in despair. "We're two of a kind, you and I."

They went down the stairs together. Spade left by the back door and crossed the courtyard to his own quarters.

He needed to talk to Alf Nash. It might be revealing to see whether the man's reactions betrayed any signs of guilt. At this time of day Alf would be at his dairy. Spade put on his hat and coat, picked up his milk jug, and went out again.

Alf was alone in the shop, counting money from his morning round. He was chubby-faced and healthy looking, as he should have been with all that butter and cheese to eat. Spade put his jug on the counter.

Alf dipped a measuring jug into a bucket of milk. Spade waited until he was concentrating on pouring from his jug into Spade's, then said: "Did you hear they arrested Jeremiah?" He watched Alf's face closely as he waited for the answer.

Alf spoke in a firm voice without hesitation. "I heard it a dozen times on my round. Everyone's talking about it." He finished pouring and said: "A penny, please, Spade." His expression was impassive, but he did not meet Spade's eye.

Spade handed over a coin.

He thought Alf was guilty, but he wanted to be more sure, and suddenly he thought of a way. He leaned over the counter and spoke confidentially. "They found only one pamphlet, the original from London."

"So I hear."

"Fortunately, Jeremiah finished printing the copies yesterday and stashed them in my warehouse." This was a lie.

Alf looked directly at him for the first time. "In your warehouse? That was clever."

Alf believed the lie, Spade thought with satisfaction. "We've outwitted that swine Hornbeam," he said. Then he elaborated on the lie. "We'll have all the copies we need for our meeting."

"Excellent news," Alf said, but his tone was emotionless and Spade was sure he was acting.

Spade picked up his jug and went to the door. He had one more thing to say. He turned back. "Don't tell anyone what I just said, will you."

"Of course not," said Alf.

"Don't even discuss it with other committee members. Walls have ears."

"My lips are sealed," said Alf.

In the hour before noon a crowd gathered in the market square for the flogging, despite the rain. Goods were laid out on the stalls, and the Bell tavern was open, but people did not have much money to spend. Nevertheless the square became packed, except for a space around the whipping post, which people shunned as if it might be contaminated and they feared infection.

The Kingsbridge executioner stood by the post with his whip in his hand. His name was Morgan Ivinson, and flogging was one of his duties. He was an unpopular man who did not care for popularity, which was just as well, because no one wanted to be friends with an executioner. He was paid a pound a week plus a pound for every execution—very good wages for little work.

He got two shillings and six pence for a flogging.

Jeremiah was brought from Kingsbridge Jail, which stood next to the Guild Hall. Naked from the waist up, his hands tied in front, he was marched down Main Street by two constables. As the people in the square caught sight of him a sympathetic murmur rose up.

If the convicted man was a burglar or a footpad the

crowd would jeer at him, yelling insults and even throwing rubbish: they hated thieves. But this was different. They knew Jeremiah and he had done no harm to them. He had read a pamphlet that advocated reform, and most of them believed that reform was long overdue. So there was not much mockery, and when some lads near the post began to catcall they were told to shut up by others in the crowd.

Spade was standing on the cathedral steps, looking over the scene. Next to him, Joanie was carrying what looked like a large clean bedsheet. Spade said: "What's that for?"

"You'll see," said Joanie.

Sal was there, too. She said: "Tell me, Spade, who betrayed us? Somebody told Hornbeam that Jeremiah was going to print that pamphlet. Who was it?"

"I don't know," said Spade. "But I'm going to find out."

Jarge said: "When you do, let me know."

"What will you do?"

"Explain to the man the error of his ways."

Spade nodded. He knew what Jarge's explanation would involve, and it was not quiet words of wisdom.

Sheriff Doye officiously shoved his way through the crowd. The constables brought Jeremiah to the whipping post, a crude structure of three wooden beams in the shape of a door frame. Hornbeam and Riddick brought up the rear, as the justices who had imposed the sentence.

Jeremiah was placed in the timber rectangle like a figure in a picture frame. His hands were tied to the crosspiece above his head, exposing all of his back.

The whip was the standard cat-o'-nine-tails, the destructive power of its nine thongs increased by the stones and nails embedded in the leather. Ivinson shook it, as if testing its weight, and straightened the thongs carefully.

Every town and village had such an implement. So did every ship in the Royal Navy and every unit in the army. It was thought to be essential to law and order and military discipline. People said it deterred crime and misbehavior. Spade doubted that.

A clergyman came out of the cathedral. Spade, Jarge, Sal, and Joanie stepped out of his way. Spade did not know the man but he was quite young and was probably a junior. The bishop would not lower himself to attend this routine punishment, but the church had to show that it approved of what was happening. The crowd spotted the clerical robes and quietened a little, and the clergyman loudly intoned a prayer and asked God to forgive the crime of the guilty man. Not many people said amen.

Hornbeam nodded to Ivinson, who positioned himself behind Jeremiah and to the left so that his right arm could swing back widely.

The crowd went quiet.

Ivinson struck.

The sound of the whip on skin was loud. Jeremiah made no noise. Red welts appeared on his back but no blood was drawn.

Ivinson drew back his arm and struck again. This time, pinpricks of blood showed.

Ivinson moved slowly: the punishment was not supposed to be quick. If he tired the torture would simply go on longer. He drew back his arm a third time, and struck a third time, and now Jeremiah began to bleed in several places. He let out a groan.

The whipping went on. More cuts appeared on Jeremiah's back. For variety, Ivinson struck his legs, shredding his trousers and revealing his bottom.

Sheriff Doye called out: "Ten." It was his job to count the strokes.

Jeremiah's back was soon all bloody. Now the whip landed not on skin but on the flesh beneath, and he began to cry out in pain. The sheriff said: "Twenty." The agony became tedious to watch, and some spectators moved away, repelled and bored, too, but most stayed to see it through to the end. Jeremiah began to scream each time the whip landed, and between strokes he uttered a horrible sound that was half sobbing and half moaning.

"Thirty."

Ivinson was tiring now and taking longer between lashes, but he seemed to hit just as hard. When he lifted the whip, it shed pieces of skin and flesh, and the spectators cringed back, revolted by the bits of a human being falling on them like living rain.

Jeremiah was naked now but for his boots and the leather belt. He was losing the ability to scream and instead cried like a child.

"Forty," said Doye, and Spade thanked God it was coming to an end.

At forty-five, Jarge said to Joanie: "Now."

Spade watched as the two of them, brother and sister, pushed through the crowd toward the whipping post.

Jeremiah's eyes were closed, but he was still crying.

The last stroke was made and Doye said: "Fifty."

Jarge stood in front of Jeremiah. The constables untied his hands and he collapsed, but Jarge held him upright. Joanie unfolded the bedsheet and draped it over the ruin of Jeremiah's back. Jarge turned him around, then Joanie wound the sheet around Jeremiah's front to hide his nakedness. Jarge turned him around again, stooped and let the half-conscious man fall across his shoulder, and stood upright.

Then he carried Jeremiah home to his wife.

Two days later Spade was awakened by a loud knocking on his warehouse door at dawn.

He knew who it was. Less than forty-eight hours earlier he had told Alf Nash that subversive leaflets were concealed here in the warehouse. Alf had believed the lie, and—as Spade had intended—had passed the false intelligence to Hornbeam, who had told Sheriff Doye. It was the sheriff's peremptory knock that had sounded.

Alf was the traitor, and had fallen into the trap.

Spade called out: "I'm coming!" But he took his time putting on his trousers and boots, shirt and waistcoat. He was not going to confront authority half dressed. It was important to look respectable.

The knocking was repeated, louder and more insistent. "Be patient!" he shouted. "I'm coming!" Then he opened up.

As he expected, he saw Hornbeam, Riddick, Doye, and Davidson. Doye said: "The justices have been informed that seditious and treasonable printed material is stored on these premises."

Spade turned to Hornbeam, who was glaring at him with an expression that reminded Spade of the phrase *if looks could kill*. "You are most welcome, Alderman."

Hornbeam looked puzzled. "Welcome?"

"Of course." Spade smiled. "You will search the premises thoroughly and clear my name of this filthy rumor. I will be most grateful." He saw Hornbeam's features shift with unease. "Please come in." He held the door and stood back as they trooped through.

They began to look around. "You'll need some light," Spade said, and he began to light lamps, giving one to each of the four men. They all looked uncomfortable. They were used to resentment and obstruction from people whose homes were being searched, and they could not understand Spade's amiable reaction.

They examined bales of cloth in the warehouse, pulled the blankets off Spade's bed, and inspected Spade's loom and those of his other weavers, as if hundreds of leaflets might have been concealed in the warp and weft.

Eventually they gave up. Hornbeam was so angry and frustrated that he looked as if he would burst.

Spade walked the party to the street. It was full light now, and there were people in the High Street, going to work and opening shops. Spade insisted on shaking hands with the furious Hornbeam, thanking him for his courtesy in a loud voice to attract the attention of passersby. In a short time everyone in town would know that Hornbeam had searched Spade's warehouse and found nothing.

Spade returned to his room and made breakfast. As he was washing his plate, Jarge came in. "I heard all about it," he said. "Why did Sheriff Doye think you had subversive pamphlets?"

"Because Alf Nash told him so."

Jarge was struggling to understand. "But you didn't have them."

"Of course not."

"So why did Alf think you did?"

"Somebody told him so."

"Who did?"

"I told him."

"But . . ." Jarge looked perplexed. "Wait a minute."

Spade smiled, watching him work it out. Eventually enlightenment dawned. "You're a sly dog, Spade."

Spade nodded.

Jarge said: "This proves that Alf Nash is a traitor. Therefore, he must be the one who informed on Jeremiah."

"That's what I think."

Jarge looked grim. "I believe I know what needs to be done next."

"I'm sure you do," said Spade.

CHAPTER 14

At the breakfast table, Hornbeam was speculatively eyeing Isobel Marsh.

She was known as Bel, but she was not beautiful. However, she was lively, and Hornbeam's family liked her. Bel had stayed over last night. At breakfast, Deborah and Bel were looking at prints in a magazine called *The Gallery of Fashion*, and laughing at what they considered to be ridiculous hats, wide-brimmed and festooned with ribbons, feathers, and brooches.

Howard was laughing with them, and that was what had caught Hornbeam's attention. Now he studied Bel more closely. She had bright blue eyes and a full red mouth, with lips that struggled to close over very prominent front teeth. She might do very well as a bride for Howard.

Her father, Isaac Marsh, had the best-run dyeing business in town. He employed a dozen or so hands and made plenty of money. Some years ago Hornbeam had made discreet inquiries about whether Marsh might want to sell the business. It would have made a splendid addition to Hornbeam's empire. But the answer had been no.

However, Bel was an only child. If she married Howard they would inherit the dye shop. And it would effectively become Hornbeam's.

As he watched the young people at the table, Howard said: "It looks like a family of pigeons are nesting in that hat!" The girls giggled and Bel playfully smacked Howard's arm. He pretended that it had hurt and said his arm was broken, and Bel laughed again. She seemed to like Howard.

Hornbeam had never before seen Howard flirting. The boy was good at it, in his way. He had not got that from his father. Well, well, thought Hornbeam, maybe I'll get the dye shop after all.

His wife, Linnie, asked the footman for more milk. Wearing his usual tragic face, Simpson said: "I'm sorry, madam, but just at the moment there is no more milk."

That irritated Hornbeam. Could all these servants between them not manage to organize enough milk for the family breakfast? He said crossly: "How can we have run out of milk?"

"Nash did not deliver this morning, sir, so I've had to send the maid to the dairy. She should be back any minute now."

Linnie said: "That's all right, Simpson, we can wait a few minutes."

"Thank you, madam."

Hornbeam did not like Linnie's way of being forgiving to the servants, but he said nothing because he was thinking about something more important. Simpson's announcement had rung an alarm bell. Alf Nash had not delivered milk this morning. Why?

Hornbeam was troubled by the negative result of his search of Spade's warehouse. He suspected that the cunning Spade had moved the offending leaflets, probably after getting a tip-off. But who could have warned him? Hornbeam had not yet figured this out. Meanwhile, this was a new development. What had happened to keep Nash from his round this morning?

Hornbeam was worried. He stood up. Linnie raised an eyebrow: he had not finished his coffee. "Something I need to take care of," he muttered by way of explanation, and he left the room.

He put on his coat and hat and a pair of riding boots to keep his legs dry, then left the house. He hurried anxiously through the rain to the dairy and stepped inside gratefully. There was a small crowd of people, mostly servants from the big houses north of High Street, all carrying jugs of various sizes. His maid Jean was among them, but he did not acknowledge her.

Nash's sister, Pauline, was behind the counter, briskly serving the unusual number of customers as fast as she could. Hornbeam pushed his way to the front. "Good morning, Miss Nash."

She gave him a cool look. "Good morning, Alderman. I'm sorry you haven't had your delivery—"

"Never mind that," he said impatiently. "I'm here to speak to Nash."

"I'm afraid he's in bed ill. Would you like some milk? I can lend you a jug—"

Hornbeam was in no mood to take insolence from a woman. He raised his voice. "Just take me to him, will you?"

She hesitated, looking insubordinate, but she did not have the courage to defy him. "If you insist," she said sulkily.

He stepped around the counter. Pauline abandoned her customers and led him into the living quarters. He followed her up the stairs. She opened a door and looked in. "Alderman Hornbeam is here, Alfie," she said. "Do you feel up to seeing him?"

Hornbeam pushed past her. The bedroom was instantly recognizable as Nash's by the smell of curdled milk. It was decorated simply in plain colors and lacking any feminine touches such as cushions, ornaments, or embroidered fabrics. Although Nash was in his thirties, he was still single.

He was lying on top of the bedclothes, and Hornbeam was shocked to see that he was dressed mostly in bandages. One leg and one arm were strapped in splints, and there was a dressing around his head. Blood was seeping through in patches. He looked terrible.

He spoke thickly, as if his mouth was hurting. "Come in, Mr. Hornbeam."

Pauline stood at the door with her hands on her hips and said to Hornbeam: "This is your fault."

Hornbeam was angered. Keeping his temper, he said coldly: "That will be all, Miss Nash."

She ignored that. "I hope you're here to make amends for what you've done."

"I've done nothing."

Nash said: "Go back to the shop, Pauline. You're losing money, standing there."

Looking cross, she left the room without curtsying.

Hornbeam said to Nash: "What the devil happened to you?"

Nash did not turn to look at Hornbeam—perhaps it hurt to move his head. With his gaze fixed on the ceiling he said: "This morning before dawn, when I went out to the cowshed to start work, I was attacked by three men with masks on their faces and cudgels in their hands."

This was what Hornbeam had feared. And he felt sure Spade was behind it. "You've seen the surgeon, evidently."

"He says I've got a broken arm and a cracked shin."

"You seem very calm."

"I was the opposite of calm until he gave me laudanum."

Laudanum was opium dissolved in alcohol.

Hornbeam pulled up a chair and sat close to Nash. Suppressing his rage, he spoke in a measured voice. "Now, think carefully," he said. "Although they had masks, did any of the men seem familiar?" He did not imagine that Spade was among them: the man was too sly for that. But perhaps the perpetrators were men who could be linked with Spade.

"It was dark," Nash said in a tone of hopelessness. "I hardly saw a thing. In no time I was on the ground. All I could think of was getting away from those cudgels."

"What did you hear?"

"Just grunts. None of them spoke."

"Didn't you cry out?"

"Yes, until they smashed my mouth."

"So you can't identify them."

Nash was indignant. "Yes, I can. They were the people who formed the Socratic Society."

"Of course they were."

"They're furious because of Hiscock's flogging and somehow they know I was responsible. Even so, they might have accepted a dozen lashes. But you went too far."

Hornbeam ignored the criticism. "We can't establish guilt if you didn't recognize anyone. You can't get up in court and say they beat you up because you were spying on them for me."

"So I'm supposed to do nothing? What shall I tell Sheriff Doye? He's bound to come here asking."

"Don't worry about Doye. Just tell him you were set upon by men in masks. Did they steal anything?"

"They took my bag of change, all pennies and halfpennies. It didn't amount to five shillings."

"Men have been killed for less than five shillings. That will do as a story for the *Kingsbridge Gazette*. But in truth your assailants didn't want the money. They took it just to make the assault look like a robbery and divert suspicion from the Socratic Society."

"Nobody will be fooled."

"No, but it makes our case hard to prove. Which means we must deal with it another way."

There was silence for a minute or two while Hornbeam thought, then he said: "That devil Spade did this, you know. He must be the one who found you out as a spy."

"What makes you think that?"

Hornbeam began to see the picture. "He told you the pamphlets were at his warehouse. He didn't tell anyone else. When I showed up there to search for them, that proved that you had told me, so you must be the spy."

"And the pamphlets were never there."

"They may not even have been printed."

"It was a trap."

"And we fell into it." Spade was devilish clever, Hornbeam thought angrily. He would have to be crushed. Yes, he thought, like a beetle under my heel.

"My spying days are over," Nash said.

"Absolutely. You're no use to me now."

"I can't say I'm sorry. But you'll have to help me with money. The surgeon says it will be months before I can do my round again."

"Get someone else to deliver the milk."

"I will. But I'll have to pay him, probably twelve shillings a week."

"I'll cover that as long as you're disabled."

"And there's the surgeon."

Hornbeam did not see how he could avoid paying these expenses. If he refused, Nash would complain all over town, and the whole story would come out, how Hornbeam set a spy to betray the Socratic Society. That would look very bad. "All right."

But money was not Hornbeam's main worry. He had been outwitted by Spade, which made him mad with vexation. He had to do something.

He stood up. "Let me know when you've found someone to do the milk round, and I'll send the money." He went to the door, eager to get away before Nash could think up any more demands. He glanced back: Nash lay still, staring at the ceiling, white as a corpse. Hornbeam went out.

He brooded as he walked through the rain. He had the feeling that he was losing control of events, and that unnerved him. Twice now he had tried and failed to put an end to the Socratic Society: first Alderman Drinkwater had refused to ban the group, and now punishing Hiscock had backfired.

The real trouble, he thought in frustration, was that the law was too vague and feeble. The country needed a tougher ban on sedition. There was talk in the newspapers of stronger treason laws. Members of Parliament should stop talking, get off their backsides, and do something. What was Parliament for if not to keep the peace and crush troublemakers?

The member of Parliament for Kingsbridge was Viscount Northwood.

Northwood had never taken his parliamentary duties very seriously, and now that the country was at war and the militia was active he had a good excuse. However, he still went to Westminster from time to time, so perhaps he could be persuaded to support new laws against groups like the Socratic Society.

Hornbeam went to the market square and entered Willard House.

Stamping his wet boots in the hall to shake off the rain, he spoke to a sergeant with graying hair. "Alderman Hornbeam to see Colonel Northwood immediately."

The sergeant said haughtily: "I'll inquire whether the colonel is free."

Typical of a lowborn upstart, Hornbeam thought. The man had probably been a butler before getting conscripted into the militia. "What's your name?" Hornbeam said.

The man clearly did not like being questioned, but was not brave enough to stand up to an alderman. "Sergeant Beach."

"Carry on, Beach."

Northwood was a Whig, and they were more liberal than the Tories, Hornbeam reflected while he waited. However, Northwood had a reputation for military efficiency, and that usually went with a strict attitude toward insubordination. On balance, there was a good chance Northwood would be against the Socratic Society.

He decided not to mention what had happened to Alf Nash. He should avoid looking as if he was on a personal vendetta. Better to present himself as a citizen concerned with the general welfare.

Sergeant Beach returned promptly: it seemed that Northwood had a sense of Hornbeam's status, even if his sergeant did not. A few moments later Hornbeam was shown into a spacious room at the front of the house, with a blazing fire and a view of the west front of the cathedral.

Northwood sat behind a large desk. To one side stood a young man in lieutenant's uniform, evidently an aide. To Hornbeam's surprise Jane Midwinter, the handsome daughter of the rogue canon, was also there, wearing a red coat like a soldier. She was sitting on the edge of Northwood's desk as if she owned it.

When she saw Hornbeam she stood up and curtsied, and he bowed politely. He recalled hearing Deborah and Bel talking about Jane, saying that she had set her cap at Northwood, so presumably she was here to progress her scheme of winning his heart. Midmorning was not the usual time for social calls, but perhaps Jane Midwinter was one of those beautiful women who thought they could do anything.

The girls thought Jane had no chance of hooking the viscount because her father was a Methodist. Looking at the dopey expression on Northwood's face now, Hornbeam had a feeling they might be wrong.

He hoped she was not going to stay. To his relief she walked to the door, blew a kiss at Northwood, and went out.

Northwood reddened and looked awkward, then said: "Sit down, Alderman, do."

"Thank you, my lord." Hornbeam took a chair. Northwood's vulnerability to Jane suggested that he had a soft side. This was not good news. The times demanded hard men.

The times always demanded hard men.

"May I offer you some refreshment?" Northwood said politely. "It's a foul day out there."

There was a tray on Northwood's desk bearing a coffee pot and a jug of cream. Hornbeam remembered that he had not finished his breakfast. "A cup of coffee would be most welcome, especially if it had a splash of cream in it."

"By all means. A clean cup, Sergeant, at the double."

"Right away, sir." Beach went out.

Northwood was courteous but brisk. "Now, Alderman, I imagine your visit has a purpose?"

"I trust the cloth I've been supplying for militia uniforms has been perfectly satisfactory?"

"I believe so. There have been no complaints."

"Good. I know you delegate the responsibility for purchasing, but if for any reason you wanted to speak to me about the cloth, naturally I'd be glad to do anything I can for you."

"Thank you," said Northwood with a touch of impatience.

Hornbeam quickly switched to his real purpose. "However, I've come to see our member of Parliament, rather than the commanding officer of our militia. I trust that's all right."

"Of course."

"I'm concerned about the Socratic Society that has been formed by Spade—David Shoveller—and some of the lower elements in the town. I think its true aims are subversive."

"Oh? I went to their first meeting."

That was a setback.

Northwood went on: "It was rather good. And quite harmless."

"That's a measure of how sly Spade is, my lord. They have lulled some of us into a false sense of security."

Northwood did not like the implication that he had been fooled, "I see no indication that they might be violent."

"I happen to know that their second meeting will be about reform of Parliament."

Northwood was not overly impressed. "That's a different matter, of course," he said, but he did not seem very worried. The sergeant brought a china cup and saucer, poured coffee and cream, and handed it to Hornbeam, while Northwood went on: "It all depends on what's said. But we certainly can't ban the meeting in advance. Merely planning a meeting to discuss Parliament isn't against any law."

"That's the problem," Hornbeam said. "It *should* be against the law. And I hear that there is much talk in Westminster of toughening up the laws on sedition."

"Hmm. You're right about that. Prime Minister Pitt wants to clamp down. But Englishmen are entitled to their opinions, you know. We're a free country, within reason."

"Indeed. And I'm a strong supporter of freedom of speech." This was the opposite of the truth, but it was a good thing to say. "However, we're at war, and the country needs to be united against the damned French."

Northwood shook his head. "You can go too far with repression, you know."

That had never worried Hornbeam. "I don't see just what you mean."

"Well, I'm sure you've heard what happened to Alf Nash, the dairyman."

Hornbeam was startled. How did Northwood know about that already? "What has that got to do with anything?"

"People are saying that Nash accused the printer who was flogged, and was beaten in revenge."

"That's outrageous!" protested Hornbeam, knowing full well that it was true. Spade and his friends had already put this story out around town, Hornbeam guessed.

"I have men flogged sometimes," Northwood said. "It's an appropriate punishment for thievery or rape. But a dozen or so lashes is plenty. The man is hurt and humiliated in front of his friends, and he vows never to take that risk again. However, sentences of fifty lashes or more are seen as vicious cruelty, and arouse sympathy for the offender. The man becomes a hero. He shows the scars like campaign medals. The punishment backfires."

Hornbeam saw that he was getting nowhere. "Well,

all I can say is that Kingsbridge traders on the whole would like to see subversive meetings banned."

"I'm not surprised. But we also have a duty to our inferiors, don't we? A horse that never leaves the stable soon loses its strength."

Hornbeam was wasting his time. He stood up abruptly. "Thank you for seeing me, my lord."

Northwood did not stand. "Always a pleasure to talk to one of my more prominent constituents."

Hornbeam left with a foreboding that amounted almost to panic. He had now suffered three defeats. The forces of disorder had allies in unexpected places.

He needed to think, and he did not want to go to his home where he might be interrupted by everyday problems. He crossed the market square and went into the cathedral. The quiet atmosphere and the cool gray stones helped him concentrate.

The heart of the problem was complacency. People saw no danger in a club for workers who sought knowledge. Hornbeam knew better. But he needed to shake others out of their torpor. Any group that encouraged hands to speak freely was opening a door. Insurrection was never far below the surface.

If the next meeting of the society should turn violent, it would prove his point.

Perhaps that could be arranged.

Yes, he thought, this could be the answer.

An outbreak of violence at the meeting would turn the town against the society. There might be arguments about who started it, but few people would care. Their attachment to free speech would not survive a few broken windows.

But how to organize it?

His mind immediately went to Will Riddick. Although the Riddicks were gentry, Will consorted with Kingsbridge lowlife. He spent a lot of time at Sport Culliver's notorious house. He would know a few ruffians.

Hornbeam went out into the rain yet again and made his way to Riddick's house.

Riddick's butler took Hornbeam's wet coat and hat and hung them near the hall fire. "Squire Riddick is at breakfast, Alderman," he said.

Hornbeam looked at his pocket watch. It was approaching midday. This was a late breakfast.

The butler opened a door and said: "Are you able to see Alderman Hornbeam, sir?"

Riddick's voice came: "Send him in."

Hornbeam went into the dining room and saw that Riddick was not alone. Sitting beside him was a young woman in a nightdress and wrapper, her long black hair unbrushed. In front of them was a plate of marrow bones, split and grilled, and the two of them were spooning out the marrow and gobbling it with relish. "Come in, Hornbeam," said Riddick. "Oh, by the way, this is . . ." He seemed unable to remember the girl's name.

"Mariana," she said. She gave Hornbeam an arch look. "I'm Spanish, you see."

About as Spanish as my arse, Hornbeam thought.

"Have a bone," Riddick said hospitably. "They're delicious." He took a long drink from a tankard of ale. His eyes were bloodshot.

"No, thank you," said Hornbeam. He turned to the butler, who was about to leave the room. "But I'd appreciate a cup of strong coffee with cream."

"Right away, sir."

Hornbeam sat down. He was uncomfortable at the same table as Mariana. He thought prostitution was disgusting. But he needed Will's help. "I've been trying to organize a ban on this so-called Socratic Society started by Spade."

"And that mad cow Sal Clitheroe."

"Yes. Alf Nash has been beaten up, and Viscount Northwood, our member of Parliament, declines to help."

"But you've got a plan, haven't you?" Riddick said knowingly.

"Oh, look," said Mariana. "I've spilled marrow on my chest. Can you help me get it off, Willy?"

Riddick picked up a napkin and wiped the visible tops of her breasts.

"Why don't you use your tongue?" said Mariana.

This was too much for Hornbeam. "Look, Will, can we talk in private?"

"Of course," said Riddick. "Off you go, sweetheart."

Mariana got up, pouting.

"I'll use my tongue on you later, darling," Riddick said.

"I'll be waiting."

When the door closed, Hornbeam said: "It's about time you gave up this sort of thing. You're getting married soon—to my daughter."

Riddick looked embarrassed. "Of course, of course," he said. "In fact I was really just saying goodbye to Mariana."

"Good." Hornbeam did not believe that for a second. But he did not press the point. He was not willing to jeopardize the fat profits he was making with Riddick's help.

"I'll be a model husband," Riddick vowed. "The bachelor life is over for me."

"I'm very glad to hear it. Having a whore at your breakfast table is really beyond the bounds of respectable behavior."

The butler came in with Hornbeam's coffee.

Riddick said: "Tell me about your plan."

"The people likely to go to Spade's meetings are already sympathetic. There may be no one to present a different point of view. What they need is some vigorous opposition."

"Vigorous?"

Riddick caught on fast, Hornbeam reflected. "I've no doubt there are many stoutly patriotic lads in town who would be outraged by the sort of nonsense spouted by Spade and Sal."

Riddick nodded slowly.

"I imagine you might know some of those lads."

"I certainly know where to find them. The Slaughterhouse Inn, down at the waterfront, would be the place to start."

That sounded good. "Do you think you could get some of them to come along to the next meeting?"

"Oh, yes," said Riddick with a grin. "They'll be very willing."

CHAPTER 15

Amos ran into Rupe Underwood on the High Street and realized they had not met for a while. The Methodists had at last split from the Church of England, and Rupe was probably among those who decided to stick with the established church. Amos asked him directly. "Have you given up on us Methodists?"

"I've given up on Jane," Rupe said sourly. He tossed his head to get the hair out of his eyes. "Or, rather, she's given up on me."

This was important news to Amos. "What's happened?"

Rupe's handsome face twisted in a grimace of disappointment and resentment. "She has jilted me, that's what. So you can have her. I won't even be jealous. She's all yours, as far as I'm concerned."

"She canceled the engagement?"

"We were never formally engaged. We had an 'understanding.' Now we don't. Goodbye, she said, and God bless you."

Amos felt sorry for Rupe, but at the same time he could not help being filled with hope. If Jane no longer wants Rupe, is there a chance that she might want me? He hardly dared to think about it. "Did she say why she was breaking it off?"

"She didn't tell the truth. She says she has realized that she doesn't love me. I'm not sure she ever did. The truth is that I haven't got enough money."

Amos still did not understand. "But something must have happened to change her feelings."

"Yes. Her father resigned from the Anglican clergy. He's no longer a canon of the cathedral."

"I know, but—" Then it hit him. "Now he's poor."

"He'll be living on whatever the Methodist congregation can scrape together to pay him. No more fancy clothes for Jane, no maids to dress her and do her hair, no more embroidered undergarments."

Amos was shocked by the mention of undergarments. Rupe could not know anything about Jane's undergarments, could he? But they had been a sort of couple for a long time. Perhaps she had permitted liberties.

Surely not.

Amos decided not to think about it. "Has she fallen for someone else?" he asked.

"Not as far as I know. She flirts with everybody. Howard Hornbeam is probably the richest bachelor in Kingsbridge—perhaps she'll set her cap at him."

It was possible, Amos thought. Howard was not very bright, and certainly not handsome, but he was amiable, unlike his father. "Howard's a couple of years younger than Jane, I think," he said.

"That won't hold her back," said Rupe.

On Sundays, after the morning services in the town's churches and chapels, some Kingsbridge folk were in the habit of visiting a graveyard. Amos occasionally felt the impulse to spend a few minutes remembering his father, and went from the Methodist Hall to the cathedral cemetery.

He always paused at the tomb of Prior Philip. It was the largest monument there. Philip, a twelfth-century monk, was a figure of legend, though not much was known about him. According to Timothy's Book, a history of the cathedral started in the Middle Ages and added to later, Philip had organized the rebuilding of the cathedral after it was destroyed in a fire.

Amos looked away from the monument and saw Jane Midwinter at another grave a few yards away, dressed in somber gray. Since his conversation with Rupe he had been hoping for a chance to talk to her. This was a most inappropriate moment, but he could not resist the temptation. He went to stand beside her and read the tombstone:

> Janet Emily Midwinter
> 4th April 1750
> to
> 12th August 1783
> Beloved wife of Charles
> and mother of Julian, Lionel, and Jane
> "With Christ, which is far better"

He tried to picture Jane's mother, but it was hard. "I hardly remember her," he said. "I must have been ten when she died."

"She loved pretty clothes, and parties, and gossip. She liked noblemen and women. She would have loved to meet the king." Jane's eyes were moist. Something clutched at his heart. But was she putting on an act? She often did.

He stated the obvious: "And you're like your mother."

"And my brothers aren't." Julian and Lionel were away at Scottish universities. "They're both like my father, all work and no play. I love my father, but I can't lead his kind of life."

She was in an unusual mood, he thought; he had never known her to be this honest about herself.

She said: "And the trouble with Rupe is that he, too, is like my father."

Most Kingsbridge clothiers were like that. They worked hard and had little time for leisure.

Amos had a flash of insight. "I suppose I am, too."

"You are, too, dear Amos, though I have no right to criticize you. Where is your father's grave?"

He offered her his arm and she rested one hand lightly

on his sleeve, friendly but not intimate, as they crossed the graveyard.

She had never spoken so affectionately to him, yet she was explaining why she would never be his sweetheart. I don't understand women, he thought.

They came to his father's grave. He knelt beside the tombstone and removed a scatter of debris from the ground: dead leaves, a scrap of rag, a pigeon's feather, a chestnut shell. "I suppose I'm like my father, too," he said, and stood up.

"In that way, perhaps. But you're so high-minded. It makes you formidable."

He laughed. "I'm not formidable, though I'd quite like to be."

She shook her head. "Put it this way: I wouldn't like to be your enemy."

He looked into her wide gray eyes. "Nor my wife," he said sadly.

"Nor your wife. I'm sorry, Amos."

He longed to kiss her. "Yes," he said. "I'm sorry, too."

The Kingsbridge Theatre looked like a grand town house, classical in style, with rows of identical windows. The interior was a large hall with benches on a flat floor, and a raised stage at one end. Against the wall were balconies held up by wooden posts. The most costly seats were on the stage, and it seemed to Amos that the expensively dressed rich people there were part of the show.

The first play of the evening was *The Jew of Venice*, and a painted backdrop showed a waterside city with ships and boats. Elsie came and sat next to Amos. They had been running the Sunday school together for more than two years, and they were close friends now.

Amos had never watched a Shakespeare play. He had seen ballet, opera, and pantomime at the theater, but this was his first drama, and he was looking forward to it eagerly. Elsie had seen Shakespeare before and had read this particular piece. "It's really called *The Merchant of Venice*," she said.

"I expect they sell more tickets if they say *Jew* instead of *Merchant*."

"I suppose so." There were Jews in Combe and Bristol, mostly involved in the re-exporting trade, buying tobacco from Virginia and selling it on the European continent. A lot of people hated them but Amos could not see why. They believed in the same God as Anglicans and Methodists, didn't they?

"People say Shakespeare is hard to understand," Amos said.

"Sometimes. The language is old-fashioned, but if you listen carefully it will touch your heart all the same."

"Spade says it can be violent."

"Yes, bloodthirsty now and again. There's a scene in *King Lear* . . ."

Amos saw Jane Midwinter coming in.

Elsie abandoned the subject of Shakespeare. "You know Jane has broken with poor Rupe Underwood," she said.

"Yes. He's very bitter about it."

"What does she think she's doing? She's kept that wretched man hanging on for two years and now she's just dismissed him like a bad servant."

"Rupe isn't very rich, and she wants to live comfortably. Lots of people want that."

"I might have known you'd make excuses for her," Elsie said. "That girl doesn't know the meaning of love."

Amos shrugged. "I'm not sure I do."

"It's an unlucky man who falls for Jane."

Elsie's criticism of Jane was making Amos uncomfortable. He said: "Jane is one of those women who is liked by men and disliked by women, I don't understand why."

"I do."

The audience went quiet and Amos pointed to the stage, relieved to escape the argument. Three actors had appeared, and now one of them said: "In sooth, I know not why I am so sad."

"I know why I'm sad," Elsie said.

Amos wondered what she meant, but he got caught up in the play. When Antonio explained that all his wealth was invested in ships currently at sea, Amos murmured to Elsie: "I appreciate what that's like, having valuable goods in transit, being worried sick about whether they're safe."

He felt restless in the second scene, when Portia complained about not being allowed to choose a husband for herself, but having to marry the winner of a contest having to do with choosing the right box out of three, one of gold, one of silver, and one of lead. "Why would her father do such a thing?" he said. "It makes no sense."

"It's a fairy tale," Elsie said.

"I'm too old for fairy tales."

The whole thing came alive when Shylock appeared in the third scene. He stormed onto the stage wearing a false nose and a wig that looked like a bright red bush, and when the audience booed he rushed to the front of the stage and snarled at them. At first they laughed at him. Then came the moment when he agreed to lend Antonio three thousand ducats, on condition that if Antonio failed to reimburse him on time he would pay a forfeit. "Let the forfeit be nominated for an equal pound of your fair flesh, to be cut off and taken in what part of your body it pleaseth me," Shylock said with sly malice.

"He'll never agree to that," Amos said, then he gasped when Antonio said: "Content, i'faith, I'll seal to such a bond."

During the intermission there was a ballet, but much of the audience ignored it, choosing instead to stretch their legs, buy food and drink, and chat to their friends. Elsie disappeared. The sound of conversation among so many people rose to a roar. Amos noticed that Jane made a beeline for Viscount Northwood. She was a shameless social climber, but Henry Northwood did not seem to mind. Amos moved closer to hear what Jane was saying.

"My father says we shouldn't hate Jews," Jane said. "What do you think, Lord Northwood?"

"I can't say I care for foreigners of any type," he replied.

"I agree with you," said Jane.

Jane would agree with anything Northwood said, Amos thought sourly. She didn't really hate Jews, she just loved noblemen.

"English is best," Northwood said.

"Oh, yes. All the same, I'd like to travel. Have you been abroad?"

"I spent a year on the continent. Picked up a few words of French and German, and bought some pictures in Italy."

"Lucky you! Are you a lover of painting?"

"In my simple soldierly way, you know. Anything with horses in it, or dogs."

"I'd love to see your pictures one day."

"Oh, well, of course, yes, but they're at Earlscastle, and I've so much to do here in Kingsbridge. You see, the militia, even though it doesn't serve overseas, has taken over the defense of our country so that the regular army is free to fight abroad." Suddenly Henry was loquacious, Amos observed, now that the subject was military. Henry added· "But that depends on the militia being ready to fight, you see."

Jane did not want to talk about the militia. "I've never been to Earlscastle," she said.

Amos did not linger to hear Henry's response to this heavy hint, because the play was recommencing. He hurried back to his seat. As he sat down Elsie said: "Will you walk me home afterward?"

"Of course," he said.

She seemed very pleased, although he could not imagine why.

He was rapt by Shylock and annoyed by the lovers in Belmont, but he had never seen anything like this, and at the end he wanted to go to more Shakespeare plays. "I may need you to explain things to me," he said to Elsie, and once again she looked pleased.

As they were leaving he said: "Could Jane marry Northwood? Isn't she too low on the social scale? He's going to be the earl of Shiring when his father dies, and she's the daughter of a mere clergyman, and a Methodist at that. The countess of Shiring has to meet the king sometimes, doesn't she? You know more about that sort of thing than I do."

It was true. As daughter of the bishop Elsie was closer to the nobility than to the clothiers. She probably could have married Northwood herself, though Amos felt sure she had no wish to. And she picked up all the gossip from visitors to the bishop's palace. "It would be difficult, but not impossible," she said. "Noblemen do sometimes marry unsuitable girls. But for years now it's been understood that Henry will marry his second cousin Miranda, the only child of Lord Combe, and thereby amalgamate two estates."

"But an understanding can be annulled," Amos said. "Love conquers all."

"No, it doesn't," said Elsie.

Three children from the same family were buried in St. Luke's graveyard on a cold, wet morning in September. All three had been regular pupils at Elsie's Sunday school, and she had watched them become more pale and scrawny each week. One thick slice of cake had not been enough to save them.

Their father had operated a fulling engine in Kingsbridge until, one day, a loose hammer head had become detached, flown off its shaft, and hit him on the head, killing him. After that his wife and children had moved into a cheap cellar room in a crumbling house, and the mother had tried to make a living as a seamstress, leaving the children alone in the cellar while she went out looking for people who needed some sewing done quickly and cheaply. The children had fallen ill with the kind of coughing and wheezing ailment that afflicted people in damp cellars, and having so little strength they had all succumbed in a single day. Now their mother sobbed at the graveside, her head covered with a cotton rag because she did not have a hat. The hymn was "The Lord's My Shepherd," and Elsie had the sinful thought that the shepherd had failed to take care of these three lambs.

St. Luke's was a small brick church in a poor neighborhood, and the vicar had roughly darned black stockings on his skinny legs. A surprising number of people stood around the grave, most of them shabbily dressed. They sang without enthusiasm, perhaps thinking that the shepherd had not done much for them either.

Elsie wondered whether their grief would one day turn to anger and, if so, how soon.

She herself felt anguished and at the same time helpless. She thought how she might have taken those three children home and fed them in the palace kitchen every day, and in the next moment she realized this was a hopeless fantasy. But she had to do something.

As the pitifully small coffins were lowered into the grave, Amos Barrowfield came and stood beside Elsie. He wore a long black coat and sang the hymn in a strong baritone. His face was wet, with tears or rain, or both.

His presence calmed and consoled Elsie. She forgot that she was cold and wet and miserable. He did not make problems go away, he just made them seem smaller and more manageable. She slipped her arm through his and he squeezed her hand against his chest in a sympathetic gesture.

When the burial was over they walked away from the grave together, still arm in arm. "This will happen again," she said to him in a low voice. "More of our children will die."

"I know," he said. "Cake isn't enough."

"Surely we could give them something more . . ." She was thinking aloud. "Like broth. Why not?"

"Let's consider how we could do that."

She loved this about him. He acted as if anything were possible. Perhaps this was because he had overcome such difficulties after his father died. The experience had left him with a positive attitude that matched her own.

She said: "Instead of baking pound cakes, our supporters could make broth with peas and turnips."

"Yes, and cheap cuts of meat like mutton neck." Amos pulled the end of his nose, a sign that he was thinking. "Will they do it?"

"It depends who asks them. Would Pastor Charles approach the Methodists?"

"I'll ask him."

"And I'll work on the Anglicans."

"We could go around the bakers on Sunday mornings and ask for the stale bread they haven't sold on Saturday."

"They sell their surplus cheaply last thing on Saturday—but they probably still have some left."

"Anyway, we can ask them."

They were now outside the bishop's palace, and they halted. Elsie said eagerly: "Shall we try it?"

Amos nodded solemnly. "I think we must."

She wanted to kiss him, but instead she detached her arm. "Next Sunday?"

"Of course. The sooner the better."

They parted company.

She did not want to enter the palace immediately, so she went into the cathedral, always a good place to think. There was no service taking place. She needed to work out the details of the new feeding program, but her mind was full of Amos. He had no idea how much she loved him: he thought they were just friends. And he was stupidly obsessed with Jane Midwinter, a girl who did not return his love and in any case was so much less than he deserved. Elsie wanted to pray, to ask God to make Amos love her and forget Jane, but it seemed too selfish for prayer, not the kind of thing you should ask God to arrange.

In the south aisle she passed two men arguing. She recognized Stan Gittings, a chronic gambler, and Sport Culliver, owner of the largest gambling den in town. Neither man was a regular churchgoer, so they had probably come in to argue out of the rain. This was not surprising. People often came here to discuss a problem, a deal, or even a love affair. In this case the issue seemed to be money, but she paid little attention.

She noticed someone she did not recognize kneeling in front of the high altar. The man looked young. He was wrapped in a big overcoat that hid the clothes underneath, so Elsie could not tell whether he was a clergyman. His face was raised but his eyes were closed, and his lips were moving in intense silent prayer. She wondered who he was.

She was going to sit down quietly in the south transept, but the argument in the aisle became heated. The men's voices were raised and they had adopted aggressive stances. She considered intervening, to suggest they move outside, but on reflection she decided they were less likely to come to blows if they stayed in the church, so abandoned her idea of a quiet moment and headed out, walking past them without speaking.

Behind her, Culliver shouted: "If you bet with money you haven't got, you must take the consequences!"

A moment later another voice was raised in high indignation, saying: "I command you to leave this holy place immediately!"

She turned and saw the young man who had been

praying at the high altar. He was striding toward the two quarrelers, his face—rather handsome, she noticed—pink with outrage. "Out!" he said to Gittings and Culliver. "Out now!"

Gittings, a scrawny man in worn clothes, looked shamefaced and was about to scurry away, but Culliver was not so easily intimidated. Not only was he tall and heavily built, he was also one of the wealthiest people in town. He was not a man to be pushed around. "Who the devil are you?" he said.

"My name is Kenelm Mackintosh," said the young man with a touch of pride.

He was expected, Elsie knew. The resignation of Canon Midwinter had triggered a series of promotions among the cathedral clergy that had left a vacancy in the bishop's personal staff, and Elsie's father had appointed a distant relative, a young clergyman recently graduated from Oxford University. So this was him. He must have just got off the stagecoach.

He quickly unbuttoned his coat to reveal clerical robes beneath. "I am the aide to Bishop Latimer. This is the house of God. I order you to take your quarrel elsewhere."

Culliver noticed Elsie for the first time and said to her: "Who does he think he is? Little whippersnapper."

"Go home, Sport," Elsie said quietly. "And if you let Sid Gittings gamble on credit you must take the consequences."

Sport was clearly furious at this scornful remark from a young woman, and he looked as if he was about to argue; then he thought better of it, and, after a pause, the two men sloped off, heading for the south porch door.

Elsie looked with interest at the newcomer. He was about her age, twenty-two, and good-looking enough to be a girl, with a shock of fair hair and interesting green eyes. And he had guts, to stand up to a big bully such as Culliver. But his face wore a dissatisfied expression: clearly he was not content with the way the confrontation had ended.

Elsie said: "They don't mean any harm."

"I was able to deal with them myself," Mackintosh said haughtily, "but all the same I thank you."

Touchy, she thought. Never mind.

"They seem to regard you as a person of authority," he went on, clearly surprised that a mere girl had been able to quell two angry men.

"Authority?" she said. "Not really. I'm Elsie Latimer, the bishop's daughter."

He was disconcerted. "I beg your pardon, Miss Latimer. I had no idea."

"Nothing to apologize for. And now we've been introduced. Have you met the bishop yet?"

"No. I sent my trunk to the palace and came straight here to give God thanks for a safe journey."

Very devout, she thought; but is it real, or for show? "Well, let me take you to the bishop."

"Gladly."

They left the cathedral and crossed the square. "I was told you were Scottish," she said.

"Yes," he replied stiffly. "Does it matter?"

"Not to me. I'm just surprised you don't have the accent."

"I got rid of it at Oxford."

"Deliberately?"

"I wasn't sorry to lose it. There's a certain amount of prejudice in the university." The words were mild but there was an undertone of bitterness.

"I'm sorry to hear that."

They entered the palace and Elsie showed him to her father's study, a comfortable room with a big fire and no desk. "Mr. Mackintosh has arrived, Father," she said.

"His luggage is here already!" The bishop got up from an upholstered chair and shook hands enthusiastically. "Welcome, dear boy."

"I'm greatly honored to be here, my lord bishop, and I humbly thank you for the privilege."

The bishop looked at Elsie. "Thank you, my dear," he said, dismissing her.

She did not leave. "I've just been to the funeral of three Sunday school children, all in the same family. Their father died, their mother struggled to feed them, they caught a chill in the damp room where they lived, and they all died in a day."

The bishop nodded. "They are now with their heavenly father," he said.

His complacency angered Elsie. In a raised voice she said: "Their heavenly father might ask why their neighbors did nothing to help them. Jesus said: 'Feed my lambs,' as I'm sure you'll remember."

"I think you'd better leave the theology to the clergy, Elsie," he said, and he winked conspiratorially at Mackintosh, who responded with a sycophantic smile.

"I will," she said, then she added defiantly: "And I'm going to feed nourishing broth to the Lord's lambs."

"Are you, indeed?" he said skeptically.

"Or at least those who come to my Sunday school."

"And how will you do that?"

"Our kitchen is plenty big enough and you'll hardly notice the increase in the grocery budget."

He was taken aback. "Our kitchen? Are you seriously proposing to feed the town's poor children out of our kitchen?"

"Not ours alone. The supporters of the Sunday school will do the same."

"This is preposterous. The food shortage is national. We can't feed everyone."

"Not everyone, just my Sunday school pupils. How can I tell them to be good and kind like Jesus, then send them home hungry?"

The bishop turned to the newcomer. "What do you think, Mr. Mackintosh?"

Mackintosh looked uncomfortable: he did not like being asked to arbitrate between Elsie and her father. After a hesitation he said: "The only thing I'm sure of is that it's my duty to be guided by my bishop, and I imagine the same goes for Miss Latimer."

He was not as brave as Elsie had thought. She said: "The Methodists are particularly keen on the idea." This was hope rather than fact, but she told herself it was a white lie.

Her father reconsidered. He would not want to appear ungenerous by comparison with Methodists. "How many children attend the Sunday school?"

"Never less than a hundred. Sometimes two hundred."

Mackintosh was surprised. "My word! It's normally twelve children in a small room."

The bishop said to Elsie: "And you and your Methodist friends want to feed them all?"

"Of course. But there are many Anglicans among our supporters."

"Well, you'd better talk to your mother and find out what she thinks our kitchen can manage."

Elsie kept her face rigid, to avoid smiling triumphantly. "Yes, Father," she said.

CHAPTER 16

When Sal first floated the idea of the Socratic Society she had not imagined that it would become such a big thing. She remembered how casually she had said: "We ought to be doing that—studying and learning. What's this Corresponding thing you said?" She had pictured a dozen or so people in a room over a tavern. The success of the Roger Riddick lecture had changed her view. More than a hundred people had attended, and the event had been written up in the *Kingsbridge Gazette*. And the triumph was her triumph. Jarge and Spade had been encouraging and helpful, but she had been the driving force. She was proud of what she had done.

But now she felt the society was only a first step. It was part of a movement taking place in the whole country, working people educating themselves, reading books and attending lectures. And there was a purpose behind the movement. They wanted to have a say in the way their country was governed. When there was war, they had to fight, and when the price of bread shot up they went hungry. We suffer, she reasoned, so we should decide.

What a long way I've come from Badford, she thought.

A month later, the second meeting of the society seemed even more important. Kingsbridge workers were angry about rising prices, especially for food. In some towns there had been bread riots, often led by women desperate to feed their families.

The meeting was scheduled for a Saturday, when people finished work a couple of hours early. A few minutes before it started, Sal and Jarge went to Pastor Charles Midwinter's home to meet the visiting speaker, the Reverend Bartholomew Small.

Pastor Midwinter had moved out of the canon's house, a mansion that was almost a palace. His new home, conveniently near the Methodist Hall, was not much bigger than a worker's cottage. It must have felt like a comedown, Sal thought, especially for Jane, who yearned for the good things in life.

In the sitting room Midwinter offered them sherry. Sal was not comfortable and Jarge was worse. They had dressed as well as they could but their shoes were patched and their clothes were faded. However, the pastor gave them a big buildup: "Reverend Small, these two people are the intellectual leaders of the Kingsbridge laboring folk."

Small said: "I'm honored to meet you both." He was a slim man with a soft voice, and looked just as Sal had always pictured a professor: gray haired, wearing spectacles, with a stoop from years of poring over books.

Jarge said: "Truth be told, Reverend, Sal here is our intellectual."

The praise embarrassed Sal. I'm no intellectual, she thought. But never mind, I'm learning.

Small said: "Tell me, how many people do you expect in the audience tonight?"

Sal said: "A couple of hundred, give or take."

"So many! I'm used to a dozen or so students."

He was slightly nervous, which surprised Sal, and at the same time made her more confident.

Pastor Midwinter drained his sherry glass and stood up. "We mustn't be late," he said.

They walked up Main Street, where streetlamps made the falling rain gleam. As they approached the Assembly Rooms, Sal was shocked to see a dozen or so men of the Shiring Militia outside the building, wet but smart in their uniforms, armed with muskets. Spade's brother-in-law, Freddie Caines, was among them. Why were they here?

She was horrified to see Will Riddick with them, wearing a sword, evidently in charge.

She stood in front of him with her hands on her hips. "What's this?" she said. "We don't need you and your soldiers."

He stared back at her. His expression mingled contempt with a hint of fear. "As a justice of the peace, I have brought the militia here to deal with any trouble," he said smugly.

"Trouble?" she said. "This is a discussion group. There will be no trouble."

"We'll see about that."

A question occurred to her, and she frowned. "Why isn't Viscount Henry Northwood here?"

"Colonel Northwood is out of town today."

That was a shame. Northwood would never have done something as provocative as this. Will was malicious as well as stupid. And he hated Sal personally.

But there was nothing she could do.

Walking into the building, she saw Sheriff Doye and Constable Davidson standing just inside the entrance, trying to look as if they did not know how unpopular they were.

The seats were in rows facing a lectern. There was a big turnout, Sal saw, more than had come to the first meeting. A lot of artisans—weavers and dyers, glovers and shoemakers—were mixed in with the millhands. Spade was sitting at the back with the bell ringers.

The printer Jeremiah Hiscock was there, though clearly he had not recovered fully from the flogging: he was pale and seemed nervous, and the bulky look of his coat suggested heavy bandages still on his back. His wife, Susan, sat beside him, with a defiant air, as if daring anyone to call her husband a criminal.

Susan and Sal were among only a handful of women in the room. It was often said that politics should be left to men, and some women believed it, or pretended to.

The audience included a group of young men Sal had seen hanging around the Slaughterhouse Inn, down by the river. She murmured to Jarge: "I don't like the look of those lads."

"I know them," Jarge said. "Mungo Landsman, Rob Appleyard, Nat Hammond—they want watching."

Sal and Jarge sat in the front row with Midwinter and the Reverend Small. A minute later Spade got up and came to the lectern. There was a murmur of surprise: Spade was smart, everyone knew, and he read the newspapers, but still, he was only a weaver.

He held up a copy of *Reasons for Contentment: Addressed to the Labouring Part of the British Public*. "We should pay close attention to what Mr. Paley says," he began. "He is very wise about how we should manage our affairs here in the west of England, because he is an archdeacon . . . of Carlisle." There was a ripple of laughter. Carlisle was on the Scottish border, some three hundred miles from Kingsbridge.

He went on in the same vein. Sal had looked through Paley's pamphlet, and she knew it contained pompous and condescending remarks about laboring people. Spade read out the worst of them in a deadpan voice, and with every quotation the laughter grew louder. He began to play to the audience, pretending he was puzzled and offended by their reaction, which made them laugh all the more. Even Tories were amused, and there was no hostility, no heckling. Midwinter whispered to Sal: "This is going well."

Spade sat down to cheers and applause, and Midwinter introduced the Reverend Small.

Paley was a philosopher, and so was Small; and Small's approach was academic. He did not mention the French revolution or the British Parliament. His arguments were about the right to govern. Kings were chosen by God, he admitted, but so were dukes and bankers and shopkeepers, and none of them were perfect, so no one ruled by divine right. The audience became restive, fidgeting and making remarks to one another. Sal was disappointed, but at least Small had said nothing inflammatory.

Suddenly someone jumped up and shouted: "God save the king!" It was Mungo Landsman, Sal saw.

"Oh, hell," she said.

Several men in the audience did the same, standing up and shouting, "God save the king!" then sitting down.

It was the group from the Slaughterhouse, Sal noted, but there seemed to be more than the three Jarge had named. She was seized by consternation. What was happening? Small had said nothing about King George specifically, so they could hardly have been inflamed by his speech. Had they planned to do this regardless of what was said? Why would they come just to disrupt the meeting?

Small continued with his speech, but soon he was interrupted again. "Traitor!" someone shouted, then: "Republican!" and "Leveler!"

Sal turned in her seat. "You can't know what he is if you don't listen to him," she called angrily.

"Whore!" they shouted, then: "Papist!" and "Frenchwoman!"

Jarge stood up and walked slowly to the back, near the shouters. He was joined by his friend Jack Camp, who was even bigger. They did not speak to the troublemakers, but stood with their arms folded, looking to the front.

Midwinter murmured: "This is not good, Sal. Perhaps we should close the meeting now."

Sal was dismayed. "No," she said, though she was worried. "That would be giving in to them."

"There could be a worse outcome."

Sal felt he might be right, but she could not bear to admit defeat.

Small continued, but not for long. The shouting resumed, and Sal said: "It's as if they actually want a fight!"

"This was all prearranged, I'm sure," Midwinter said. "Someone is determined to discredit the society."

Sal had a sick feeling that he was right. The Slaughterhouse lads were not responding to what was said, they were following a predetermined plan.

And Riddick knew about it, she realized; that was why he had come with the militia. There was a plot.

But who had made the plan? The men who ruled the town disapproved of the society, but would they really try to arrange a riot? She said: "But who would have done it?"

"A frightened man," said Midwinter.

Sal did not know what he meant.

People sitting near the shouters began to get up and move away, no doubt nervous about what might happen next.

The Reverend Small abandoned his lecture and sat down.

Midwinter stood up and said loudly: "We will now have a short break, followed in a quarter of an hour by a discussion."

Sal hoped that would calm everyone, but it made no difference, she saw with despair. People began to rush for the doors. Sal kept her eyes on the Slaughterhouse mob. They stayed where they were, looking pleased at the panic they had caused.

Sal saw a fleeing woman stumble into Mungo Landsman. He staggered, then punched her face. Blood spurted from her nose. Jarge then hit Mungo. In no time half a dozen people were fighting.

Sal would have liked to floor some of these troublemakers but she resisted the temptation. Where was Sheriff Doye? A moment after this question occurred to her, she saw Doye entering by the far door. Why had he gone out? The answer came a second later: he was followed in by Will Riddick and the militia. The soldiers, plus Constable Davidson, started breaking up the fights, arresting men, tying them up and making them lie on the floor.

Seeing this, most of the brawlers forgot their grievances and fled.

Sal said: "I'm going to make sure they arrest those ruffians from the Slaughterhouse." She walked determinedly toward the soldiers.

Will Riddick stood in her way. "Keep out of this, Sal Clitheroe," he said. With a mean grin he added: "I don't want you to get hurt."

Sal said: "As you were outside the building you can't know who started this, but I can tell you."

"Save it for the justices," said Riddick.

"But you are a justice. Don't you want to know?"

"I'm busy. Get out of my way."

Sal began to make a mental note of all those arrested. Some were from the Slaughterhouse mob, but others were their victims. Jarge was among them.

Riddick made them all stand up. They were tied together and marched out. Sal and Midwinter followed. They went to the Kingsbridge Jail, just across the street from the Assembly Rooms. The prisoners were received by Gil Gilmore, the jailer. As they disappeared into the darkness of the prison, Sal said to Riddick: "You'd better see that all those you've arrested are brought before the justices. Make sure none are released for reasons of favoritism."

Sal could tell from Riddick's expression that he was planning exactly that. "Don't you worry," he said airily.

Midwinter said: "Evidence of bias on your part would undermine the prosecution of them all, wouldn't it?"

"Just leave the law to me, Pastor. You concentrate on the theology."

The justices gathered on Monday morning in the anteroom next to the council chamber. Hornbeam was pleased that the second meeting of the Socratic Society had turned into a brawl—as he had planned—but he did not rest. He had spent Sunday preparing for the trial, laying the groundwork for conviction and harsh sentences.

All jurors were men aged between twenty-one and seventy who owned property in Kingsbridge worth at least forty shillings a year rent. Men in this group were also entitled to vote, and the rule was called the forty-shilling franchise. They constituted the ruling elite of the town, and in general they were not slow to find workers guilty.

It was the sheriff's duty to empanel the jury, and he was supposed to select men randomly. However, some of those eligible were unreliable, in Hornbeam's view, so he had had a word with Doye and told him to exclude Methodists and other nonconformists, who might sympathize with people trying to hold a discussion group. Doye had agreed without demur.

Hornbeam was only disappointed that Spade had not been arrested.

Alderman Drinkwater was the chairman of justices, and he would preside. Hornbeam feared Drinkwater would be lenient, but hoped Will Riddick might compensate for Drinkwater's indulgence.

While the justices waited for the accused to be brought from the jail, Hornbeam was reading *The Times*, pretending to be relaxed. "The royalists have been defeated in France—again," he said. "I know nothing about this young general Napoleon Bonaparte. Has anyone heard of him?"

"Not I," said Drinkwater, adjusting his wig in a looking glass.

"Nor me," said Riddick, who did not read the papers much.

"He sounds like the very devil," Hornbeam went on. "He deployed forty cannons on the streets of Paris and wiped out the royalists with grapeshot, it says here. Carried on even after his horse was shot from under him."

Drinkwater said: "I don't like to hear of men being shot with cannons. To me it seems ungentlemanly. Battle should be man to man, pistol to pistol, sword to sword."

"Maybe so," said Hornbeam. "All the same, I wish General Bonaparte was on our side."

The clerk looked in and said the court was ready.

"Very good, tell them to be silent," said Drinkwater.

The three justices entered the courtroom and took their seats.

The room was full. There were a dozen defendants, numerous witnesses, and all their families and friends, plus others who came simply because it was a big event in town. To one side the jury sat on benches. Everyone else was standing.

There were no lawyers in the room other than the clerk to the justices, Luke McCullough. Lawyers rarely appeared before justices, except perhaps in London. In most cases the victim of the crime was also the prosecutor. Today, as the brawl had been a public event, Sheriff Doye would prosecute.

Doye announced the names of those accused of common assault, including Jarge Box, Jack Camp, and Susan Hiscock. The list did not include the Slaughterhouse lads: Mungo Landsman, Rob Appleyard, and Nat Hammond. Hornbeam had told the sheriff to release them without charge. However, they were in the room as witnesses.

Riddick murmured to Hornbeam: "A pity that bitch Sal Clitheroe wasn't arrested."

Drinkwater said: "One of the defendants, Jarge Box, was also among the organizers of the event, so let's hear his case first."

Hornbeam realized he was not the only one who had made plans for this trial. He was surprised that Drinkwater had shown so much foresight. But perhaps Drinkwater had discussed the case with his more intelligent son-in-law, Pastor Midwinter, who would have suggested the best way to deal with it. And Jarge Box seemed to have been briefed, too, for he did not look surprised to be called first.

Box was charged with assaulting Mungo Landsman, and pleaded not guilty. Landsman swore to tell the truth and said that Box had knocked him down, then kicked him. Box was asked if he had anything to say.

"If it please Your Worships, I would like to tell you what happened," he said; and Hornbeam felt sure that sentence had been rehearsed. Also, Box was dressed in a respectable coat and decent shoes, which were certainly borrowed for the occasion.

Drinkwater said: "Yes, all right, go ahead."

Box was made nervous by the formal court setting, but he overcame his anxiety and began with confidence. "The meeting was peaceful and quiet for nigh on an hour before trouble broke out," he said. "Reverend Small from Oxford—"

Hornbeam interrupted. "Small was not the only speaker, was he?"

This put Box off his stride. He took a moment to collect his thoughts, then said: "Spade spoke. David Shoveller, that is."

"On what subject?" Hornbeam asked.

"Um, Archdeacon Paley's book for the laboring people."

"Isn't it true that he made the audience laugh?"

"He only read out bits from the book."

"In a funny voice?"

"In his normal voice."

Drinkwater said: "Well, if people laugh when the book is read out, perhaps it's the fault of the author, not the reader." There was a titter from the spectators. "Carry on, Box."

Box was encouraged. "Reverend Small was speaking about monarchs in general, nothing about King George himself, when Mungo Landsman got up and shouted out: 'God save the king.' Some others then stood and shouted the same. We couldn't understand what had offended them. It seemed like they had come to the meeting intending to cause trouble. We wondered if someone had paid them to do it."

From among the spectators came a shout: "Too true!"

It was a woman's voice, and Riddick muttered: "That's the Clitheroe woman."

Box went on: "Mr. Small continued his talk but they interrupted him again, shouting that he was a traitor, a republican and a leveler. Mrs. Sarah Clitheroe said they could not know what he was unless they listened to him, but they shouted that she was a whore, which is a wicked lie."

Hornbeam interrupted again. "Are you talking about Sal Clitheroe?" It was said she was the real organizer of the society.

Box said: "Yes."

Hornbeam looked directly at Sal as he said: "The woman who was banished from the village of Badford for assaulting the squire's son?"

Box was put on the defensive, and there was a pause before he answered: "Riddick killed her husband."

Will Riddick spoke from the bench. "I most certainly did not."

Drinkwater said impatiently: "We're not here to try that case. Carry on with your evidence, Box."

"Yes, Your Worship. Me and Jack Camp went and stood near the troublemakers, but that did no good. The noise was so bad the speaker couldn't go on, and Pastor Midwinter called for a break, hoping Mungo and his friends would shut up or leave, so we could have a quiet discussion and learn something. But a lot of people rushed to the doors, I think the shouting got them scared, like, and they just decided to go home."

Hornbeam interrupted a third time. "Get to the point, man. Did you assault Mungo Landsman?"

Jarge was not so easily deflected from his story. He said: "Lydia Mallet was trying to leave when she bumped into Mungo, so he punched her in the face."

Drinkwater said: "Is Lydia Mallet here?"

A young woman stepped out of the crowd. She was pretty, except that her nose and mouth were red and swollen.

Drinkwater said: "Did Mungo Landsman do that to you?"

She nodded.

He said: "Please say yes, if that's what you mean."

"Yeth," she said, and everyone laughed. "Thorry, I can't thpeak right," she added, and there was more laughter.

Drinkwater said: "I think we'll take that as corroboration." He looked at the sheriff. "If this account is accurate, it's surprising that Landsman is not among those charged."

Sheriff Doye said: "Lack of evidence, Your Worship."

Drinkwater was clearly dissatisfied, but chose not to take it further. "What happened next, Box?"

"I knocked Mungo down."

"Why?"

Jarge answered indignantly. "He punched a woman!"

Hornbeam said: "And why did you kick him?"

"To make him stay down."

Drinkwater said: "You shouldn't have done that. It's taking the law into your own hands. You should have reported Landsman to the sheriff."

"Phil Doye had gone outside to fetch the militia!"

"You could have reported it later. That's enough from you, Box, I think we've got all the information we need."

Hornbeam was annoyed by the way the trial was going. He would not have let Box tell a long story about how the violence was provoked. It might make the jury sympathetic. And Drinkwater was clearly annoyed that the Slaughterhouse lads had been let off.

As usual, the court would hear all the cases before asking the jury for its verdicts. It was not a good practice: by the end of the day they had forgotten much of what they had heard. On the other hand, when they were uncertain they usually erred on the side of guilty verdicts, which Hornbeam thought was a good thing, since in his view just about everyone who got into trouble with the law deserved punishment.

The cases were repetitive. A had punched B because B had shoved C. Every accused person claimed provocation. None of the injuries was very serious: bruises, cracked ribs, a tooth knocked out, a wrist sprained. In each case, Drinkwater was at pains to point out that provocation did not justify violence. At the end the jury found them all guilty.

It was time for the justices to decide on punishment. They spoke quietly to one another. Hornbeam said: "A clear case for flogging, I would say."

"No, no," said Drinkwater. "I think we should give them all a day in the stocks."

Hornbeam murmured: "With the option of a ten-shilling fine instead, I suggest." He wanted to be able to save selected men.

"No," said Drinkwater firmly. "They should all be the same. I don't want half of them in the stocks and the other half walking around town just because someone paid their fine."

That was exactly what Hornbeam had been planning, but he knew when he was defeated, so he just said: "Very well."

As always, he had a fallback plan.

Hornbeam despised laboring men, especially in a crowd, and the worst crowd of all was the London mob. Yet even he was shocked by the news in the next morning's paper. As the king was on his way to Parliament his carriage had been attacked by hooligans chanting: "Bread and peace!" Stones had smashed the carriage window.

They stoned the king! Hornbeam had never heard of such an insult to the monarch. This was high treason. And yet, even while he was fuming with indignation, he realized this news might help him today, when he met with the lord lieutenant, the earl of Shiring. He folded the newspaper carefully and tucked it inside his coat. Then he went out.

He was proud of the carriage that stood at the front door. It had been made for him by the royal coachmaker, John Hatchett, in Long Acre, London. As a boy he had seen vehicles like this and longed for one. It was a model called a Berline, fast but stable, less likely to overturn at speed. The body was blue with gold-colored coachlines, and the paintwork gleamed with varnish.

Riddick was already inside. They were going to Earlscastle together. The lord lieutenant would surely find it hard to ignore a complaint by two justices.

They drove through the market square, already busy though it was early. Hornbeam stopped the carriage so that they could look at the people being punished.

The contraption called the stocks clamped the legs, forcing the offender to sit in an uncomfortable position on the ground all day. It was more humiliating than painful. This morning all twelve people found guilty by the justices were on display in the rain.

Often offenders were mocked and abused, helpless to resist. Ordure from dunghills might be thrown at them. Actual violence was prohibited, but the line was narrow. However, today the people in the square showed no hostility. It was a sign that they sympathized.

Hornbeam did not care. He had no wish to be popular. There was no money in that.

He looked at Jarge Box, the ringleader, and his sister, Joanie, side by side. They did not appear to be suffering much. Joanie was chatting to a woman with a shopping basket. Jarge was drinking ale from a tankard, presumably brought to him by a well-wisher.

Then Hornbeam noticed Sal Clitheroe, the organizer,

who had not even been charged. She stood beside Box holding a heavy wooden shovel on her shoulder. She was there to defend Box if necessary. Hornbeam doubted that anyone would challenge her.

It was all very unsatisfactory.

Riddick commented: "The real culprits are the organizers, and they aren't there."

Hornbeam nodded agreement. "When we return from Earlscastle this afternoon we should have firmer control of the courts in the town."

He told the coachman to drive on.

It was a long journey. Riddick proposed a few hands of faro, but Hornbeam declined. He did not enjoy games, least of all the kind in which a man could lose money.

Riddick asked him how well he knew the earl. "Hardly at all," he said. He recalled an older version of Viscount Northwood, with the same big nose and sharp eyes, but a bald head instead of brown curls. "I've met him on ceremonial occasions, and he interviewed me before making me a justice. That's about it."

"The same with me."

"He doesn't understand business, of course, but few of these noblemen do. They think wealth comes from the land. They're still in the Dark Ages."

Riddick nodded. "The son has a soft streak. He's inclined to talk about England being a free country. I don't know whether the old man is the same."

"We're going to find out." A lot was at stake. If the meeting went well, Hornbeam would return to Kingsbridge considerably more powerful.

Several hours later they saw Earlscastle. It was no longer a castle, although a short section of defensive wall remained, with its battlements and arrow-slit windows. The modern part of the dwelling was made of red brick with long leaded windows, and featured many tall chimneys sending smoke into the rain clouds above. Rooks in the high elms cawed scornfully as Hornbeam and Riddick got down from the carriage and hurried inside.

"I hope the earl is going to offer us dinner," said Riddick as they took off their coats in the hall. "I'm starving."

"Don't count on it," said Hornbeam.

The earl greeted them in his library, rather than the drawing room, a sign that they were below his social level, and that consequently he considered this a business meeting. He was wearing a plum-colored coat and a silver-gray wig.

Hornbeam was surprised to see Viscount Northwood there, out of uniform and wearing riding clothes. This must have been where he was on the evening of the Socratic Society meeting. His presence was an unwelcome surprise. He was unlikely to approve the scheme Hornbeam was going to propose.

There was a good blaze in the enormous fireplace. Hornbeam was glad of it, for the coach ride had been cold.

A footman offered them sherry and biscuits. Hornbeam declined, feeling he needed his wits about him.

He told the story of the Socratic Society meeting: a revolutionary speaker, a protest by citizens loyal to the king, intimidation by republican bruisers, and a riot.

The earl listened attentively, but Northwood's face showed skepticism, and he said: "Was anyone killed?"

"No. Several were injured, though."

"Seriously?"

Hornbeam was about to say yes, untruthfully, then it occurred to him that Northwood might have received a report from his aide-de-camp, Lieutenant Donaldson. He had to admit the truth. "Not very," he said.

"More of a brawl than a riot, then," said Northwood, echoing what Drinkwater had said in court. Yes, the viscount had definitely been briefed by someone.

"Twelve people were brought before the justices," Hornbeam said. "Alderman Drinkwater presided, and that was where things started to go wrong. First he downgraded the charges from riot to assault. The jury were sensible, and found all twelve guilty. But Drinkwater insisted on light sentences. They were all given a day in the stocks. They're there now, chatting to passersby and being brought tankards of ale."

Riddick added: "It makes a joke of justice."

The earl said: "You feel this is serious."

"We do," said Hornbeam.

"What do you think should be done?"

Hornbeam took a breath. This was the crucial moment. "Alderman Drinkwater is seventy," he said. "Age is not everything, of course," he added hastily, remembering that the earl was in his late fifties. "However, Drinkwater has entered that benign phase of maturity in which some men become all-forgiving—an attitude suitable in a grandfather, perhaps, but not the chairman of justices."

"Are you asking me to dismiss Drinkwater?"

"As a justice, yes. Of course he will remain an alderman."

Northwood put in: "I suppose you want to be chairman in Drinkwater's place, Hornbeam, do you?"

"I would humbly accept the post if offered."

Riddick said: "Alderman Hornbeam is the obvious choice, my lord. He's the leading clothier in town and will surely be mayor sooner or later."

That's it, thought Hornbeam; that's our case. Now we'll see how it's been received.

The earl looked doubtful. "I'm not sure that what you've told me justifies dismissal. It's quite a drastic step."

Hornbeam had been afraid of this.

Northwood said: "Let's not make a mountain of a molehill. An Englishman is entitled to his opinions, and the Kingsbridge Socratic Society is a debating group. A few bloody noses don't make a revolution. I don't believe the society poses the least threat to His Majesty King George or the British constitution."

Wishful thinking, Hornbeam thought, but he did not dare to say it.

There was a silence. The earl seemed adamant and his son looked pleased with the way the conversation was turning out. Riddick looked baffled. He was no genius, and he had no idea what to do next.

But Hornbeam had a card up his sleeve, or rather in his pocket. "I wonder, my lord, whether you have seen a newspaper today." He took out *The Times*. "It is reported that the king was stoned by the London mob."

The earl said: "Good gracious!"

Riddick said: "I didn't know that."

Northwood said: "Is this true?"

"They chanted 'Bread and peace,' according to this report." Hornbeam unfolded the paper and handed it to the earl.

The earl read a few lines and said: "They broke the windows of his carriage!"

"Perhaps I'm overreacting," Hornbeam said disingenuously. "But I do think those of us in authority in the land need to take firmer action against agitators and revolutionaries."

The earl said: "I'm beginning to think you're right."

Northwood was silent.

Riddick said: "Those people are fiends."

Hornbeam said: "This is how revolutions begin, isn't it? Subversive ideas lead to violence, and violence escalates."

"You may be right," said the earl.

He was softening, Hornbeam thought, but the son was an obstacle.

A young woman came into the room, expensively dressed in riding costume, with a pretty little hat. She curtsied to the earl and said: "I apologize for interrupting you, Uncle, but the riding party is waiting for my cousin Henry."

Northwood stood up. "I beg your pardon, Miss Miranda. An important conversation . . ." He was clearly reluctant to leave.

But the earl said: "You're excused, Henry. Thank you for your help."

Hornbeam realized that the woman was Henry's cousin Miranda Littlehampton. It was said that they were unofficially engaged. Hornbeam was no expert on romance, but it seemed to him that Miranda was keener than Henry.

However, Henry left, and that was a stroke of luck for Hornbeam.

"Pretty girl," said Riddick admiringly.

Shut up, you fool, Hornbeam thought. The earl doesn't want your approval for his future daughter-in-law. Hastily he said: "I thank Your Lordship for receiving me and Squire Riddick today. We both appreciate the privilege, and we know this conversation has been of the highest importance to your county and especially the city of Kingsbridge."

It was pure flannel, but it moved the earl's attention from Riddick's crass remark about Miranda. "Yes," the earl said. "I thank you for bringing this to my notice. I think I must do as you suggest, and tell Drinkwater it's time for him to retire."

Ah, success, thought Hornbeam with profound satisfaction, keeping his face woodenly expressionless.

"I'll write to Drinkwater," the earl went on.

Hornbeam said eagerly: "If you would like me to deliver the letter . . ."

"I think not," the earl said severely. "Drinkwater might take that as a discourtesy. I'll give the letter to Northwood."

Hornbeam realized he had been too hasty in his triumph. "Yes, my lord, of course, foolish of me."

"I imagine you're keen to get back on the road. It's a long ride to Kingsbridge."

The earl's tone did not invite discussion. And he was not going to ask his visitors to stay for dinner. Hornbeam stood up. "With your permission, my lord, we'll take our leave."

The earl reached for a bellpull, and a minute later a footman appeared. Hornbeam and Riddick bowed and went into the hall. The earl did not follow.

They put on their coats and stepped outside. Hornbeam's carriage was waiting, glistening with rain. They got inside and the horses pulled away.

Riddick said: "I have to hand it to you, Hornbeam, you're a clever swine."

"Yes," said Hornbeam, "I know."

CHAPTER 17

The hands were paid on Saturday afternoon at five o'clock, when work stopped at the mills. Although they all worked set hours, the amount they got paid depended on how much yarn they had made. Sal and Kit usually produced enough to earn about twelve shillings. Three years ago this would have made her feel rich, but since then, bad harvests had pushed up the price of food and war taxes had made other necessities dearer. Now twelve shillings would barely last the week.

Sal and Joanie immediately went to pay their rent, trudging through a drizzling rain, trailed by Kit and Sue. A home with a fireplace was even more important than food. You would die of cold faster than you would starve to death. Getting into arrears with rent was the first step on the downward slope to utter destitution.

Their house was owned by the cathedral, but the rent office was in the poor neighborhood where they lived. Their rent was a shilling a week, and Sal paid five of the twelve pence, as she occupied a bit less than half the building. They handed over their money, then walked to the marketplace. It was already dark, but the stalls were bright with lamplight.

Sal asked a baker for a standard four-pound loaf, and he said: "That will be one shilling and two pence."

Sal was outraged. "It was a shilling and a penny yesterday—and seven pence only a year ago!"

The baker looked weary, as if he had been listening to the same lament all day. "I know," he said. "And flour used to be thirteen shillings a sack, and now it's twenty-six. What am I supposed to do? If I sell below cost I'll be broke in a week."

Sal was sure he was exaggerating, but all the same she saw his point. She bought a loaf, and Joanie did the same, but what would they do if it went up more?

This was not just a Kingsbridge problem. Spade said it was happening all over the country. In some towns women had rioted, often starting at the door of a shop.

In the indoor market on the south side of the cathedral was a butcher with a mouthwatering display—joints of beef, pork, and mutton—but it was all too dear. Sal looked for pheasant or partridge, skinny game birds with chewy meat that would have to be stewed. They were usually available at this time of year, but today there were none. "It's the weather," said the butcher. "These dark, rainy days the woodsmen can't see the birds, let alone catch the buggers."

Sal and Joanie looked at cured and smoked meat, bacon and salt beef, but even they were dear. In the end they bought salt cod. "I don't like it," Sue whined, and Joanie said brusquely: "Be grateful—some children have nothing but porridge."

On their way home they passed the Assembly Rooms, where a party was about to begin. Carriages were drawing up at the front, and the ladies were trying to keep their fabulous gowns dry as they rushed into the building. At the back, the kitchen was taking in last-minute deliveries: huge sacks of loaves, whole hams, and barrels of port. Some people could still afford such things.

Joanie spoke to a porter who was carrying a basket of oranges from Spain. "What's the party for?"

"Alderman Hornbeam," said the man. "A double wedding."

Sal had heard about it. Howard Hornbeam had married Bel Marsh and Deborah Hornbeam had married Will Riddick. Sal felt sorry for any girl who married Will Riddick.

"It's going to be a huge party," said the porter. "Couple of hundred people, we're expecting."

That number would include more than half the town's

voters. Hornbeam was now chairman of justices and would surely stand for mayor one day. In some towns the post of mayor was rotated annually among the aldermen, but in Kingsbridge the mayor was elected and remained in office until he retired or was thrown out by the aldermen. Right now Mayor Fishwick was in good health and popular. But Hornbeam would be playing a long game.

They made their way home. Sal put out the bread and salt fish in the kitchen. Later they would let the fire die and go to the Bell, taking the children. By saving money on firewood they could afford a mug of ale. That thought cheered her. And tomorrow was a day of rest.

Joanie shouted upstairs for Aunt Dottie. Jarge came into the kitchen and they sat around the table as he sliced the fish. Dottie did not appear, so Joanie said to Sue: "Run upstairs for your auntie. She's probably sleeping." Sue stuffed bread into her mouth and went upstairs.

A minute later she came back and said: "She won't speak."

There was a moment of silence, then Joanie said: "Oh, Jesus."

She hurried up the stairs, followed by the others, and they all crowded into Dottie's attic room. The old lady was on her back on the bed. Her eyes were open wide, but she was seeing nothing. Her mouth was open, too, though she did not breathe. Sal had seen death and knew what it looked like and she had no doubt that Dottie had passed away. Joanie was silent, but tears streamed down her face. Sal felt for a heartbeat, then for a pulse, but she was going through the motions. As she handled the body she realized that Dottie had become very thin. She had not noticed that, and she felt guilty.

This was what happened when food was in short supply, Sal knew: it was the very young and the very old who died.

The children were wide-eyed with shock. Sal thought

of sending them out of the room, then decided they should stay. They would see plenty of dead people in their lives, so they might as well get used to it early.

Dottie had been Joanie's mother's sister, and had raised Joanie after her mother died. Now Joanie was grief-stricken. She would recover, but for a while Sal would have to take charge. Dottie had been Jarge's aunt, too, but the two of them had never been close. Anyway, much of what needed to be done was women's work.

Sal and Joanie would have to wash the body and wrap it in a winding sheet—a burdensome expense to add to all the price rises. Then Sal would go to the vicar of St. Mark's and talk about the funeral. If it could be held tomorrow, Sunday, then all of them could work normally on Monday and avoid losing pay.

"Jarge," Sal said, "would you give the children their supper while Joanie and I take care of poor Dottie's body?"

"Oh!" he said. "Ah, yes. Come on downstairs with me, you two."

They went out.

Sal rolled up her sleeves.

Elsie and her mother, Arabella, sat at the side of the ballroom, watching the dancers surge and ebb in the gavotte. The women had billowing skirts, swooping sleeves, and puffed ruffles, all in bright colors, plus high towers of beribboned hair, while the men were armored in tight waistcoats and stiff-shouldered tailcoats. "It seems odd to be dancing," Elsie mused. "We're losing the war, the people can hardly afford bread, and the king has been stoned in his carriage. How can we be so frivolous?"

"This is when people need frivolity the most," said her mother. "We can't think about misery all the time."

"I suppose. Or perhaps the people here don't care about the war, the king, or the hungry mill hands."

"That might be a nice way to live, if you could manage it. Happy apathy."

Not for me, Elsie thought, but she decided not to say it. She loved her mother, but they did not have much in common. She had little in common with her father either. Sometimes she wondered where she had come from.

She thought about what kind of children might be produced by the two pairs of newlyweds now on the dance floor. Howard Hornbeam's offspring would probably be plump and lazy, as he was. "Howard looks bewildered but happy," she remarked.

"It was a short engagement, and I hear he didn't have much say in the choice of a bride," said Arabella. "He's entitled to be bewildered."

"He seems content with his bride, anyway."

"Despite her rabbit teeth."

"He may be thinking how much worse it could have been. Alderman Hornbeam could have chosen someone horrible for him."

"And Bel Marsh may be grateful for the same reason. Howard's a nice boy, and not a bit like his father."

Elsie nodded agreement. "Bel looks quite pleased with herself." She turned her attention to the other couple, who seemed more solemn. Squire Riddick would neglect his children, she felt sure, and they would be better for that. She said: "I'm sure Riddick just wants someone to manage his household for him, so that he can spend all his time drinking and gambling and whoring."

"He may find that Deborah has her own ideas about that. Look at her chin. It's a sign of determination."

"I do hope so. I'd love to see Riddick struggling to cope with a strong woman."

Kenelm Mackintosh came and sat beside Elsie. "What a pleasant occasion this is," he said. "Two couples finding happiness in holy matrimony."

Time will tell whether they find happiness, Elsie thought. She said: "Is matrimony holy when the marriage has been arranged by the parents?"

He hesitated, then said: "It's God's choice that matters."

That was an evasive answer, but Elsie did not say so.

The gavotte ended and a minuet was announced. This was danced in couples. The dyer Isaac Marsh, father of Bel, now appeared and asked Arabella to dance. "Delighted," she said, standing up. This often happened. Arabella was probably the most attractive middle-aged woman in Kingsbridge, and a lot of men took the opportunity of stepping out with her. She liked the attention and admiration, so she usually said yes.

Elsie said to Mackintosh: "What would you hope for in marriage?"

"Someone to support my sacred calling," he said promptly.

"Very wise," she said. "Married people should support each other," she added, making it a two-way process.

"Exactly." He did not notice that she had modified his idea. "How about you? What would you want from a marriage?"

"Children," she said. "I picture a big house full of children—four, maybe five, all healthy and happy, with toys and books and pets."

"Well, that is certainly God's will. Of course, you wouldn't continue to run the Sunday school after marriage."

"I most certainly would."

He raised his eyebrows. "Wouldn't you devote yourself to your husband?"

"I think I could manage both. And, after all, the Sunday school is God's work."

He nodded reluctant agreement. "It is, yes."

The conversation had taken a turn to the personal, Elsie thought. She had meant only to challenge his glib presumption that marriage meant happiness, but he had swerved into whether she would continue her work after the wedding, and how she would devote herself to her husband. It was almost as if he was considering her as a possible wife.

Before she could react to that, she saw the man she would marry in a heartbeat. Amos was wearing a new dark red tailcoat and a pale pink waistcoat. Elsie realized he had not previously met Mackintosh, so she introduced them.

Mackintosh said: "I've heard a lot about you, of course. Miss Latimer spends a great deal of time with you." His tone as he said this was faintly disapproving.

"We run the Sunday school together," Amos said. "By the way, I think you might know my friend Roger Riddick. He's just graduated from Oxford, as I believe you have."

Mackintosh looked wary. "I did come across Riddick once or twice, yes."

"He's off to Berlin in January."

"I'm afraid he and I moved in different circles."

"I'm sure." Amos laughed. "Roger is an inveterate gambler—not a good pastime for a theology student. But he's a brilliant engineer."

"Tell me," Mackintosh said, "what preparation did you have for teaching Sunday school?"

Amos had had none, of course, and Elsie felt that Mackintosh had been tactless.

Amos hesitated, then said: "Looking back at my own schooling, I think the best teachers were those who could speak clearly. Muddled minds produce confusing sentences. So I do my best to make everything easy to understand."

Elsie added: "Amos is very good at that."

Mackintosh said stubbornly: "But you haven't made any systematic examination of the scriptures."

Elsie realized that Mackintosh was trying to establish superiority. He had commented that Elsie spent a lot of time with Amos. Perhaps he regarded Amos as a rival for her affections.

If he thought that, he was dead right.

"But I know the scriptures well," Amos said spiritedly. "I attend a Methodist Bible study class once a week, and have done for years."

"Ah, yes," said Mackintosh with a condescending smile. "Methodist Bible study."

He was underlining the fact that he had studied at a university and Amos had not. Young men were like this, Elsie knew. Her mother, who could be vulgar at times, had told her that this kind of argument between two males was called a pissing contest.

Her father appeared, walking slowly, as if tired, and Elsie wondered anxiously if he was unwell.

Mackintosh sprang eagerly to his feet. "My lord," he said.

"Be a good fellow and find the archdeacon for me, would you?" said the bishop. He seemed short of breath. "I need a word with him about the services tomorrow."

"Right away, my lord bishop." Mackintosh hurried away and the bishop moved on.

Amos said to Elsie: "Roger told me that Mackintosh wasn't very popular at Oxford."

"Did he say why?"

"The man is a sycophant, always trying to win the favor of important people."

"He's ambitious, I think."

"You seem to like him."

Elsie shook her head. "Neither that nor the opposite."

"You have nothing in common with him."

This line of talk displeased Elsie. She frowned. "Why are you running him down to me?"

"Because I know what the sly dog is up to."

"Do you?"

"He wants to marry you because it will help his advancement."

This infuriated her. "Is that the reason? Well, well."

Amos did not notice her reaction. "Of course. The son-in-law of a bishop can hardly fail to gain promotion within the church."

Elsie was riled. "You're sure of that."

"Yes."

"You don't think it's possible that the Reverend Mackintosh has simply fallen in love with me."

"No, of course not."

"What makes you think it so unlikely that a young man would fall for me?"

Amos seemed to realize the implication of what he had been saying. He was indignant. "That's not what I meant."

"You seemed to think it."

"You don't know what I think."

"Of course I do. Women always know what men are thinking."

Jane Midwinter appeared, dressed in black silk. "I haven't got anyone to dance with," she said.

Amos leaped to his feet. "You have now," he said, and he led her away.

Elsie wanted to cry.

Her mother returned to her seat. Elsie asked her: "Is Father all right? He seemed a bit weak. I wondered if he was ill."

"I don't know," said Arabella. "He says he's fine. But he's very overweight, and the least effort seems to tire him."

"Oh, dear."

"Something else is bothering you," Arabella said perceptively.

Elsie could not hide things from her mother. "Amos has annoyed me."

Arabella was surprised. "That's unusual. You're fond of him, aren't you?"

"Yes, but he wants to marry Jane Midwinter."

"And she has her heart set on Viscount Northwood."

Elsie decided to tell her mother about Mackintosh. "I think Mr. Mackintosh wants to marry me."

"Of course he does. I've seen how he looks at you."

"Really?" Elsie had not noticed. "Well, I could never love him."

Arabella shrugged. "Your father and I never had a grand passion. He's awfully pompous, but he's given me comfort and stability, and I like him for that. For his part, he thinks I'm something special, bless him. But on both sides it's not the kind of love that cries out urgently to be consummated . . . if you know what I mean."

Elsie did. The conversation had become intimate. She was embarrassed but fascinated. She said: "And now? Are you glad you married him?"

Arabella smiled. "Of course!" She reached out and took Elsie's hand. "Otherwise," she said, "I wouldn't have you."

No one worked on a holy day. The important religious festivals were days of rest for the Kingsbridge hands. They had Good Friday, Whit Monday, All Saints' Day, and Christmas Day, plus one that was celebrated only here: St. Adolphus Day, late in the year. Adolphus was the patron saint of Kingsbridge Cathedral, and a special fair was held on his day.

A light rain was falling, not as bad as the recent torrents. Around this time of year farmers had to decide how many of their livestock they could afford to keep through the winter, then they would slaughter the rest; so the price of meat usually dipped. Also, most farmers had kept back some of their grain harvest to sell later when the summer plenty had shrunk.

Sal, Joanie, and Jarge went to the market square, hoping to find bargains, perhaps some cheap beef or pork, and the children came along for the excitement.

But they were disappointed. There was not much food for sale and nothing was cheap. The women were angered by the prices. They could hardly bear the fear that they might not be able to feed their families. Women who could not name the prime minister said he should be thrown out. They wanted the war to be ended. Some of them said the country needed a revolution, like the ones in America and France.

Sal bought some tripe, from the stomach of a sheep, which had to be boiled for hours to make it soft enough to chew, and had no flavor unless cooked with onions. She wished she had just a little real meat for Kit; he was such a little boy and he worked so hard.

On the north side of the square, next to the graveyard, grain was being auctioned. Behind the auctioneer, sacks were piled high, each pile belonging to a different seller. Sal heard bakers muttering angrily about the prices being fetched. One said: "If I paid that much for grain, my bread would cost more than beef!"

"Today's largest lot, a hundred bushels of wheat," said the auctioneer. "What am I bid?"

"Look over there," said Joanie. "Behind that woman in the red hat." Sal scanned the crowd. Joanie said: "Is that who I think it is?"

"Are you talking about Alderman Hornbeam?"

"I thought it was him. What's he doing at a grain auction? He's a clothier."

"Perhaps he's just curious—same as us."

"Curious as a snake."

As the price of the lot rose, a discontented muttering spread through the crowd. They would never be able to afford bread made from this wheat.

Joanie said: "The farmer who's selling this lot is making a great deal of money."

Something clicked in Sal's brain, and she said: "It might not be a farmer."

"Who else would have wheat to sell?"

"Someone who bought it from a farmer at harvest time and hoarded it until the price went sky-high." She recalled a word from a newspaper. "A speculator."

"Eh?" said Jarge, struck by this thought. "Isn't that against the law?"

"I don't think so," said Sal.

"Then it damn well ought to be."

Sal agreed with that.

The grain was sold at a price beyond her imagining. It was also beyond the means of any Kingsbridge baker.

Several men started to pick up the sacks and load them onto a handcart. Each sack held a bushel and weighed about sixty pounds, so the men worked in pairs, each grasping one end of the sack, then together swinging the sack onto the cart. Sal did not recognize any of them. They had to be out-of-towners. "I wonder who bought the grain," Sal said aloud.

A woman in front of her turned around. Sal knew her vaguely; her name was Mrs. Dodds. "I don't know," she said, "but that man in a yellow waistcoat talking to the auctioneer now is Silas Child, the grain merchant from Combe."

Joanie said: "Do you think he's the buyer?"

"Seems likely, doesn't it? And those men picking up the sacks are probably his bargees."

"But that means the grain will go out of Kingsbridge."

"It does."

"Well, that's not right," said Joanie angrily. "Kingsbridge grain shouldn't go to Combe."

"It may be going farther than that," said Mrs. Dodds. "I've heard it said that our grain is being sold to France, for the French are richer than us."

"How can people sell grain to the enemy?"

"Some men will do anything for money."

Jarge said: "That's the truth, devil take 'em."

The handcart was loaded quickly, and two men took it away, each holding one handle. The cart turned into Main Street, the men leaning back and heaving on the handles to prevent it running away down the slope.

Sal said: "Kit and Sue, follow that cart, see where it goes, then run back here as fast as you can and tell me."

The children raced away.

Sime Jackson appeared and said to Sal: "That load of a hundred bushels is going to France, people are saying." The notion had spread through the crowd already.

Some of the women clustered around the second cart, haranguing the men. At a distance, Sal heard the words *France* and *Silas Child*, and then someone shouted, "Bread and peace!" That was the slogan they had yelled at the king in London.

Silas Child, in his yellow waistcoat, was looking worried.

Hornbeam had vanished.

Kit and Sue returned, breathless from running up Main Street. "The cart went to the riverside," Kit said.

Sue added: "They're putting the sacks on a barge."

Kit said: "I asked whose barge it is and a man said Silas Child's."

"That settles it," said Sal.

Mrs. Dodds had been listening to Kit. Now she turned to a neighbor. "Did you hear that?" she said. "Our grain is being loaded onto a Combe barge."

The neighbor turned to another woman and repeated the news.

Joanie said: "I'm going to the riverside to see for myself." Sal wanted to counsel caution, but Joanie was headstrong, like her brother, Jarge. She started across the square without waiting to consult. Sal, Jarge, and the children followed. Mrs. Dodds came after them, and others in the crowd had the same idea. They started chanting: "Bread and peace."

Sal saw Will Riddick, clearly in a hurry, entering Willard House, the militia headquarters. As she passed the front window she saw Hornbeam standing inside, looking out with a worried frown.

Hornbeam was in Northwood's office. He said to Riddick: "You have to stop this now."

"I'm not sure how—"

"Whatever it takes. Muster your militiamen."

"Colonel Northwood gave the men the day off for St. Adolphus."

"Where the devil is Northwood?"

"Earlscastle."

"Still?"

"Yes. A lot of the men are right outside here, in the square, with their girlfriends."

It was true. Hornbeam stared out, burning with frustration. The militiamen were in their uniforms—they were not affluent enough to keep two sets of clothes—but they were enjoying the holiday just like everyone else. "Some towns are guarded by militia from a different county," he said. "It's a better system. It discourages this kind of fraternization. The men are more willing to get tough with troublemakers they don't know."

"I agree, but Northwood won't have it," said Riddick. "He says it goes against the tradition."

"Northwood is a damn fool."

"And the duke of Richmond is against it, too. He's master general of the ordnance. He says it makes recruitment difficult—men don't want to be taken far from their homes."

Hornbeam knew he could not fight against dukes and viscounts—at least not until he became a member of Parliament. "Just go out there and tell them to form up," he said to Riddick.

Riddick hesitated. "They won't like it."

"They'll have no choice but to do what they're told. And this is shaping up to be a riot."

Riddick could not disagree. "Very well," he said. He went into the hall, and Hornbeam followed.

Sergeant Beach was in the hall. "Sir?"

"Go round the square and speak to all the men in uniform. Tell them to come here. Issue them with muskets and ammunition. Then form them up at the riverside."

The sergeant looked uncomfortable, and seemed about

to protest, then he caught Hornbeam's eye and changed his mind. "Right away, sir." He went out.

Young Lieutenant Donaldson came down the stairs. Riddick said: "Break out muskets and ammunition."

"Yes, sir."

Two soldiers came in from the square, looking sulky. Riddick said: "Button up your tunics, both of you. Try to look like soldiers. Where are your hats?"

One of them said: "I didn't wear mine, sir." He added resentfully: "Today is a holiday."

"It was. Not any longer. Smarten up. Sergeant Beach will give you a gun."

The second man was Freddie Caines, who—Riddick recalled—was related to that troublemaker Spade. Caines said: "Who are we going to shoot, sir?"

"Whoever I tell you to shoot."

Caines clearly did not like that idea.

Donaldson returned with muskets and ammunition. Hornbeam was not a military man but he knew that the standard flintlock muskets were smoothbore, not very accurate. In some regiments, sharpshooters were issued with rifles, which had a spiral groove inside the barrel to spin the bullet and make it fly straight; but most soldiers normally shot at a large mass of enemy troops, and accuracy was not a priority.

Today the enemy would be a crowd of civilians—mostly women—and, again, accuracy would not be needed.

Donaldson gave each man a gun and a handful of paper cartridges. They put the ammunition in the waterproof leather cases they wore on their belts.

Two more men came in from the square, and Riddick repeated his instructions. Others followed, then Sergeant Beach returned. "That's the lot, sir," he said.

"What?" Only fifteen or twenty men had come into the hall. "There were at least a hundred in the square!"

"To be frank, Major, when they saw what was happening a lot of them sort of melted away."

"Make a list of their names. They shall all be flogged."

"I'll do my best, sir, but I couldn't name the men I didn't speak to, if you see—"

"Oh, shut your stupid mouth. Summon everyone in this building, officers and men. We'll pick up more on the way to the waterfront."

"This is poor discipline!" Hornbeam said in frustration.

"I don't understand it," Riddick said. "I make a point of ordering at least one flogging a week, to keep the men in line. I never had much trouble with the villagers of Badford. What's wrong with these militiamen?"

Donaldson said: "Major, should someone read the Riot Act?"

"Yes," said Riddick. "Send a man to fetch the mayor."

The crowd made slow progress down Main Street. Everyone watched them go by and some joined in. Sal was amazed at how fast the mob grew. Before they were halfway to the river they were at least a hundred, most of them women. Sal heard a man among the watchers shout: "Fetch the militia!" She began to think that what she was doing might not be wise. Of course they were entitled to know where the grain was going—but the crowd was in a mood to do more than ask polite questions.

She worried about Jarge. He had a good heart but a quick temper. She said: "Don't do anything rash, please."

He gave her a black look. "It's not for a woman to give a man advice."

"I'm sorry, but I don't want to see you flogged like Jeremiah Hiscock."

"I can take care of myself."

She asked herself why she was so concerned. He was her best friend's brother, but that did not make her responsible for him.

Joanie had forged ahead and was leading the pack. Sal looked around and made sure the children were close behind.

They reached the river and turned west along the waterfront until they came upon the handcart parked in front of the Slaughterhouse tavern. It was already half unloaded. A bargee hoisted a sack onto his shoulder, then walked across a short, narrow plank to the deck. A second man made the return journey. It was heavy work, and the men looked strong.

Joanie stood in front of the cart, hands on hips, chin jutting forward aggressively. The bargee said: "What's the matter with you?"

"You have to stop work," she said.

He looked puzzled, but gave a scornful laugh and said: "I work for Mr. Child, not you."

"This is Kingsbridge grain, and it can't go to Combe, nor to France neither."

"That's none of your business."

"It is my business, and you can't load that barge."

"Who's going to stop me—you?"

"Yes. Me and all these others."

"A bunch of women?"

"Exactly. A bunch of women who won't send their children hungry to bed. They're not going to let you take this grain away."

"Well, I'm not going to stop working." He bent to a sack.

Joanie put her foot on the sack.

The man drew back his fist and punched the side of her head. She staggered away. Sal cried out, enraged.

He bent to the sack again, but before he could pick it up, he was set upon by half a dozen women. He was a strong man, and he struggled energetically, throwing powerful punches that felled two or three women—who were immediately replaced by others. Sal was about to join in but she was not needed: the women grabbed his arms and legs and wrestled him to the ground.

His coworker, coming off the barge for another sack,

saw what was happening and joined in the brawl, hitting the women and trying to pull them off his mate. Two more bargees jumped on land and entered the fray.

Sal turned and saw Kit and Sue behind her. With a swift movement she picked both up and pushed through the crowd with one under each arm. A moment later she spotted a kindly neighbor, Jenny Jenkins, a widow with no children who was fond of Kit and Sue. "Jenny, will you take them home where they'll be safe?"

"Of course," Jenny said. She took each child by the hand and walked away.

Sal turned to see Jarge right behind her. "Well done," he said. "Good thinking."

Sal was looking past him. Thirty or forty militiamen were arriving, led by Will Riddick. Spade's brother-in-law, Freddie Caines, was among them. The soldiers were laughing at the waterside scene, cheering the Kingsbridge women who were beating up the Combe bargees. She heard Riddick roar: "What the hell are you men doing? Form up!"

The sergeant repeated the order, but the men ignored him.

At the same time, the bargees who had been up in the square, loading carts, came running down Main Street, shoving brutally through the crowd, no doubt coming to the rescue of their fellows at the waterfront. Some had improvised weapons, lengths of wood and sledgehammers and the like, that they used mercilessly to beat people out of their way.

In front of the Slaughterhouse, Mayor Fishwick was reading the Riot Act. No one was listening.

Sal heard Riddick yell: "Shoulder arms!"

She had heard this instruction before. The militiamen spent days drilling in a field across the river, not far from Barrowfield's Mill. There were something like twenty different movements in the firing routine. After *Shoulder arms* came *Order arms*, then *Support arms* and *Fix bayonets*, and after that she forgot. The men had done it so often that their movements became automatic, like Sal's when she was operating the spinning jenny. The theory, Spade had told Sal, was that in battle they would follow the routine, regardless of the chaos around them. Sal wondered whether that really worked.

Sal could see that today the men were reluctant, their movements slow and uncoordinated; but they did not disobey.

Each man bit the end off a paper cartridge and poured a little powder into the priming pan. Then he inserted the main part of the cartridge into the barrel and packed it tight, using the ramrod slung under the barrel. Kit, who was interested in every kind of machine, had told Sal that the firing mechanism would strike a spark that lit the priming powder, which would flash into the touchhole to ignite the large gunpowder charge and send the ball hurtling through the air.

Surely, Sal thought, Kingsbridge lads like Freddie Caines won't shoot their own womenfolk?

She kept her eye on Riddick but spoke quietly to Jarge. "Can you find me a stone?"

"Easy."

The street was cobbled, and the iron wheels of carts coming to the waterside constantly damaged the surface and loosened the mortar. Repairs were continual but there were always loose stones. Jarge passed her one. The smooth round surface fitted comfortably into her right hand.

She heard Riddick shout: "Make ready!"

This was the penultimate movement, and the men stood stiffly upright with rifles pointing to the sky.

Then: "Fire!"

The men aimed their muskets at the crowd, but no one fired.

"Fire!" Riddick said again.

She saw Freddie start fiddling with his gun, opening the firing mechanism, examining the priming pan, and others quickly followed his example. There were many reasons why a gun might fail to fire, Sal knew: the flint did not strike a spark, the gunpowder was damp, the priming powder lit but the flash failed to pass through the touchhole.

But it was virtually impossible for accidents to happen to twenty-five guns simultaneously.

This could not be happening.

Sal heard Freddie say: "Everything's damp, Sergeant. It's the rain. Wet gunpowder's no good."

Riddick was red in the face: "Rubbish!" he yelled.

The sergeant said to Riddick: "They won't fire on their own friends and neighbors, you see, sir."

Riddick was incandescent with rage. "Then I'll fire!" he said. He snatched a musket from one of the men. As he aimed it, Sal threw the stone. It hit Riddick squarely on the back of his head. He dropped the musket and crumpled to the ground.

Sal gave a sigh of utter satisfaction.

Then Jarge shouted: "Look out, Sal!"

Something hit her on the head, and she blacked out.

Sal came round lying on a hard surface. Her head hurt. She opened her eyes and saw the underside of a thatched roof. She was in a large room. There was a smell of stale beer, cooking, and tobacco. She was in a tavern, on a table. She turned her head to look around, but it was too painful.

Then she heard Jarge say: "Are you all right, Sal?" For some reason his voice was heavy with emotion.

She tried turning her head again, and it was less agonizing this time. She saw Jarge's face, above her and to the side. "I've got a terrible headache," she said.

"Oh, Sal," he said, "I thought you were dead." And to her astonishment he burst into tears.

He bent to her and laid his head next to hers. Slowly, thoughtfully, she put her arms around his big shoulders and drew him to her chest. She was surprised by his reaction. She had thought, three years ago, that he might have wanted to marry her, but she had discouraged him, and she had imagined that his ardor had faded away.

Apparently not.

He wept quietly, and his tears wet her neck. "A bargee hit you with a length of two-by-four," he said. "I caught you before you hit the ground." His voice dropped to a whisper. "I was afraid I'd lost you."

She said: "They'll have to hit harder than that to kill me."

A woman's voice said: "Have a drink of this."

Sal turned her head carefully and saw the landlord's wife holding a glass. The landlord of the Slaughterhouse was a ruffian, but his wife was all right. "Help me sit up," Sal said, and Jarge got one strong arm under her shoulders and raised her to a sitting position. She felt a bit dizzy for a moment, then her head cleared and she took the glass. It smelled like brandy. She sipped, felt better, then swallowed it all. "That's the ticket," she said.

Jarge said: "Our Sal." He was laughing and crying at the same time.

He gave the landlady a coin and she took the glass away.

Sal said to Jarge: "I dealt with Will Riddick didn't I?"

He laughed. "You did."

"Did anyone see?"

"They were all too busy getting out of the way of them bargees."

"Good. What's happening now?"

"Things are quieting down, by the sound of it."

Sal listened. She could hear women and men shouting, sometimes angrily, but it did not sound very riotous: no screams, no breaking glass, no sounds of destruction.

She swung her legs around and put her feet on the floor. Again she felt dizzy, again it passed quickly. "I hope Joanie's all right."

"Last I saw, she was the one calming everybody."

Sal put her weight on her feet and felt fine. "Take me out the back way, Jarge, so I can get steady on my legs."

He put an arm around her shoulders, supporting her weight, and she wrapped her arm around his waist. They walked slowly through the back door and into the yard. They passed the open door of the barn.

Sal was seized by a strong impulse. She turned her body into Jarge's and put both arms around him. "Kiss me, Jarge," she said.

He bent his head to hers and kissed her with surprising gentleness.

It was more than three years since she had kissed a man like this, and she realized she had forgotten how good it was.

She broke the kiss and said: "I've been drinking brandy—you could get drunk on my breath."

"I could get drunk just looking at you," he said.

She studied his face. There was tenderness in his gaze. "I've underestimated you, Jarge," she said, then she kissed him again.

This time it was urgent, sexual. He touched her neck, and her breasts, then pushed his hand between her legs. She felt a surge of desire, and she realized that in the next few seconds he would want to be inside her, and she would want it, too.

She pushed him away, looked around the yard, and said: "In the barn."

They stepped inside and Jarge closed the door. In the gloom Sal made out beer barrels and sacks of potatoes, and a bored horse in a stall. Then she had her back to the wall and Jarge was pulling up her dress. Beside her stood a wooden crate of empty bottles, and she lifted one leg and rested her foot on it. She was wet inside, soaking wet, and he slid into her effortlessly. Now she remembered how very satisfying it was to feel filled up that way. He said: "Aah," and his voice throbbed. They moved together slowly, then faster.

The end came quickly, and she bit his shoulder to stop herself crying out. Then they stayed locked together, arms around each other, holding each other close. After a few moments she started to move again, and in seconds she felt the spasms of pleasure renewed, sharper this time.

It happened a third time, and then she was too exhausted to stand, and she broke the embrace and sank to the floor, where she sat with her back against the barn wall. Jarge slumped beside her. As she caught her breath she noticed him rubbing his shoulder and remembered biting him. "Oh, no, did I hurt you?" she said. "I'm sorry."

"You haven't got anything to be sorry about, I'll swear," he said, and she giggled.

She noticed the horse looking at her with idle curiosity.

Somewhere nearby a collective shout rose from a crowd, and Sal was brought back to the present. "I hope Joanie's all right," she said.

"We better go and see."

They got to their feet.

Sal felt dizzy again, but this time it was from the sex, and she recovered fast. All the same she held Jarge's arm as they walked around the side of the tavern and emerged on the waterfront.

They found themselves at the back of a crowd looking toward the river. To one side stood a small troop of the Shiring Militia, in uniform and holding their muskets, but looking rebellious and sulky. Will Riddick was sitting on a doorstep and someone was examining the back of his head. Clearly his men had continued to refuse to attack. In some towns, she had heard, the militia actually sided with rioting housewives and helped them steal food.

The bargees were not in sight.

At the front was Joanie, standing on something and shouting. "We are not thieves!" she yelled. "We are not going to steal the grain!"

The crowd muttered discontentedly, but they continued to listen, waiting to see what she would say next.

Jarge and Sal pushed their way to the front. The grain had been unloaded from the barge, and Joanie was standing on a pile of sacks.

"I say, Kingsbridge bakers can buy this grain—at the price it fetched before the war," Joanie shouted.

Jarge said quietly: "What's the point of that?" But Sal had a notion where Joanie was going with this.

"On condition," Joanie added, "on condition they promise to sell a four-pound loaf for the old price—seven pence!"

The crowd approved of that.

"Any baker who tries to break this rule will receive a visit . . . from some Kingsbridge women . . . who will explain to him . . . what he ought to do."

A cheer went up.

"Someone find Mr. Child. He won't be far away. He's wearing a yellow waistcoat. Tell him to come and collect his money. It won't be as much as he paid for it, but it's better than nothing. And, bakers, line up here, please, with your money in your hands."

Jarge was shaking his head in amazement. "My sister," he said. "One of a kind."

Sal was worried. "I hope she doesn't get into trouble for this."

"She's prevented the crowd stealing the grain—the justices ought to give her a reward!"

Sal shrugged. "Since when have they been fair?"

Several Kingsbridge bakers made their way to the front of the crowd. Silas Child's yellow waistcoat appeared. There was a discussion, and Sal guessed it was about the exact price of a bushel of grain three years ago. However, the matter seemed to get resolved. Money changed hands, and bakers' apprentices began to walk away with sacks of grain on their shoulders.

"Well," said Jarge, "looks like it's all over."

"Don't be so sure," said Sal.

Next day, in petty sessions before the justices, Joanie was accused of riot—a capital offense.

No one had expected this. She had been the one to say the mob could not steal the grain—and yet she faced the death penalty.

Today's hearing could not find her guilty. The justices could not decide a capital case. They could only convene a grand jury to either commit Joanie for trial at the higher court, the assizes—or dismiss the charge.

"They can't commit you," Jarge said to Joanie, who had a huge bruise on the left side of her face.

Sal, who had a lump on her head, was not so sure.

Poor Freddie Caines had been flogged at dawn for leading the militiamen's mutiny. Spade had told Sal that Freddie had volunteered for the regular army, so that he would be pointing his gun at England's enemies, not at his neighbors. He would join the 107th (Kingsbridge) Foot Regiment.

Hornbeam presided as chairman of justices. Will Riddick sat beside him. There was no doubt about whose side they would take, but they did not have the final say: the decision would be made by the jury.

Sal was pretty sure Hornbeam had not realized that Jarge was one of his weavers. Hornbeam had hundreds of hands and he would not know them all, or even most. If he did find out he might sack Jarge. Or he might decide it was better to have him in the mill weaving than outside making trouble.

Sheriff Doye had impaneled the jurors, and Sal studied them as they took the oath. They were all prosperous Kingsbridge businessmen, proud and conservative. Plenty of townsmen who qualified to be jurors were liberal minded—some were even Methodists: Spade, Jeremiah Hiscock, Lieutenant Donaldson, and others, but no men of that type were sworn in. Clearly Hornbeam had got Doye to fix the jury.

Joanie pleaded not guilty.

The first witness was Joby Darke, a bargee, who said that Joanie had attacked him, and he had defended himself. "We had loaded about half the sacks onto the barge, then she showed up with the mob and tried to stop me doing my job," he said. "So I pushed her out of the way."

Joanie interrupted. "How do you say I did that?" she said. "How did I stop you?"

"You stood in front of me."

"I put my foot on a sack of grain, didn't I?"

"Yes."

"Did that hurt you?"

The people in the courtroom laughed.

Darke was embarrassed. "Course not."

Sal began to feel more optimistic.

Joanie touched her bruise. "So why did you punch my head?"

"I never."

Several people in the courtroom shouted: "You did! You did!"

Hornbeam said: "Quiet!"

Spade stepped forward. "I saw it," he said. "I'll swear that Joby Darke punched Joanie in the head."

Good for you, Spade, thought Sal. He was one of the clothiers but he stuck up for the hands.

Hornbeam was irritated. "When I want you to speak, Shoveller, I'll tell you. Carry on, Darke. What happened next?"

"Well, she fell down."

"And then?"

"Then I was attacked by half a dozen women."

Someone shouted: "Lucky you!" and everyone laughed.

Hornbeam said: "Who was the leader of these women?"

"It was her, Joanie, the one that's accused."

"She led the mob from the market square to the riverside?"

"Yes, she did."

That was true, Sal thought.

"So she was the instigator of the riot."

That was an exaggeration, but Darke said yes.

Joanie said: "How many times did I punch you, Joby?"

He grinned. "If you did, I never felt it," he said boastfully.

"But you still say I started a riot?"

"You brought all those other women."

"And they beat you up?"

"Not exactly, but I couldn't get them all off me!"

"They didn't beat you up, then."

"They stopped me doing my job."

"So you keep saying."

"And you led them."

"What did I say, to make them come to the riverside?"

"You said: 'Follow me,' and that kind of thing."

"When did I say that?"

"I heard it when I was leaving the market square."

"And you say I made the women follow you."

"Yes."

"And then I stopped you working."

"Yes."

"But you said that you unloaded half the sacks before I arrived with the women."

"That's right."

"So you must have left the market square well ahead of the women."

"Yes."

"So how could you hear me telling them to follow me, when you were already at the waterfront unloading sacks?"

Jarge said loudly: "Aha!"

Hornbeam frowned in his direction.

Darke said: "Maybe you took a long time to persuade them."

"The truth is that you never heard me tell them to follow me, because I never did. You're making it up."

"No, I'm not."

"You're a liar, Joby Darke." Joanie turned her back on him.

She had done well, Sal thought, but had she convinced the jury?

The other bargees told similar stories, but they could only say that the women had attacked them and they had fought back; and Sal thought that Darke's confused testimony made all of them seem unreliable.

Joanie then told her own story, emphasizing that her main role had been to prevent the crowd helping themselves to the sacks of grain.

Hornbeam interrupted her. "But you sold it!"

That was irrefutable.

"At a fair price, yes," said Joanie.

"The price of grain is set by the market. You can't decide it."

"But I did yesterday, didn't I?"

The spectators laughed.

Joanie added: "And I gave the money to Mr. Child."

"But it was a lot less than he paid for it."

"And who sold him grain at such a high price? Was it you, Alderman Hornbeam? How much profit did you take?" Hornbeam was trying to interrupt her but she raised her voice above his. "Perhaps you should give that money back to Mr. Child now. That would be justice, wouldn't it?"

Hornbeam flushed with anger. "You be careful what you say."

"I beg your pardon, Your Worship."

"There's not much difference between what you did and stealing."

"There is. I didn't profit. But that doesn't matter, does it?"

"Why on earth not?"

"Because I'm not charged with stealing. I'm charged with riot."

That was clever, Sal thought. But will it do any good? The masters don't like hands to be too smart. I'm not paying you to think, they liked to say; I'm paying you to do as you're told.

Joanie said: "I expect Luke McCullough will confirm what I say."

McCullough, the clerk, said sourly: "I don't answer questions from the accused."

All the same, Hornbeam was flustered. He had taken the questioning in a wrong direction. He said: "You started a riot, you stole Mr. Child's grain, and then you sold it."

"And gave the money to Mr. Child."

"Do you want to call any witnesses?"

"I certainly do."

Sal testified, then Jarge, then Mrs. Dodds, and several others. They all said that Joanie had not told people to follow her, had not attacked anyone, and had prevented the grain from being stolen.

The jury retired to a side room.

Sal, Jarge, and Spade huddled with Joanie. She had the same worry as Sal. "Do you think I was too clever?"

"I don't know," said Spade. "You can't be meek and mild—that just makes them think you're guilty and remorseful. You've got to show some spirit."

Jarge said: "The jury are all Kingsbridge men—they ought to know it was wrong, selling the grain out of our town when we've got people who can't feed their selves."

Spade said: "One thing they're all agreed on is their right to make a profit, regardless of who suffers."

"That's the bloody truth," said Jarge.

The jury came back in.

Sal spoke in a low voice. "Don't get yourself flogged, now, Jarge."

"What are you talking about?"

"If it goes against Joanie, don't shout out or threaten the jury or the justices. You'll only get punished. That pig Riddick would love to see you whipped. Keep your mouth shut, whatever happens. Can you do that?"

"Course I can."

The jury stood in front of the justices.

Hornbeam said: "What is your decision?"

One of them said: "She is committed for trial at the assizes."

There was a shout of protest from the crowd.

Sal looked at Jarge. "Keep still and calm, now."

Jarge just said quietly: "Damn their eyes."

CHAPTER 18

Sal lay in bed with Jarge's arms around her and her head on his shoulder. Her breasts were squashed against his chest, which rose and fell with panting. Apart from their breathing there was no noise in the house: Kit and Sue were sleeping soundly upstairs. Outside in the street, some distance away, two drunk men were arguing, but otherwise the town was quiet. Sal's neck was damp with perspiration, and the sheets felt rough on her bare legs.

She was happy. She had missed this, almost without realizing it: the comfort of intimacy with a man, the sheer delight of making love. After Harry was killed she had lost interest in romance. However, in time, imperceptibly, she had become more and more fond of big, strong, passionate, impetuous Jarge, and now she was glad to be in his arms. Since the day of the riot, and their sudden folly in the barn behind the Slaughterhouse, she had slept with him every night. Her only regret was that she had not done this sooner.

As her breathing slowed, and the euphoria faded, she thought about poor Joanie, lying in Kingsbridge Jail. Joanie had a blanket, and Sal took food to her every day, but the building was cold and the beds were hard. It made Sal angry. The men profiting from high prices should be the ones committed to the assizes.

There was no telling what might happen in a trial, but the hearing at petty sessions had gone badly, and that was a dismal omen. Surely, Sal thought, they would not hang her? But they might. There was a new atmosphere since the stoning of the king's carriage and the food riots: the British ruling elite were in an unforgiving mood. In Kingsbridge, shopkeepers gave no credit, landlords evicted late-paying tenants, and justices handed down harsh sentences. Hornbeam and Riddick were cruel men anyway, but right now they had the support of many of their fellow businessmen. As Spade kept saying: the masters were scared.

Sal was also worried about money. Joanie was not earning, nor was Sue, but both still had to be fed. Sal had rented the attic to a widow, but she paid only four pence a week as it was a single room with no fireplace.

Sal sighed, and Jarge heard her. "Tell me what you're thinking," he said. He could be sensitive occasionally.

"That we don't have enough money."

She felt his shrug. "Nothing new, then," he said.

She asked him the same question. "What are you thinking?"

"That we should get married."

That surprised her, though on reflection it should not have. They were living together as husband and wife, and taking care of his niece as well as her son; they acted like a family.

Jarge said: "Us laboring people aren't strict about such things, but before too long our friends and neighbors will expect you and me to make things regular."

It was true. Word got around, and at some point the vicar would appear on the doorstep to point out that they needed God's blessing on their togetherness. But did she want that? She was happy, for now, but was she confident enough to tell the world that she belonged to Jarge?

He said: "And besides . . ." Then he hesitated, shifted his position uneasily, and scratched his thigh, signs she knew to mean that a man was trying to express unfamiliar emotion.

She encouraged him. "Besides what?"

"I'd like to marry you because I love you." Embarrassed, he added: "There, that's it, I've said it now."

This did not surprise her, though it moved her. However, she had not thought much about her future with

Jarge. He could be kind, and he was loyal to his friends and family, but he had a violent streak that gave her pause. Violence was common in strong men who were trodden down by the world and baffled by its injustice, she had observed. And the law gave women little protection.

She said: "I love you, too, Jarge."

"Well, that's agreed, then!"

"Not quite."

"What are you talking about?"

"Jarge, my Harry never hurt me."

"So . . . ?"

"Some men, many men, feel that marriage means they can chastise a woman . . . with their fists."

"I know."

"You know, but what do you think about it?"

"I have never hurt a woman and I never will."

"Swear that you'll never hurt me or Kit."

"Don't you trust me?" He sounded pained.

She persisted. "I won't marry you unless you make a solemn promise. But don't promise unless you really mean it."

"I will never hurt you or Kit, and I really mean that, and I swear it, so help me God."

"I'll marry you, then, and gladly."

"Good." He turned on his side to embrace her with both arms. "I'll see the vicar about reading the banns." He was happy.

She kissed his mouth and touched his soft cock. She intended an affectionate pat, but it fattened quickly in her hand. "Again?" she said. "Already?"

"If you like."

"Oh, yes," she said. "I like."

After the Communion service in the Methodist Hall, Pastor Charles Midwinter made an announcement. "In the past few days, Prime Minister Pitt has created two new laws that we need to know about," he said. "Spade is going to explain them."

Spade stood up. "Parliament has passed the Treason Act and the Seditious Meetings Act. They make it a crime to criticize the government or the king, or to call a meeting for the purpose of criticizing the government or the king."

Amos knew this and he was against it. His attachment to a nonconformist religion had made him passionate about freedom of speech. No one had the right to stop another man's mouth, he thought.

Others in the congregation had not thought about the new laws, and Spade's blunt summary caused a hubbub of indignation.

When the noise died down Spade said: "We don't know exactly how they will apply these laws, but in principle at least, a meeting such as the Socratic Society's discussion of Archdeacon Paley's book would be illegal. The court would not have to prove there was a riot, just that there was criticism."

Lieutenant Donaldson said: "But we're not serfs! They're trying to go back to the Middle Ages."

Rupe Underwood said: "It's more like the Reign of Terror in Paris, when they executed anyone suspected of not being in favor of the revolution."

"Quite," said Spade. "Some of the newspapers are calling it Pitt's Terror."

"How on earth do they justify such a law?"

"Pitt made a speech saying that the people should look to Parliament, and Parliament alone, for the redress of such grievances as they might have to complain of, with a confident reliance of relief being afforded them."

"But Parliament doesn't represent the people. It represents the aristocracy and the landed gentry."

"Indeed. Myself, I thought Pitt's speech was laughable."

Susan Hiscock, the wife of the printer who had been

flogged, said: "Are we criminals just for having this discussion?"

"In short, yes," said Spade.

"But why have they done this?"

"They're scared," he said. "They can't win the war and they can't feed the people. Kingsbridge is not the only town to have had a food riot. It terrifies them when a crowd chants 'Bread and peace,' and throws stones at the king. They think they will all be guillotined."

Pastor Midwinter stood up again. "We're Methodists," he said. "That means we believe that everyone has the right to their own beliefs about God. That's not illegal, yet. But we need to be careful. Whatever we may think about Prime Minister Pitt and his government, and the war, we should keep our opinions to ourselves, at least until we know how the new laws will operate."

Spade said: "I agree with that."

Spade and Midwinter were the two most respected men in Kingsbridge liberal circles, and the congregation accepted what they had said.

The meeting broke up, and Amos approached Jane Midwinter. She no longer had new clothes every few months, now that her father was a simple pastor rather than a cathedral canon, but she still managed to look irresistible in her coat of British red and a military-looking hat.

For once she had not hurried away after the service. Normally she contrived to be crossing the square just as the Anglican congregation came out of the cathedral, so that she could flirt with Viscount Northwood. But he was at Earlscastle. "Your friend Northwood missed the riot," Amos said.

"I'm sure there wouldn't have been a riot if the viscount had been in charge of the militia," she said. "Instead of that fool Riddick."

Riddick was a fool, Amos agreed, but he was not sure Henry or anyone else could have prevented the riot. "Why did he go to Earlscastle anyway?"

"I expect he wanted to tell his father that he does not wish to marry his horsey cousin Miranda."

"Did he say that to you?"

"Not in so many words."

"Do you think he wants to marry you?"

"I'm sure of it," she said gaily, but Amos did not believe her.

He looked into the silver mist of her eyes and said: "Do you love him?"

She might reasonably have said that it was none of Amos's business, but she answered the question. "I will be very happy married to Lord Northwood," she said. The defiant note told Amos that she was asserting something she was not sure about. "I shall be a countess, and my friends will all be noblewomen. I will have beautiful clothes and wear them to marvelous parties. I will be presented to the king. He will probably ask me to be his mistress, and I will say: 'But, Your Majesty, surely that would be a sin?' and pretend to be regretful."

Jane had never embraced the Methodist virtues of modesty and self-denial, so this kind of talk did not shock Amos. She followed her father's religion without serious commitment. If she married Northwood she would go back to the Church of England in a heartbeat.

He said: "But you don't love Northwood."

"You sound like my father."

"Your father is the best man in Kingsbridge, and the comparison honors me unduly. But I still say you don't love Northwood."

"Amos, you're a sweet man, and I'm fond of you, but you don't have the right to badger me."

"I love you. You know that."

"How miserable we would be together, a worker bee married to a butterfly."

"You could be the queen bee."

"Amos, you can't make me a queen."

"You're already queen of my heart."

"How poetic!"

I'm making a fool of myself, he thought. But the fact remains that Northwood hasn't proposed to her. He hasn't even invited her to meet his father.

It may never happen.

Sal and Jarge got married in St. Luke's Church on a Saturday evening after work. They had no money for a celebration, so they took only Kit and Sue to church with them. However, to Sal's surprise Amos Barrowfield and Elsie Latimer showed up and signed as witnesses. Then Amos surprised her by saying that a gallon of ale and a small barrel of oysters was waiting outside.

Sal said: "Would it be all right if we shared them with Joanie?"

"Perfectly all right," said Amos. "I'll give Gil Gilbert a shilling and offer him a cup of ale and he'll be happy to let us in."

The wedding party left the church and walked to the jail. It was two big old houses knocked into one, with bars on the windows and locks on all the doors. Gil cheerfully showed them to Joanie's small room. The floorboards were uneven, there was mold on the walls, and the fireplace was cold and empty, but no one cared. They were five adults and two children, and they soon warmed the place. Amos poured ale for everyone, and Jarge opened the oysters with his pocketknife. Gil offered to sell them a loaf of bread to go with the feast, and asked the outrageous price of two shillings, but Amos paid it anyway, saying: "Let him make a bit of extra money."

"My brother," said Joanie, raising her tankard in a toast. "I thought he'd never find a good woman, but he picked the best of the lot, God bless him."

Jarge said: "I did, didn't I? Now who's going to say I'm not clever?"

Amos said: "It's a match—two people with strong

arms and kind hearts. And Kit is the cleverest boy in the Sunday school."

Elsie added hastily: "And Sue is the most popular girl in school."

Sal was euphoric. She had been anticipating a quiet evening at home, with stewed neck of mutton, and instead there was a banquet. "I bet noblemen's weddings aren't this much fun," she said. "With all their stiff clothes and nice manners."

Joanie said: "My good woman, I would have you know that I am the Lady Johanna, the duchess of Shiring."

Kit and Sue squealed with laughter.

Sal played along. She curtsied, then said: "I am honored by your condescension, Duchess Johanna, but I must point out that I am the countess of Kingsbridge, and nearly as good as what you are."

Joanie turned to Jarge and said: "You there, open me another oyster."

Jarge said: "My dear duchess, you have mistook me for a butler, but I am in fact the bishop of Box, and cannot open oysters with my lily-white hands." He showed his palms, which were brown, scarred, and not perfectly clean.

Sal, giggling, said: "Dear bishop, I find you very attractive, give me a kiss."

Jarge kissed her and they all clapped.

Sal looked around the room and realized that all the important people in her life were here: her child, her husband, her best friend, her friend's child, the woman who was teaching Kit, and Amos, the master who had always brought her good fortune. There were cruel and wicked people in Kingsbridge and the world, but everyone in this room was good. "This must be what heaven is like," she said.

She swallowed another oyster and drank a long draft of ale, then she said: "And I doubt whether there's anything in heaven that tastes better than oysters with ale."

Kingsbridge was proud of being an assize town. It was a mark of distinction and an acknowledgment that this was the most important place in the county of Shiring. The twice-yearly visit of a judge from London was a big event in the social calendar, and he always had more invitations than he could accept.

The council welcomed him with a magnificent Assize Ball. The aldermen were not spendthrift, however: tickets were costly and the ball made a profit.

Hornbeam's house was only a quarter of a mile from the Assembly Rooms, and the evening was fine, so he and his family walked. The endless rain of the summer and autumn had stopped, thankfully, though it was far too late to rescue the harvest.

There were three couples in the Hornbeam party: himself and Linnie, Howard and Bel, and Deborah with Will Riddick. The young men wore white gloves and glossy boots, and their cravats were tied in huge bows that looked foolish to Hornbeam. The young ladies' necklines were lower than he liked, but it was too late now to make them change.

Outside the porticoed entrance stood a crowd of townspeople, mostly women with shawls wrapped around cold shoulders, watching the arrival of the rich folk. They cooed at displays of jewelry and clapped for any particularly extravagant outfit: a bright yellow cloak, a white fur, a tall hat with feathers and ribbons. Hornbeam ignored the rabble and fixed his gaze straight ahead, but his family waved and nodded to acquaintances as they passed through the admiring throng.

Then they were inside. A small fortune had been spent on candles, and the whole place was brightly lit, revealing a host of magnificently dressed women and splendid men. Even Hornbeam was impressed. Kingsbridge clothiers and their families wore their best fabrics for such events. The men were in tailcoats of purple, bright blue, lime green, and rich chestnut. The women wore bold checks and bright stripes, pleats and gathers and sash belts, and yards of lace. It was a massive advertisement for the town's collective genius.

People were lining up for the contradance, in which the lead couple kept changing. Hornbeam noticed that Viscount Northwood was taking part. Surprisingly, Northwood looked as if he had already drunk quite a lot of champagne.

Deborah said: "I hope this band can play a waltz."

"Out of the question," said Hornbeam immediately. He had never seen a waltz but he had heard about the new dance craze. "This is the Assize Ball, a respectable event organized by the borough council. We'll have no obscene dancing."

Deborah usually gave in to her father, but now she pushed back. "There's nothing obscene about it! People in London do it all the time."

"This is not London, and we don't permit dances in which people hug one another . . . frontally. It's disgusting. They might not even be married!"

Howard grinned and said: "You know, Father, you can't actually get pregnant waltzing." The others laughed loudly.

Hornbeam was irritated. "That's not a very helpful remark, Howard, especially in front of the ladies."

"Oh. Sorry."

Deborah said: "Father, you're talking like an old clothier who won't use the newfangled machinery. You should keep up with the times!"

Hornbeam was stung. He did not think of himself as a stick-in-the-mud. "That's a ridiculous comparison," he said crossly. Deborah was the only one in the family who could stand up to him in an argument.

"Perhaps just one or two waltzes?"

"There will be no waltzing."

The youngsters gave up and joined in the contradance.

Hornbeam saw, with a grimace of distaste, that Amos Barrowfield was taking part.

There was always something to spoil his mood.

After the wedding party, Sal sat at the kitchen table with a borrowed quill and a little ink and opened her father's Bible. She wrote the date, then the word *Marriage*, then she said: "How do you write *Jarge*?"

"What are you doing?" said Jarge.

"I'm putting our wedding in the family Bible."

He looked over her shoulder. "That's a fine book," he said.

It was old, Sal reflected, but it had a good brass clasp and was printed with clear letters that were easy to read.

"Must have cost a bit," Jarge said.

"Probably," she said. "My grandfather bought it. How do you spell your name?"

"I don't know that I've ever seen it wrote down."

"So, if I write it wrong you won't know."

He laughed. "Nor care, neither."

Sal wrote:

Jarj Boks and Sarah Clitheroe

"Very good," said Jarge.

It did not look right to Sal, but it was done now. She blew on the ink to dry it. When it stopped glistening and turned to a dull unreflective black, she closed the book.

"Now," she said, "let's go and watch the guests arriving at the ball."

Elsie was not much of a dancer but she liked dancing with Amos, who was graceful and precise. The contradance was energetic, and at the end they left the floor, panting with effort.

The Assembly Rooms looked very different tonight than when Elsie used them for her Sunday school. This was how the place was intended to be, full of music and chatter, with corks popping and glasses being filled and emptied and rapidly refilled. But she preferred it when the only occupants were poor children determined to learn.

She said to Amos: "Well, now I've been to jail. That's a first."

He laughed. "I've known Sal a long time. She really loved her first husband, Harry, and I'm glad to see her happy again."

"You're a kind man, Amos."

"Sometimes."

She knew that Amos was embarrassed by compliments, so she quickly changed the subject. "I'm sorry the Socratic Society has been wound up."

"Spade and Pastor Midwinter think it's for the best."

"A great shame."

"There's a little money left over, and they're going to use it to start a book-sharing club."

"Well, that's something, though it will do no good to those who can't read."

"On the contrary, men join in order to learn to read." He looked over her shoulder and his face changed.

She turned to see what had caught his attention. Jane Midwinter was talking to Northwood. I might have guessed, Elsie thought. She heard Jane say: "Come to the buffet and get something to eat before you drink any more champagne. I don't want you to disgrace yourself." It was the kind of thing a wife might say, or a fiancée.

Elsie turned back to Amos and said: "What will you do if Jane marries Northwood?"

"She won't. The earl won't permit it."

She persisted. "But what would you do, if it happened?"

"I don't know." Amos looked uncomfortable. "Nothing, I suppose." He brightened. "There's a war on, and Northwood will have to fight sooner or later. If he's killed in battle, Jane will be single again."

That was heartless, which was uncharacteristic for Amos. "So you would just wait and hope."

"Something like that. Excuse me." He left her and followed Jane and Northwood.

Despair settled over Elsie. There was no hope for her. Amos would remain faithful to Jane even if she married someone else.

It was time Elsie faced reality.

I'm twenty-two years old and single, she thought. All I want is a house full of children. Bel Marsh is now Bel Hornbeam, and Deborah Hornbeam is now Deborah Riddick, and they'll probably have children soon, while I'm still holding on for a man who loves someone else.

I'm not going to turn into an old maid. I must forget about Amos.

She got a glass of champagne to cheer her up.

Arabella Latimer looked ravishing in a russet-colored dress made of one of Spade's cashmeres. The gathered bodice and high waist emphasized her generous bust. Spade could hardly take his eyes off her. He said: "If I can get the band to play a waltz, will you dance it with me?"

"I'd love to," she said. "But I don't know how."

"I'll teach you. I learned in London. It's easy. There'll be lots of people learning—it hasn't been danced before in Kingsbridge."

"All right. I hope the clergy won't be scandalized."

"They like being scandalized. It gives them a thrill."

Spade went to the bandstand, and, when the current dance ended, he showed the bandleader a silver crown piece, the equivalent of five shillings, and said: "Can you play a waltz?"

"Of course," said the bandleader. "But I don't think Alderman Hornbeam will like it."

That annoyed Spade, but he forced a smile. "Mr. Hornbeam doesn't always get his way," he said with suppressed irritation. He held up the coin. "Up to you," he said.

The bandleader took the money.

Spade returned to Arabella. "It goes *one* two three, *one* two three. You step back with your left foot, then sideways and back with your right, then draw your feet together, like those foreigners who click their heels as they bow." He stood in front of her, not touching, and they did the steps together.

Arabella got the idea quickly. "It really isn't difficult," she said. She was bright-eyed and eager, and Spade began to think she might be as much in love with him as he was with her.

No one paid them much attention. At balls such as this people were often seen teaching each other the complicated steps of strictly choreographed dances such as the cotillion, which involved four couples in a square who touched only each other's hands.

An allemande came to an end, and there was a pause in the music. Normally the bandleader would announce the next dance, so that people could get ready, but this time he did not, perhaps fearing that the waltz might be stopped before it got started, and he would have to give back his five shillings. The music began with no announcement, but the bumpety-bumpety rhythm was unmistakable. People in the crowd looked puzzled by the unfamiliar music.

"Here we go," said Spade. "Put your right hand on my left shoulder." He put his hand on her waist, which was softly rounded and slightly warm. He held her other hand at shoulder level. Their bodies touched.

"This is very intimate," she said. It was not a complaint.

Spade took the first step and she fitted in smoothly. In no time they were waltzing as if they had done it many times before.

"We're the only ones dancing," said Arabella.

Spade noticed that the hubbub of conversation and laughter had died down somewhat, and a lot of people were watching him with the bishop's wife. He began to wonder whether this had been a mistake. He did not want Arabella to get into trouble with her husband.

He noticed Hornbeam staring at him with a furious expression.

Arabella said: "Oh, dear, everyone's looking at us."

Spade had his love in his arms and he did not want to stop dancing. "To hell with them all," he said.

She laughed. "You fool, I adore you."

Then Deborah Hornbeam dragged Will Riddick onto the floor, and Deborah's brother, Howard, followed with his new wife, Bel; and both couples began to waltz.

"Thank heaven for that," said Arabella.

Spade looked at the young Hornbeams and said: "They've been practicing at home. I bet Hornbeam didn't know about it."

More couples joined in, and soon a hundred people were waltzing, or trying to. Feeling more confident, Spade pulled Arabella's body closer, and she responded, pressing herself against him as they spun around the floor. She whispered in his ear: "Oh, my, this is like fucking."

Spade smiled happily. "If you think fucking is like this," he murmured, "you haven't been doing it right."

The waltz came to an end and the bandleader announced a cotillion. Kenelm asked Elsie to partner him, and she agreed. He led her well, and she thought her clumsiness did not show much. Afterward he said: "Let's get champagne."

It was her third glass, and she was relaxed. She said: "Did you dance much at Oxford?"

Kenelm shook his head. "No women." Then he added: "None that an aspiring clergyman would dance with, anyway."

"Stop it," she said.

"Stop what?"

"Being judgmental. It's charmless. You're a clergyman, everyone assumes that you have no interest in unsuitable women. You don't have to underline it."

He frowned resentfully, and seemed about to argue; then he hesitated and looked thoughtful.

Amos liked dancing, and he knew how to waltz, but he did not join in. He was following Jane and Northwood. He knew he was behaving badly, but they did not observe him, because they were wrapped up in each other. No one else had noticed, either; not yet, anyway.

They went to the buffet, then joined in the dancing, and then moved to the promenade walk. Finally they passed through the doors into the lamplit garden.

The night air was cold and there were few people outside. Amos tasted mist.

Jane had put on a cloak against the chill. They strolled up and down. Northwood's steps were a bit erratic; Jane was completely in command of herself. It was hard to see their faces in the gloom, but their heads tilted close, and their conversation was clearly intense.

Amos leaned against the outer wall of the building, like a man in need of fresh air. Something big was going on between Jane and Northwood, something beyond flirting.

Then they vanished.

They had slipped behind a clump of tall bushes, he realized. Now they were out of everyone's sight. What were they doing? He had to know. He crossed the lawn. He could not help himself.

When he got close he found he could glimpse them through the shrubbery. They were embracing and kissing, and he heard Northwood groan in passion. He felt furious, and at the same time he was ashamed to be a voyeur. Northwood was doing things Amos had dreamed about. He was torn between the impulse to attack Northwood and the urge to walk away unnoticed.

He saw Northwood's hand close over Jane's breast.

He stepped closer.

"No," said Jane quietly, and she took Northwood's hand away.

Amos stood still.

Holding both Northwood's hands in her own, Jane said: "The man I marry may stroke my breasts any time he likes—and I will be happy to let him."

Amos heard Northwood gasp.

Then Northwood said: "Marry me, Jane."

"Oh, Henry!" she said. "I will!"

They kissed again, but Jane broke the embrace. She took Northwood's hand and led him out from behind the bushes. Amos quickly turned around and pretended to be strolling idly by.

Jane was not fooled. "Amos!" she said. "We're engaged!"

She did not stop, but led Northwood inside; and Amos followed.

Holding Northwood's arm firmly, Jane approached her father, Pastor Midwinter, who was talking to Alderman Drinkwater and the two Hornbeam girls, Deborah and Bel. "Father," said Jane, "Henry has something to say to you."

This could mean only one thing, especially as Jane had used Northwood's first name. Both Deborah and Bel squealed with delight.

Northwood was tipsy, but his good manners came to his rescue, and he said: "Sir, may I have your permission to ask your daughter for her hand in marriage?"

The pastor hesitated. Amos's last hope was that Midwinter would make an excuse, and tell Northwood to come and call on him tomorrow, so that they could discuss the proposal properly.

But Drinkwater, who was Jane's grandfather, could not contain his joy. "How splendid!" he said.

Bel Hornbeam said loudly: "Jane's marrying Viscount Northwood! Hurrah!"

Midwinter was obviously unhappy with the way this was being done. However, if he refused his daughter she would be shamed. After a long pause he finally said to Northwood: "Yes, my lord, you may ask her."

"Thank you," said Northwood.

Deborah Riddick murmured admiringly: "Well done, Miss Midwinter." She obviously realized that the whole thing had been cleverly managed by Jane.

Jane took Northwood's hand, faced him, and said: "It will be my life's work to make my wonderful husband happy."

Amos turned away, walked out of the building, and headed for home.

Elsie saw Amos leave, and knew from his demeanor that something bad had happened. It did not take her long to find out what. Within minutes there was an atmosphere of excitement in the room, people talking animatedly, their voices sounding surprised and a bit scandalized. Then Kenelm Mackintosh approached her and said: "Northwood has proposed marriage to Jane Midwinter, and Jane has accepted him."

"Well, well," said Elsie. "So Jane has got the man she wanted." *And I have not.*

"Aren't you surprised?"

"Not very. Jane has been working hard at this for months."

"But her father is a Methodist—and Northwood's going to be the earl of Shiring!"

"And Jane will be the countess."

"I worry that Methodism is coming to be seen as a normal part of English Christianity."

"Why not? Protestantism has become a normal part of European Christianity."

He was temporarily floored by this riposte. Elsie enjoyed watching him flounder for an answer. And he was awfully good to look at.

At last he said: "Sometimes you can be terribly flippant."

"Why, Mr. Mackintosh, you sound almost as if you're getting used to me."

He gazed at her for a moment. "You're very clever."

"My word—such a compliment—especially coming from a man!"

"Flippancy again."

"I know."

"Despite that, I admire you."

That was code. It meant: *I'm falling in love with you.* She suppressed the urge to mock. She had guessed that he was developing a tendresse for her, and a genuine feeling should not be ridiculed. On the other hand, he had never looked at her with the raw desire she had seen when Amos looked at Jane. She could not help remembering what Amos had said: *He wants to marry you because it will help his advancement. The son-in-law of a bishop can hardly fail to gain promotion within the church.* She said: "Are you ambitious?"

"Ambitious to do God's work, yes. And my wife will have the joy of helping me to serve him."

His words were clichés, but he seemed sincere. She said: "To do God's work, yes, but in what capacity?"

"If it's his will, I believe I might toil as a bishop. I've had the necessary education, and I'm dedicated and hardworking."

"Would you say you're proud?"

He was uncomfortable under this interrogation, but he suffered it doggedly. "I have had occasion to confess the sin of pride, yes."

That was honest.

She said: "I love children. Do you?"

"I've never had the chance. I have no sisters and just one brother who is twelve years older than I. My earliest memory is of him leaving home—and leaving Scotland. He went to take up a job in Manchester, as I left to go to Oxford. There's not much in Scotland for aspirant young men."

"For some people, God's work may be teaching."

"I agree. 'Suffer little children, and forbid them not, to come unto me, for of such is the kingdom of heaven,' Jesus said."

"You try to help in the Sunday school, but you're never at ease with the little ones."

"Perhaps you could teach me."

This was the first time she had known him to show humility. There was a decent man in there somewhere.

Mackintosh said: "I have spoken to your father."

She felt panicky. He was now going to propose to her, and she did not know how to answer him. She looked around the room and said: "I don't see my father."

"He left. He wasn't feeling well. I'm a bit worried about his health."

Playing for time, Elsie said: "And my mother?"

"She said she would find someone to walk her home, and he was not to worry."

"Oh, good."

"I told your father that I had come to love you . . ."

"I am honored." It was a formal sentence that did not commit her one way or the other.

". . . and I said I had some slight hope that you might become fond of me."

I don't know, she thought, I really don't know.

"Miss Latimer—or may I say my dearest Elsie—will you marry me?"

There it was, and now she had to make a lifetime decision.

As surely as it was possible to know another person's

heart, she knew that Amos would never marry her. And in the last few minutes she had seen a side of Mackintosh that he had never shown her before. He might turn into a good father, after all.

She would never love him passionately. But her parents' marriage had been like that. And when she had asked whether her mother was glad she had married her father, her mother had said: *Of course! Otherwise I wouldn't have you.* That's how I would feel, Elsie thought; glad of the marriage because of the children.

If I was eighteen I'd say no. But I'm twenty-three. And I haven't got Jane's way with men. I can't put my head on one side, and smile shyly, and speak in a low, intimate voice so they have to lean closer to hear. I've tried, and I just feel dishonest and foolish. But I want someone to kiss me at night, and I long to bear children and love them and raise them to be good and clever and kind. I don't want to grow old alone.

I don't want to be an old woman with no children.

"Thank you for honoring me, Kenelm," she said. "Yes, I will marry you."

"Praise God," said Kenelm.

Spade used his personal key to unlock the door in the north porch of the cathedral. He stepped in, and Arabella followed him. It was colder inside than out. When he closed the door he could see nothing. Working by touch, he found the keyhole and locked the door.

"Hold my coattails and follow me," he said to Arabella. "I think I can find my way in the dark."

Holding his arms out in front of him like a blind man, so that he would not walk straight into a pillar, he headed west, trying to go in a straight line. After a few seconds he realized he could just about see the windows, dark gray pointed shapes against the pitch black of the masonry. When he drew parallel with the last window he knew he was just two or three steps from the end wall. His hands touched the cold stones and he turned. He followed the wall around the corner to the narthex, a lobby beneath the bell tower. He found a door and unlocked it. When they were inside he locked it again.

They climbed the spiral staircase to the rope room.

Arabella said: "I can't see a thing!"

He took her in his arms and kissed her. She kissed him back enthusiastically, holding his head in her hands, digging her fingers into his hair. He touched her breasts through her dress, relishing their weight, their softness, and their warmth.

She said: "But I want to see you."

"I left a bag after practice last Monday," said Spade, breathing hard. "Just stand still while I find it." He crossed the floor, treading on the mats and feeling the dangling ropes brush his coat. He got down on his knees and felt around until he touched the leather satchel he had stashed here. He took out a candle and a tinderbox, then lit the candle. There were no windows in the rope room, so the light could not be seen from outside.

He turned and looked at her. In the candlelight they smiled at each other.

"You planned this," said Arabella. "Clever you."

"It was more like a daydream than a plan."

As the wick burned brighter, he dripped wax on the floorboards, then fixed the base of the candle into the melt and held it there until the wax hardened enough to hold it in place.

She said: "Let's lie on the floor. I don't care if it's uncomfortable."

"I have a better idea." On the floor were the mats used by the ringers, their purpose to reduce wear on the ropes as they brushed the floor. He picked up several mats and arranged them in a pile to make a bed.

"You thought of everything!"

"I've been picturing this moment in my mind for months."

She giggled. "Me too."

He lay down and looked up at her.

To his surprise, she stood over him and raised the skirt of her dress until it was around her waist. Her legs were white and shapely. He had wondered whether she might be wearing underdrawers, a risqué new fashion, but she was not, and the hair at her groin was a dark red-brown. He wanted to kiss it.

His erection made a bulge in the front flap of his breeches, and he felt embarrassed—which was silly, he realized, but there it was.

Arabella was far from embarrassed. She knelt astride his legs and unbuttoned his flap, freeing his cock. "Oh, how nice!" she said, and she took it in her hand.

"I'm about to explode," Spade said.

"No, wait for me!" She moved over him and slid it inside her. "Don't push, not yet." When it was all the way in she bent forward, grasped his upper arms, and kissed him. Then she lifted her head, looked into his eyes, and began to move slowly. He held her hips and moved in rhythm.

"Keep your eyes open," she said. "I want you to watch me."

Not a difficult task, he thought, with her reddish hair flying and her orange-brown eyes wide, her mouth open and her wonderful bust rising and falling as she panted. What did I do to deserve this marvelous woman?

He wanted it to go on forever, but he was not sure he could last another minute. However, she was the one who lost control. She gripped his arms so hard that it hurt, but he hardly cared because he, too, was carried away, and the end came for both of them. "So good," she said as she collapsed on his chest. "So good."

He put his arms around her and stroked her hair.

After a minute she said: "I'm glad you have the keys."

That struck him as funny, and he chuckled. She laughed, too.

Then she gasped. "The things I said to you! The things

I did! I don't normally . . . I mean I never before . . . oh, damn, I'm going to shut up."

After another minute she said: "I wanted it to go on longer, but I couldn't wait."

"Don't worry," he said. "There's always tomorrow."

At the assize court, the prosecution evidence against Joanie was the same, but the defense was better, Sal thought. Amos Barrowfield swore that Joanie had worked for him for years, and had always been honest and respectable, had never been violent, and would not have incited people to riot. Similar testimony came from other Kingsbridge worthies: Pastor Midwinter, Spade, and even the vicar of St. Luke's. And Silas Child admitted that Joanie had given all the money to him.

The jury was out for a long time. This was not surprising. The petty sessions jury had been deciding only whether to commit her to the assizes. This jury was making a life-or-death decision.

Sal talked to Spade. "What do you think?"

"The fact that she gave the money to Child is a big factor in her favor. What's against her is the mob that stoned the king's carriage."

Jarge, standing with Sal, said: "That wasn't Joanie's fault!"

"I don't say it's fair, but the attack on the king has put them all in a mood to be harsh."

By that he meant the death sentence, Sal knew. "Pray God you're wrong," she said fervently.

"Amen," said Spade.

For the spectators in the courtroom, the trial was not the only topic of conversation. Many were talking about the two engagements that had been made at the Assize Ball. Northwood and Jane were the big news. Yesterday, Jane Midwinter had attended Communion at the cathedral, rather than at the Methodist Hall, and had sat with

Northwood, as if they were already married. Then Pastor Midwinter had invited Northwood to Sunday dinner at his modest house, and Northwood had gone. However, everyone was waiting for the reaction of Northwood's father, the earl of Shiring. He would probably object—though in the end he could not stop his twenty-seven-year-old son marrying the bride of his choice.

Elsie Latimer and Kenelm Mackintosh were not so remarkable, though a few people were surprised that Elsie had said yes.

Both weddings would surely take place in the cathedral. Sal looked at Jarge and smiled wryly when she thought how different those weddings would be from hers. But she would not have changed anything about her own wedding even if she could.

If I said that aloud no one would believe me, she thought.

The jury came back in, and the clerk asked the foreman whether they found Joanie guilty or not guilty.

"Guilty," said the foreman.

Joanie staggered and seemed about to fall, but Jarge held her up.

There was an indignant noise from the public.

Sal saw Will Riddick smile. I wish I'd killed him with that stone, she thought.

"Prisoner in the dock," said the judge. "You have been found guilty of a crime that renders you liable to the death penalty."

Joanie was white with dread.

"However," the judge went on, "your fellow townspeople have argued strongly for leniency, and the merchant Silas Child has testified that you gave him all the money you received by selling the stolen grain."

Surely, Sal thought, this means she won't hang. But what will her punishment be? Flogging? Hard labor? The stocks?

"Because of that, I will not condemn you to death."

Jarge said: "Oh, thank God."

"Instead, you will be transported to the penal colony of New South Wales in Australia for fourteen years."

Jarge shouted: "No!"

He was not alone. The crowd was outraged, and there were more shouted protests.

The judge raised his voice. "Clear the court!"

The sheriff and the constables began to push people out. The judge disappeared through the door to the anteroom. Sal held Jarge's arm and talked to him to distract him from thoughts of violence. "Fourteen years, Jarge—she'll only be forty-four."

"They hardly ever come back even when their sentence is up, you know that. When it was America few returned, and Australia's farther away."

Sal knew he was right. When the sentence ended prisoners had to pay for their passage home, and it was nearly impossible for them to earn enough money out there. In almost all cases, transportation was effectively banishment for life. "We can hope, Jarge," said Sal.

His anger was turning to grief. Near to tears, he said: "And what about little Sue?"

"She'll be left behind. No one would want to take a child to a penal colony, and anyway it's not allowed."

"She'll have no mother or father then!"

"She'll have you and me, Jarge," Sal murmured solemnly. "She's our child now."

Kit knew something terrible had happened, but for several days he could not get any adult to reveal the details. Then one morning at breakfast his mother said: "Kit and Sue, I'm going to try to explain to you what's going to happen today."

At last, Kit thought. He sat upright, interested.

"Sue, your mum has to go away this morning."

Sue said: "Why?"

Kit, too, wanted to know that.

Sal said: "The judge thought she did something wrong when she stopped the men loading the sacks of grain onto Mr. Child's barge."

Kit knew about this. He said stoutly: "It was Kingsbridge grain, it shouldn't have been sent away."

Jarge said: "That's what we all thought, but the judge saw it differently, and he's the one with the power."

Sue said: "Where is Mummy going?"

Sal said: "New South Wales, in Australia."

"Is it far?"

Kit knew the answer to this. He collected such facts. "It's ten thousand miles," he said, proud of his knowledge. But Sue looked puzzled, as if she couldn't understand what ten thousand miles was. He added: "It takes half a year for the ship to get there."

"Half a year!" She understood that, and she began to cry. "But when will she come back?"

Sal said: "It will be a long time. Fourteen years."

Kit said to Sue: "You and me will be grown-up by then."

Sal said: "Kit, let me answer the questions, please."

"Sorry."

"In a minute we're going to the riverside to wave goodbye. She will go in a barge to Combe, then board a big ship for the long journey. Now, the sheriff has said that we can't hug or kiss her, in fact we mustn't try to touch her."

Sue sobbed: "It's not fair!"

"It certainly is not. But we'll get into big trouble if we try to break the rules. Do you understand?"

"Yes," said Sue.

"Kit?"

"Yes."

"Then we can go."

They put on their coats.

Kit knew what was happening but did not really understand it. No one he knew thought that Joanie was a criminal. How could the judge have done such a wicked thing?

There was a crowd at the riverside. Kingsbridge people had been transported before, but they had been thieves and murderers. Joanie was a woman and a mother. He sensed the rage in the people who stood around him in their threadbare coats and old hats, huddled together in a light rain, resentful but helpless.

Joanie appeared, escorted by Sheriff Doye, and a muted rumble of hostility arose from those waiting. Kit saw that Joanie's ankles were hobbled by a chain, which made her walk with unnaturally small steps. Sue saw the same thing, and cried: "Why are her feet chained up?"

Kit said: "To stop her running away."

Sue burst into tears.

Sal said angrily: "Kit, I told you to let me answer the questions. You upset her."

"Sorry." I was only telling the truth, he thought, but his mother was not in a mood to be argued with.

Someone started clapping, and others joined in. Joanie seemed suddenly to notice the crowd, and her posture changed. She could not alter her peculiar walk, but she straightened her back and held her head high, and looked from side to side, nodding to people she knew. Kit thought vaguely that this was better for Sue. The worst thing must be to see her mother looking abject.

The applause grew as Joanie approached the barge.

Kit took Sue's hand, to comfort her. His mother took the other hand, probably to restrain her if she tried to run to Joanie.

Joanie crossed the gangplank and stepped onto the deck of the barge.

Sue screamed, and Sal swiftly picked her up. Sue's arms and legs thrashed, but Sal held her tightly.

A bargee untied the ropes and pushed off from the quay. The current gently eased the barge downstream, strong but unhurried.

On deck, Joanie turned to face the shore and the watching crowd. Kit wondered how she could be so still and quiet, just looking. She was leaving her family and the place where she had spent her whole life, and going to somewhere new on the other side of the globe; the thought was so terrifying that Kit tried to push it out of his mind.

The current took the barge downstream rapidly. Sue's screams diminished. The crowd stopped clapping.

The barge turned around the first bend in the river and disappeared from view.

PART III

The Combination Act

1799

CHAPTER 19

Amos Barrowfield got up at four o'clock. He was alone in the house: his mother had died two years ago. He dressed quickly and left a few minutes later, carrying a lantern. It was a crisp spring morning. Despite the hour he was not the only one up. There were lights in all the poorer dwellings, and hundreds of hands were already trudging through the dark streets, heading for the mills.

Amos noticed two men standing guard outside militia headquarters, and he thought sourly that the red cloth of their uniform coats had been woven by Hornbeam.

Kingsbridge had lost its air of prosperity. People could not afford to repaint their front doors or repair broken panes of glass. Some shops had gone out of business and others had drab window displays and low stock. Shoppers bought the cheapest, not the best. Demand was slack for the high-quality clothes that Amos specialized in.

It was the war. A coalition of Britain, Russia, the Ottoman Empire, and the kingdom of Naples was attacking the French empire over much of Europe and the Middle East, and getting beaten. The French suffered occasional reverses but always bounced back. For the sake of that pointless war, Amos thought, we're all struggling to make a living. And the hands just get angrier.

Moonlight glinted off wavelets in the river. He crossed the bridge to Leper Island. There were lights in Caris's Hospital, he saw. The second span of the bridge took him to the suburb called Loversfield. There he turned left.

On this side of the river Hornbeam had built long rows of houses, side by side and back-to-back, with a water pump and a privy in the middle of each street. The houses were rented by the hands who worked at the nearby mills.

In the hilly country north and east of the town the river and its tributaries flowed fast enough to turn mill wheels and at the same time supply unlimited water for fulling and dyeing. There was no street plan here: buildings, millponds, and millraces were put up where the water flowed.

He walked upstream to his mill. Nodding to the sleepy-eyed watchman, he unlocked the door and went inside. He was lighting the lamps when Hamish Law arrived, in riding boots and a long blue cloak.

Hamish now did the job Amos had had before his father died: touring the villages and visiting the cottage workers. Hamish was always well-dressed, and went out of his way to be friendly with people. However, although good-natured he was also tough enough to stand up to ruffians on the road. In short, he was a younger version of Amos.

Together they loaded the packhorses and talked about the places Hamish would visit today and the craftspeople he would deal with. Most spinning was now done at the mill, on machines, so there were fewer hand spinners to visit; but weaving was still a manual skill, and weavers worked either at home or in mills.

"You'd better warn them there may be no work next week," Amos told Hamish. "I've got no more orders and I can't afford to stockpile cloth."

"Perhaps something will come up in the next few days," Hamish said optimistically.

"We can hope."

The hands began to arrive, eating bread and drinking from earthenware mugs of weak ale, chattering like sparrows in the morning. They always had plenty to talk about. They worked so hard and so long that it seemed miraculous to Amos that they had energy for conversation.

At five o'clock the work began. The fulling hammers

thudded, the spinning jennies bumped and whirred, and the looms clacked as the weavers threw their shuttles from right to left and back again. The banging and clattering was melodic to Amos. Cloth was being made to keep people warm, wages were being earned to feed families, profits were accumulating to keep the whole enterprise going. But soon his worries returned.

He sought out Sal Box, who was the unofficial representative of the workforce. She looked well, despite the hard times. Marriage suited her, although her husband, Jarge, seemed a bit of a thug to Amos.

The spinning engines were now driven by water power, so spinners did not have to turn a wheel by hand. This meant that an experienced spinner such as Sal could supervise three machines at a time.

They had to raise their voices to talk over the noise.

"I haven't got any work for next week," he said. "Unless I make a sale at the last minute."

"You ought to get military orders," Sal said. "That's where all the money is."

Many clothiers would take offense at advice from their hands, but not Amos. He liked to know what they were thinking. He had just learned something important: they imagined he had not bid for Shiring Militia contracts. Now he had a chance to set the record straight. "Don't think I haven't tried," he said. "But Will Riddick gives all the orders to his father-in-law."

Her face darkened. "That Will Riddick should hang."

"It's impossible to break into the business."

"That's not right."

"Don't I know it."

"There's lots of things not right in this country."

Amos said hastily: "But anyone who says so may be charged with treason."

Sal pressed her lips together in a disapproving line.

Amos noticed that Kit was not with Sal. "Where's your boy?"

"Gone to help Jenny Jenkins."

Amos looked around the room. One of the spinning engines was still and Kit was bending over it, his ginger head close to the machinery. Amos crossed the floor to find out what was going on.

Kit was fourteen years old but still very much a child, with a high voice and no trace of a beard. "What are you doing?" Amos asked him.

Kit looked anxious, fearing he was about to be reprimanded. "Tightening a spindle, Mr. Barrowfield, with my thumbnail, but it will get loose again. I hope I didn't do nothing wrong."

"No, lad, don't worry. But this isn't really your job, is it?"

"No, sir, but the women ask me."

Jenny said: "It's true, Mr. Barrowfield. Kit is so clever with the machines that we all turn to him when something goes wrong and he usually fixes it in a minute."

Amos turned to Kit. "How did you get to be good at this?"

"I been working here since I was only six, so I suppose I know the engines, sir."

Amos recalled that Kit had always been fascinated by machinery.

Kit added: "But I could do much better if I had a turnscrew instead of using my thumbnail."

"I'm sure you could." Amos was thoughtful. Normally the hands repaired the machines themselves, often taking a long time over a simple problem. A specialist to do the job would save time and increase production.

He studied this little engineer and considered making the job official. He liked to reward people who did more than was strictly necessary: it encouraged the others. He would give Kit a title and a weekly wage, he decided. He couldn't really afford generosity, but a few shillings was not going to make much difference.

First he had better square it with Sal. He did not think she would object, but with her it was wise to be sure. He returned to her station. "Kit is really very smart," he said.

Sal glowed with pride. "Truth to tell, Mr. Barrowfield, I've always believed he was destined for something grand."

"Well, this isn't very grand, but I'm thinking about making him a tackler—a full-time maintenance man."

She beamed. "That's very kind of you, sir."

"I would only be acknowledging something that's already happening."

"That's true."

"I'll pay him five shillings a week."

Sal was startled. "That's very good of you, Mr. Barrowfield."

"I like to pay people what they deserve—when I can." He studied her expression and saw relief on her face. A few extra shillings would make a big difference to her weekly budget.

He said: "If I have to close the mill next week, he can come in and run his eye over all the machines while they're idle. It's always better to prevent than to repair. Is that all right?"

"Yes, sir. I'll tell him."

"Good," said Amos. "I'll buy him a turnscrew."

Hornbeam took his son, Howard, to see his new mill.

Howard had produced a child since getting married three years ago. His wife, Bel, had given birth to a boy, and they had named him Joseph after his grandfather, which had pleased Hornbeam more than he had expected. "As long as you never call him Joey," Hornbeam had said. "I hate the name Joey. Call him Joe for short, if you must." He did not care to be reminded of the time when he had been a scrawny kid scavenging London's rubbish heaps and his name had been Joey. But he did not need to explain his feelings. His family would do what he said without asking why.

Joe was now almost two years old, and big for his

age—he would be tall, like Hornbeam himself. And he would not be called Joey.

And Hornbeam's great wealth would be passed on to a third generation. It was a kind of immortality.

Deborah and Will Riddick were childless, so far, but it was too soon to give up hope of grandchildren from them, too.

The new mill was in its finishing stages on a site where formerly there had been a piggery. Hornbeam and Howard tramped across a field of mud churned up by the wheels of carts. Builders brought in from Combe had pitched tents, built fires, and dug latrines all around. The mill would replace Hornbeam's existing three. "It will be entirely devoted to producing cloth for uniforms," Hornbeam said. "Not just for the Shiring Militia and the 107th Kingsbridge Regiment of Foot, but for a dozen other major customers."

The mill was not beside the river, but next to a small stream, for the machinery would not be driven by water. He had been keeping everything secret, not even telling his family, but it was becoming impossible to disguise the work that was going on, and he had decided to let the news out. Howard was getting briefed before anyone else. "This will be the first steam-driven mill in Kingsbridge," Hornbeam said proudly.

"Steam!" said Howard.

Steam was steadier than the river, whose force varied from day to day, and more powerful than a horse or an ox. And it was now used in hundreds of mills, especially in the north of England. Kingsbridge had been slow to catch on. But not anymore.

They went inside. It was awesome: the only building in town larger than this was the cathedral.

Workmen were whitewashing the walls and glazing the big windows—mills needed light. They held shouted conversations across the great spaces, and some sang as they worked. Men from Combe did not know who

Hornbeam was. If they had known they would have fallen silent when he passed. For once he did not mind this lapse. He was too pleased with his building.

He showed Howard the coal-burning furnace, which was the size of a small cottage. Above it was a boiler built to the same scale. Next to them stood a cylinder, as tall as Hornbeam himself, driving a flywheel, which in turn was connected to a manifold. "That manifold takes power to every part of the mill," Hornbeam said. "Now, follow me upstairs."

He led the way up. "This is the weaving room." It contained dozens of looms in four parallel rows. "You see the shafts that run the length of the ceiling? They are connected to the looms by driving belts. When the shaft spins, the belt drives the loom to perform the three actions of weaving: one, it lifts every alternate thread in the warp to open the 'shed' like a crocodile's mouth; two, it passes the shuttle through the shed, as if it were between the crocodile's teeth; and three, it presses the thread firmly into the throat of the shed, the movement they call beating up. Then it repeats the process in reverse, completing the weave."

"It's fantastic," Howard said.

"But it can't be done with water power. A power loom requires an exact and steady force, one hundred and twenty revolutions per minute, plus or minus five. Otherwise the shuttle may move too fast or not at all. The river cannot provide such exact and constant power, but steam can."

"Will we need *any* hands?"

"Yes. But one man can manage three or four power looms at a time, they tell me—sometimes more, depending on the man. We'll need no more than a quarter of our present workforce."

"I can imagine it," said Howard. "All these looms working by themselves, making money all day, with just a handful of men watching them."

Hornbeam was thrilled, but also anxious. By the time it was finished the mill would have used all the money he had saved in the last twenty years plus a substantial loan from Thomson's Kingsbridge Bank. He was confident that it would make profits: his business judgment had been proved many times. And he had the military cloth contracts sewn up. All the same, there was no business without risk.

Howard was thinking along the same lines. "What if peace breaks out?" he said.

"It's not likely," Hornbeam said. "This war has been going on for six years and there's no sign of an end to it."

On the way back they passed through the neighborhood of houses they had built for the hands. Great piles of rubbish and ordure stood in the occupied streets. Hornbeam said: "These people are filthy."

Howard said: "It's our fault, really."

Hornbeam said indignantly: "How can it be our fault that people live in dirt?"

Howard trembled, but for once he stood his ground. "These are back-to-back houses. They don't have yards."

"Ah, yes—I'd forgotten that detail. It saves us a lot of money."

"But there's nowhere to put the refuse other than the road."

"Hmm."

The builders were finishing a new street. Howard said: "I've had approaches from three people who want to open shops here."

"But we have our own shops, and they make good profits."

"The hands say our shops charge higher prices. Some of them walk to the town center rather than pay more."

"Why would we invite competitors in to reduce our profits?"

Howard shrugged. "No reason, really."

"No," said Hornbeam. "Let them pay, or walk."

The May Fair was held in a meadow next to a wood on the outskirts of town. Amos was watching the rope dancing, a show in which young women in tight clothing cavorted on a tightrope ten feet above the ground, when Jane, now Viscountess Northwood, distracted him. She was a more alluring sight than the rope dancers. She wore a straw bonnet trimmed with ribbons and flowers, and carried a little parasol—the very latest fad. She looked extraordinarily pretty.

He wondered whether there was something wrong with him. He was pretty sure it was not normal for a young man to be obsessed for seven years with one woman who plainly did not return his love.

She took his arm and they walked around together, enjoying the spring sunshine, looking at the food stalls and the beer bars, pretending not to see the prostitutes.

They stopped to watch a troupe of acrobats, and he asked her how she was. The conventional question produced an unexpectedly candid answer. "I hardly ever see Henry!" she said. "He spends all his time with the militia, training and drilling them and I don't know what. They never actually fight. I don't see the point."

"They're supposed to defend the home country, and thereby free up regular army units to fight abroad."

She did not want to hear explanations. "He insists I live at Earlscastle, where nothing ever happens. I see more of his father than of him! It will serve him right if I have an affair."

Amos glanced around, afraid someone might have overheard this most unladylike comment, but fortunately no one was nearby.

They moved on to a boxing ring where a fighter called Pegleg Punch was offering a pound to anyone who could knock him down. Despite his disability—he really did have a wooden leg—the man looked terrifying, with huge shoulders and a broken nose and scars on his arms. "I wouldn't take him on for fifty pounds," Amos said.

"I'm glad to hear it," said Jane.

Mungo Landsman, one of the toughs who hung around the Slaughterhouse, paid his shilling. He was a big lad with a mean look, and he jumped into the ring eager for a fight. Before he could put his fists up, Pegleg moved in close, punching his head and body so fast it was hard to follow the blows. When the lad fell down, Pegleg kicked him with his wooden leg, and the crowd cheered. Pegleg grinned, showing that he had lost most of his teeth.

Amos and Jane walked away. Amos wondered what a woman such as Jane was supposed to do with herself after she had married a rich but busy man. "I expect you'd like to have children," he said.

"It's my duty to produce an heir," she said. "However, the question is academic. There's not much chance of children given how little time Henry and I spend together."

Amos mulled that. Jane had got what she wanted, marriage to Henry. People had said he would never marry someone so far beneath him socially. A more suitable marriage had been arranged for him, and he must have had serious opposition from his father when he decided to repudiate that plan. She had overcome all the obstacles. But it had not made her happy.

They came to a stall where Sport Culliver, wearing a red top hat, was selling Madeira by the glass. They were walking past, but he called out to Jane. "My lady viscountess, don't drink the ordinary Madeira—that's for the common folk. I have a special brand for you." He bent down and took a bottle from under the table. "This is the best Madeira ever made."

Jane said to Amos: "I'd quite like a glass."

Amos said to Culliver: "Two, please, Sport."

Culliver poured two large glasses and handed them over. When Jane had sipped hers he said: "That'll be two shillings, then, please, Mr. Barrowfield."

Amos said: "What's in it, gold dust?"

"I told you it was the best."

Amos paid, then tasted it. The wine was all right, but it was not the best. He grinned at Sport. "If ever you want a job as a cloth salesman, come to me," he said.

"Very kind of you, Mr. Barrowfield, but I'll stick with what I know."

Amos nodded. The cloth trade was not for Culliver. There was much more money in drink, gambling, and prostitution.

They emptied their glasses and moved away from the stall, following a path toward the woods. Jane turned and spoke to a young woman behind them, and Amos realized the girl had been following them, no doubt as a chaperone. Jane said: "Sukey, I'm a bit chilly—will you fetch my wrap from the carriage?"

"Yes, my lady," said Sukey.

Jane and Amos walked on unchaperoned. Amos said: "Well, at least now you can buy all the clothes you want. You look wonderful today."

"I have rooms full of clothes, but where can I wear them? This dull event—the Kingsbridge May Fair—is the most exciting social occasion I've attended in the last three months. I expected Henry to take me to parties in London. Ha! We've never made one trip to London. He's too busy—with the militia, of course."

Northwood probably felt that Jane was too lowborn to mingle with his aristocratic friends, Amos thought; but he did not say it. "You and he must have some social life."

"Parties with officers—and officers' wives," she said scornfully. "He's never introduced me to anyone remotely royal."

That tended to confirm his suspicion.

Jane had not been brought up to prize social advancement. Her father had given up a high clerical position to become a Methodist pastor. She had abandoned the values Charles Midwinter had taught her. "You yearn for all the wrong things," Amos said.

Jane did not take criticism lying down. "And you?" she said spiritedly. "What are you doing with your life? You devote yourself to your business. You live alone. You make money, but not much. What's the point?"

He reflected on that. She was right. At first he had wanted to take over the enterprise from his father, then he had been desperate to pay off his debt, but now that he had achieved both those aims he was still working all hours. But the business did not weigh him down, in fact it gave him satisfaction. "I don't know, it seems the natural thing to do," he said.

"It's been drummed into you that a man has to work hard. But that doesn't make it true."

"There's more to it than that." This was something he had never much pondered, but now that she had asked the question he began to see the answer. "I want to prove that we can have industry without exploitation," he said. "And business without corruption."

"So it's all to do with Methodism."

"Is it? I'm not sure Methodists have a monopoly of kindness and honesty."

"You think I'm unhappy because I married the wrong man."

That was a switch. "I don't mean to criticize you . . ."

"But I'm right, am I not?"

Amos said carefully: "I certainly think you'd be happier if you had married for love."

"I'd be happier if I'd married you."

She had a way of startling him with unexpected statements. "That wasn't what I meant," he said defensively.

"It's true, though. I bewitched Henry, but the spell has worn off. You really loved me. You probably still do."

He looked around, hoping that no one was within hearing distance. He realized that they had entered the woods and were alone.

She took his silence for assent. "I thought so," she said. She stood on tiptoe and kissed his mouth.

He was too surprised to do anything. He stood still, frozen, staring at her, nonplussed.

She put her arms around him and pressed her body to his. He could feel her breasts, her belly, and her hips.

"We're alone," Jane said. "Kiss me properly, Amos."

He had daydreamed this moment more times than he could count.

But he heard himself saying: "It's not right."

"It's as right as anything in this world. Dear Amos, I know you love me. Just one kiss, that's all."

Stubbornly he said: "But you're married to Henry."

"To hell with Henry."

He took her wrists and moved her hands off his waist. "I would feel so terribly ashamed," he said.

"Oh, so now I'm something to be ashamed of."

"Only when you betray your husband like this."

She broke apart from him, turned, and walked away.

Even now, striding angrily, she looked irresistibly alluring.

He watched her go, and thought: What a damn fool I am.

One evening at eight o'clock, when Sal and Jarge were getting ready for bed, Jarge said: "There's a rumor going round that Hornbeam's new mill will have a gigantic steam engine that will operate dozens of looms, and most of us weavers will no longer be wanted, because in the new mill one man will supervise four steam looms."

Sal said: "Is that possible? Can a steam engine be a weaver?"

"I don't see how."

She frowned. "I have heard that steam looms are used in the cotton mills up north."

"I find it hard to believe," said Jarge.

Sal said: "Let's say it might be true. What are the consequences?"

THE COMBINATION ACT

"Three out of four of Hornbeam's weavers are going to be looking for work. And with things the way they are, we may not find it. But what can we do about it?"

Sal was not sure she had an answer. It seemed she had become some kind of leader of the Kingsbridge hands, but she did not know how it had happened and she did not feel qualified to fulfill the role.

Jarge said belligerently: "In the past, hands have rioted against new machines."

"And been punished for it," said Sal.

"That doesn't mean we should allow the masters to do anything they want to us."

"Let's not get carried away," Sal said pacifically. "Before we do anything, we need to find out whether the rumor is true."

"How can we do that?" said Jarge.

"We can go and take a look. The builders are camped on the site, but they won't care who looks around, as long as we don't do any damage."

"All right," said Jarge.

Sal said: "We'll go on Sunday afternoon."

Kit had never seen a steam engine, but he had heard about them, and he was fascinated. How could steam drive a machine? He understood how flowing water could turn a mill wheel, but steam was just air—wasn't it?

After dinner on Sunday, when he and Sue were about to go to Elsie Mackintosh's Sunday school, Kit's mother and Jarge got ready to go out. "Where are you off to?" Kit asked Sal.

"We're going to take a look at Hornbeam's big new mill."

"I'm coming with you."

"No, you're not."

"I want to see the steam engine."

"You can't see anything, the place is shut up."

"Then why are you going?"

Sal sighed the way she always did when he was right and she was wrong. "Do as you're told and go to Sunday school."

He and Sue left, but as soon as they were out of sight of the house Kit said: "Let's follow them."

Sue was not as bold as Kit. "We'd get into trouble."

"I don't care."

"Well, I'm going to Sunday school."

"Goodbye, then."

He watched the house from the corner, hid when the adults came out, and then walked a long way behind them, knowing roughly where they were headed. Many families strolled out into the countryside for fresh air on Sunday afternoons, so he was not conspicuous. The weather was cool, but the sun broke cheerfully through the clouds now and again, a reminder that summer was on the way.

The mills were silent, and in the Sunday quiet Kit could hear birdsong, the wind in the trees, and even the rush of the river.

On the site of the old piggery some builders were playing a football match with improvised goals, while others looked on. Kit saw Sal speak to one with a friendly face. He guessed she was telling him she just wanted to look around. The man shrugged, as if it did not matter.

The new mill was long and narrow, and made of the same stone as the cathedral. Kit watched from a distance as the grown-ups walked all the way around the building, looking in through the windows.

Kit guessed they wanted to go inside. So did he. But it seemed the doors were locked, and the ground-floor windows were shut. They all looked up: there were windows open on the upstairs floor. Kit heard Jarge say: "I think I saw a ladder at the back."

They went around the building to the side farthest from the football game. A ladder lay on the ground, its rungs stained with whitewash. Jarge picked it up and leaned it against the wall. It reached to the upstairs windows. He climbed up, and Sal stood on the bottom rung to steady the ladder.

Jarge peered through the window for a few moments, then said: "Well, I'm damned."

Sal said impatiently: "What can you see?"

"Looms. So many, I can't count them."

"Can you get inside?"

"The window opening is too small—I can't get through there."

Kit stepped out from behind a stack of timber. "I could squeeze through," he said.

Sal said: "You naughty boy! You're supposed to be at Sunday school!"

Jarge said: "He could get in, though. Then he could open a door for us."

"I should spank him," she said.

Jarge came down. "Go on, then, Kit," he said. "I'll steady the ladder."

Kit went up and scrambled through the window. Inside he stood upright and looked around in amazement. He had never seen so many looms in one place. He wanted to figure out how they worked, but he knew he should let the grown-ups in first. He ran down the stairs and found a door that was bolted on the inside but not locked with a key. He opened it up, stood aside for Jarge and Sal to come in, then closed the door quickly as soon as they were inside.

The steam engine was here on the ground floor.

Kit studied it, awestruck by its size and evident power. He identified the enormous furnace, and the boiler on top where the water would be turned to steam. A pipe took the hot steam into a cylinder. Obviously something inside the cylinder went up and down, for the top of the cylinder was connected to one end of a beam that looked like a giant scale for weighing things. As this end of the beam rose and fell, the other end would fall and rise, and in doing so turn a giant wheel.

From then on it worked like a waterwheel, he supposed.

The amazing part was that the steam was strong enough to move the heavy metal-and-wood mechanism.

Sal and Jarge went up the stairs, and Kit followed. There were four rows of looms on the upper floor, all gleaming new, with no yarn loaded yet. The steam engine must spin the big shaft on the ceiling, Kit figured; and the shaft was connected to each loom by drive belts.

Jarge was bewildered. "I just don't get it," he said, scratching his head through his hat.

Kit said: "Pull on that belt and see what happens."

Jarge looked dubious but said: "All right."

At first nothing happened.

Then there was a loud clack from the loom and one of the heddles lifted. If the yarn had been threaded into place, the heddle would have raised every alternate thread of the warp, forming the gap, or shed.

Next, there was a bang as the flying shuttle shot from one side of the loom to the other.

Kit could see the mechanism at the back, a system of cogs and rods that directed the motion to the next task.

Jarge was amazed. "It's all happening—but with no weaver!"

Another bang, and the beater thrust into the shed in the action that pushed the thread deep into the V shape.

With another loud crack one heddle dropped and the other lifted, to raise the other threads. The shuttle flew back to its original position, and the beater thrust again.

Then the process started over again.

Jarge said: "Well, how does it know what to do next?" There was a note of superstitious dread in his tone as he added: "There must be an imp working the machine."

"It's a mechanism," Kit said. "Like clockwork."

"Like clockwork," Jarge muttered. "I never really understood clocks."

Kit was astonished for a different reason. "All these

looms will work together—driven by that steam engine!"

"There's more to this than steam," Jarge said, and he looked fearful.

Sal said: "I'll wager it won't make a good smooth cloth."

Kit had noticed that the hands always said that Satan was in the machines and they would never do as good a job as a craftsman. He believed they were wrong.

Sal said thoughtfully: "Hornbeam may be a nasty devil, but he doesn't waste his money. If these machines work . . ."

"If these machines work," Jarge said, "what would be the point in being a weaver?"

"This can't be allowed," Sal said, muttering half to herself. "But what can we do?"

Jarge said: "Smash the machines. There's enough weavers, about a hundred, working for Hornbeam. If they all come here with hammers, who's going to stop them?"

Then they will be transported to Australia, like Joanie, Kit thought.

"You know what?" Sal said. "I'd like to tell Spade about this, and see what he's got to say."

Kit thought: And Spade will have a better idea than smashing everything up.

Sal sent Kit to Sunday school. "You'll be in time for the soup," she said. The discussion with Spade would be about how to take action against the masters, and she did not want a child listening to that. Kit was a bright lad but he was too young to be trusted with secrets.

Spade was just finishing his dinner, and there was bread and cheese on the table. He told his visitors to help themselves, and Jarge tucked in. Sal summarized what they had seen at the new mill.

"I've heard rumors," Spade said when she had finished. "Now I know they're true."

Sal said: "The question is, what do we do about it?"

Speaking through a mouthful of bread and cheese, Jarge said again: "Smash the machines."

Spade nodded. "That's a last resort, though."

"Well, what else is there?"

"You could start a union—a workers' combination."

Sal nodded. She had been thinking along that line, but vaguely, because she was not sure what a union was or did.

Jarge asked the question. "How would that help?"

"First of all, it means the hands all act together, which makes them stronger than they are as individuals."

Sal had not thought of this before, but it was obvious once it had been said. "Then what?"

"See if the master will talk to you. Get a sense of how determined he is."

"And if he persists in his plan?"

"What would Hornbeam do if one day none of his weavers showed up for work?"

Jarge said: "A strike! I like that idea."

Spade said: "It's happening a lot, in other parts of the country."

Sal nodded slowly. "How do the strikers live, without wages?"

"You have to raise money from other workers, to help them. Collect halfpennies and farthings in the market square. But it's not easy. The weavers would have to tighten their belts."

"And Hornbeam would not be making any profits."

"He'd be losing money every day. I've heard he took a big loan from Thomson's bank for this mill—he's paying interest on that, remember."

"All the same," said Sal, "the weavers will get hungry before Hornbeam."

Jarge said: "*Then* we smash the machines."

"It's like a war," said Spade. "At the beginning, both sides expect to win. One of them is wrong."

Sal said: "If we were going to do this, what would be the first step?"

"Talk to the other weavers," Spade said. "Find out whether they've got the stomach for a fight. If you think you've got enough support, book a room and call a meeting. You know how to organize that, Sal."

I suppose I do, Sal thought. Not that I've got much time to spare, after working fourteen hours a day and looking after two children. But she knew she could not refuse this challenge. For too long she had been outraged by the way she and people like her were treated in their own country. Now she had a chance to do something about it. She could not turn it down.

People who said things would never change were wrong. England had changed in the past, she remembered her father saying—from Catholic to Protestant, from absolute monarchy to parliamentary rule—and it would change again, if people like her insisted on it.

"Yes," she said. "I know how to organize that."

⁂

Spade was fond of his sister, Kate, but not enough to live with her. She shared the house with Becca, and Spade had his room in the workshop. They lived separate lives, but all the same their relationship was intimate. They knew one another's secrets.

On Tuesday morning at eleven o'clock he went into the house by the back entrance. He stood for a moment by the door to the shop, listening. He could hear voices. Kate and Becca often rowed, but right now their talk seemed calm. He could not hear a third voice, so they did not have a customer. He tapped on the door and looked in.

"All clear?" he said.

"All clear," Kate replied with a smile.

He closed the door and went up the stairs. At the top he turned into one of the dressing rooms.

Arabella lay on the bed.

She was naked.

How lucky I am, he thought.

He closed the door and locked it, then turned back and smiled at her. "I wish I had a painting of you like this," he said.

"Heaven forbid."

He sat on a chair and took off his boots. "I could paint you myself. I used to draw, when I was a child."

"What if someone saw the picture? The news would be around town in a flash."

"I'd hide it in a secret place, get it out at night, and look at it by candlelight." He took off his coat, waistcoat, and breeches. "Wouldn't you like a picture of me?"

"No, thanks. I want the real thing."

"I was never a pretty boy."

"It's the feel of you I like."

"So you want a sculpture?"

"A life-size statue, complete with all details."

"Like that famous Italian statue?"

"You mean Michelangelo's *David*?"

"If you say so."

"Absolutely not. It's got a tiny little willy, all shriveled up."

"Perhaps the model was cold."

"My statue would have your nice fat knob."

"And where would you hide this work of art?"

"Under my bed, of course. Then I'd take it out, like you with the picture."

"And what would you do while you were looking at it?"

She put her hand between her legs and stroked, the dark red hair showing between her fingers. "This."

He lay beside her. "Fortunately, this morning we have the real thing."

"Oh, yes," she said, and she rolled on top of him.

They had been lovers since the night of the Assize Ball three years ago. Kate's shop was their regular rendezvous. They were in love, but they could not marry, so they took what happiness they could. Spade felt little guilt. He could not believe that God would give his children overwhelming sexual desires, then torture them with frustration. As for Arabella, she seemed not to think about sin.

They were discreet. They had gone undiscovered all this time, and Spade thought they could probably carry on indefinitely.

Afterward, when they lay on their backs, side by side, panting, she said: "I was never like this, you know. The way I talk to you . . . the things I do."

"You surprised yourself." She had surprised him, too. He was younger and lower-class, and she was married.

He asked: "How did you learn the words?"

"From other girls, when we were young. But I never said them to a man, until you. I feel as if I spent my life in prison, then you let me out."

"I'm glad I did."

She became more serious. "I have something to tell you."

"Good news, or bad?"

"Bad, I suppose, though I can't bring myself to feel sorry about it."

"Intriguing!"

"I'm pregnant."

"Good God!"

"You thought I was too old. It's all right, you can say it. I thought so, too. I'm forty-five."

She was right, he had imagined she was past conceiving; but women were not all the same.

Arabella said: "Are you angry?"

"Of course not."

"What, then?"

"Don't be offended."

"I'll try."

"I'm happy . . . happier than I can tell you. I'm overjoyed."

She was surprised. "Really? Why?"

"For sixteen years I've lived with the sadness of my only child dying before he was even born. Now God is giving me another chance to be a father. I'm thrilled."

She put her arms around him and hugged him. "I'm so glad."

Spade enjoyed the blissful mood as long as he could, but they had to face the difficulties that loomed. "I don't want you to get into trouble," he said.

"I don't think that will happen. People will be too busy talking about my age to wonder who the father is." Her face showed that she was more worried than she pretended.

"What will you tell the bishop?" he asked her. "You and he don't . . ."

"Not for at least ten years."

"I suppose you could make it happen . . ."

She looked disgusted. "I'm not sure he's even able to do it nowadays."

"Then . . ."

"I don't know." She was afraid, he saw.

"You'll have to tell him something."

"Yes," she said gloomily. "I suppose I will."

A week later, in the Bell, Sal and Jarge sat down with Spade.

Spade said: "Hornbeam wants to see you—both of you."

"Why me?" said Sal. "I'm not threatening to strike."

"Hornbeam always has spies, so he knows you're helping Jarge. And Hornbeam's son-in-law, Will Riddick, has got him convinced that you're the devil in female form."

"I'm surprised he's condescending to speak to me."

"He'd rather not, but I talked him round."

"How did you manage that?"

"I told him that nine out of ten of his employees had joined your union."

This was not true. The actual figure was about five out of ten. But that had been achieved in a week, and the total was still going up.

Sal was thrilled by the success but nervous about confronting Hornbeam in person. He was a confident man, accustomed to argument, a practiced bully. How could she go up against him? She hid her trepidation with a sarcastic remark. "How kind of him to lower himself to my level."

Spade smiled. "He's not as clever as he thinks. If he was really smart he'd try to make a friend of you."

She liked the way Spade thought. He always wanted to prevent an argument becoming a contest. She said: "Should I make a friend of Hornbeam?"

"He'll never allow himself to be friendly with a mill hand—but you might disarm him. You could say that the two of you have a shared problem."

That was a good approach, Sal thought; better than a head-on attack.

The potman appeared and said: "What'll it be, Spade?"

"Nothing, thanks," Spade said. "We've got to go."

"He wants to see us right now?" said Sal.

"Yes. He's at the Guild Hall and he'll talk to you before he goes home for supper."

Sal felt flustered. "But I haven't got my best hat!"

Spade laughed. "Nor has he, I'm sure."

"All right, then," said Sal, and she stood up.

Spade and Jarge did the same. Spade said: "I'll come with you, if you like. Hornbeam will probably have someone with him."

"Yes, please."

"But you must speak for yourselves. If I speak for you it will give Hornbeam the impression that the hands are weak."

She saw the logic of that.

They walked up Main Street from the Bell to the Guild Hall. Hornbeam was waiting for them, with his daughter, Deborah, in the grand room that served as meeting room for the council as well as the courtroom. Will Riddick was there, too. It made Sal nervous to be in here with two justices. There was nothing to stop them sentencing her here and now. Her throat felt constricted and she feared she might find herself unable to speak. She guessed Hornbeam had intended something like this. He wanted to make her feel vulnerable and weak. She could tell that Jarge was even more nervous. But she had to fight back against intimidation. She had to be strong.

Hornbeam was standing at the end of the long table around which the aldermen sat for council meetings—another symbol of his power over people such as Sal. What could she do to make herself feel that she was his equal?

As soon as she had asked herself the question, she knew the answer. Before Hornbeam could speak, she said: "Let's sit down, shall we?" and pulled out a chair.

He was nonplussed. How could a mill hand invite a clothier to be seated? But Deborah took a chair, and Sal thought she saw her suppress a smile.

Hornbeam sat.

Sal decided to keep the initiative. Remembering Spade's suggestion, she said: "You and I have a problem."

He looked supercilious. "What problem could I possibly share with you?"

"Your new mill has steam-driven looms."

"How would you know that? Have you been trespassing on my property?"

"There's no law against looking through windows," Sal said crisply. "That's what glass is made for."

She heard Spade chuckle.

I'm doing all right, she thought.

Hornbeam was disconcerted. He had not expected her to be articulate, let alone witty.

Will Riddick went on the attack. "We hear you've formed a union."

"There's no law against that, either."

"There should be."

Sal turned back to Hornbeam. "Of the weavers you have now, how many are going to be told there's no more work for them when you move into the Piggery Mill?"

"It's called Hornbeam's Mill."

That might have been true, but everyone was calling it Piggery Mill. He seemed unduly angry over this detail.

Sal repeated her question. "How many?"

"That's my business."

"And if the weavers go on strike, that too will be your business."

"I shall do what I think fit with my own property."

Deborah interrupted. She looked at Jarge. "Mr. Box, you work at Hornbeam's Upper Mill."

So, they've realized that, Sal thought.

Jarge said: "You can fire me if you like. I'm a good weaver, I'll get work elsewhere."

"But I would like to know exactly what you hope for from this meeting. You surely don't expect my father to abandon the new mill and the steam engine."

Interesting, Sal thought; the daughter is more reasonable than the father.

"Yes, I do," said Jarge defiantly.

Sal said: "Our main concern is that weavers should not find themselves out of work because of your steam engine."

Hornbeam said: "A foolish idea. The whole point of the steam engine is to replace workers."

"In that case there will be trouble."

"Are you threatening me?"

"I'm trying to tell you the facts of life, but you're not listening," Sal said, and the contempt in her own voice startled her. She stood up, surprising Hornbeam again:

it would usually be he who ended a meeting. "Good evening to you." She walked out, and Jarge and Spade followed.

Outside the building, Spade said: "You were absolutely magnificent in there!"

Sal was no longer concerned about her own performance. "Hornbeam is completely stubborn, isn't he?"

"I'm afraid he is."

"So there has to be a strike."

"So be it," said Spade.

CHAPTER 20

In Arabella's garden the prickly bush of the Scotch rose—always the first to bloom—had produced a snowstorm of fragile white flowers with yellow hearts. Elsie sat on a wooden bench, breathing the cool damp air of early morning, with her two-year-old son, Stevie, on her knee. He had ginger hair that must have come from Arabella, his grandmother, bypassing dark-haired Elsie. Together Elsie and Stevie watched Arabella, kneeling on the ground in her apron, pulling weeds and dropping them into a basket. Arabella loved her rose garden. In the years since she had started it she had seemed happier—more energetic, yet calmer.

Stevie was named Stephen after his grandfather, the bishop. Elsie had nursed a secret desire to call him Amos, but had not been able to think of a plausible pretext. Now he wriggled in Elsie's grasp, wanting to help his grandmother. Elsie put him down and he toddled to Arabella. "Don't touch the bushes, they have thorns," Elsie said. He immediately grasped a twig, hurt his hand, burst into tears, and came running back to her. "You should listen to Mummy!" she said.

Arabella said quietly: "Just like Mummy never did."

Elsie laughed. It was true.

Arabella said: "How are things at your school?"

"It's such an exciting time," Elsie said.

It was no longer just a Sunday school. All the children who worked in Hornbeam's mills were now on strike, so Elsie was giving lessons every day. The parents sent the children to school for the free dinner.

"This is such a great chance for us," Elsie enthused. "It's the only time these children will ever be in full-time education, so we must make the most of it. I was afraid my supporters would say it's too much work, but they have all rallied round, bless them. Pastor Midwinter is teaching every day."

There was a pause in the conversation, then Elsie said: "Mother, I'm pretty sure I'm expecting another child."

"How wonderful!" Arabella put down her trowel, stood up, and hugged her daughter. "Perhaps it will be a girl this time. Wouldn't that be nice?"

"Yes, though I really don't mind."

"What would you call a girl?"

"Arabella, of course."

"Your father might want Martha. That was his mother's name."

"I won't fight him." After a moment Elsie added: "Not about that, anyway."

Arabella knelt down again and resumed weeding. She was in a reflective mood. "It seems to have been a fertile spring," she mused.

Elsie was not sure what she meant. "One pregnancy doesn't make a fertile spring."

"Oh!" said her mother, vaguely embarrassed. "I . . . I was thinking of the garden."

"The Scotch roses have put on a lovely show this year."

"That's what I meant."

Elsie felt that her mother was hiding something. And now that she came to think of it, she got this feeling more often nowadays. There had been a time when they told each other everything. Arabella knew all about Elsie's hopeless love for Amos. But Arabella had become less confiding. Elsie wondered why.

Before she could probe further her husband, Kenelm, appeared, washed and shaved and full of bustling efficiency.

Elsie and Kenelm were still living at the palace. There was plenty of room, and it was more comfortable than any house Kenelm could afford on his salary as the bishop's aide.

Elsie had learned, in three years of marriage, that Kenelm's great strength was assiduousness. He did everything meticulously. His work for her father was done promptly and carefully, and the bishop could hardly praise him enough. Kenelm was dutiful with their child, too. Each evening he knelt with Stevie beside the child's bed and said a prayer, though otherwise he never spoke to the boy. Elsie had seen other fathers toss their children in the air and catch them, making them squeal with delight; but that kind of thing was too undignified for Kenelm. Sex was another duty he performed conscientiously—once a week, on Saturday night. They both enjoyed it, even though it was always the same.

But the main reason for her warm feelings toward Kenelm was the little boy sitting on her lap. Kenelm had given her Stevie, and the child growing in her womb, too. Whereas Amos was still obsessed with Jane. Elsie had seen them together at the May Fair, deep in conversation, Jane dressed up to the nines and carrying a superfluous little parasol, Amos hanging on her words as if she were a prophet with pearls of wisdom dropping from her lips. If Elsie had pinned her hopes on Amos she would still be waiting. She kissed the top of Stevie's gingery head, immeasurably glad that she had him.

She still thought of Amos on Saturday nights, though.

Kenelm bowed to Arabella and said: "The bishop sends you the compliments of the morning, Mrs. Latimer, and begs to let you know that breakfast is served."

"Thank you," said Arabella, and she got to her feet.

They all went inside. Elsie took Stevie to the nursery and handed him over to the nurse. Elsie had taken an early breakfast in the kitchen, and now she put on her hat and went out, eagerly heading for the school.

Elsie could not use the Assembly Rooms for her school on weekdays, but she had rented cheaply an old building in the southwestern suburb called Fishponds. There were usually at least fifty children. Those who had not previously attended the Sunday school knew almost nothing, and their teachers had to start from scratch: the alphabet, simple arithmetic, the Lord's Prayer, and how to eat with a knife and fork.

She stood with Pastor Midwinter and watched with delight as the children arrived, chattering at the tops of their voices, scrawny and ragged, many without shoes, all with minds thirsty for knowledge as the desert for rain. She felt sorry for people who spent their lives making woolen cloth: they would never know this thrill.

Today she taught the oldest children, usually the most difficult to manage. She first taxed their brains with arithmetic: currant buns cost a halfpenny, so how many would you get for six pence? Then she taught them to write their own names and one another's. After the midmorning break she made them learn a psalm by heart and told them the story of Jesus walking on the water. They became restless in the last hour, when the building filled with the smell of cheese soup.

Amos arrived at dinnertime, immaculate as always, today wearing the dark red tailcoat that was Elsie's favorite. He helped serve the meal, then Elsie and he took a bowl each and sat apart to talk. She resisted the urge to stroke his wavy hair and was careful not to stare into his deep brown eyes. She longed to go to sleep beside him at night and wake up with him in the morning, but it would never happen. At least she had this close friendship, and for that she was grateful.

She asked him about the strike.

"Hornbeam won't negotiate," he said. "He refuses to consider changing his plans."

"But he can't run his mill with no hands at all."

"Of course not. But he thinks he can outlast the strikers. 'They'll come crawling to me, begging me to take them back,' he says."

"Do you think he's right?"

"Maybe. He's got more reserves than the workers. But they have resources of a different kind. At this time of year the woods are teeming with young rabbits and birds, if you know how to trap them. And there are wild vegetables—chickweed, hawthorn buds, lime leaves, mallow stems, sorrel."

"Thin fare."

"There are less honest ways to get by. This is not a good time to walk in the dark with money in your purse."

"Oh, dear."

"You shouldn't worry. You might be the only affluent person in town they wouldn't rob. You feed their children. They consider you a saint."

But a saint would be in love with her husband, Elsie thought; with her husband and no one else.

"In truth no one knows how this will end," Amos said. "In other strikes around the country the masters have won in some places and the hands in others."

The afternoon session was shorter and Elsie was home in time to give Stevie his afternoon snack of buttered toast. Then she joined her mother for tea in the drawing room.

Her father came in a few minutes later. He had something on his mind: Elsie could tell by the way he fidgeted. "Have you been shopping, my dear?" he said to Arabella as she handed him a cup.

"Yes."

"You favor the establishment of Kate Shoveller, I believe."

"She's the best dressmaker in Kingsbridge—in Shiring, even."

"I'm sure." He dropped a lump of sugar into his tea and stirred longer than was necessary. At last he said: "Is she still unmarried?"

"As far as I know, yes," said Arabella. "Why do you ask?"

Elsie, too, was wondering what the bishop was getting at.

"There is something odd about a healthy woman who remains single into her thirties, don't you think?"

"Is there?"

"One always wonders why."

Elsie said: "Marriage isn't for everyone. Some women don't see the point of enslaving themselves to a man for life."

The bishop was shocked. "Enslaving? My dear! Marriage is a holy sacrament."

"But it's not compulsory, is it? The apostle Paul says that it's better to marry than to burn, which is a rather half-hearted endorsement."

"How discontented you seem!"

"Mother and I are extraordinarily lucky in our husbands, of course."

The bishop was not sure whether he was being mocked. "Very good of you to say so," he said uncertainly. "In any case," he went on, "Miss Shoveller's brother is behind this strike. I wonder if you knew that."

Elsie said: "I thought Sal Box was the organizer."

"She's a woman. Spade is the brains behind her."

Elsie decided not to challenge the assumption that no woman could have an organizational brain. Instead she said: "Why would Spade want a strike? He's a clothier himself, though he still operates a loom sometimes."

"Good question. In fact there has been talk of making him an alderman. His behavior is baffling. In any event, Arabella, please do not become anything more than a customer of Miss Shoveller. I should not wish my wife to associate with such people on any terms other than the strictly commercial."

Elsie expected her mother to dispute this ruling, but she accepted it meekly. "I shan't do anything of the kind, my dear," she said to the bishop. "You need hardly have said it."

"I'm glad to hear that. Forgive me for mentioning it."

"Not at all."

There was something concealed beneath this stiffly formal exchange, Elsie felt sure. She had a notion it had something to do with Kate Shoveller's partner, Becca. She had heard girls talk about women who loved other women, in preference to men—though she could not imagine exactly what that might mean: there was, after all, a question of anatomy. And women trying on new clothes did undress in the rooms above Kate's shop. Had her father heard some absurd rumors about Arabella being involved in such activity?

The bishop finished his tea and went back to his study, and Elsie said to her mother: "What was that all about?"

Arabella made a dismissive noise. "Your father's got some kind of bee in his bonnet, but I've no idea what it is."

Elsie was not sure she believed that, but she did not pursue the question. She went upstairs to help the nurse get Stevie ready for bed. Later Kenelm arrived to say a prayer with him. While he was there the maid, Mason, looked in and said: "Mrs. Mackintosh, the bishop would like to see you in his study."

"I'll come right away," said Elsie.

Kenelm said: "What does your father want?"

"I don't know."

Mason said helpfully: "Alderman Hornbeam and Squire Riddick are with the bishop."

Kenelm frowned. "But the bishop didn't ask for me?"

"No, sir."

Kenelm was annoyed. He hated to be excluded from anything. He was oversensitive about rejection. He quickly felt disrespected, slighted, undervalued. More than once Elsie had told him that sometimes people were simply absentminded, and left him out by accident, but he never believed that.

She went downstairs to the study. Hornbeam and Riddick were wearing wigs, indicating that this was a formal visit. Riddick looked a bit drunk, which was not unusual for him at this time of the evening. Hornbeam wore his habitual look of stern resolve. They both stood up and bowed to her as she entered, and she sketched a curtsy and sat down.

"My dear," her father said, "the alderman and the

squire have something they would like to discuss with you."

"Really?"

Hornbeam said: "It's about your school."

Elsie frowned. The school was controversial only because both Anglicans and Methodists supported it, and occasionally one faction would seek to exclude the other. But neither Hornbeam nor Riddick cared about religious differences, as far as she knew. "What about my school?" she said, and she heard the hostility in her own voice.

Hornbeam said: "I believe you're giving the children of strikers free dinners."

So that was it. She remembered that attack was the best form of defense. "The town is presented with a splendid opportunity," she began. "For a limited time we have the chance to instill a little knowledge into children who otherwise spend all day, six days a week, minding machines. We must make the most of it, mustn't we?"

Hornbeam did not let her steer the conversation. "Unfortunately, you're supporting the strike. I'm sure you don't intend to, but that is the effect of what you're doing."

"What on earth do you mean?" said Elsie, though she could see where this was going, and she had a bad feeling.

"We hope that hunger will make the strikers see reason. And though they may be willing to suffer themselves, most parents cannot bear to see their children go hungry."

"Are you saying . . ." Elsie paused to take a breath. She could hardly believe what she was hearing. "Are you saying that I should stop feeding these starving children? As a way of pressuring the hands to return to work?"

Hornbeam was not moved by her incredulity. "It would be better for all concerned. By prolonging the strike you prolong the suffering."

Her father said: "Alderman Hornbeam is right, you know, my dear."

Elsie said indignantly: "Jesus told Peter: 'Feed my sheep.' Aren't we in danger of forgetting that?"

Riddick spoke for the first time. "The devil can quote scripture to his purpose, they say."

Elsie said: "Be quiet, Will, you're out of your depth."

Riddick flushed with anger. He had been insulted, but he could not think of a riposte.

Hornbeam said: "Really, Mrs. Mackintosh, we must ask you to end this interference in our business."

"I'm not interfering," she said. "I'm feeding hungry children, as is the duty of all Christians, and I'm not going to stop for the sake of clothiers' profits."

"Who supplies the food?"

Elsie did not want to answer that question, because her father did not realize how much of the children's broth came from the palace kitchen. She said: "It's donated by generous townspeople, both Anglican and Methodist."

"People such as who?"

She knew what Hornbeam was up to. "You want a list of names so that you can go round them all up and bully them into withdrawing support."

Hornbeam colored, confirming the truth of her accusation. Angrily he said: "I'd like to know who is subverting the commercial success of this town!"

There was a tap at the door and Kenelm looked in. "Is there anything I can help you with, my lord bishop?" he said, looking eager. He wanted to be in on whatever was happening.

The bishop looked irritated. "Not just now, Mackintosh," he said curtly.

Kenelm looked as if he had been slapped. After a hesitation, he closed the door. He would be angry about this all evening, Elsie knew.

The interruption had given her a moment to think, and now she said: "Alderman Hornbeam, if you're so concerned about the commercial future of this town, why don't you negotiate with your hands? You might find that you're able to reach agreement."

Hornbeam drew himself upright. "I will not be told how to run my business by the hands!"

"So this is not really about the town's commerce," Elsie said. "It's about your pride."

"Certainly not!"

"You ask me to stop feeding fifty hungry children, yet you won't lower yourself to talk to your weavers. You argue a poor case, sir."

There was a silence. Both Riddick and the bishop looked at Hornbeam for a response, and Elsie realized that they, too, thought his obstinacy was part of the problem.

She said: "Anyway, I couldn't stop the free dinners even if I wanted to. Pastor Midwinter would take over from me and continue the work. The only difference would be that it would become a Methodist school."

This was not quite true. She was the driving force behind the whole enterprise. It was by no means certain to survive without her.

However, her father believed it. "Oh, dear," he said, "we don't want a Methodist school."

Hornbeam was furious. "I see I'm wasting my time here," he said. He stood up, and Riddick followed suit.

The bishop did not want the meeting to end on such a hostile note. He said: "Oh, don't go so soon. Have a glass of Madeira."

Hornbeam was not mollified. "I'm afraid I have pressing business," he said. "Good day to you, Bishop." He bowed. "And Mrs. Mackintosh."

The two visitors went out.

The bishop said angrily: "That was frightfully embarrassing."

Elsie frowned. "Hornbeam didn't look as defeated as he should have."

Although her father was cross, he was intrigued by this comment. "What do you mean?"

"He failed in his purpose, which was to bully me. He's gone away empty-handed. Yet he didn't look beaten, did he?"

"No, I suppose not."

"I'll tell you what I think. I think he's got a fallback plan."

Kenelm came into Elsie's bedroom that night, when she had just put on her nightgown. Their rooms had a communicating door, but he normally used it only on Saturdays. She knew that love was not on his mind now.

"Your father has told me what transpired between you and Alderman Hornbeam," he said.

"He tried to make me stop feeding the children—and he failed. That sums it up."

"Not quite," Kenelm said.

Elsie got into bed. "You can get in with me, if you like," she said. "It would be more friendly."

"Don't be ridiculous, I'm fully dressed."

"Just take off your shoes."

"Stop being frivolous. I'm serious."

"When are you not?"

He ignored that. "How could you defy the most powerful man in Kingsbridge?"

"Easily," she said. "He doesn't care about hungry children. Any good Christian would defy him. He's a wicked man, and it's our duty to oppose him."

"You don't understand anything!" Kenelm was bursting with indignation. "Powerful men must be appeased, not provoked. Otherwise they will make you suffer."

"Don't be silly. What can Hornbeam do to us?"

"Who knows? You shouldn't make enemies of such men. One day the archbishop of Canterbury may say: 'I'm thinking of making Kenelm Mackintosh a bishop,' and someone may say to him: 'Ah, but his wife is something of a troublemaker, you know.' Men talk like that all the time."

Elsie was shocked. "How can you bring something like that up when we're talking about starving children?"

"I'm thinking about the rest of my life. Are my efforts to do God's work going to be held back by an unsuitable wife?"

"Your efforts to do God's work? Do you mean your career in the church?"

"They are the same thing."

"And that is more important than giving broth and bread to God's little children?"

"You always have to simplify everything."

"Hunger is simple. When you see hungry people you give them food. If that isn't God's will, nothing is."

"You think you know all about God's will."

"And you think you know better."

"I do know better. I've studied the matter with the wisest men in the land. So has your father. You're an ignorant, uneducated woman."

That was too stupid even to argue with. "Anyway, I can't close the school—it's not in my power. I told Hornbeam that."

"I don't care about the school. I don't care about the strike either. I care about my future, and I want a wife who will obey me and stay out of trouble."

"Oh, Kenelm," she said, "I think you married the wrong woman."

CHAPTER 21

On Saturday afternoon, after the mills shut down at five o'clock, Kit and his friends played football on a patch of waste ground near the new houses on the other side of the river. Kit was smaller than average; he could run and dodge but he could not kick far and was easily knocked down. All the same he enjoyed it and played enthusiastically.

When the game ended they broke up. Wandering aimlessly, Kit found himself in a street of empty new houses with doors opening directly onto the street. Out of idle curiosity he looked through a window and saw a small bare room, floorboards and plastered walls, and a staircase leading up. There was a fireplace, a small table, and two benches.

For no particular reason he tried the front door and found it unlocked. There on the doorstep he hesitated. He looked up and down the street and saw no one but a few of his football friends. He recalled a saying of Jarge's: "Curiosity killed the cat."

He slipped into the house and quietly closed the door behind him.

The place smelled of new plaster and fresh paint. He listened for a moment, but there was no sound from upstairs: he was alone. On the table were four bowls, four cups, and four spoons, made of wood, all new. It reminded him of one of his mother's stories, the tale of Goldilocks and the three bears. But there was no porridge in the bowls. The fireplace was clean and cold. The house was not yet lived in.

He went up the stairs, treading softly, just in case there should be someone up there, sleeping silently.

There were two bedrooms, each with a single window

to the street in front. He realized there were no windows at the back, and recalled hearing the phrase *back-to-back houses*. It made sense: each house shared a wall with the one behind, thereby saving bricks.

There were no beds, no silent sleepers. In one of the rooms he saw a stack of four canvas palliasses, filled presumably with straw, and a small pile of blankets. The house was ready for occupation, though barely.

Occupation by who? he wondered.

He had exhausted the interest of an empty house. He went down the stairs and out onto the street. He was shocked to see a heavyset red-faced man standing a few yards away. The man was equally shocked. They stared at one another for a moment, then the man roared angrily and stepped toward Kit.

Kit ran.

"Little thief!" the man yelled, though Kit was empty-handed.

Kit raced away, his heart pounding with fear. The fellow was probably some kind of watchman. He must have been sleeping on the job when Kit arrived, but now he was very awake. Men could run faster than boys, if they were in good shape, but in Kit's brief look this one had appeared unfit. However, when he glanced back over his shoulder he saw that the man was gaining on him. I'm going to get a beating, Kit thought, and he tried to run faster. He saw his friends scattering in panic.

Ahead of him, coming along the street, he saw a strange sight: a large wagon, pulled by four horses, packed to overflowing with men, women, and children. He passed it, then again looked behind at his pursuer. He saw the man stop, breathing hard, and lean on the side of the wagon to speak to the driver.

Kit wondered if he had been saved.

He slowed his pace but ran on until he was at a safe distance. Then he stopped and turned around, panting.

The people on the wagon were all strangers, and they looked about them with eager interest. Kit could hear them talking but did not understand what they said. Some of the words were recognizable but they were spoken in a strange accent.

The newcomers began to climb down from the wagon, carrying bundles and bags. They seemed to be in families: husband, wife, and children, plus a handful of young men, about thirty individuals altogether. As Kit watched, a second wagon appeared, similarly loaded.

Sixty people, Kit thought, doing arithmetic in his head as usual; fifteen or twenty families.

Then a third wagon arrived, and a fourth.

The red-faced man had now forgotten Kit and was busy directing people into houses. They did not always understand what he was saying, and he responded by shouting at them. One of the newcomers seemed to be their leader, a tall man with a shock of black hair. He spoke to the group, apparently interpreting what the red-faced man said.

The families began to disperse, and the leader walked toward Kit, accompanied by a woman and two children. Kit decided to speak to them. "Hello," he said.

The man said something Kit did not understand.

Kit said: "Who are you?"

The reply sound like: "Oy ma waver."

Kit thought for a moment. "You're a weaver?"

"That's what I said. We're all weavers."

"Where have you come from?"

The man said something that sounded like *doubling*.

"Is it far?"

The man replied, and this time Kit understood, getting used to the accent. "Three days on a ship to Bristol, then a day and a half in that wagon."

"Why have you come to Kingsbridge?"

"Is that what this place is called?"

"Yes."

"The mill in our village closed down, and we had no work. Then a man came and said we could work at a mill in England. Who are you, little man?"

"My name is Christopher Clitheroe, and they call me Kit." Proudly he added: "I'm the tackler at Barrowfield's Mill."

"Well, Kit the tackler, I'm Colin Hennessy, and I'm glad to meet you."

The family went into the house. All the front doors had been unlocked and were ready, Kit realized, and that was why he had been able to get in. Looking through the open door, he saw the children racing around excitedly. The wife appeared pleased.

Kit felt this was an important event, though he could not figure out quite why. He headed home, excited to be the bringer of news.

His mother was making supper, gruel with wild onions. Jarge was sitting down with a flagon of ale. He was on strike, and Kit had heard Sal say: "Idleness is bad for Jarge—he drinks too much."

Kit said to them: "I saw something strange."

Jarge took no notice, but Sal said: "And what was that?"

"You know the new houses?"

"Yes," Sal said. "Over by Piggery Mill."

"They're finished. I had a look inside one. It was all ready for people, with mattresses and a table and cups."

His mother frowned. "It's not like Hornbeam to give his tenants free gifts."

Kit decided to skip over the episode with the watchman. "Then this wagon came along full of people who talked funny."

Sal put down the spoon she was using to stir the gruel, then turned to look at Kit. "Really?" she said. Her attitude told him that he was right to think this news was important. "How many people?"

"About thirty. And then three more wagons came."

Jarge put down his tankard. "Why, that's more than a hundred people."

"A hundred and twenty," Kit said.

Sal said: "Did you speak to them?"

"I said hello to a tall man with black hair. He said they had been three days in a ship."

"Foreigners," said Jarge.

Sal said: "Did you ask where they came from?"

"It sounded like *doubling*."

"Dublin," said Sal. "They're Irish."

"He said he was a weaver, but the mill in his village closed."

Sal said: "I didn't know they had mills in Ireland."

"They do," said Jarge. "The Irish sheep have long, soft fleeces that make a nice warm tweed called Donegal."

Kit added: "They're all weavers, he said."

"By the deuce," Jarge said, "Hornbeam has brought in scabs."

"Scabs?" said Kit, puzzled. Scabs were what he got on his knees after falling.

"Strikebreakers," Sal explained: "Hornbeam will put them to work in his mills."

"Yes," said Jarge grimly. "If they live that long."

On Sundays Jane went to Communion in the cathedral. Amos wanted to speak to her, so he skipped the service in the Methodist Hall and waited outside the cathedral until the Anglican congregation emerged.

Jane was dressed in a coat of somber navy blue and a plain hat, suitable for church. She looked rather solemn, but brightened when she saw Amos. Viscount Northwood was not far behind her, but he was deep in conversation with Alderman Drinkwater.

Amos said to Jane: "It said in *The Times* a few days ago that the duke of York is planning radical reforms of the British Army."

"My, my," said Jane. "You do know how to sweet-talk a girl, don't you?"

Amos laughed at himself. "Sorry," he said. "How are you? I love your hat. That dark navy really suits you. Now, have you heard about the army reforms?"

"All right. I know you in your dog-with-a-bone mood. Yes, I know about the army reforms—Henry talks about little else at the moment. The duke wants every enlisted man to have a greatcoat. It sounds very sensible to me. How can they fight if they're freezing cold?"

"The duke also thinks the army pays too much for its supplies. The militia is being robbed, he thinks, and he's right. Those greatcoats will cost three or four times what they should."

"I hope you're not going to become as boring as my husband."

"This is not boring. Who's responsible for purchasing on behalf of the Shiring Militia?"

"Major Will Riddick. Oh, I think I see what you're getting at."

"From whom does Riddick buy all the cloth for uniforms?"

"From his father-in-law, Alderman Hornbeam."

"Six years ago, before Riddick married into the Hornbeam family, I bid for an army contract. Will agreed my price, then asked me for a bribe of ten percent."

Jane was shocked. "Did you report him?"

"No." Amos shrugged. "He would have denied it, and I couldn't prove it, so I did nothing."

"Then why are you telling me?"

"In the hope that you might tell your husband."

"But you still can't prove anything."

"No. But you know my beliefs. I wouldn't lie."

"Of course. But what do you want Henry to do? If you can't prove corruption, he can't either."

"He doesn't need to prove anything. He's the commanding officer. He can simply assign Major Riddick to a different role—master of firearms, for example—and pick someone else to supervise the purchasing."

"What if the new man is just as corrupt as Will?"

"Tell Henry to appoint a Methodist."

Jane nodded thoughtfully. "He might do that. He says the Methodists make good officers."

Henry Northwood separated from Alderman Drinkwater and came to his wife's side. Amos bowed to him. The viscount said: "What do you think of this strike, Barrowfield?"

"The clothiers must make a profit, and the hands must have a living wage—it's really not so difficult, my lord. But greed and pride get in the way."

"You think the masters should give in?"

"I think both sides should compromise."

"Very sensible," said Northwood, and he took Jane's arm proprietorially and led her away.

The Irish started work at Hornbeam's mills on Monday. That evening after ringing practice there was a meeting in the back room of the Bell. The room was large but tonight it was crammed: most of the striking weavers were there, with Sal, Jarge, and Spade, too.

No one was drinking much. There was an air of tense anticipation. Something had to happen, though no one was sure what. Some of the weavers were carrying stout sticks, wooden shovels, and mallets.

Sal wanted to avoid violence.

Jarge was in favor of battle. "A hundred of us, outside Piggery Mill tomorrow at half past four in the morning, armed with cudgels. Anyone who tries to go into the mill gets a beating. Simple as that."

Jarge's pal Jack Camp, also a weaver at Hornbeam's Upper Mill, said: "That's the way," and an angry murmur indicated much support for this approach.

Sal said: "And then what?"

"Hornbeam will have to give in," Jarge said.

Spade said: "Is he a giving-in type of man, do you think, Jarge? Mightn't he call out the militia?"

Jarge laughed. "That won't do him no good. The militiamen are our friends and neighbors."

"True, they refused to fire on women at the bread riot," Spade conceded. "But can we be sure the same would happen again? What if, instead of shooting, they start arresting people?"

Jarge was scornful. "They'll have trouble arresting me."

"I know," said Spade. "So there would be a fight, three or four soldiers against you."

"Against me and my friends."

"And then more soldiers would join in, and more of your friends."

"Very likely."

"And that would be a riot."

"Well . . ."

Spade pressed his point. "And, Jarge, I'm sorry to mention this, but your sister, Joanie, was convicted of riot, narrowly escaped hanging, and got transported to Australia, and may never come back."

"I know," said Jarge, irritated that he was losing the argument.

Spade was relentless. "So, if the hands follow your plan, how many more of you do you think will end up transported or hanged?"

Jarge became indignant. "What are you saying, Spade—that we should just sit here and do nothing?"

"Give it a week," Spade said.

"What for?"

"To see what happens."

There was a rumble of discontent, and Sal said: "Listen to him, listen. Spade always makes sense."

Jarge said worriedly: "Nothing's going to happen if we just wait."

"Don't be so sure." As always, Spade's tone was mild, reasonable. "Look, what have you got to lose? Wait a week. A lot can happen in a week. Let's all meet again here on Saturday night, after supper. If I'm wrong and nothing has changed, that will be the time to plan something more drastic."

Sal nodded approval. "No unnecessary risks."

"Meanwhile," said Spade, "stay out of trouble. If you see an Irishman, walk away from him. You're mill hands. By the unwritten laws of England, you're guilty until you prove yourself innocent."

Jarge accepted the decision of the group, but he did not like it. Sal watched with trepidation as he became angrier and drank more. On Tuesday evening when she finished work she saw him outside Hornbeam's new mill, watching the Irish leaving. But he did not speak to anyone and he walked home with Sal.

"Why are we at war with Bonaparte and the French?" he said. "We should be fighting Hornbeam and the Irish."

Sal agreed with him. "Bloody right," she said. "But we have to be clever. Hornbeam is sly, and all his sort are the same. We mustn't let the bastards outsmart us."

Jarge looked mutinous and made no reply.

The fact that he was not working made his mood worse. Having nothing to do he spent his days in the alehouse. When Sal came home on Thursday evening she saw that her father's Bible was missing. "He's pawned it," she said to herself. "He's pawned it, and he's spending the money on drink." She sat on her bed and cried a for a while.

But she had children to look after.

As she was giving them their supper—cheap stale bread and pork dripping—Jarge staggered in, stinking of ale, bad-tempered because he had no money for more. "Where's my supper?" he said.

Sal said: "Where's my father's Bible?"

He sat at the table. "I'll get it back after the strike is

over, don't worry." He spoke as if it was not very important, which made her angrier.

She cut a slab of bread, smeared it with dripping, and put it in front of him. "Get that inside you to soak up some of the ale."

He took a bite, chewed, swallowed, and made a face. "Bread and dripping?" he said. "Why is there no butter?"

"You know why there's no butter," Sal muttered.

Kit piped up: "Because there's a strike on, didn't you know?"

That annoyed Jarge. "Don't you cheek me, you little turd," he said, slurring his words. "I'm the master of this house, and don't you forget it." And with that he smacked the side of Kit's head so hard that the boy fell off his chair onto the floor.

That broke Sal's self-control. A memory came back to her, as vivid as if it had been yesterday, of six-year-old Kit lying in bed at Badford manor house, with a bandage around his head, after Will Riddick's horse had cracked his skull; and rage boiled up volcanically inside her. She stepped toward Jarge, mad with fury. He saw her expression and quickly stood up, shock and fear on his face; then she was on him. She kicked him in the balls, and she heard Sue scream but took no notice. When Jarge's hand covered his groin she punched his face twice, three times, four. She had big hands and strong arms. He backed away, yelling: "Get away from me, you mad cow!"

She heard Kit yelling: "Stop, stop!"

She punched Jarge again, high on his cheekbone. He grabbed her arms, but he was drunk and she was strong, and he could not hold her. She punched his stomach and he bent over in pain. She kicked his legs from under him, and he went down like a felled tree.

She snatched up the bread knife from the table and knelt on his chest. Holding the blade to his face, she said: "If you ever touch that boy again, I swear I'll cut your throat in the middle of the night, so help me God."

She heard Kit say: "Ma, get off him."

She stood up, breathing hard, and put the knife in a drawer. The children were halfway up the stairs, open-mouthed, staring at her in awe and fear. She looked at Kit's face. The left side was red and beginning to swell. She said: "Does your head hurt?"

"No, it's my cheek," he said.

The two children stepped cautiously down the stairs.

Sal hugged Kit, feeling relieved: she was always fearful of his hurting his head.

Her knuckles were bruised and the ring finger of her left hand felt sprained. She rubbed her hands together, easing the pain.

Jarge clambered slowly to his feet. Sal glared at him, daring him to attack her. His face was all cuts and bruises but he showed no sign of fight. His body was slumped and his head bowed. He sat down, folding his arms on the table, and lowered his face to his forearms. He trembled, and she realized he was weeping. After a while he lifted his head a little and said: "I'm sorry, Sal. I don't know what came over me. I never meant to hurt the poor boy. I don't deserve you, Sal. I'm not good enough. You're a good woman, I know it."

She stood with her arms folded, looking at him. "Don't ask me to forgive you."

"I won't."

She could not help feeling a twinge of pity. He was abject, and he had done Kit no real harm. But she felt the need to draw a line. Otherwise Jarge might think he could hit Kit again, and apologize again. She said: "I need to know this will never happen again."

"It won't, I swear." He wiped his face with his sleeve and looked at her. "Don't leave me, Sal."

She regarded him for a long moment, then made up her mind. "You'd better have a lie down, and sleep off all that ale." She took hold of his upper arm and encouraged him to stand. "Come on, upstairs with you." She took him into the bedroom they shared and sat him on the edge of the bed. She knelt and pulled off his boots.

He swung his legs onto the bed and lay back. "Stay with me a minute, Sal."

She hesitated, then lay down beside him. She slid her arm under his head and pillowed his face on her bosom. He fell asleep in seconds, and his whole body went limp.

She kissed his battered face. "I love you," she said. "But I won't forgive you a second time."

Saturday was a fine day, and the sun was still shining at half past five when Hornbeam took the air in the garden of his house. He had had a good week. All his mills were working with Irish labor, and some of the newcomers were being trained on the steam looms. He had eaten a good dinner and now he was smoking a pipe.

But his tranquility was disturbed by a message from his son-in-law, Will Riddick. The messenger was a young militiaman in uniform, perspiring and breathless. He stood at attention and said: "Alderman Hornbeam, sir, begging your pardon, Major Riddick presents his compliments, and begs you to meet him outside the Slaughterhouse Inn as soon as possible."

Hornbeam said: "Has something happened?"

"I don't know, sir, I was just told the message."

"All right. Follow me."

"Very good, sir."

Hornbeam went into his house and spoke to the footman, Simpson. "Tell Mrs. Hornbeam that I've been called away on business." Then he put on his wig, looking in the hall mirror to adjust it, and stepped outside.

It took him and the messenger only a few minutes to walk briskly down Main Street to the Lower Town. Before they reached the Slaughterhouse Hornbeam saw why Riddick had summoned him.

The Irish were coming to town.

Hornbeam stared at them walking across the bridge, bringing their children. They each had only one set of clothes but, like Kingsbridge mill hands, they dressed up with a bright scarf, a hair ribbon, a sash, or a jaunty hat. Hornbeam had imported a hundred and twenty people from Ireland and it looked as if all of them were out for pleasure tonight.

He wondered how the locals would react.

The messenger led him to the Slaughterhouse, the largest of the waterfront taverns. A crowd of drinkers stood outside, enjoying the sun. The place was busy, and many of the Irish had already arrived and were quaffing from tankards. They were distinguishable by their subtly different clothes, tweed with random colors in the weave rather than the ordered stripes and checks of West of England cloth.

The messenger guided Hornbeam inside, where he spotted Riddick, holding a tankard. Hornbeam said: "I should have anticipated this."

"Me too," said Riddick. "They've just been paid and they want to enjoy themselves."

"But there seems to be no hostility between the locals and the newcomers."

"So far."

Hornbeam nodded. "We should muster a squad of militia just as a precaution."

Riddick spoke to the messenger. "My compliments to Lieutenant Donaldson, and will he be pleased to muster companies one, two, and seven immediately, but hold them at headquarters pending further orders."

The young man repeated the message accurately, and Riddick sent him off.

Hornbeam was worried. If there was trouble it would be blamed on the Irish, and there might even be pressure on him to get rid of them. That would leave him at the mercy of the damned union.

He needed to look around. "Let's take a stroll," he said. Riddick emptied his tankard and they went outside.

There was another, smaller pub a few steps away, its signboard a picture of a swan. "The White Swan," Riddick said. "Humorously referred to as the Mucky Duck."

They looked inside. The strangers were sitting and standing with the locals, and no one was making trouble.

Street hawkers were selling hot and cold snacks: baked apples, nuts, hot pies, and gingerbread. At the dockside a barge was unloading barrels of winkles, tiny edible sea snails that had to be prized out of their shells with a pin, and a man was already boiling them in a bucket over a coal fire. Hornbeam did not want any but Riddick bought a cone, sprinkled with vinegar, and ate them as he walked, dropping the shells on the ground.

He and Hornbeam toured the district. They looked into taverns, gambling dens, and brothels. The pubs were all very basic, with crude homemade furniture. They mainly sold ale and cheap gin. The Irish would not be at the gaming tables: they did not have enough money, Hornbeam assumed. Bella Lovegood, who was getting older, was madam of her own place now, and four or five of the young Irish men were there, waiting patiently for a turn with a girl. There were no Irish in Culliver's house, doubtless because it was too expensive for mill hands.

By the time they found themselves back at the Slaughterhouse, the sun was beginning to sink downriver, and the drinkers were getting noisier. The messenger was waiting to tell them that Lieutenant Donaldson had mustered the three companies. Riddick said: "Stay close to me now—there may be another message."

The mood in the tavern was boisterous, but there was no sign of tension. Riddick got another tankard and Hornbeam a glass of Madeira, and they took their drinks outside where the air was still warm but fresher. Hornbeam began to feel that things would be all right.

One or two people were becoming irritated with the children. They seemed especially energetic, racing around playing games of chase. Occasionally one would crash into a grown-up and dodge away without apology. "I wonder," Hornbeam said fretfully, "whether we should suggest that people keep their children under control or, better, take them home to bed."

A gingerbread man appeared and sold thick slices of his sweet cake to the drinkers outside the Slaughterhouse. Hornbeam saw a boy of about eight snatch a piece from the hand of a young woman and stuff it straight into his mouth. But he was not quick enough, and the woman's companion grabbed the child's arm. "Little thief!" the man shouted. The boy tried to pull away but could not escape the man's grip, and he began to screech. People turned to look.

Hornbeam recognized the man holding the child as Nat Hammond, one of the young hooligans who patronized the Slaughterhouse. Hammond had appeared before the justices two or three times on assault charges.

A moment later an Irishman approached Hammond and said: "Leave little Mikey be."

Hornbeam heard Riddick mutter: "Oh, damn."

Hammond shook the boy and said aggressively: "Is this yours?"

The Irishman said: "You will let my boy go—or you'll suffer the consequences."

Riddick spoke to the messenger. "Run to headquarters and tell Donaldson to get the militia down here fast."

The child Mikey was emboldened by the arrival of his father and he gave his captor a terrific kick. Hammond shouted with surprise and pain, and smacked Mikey's face, at the same time letting go of his arm. The child fell to the ground, bleeding from his little snub nose.

The father jumped at Hammond and punched him in the belly. As Hammond doubled over, the Irishman said: "Now see if you'd like to smack my nose, instead of a little boy's."

Riddick took Hornbeam's arm. "Let's stand clear," he said. Hornbeam complied nimbly.

As they backed away, two men—one local, one Irish—intervened between the two fighters, but immediately started hitting each other. More men joined in. Each began by trying to pull fighters apart, and each quickly got into a scrap of his own. Some of the women came to the rescue of their men and joined the fray. The shouting reached uproar level and drew people from inside the Slaughterhouse and the Mucky Duck. The man selling winkles tried to keep people away from his barrel but, since the technique he used was to punch them, he was soon himself embroiled, and the barrel was knocked over. It rolled away, spilling winkles and seawater across the cobblestones.

To Hornbeam's dismay there were soon at least fifty people fighting. He looked along the street but saw no sign of the militia. He cast about desperately for some way he could stop this, but anything he or Riddick did would only involve them in the fighting.

This was going to discredit the Irish strikebreakers and Hornbeam himself. It was a disaster, and—he saw now—it was spreading along adjacent streets, drawing people out of other taverns. He might even be forced to send the Irish home.

This will please the striking hands, he thought angrily.

At last Donaldson arrived with the militia. Some carried their muskets but others were unarmed. Donaldson ordered the armed men to stand well back from the crowd with their weapons ready, and told the others to arrest anyone who was fighting.

Hornbeam would have liked to see the militia open fire, but he realized this would do him even more harm.

The militia began pulling people out of the scrum and tying them up. This had some effect, Hornbeam saw: some brawlers disentangled themselves from their opponents and hurried away before they too were seized.

Hornbeam said to Riddick: "We have to blame this

on the new union. Make sure you arrest any strikers you can see."

"I wouldn't know them."

"Then look for the ringleaders—Jarge Box, Jack Camp, Sal Box, or that fellow Spade." Hornbeam knew he could find men to swear that the strike leaders deliberately provoked the trouble.

"Good plan," said Riddick, and gave orders to a corporal.

With luck they would pick up some of the strikers anyway, he thought.

Soon he could see that the battle was coming to an end. More people were running away than fighting. Many of those still in view were on the ground, nursing injuries. He guessed that those Irish who had escaped arrest had gone back over the bridge.

Now Hornbeam had to find a way to limit the damage.

"How many have you arrested?" he asked Riddick.

"Twenty or thirty. They're locked in the Slaughterhouse barn for the moment."

"Take them to Kingsbridge Jail. Get all the names and other details and come to my house. We'll let the Irish go. I'll hold petty sessions early tomorrow, even though it's Sunday. I'll hand out tough sentences on the strikers and their leaders and go easy on the rest. I want people in Kingsbridge to understand that this was caused by the union, not by the Irish."

"Good plan."

Hornbeam took his leave and went home to await the next stage.

A small boy rushed into the Bell, ran up to Spade, and said: "The men are fighting the scabs down at the Slaughterhouse! The militia are arresting people!"

"Right!" said Jarge, standing up. "We better get down there damn quick."

Spade said firmly: "Sit down, Jarge."

"What—are we going to sit here drinking ale while our neighbors are fighting the scabs? Not me!"

"Just think for a minute, Jarge. If we go there, some of us will be arrested."

"Well, that's not the worst thing in the world."

"And then we'll be hauled up before the justices. And the justices will say the riot wasn't the fault of the Irish, because it was started by the strikers."

"They'll probably say that anyway, won't they?"

"They can't, because we're all here. Just about all of Hornbeam's weavers have been with us all evening, drinking ale. And there's a hundred people here who can swear to it, including the landlord, whose uncle is an alderman."

"So . . . so . . ." It took Jarge a minute to figure this out. "So they'll have to blame the scabs."

"Exactly."

Jarge thought some more. "Did you know this was going to happen, Spade?"

"I thought it was likely."

"That's why you didn't want us to go to Piggery Mill last Monday."

"Yes."

"That's why you made us all meet here tonight."

"Yes."

"By the deuce." Jarge laughed. "I've said it before, Spade—you're a bloody sly one."

On Sunday morning after church the mayor, Frank Fishwick, organized an impromptu meeting at the Guild Hall. All the leading clothiers were invited, Anglican and Methodist. Both Hornbeam and Spade were there.

Spade knew that he had been invited not because he was one of the wealthiest but because he was close to the hands. He could tell the others what their workers were saying and doing.

Mayor Fishwick was in his fifties and stout, with a grizzled beard. He had a calm authority. He believed his job was to make sure Kingsbridge clothiers could do business unimpeded—he had no time for foolish notions about the rights of man—but he was not as combative as Hornbeam. Spade was not sure which way Fishwick would jump today.

Fishwick began by saying: "One thing I'm sure we can all agree upon. We cannot have running battles in the streets of Kingsbridge. We must put a stop to this immediately."

Hornbeam went on the attack right away. "My Irish hands were peacefully spending their well-earned wages on Saturday night when they were set upon by thugs. I know. I was there."

People looked at Spade, expecting him to contradict Hornbeam, but he remained silent.

As he hoped, someone else countered Hornbeam. It was Amos Barrowfield, a quiet chap who occasionally surprised everyone by having strong views. "I don't much care who started the fighting," he said crisply. "This riot happened because more than a hundred foreigners were brought to Kingsbridge to break the strike."

Hornbeam said angrily: "I was completely within my rights!"

"I can't deny that, but it doesn't get us anywhere, does it?" Amos replied. "What will happen next Saturday, Hornbeam? Can you suggest how we might prevent a recurrence?"

"I most certainly can. Last night's fight was deliberately provoked by the union that has been formed by discontented weavers. They must be suppressed."

"Interesting," Amos replied. "If that is so, then of course the offenders must be brought to justice. But I believe you held court this morning to deal with those arrested last night, and—"

"Yes, but—"

"Allow me to finish what I was saying," Amos said in a raised voice. "I insist on being heard."

"Let him say his piece, Hornbeam," Fishwick said firmly. "We're all equals here."

Spade was pleased. That intervention was a sign that Hornbeam was not going to have everything his own way.

"Thank you, Mr. Mayor," said Amos. "Hornbeam, your fellow justices weren't informed of this morning's session so couldn't attend, but I understand that the accused men did not include any of your weavers nor any of the presumed organizers of the union."

"They were very sly!" said Hornbeam.

"So sly, perhaps, that they cleverly did not riot, and therefore are innocent."

Hornbeam reddened with anger but was momentarily lost for words.

Spade judged it was time for him to speak. "I can confirm that, Mr. Mayor," he said. "If I may?"

"Please, Mr. Shoveller."

"The strikers and a few of their supporters met last night to discuss the issues facing them. I happened to be at the Bell and can confirm that they were in the room all evening. They were informed of the riot, and agreed to take no action. They remained at the inn until well after the trouble was over. The landlord of the inn, his staff, and about a hundred customers can bear witness to that. So we may be quite confident that the strikers and their supporters had nothing to do with it."

"They could still have organized it," said Hornbeam.

"Perhaps," said Amos. "But there's no evidence for that. And we can't act on mere supposition."

"In that case," said Fishwick, taking charge of the discussion again, "perhaps we can talk about what we might do to bring the strike to an end and prevent further conflict of this kind in our town. Obviously we can't ask our friend Hornbeam not to use his new steam looms—we can't hold back progress."

Hornbeam said: "Thank you for that, at least."

Fishwick went on: "But perhaps there might be some lesser concession that would persuade the hands. Mr. Shoveller, you may be more in touch with the workers than I am. What do you think might persuade them back to work?"

"I can't speak for them," Spade said, and he sensed the disappointment in the group. "However, perhaps I can suggest a way forward."

"Go ahead, please," said Fishwick.

"A small group of clothiers, say three or four people, might be appointed to meet with representatives of the hands. Perhaps we could explain to them which demands are impossible and which may be possible. Armed with that kind of understanding, our group could report back to Mr. Hornbeam, and the hands' representatives to them, and we might be able to reach agreement."

All the clothiers were accustomed to negotiation in business, and they understood the language of haggling and compromise. Around the table there were murmurs and nods of agreement.

Encouraged, Spade added: "Obviously the group would not have the power to make decisions on Mr. Hornbeam's behalf, nor indeed on behalf of the hands. All the same it needs some authority, and to that end I suggest that you, Mr. Mayor, should be its leading member."

That, too, met with approval. Fishwick said: "I'm at your service, of course. And, Mr. Shoveller, you would clearly be a great help to the group."

"Thank you. I'm happy to do what I can."

Someone said: "And Mrs. Bagshaw."

Spade approved. Cissy Bagshaw was the only female clothier, running the business she had inherited when her husband died. She was intelligent and open-minded.

Fishwick said: "And Mr. Barrowfield, perhaps?"

Once again there was agreement.

"Very good," said Fishwick. "And with your agreement, gentlemen and lady, I would like us to start work today."

And so, Spade thought with satisfaction, the union achieves official recognition.

I wonder what Hornbeam will do next?

"Do other men do this?" Arabella asked Spade.

"I don't know," he said.

He was combing her pubic hair.

She said: "No man has ever looked at me there."

"Oh? But you managed to conceive Elsie . . ."

"In the dark."

"Do bishops have to do it in the dark?"

She giggled. "It's probably a rule."

"So I'm the first man to see this glorious golden red."

"Yes. Ouch! Don't tug."

"Sorry. I'll kiss it better. There. But I have to get the tangles out."

"You don't have to, you just like to."

"Should I give you a parting?"

"That would be so vulgar."

"If you say so. There, that's much neater." He sat up on the bed beside her. "I'm going to keep this comb forever."

"You don't think I'm ugly down there?"

"On the contrary."

"Good." She paused, and he realized she had something on her mind. "Um . . . I need to tell you . . ." She hesitated. "I slept with him the night before last."

Spade raised his eyebrows.

"He drank a lot of port that evening, as well as brandy last thing. I had to help him undress. Then he practically fell into bed and started to snore. I saw my chance."

"You got in with him."

"Yes."

"And..."

"And he did nothing all night but fart."

"Oh, disgusting."

"He was astonished when he woke up and found me in bed with him. It's been years since the last time we slept together."

Spade was fascinated but apprehensive. What had she done? He was afraid that some drama between Arabella and the bishop would spoil everything. "What did he say?"

"He said: 'What are you doing here?'"

Spade laughed. "What a question for a man to ask his wife in bed! How did you answer?"

"I said: 'You were very insistent last night.' I tried to look, you know, bashful."

"That must have been something to see. I can't imagine it."

Arabella did a very good imitation of a girl being coy, saying: "Oh, Mr. Shoveller, you make me blush."

Spade chuckled.

She went on: "Then he wanted to know what had happened. He said: 'Did I actually...?' and I said: 'Yes.' That was a lie. Then, to make it more plausible, I said: 'Not for long, but long enough.'"

"Did he believe you?"

"I think so. He looked shocked, then said he had a headache. I said I wasn't surprised, after the brandy on top of the port."

"What did you do?"

"I went to my room, called the maid, and told her to send the footman to the bishop with a large pot of tea."

"So now, when you tell him you're pregnant..."

"I'll remind him of that night."

"You only did it once."

"Every pregnancy is the result of one act of intercourse."

"Will he be fooled?"

"I think so," she said again.

The clothiers met again a week later, in the same place at the same time.

Spade felt that the fact of an agreement would be more important than its terms. It would establish the union as useful to both masters and hands.

Mayor Fishwick reported on the discussions. "First of all," he said, "the hands made two demands which, we had to tell them, the masters would never agree to."

This way of presenting the information had been Spade's idea.

"They asked for the Irish to be sent away."

Hornbeam said: "Out of the question."

Fishwick ignored the interruption. "We explained that this is up to Alderman Hornbeam. Although some clothiers might agree that the Irish should go home, we don't have the power to command Mr. Hornbeam."

Someone muttered: "Too true."

"Second, they demanded that hands thrown out of work should be given parish relief without having to enter Kingsbridge workhouse."

The hands hated the workhouse. It was cold and uncomfortable, and most of all it humiliated its residents. It was not much different from a prison.

"Once again," Fishwick said, "we had to explain that we have no jurisdiction over parish relief, which is controlled by the church."

Spade had proposed this approach because he knew the clothiers would be reassured to hear that the group had stoutly resisted some of the hands' demands. It would make them more compliant when they heard the rest.

"Now I come to a third demand, which I recommend we accept," Fishwick went on. "They want hands who are displaced by machines to be given priority for alternative work. If we agree, the council of aldermen—of which most of us here are members—might pass a resolution saying that this is the required procedure in Kingsbridge. This would ease the present crisis and make it easier for all of us to introduce new machinery in the future."

Spade was watching the faces, and he saw that most agreed with this.

"In order that this system may work smoothly, two further suggestions were made. One, that before new machinery is installed the master should explain it to the hands and discuss how many people will work on the machine and how many will be displaced by it."

Hornbeam was predictably scathing. "So I have to consult with the hands before I buy a new machine? Ludicrous!"

Amos said: "Some of us do this anyway. It oils the wheels."

Hornbeam snorted in disgust.

"And two," Fishwick continued, "that representatives of masters and hands should monitor compliance by the two sides in the future so that any trouble may be resolved before it becomes a dispute."

This was a new idea, quite at odds with the way most of them were used to relating to their hands. However, only Hornbeam spoke against it. "You will make masters out of the hands," he said in a tone of scorn. "And hands out of the masters."

Fishwick looked exasperated. "The people around this table aren't fools, Hornbeam," he said with irritation. "We can manage a relationship of cooperation without becoming slaves."

There was a murmur of agreement.

Hornbeam threw his hands up in a gesture of defeat. "Go ahead," he said. "Who am I to stand in your way?"

Spade was satisfied. This was the outcome Sal and Jarge were expecting, and it would end the strike. The union had become an established part of the Kingsbridge cloth business. But he had one more thing to say. "The hands are pleased to have reached an agreement, but they did make it clear that there must be no attempt to punish strike leaders. That, I fear, would completely undermine the deal."

There was a silence while they digested that.

Then Mayor Fishwick said: "That concludes our business for today, gentlemen and lady, and I wish you all a hearty Sunday dinner."

As they all made ready to leave, Hornbeam threw a parting shot. "You've all surrendered to this union. But it's only temporary. Trade unions will shortly be made completely illegal."

There was an astonished silence.

"Good day to you all," he said, and he left the room.

CHAPTER 22

Most of the clothiers thought Hornbeam was talking rubbish for the sake of bravado. Spade disagreed. Hornbeam would not tell a lie that could easily be found out, for that would make him look foolish. There had to be something in what he was saying. Any threat from Hornbeam was worrying. So Spade went to see Charles Midwinter.

The pastor thought that Methodists ought to be well-informed about their country's affairs, even if they could not afford to buy newspapers and journals, so he subscribed to several publications and kept them for a year in the reading room of the Methodist Hall. Spade went there to look through back numbers. He told Midwinter what Hornbeam had said, and Midwinter helped him search for some mention of a law against trade unions. They sat on opposite sides of a cheap table, in a small room with a big window, and paged through newspapers, starting with the most recent.

The search did not take long.

They learned that on June 17—the previous Monday—Prime Minister William Pitt had announced the Workmen's Combination Bill, which would make it a crime for workmen to get together—"combine"—to ask for higher wages or otherwise interfere with the masters' freedom to do as they pleased. The bill was said to be a response to the current plague of strikes. Spade thought that *plague* was an exaggeration, but it was true there had been much unrest in industries blighted by wartime taxes and trade restrictions.

The reports were brief and details were few, which was probably why Spade had failed to spot the danger in his daily reading, but a careful perusal showed clearly that trade unions would be illegal.

And that would change everything. The hands would be an army with no guns.

The bill had been presented to Parliament on the following day and had its "second reading" in the House of Commons—meaning it had met with approval—a day later.

"My word, that's quick," said Midwinter.

"The bastards are rushing it through," Spade said.

In accordance with parliamentary procedure, the bill had then been sent to a committee charged with examining it in detail and reporting back.

"Do you know how long that takes?" Spade asked.

Midwinter was not sure. "I think it varies."

"This is important. We may not have much time. Let's ask our member of Parliament."

"I'm not a voter," said Midwinter, who was not a property owner, and therefore failed the test of the forty-shilling franchise.

"But I am," said Spade. "And you can come with me."

They left the hall. The June sun was warm on their faces as they walked briskly to the market square and turned into Willard House.

Viscount Northwood was just finishing his midday dinner, and he offered them a glass of port. There were nuts and cheese on the table. Midwinter declined the port but Spade accepted. It was very good, smooth and sweet with a stimulating bite of brandy in the satisfying finish.

Spade told him about Hornbeam's jibe and what they had subsequently discovered from last week's papers. Northwood was surprised to learn about the Combination Bill, but then he had never been conscientious about his parliamentary duties.

"I don't like the sound of this," he said. "I can see why you're concerned. Of course, disruption of business must be avoided, we all know that, but to completely prohibit the hands from getting together amounts to bullying. I hate bullies."

Spade said: "And here in Kingsbridge the union has actually helped bring the strike to an end."

"I didn't know that," Northwood said.

"It's only just happened. But believe me, without a union there will be more industrial strife, not less."

"Well, I must find out more about this Combination Bill."

It was bad manners to ask a nobleman to hurry, but all the same Spade said: "How long might that take, my lord?"

Northwood raised an eyebrow but decided not to take offense. "I'll write today," he said. "My man in London will send me the details."

Spade persisted. "I can't help wondering how long the committee will take to report back."

"Given the government's evident hurry, it will probably be just a few days."

"Is there anything we can do to persuade Parliament to reconsider?"

"As workmen can't vote, the usual way for them to try to influence Parliament is to present a petition."

"I'll start work on that today."

The following Friday Northwood got a reply to his letter. It came in the form of a short, round, bald man called Clement Keithley. He explained to Spade, sitting in Northwood's office opposite the cathedral, that he was a lawyer working as an assistant to Benjamin Hobhouse, MP. Hobhouse knew Kingsbridge because his father had been a Bristol merchant.

Keithley, who had been at Bristol Grammar School with Hobhouse, said with pride that Mr. Hobhouse had spoken vehemently against the Combination Bill, but his opposition had not been enough to kill the bill, which would now be considered by the upper chamber, the House of Lords.

"Mr. Pitt's government is in a terrific rush about this, aren't they?" said Northwood.

"Indeed they are, my lord, and there has been no time for their opponents to organize petitions."

Spade said: "We have a petition with several hundred signatures already."

"Then we must get some more, and present it to the House of Lords." Keithley turned to Northwood. "My lord, would you be kind enough to call a public meeting for this matter to be explained to your constituents?"

"A very good idea. When?"

"Today or tomorrow. We cannot delay."

"Well, I'm sure it could be arranged for tomorrow."

Spade said: "Let me go now and make sure the Assembly Rooms are available."

"If you would," said Northwood.

"And perhaps Mr. Keithley would like to come with me, and look at the place where he will be speaking."

"Yes, I would," said Keithley.

They left. Outside the building, Keithley paused to take in the cathedral. It always looked its best in sunshine, Spade thought. "I remember this," Keithley said. "I must have come here as a boy. Magnificent. And all made without machines."

Spade said: "I'm not against machines, as such. Anyway, they can't be stopped. But we can ease the pain."

"Exactly."

They walked up Main Street to the Assembly Rooms at the crossroads. The door was open. Inside, a handful of people were doing cleaning and maintenance. Spade led Keithley to the manager's office. Yes, the main hall was free on Saturday evening, and of course the manager would be delighted to host Viscount Northwood for a political meeting.

They paused in the ballroom. Sunlight through the windows gilded the dust thrown into the air by the cleaners. Spade said: "Plenty of space, as you can see. There are about two hundred voters in Kingsbridge, but I assume we will let the hands attend as well."

"Oh, definitely. Your MP must witness the strength of

feeling when working people learn what is being plotted against them. How many hands are there in Kingsbridge?"

"In the woolen mills, about a thousand."

"Encourage them to come."

"I'll spread the word."

"Splendid. I suggest you collect signatures for your petition immediately after the meeting, and I'll take the lot up to London on Sunday."

"In your honest opinion," Spade said, "what chance do we have of stopping the bill?"

"It can't be stopped," Keithley said. "Just like the machines. All we can hope to do is get it modified. Ease the pain, as you put it."

That was disappointing. Spade felt angry. I would like to be in Parliament, he thought. I'd shake the buggers up.

Sal thought the emissary from London seemed unimpressive. Good speakers were often striking looking, like Charles Midwinter, but Keithley was the opposite. She hoped he would not be like the Reverend Bartholomew Small, who had bored everyone. She wanted the hands to get fired up.

However, the meeting attracted a big crowd. Sal saw most of the major clothiers and several hundred mill hands. The seats were full and people were standing at the back. At the front was a platform with a table. Viscount Northwood sat behind the table in the center, clearly in charge. Mayor Fishwick was on one side of him, and Keithley on the other, with Spade at the end of the row. Sal was seated in the audience: despite her key role in the strike, no one would expect a woman to be on the platform.

To one side of the room, Elsie Mackintosh sat at a table with paper, pens, and ink, ready to collect signatures for the petition later.

Northwood opened the meeting. He was well-meaning,

but he could not help sounding as if he were giving his troops a pep talk before a battle. "Now pay attention, everyone. We're here to learn about an important bill now before Parliament, so you must all listen carefully to what is said by Mr. Keithley, who has come all the way from London to address us."

Keithley was more relaxed. "If this bill is passed in its present form, it will change the lives of every working man, woman, and child in our country," he said. "So if anything isn't clear, please stand up and say so, or ask a question for clarification. I don't mind being interrupted."

This was a better style for the hands, Sal knew: they responded well to informality.

Keithley began with the rushed passage of the bill through Parliament. "Announced by the prime minister on the Monday before last, first reading the next day; second reading the day after that. The committee reported a hasty seven days later, which was last Wednesday; and it will be before the House of Lords the day after tomorrow. However, they're not in such a hurry to listen to the workingmen and -women of the nation they rule. Parliament has not yet found time to consider a petition opposing the bill from the calico printers of London."

Someone called out: "Shame on them."

"And what does this bill say?" Keithley lowered his voice dramatically. "My friends, listen very carefully." Then he spoke in a crescendo. "It says that any workman who gets together with another—just one!—to ask for a wage increase has committed a crime *and may be punished with two months' hard labor!*"

There was a shout of protest from the crowd.

Keithley was more impressive than he looked, Sal thought gratefully. She had underestimated him.

A harsh, penetrating voice said: "Just a minute."

Sal looked for the source and saw Hornbeam standing up.

She noticed Spade whispering to Keithley, and guessed he was explaining who the interrupter was.

Hornbeam said: "Allow me to point out that the bill equally forbids combinations of masters."

"Thank you for that interjection," said Keithley. "I'm told I have the honor to address Alderman Hornbeam, is that right?"

Hornbeam said: "Yes."

"And you're a clothier, Mr. Hornbeam."

"Yes."

"And a justice of the peace."

"Yes."

"You used the word *equally*, but let us look closer." Keithley turned away from Hornbeam to the crowd. "This bill, my friends, will allow Mr. Hornbeam to accuse any two of his hands of combination. He will then be able to try their case on his own *with no second justice and no jury*. Finding them guilty, he may sentence them to hard labor—all without consulting a single other person in the world."

There was a rumble of indignation from the audience.

"Note the following contrast," Keithley continued. "Masters accused under this bill will have to be tried by at least two justices and a jury."

Sal said loudly: "That's not justice!" People around her voiced their agreement.

"And that is not the only inequality," said Keithley. "Workingmen may be questioned about conversations with their workmates, and it will be a crime to refuse to answer. *You will be obliged to testify against yourselves and your workmates—or go to prison for refusing so to do.*"

Hornbeam stood up again. "I believe you are a lawyer, Mr. Keithley, so you must know that combination, or conspiracy, is notoriously hard to prove. This clause is essential to the working of the bill. The accused men must provide the evidence themselves—otherwise no prosecution would ever succeed."

"Thank you for pointing that out, Mr. Hornbeam. I will repeat your argument, for it is very important. My friends, Mr. Hornbeam correctly states that it is difficult to prove conspiracy unless the accused are made to testify against themselves. And that is why the clause is essential. Perhaps, my friends, that is also why this clause applies *only to workingmen and not to their masters!*"

They roared their indignation.

Sal realized that Hornbeam had never come up against someone of Keithley's caliber. This was a man with formidable skill in debate—he was better even than Spade, who was the best in Kingsbridge. Hornbeam normally got his way by intimidation, not argument. Today he was outclassed.

Hornbeam said desperately: "There's provision for appeal."

"Thank you, Mr. Hornbeam. You are making my speech for me. Mr. Hornbeam reminds me that a worker convicted under this law can appeal against his conviction. That's fair, isn't it? All he needs to do is *to pay twenty pounds.*"

The crowd burst out laughing. No mill worker had ever held twenty pounds in their hands.

"If by some mischance that worker does not happen to have twenty pounds put by . . ." Now the laughter had a jeering quality, and Hornbeam reddened. He was being humiliated publicly.

"Perhaps that worker could get a group of supporters together to try to raise the twenty pounds. It's a lot of money, but they might manage it—except that by doing that *they would be entering into a combination and therefore they would be breaking the law!*"

Someone shouted: "So they've got us coming and going!"

"One more thing," Keithley said. "Some of you may have paid money into a fund held by a trade union or similar group." Sal nodded. The union had collected money to support the strikers. Because the strike had ended quickly, there was some left.

Keithley said: "And what do you think the bill says?"

He paused dramatically. "The government will take that money!"

"Bloody thieves!" someone shouted.

Hornbeam stood up, left his place, and walked toward the exit.

Keithley pointed at him and said: "That is Mr. Hornbeam's idea of justice."

Hornbeam's face was now flaming red.

As Hornbeam disappeared through the door, Keithley said: "It also seems to be the prime minister's idea of justice. But it is not my idea of justice, and I suspect it is not yours."

Shouts of agreement came from the audience.

"If it is not your idea of justice, you may like to sign the petition." Keithley pointed to Elsie at the side of the room. "Mrs. Mackintosh has paper and ink. Please write your name, or make a cross and allow Mrs. Mackintosh to write your name." People began to stand up and make their way to Elsie's table. Keithley raised his voice. "Tomorrow I will carry your petition to London and do my utmost to persuade Parliament to take notice of it."

The line that formed at Elsie's table already included more than half the audience.

Sal was deeply satisfied. The legislation had been explained vividly. No one was in any doubt about its vicious intent.

Frank Fishwick stood up to speak. "As mayor of Kingsbridge, I would like to thank Mr. Keithley," he began.

No one was listening, and Mayor Fishwick gave up.

Spade was pleased. The government had tried to slip the new law through without the people noticing, but they had failed. Keithley had made the danger crystal clear and the bill would not pass without trouble.

While hundreds of hands were patiently queueing to

sign, Keithley said to Spade: "Would you be able to come to London with me tomorrow?"

Spade was surprised, but after a moment's thought he said: "Yes. Not for long, but I could go."

"It may be useful to have a Kingsbridge man on hand in case a parliamentary committee should wish to take evidence straight, as it were, from the horse's mouth."

"Very well."

Charles Midwinter approached, and Spade introduced him. "Pastor Midwinter is treasurer of the union formed by Hornbeam's weavers," he explained.

They shook hands, and Charles said: "A question, if I may, Mr. Keithley?"

"Of course."

"I'm holding ten pounds belonging to the union—all donated by sympathetic Kingsbridge folk. Is there anything I can do to keep it out of the hands of the government?"

"Yes," said Keithley. "Form a friendly society."

Friendly societies were popular. A group of people each put in a small weekly subscription, and when one of them was sick or unemployed the club paid out a modest living allowance. There were hundreds of such societies in England, perhaps thousands. The authorities encouraged them, for they supported people who might otherwise apply for parish relief.

Keithley said: "Make all the union members also members of the friendly society, then transfer the union's money to the society. Then the union has no money for the government to grab."

Midwinter smiled. "Very shrewd."

Keithley added: "Also, a friendly society may discreetly perform many of the functions of a trade union. For example, the society might hold discussions with the masters about new machinery, on the grounds that it affects the society's outgoings."

Spade liked that idea, but he saw a snag. "What if we succeed, and the Combination Bill fails?"

"Then just tear up the document transferring the money."

"Thank you, Mr. Keithley," said Midwinter.

Spade said: "How useful it is to have a lawyer on hand."

Spade was friendly with one of his best customers in London, Edward Barney, a young cloth merchant. Spade had brought with him a trunk full of samples, so as to justify the expense of the trip by making some sales. He visited Edward's warehouse in Spitalfields, where costly specialist fabrics such as watered silks, velvets, cashmeres, and unusual blends were displayed at the front near the door, and bales of everyday serge and linsey-woolsey stood on racks at the back.

Edward invited Spade to stay at the apartment over the warehouse. Spade accepted eagerly: he disliked lodging in taverns, which were never very comfortable or clean.

The Workmen's Combination Bill made no progress in Parliament for a week. While Spade was waiting he called on all his regular customers in London. Business seemed to be recovering: exports to America were making up for the fall in European trade.

When he ran out of customers to visit he talked to Edward's father, Sid. Although only forty-five, Sid had retired from the business with arthritis, and sat all day amid cushions piled under his twisted limbs. He liked talking to someone who could take his mind off his discomfort.

Spade told him all about the Combination Act and Kingsbridge's reaction to it.

"I knew a lad called Hornbeam," Sid said. "Joey Hornbeam. He was an orphan. We were all very poor, but I raised myself up. So did Joey."

Spade was curious to know more about the background of Kingsbridge's richest businessman. "How did he do it?"

"Same way I did, though in a different firm: started out sweeping the floor, became a messenger, kept his eyes open and his wits about him, learned everything there was to know about the cloth business, and waited for an opportunity. There our paths diverged. I married my boss's daughter. Dear Eth gave me Edward and four daughters before she died, rest her soul."

"And Hornbeam?"

"He started his own firm."

"Where did he get the money?"

"No one was sure. After a while he sold up and left London. Now I know where he went: Kingsbridge."

"Was he some kind of swindler?"

"Probably. I wouldn't hold it against him. He came from St. Giles, a neighborhood where there's no law, no right or wrong."

Spade nodded. "What was he like, back then?"

"He was hard," Sid said. "Hard as nails."

"He still is," said Spade.

The House of Lords met in the medieval Queen's Hall within the Palace of Westminster, and had done so—Keithley informed Spade—since before Guy Fawkes attempted to blow the place up with gunpowder. Visitors could enter the room but had to remain behind a railing, called the bar. Spade stood with his elbows on the bar while the lords debated the Combination Bill. He had never before seen more than one or two aristocrats in a room: here there were dozens, plus bishops. He was naturally interested in their clothes, which were made of good cloth and well cut. Their speeches were not so impressive. Their sentences were unnecessarily complicated, and he had to simplify them in his mind before he could grasp the arguments. Perhaps that was how the upper classes liked to talk.

Several people stood up in favor of the bill, saying that "unlawful" combination between workers was becoming more common and threatened serious mischief. "Claptrap," said Spade under his breath. There were not enough unions. Millions of hands had no protection from the rapacity of masters.

What the House of Lords really feared, Spade had no doubt, was a revolution like the one in France.

Keithley spoke in a familiar way to a man standing, like Spade, with his elbows on the bar. After a short conversation he returned to Spade's side and said: "Lord Holland should be speaking next but one." Holland was the only peer expected to speak against the bill.

"Who was that man you talked to?"

"A newspaper reporter. They know everything."

Spade studied the man. "Where's his notebook?"

"Forbidden," said Keithley. "Taking notes is against the rules of the house."

"So he has to remember everything."

"As much as he can. If ever you hear a peer or an MP complaining about inaccurate newspapers, ask them why they won't let reporters take notes."

"Seems foolish."

"This place has far too many foolish rules."

Once again Spade felt the urge to become a member of Parliament and campaign for reform.

Keithley pointed out Lord Holland, a handsome man in his midtwenties with thick black eyebrows and curly black hair just beginning to recede at the temples. Although he owned slaves in Jamaica, he was in other respects liberal. "Married to a divorced woman," Keithley murmured disapprovingly; Spade, being the lover of a married woman, could not share his disapprobation.

A few minutes later Holland was on his feet, and he spoke with passion. "The bill is unjust in principle and mischievous in tendency," he said.

Good start, Spade thought.

"The object of the bill is to prevent combinations among workmen; but its great, and peculiar, feature is that it changes trial by jury to summary jurisdiction. We must ask whether the bill, if likely to destroy combinations, is also likely to be productive of consequences equally dangerous to society."

This was all a bit abstract, to Spade; too distant from the everyday lives of the people at whom the bill was targeted.

"The two parties do not meet on equal terms; the inequality is in favor of the masters. They have the advantage of their workmen, by being able to hold out longest; they have better opportunities of prejudicing mankind in their favor; they are smaller in number, and consequently better able to concentrate and combine their strength—and to defeat detection."

Holland used a lengthy and confusing comparison with gamekeepers and poachers to illustrate the simple point that masters and hands had opposing interests, and therefore justices who were also manufacturers could not possibly be objective as judges in trials of their workers, or their friends' workers. "It is always in the interest of the master to impute a conspiracy to his workmen, even if they have a perfectly fair case for a raise in wages."

"Bloody right," Spade said under his breath.

Holland pointed out that the bill cast its net too wide. "A person might be prosecuted as concerned in a combination for merely giving friendly and well-intended advice!"

He finished by proposing a delay of three months so that the bill could be given better consideration.

No one supported him. The proposers of the bill did

not trouble to reply to his speech. His suggestion of a delay was rejected.

No petitions were considered.

The bill was then put to a vote. So few men shouted "No" that a count was unnecessary.

Two days later the bill was approved by the king and became law.

CHAPTER 23

Elsie wondered why her mother looked anxious. They were at breakfast in the palace. Arabella had a slice of toast on her plate that she had buttered but was not eating. There was a little frown between her red-brown eyebrows. Otherwise she looked fine. She had put on weight lately, but she seemed to have a glow of health. What was bothering her?

The bishop was tucking into sausages and reading *The Times.* "An Anglo-Russian force has invaded the Netherlands," he said. He liked to tell his wife and daughter what was happening in the world. "That part of the Netherlands was conquered by the French, who decided to call it the Batavian Republic."

Elsie had the *Kingsbridge Gazette* in front of her. "It says here that the 107th Foot—that's the Kingsbridge regiment—is part of that force. Some of my former Sunday school pupils are in the regiment. I hope they'll be all right."

Arabella said: "Freddie Caines must be there."

The bishop said: "Who is Freddie Caines?"

"Oh . . . he used to be in the militia here. I don't remember how I met him. A sweet boy."

Elsie said: "I remember. He's Spade's brother-in-law."

Arabella said: "I had forgotten that."

It was a fine September morning, and the sun was shining through the windows of the breakfast room. Kenelm stood up and said: "Please excuse me. A carpenter is due to install a new door in the north porch—the old one has rotted away—and I need to make sure he puts it in the right place." He left.

Elsie had already spent two hours in the nursery, washing and dressing Stevie—now two years old—with the help of the nurse. Later today she was giving a tea party for supporters of her school, who had stood by her during the strike. She was about to excuse herself when her mother said: "I have some rather surprising news."

Elsie sat down again and said: "That's exciting."

The bishop was not excited. "What news?" he said indifferently.

Arabella said: "I'm expecting a baby."

Elsie stared at her mother in astonishment. She was forty-five! And the bishop was seventeen years older at sixty-two. He was also overweight and far from agile. Furthermore, Elsie had not seen her father touch her mother affectionately for many years. She almost said *How did that happen?* But she stopped herself in time and said: "When?"

"December, I think," said Arabella.

The bishop was stunned. He said: "But, my dear . . ."

"You must remember. It was around Easter."

He said: "This year Easter Sunday was the twenty-fourth day of March." He seemed glad to have a mundane piece of information to cling to while this earthquake was shaking his world.

Arabella said: "I remember it well. You were full of the joys of spring."

He was embarrassed. "Not in front of others, please!"

"Oh, don't be silly, Elsie's a married woman."

"All the same . . ."

"You enjoyed a particularly fine port that evening."

"Oh!" He seemed to remember.

"You did seem a bit surprised to wake up and find me in your bed, I recall."

"Was that as long ago as Easter?"

"Yes, I think so," said Arabella, but Elsie saw a look of anxiety in her mother's golden eyes, and she knew then that something was wrong. Arabella was acting a part. She might well have been happy to be pregnant, but she was terribly worried about something. What, though? It made no sense.

The bishop's attitude was also unexpected. Why was he not delighted? A child, at his age! Men were usually proud of their ability to sire children. Kingsbridge people would soon be nudging one another in the cathedral and whispering *There's life in the old dog yet*.

An astonishing thought crossed Elsie's mind: was it possible that the bishop thought the child was not his?

The notion seemed laughable. Women of Arabella's age did not commit adultery. At least, Elsie did not think so. Didn't they lose interest in all that sort of thing? Elsie did not really know anything about it.

And suddenly she remembered a conversation with Belinda Goodnight, the town gossip. "What's this I hear about your mother?" Belinda had said to Elsie in the cathedral one Sunday. "She seems to have become awfully friendly with Spade."

Elsie had burst out laughing. "My mother?" she had said. "Don't be silly."

"Someone told me she's always in his sister's shop."

"Like every fashionable woman in Kingsbridge."

"Oh, well, I'm sure you're right," Belinda had said.

Elsie had been sure she was right, until now.

Was this why Arabella had been anxious about revealing something that ought to have been joyful news? If the bishop believed her to have been unfaithful, his wrath would be monstrous. He had a vengeful streak that was quite frightening. He had once locked Elsie in her room and fed her on bread and water for a week, for some offense that she had now forgotten. Her mother had cried, but that had had no effect on the bishop's obduracy.

She looked hard at her father now, trying to read his mind. He had been startled at first, then embarrassed. Now, she thought, he was puzzled. She guessed he found it hard to believe that he had had sexual intercourse for the first time in many years and then forgotten about it. On the other hand, he must have been well aware that he occasionally drank more port than was wise, and everyone knew that caused a man to forget what he had done.

And he admitted he remembered the morning after. They had woken up in bed together. Did that not settle the matter? Not quite, she realized. A woman who had been made pregnant by her lover might sleep with her husband to persuade him that the child was his. Could Arabella have been so devious? she wondered. My mother?

A desperate woman might do a lot of things.

Sal was pleased with the way things were going. Although the union had been forced to close down by the Combination Act, the friendly society had taken its place, and had become citywide. Representatives from the mills now collected weekly subscriptions to "the friendly," and they met periodically to discuss the affairs of the society and related topics. Already two clothiers introducing new machinery had found it suited them to approach the representative of the friendly to discuss the changes in advance.

The Irish workers had settled into Kingsbridge, and no one could remember why there had ever been fights. They patronized two or three waterfront taverns, which had become known as Irish pubs and were glad of the business. Colin Hennessy, the Irishman Kit had met the day they arrived, was the representative of the friendly at Piggery Mill.

One night in October Colin appeared in the Bell, where Sal was sitting with Jarge and Spade. Sal liked Colin. He was her kind of man: big and strong and unafraid. Spade bought him a tankard of ale. He took a long draft, wiped his mouth with his sleeve, and told them why he had sought them out. "Hornbeam has bought a new machine, a giant scribbling engine."

Sal frowned. "This is the first we've heard of it."

"I found out only today. They were making space for it to arrive tomorrow."

"So he hasn't discussed it with the hands."

"Not at all."

Sal looked at Spade. "He's ignoring the agreement."

Jarge said: "We'll have to go back on strike."

Jarge was a lot like Hornbeam, Sal reflected; ever in favor of the most aggressive response. Men like that believed that belligerence would always win the day, despite all evidence to the contrary.

Spade said: "You might be right, Jarge, but first we need to talk to Hornbeam and find out what's on his mind. Why has he done this? It's hard to see what he might gain, other than a lot of trouble."

Jarge said: "He won't tell you the truth."

"But you can learn something just by studying which lies a person chooses to tell."

Jarge backed down. "That's true, I suppose."

Spade said: "Sal, you and I should go and see Hornbeam, as we're in the team assigned to monitor compliance. And we should take Colin with us because he can testify that Hornbeam has broken the agreement."

Sal said: "Agreed."

"When shall we go?"

"Now," said Sal. "I can't spare the time out of the working day."

Colin looked a bit startled, but he said: "All right, then," and emptied his tankard.

They left Jarge and walked to the select neighborhood north of High Street. Hornbeam's front door was opened by a footman who looked disdainfully at them, then recognized Spade. "Good evening, Mr. Shoveller," he said warily.

Spade said: "Hello, Simpson. Please tell him I'd be grateful for a few minutes of his time on a matter of considerable importance."

"Very good, sir. Please step into the hall while I find out whether Alderman Hornbeam is at home."

They went inside. Sal found the hall dark and depressing. There was a fireplace with no fire, and a tall clock that ticked importantly. In the portrait over the fireplace, Hornbeam glared malevolently at anyone who dared to enter his home. What was the point of a great big house if you lived without light and warmth? Sometimes rich people really did not know how to spend their money.

Simpson came back and showed them into a rather small room that appeared to be Hornbeam's study or office. It was as unwelcoming as the hall. Hornbeam was behind a big desk, dressed in a coat of a rich dark-brown cloth. He said curtly: "What is it, Shoveller?"

Spade was not willing to dispense with the courtesies. "Good evening, Alderman," he said.

Hornbeam did not ask them to sit down. He looked hard at Colin, then returned his gaze to Spade. "What's that man doing here?"

Spade would not let Hornbeam steer the conversation. Ignoring the question, he said: "You've bought a new scribbling engine."

"What's that got to do with you?"

"Mrs. Box and I are among those tasked with monitoring compliance with the agreement that ended the strike caused by your steam looms."

Hornbeam bristled. "Caused by interference from outsiders."

Spade continued to ignore Hornbeam's quarrelsome interruptions. "We're hoping to avoid another strike."

Hornbeam laughed scornfully. "Then don't call one!"

Spade did not respond to that. "You'll remember, Hornbeam, that the clothiers collectively agreed to consult the hands when introducing important new machinery, to avoid the unrest that is so often caused by unheralded change."

"What do you want from me?"

"We want you to inform your hands about the new machine, tell them how many people will work on it and how many will be displaced by it, and discuss the consequences."

"You shall have my answer tomorrow."

There was a silence. Sal realized that was intended to be the end of the meeting. After an awkward pause, the three visitors left the room.

Outside the house, Spade said: "That wasn't as bad as I expected."

Colin said: "What? He was as mean as a cat! He looked as if he would cheerfully hang us all."

"Yes, and by the end I was expecting a flat refusal—but then he told us to wait until tomorrow. That suggests he's going to think it over. Which is more promising."

"I don't know," said Sal. "I think he's got something up his sleeve."

Sal was dreaming that Colin Hennessy was making love to her, his black hair falling forward over his face as he gasped with pleasure, when she was awakened by a banging on the house door. She felt guilty when she looked at her husband next to her. What a good thing others could not know what you dreamed about.

She thought the banging was the knocker-up, who ran through the streets waking mill hands around four o'clock in the morning. But the sound was repeated, as if someone wanted to come in.

Jarge went to the door in his underwear, and she heard him say: "What bloody time is it?"

Then a voice said: "Now don't you give me any trouble, Jarge Box. It's your wife I want, not you."

It sounded like Sheriff Doye, Sal thought, and she was struck with fear. Doye himself did not frighten her, but he represented the arbitrary power of ruthless men such as Hornbeam. She was frightened of Hornbeam.

She got out of bed and pulled her dress over her head.

She stepped into her shoes and splashed water on her face. Then she went to the door.

Doye was with the constable, Reg Davidson. Sal said: "What the hell do you two want with me?"

"You got to come with us," said Doye.

"I've done nothing wrong."

"You're accused of combination."

"But the union has been shut down."

"I don't know anything about that."

"Who has accused me?"

"Alderman Hornbeam."

She felt a shiver of dread. So this was what Hornbeam had meant when he said *You shall have my answer tomorrow.* "This is ridiculous," she said, but it was not ridiculous, it was scary.

She put on her coat and went out.

Doye and Davidson took her through cold, dark streets to the town center. She thought with horror of the possible punishments she faced: flogging, the stocks, prison, or hard labor. Women sentenced to hard labor were made to do work called hemp beating: for twelve hours a day they used sledgehammers to pound soaked hemp, separating the fibers from the woody core so that they could be turned into rope. It was backbreaking work. But she did not see how she could possibly be found guilty.

She assumed they were going to Hornbeam's house, but to her surprise she was led to Will Riddick's mansion. "What are we doing here?" she said.

"Squire Riddick is a justice," said Doye.

Hornbeam was dangerous and Riddick was his puppet. What were they up to? This was bad.

The hall of Riddick's house smelled of tobacco ash and spilled wine. A mastiff was chained up in a corner, and barked at them. Sal was surprised to see Colin Hennessy there, sitting on a bench, and she remembered her dream with embarrassment. Colin was being guarded by a constable, Ben Crocket.

Sal said to Colin: "This follows from our visit to Hornbeam last night."

"I thought we were doing what the clothiers agreed to," said Colin.

"We were." Sal was puzzled as well as afraid. She turned to Doye. "Obviously Hornbeam told you to arrest us."

"He's the chairman of justices."

That was true. This was not Doye's fault. He was just a tool.

Sal sat beside Colin on the bench. "What now, then?" she asked Doye.

"We wait."

It was a long wait.

The house came awake gradually. A grumpy footman cleaned the fireplace and built a new fire but did not light it. Alf Nash delivered milk and cream to the front door. Daylight filtered through a dirty window into the hall, along with the sounds of the city: horses' hooves, cartwheels on cobblestones, and the morning greetings of men and women emerging from their houses and heading for work.

Sal smelled bacon frying, and realized she had had nothing to eat or drink today. But no one offered refreshment, even to the sheriff.

Just as a clock somewhere in the house was striking ten, Hornbeam appeared. The grumpy footman let him in. He said nothing to those in the hall, but followed the footman upstairs.

However, a few minutes later the footman came to the top of the stairs and said: "All right, come on."

Riddick's footman was an oaf. Sal wondered whether footmen mirrored their masters, as dogs did.

They climbed the stairs and were shown into a large drawing room. It had not yet been cleared of the debris of last night's revels, and there were unwashed wineglasses and coffee cups all around. Sal reflected that Riddick's wife, Hornbeam's daughter, Deborah, seemed not to have changed Riddick's way of life much.

Riddick himself sat in an upright chair, wearing civilian clothes and a wig, though looking as if he had not yet recovered from the previous evening's carousing. Hornbeam was on a sofa, straight-backed and stern. Between the two of them a man Sal did not know sat at a small table with paper and ink, presumably a clerk.

Riddick said: "Sheriff Doye, give the names of the accused and the charge."

Doye said: "Colin Hennessy and Sarah Box, both mill hands of Kingsbridge, are accused by Alderman Hornbeam of combination."

The clerk wrote quickly with a quill pen.

Sal realized this was being carefully staged to look like a fair trial.

Riddick said: "What do the accused say to the charge?"

Colin said: "Not guilty."

Sal said: "There is no combination. The union has been dissolved. We were carrying out the wishes of the clothiers, not conspiring against them."

Riddick said: "Alderman Hornbeam, what are the facts?"

Hornbeam spoke in a flatly emotionless tone. "Box and Hennessy came to my house yesterday at about eight o'clock in the evening. They said I had bought a large new scribbling machine and I needed the permission of my hands to install it. They threatened a strike if refused."

Riddick said: "Well, it looks to me as if they combined to interfere with trade in a way that clearly violates the Combination Act."

Sal said: "No, it doesn't."

"Sal Box, I knew you in Badford, when you were Sal Clitheroe, and you were a troublemaker then."

"And you were a violent drunk. But we aren't in Badford now, we're in Kingsbridge, and the clothiers of Kingsbridge have an agreement with the hands. The agreement ended the strike and Hornbeam's mills reopened. But he won't keep to the agreement. He is like a man who prays for the Lord's help but afterward won't go to church. Last night, Colin and I told him he was breaking the agreement, and I said that keeping the agreement was the best way to avoid strikes. That's not a threat, that's a fact, and there's no law against facts."

"So you admit that you combined, and you admit that you tried to interfere with Alderman Hornbeam's business."

"When you tell a fool that he's doing something harmful to himself, is that interference?"

Will did not answer that question. "I find you both guilty," he said. "And I sentence you to two months' hard labor."

CHAPTER 24

Dear Spade,

Well, here I am in the Netherlands, and I have had my first experience of battle, and I am still alive and not badly wounded. The rest of the news is all bad.

We mustered in Canterbury, and I must say their cathedral is even bigger than ours in Kingsbridge. A lot of the lads had joined up from the militia like me, so we were mostly "green" as they say, meaning we had not done any real fighting. Well, that did not last long.

We landed at a place called Callantsoog, funny names they have here, and right away the enemy came at us over the sand dunes. Well, I was so scared I would have ran away but behind me was only the sea so I had to stand and fight. Anyway our ships fired all their cannons over our heads and into the enemy and it was them as ran away.

They left us some nice empty fortresses that we moved into, but not for many days. Soon we had a fight at Krabbendam where the French general was a man called Marie Anne, you see what I mean about names, anyhow he can't have been much good because we won.

Then the duke of York arrived with some reinforcements and we thought we were sitting pretty. We marched to a city called Hoorn and took it but soon we left it and went back to where we had started, this kind of thing happens a lot in the army, good thing you don't run your business that way Spade ha ha.

We had a bad time marching along a narrow beach where we had no fresh water, we were fired on by the French, not sure whether we would die of thirst or bullets. My pal Gus was shot in the head and died, you make friends fast in the army but you can lose them just as quick. Then it got dark, and we were told the enemy had retreated, I don't know what we did to scare them off!

Disaster struck at the town of Castricum. It was pissing with rain but that was not our biggest problem unfortunately. The French attacked with bayonets which was very bloody and we ran. We were chased by the French cavalry. I was bleeding from a cut on my arm and would certainly have been killed but for some light dragoons who sprang up from a sort of valley in the dunes and sent the Frenchies back.

We lost a lot of men in that battle and the duke decided to withdraw so there was a truce and he has gone back to London. I think this means we have been defeated.

We are on the coast waiting for ships to take us away. No one knows where we will be going, but I'm hoping for home so perhaps you will soon be able to drink a tankard in the Bell Inn with me—

Your affectionate brother-in-law Freddie Caines.

Hornbeam watched the giant scribbling engine at work. It was a marvel. Driven by steam, it never took a break, never went to the privy, never fell ill. It never got tired.

He was not bothered by the deafening clatter of machinery: it was making money for him. He did not even mind the smell of the hands, who did not own bathtubs and would not know what to do with one. It was all money.

The new mill had doubled his capacity. On his own, he could now supply all the cloth required by the Shiring Militia, and handle plenty of other business as well.

He just hoped that peace would not break out.

This pleasant moment of contemplation came to an end with the sudden appearance of Will Riddick, in uniform, looking angry. "Damn it, Hornbeam," he said, shouting over the noise. "I've been moved."

"What?"

"I've been put in charge of training."

"Come outside."

They went down the stairs and out into the chill November air. Children too young to work were playing in the mud around the mill. There was a smell of coal smoke from the boilers. "That's better," said Hornbeam. "Why do you not want to be in charge of training?"

"Because I'm no longer involved in purchasing."

"Oh." That was a problem. Both Hornbeam and Riddick had profited from Riddick's position as chief buyer for the militia. They would lose a lot of money if he was moved from the post. "What brought this on?"

"The duke of York."

"What's he got to do with anything?"

"He's in charge of the British Army now."

Hornbeam remembered reading something in *The Times*. "The French just defeated him in the Netherlands."

"Yes, but people say he's a better manager than fighter. At any rate, Northwood met him in London and is now full of enthusiasm for new ways of doing things:

warm coats for all troops, more rifles, less flogging, and—here's the thing—better purchasing."

"And by 'better,' the duke means . . ."

"He's made inquiries and discovered that too many quartermasters buy everything from their friends and family."

"Oh, dear."

"Northwood said to me: 'Of course, I'm sure you don't favor your family, Riddick, but all the same it looks bad when you buy from your father-in-law.' Sarcastic swine."

"And who's in charge of purchasing now?"

"Archie Donaldson. He's been promoted to major."

"Do I know him?"

"He's Northwood's right-hand man. Sits in the office with him half the day."

"What does he look like?"

"Young, fresh-faced . . ."

"I remember."

"He's a Methodist."

"That makes it worse." Hornbeam was thoughtful for a minute. Then he said: "Walk with me back into town."

He wrestled with the problem as they went through the new streets of mill hands' houses and along one side of a cabbage field to the bridge. People were conscripted into the militia, but there remained an element of choice: you could pay someone to take your place. Donaldson had not done so. That meant that he was either too poor to pay a substitute or too high-minded to shirk his patriotic duty. If he was poor he could be bribed. If he was high-minded that might not be possible. Although every man had his price—didn't he?

"You should congratulate Donaldson," Hornbeam said as they walked up the cobbles of Main Street.

Riddick was indignant. "Congratulate the wretch?"

"Yes. Say that you've had a good run and it's time for someone else to take over. Tell him how glad you are that he's got the job."

"But that's completely untrue."
"When has truth ever bothered you?"
"Huh."

They drew level with Drummond's Fine Wines, and Hornbeam steered Riddick inside. Alan Drummond was behind the counter, a balding man with a red nose. After the usual courtesies Hornbeam said: "Bring me pen and ink and a sheet of good letter paper, Drummond, would you?"

The man obliged.

"Send a dozen bottles of a good midpriced port to Major Donaldson of the militia, and charge it to my account."

"Donaldson?"

Riddick said: "He lives in West Street."

Hornbeam wrote: "Congratulations on your promotion. With the compliments of Joseph Hornbeam."

Riddick read it over his shoulder and said: "Very clever."

Hornbeam folded the sheet and handed it to Drummond, saying: "Send this note with it."

"Very good, Mr. Hornbeam."

They left the shop.

"I'll do as you suggest, and butter him up," said Riddick. "We'll get him on our side."

"I hope so," said Hornbeam.

The following morning the wine was dumped on Hornbeam's doorstep with a note:

"Thank you for your kind congratulations, which are much appreciated. I regret I cannot accept your gift. Archibald Donaldson (Major)."

Elsie took a pound of bacon, a small wheel of cheese, and a dish of fresh butter from the palace kitchen. By arrangement she met Spade in the market square. He was carrying a ham. They walked up Main Street and into the poorer northwest quarter of Kingsbridge, heading for the home of Sal Box, who was in prison doing hard labor. They wanted to make sure her family were all right.

"I can't believe I didn't see it coming," Spade said. "It just never occurred to me that Hornbeam would use the Combination Act in that way."

"It seems almost too outrageous even for him."

"Exactly. But I should have known better. And Sal's suffering because of my lapse."

"Don't torture yourself. You can't think of everything."

It was half past seven on a Monday evening. They found Jarge and the children at the table eating oatmeal. "Don't let me interrupt your supper," Elsie said, putting her gifts on the sideboard. "I came to see how you're getting on, but you seem fine."

"We miss Sal, but we're managing," said Jarge. "What you've brought us is much appreciated, though, Mrs. Mackintosh."

Sue said: "I cooked supper. I put dripping in the gruel to make it taste better." She was fourteen, the same age as Kit. She was growing up before him, and had the hint of a womanly figure.

"They're good children," said Jarge. "I wake them in the morning and make sure they have something to eat before they go to work. We can have bacon for breakfast tomorrow, thanks to you. It's a long time since we've tasted bacon."

"I don't suppose you know how Sal is faring."

Jarge shook his head. "No way to find out. She's strong, but beating hemp is wicked hard work."

"I pray for her every night."

"Thank you."

"Will you go to bell-ringing practice tonight?"

"Yes, and I'd better make haste—they'll be waiting for me."

"Is there someone to keep an eye on Kit and Sue?"

"Our tenant, Mrs. Fairweather—she rents the attic. She's a widow, and her two children died in the food shortage four years ago."

"I remember."

"Not that they're any trouble. They'll go to bed after supper and sleep until morning."

It was hardly surprising, Elsie thought, after they had worked for fourteen hours. All the same, Jarge was taking good care of those two youngsters, neither of whom was his child: Kit was his stepson and Sue his niece. He was a good man at heart.

She and Spade left. As they walked back to the town center, Spade said: "I learned something about Hornbeam's past, last time I was in London. He was orphaned at a young age and had to make his own way in the world. He got a job with a cloth merchant as a messenger, then learned the trade and worked his way up."

"You'd think he'd have more feeling for the poor."

"Sometimes it works the opposite way. I think he's terrified of falling back into the poverty of his childhood. It's not rational, it's probably a feeling he can't shake. No amount of money will ever be enough to make him feel safe."

"Are you saying you feel sorry for him?"

Spade smiled. "No. At the end of the day, he's still a spiteful bastard."

They parted company in the market square. When Elsie entered the palace she felt immediately that something was going on. The house was strangely quiet. No one was talking, or clattering saucepans, or sweeping or scrubbing. Then she heard a cry from upstairs that sounded like a woman in pain.

Was her mother giving birth? It was only November—she had said December. But perhaps she had miscalculated.

Or she might have lied.

Elsie raced up the stairs and burst into Arabella's bedroom. Mason, the maid, was sitting on the edge of the bed holding a white towel. Arabella lay in bed, covered only by a sheet, her legs spread wide with her knees pointed up at the ceiling. Her face was red with effort and wet with tears or sweat or both. Mason wiped her cheeks tenderly with the towel and said: "Not long now, Mrs. Mackintosh."

Mason had been with Arabella when Elsie herself was born, she knew. She remembered Mason taking care of her when she was very small. She recalled her astonishment on discovering that Mason had another name—Linda. Mason had also helped at the birth of Elsie's own child, Stevie, and she would attend the delivery of the child Elsie was now carrying. Her presence was a comfort.

Arabella seemed to experience a moment of relief. "Hello, Elsie, I'm glad you're here," she said. "For the love of Christ don't tell me to push." Then another spasm gripped her, and she cried out. Elsie took her hand, and Arabella grasped it so hard that Elsie thought her bones would break. Mason passed Elsie the towel, and Elsie took it with her free hand and mopped her mother's face.

Mason lifted the sheet. "I can see the baby's head," she said. "It's almost over."

Except it's only just beginning, Elsie thought. Another human being is struggling to start the journey of life, heading for love and laughter and bloodshed and tears.

Arabella's grip eased and her face relaxed but she did not open her eyes. She said: "It's a good thing fucking is so great, otherwise women would never subject themselves to this."

Elsie was shocked to hear her mother talk that way.

Mason said apologetically: "Women say strange things in the pain of childbirth."

Then Arabella tensed again.

Mason, still looking under the sheet, said: "This could be the last one."

Arabella made a sound that was part grunt of effort, part scream of agony. Mason threw back the sheet and reached between Arabella's thighs. Elsie saw the baby's head emerge, and heard Arabella groan. Mason said: "There, little one, come to Auntie Mason, oh, what a dear beautiful little thing you are." The baby was covered in mucus and blood, with a cord still attaching it to its mother, and its face was set in a grimace of discomfort, but even so, Elsie agreed that it was beautiful.

"A boy," said Mason. She turned the baby over, easily holding him in her left hand, and smacked his bottom. He opened his mouth, took his first breath, and let out a howl of protest.

Elsie realized she had tears streaming down her cheeks.

Mason put the baby down on his back and went to the bedside table where there was a folded shawl, a pair of scissors, and two lengths of cotton. She tied two knots around the cord, then cut between the knots. She wrapped the baby in the shawl and handed him to Elsie.

Elsie took him carefully, holding his head up, and hugged him to herself. She was swamped by a feeling of love so powerful that it made her weak.

Arabella sat up in bed, and Elsie passed the baby to her. She pulled down the front of her nightdress and put him to her breast. His mouth found the nipple, his lips closed over it, and he began to suck.

"You have a son," said Elsie.

"Yes," said Arabella. "And you a brother."

Amos found it hard to understand what was happening in Paris. It seemed there had been some kind of coup on November 9, which was Brumaire 18 in the revolutionary calendar. General Bonaparte had invaded the French parliament with armed troops and appointed himself first consul of France. The English newspapers seemed not to know what *first consul* meant. The only thing certain was that events were being driven by Napoleon Bonaparte and no one else. He was the greatest general of his time and hugely popular with the French people. Perhaps he would end up as their king.

More important for Amos, the end of the war was not in sight. That meant continuing high taxes and scarce business.

When Amos had read the newspaper he went to militia headquarters in Willard House.

Viscount Northwood had done what Amos had suggested to Jane. Amos had not been confident that Jane would pass his suggestion on, or that Northwood would consider it. But Northwood had moved Will Riddick to a different post and put a Methodist in charge of purchasing, as Amos had recommended.

Amos wondered about that marriage. Northwood was obviously capable of desire—he had undoubtedly fallen madly in love with Jane, though it had not lasted. However, there were no rumors about another woman in Northwood's life—nor, for that matter, about Northwood and men. He never went to Culliver's brothel. Jane's rival was the army, it seemed. Running the militia consumed Northwood. It was all he really cared about.

The replacement of Riddick by Donaldson presented an opportunity to Amos, and to other Kingsbridge clothiers. The military's need for cloth was the only steady demand these days. Amos entered the headquarters building full of hope. Even a share of the militia's business could set his enterprise on a stable footing for the first time.

He went to the upstairs office formerly occupied by Riddick. He found Donaldson seated behind Will's old desk. A window was open, and the smell of tobacco ash and stale wine had gone. A small black Bible was placed rather ostentatiously on the desk.

Amos and Donaldson were not friends, but they knew each other from Methodist meetings. In discussions, Donaldson often put forward a dogmatic point of view based on scrupulously literal interpretation of scripture. Amos thought that was a bit juvenile.

Donaldson waved him to a chair.

"Congratulations on your promotion," Amos said. "I and many other people are delighted that Hornbeam no longer has a stranglehold on the supply of cloth to the militia."

Donaldson did not smile. "I don't want there to be any misunderstanding between us," he said severely. "I intend to act solely in the interest of His Majesty's militia."

"Of course—"

"You're quite right to suppose that I will not favor Alderman Hornbeam."

"Good."

"But please understand that I won't favor anyone else either, and that includes my fellow Methodists."

Donaldson was being unnecessarily emphatic. Amos had expected him to be scrupulous, but did not want him to go too far. He spoke with equal firmness. "But I'm sure you won't exclude Methodists, merely to avoid a superficial appearance of favoritism."

"Certainly not."

"Thank you."

"In fact, my orders from Colonel Northwood are to divide the business between Anglican and Methodist clothiers, rather than place it all with one manufacturer."

Amos could not ask for more. "That suits me perfectly," he said. He took a sealed letter from inside his coat and put it on the desk. "So here's my bid."

"Thank you. I will treat it as I would anyone else's."

"That's exactly what I would expect from a Methodist," said Amos, and he took his leave.

Arabella's baby was christened by the bishop in the cathedral on a cold winter morning.

Elsie studied her father's face. He showed no emotion.

She was not sure how he felt about his second child. Many men were a bit awkward around babies, especially men of high dignity such as the bishop. All the same it was noticeable that he had never held or kissed the baby boy, or even smiled at him. Perhaps he was embarrassed about fathering a child so late in life. Or perhaps he was not sure he was the boy's father. Anyway, he carried out the ceremony solemnly but lugubriously.

No one knew what name he would give the child. He had refused to discuss it, even with his wife. Arabella had told him she liked David, but he had not said yes or no.

Baptism was normally a family ceremony, but a bishop's child was special, and a crowd gathered around the ancient stone font in the north aisle of the nave, all wearing their warmest winter coats. The most important people in Kingsbridge were there, including Viscount Northwood, Mayor Fishwick, Alderman Hornbeam, and most of the senior clergy. Many brought costly silver christening gifts: mugs, spoons, a rattle.

Elsie stood next to Kenelm, with two-year-old Stevie in her arms. On her other side was Amos, and when their shoulders touched she felt the old familiar ache of longing.

At the back of the group were Spade, his sister Kate, and Kate's partner, Becca—the three people, thought Elsie, who were mainly responsible for Arabella's being so well-dressed.

The mood was subdued, a bit wary: no one was sure how heartily to congratulate the bishop, since he himself showed little sign of a father's joy and pride.

The baby had a lot of dark hair. He wore a white christening gown lavishly trimmed with lace, the garment that Elsie herself had been christened in, as had her son, Stevie. After today it would be carefully washed and pressed and folded away in a muslin bag for another child. That would surely be Elsie's next, due in the New Year. She had told only a few people, not wanting to steal the limelight from her mother; but her pregnancy would soon be evident, even under discreetly draped clothing.

Kenelm was relating to Stevie more, Elsie mused during the prayers. He actually spoke to the little boy sometimes. Now that Stevie could walk and talk, Kenelm made efforts to train him. "Don't put your finger in your nose, boy," he would say. And he gave him information. "That horse isn't brown, it's bay, look at its black legs and tail." She reminded herself that people had different ways of showing love.

The ceremony was not long. At the end, while Arabella held the baby, the bishop poured a trickle of water on the tiny head. The baby cried immediately and loudly—the water was cold. The bishop said: "In the name of the Father, the Son, and the Holy Spirit, I baptize you . . . Absalom."

There were half-muffled grunts of surprise and gasps of shock at the name. It was a strange choice. As he said the final amen, Arabella glared at him and said: "Absalom?"

"The father of peace," said the bishop.

Well, yes, Elsie thought; in Hebrew *Absalom* meant "father of peace"—but that was not what he was known for. One of the sons of King David, Absalom had murdered his half brother, revolted against his father, declared himself king, and died after a battle with his father's army.

The name, Elsie realized, was a curse.

CHAPTER 25

Hornbeam's grandson, Little Joe, reminded him of someone. Joe was two and a half, tall and confident, and in that, he resembled his grandfather; but there was something else. Hornbeam did not coo over babies, as his wife and daughter did, but he studied the boy as the women fussed, and something in the babyish face tugged at Hornbeam's flinty heart. It was the eyes, he decided. The boy did not have Hornbeam's eyes, which were deep-set under formidable brows that shadowed his feelings. Joe's eyes were blue and candid. He might never dominate others by sheer force of character, as Hornbeam did, but he would get his way by charm. There was something familiar about those innocent eyes, but Hornbeam could not say why—until he realized, with a shock, that when he looked at Joe he saw his long-dead mother. She had had eyes like that. Hornbeam hastily pushed the thought out of his mind. He did not like to be reminded of his mother.

He put on his coat, left the house, and walked to Willard House, where he asked to see Major Donaldson.

Donaldson looked boyish but, Hornbeam reckoned, he must have brains, otherwise Northwood would not have had him as a right-hand man for so long. It would be wise not to underestimate him. Hornbeam noticed but did not comment on the Bible displayed on the desk. Some Methodists wore their religion like a badge. Hornbeam thought religion was all right as long as it was not taken too seriously. He would keep that belief to himself during this meeting.

He began by saying: "I've already sent you a written bid for your current cloth requirements, but I thought it would be a good idea to chat to you a bit."

Donaldson replied tersely: "Go on."

"Your military career has been impressive, and—if I may say so without condescension—you're clearly a very capable man. But you haven't any experience of the cloth trade, and you may perhaps find it helpful if I give you some hints."

"I should be most interested. Please sit down."

He took the chair in front of the desk. So far, so good.

He said: "In every business there are formal and informal ways of doing things."

Donaldson said warily: "What do you mean, Alderman?"

"There are the rules, and then there is the way everybody actually does things."

"Ah."

"For example, we put in bids to you, and you give the order to the bidder with the lowest price, in theory; but in practice that's not the whole story."

"Is it not?" The tone of Donaldson's voice gave no hint of how he felt.

Hornbeam was not sure he was getting his message across, but he pressed on. "In reality, we operate a special discount system."

"And what is that?"

"You accept my bid of, say, a hundred pounds, but I give you an invoice for one hundred and twenty. You pay me a hundred pounds, which leaves you with a surplus of twenty pounds which, being already accounted for in your records, can therefore be used by you for other purposes."

"Other purposes?"

"You may put the money aside for the widows and orphans of men killed in combat, for example. Or you could buy whiskey for the officers' mess. It forms a kind of discretionary fund, for worthwhile expenditure that perhaps should not actually appear in the accounts ledger. Of course you never have any need to tell me—or anyone else—how you have spent it."

"The accounts therefore become deceitful."

"You might look at it that way, or you might see it as a way of oiling the gears of the machine."

"I'm afraid I don't take that view, Mr. Hornbeam. I will not be involved in deceit."

Hornbeam made his face a mask. This was a major setback. He had feared it but had not really thought it would happen. Donaldson could make a fortune but he was not going to take the opportunity. It was incomprehensible.

Hornbeam immediately backtracked. "Of course, you must do as you think fit." The contract could still be won. "I will be happy to do business with you in any way you require. I hope my written bid finds favor."

"In fact it doesn't, Mr. Hornbeam. I've already reviewed the bids with Colonel Northwood and I'm afraid you have not won the contract."

Hornbeam felt as if he had been punched in the stomach. His mouth fell open. It took him a moment to recover, then he said: "But I've built a new mill to fulfill your requirements!"

"I wonder why you were so sure you'd get the contract."

"Who did you give it to? One of your fellow Methodists, I suppose!"

"I'm not obliged to tell you, but I have no reason not to. The contract was divided between the two best bids. One of the successful bidders is a Methodist—"

"I knew it!"

"—and the other a staunch Anglican."

"Who are they? Give me the names!"

"Please don't try to bully me, Mr. Hornbeam. I understand that you're disappointed, but you can't come to my office and insult me, you know."

Hornbeam controlled his rage. "Forgive me. But if you would kindly tell me who the successful bidders are, I should be grateful."

"The Anglican is Mrs. Bagshaw, and the Methodist is Amos Barrowfield."

"A woman and a jumped-up jackanapes!"

"By the way, neither of them mentioned the special discount system."

Hornbeam had been played for a fool. Donaldson had let him burble on, knowing that the issue was already decided, until Hornbeam revealed the system of bribery he had operated with Riddick. Did Donaldson—or Northwood—intend to prosecute Hornbeam? But there was no evidence. He could deny this conversation or say there had been a misunderstanding. No, there was little real danger of a court case. But he had lost the contract. He would struggle to keep his new mill busy. He would lose money.

He was ready to strangle Donaldson. Or Barrowfield. Or the widow Bagshaw. Preferably all three. He needed to kill someone, or break something. He was boiling over with fury and had no one to take it out on.

He stood up. Through gritted teeth he said: "Good day to you, Major."

"Good day, Alderman."

There was even a hint of sarcasm in the way Donaldson said *Alderman*.

Hornbeam left the room and stamped out of the building. People moved out of his way as he marched up the cobbled street, glaring at everyone and no one.

He had been defeated and humiliated.

And for once he had no fallback plan.

"Just fancy that!" said Elsie, reading the *Kingsbridge Gazette* at the breakfast table. "Mr. Hornbeam didn't get the contract for red cloth for militia uniforms."

Arabella said: "Who did?"

"Two people, it says here: Mrs. Cissy Bagshaw got half, and Mr. Amos Barrowfield the other half. And the expensive cloth for officers' uniforms will be supplied by Mr. David Shoveller."

The bishop looked up from his *Times*. "David Shoveller?"

"The one everybody calls Spade." As Elsie said this she caught her mother's eye. Arabella suddenly looked frightened.

The bishop said: "I had forgotten that his real name is David."

Elsie shrugged. "Most people don't know." Her father seemed unaccountably struck by this insignificant fact.

She looked again at her mother. Arabella's hand was shaking as she stirred sugar into her tea.

The bishop said: "Arabella, my dear, you like the name David, do you not?" Elsie was worried by the look in his eye.

Arabella said: "Many people like it."

"A Hebrew name, of course, but popular in Wales, where their patron is Saint David. They shorten it to Dai, though not when referring to the saint, naturally."

Elsie could tell that something dramatic was going on here, under the blanket of a mundane discussion, but she could not figure out the underlying issue. Who cared if Arabella liked the name David?

When the bishop spoke again there was a look of spite on his face. "In fact, I seem to remember that you wanted to call your son David."

Why did he say *your* son?

Arabella lifted her gaze and looked directly at him. Defiantly she said: "It would have been better than Absalom."

Elsie began to understand. The bishop thought he was not the father of Absalom: he had always been puzzled by the story of his drunken night last Easter. Arabella had wanted to call the boy David—which was Spade's real name. Belinda Goodnight had said that Arabella was surprisingly friendly with Spade.

The bishop thought Spade was the father of Absalom.

Spade? If Arabella had committed adultery, would it be with Spade?

The bishop seemed to have no doubts. He stood up, his eyes blazing. Pointing a finger at Arabella, he said: "You will be punished for this!" Then he left the room.

Arabella burst into tears.

Elsie sat beside her and put her arm around her, smelling her orange blossom perfume. "Is it true, Mother?" she said. "Is Spade the real father?"

"Of course!" said Arabella, sobbing. "The bishop couldn't possibly have done it and I was a fool to pretend. But what else could I do?"

Elsie almost said *But you must be ten years older than Spade* but she realized that would not be helpful. All the same she thought it, and more. Her mother was the bishop's wife, one of the leading ladies in Kingsbridge society, and the best-dressed woman in town: how could she be having an affair? An adulterous affair with a younger man? With a Methodist?

On the other hand, Elsie thought, he was charming and amusing, he was intelligent and well-informed, he was even handsome in a craggy way. He was well below Arabella on the social ladder, but that was the least of the rules she was breaking.

But where did they go to be together? Where did they do the thing that adulterers do? Suddenly Elsie remembered the changing rooms in Kate Shoveller's shop. She immediately felt sure that was the place. Those upstairs rooms had beds in them.

She was seeing her mother with new eyes.

The sobs died down. Elsie said: "Let me help you upstairs."

Arabella stood up. "No, thank you, my dear," she said. "There's nothing wrong with my legs. I'll just lie down quietly for a while."

Elsie went with her into the hall, then watched her go slowly up the stairs.

This was the day Sal was getting out of jail, Elsie remembered. She wanted to see Sal, to make sure she was all right. She could leave her mother now.

She put on her coat—made by Kate and Becca from cloth woven by Spade, she recalled. She went out into a rainy morning and walked briskly to the northwest quarter, heading for the Box family home. On the way she was assailed by an unwelcome image of her mother kissing Spade in a changing room. She pushed it out of her mind.

Sal was not all right. When Elsie walked in she was sitting in the kitchen with her elbows on the table. She was thin, tired, and dirty. Kit and Sue stood staring at her: both children had been shocked and silenced by the change in her appearance. There was a cup of ale in front of her but she was not drinking. She must be hungry, Elsie reasoned, but too exhausted to move.

Jarge said: "She's done in, Mrs. Mackintosh."

Elsie sat beside Sal. "You need to rest and eat to rebuild your strength," she said.

Sal spoke listlessly. "I'll rest today, but I must go to work tomorrow."

Elsie said: "Jarge, get some mutton from the butcher and make a fatty broth for her to drink." She took a sovereign from her purse and put it on the table. "And some bread and fresh butter. When she's got food inside her she'll sleep."

"You're very kind," said Jarge.

Elsie said to Sal: "It must have been brutal, doing hard labor."

"Hardest work I've ever done. Women faint from weakness, but they're whipped until they come round and stand up and start again."

"And the men in charge—how did they treat you?"

Sal's eyes flashed a warning to Elsie. It was a split-second look, and Jarge did not see it, but Elsie guessed its meaning: the jailers had abused the women. Sal did not want Jarge to know that. If he found out he would probably kill one of the jailers, and then he would be hanged.

Sal covered the brief silence. "They were hard taskmasters," she said.

Elsie took Sal's hand and squeezed it. Sal squeezed back briefly. It was women's code. They would keep the secret of the prison rape.

Elsie stood up. "Food and rest," she said. "You'll be your old self soon." She went to the door.

Jarge said: "You're an angel, Mrs. Mackintosh."

Elsie went out.

She walked back to the town center in the rain, reflecting grimly on the cruelty of human beings to one another, and how one gold coin could seem, to a poor man such as Jarge, to be a miracle wrought by an angel.

She continued to be worried about her mother. What was going on at home? What punishment did her father envisage? Would he lock Arabella up for a week with only bread and water, as he had Elsie?

When she returned to the palace, her mother was not in the morning room and her father was not in his study. She went to her mother's bedroom and found her sitting on the bed weeping bitterly. "What is it, Mother?" said Elsie. "What has he done now?"

Arabella seemed unable to reply.

A terrible thought crossed Elsie's mind. Surely her father would not harm the baby? She said: "Is Absalom all right?"

Arabella nodded.

"Thank God. But where is my father?"

Arabella managed: "Garden."

Elsie ran down the stairs and through the kitchen, where the servants were looking subdued and scared. She stepped out through the back door and looked around. She could not see her father but could hear voices. She crossed a lawn and passed under the basketwork arch that carried a hundred roses in summer but now, in winter, held only bundled twigs. Then she entered the rose garden.

She was shocked by the sight that greeted her.

The square of low rose trees in the middle had been dug up, and the ruined stalks now mingled with excavated earth. On the far side, the trellis had been ripped off the old wall and thrown to the ground, and the rose trees that had decorated it had been uprooted and tossed aside. A cold drizzle fell dismally on the turned clods. Two gardeners with spades were energetically leveling the area, supervised by the bishop, who had mud on his white silk stockings. He saw Elsie and grinned with a delight that seemed to her borderline manic. "Hello, daughter," he said.

She said incredulously: "What are you doing?"

"I thought we'd have a vegetable plot," he crowed. "Cook loves the idea!"

Elsie struggled not to cry. "My mother loves her rose garden," she said.

"Ah, well, we can't have everything we want, can we? Besides, she's going to be too busy looking after her new baby to do any gardening."

"You're a very cruel man."

The gardeners heard this and looked startled. Nobody criticized the bishop.

He said to her: "You should be careful what you say—especially if you want to continue to feed your Sunday school children at my expense."

"My school! How can you threaten that?"

He crossed the ground to where she stood, and lowered his voice so that no one else could hear. "I have taken from your mother something she loved, because she did the same to me."

"She never took anything from you!"

"She took what I valued most—my dignity."

That was true, Elsie realized. She was struck dumb by the revelation. What he was doing was cruel, that was undeniable; but now she understood why he was doing it.

He went on: "So don't speak disrespectfully to me in front of gardeners, or indeed anyone else, or I will teach you how it is to lose what you most prize."

With that he turned away from her and went back to the gardeners.

Spade was at his loom, setting it up for a complex striped fabric, when Kate appeared and said: "There's a surprise waiting for you over at the house." He stood up and, leaving Kate behind in his hurry, crossed the yard, entered the house, and ran up the stairs. When he entered the room Arabella was waiting for him, as he had expected—but not alone.

She was holding the baby.

He put his arms around them both, kissed Arabella's mouth, then looked at the child. At the christening in the cathedral he had not been able to get a clear sight. There had been a press of important people crowding around the font, and he had not wanted to call attention to himself by pushing his way to the front. Now he feasted his eyes. "Absalom," he said.

"I'm calling him Abe," said Arabella.

"Abe," Spade repeated.

"I will never use the name Stephen christened him with. I refuse to let him live under a curse."

"Good," said Spade.

The baby's eyes were closed and he looked peaceful.

"He's got your hair," said Arabella. "Dark and curly, and lots of it."

"I wouldn't have minded if he had yours. What color are his eyes?"

"Blue, but most babies have blue eyes. A lot of them change after a while."

"I never think babies are pretty—but Abe is beautiful."

"Do you want to hold him?"

Spade hesitated. He had no experience of this. "Can I?"

"Of course. He's yours."

"All right."

"Put one hand under his bottom and the other behind his head, and that's all you need to do."

Spade obeyed the instructions. Abe was almost weightless. Spade pressed the baby to his chest and inhaled a warm, clean aroma. Powerful emotions possessed him: he felt deeply proud, loving, and protective. "I've got a child," he marveled. "A son."

After a while he asked Arabella: "How are things at home?"

"The bishop has taken his revenge. He has destroyed my rose garden."

"I'm so sorry!"

"So am I." She shrugged. "But I've got you, and I've got Abe. I can do without roses." All the same she looked sad.

Spade kissed Abe's head. "It's very strange," he said.

"What is?"

"This little boy has caused a lot of trouble on his entrance into this world, and there's probably more coming. But you and I hardly care. We're both thrilled to have him, and we adore him. We'll cheerfully dedicate our lives to taking care of him. It's good—but it's strange."

"Perhaps that's the way God works," said Arabella.

"Must be," said Spade.

PART IV

The Press Gang

1804–1805

CHAPTER 26

In the autumn of 1804 Amos took a barge from Kingsbridge to Combe. It was a leisurely journey downstream, though on the return the bargees would have to row against the current.

When he sailed into Combe Harbour he had an unpleasant surprise. On the headland there was a new building: a squat, round fortress, shaped like a beer tankard with the bottom wider than the top. It was nasty looking and scary, reminding him somehow of those boxers who offered to take on all comers at fairgrounds.

Hamish Law was with him. Now that the business was using fewer cottage workers and more mill hands, Hamish had less traveling to do, and he had become Amos's assistant on the sales side. Kit Clitheroe played a similar role on the production side.

Standing on the deck next to Amos, Hamish said: "What the hell is that?"

Amos thought he knew the answer. "It must be a Martello tower," he said. "The government is supposed to be building a hundred of them all along this coast, to defend us against the French invasion."

"I've heard of them," said Hamish. "I just didn't expect it to look so bloody ugly."

Amos recalled what he had read in the *Morning Chronicle*. A Martello tower had walls eight feet thick and a flat roof with a heavy cannon that could be turned through a complete circle to fire in any direction. Each tower was staffed by an officer and twenty men.

For months Amos had been reading about the threatened French invasion. He had been worried in a general way when he read that the ruler of France, Napoleon Bonaparte, had mustered two hundred thousand troops at Boulogne and other ports and was assembling an armada to bring them across the English Channel. But the grim sight of a fortress guarding Combe Harbour made the whole thing suddenly more real.

Bonaparte had plenty of money to pay for the invasion. He had sold to the United States a vast unprofitable territory the French had called Louisiane, which stretched from the Gulf of Mexico all the way to the Great Lakes on the Canadian border. President Thomas Jefferson had doubled the size of the USA at the cost of fifteen million dollars. Bonaparte was spending it all to conquer England.

Paradoxically, trade with the European continent went on, thanks to the Royal Navy, which patrolled the channel. France was out of bounds, and the French had conquered the Netherlands, but ships from Combe could still sail to cities such as Copenhagen, Oslo, and even St. Petersburg.

Amos was bringing a consignment of cloth to Combe for onward shipment to a customer in Hamburg. He would be paid with a letter of exchange. His customer would pay the price of the cloth to a German banker called Dan Levy, and Amos would collect his money from Dan's cousin Jonny, who had a bank in Bristol.

Meanwhile, back in Kingsbridge, Amos now had two mills. His business with the army had grown, and his original mill had become overcrowded, so he had bought a second, called Widow's Mill, from Cissy Bagshaw, who was retiring. Half a year ago he had made Kit Clitheroe manager of both mills. Kit was very young for the job, but he understood the machinery and got on well with the hands: he was easily the most competent deputy Amos had ever had.

The Combe waterfront was busy. Porters and carters came and went, and ships and barges unloaded and reloaded, in the never-ending process that made Britain the richest country in the world.

The bargees found the vessel Amos was looking for,

the *Dutch Girl*, and moored alongside. Amos went ashore and Hamish began to unload Amos's bales of cloth. Kev Odger, master of the *Dutch Girl*, appeared. Amos had known him for years and trusted him, but nevertheless they counted the bales together, and Odger opened three at random to check that they were white wool serge as specified in the manifest. They signed two copies of the bill of lading and took one each.

Odger asked him: "Are you staying overnight?"

"It's too late to head back to Kingsbridge today," Amos replied.

"Then watch out for the press gang this evening. I lost two good men last night."

Amos understood. Britain was in constant need of men for the navy. The militia, the home defense force, had no shortage, for it had the power to conscript men whether they liked it or not. There was no conscription into the regular army, but poverty-stricken Ireland supplied about a third of army recruits, and the criminal courts accounted for most of the rest, for they could sentence an offender to military service as a punishment. So the biggest problem was the navy that kept the seas free for British trade.

Sailors were paid little, and frequently late, too, and life at sea was brutal, with flogging an everyday punishment for minor offenses. One-tenth of the navy now consisted of convicts taken from Irish prisons, but that was not enough. Rather than reform the navy and pay sailors properly, a government with taxpayers' interests at heart simply forced men into the navy. In England, teams called press gangs kidnapped, or "impressed," able-bodied men in coastal towns, took them aboard ships, and kept them tied up until they were miles from land. The system was hated, and often led to rioting.

Amos thanked Odger for the warning and went with Hamish to Mrs. Astley's lodging house, where Amos always stayed when he had to spend a night in Combe. It was a normal town house, but packed tight with beds, one or two in the smaller rooms and several in the larger. The hostess was a smiling Jamaican woman whose girth was a good advertisement for her cooking.

They were in time for dinner. Mrs. Astley served a spicy fish stew, with fresh bread and ale to drink, for a shilling. At the communal table Amos sat next to a young man who recognized him. "You don't know me, Mr. Barrowfield, but I'm from Kingsbridge," he said. "My name's Jim Pidgeon."

Amos did not recall seeing him before. He said politely: "What brings you to Combe?"

"I work on the barges. I know the river pretty well between Kingsbridge and Combe."

Another lodger, a man with a withered right arm who was humorously called Lefty, was raging against the French between mouthfuls. "Godless, bloodthirsty, ignorant men, they have murdered the flower of the French nobility, and they want to murder ours, too," he said, and slurped from his spoon.

Hamish took the bait. "We were at peace for fourteen months," he said. The Treaty of Amiens had been signed in March 1802, and affluent English shoppers and tourists had flocked back to their beloved Paris; but Britain had ended the truce in May last year.

"The French attacked us again," said Lefty.

"Funny you should say that," Hamish replied. "According to the newspapers, we declared war on the French, not the other way about."

"Because they invaded Switzerland," said Lefty.

"No doubt they did, but is it a reason to send Englishmen to their deaths? For Switzerland? I only ask the question."

"I don't care what you say, I hate the fucking French."

A voice came from the kitchen: "No foul language, gentlemen—this is a respectable house."

The belligerent Lefty submitted to her authority. "Sorry, Mrs. Astley," he said.

Dinner was over soon after that. As the men were

leaving the table, Mrs. Astley came in and said: "Have a pleasant evening, gentlemen, but remember my rule: the door is locked at midnight, and no refunds."

Amos and Hamish strolled around the town. Amos was not worried about the press gang. They did not take well-dressed middle-class gentlemen.

Combe was a lively place, as port towns usually were. Musicians and acrobats performed on the streets for pennies; hawkers sold ballads and souvenirs and magic potions; young women and men offered their bodies; pickpockets robbed sailors of their wages. Amos and Hamish were not tempted by the many brothels and gambling houses, but they did sample the ale in a few taverns, and ate oysters from a street stall.

When Amos announced that it was time to return to Mrs. Astley's place, Hamish begged for one more tankard, and Amos indulged him. They went to a tavern near the waterfront. Inside were a dozen or so men drinking beer, and a sprinkling of young women. Amos spotted Jim Pidgeon there, enjoying a friendly conversation with a girl in a red dress.

"Nice place," said Hamish appreciatively.

"No, it's not," said Amos. "Look at that young fellow Jim from Kingsbridge. He's very drunk."

"Lucky him."

"Why do you think that girl is being nice to him?"

"I expect she likes him."

"He's not handsome and he's not rich—what does she see in him?"

"There's no accounting for women's choices."

Amos shook his head. "This is a crimping house."

"What does that mean?"

"She's put gin in his beer without him noticing. Any minute now she'll take him into the back room, and he'll think it's his lucky night. But it's not, because the press gang will be waiting. They'll take him aboard a ship and lock him in the brig. Next time he sees daylight he'll be a sailor in the Royal Navy."

"Poor bastard."

"And the girl will get a shilling for her help."

"We better save him."

"Yes." Amos went up to Pidgeon and said: "Time to go home, Jim. It's late and you're drunk."

"I'm all right," said Jim. "I'm just talking to this girl. Her name is Mademoiselle Stephanie Marchmount."

"And mine's William Pitt the Younger," said Amos. "Let's get going."

The woman who called herself Stephanie said: "Why don't you mind your own bloody business?"

Amos took Jim firmly by the arm.

Stephanie screeched: "Leave him be!" She flew at Amos and scratched his face.

He batted her hand aside.

Three men were standing nearby, talking to another pretty girl. One of them turned and said: "What's going on?"

"My friend is drunk," said Amos, hand to his bleeding cheek. "We're going home before the press gang gets him. And you might think about doing the same."

"Press gang?" the man said. He was fuddled, but enlightenment slowly dawned on his face. "Is the press gang here?"

Amos looked toward the back of the room and saw three tough-looking men coming in, led by a fourth in the uniform of a naval officer. "Look there," he said, pointing. "They just walked in."

Stephanie waved to them. The men moved fast, as if repeating actions they had taken many times, and in a second they were at her side. She pointed to Jim.

The officer said: "Stand aside, you men."

One of the toughs grabbed Jim, who was helpless to resist. Hamish hit the second tough with a mighty roundhouse punch, knocking him down. The third man punched Amos in the belly, a hard blow accurately directed, and Amos doubled over in agony. The man came at him with a flurry of punches. Amos was tall and strong, but he was no street fighter, and he struggled to protect himself, backing away through the crowd.

But the bystanders were not neutral. The press gang was every man's enemy. Those nearest to Amos joined in the fight. They attacked the man punching Amos and drove him back.

That gave Amos a moment to take stock. The fighting had become general, men yelling and lashing out indiscriminately while women screamed. Hamish had grabbed Jim and was trying to separate him from his captor. Amos went to Hamish's assistance but a bystander saw his fine clothes, assumed he was on the side of the press gang, and threw a wild punch at him. It was a lucky blow and caught him under the chin. He blacked out for a moment and found himself on the floor. It was no place to be in the middle of a riot, but he was too dazed to stand.

He managed to struggle to his knees, then someone grabbed him under the arms, and he saw the welcome face of Hamish. Then Hamish hauled him up and slung him over one wide shoulder. Amos went limp, giving himself up to fate. His feet bashed against people's bodies as Hamish thrust his way through the crowd. A few seconds later he breathed cold fresh air. Hamish carried him some distance, away from the tavern, then set him on his feet leaning against a wall.

"Can you stand?" Hamish said.

"I think so." Amos's legs felt weak but he remained upright.

Hamish laughed. "That was quite a ruckus." He had clearly enjoyed it. "The Stephanie woman spoiled your face, though. You used to be quite handsome."

Amos's hand went to his cheek and came away bloody. "I'll heal," he said. "Where's Jim Pidgeon?"

"I had to leave him behind. I couldn't carry you and fight the press gang at the same time."

"I hope he got away," said Amos.
"I suppose we'll find out tomorrow at breakfast."
Next morning there was no sign of Jim Pidgeon.

Elsie put her three sons to bed one by one. This was her favorite time of day. She loved the quiet time with the children, and she also looked forward to the moment when they were all asleep and she could rest.

She began with the littlest, Richie, who was two years old. He was blond, like Kenelm, and promised to be handsome. She knelt by his cot and said a short prayer. When it ended he said "Amen" with her. It was one of his few words, along with *mama, poo-poo,* and *no.*

Billy was next. He was four, and a bundle of energy. He could sing, and count, and contradict his mother, and run, though not fast enough to escape from her. He said the Lord's Prayer along with her.

Finally she came to her firstborn, Stevie, seven. His fluffy ginger hair had darkened a little and become more like Arabella's auburn. He was reading a lot and could write his name. He said his prayers without guidance from Elsie, and it was she who said "Amen" with him.

Kenelm had always done this with Stevie, but now that they had three children he found that it took up too much time.

She left the boys in the care of the nurse, who slept within earshot of them. On the landing she met her mother coming out of the bishop's room.

Elsie's parents had barely spoken to one another for five years, until the bishop had fallen ill this past summer, at the age of sixty-seven. He suffered chest pains and was short of breath, so much so that any effort exhausted him, and he no longer got out of bed. So Arabella had begun to nurse him.

Now Elsie and her mother walked down the stairs together and went into the dining room for supper. There was hot soup, a cold game pie, and cake. A jug of wine stood on the table, but both women drank tea.

Kenelm was at a meeting in the vestry and had said he would be late, so they started without him.

Elsie asked how her father was.

"A little weaker," Arabella said. "He complains that his feet are cold, even though there's a blazing fire in the room. I took him some clear soup for supper, and he drank it. He's sleeping now. Mason's with him."

"Why do you take care of him? Mason could do it on her own."

"A question I often ask myself."

Elsie was not satisfied with that. "Is it because you're thinking of the afterlife?" Elsie had been on the point of saying *the Day of Judgment* but had felt it was too harsh.

"I don't know much about the afterlife," Arabella said. "Nor do the clergy, though they pretend to. Happily married couples think they'll be together in heaven, but what about a widow who marries a second time? She may have two husbands in heaven. Will she have to choose between them, or can she have both?"

Elsie giggled. "Mother, don't be silly."

"I'm just pointing out the foolishness of what people believe."

"Are you still in love with my father?"

"No, and I probably never was. But that wasn't his fault. We were both responsible for the things that happened to us. I should never have married him, of course, but it was my decision. He asked me, and I could have said no. I would have, if my pride had not been wounded by the boy who rejected me."

"Some rebound marriages work out well enough."

"The trouble was that your father was never really interested in me. He wanted a wife, for convenience and because it's thought to prove that a clergyman isn't, you know, a molly."

"Is Father a molly?"

"No, but his inclination in the other direction is not

very strong. After you were born we made love rather infrequently. And eventually, you see, I found someone who could hardly keep his hands off me because he loved me so much, and I realized that that was how it ought to be."

That's not how it is for me, Elsie thought sadly. But I'm sure it could be—with Amos. She drank some soup and said nothing.

Arabella said: "I don't want him to die hating me. I don't want to stand by his grave cursing him. So I think about the early days, when he was slim and handsome and not so pompous, and I was at least fond of him. And perhaps he'll forgive me before the end."

Elsie did not think her father was the forgiving type, but that was another thought she kept to herself.

The confessional atmosphere evaporated when Kenelm walked in. He sat at the table and poured a glass of Madeira. "What are you two looking so solemn about?" he said.

Elsie decided not to answer. Instead she said: "How was your meeting?"

"Very straightforward," he replied. "It was an organizational discussion. I had cleared everything beforehand with the bishop, so I could tell the clergy what he wanted them to do. When they disagreed, I said I would speak to the bishop about it again, but I did not think he would change his mind."

Arabella said: "Are you sure the bishop even understands what you say to him?"

"I believe so. At any rate, between us we make sound decisions." Kenelm took a slice of the game pie and began to eat.

Arabella stood up. "I'm going to retire. Good night, Kenelm. Good night, Elsie." She left the room.

Kenelm frowned. "I hope your mother isn't displeased with me for some reason."

"No," said Elsie. "But I suspect she thinks the bishop

is not really capable of making decisions, and that in truth you're running things now."

Kenelm did not deny it. "And if that were true, would it matter?"

"A hostile observer might say that what you're doing is deceitful."

"Hardly," said Kenelm with a little laugh, pretending that the suggestion was fanciful. "In any case, what's essential is to keep the diocese running smoothly while the bishop is indisposed."

"He may never get better."

"All the more reason to avoid a row among the clergy over who's going to be acting bishop in the interim."

"Sooner or later people will realize what you're up to."

"All the better. If I show myself capable of the job, then when your father is at last called home to be with the Lord, the archbishop should appoint me bishop in his place."

"But you're only thirty-two years old."

Kenelm's fair cheeks darkened with anger. "Age should have nothing to do with it. The post should go to the ablest man."

"There's no doubt of your competence, Kenelm. But this is the Church of England, and it's run by old men. They may think you're too young."

"I've been here nine years and I've proved my worth!"

"And everyone would agree." This was not really true—Kenelm had clashed with some of the senior men who disliked his bumptious confidence—but she was trying to soothe his outraged feelings. "I just don't want you to be too disappointed if the decision doesn't go your way."

"I really don't think there's much chance of that," he said with finality, and Elsie said no more.

He finished his supper and they went upstairs together. He followed her into her bedroom, then went through the communicating door into his own room. "Good night, dear," he said as he closed the door.

"Good night," said Elsie.

When the bishop died, Elsie was surprised by her grief. Her relationship with her father had been fraught, and she had not expected to shed tears. It was not until the undertakers had done their work, and she looked at his cold body in the coffin, dressed in his episcopal robes and a full wig, that sadness overwhelmed her, and she sobbed. She found herself thinking of scenes from her childhood that she had not recalled to mind for twenty-five years: her father singing to her, children's hymns and folk songs; telling her bedtime stories; saying how pretty she looked in her new clothes; teaching her to recognize the first letter of her name on carved inscriptions in the cathedral. At some point those intimacies had come to an end. Perhaps it was when she changed from a sweet little girl to a challenging, argumentative adolescent.

"All the good times," she said to her mother. "Why did I forget them for so long?"

"Because bad memories poison good," said Arabella. "But now we can look at his life as a whole. He was kind at some moments and cruel at others. He was clever but narrow-minded. I can't think of a single occasion when he lied to me, or to anyone else for that matter—though he could deceive by silence. Every life is that kind of patchwork, under scrutiny, unless you're a saint."

Amos said he understood how Elsie felt. Chatting at Sunday school, while the children ate their free dinner, he talked about the death of his own father twelve years ago. "When I saw him pale and still I was just seized with a fit of weeping, overwhelmed by it, I couldn't stop crying. And yet at the same time I knew he had treated me badly. I remembered that, and it made no difference. I couldn't understand it—still can't."

Elsie nodded. "The attachment goes too deep to be altered by circumstances. Grief isn't rational."

He nodded and smiled. "You're so wise, Elsie."

And yet you prefer that flibbertigibbet Jane, she thought.

The bishop left four thousand pounds in his will, divided equally between his wife and daughter. Arabella could live modestly on her inheritance. Elsie would use hers for the Sunday school.

The archbishop did not come to Kingsbridge for the funeral, but sent his right-hand man, Augustus Tattersall. He stayed at the palace. Elsie was impressed by him. She had met two previous emissaries of the archbishop and found both of them arrogant and overbearing. Tattersall was an intellectual, a man of considerable influence, but he carried his distinction lightly. He spoke softly and was carefully courteous, especially to those in his power; but there was no sign of weakness, and he could be very firm when talking about what the archbishop wished. It occurred to her that Amos would have been like this if he had become a clergyman—except that Tattersall was not so handsome.

During past visits Elsie had been embarrassed by how obviously Kenelm strove to impress senior clergymen, constantly saying how much the bishop depended on him and hinting that he could run things better. She understood that Kenelm wanted to progress in the church, but she felt that holders of high office in the church might have been more impressed by a subtler approach.

Kenelm told Elsie he was confident, but he was bursting to hear the news from Tattersall. However, Tattersall kept them all in suspense and said nothing about it while the funeral arrangements were made.

With great ceremony the bishop was laid to rest in the graveyard on the north side of the cathedral. Tattersall had scheduled a meeting of the chapter immediately afterward. But he asked to speak to Arabella, Kenelm, and Elsie before the chapter, which was thoughtful of him, Elsie felt.

They sat in the drawing room. Tattersall spoke briskly. "The archbishop has decided that the new bishop of Kingsbridge will be Marcus Reddingcote."

Elsie shot a look at Kenelm. He went pale with shock. She felt a wave of compassion. This had meant so much to him.

Tattersall said to Kenelm: "I think you knew Reddingcote at Oxford. He was a teacher there at the time."

Elsie had heard of Reddingcote, a conservative intellectual who had written a commentary on Luke's gospel.

Kenelm found his voice. "But why not me?"

"The archbishop is well aware of your abilities, and feels you have a great future ahead. With a few more years' experience you may be ready to take on a diocese. Right now you're too young."

"Plenty of men my age have become bishops!"

"Not plenty. A few, yes, and they have generally been the second or third sons of wealthy noblemen, I'm sorry to say."

"But—"

"Moving on," Tattersall said firmly, "the dean of Kingsbridge is soon to retire, and the archbishop is promoting you, Mr. Mackintosh, to be dean."

Kenelm was not mollified. It was a desirable promotion, but he yearned for more. However, he managed to say: "Thank you."

Tattersall stood up. "Reddingcote is eager to come here immediately," he said. "You should take over the deanery as soon as the present dean moves out."

Elsie felt that her life was changing too fast. She wanted to pause it and take stock.

Tattersall looked at his watch. "I'll address the chapter in fifteen minutes. I assume you'll join me there, Mr. Mackintosh."

Kenelm looked as if he wanted to say *Go to hell*, but after a pause he nodded obediently. "I'll be there."

Tattersall went out.

Elsie said chirpily: "Well, so we're moving into the

deanery! It's a very nice house—smaller than this palace, of course, but probably more comfortable. And it's in Main Street."

Kenelm said bitterly: "Nine years of fetching and carrying for the bishop and all I get is a deanery."

"It's a quick promotion by the standards of ordinary clergymen."

"I'm not an ordinary clergyman."

He had expected special treatment because he was the son-in-law of a bishop, Elsie knew. But the bishop was dead and Kenelm had no other influential connections. Sadly she said: "You thought you'd get special treatment by marrying me."

"Ha!" he said. "That was a mistake, wasn't it?"

It was a slap in the face, and Elsie was silenced.

Kenelm left the room.

Arabella said: "Oh, dear, that was unkind—but I'm sure he didn't mean it. He's upset."

"I'm sure he did mean it," said Elsie. "He needs someone to blame for his disappointment."

"Well, he didn't get his wish, but you got yours. You have Stevie, Billy, and Richie. And I have Abe. We'll move into the deanery and have a house full of children. Life could be worse!"

Elsie got up and hugged her mother. "You're right," she said. "Life could be a lot worse."

CHAPTER 27

Hornbeam's daughter, Deborah, had a magazine beside her plate. She was jotting numbers on a scrap of paper, using a pencil, concentrating hard while her tea went cold. On the page were geometric drawings, triangles and circles with tangents. Hornbeam was intrigued. "What are you doing?"

"It's a maths puzzle," she said without looking up. She was completely absorbed.

He said: "What's the magazine?"

The Ladies' Diary: or, Woman's Almanack.

He was surprised. "They have maths puzzles in a women's magazine?"

She looked up at last. "Why not?"

"I wouldn't have thought women could do maths."

"Of course we can! You know I've always liked numbers."

"I thought you were exceptional."

"A lot of women pretend they don't understand numbers because they've been told that boys don't like clever girls."

That was a novel idea to Hornbeam. "You're surely not saying that underneath they're as clever as men."

"Oh, no, Father, definitely not."

She was being sardonic. Not many people had the nerve to disagree with Hornbeam, let alone mock him, but Deborah was one of the few. There was no danger of her pretending to be stupid. She was bright and he enjoyed arguing with her.

Her husband was not beside her. Will Riddick had gone wrong. He had lost his source of wealth when he had been moved from his position as head of purchasing for the Shiring Militia. He still had his rents from Badford and his army pay, but that was nowhere near enough to maintain his way of life—especially the gambling—and he was broke. Hornbeam had loaned him a hundred pounds, for Deborah's sake, but Riddick had not paid it back; in fact three months later he had asked for more. Hornbeam had refused. Now Riddick had left his Kingsbridge house and gone back to Badford village. Deborah had refused to go with him, and Riddick seemed not to care. They had no children, so the separation was uncomplicated.

It was not what Hornbeam would have wished, but he liked having Deborah living with him.

The clock chimed half past nine, and Hornbeam stood up. "I must go and deal with the poor of Kingsbridge," he said with distaste, and he left the room.

In the hall his grandson, Joe, was playing with a wooden sword, fighting an imaginary enemy. Hornbeam looked fondly at the boy and said: "That's a big sword for a six-year-old."

"I'm nearly seven," said Joe.

"Oh, that makes it completely different."

"Yes," said Joe, oblivious of sarcasm. "When I grow up I'm going to kill Bonaparte."

Hornbeam hoped the war would be over before Joe was old enough to join the army, but he said: "I'm glad to hear it. We'll be well rid of Bonaparte. But what will you do after that?"

Joe looked at his grandfather with innocent blue eyes and said: "I shall make a lot of money, like you."

"That strikes me as a very good plan." And you will never know the hardship I suffered as a boy, Hornbeam thought. That is my great consolation in life.

Joe resumed fencing, saying: "Get back, you French cowards."

The French were anything but cowards, Hornbeam reflected. For twelve years they had resisted all English attempts to crush their revolution. But that was too subtle a thought to share with a patriotic six-year-old, even one as bright as Joe. Hornbeam put on his coat and went out.

He had recently been made overseer of the poor in Kingsbridge. It was a job few people wanted, involving a lot of work for little reward, but Hornbeam liked to have the reins of power in his hands. Poor Relief was distributed by the parish churches, but the system was monitored by the overseer. It was important to make sure the ratepayers' money was not going to idlers and wastrels. Hornbeam visited each parish once a year, and sat in the vestry with the vicar, listening to sob stories from men and women who could not feed themselves and their families without help from those who were not so improvident.

Today he went to St. John's, south of the river, formerly a semi-rural parish, now the crowded neighborhood of houses built by Hornbeam and his son, Howard, for the hands working in the riverside mills.

The vicar of St. John's, Titus Poole, was a thin, intense young man with a soulful look. Hornbeam was wearing a wig to enhance his dignity and authority, but Poole was not. He was probably one of those people who thought wigs were unnecessary and cost too much and looked silly. Hornbeam despised him. The worst kind of softhearted clergyman, he was so keen to help people that he never thought of teaching them to help themselves.

In the first few minutes they granted relief to several undeserving cases: a man with bloodshot eyes and a red nose who clearly had enough money to get drunk; a woman who was fat despite the poverty she claimed; and a girl with three children who was a known prostitute and had appeared before Hornbeam at petty sessions more than once. Hornbeam would have clashed with Poole over every case, except that there were rules, and it was the duty of both men to follow them. That enabled them to reach agreement—until Jenn Pidgeon arrived.

She began speaking as she walked in. "I need help to

feed my boy. I'm penniless and it's not even my fault. A four-pound loaf is more than a shilling now and what else can people eat?" She was angry and articulate and showed no fear.

Poole intervened. "Speak when you're spoken to, Mrs. Pidgeon. Alderman Hornbeam and I will ask you questions. All you have to do is answer truthfully. You say you have a son?"

"Yes, Tommy, fourteen years old, and he looks for work every day, but he's small and not very strong. Sometimes people pay him to run errands or sweep up."

She was about thirty, wearing a threadbare dress and shawl with moth holes. On her feet she had wooden clogs. She looked half starved, Hornbeam observed. That was in her favor. His wife, Linnie, said that fatness was an illness with some people. Hornbeam thought they were just greedy.

Poole said: "And where do you live?"

"At Morley's farm, but not in the house, there's a kind of shed up against the barn wall, they call it a lean-to, it's got no chimney but there's a smoke hood, they let me have it for a penny a week, and they gave me a straw mattress for the two of us to sleep on."

Hornbeam said disapprovingly: "You sleep in the bed with your fourteen-year-old boy?"

"Only way to keep warm," she said indignantly. "That shed is drafty."

She's not too hungry to argue with me, Hornbeam thought sourly.

Poole said: "What work do you do?"

"Anything I can get. But they don't need help on the farm in the winter, and the mills are short of orders because of the war, and I used to be a shopgirl but the shops in Kingsbridge aren't hiring—"

Hornbeam interrupted her. He did not need an explanation of unemployment in Kingsbridge. "Where is your husband?"

He expected her to say that she did not have one, but

he was wrong. "He was took by the press gang, may they all burn in hell."

That was borderline seditious, and Poole said: "Steady on."

She did not appear to hear his warning. "I was never poor before. When me and Jim came here from Hangerwold he got work on the barges and we didn't have much but I never got into debt, not for one single penny." She looked directly at Hornbeam. "Then your prime minister sent thugs to tie Jim up and throw him on board a ship and make him go to sea for God knows how long and leave me on my own. I don't want Poor Relief, I want my husband, but you people stole him away!" She began to cry.

Poole said: "It won't help you to abuse us, you know."

Her sobs stopped abruptly. "Abuse? Have I said anything untrue?"

The woman was impudent, Hornbeam thought with irritation. Most applicants at least had the common sense to be deferential. This one deserved to go hungry as a punishment for her cheek. He said: "You say you're from Hangerwold?"

"Yes, me and Jim. It's in Gloucestershire. Jim had an aunt here in Kingsbridge. She's dead now though."

"Surely you know that Poor Relief is available only in the parish where you were born?"

"How can I go to Gloucestershire? I've got no coat and my boy has no shoes, and I've got no home there and no money for rent."

Poole spoke to Hornbeam in a low voice. "We generally pay out in circumstances such as these. She's obviously done everything she can."

Hornbeam was disinclined to bend the rules for this insubordinate woman, who seemed to think she was his equal. "You say your husband was press-ganged?"

"So I believe."

"But you're not sure."

"They don't inform the poor wives. But he went to

Combe on a barge, and that evening the press gang raided the town, and my Jim never came home, so we know what happened, don't we?"

"He may simply have run off."

"Some men might, but not Jim."

Poole lowered his voice again. "This is a quibble, Mr. Hornbeam."

"I disagree. The husband may be dead. She must return to her birthplace."

Anger flashed in the vicar's eyes. "She'll probably die on the way."

"We can't change the rules."

Poole spoke forcefully. "Hornbeam, this woman is quite clearly the innocent victim of a government that allows the navy to kidnap men such as her husband! The press gang may perhaps be a regrettable necessity, especially in time of war, but we can at least do something for the families of victims so that the children don't starve."

"But that's not what the rules say."

"The rules are cruel."

"That's as may be. We still have to follow them." Hornbeam looked at Jenn Pidgeon and said: "Your application is refused. You must apply at Hangerwold."

He expected the woman to sob, but he was surprised. "Very well, then," she said, and she walked out with her head held high.

It was as if she had a fallback plan.

Elsie loved her new house. Instead of the grand echoing chambers of the bishop's palace, the deanery had human-sized rooms, warm and comfortable, with no marble floors on which children might slip and fall and bang their heads. The family had simpler meals and fewer servants, and no obligation to entertain visiting clergymen.

Arabella liked it, too. She was in mourning, and would continue so for a year; and the color black against her fair complexion made her look pale and slightly ill, like the beautiful heroine of one of the Gothic romances that she liked to read; but she was happy, Elsie could tell. She walked as if she had shed a burden. She often went shopping, sometimes taking five-year-old Abe with her, but she usually came back without having bought anything, and Elsie assumed she was surreptitiously seeing Spade. They were both single now, but they still had to be discreet, for it would have been shocking for a woman of her status to be openly courting while still in mourning. Nevertheless their relationship was the worst-kept secret in Kingsbridge, known by everyone who had an ear to the ground.

No doubt some people wondered whether Spade was the father of Abe, especially since the destruction of the rose garden—that story had kept Belinda Goodnight and her friends chattering for weeks—but no one except Arabella would ever know for sure. Anyway, there was a general feeling that such questions were better left unasked. Perhaps, Elsie speculated, other married women had babies whose paternity was questionable, and they feared that gossip about one might lead to gossip about others.

The new bishop was settling in well. Marcus Reddingcote was a traditionalist, which was what most of Kingsbridge expected a bishop to be. His wife, Una, had a stiffly superior air, and seemed to find her palace predecessors a bit raffish. When Elsie had said that she ran the Sunday school, Una had said in amazement: "But why?" And she had been visibly shocked to meet Abe and realize that the forty-nine-year-old Arabella had a child of only five.

Elsie envied her mother's passionate romance. How wonderful it must be, she thought, to love someone with all your heart, and to be loved the same way in return.

One morning Elsie looked out of the window and saw

crowds of people walking along Main Street, heading for the square, and she remembered that today was St. Adolphus Day. The mills were closed and there was a special fair in the marketplace. She decided to take her eldest, Stevie, and Arabella said she would take Abe.

The November sun was weak and the air was cold. They dressed in warm clothes with colorful additions: Elsie had a red scarf and Arabella a green hat. Many others did the same, and the square was full of bright hues against the gray stone backdrop of the cathedral. The stone angel on the tower, said to represent the nun Caris who had founded the hospital, seemed to look down benevolently on the townspeople.

Elsie told Stevie to hold her hand tightly and not to wander off and get lost. In truth she was not very worried: many children would get separated from their parents today, but they would not go far, and all would be found with the help of a friendly crowd.

Arabella wanted some white cotton for a petticoat. She located a stall selling a fabric she liked at a reasonable price. The stallholder was serving a poor woman who was haggling over the price of a length of coarse linen, so they waited. Elsie looked at a display of embroidered handkerchiefs. A skinny boy of about fourteen was studying the many different shades of silk ribbon on a tray, which Elsie thought was unusual: she had taught many fourteen-year-old boys and had never met one who was interested in ribbons.

Out of the corner of her eye she saw him casually pick up two reels, put one back, and slip the other inside his ragged coat.

She was so surprised that she froze, silent, hardly able to believe her eyes. She had seen a thief in the act of stealing!

The customer decided not to buy the linen, and the stallholder said: "What can I do for you today, Mrs. Latimer?"

As Arabella began to tell him what she wanted, the boy thief turned away from the stall.

Elsie should have shouted: "Stop, thief!" But the lad was so small and thin that she could not bring herself to denounce him.

However, someone else had seen the theft. A burly man in a green coat grabbed him by the arm and said: "Just a minute, you."

The boy wriggled like a trapped snake but he could not escape the man's grip.

Arabella and the stallholder stopped their conversation and stared.

"Let's see what's inside your coat, shall we?" said the man.

The boy yelled: "Get off me, you bully! Pick on someone your own size!" People around stopped what they were doing to watch.

The man thrust his hand inside the ragged coat and brought out a reel of pink silk ribbon.

The stallholder said: "That's mine, by God!"

The man in the green coat said to the boy: "You're a little thief, ain't you?"

"I never done nothing! You put that there, you great big lying toad."

Elsie could not help liking the boy's spirit.

The man asked the stallholder: "How much do you charge for a ribbon like this?"

"The whole reel? Six shillings."

"Six shillings, you say?"

"Yes."

"Very good."

Elsie wondered what was so significant about the price, that it had to be repeated.

The stallholder said: "And I'll have it back, please."

The man hesitated and said: "You will give evidence in court?"

"Of course."

The reel was handed over.

Elsie said: "Wait a minute. Who are you?"

The man said: "Good day to you, Mrs. Mackintosh.

I'm Josiah Blackberry. There's been an outbreak of thieving in Kingsbridge lately, and the borough council has asked me and a few others to keep an eye on suspicious characters at the market today. I take it you saw this boy pocket the ribbon."

"Yes, but I question why. Boys do not generally want pink ribbons."

"Perhaps not, but all the same I must take him to the sheriff."

Elsie said to the boy: "Why did you take that ribbon?"

His defiance, which had been ignited by rough words, now melted, and he seemed on the verge of tears. "My mother told me to."

"But why?"

"Because we have no bread. She can sell it and then we can eat."

Elsie turned to Josiah Blackberry. "This child needs food."

"I can't help that, Mrs. Mackintosh. The sheriff—"

"You can't help him, that's true, and nor can the sheriff, but I can. I will take him home and feed him." Elsie turned to the boy. "What's your name?"

"Tommy," he said. "Tommy Pidgeon."

"Come with me and I'll give you something to eat."

Blackberry said: "All right, but I must stay with him. I have to deliver him to the sheriff. What he stole is worth more than five shillings, and you know what that means."

"What does it mean?" said Elsie.

"It means he may be hanged."

When Roger Riddick walked into Barrowfield's New Mill, Kit recognized him instantly. Roger's face had lost that boyish glow—he must be past thirty now, Kit reckoned—but he still had an impish grin that made him seem younger.

Over the years Kit had picked up scraps of news about Roger going from one university to another, studying and sometimes lecturing, and had thought he must end up teaching, probably at one of the Scottish universities that specialized in maths and engineering. But here he was back in Kingsbridge.

However, Roger did not recognize Kit.

When Kit approached him, Roger said: "Are you the manager?"

Kit nodded.

"I'm looking for Mr. Barrowfield."

"I'll take you to him," Kit said, smiling warmly.

"Who are you?" Roger said.

"Have I changed that much, Mr. Riddick?"

Roger looked hard at him for a moment, then his face broke into a big smile. "Oh, my soul! You're Kit!"

"I am," said Kit, and they shook hands enthusiastically.

"But you're a man!" said Roger. "How old are you?"

"I'm nineteen."

"Goodness, I've been away a long time."

"You have. We've missed you. Come this way."

Kit took Roger to the office. Amos was delighted to see his old school friend after so many years. Together the three of them toured the mill, which was the one Amos had bought from Mrs. Bagshaw.

The old mill produced only military cloth now, but this one was more varied. Half a dozen weavers on the top floor made special fabrics that sold for high prices, such as brocade, damask, and matelassé, with complex multicolored patterns.

Roger looked intently at one of the looms. Each warp thread passed through a loop in a metal control rod that had a hook on the other end. Making simple cloth, a weaver would use the hooks to lift every other thread, then shoot the shuttle through the gap, called the shed. He would lift the alternate threads for the return shot, making a plain in-and-out weave. With patterns, such as stripes, the rods had to be lifted a few at a time in a sequence that might go twelve up, twelve down, six up, six down, and so on. This job was done by a secondary weaver called a draw boy, often sitting on top of the loom. The more elaborate the pattern, the more times weaving had to pause while the changes were made. The operators had to be skilled and diligent, and the process was time-consuming.

Roger spent several minutes watching Amos's most experienced men, then he took Amos and Kit aside so that they could not be heard by the hands. "There's a man in France who has thought of a better way to do this," he said.

Kit felt excited. He shared Roger's love of machines. It was Roger who had first shown Amos a spinning engine. "Go on," Amos said.

"Now," said Roger, "each time the pattern changes, the draw boy has to lift a different selection of control rods, according to the instructions of the designer—you, in this case, I presume."

Amos nodded.

"The new idea is that all the control rods are pushed up against a large card, made of pasteboard, that has holes punched in it according to your design. Where there is a hole, the rod passes through; where not, it is deflected. This replaces the lengthy process of the draw boy moving the control rods one at a time. When the pattern of stripes or checks changes, a different card comes into play, with holes in different places."

Kit thought about that. The concept was blindingly plain. "So . . . you can change the pattern as often as you like just by switching cards."

Roger nodded. "You were always quick to pick up these things."

"And you can have as many cards as you like."

Amos said: "This is brilliant. Who on earth thought of it?"

"A Frenchman called Jacquard. It's the very latest thing. You can't even buy such a machine in England. But it will come, sooner or later."

Kit was dazzled. Amos would be able to make fancy fabrics twice as fast, maybe even quicker. If this machine was real, and if it worked, Amos had to have one—or several, more likely.

Amos, too, had seen that. He said: "As soon as you hear of one for sale . . ."

"You'll be the first to know," said Roger.

Sal had changed, Spade thought, since she came out of prison. She was thinner, less jolly, tougher. Perhaps it was the hard labor that had altered her, but he suspected something else had happened in that jail. He did not know what and he did not ask: she would tell him if she wanted him to know.

The day before the trial of Tommy Pidgeon, Spade sat with Sal in the back room of the Bell, on a dark winter evening, both drinking ale from tankards. The case was discussed in every house in Kingsbridge. Petty theft was commonplace, but Tommy was only fourteen, and looked younger. And he had committed a capital offense. No one could remember seeing a child hanged.

"I hardly knew the Pidgeon family," Spade said.

"They lived near me and Jarge," said Sal. "They didn't have much, but they kept their heads above water until Jim disappeared. After that Jenn couldn't pay the rent, so she was evicted, and I never knew where she went."

"I didn't even know Jim had been impressed."

"Jenn complained bitterly about it to anyone who would listen, but there are so many women in the same plight that she didn't get much sympathy."

"My guess is that about fifty thousand men have been forced into it," Spade said. "According to the *Morning Chronicle* there are about one hundred thousand men in the Royal Navy and something like half of them were impressed."

Sal whistled. "I didn't know it was that many. But why didn't Jenn get Poor Relief?"

"She applied, in the parish of St. John, where she lives," said Spade. "The vicar there is Titus Poole, a decent man, but apparently Hornbeam was sitting in as overseer of the poor and he overruled Poole and said Jenn was not entitled."

Sal shook her head in disgust. "The men who rule this country," she said. "How low will they go?"

"What are people in town saying about Tommy now?"

"There are two camps, so to speak," said Sal. "One says a child is a child, the other says a thief is a thief."

"I suppose most of the mill hands are in the sympathetic camp."

"Yes. Even in good times, we know that things can change and destitution can come to us very quickly." She paused. "You know Kit is making good money now."

Spade did know. Kit was earning thirty shillings a week as Amos's mill manager. "He deserves it," Spade said. "Amos values him highly."

"Kit isn't spending half of it. He knows that money may come and go. He's saving in case of bad times."

"Very wise."

She smiled. "He did buy me a new dress, though."

Spade reverted to the Pidgeon case. "I can't believe they'll hang little Tommy."

"I can believe anything of that lot, Spade. People like you ought to be justices and aldermen, and members of Parliament. Then we might see a change for the better."

"Why not people like you?"

"Women? We can dream. But for now, seriously, Spade, you're a leader in this town."

This was perceptive of Sal. Spade had thought about standing for election as member of Parliament. It was the only way to change things. "I'm thinking about it," he said.

"Good."

Quarter sessions began the next day. The council room of the Guild Hall was packed full. Hornbeam was on the bench, as chairman of justices, holding a scented handkerchief to his face to take away the smell of the crowd. Two other justices were with him, one on each side, and Spade hoped they would have a softening influence. The clerk, Luke McCullough, sat in front of them, his job to advise them on the law.

The justices dealt briskly with several cases of violence and drunkenness, then Tommy Pidgeon was brought in. Jenn had washed his face and cut his hair, and someone had loaned him a clean shirt that was too big and made him look even smaller and more vulnerable. Now that Spade had a son of his own—Abe, aged five, unacknowledged but much loved—he felt keenly that children needed to be cherished and protected. He hated to see Tommy exposed to the unforgiving wrath of the law.

As always, the jury was drawn from the forty-shilling franchise, the substantial property owners of the town. Spade knew most of them. They believed their duty was to safeguard the town from theft and anything else that might threaten their ability to do business and make money. They would decide whether the case against Tommy was strong enough for him to be sent to the assize court for trial. Only the assizes could deal with a hanging offense.

Josiah Blackberry was the main witness. He was self-important, but Spade believed he was honest, and he told his story plainly. He had seen the boy steal the ribbon, so he had seized him and held him.

Elsie Mackintosh was called to corroborate the evidence. She said much the same, and the case was made. But when Hornbeam thanked her for her testimony she said: "I have told the truth, but not the whole truth."

The room went quiet.

Hornbeam sighed, but he could not ignore her. "What do you mean, Mrs. Mackintosh?"

"The whole truth is that this boy was starving, because his father had been taken by the press gang and his mother had been denied Poor Relief."

There was a murmur of indignation.

Spade saw Hornbeam's face set in a mask of suppressed anger. "We're not here to discuss Poor Relief."

Elsie turned to the accused child. "Why did you take the ribbon, Tommy?"

There was dead silence as the court waited for the answer.

Tommy said: "So my mother could sell it and buy bread, for we had nothing to eat."

Somewhere in the room a woman sobbed.

At last Elsie turned to the jury. "If you send this boy to the assizes, you will be killing him," she said. "Take a good long look at him now. See the frightened eyes, and the cheeks that have never yet needed shaving. I promise you, you're going to remember that face for the rest of your lives."

Hornbeam said: "Mrs. Mackintosh, you have testified that the father of the accused was taken up by the press gang."

"Yes."

"How do you know?"

"His wife told me."

Hornbeam pointed at Jenn. "Mrs. Pidgeon, did you see your husband being taken up?"

"No, but we all know what happened."

"But you were not there."

"No, I was here, in Kingsbridge, looking after the little boy you want to hang."

The crowd rumbled angrily.

Hornbeam insisted: "So no one knows for sure that Jim Pidgeon was press-ganged."

Jenn remained silent.

Then Hamish Law stepped forward. "I was there," he said. "I went into a pub in Combe and there was Jim, so drunk he was nearly asleep."

Some in the audience laughed.

Jenn protested: "He was never a drunkard."

"There was a young woman there who was probably putting gin in his beer."

"That I can believe," said Jenn.

Hamish went on: "I was with Mr. Barrowfield, my employer, who explained to me that it was a crimping house, where girls get men drunk, then hand them over to the press gang for a shilling. We decided to take Jim away from there. But all of a sudden in came a naval officer with three ruffians who laid into us. Seems they had set a trap for Jim and we'd spoiled their game."

Hornbeam said: "Did you try to prevent Pidgeon being impressed?"

Spade hoped Hamish would not admit to that, because it was a crime.

"I did not. I saw that Mr. Barrowfield was down on the ground so I picked him up and carried him out of harm's way."

Amos stepped forward and said: "Everything Hamish Law has said is true."

"Very well," said Hornbeam with irritation. "Let us assume that Jim Pidgeon was press-ganged. It makes little difference. No one believes that the families of impressed men have a license to steal from the rest of us." He paused, and Spade saw that he was struggling to keep his face impassive. "Many people are hanged for stealing every year—men and women, young and old." Hornbeam's shaking voice betrayed some repressed emotion. "Most of them are poor. Many of them are fathers and mothers."

He seemed to be having difficulty speaking, and some of the onlookers frowned in puzzlement as the granite façade threatened to crack. "We cannot show mercy to one thief, no matter what pitiful story he tells. If we forgive one we must forgive them all. If we forgive Tommy Pidgeon, all the past thousands who have been hanged for the same crime will have died in vain. And that would be ... so unjust."

He paused, regaining his composure, then said: "Gentlemen of the jury, the accusation has been proved by witnesses. The excuses offered are irrelevant. It is your duty to commit Tommy Pidgeon for trial at the assize court. Please indicate your decision."

The twelve men conferred briefly, then one stood up. "We commit the accused to the assizes." He sat down again.

Hornbeam said: "Next case."

Yes, Spade thought; things really have to change.

CHAPTER 28

One Monday in January Sal arrived at the market square early, while the ringers were still practicing and the sound of the bells could be heard throughout the town and beyond. They were learning a new pattern—or "change," as they called it—and Sal could hear the uncertainty in their timing, though the sound was pleasant enough. Instead of waiting in the Bell Inn she decided to join the ringers.

She entered the cathedral by the north porch. The church was in darkness except for a few candle flames that seemed to tremble with the chimes. She made her way to the west end, where a small door in the wall opened onto spiral steps that led up to the rope room.

The ringers were sweating in their waistcoats with their shirtsleeves rolled, their coats in a pile on the floor. They stood in a circle so that each could see all the others, which was essential for precise timing. They hauled ropes that dangled through holes in the ceiling. Apart from the holes, the ceiling was a heavy wood barrier that reduced the sound, enabling the men to speak to one another. Spade was ringing number 1 and calling instructions. On his right was Jarge ringing number 7, the largest bell.

They were dedicated to their art but not very reverent, and despite the sanctity of the place, there was a lot of swearing when they made mistakes. They still had not mastered the new change.

A bell took about as long to swing as it took a man to say *archbishop one, archbishop two*. The period could be reduced or extended but not by much. In consequence, the only way to vary the tune was by two adjacent ringers exchanging their places in the sequence. So 2 could swap with 1 or 3, but not with any other bell.

Spade's instructions were simple: he would just call out the two numbers that had to swap. The ringers had to be alert to his instructions, unless they were familiar with the sequence and knew what was coming. The complicated part was the plan, varying the sequence so that the changes were pleasing and the tune eventually returned to the simple round with which it had begun.

Sal had been there a few minutes when the new sequence went wrong and broke down before the end. The ringers laughed and pointed at Jarge, who was cursing his own clumsiness. Spade said: "What happened to your hand?" Then Sal noticed that Jarge's right hand was reddened and swollen.

"An accident," Jarge said grumpily. "A hammer slipped."

Jarge did not use hammers in his work, and Sal suspected he had been in a fight.

"I thought I could manage," Jarge said. "But it's been getting worse."

Spade said: "We can't ring seven bells with six men."

Sal was seized by an impulse. "Let me try," she said. She regretted it immediately. She was going to make a fool of herself.

The men laughed. Jarge said: "A woman can't do it."

That stiffened her nerve. "I don't see why not," she persisted, even though she was already regretting her daring. "I'm strong enough."

"Ah, but it's an art," he said. "The timing is everything."

"Timing?" Sal was indignant. "What do you think I do all day? I operate a spinning engine. I turn the wheel with one hand while I move the clamp to and fro with the other, all the while trying to avoid snapping the thread. Don't talk to me about timing."

Spade said: "Let her try, Jarge. Then we'll find out who's right."

Jarge shrugged and stepped away from his rope.

Sal wished she had not been so reckless.

Spade said: "We'll do the simplest possible sequence: a plain round, then number one—that's me—changes one place every time until we're back where we started."

Oh, well, here goes, thought Sal. She grasped Jarge's rope. The end lay on the mat at her feet in an untidy coil.

Spade said to her: "The first pull is short, the second is long. Get the bell swinging well, and eventually you'll find it stops at the top of its own accord."

Sal wondered how that was achieved—some kind of braking mechanism? Kit would know.

"You begin, Sal, and we'll join in once you've got going," Spade said, giving her no time to puzzle out the machinery. "Don't stand on your rope, though, it'll throw you arse over tit." The men laughed at that, and she stepped back.

The pull was heavier than she had imagined, but the bell rang, and then, before she expected it, the bell swung back, pulling its rope up, unraveling the coil on the mat. If she had been standing on it she would have been tumbled.

When the rope stopped rising she pulled again, harder. Although she could not see the bell she felt its pendulum rhythm, and she quickly understood that she had to pull hardest when the bell felt heaviest.

Then it stopped.

Before she was ready Spade rang, quickly followed by the man on his left. The sequence went around the ring impossibly fast. The man to her right, ringing number 6, was one of Spade's weavers, Sime Jackson. As soon as Sime pulled on his rope, Sal did the same, heaving with all her might.

Number 7 rang too soon after number 6. She had been over-hasty. She would get it right next time.

Next time she was too slow.

She could follow the changes well enough: number 1 rang one beat later every row. But the time between pulls on the rope had to be exactly the same as the time between previous rings, and that was the difficult part. She was concentrating hard and still not getting it quite right.

All too soon they were playing the last row, in which the sequence returned to 1-2-3-4-5-6-7. She nearly got it right, but not quite. She had failed. More fool me, she thought, for imagining I could do it.

To her surprise the men clapped.

"Well done!" said Spade.

Jarge said grudgingly: "I expected it to be a lot worse."

Sal said: "I thought I got it wrong every time."

"You did, slightly," said Spade. "No one outside will have noticed. But you heard it, which shows that you have the ear."

Sime said: "Perhaps she should join the group!"

Spade shook his head. "Women aren't supposed to be ringers. The bishop would have a seizure. Keep this to yourself."

Sal shrugged. She did not want to be a ringer. She was satisfied to have proved that a woman could do it. You fight the battles you can win, and walk away from the rest.

"I think that's it for the night," Spade said. As the men put their coats on he handed out the wages, supplied by the cathedral chapter, a shilling each, good money for an hour's work. They got two shillings for ringing on Sundays and holy days.

Jarge said to Sal: "I ought to give you a penny out of mine."

Sal said: "You can buy me a tankard of ale."

Amos was working in the shop late in the evening, writing numbers in a large ledger by the light of several candles, when someone knocked at the door. He looked through the window but could see nothing, despite the streetlights, because the glass was obscured by heavy rain.

He opened the door and saw Jane there. She looked so bedraggled that he burst out laughing.

"What's so funny?" she said, irritated.

"I'm sorry, please come in, you poor thing." She entered

and he re-locked the door. "Follow me, and I'll find you a towel or two." He led her to the kitchen, where the fire was still blazing. She took off her coat and hat and threw them on a chair, a gesture that seemed to him intimately domestic, almost as if she lived here, and that gave him a special thrill. She was wearing a pale gray dress. He found towels in the adjacent laundry and helped her get dry.

"Thank you," she said. "But what made you laugh?"

"It's just that you're the best-dressed woman I've ever seen, but when I opened the door you looked like a drowned cat."

She laughed, too, then.

He said: "But why are you here? The righteous folk of Kingsbridge would be scandalized to know that you and I were alone in this house." In truth Amos himself was uncomfortable, although somehow thrilled as well. He had never been alone with a woman before. However, she would surely leave soon.

Jane said: "I got so bored at Earlscastle that I came to Kingsbridge in a carriage. But my husband is camping out with the militia on a training exercise. All the servants have gone to the tavern and the only person in the house is a corporal on guard duty in the hall. The place is cold and there's no one to make me supper. I was so miserable and lonely that I had to get out of there. And so here I am."

Amos realized she wanted him to offer her supper. Well, he could do that. The righteous of Kingsbridge would be even more shocked if they knew, but they would never know. "I can certainly give you something to eat. I haven't had my supper yet. I'll just heat up the pea soup. I have a housekeeper, but she doesn't live in."

"I know," said Jane.

So she had expected him to be alone.

He had almost no experience of women. He had walked out with three different girls, in the last few years, but it had come to nothing: he was too obsessed with Jane. Finding himself alone with a married woman he really had no idea what he was supposed to do.

Well, he knew how to be hospitable: at least he could do that with confidence.

A cooking pot full of soup stood on the sideboard. He put it on the range over the fire to warm. The table was already set with bread, butter, and cheese, and a bottle of port wine. He laid a place for her and poured two glasses of port.

Jane said: "This is a big house for one person. You should take a mistress."

She often made risqué remarks. He smiled and said: "I don't want a mistress. I'm not a Methodist for nothing."

"I know." She shrugged and changed the subject. "How is little Kit Clitheroe getting on as your manager?"

"He's very good. He understands the machines better than I do, and the hands love him. And he's not so little anymore."

"He's had a nice pay increase."

"He's worth double."

They chatted amiably for a while, then settled down to eat. When they had finished Jane said: "That was just what I needed. Thank you."

"If I'd known you were coming I'd have laid on something fancier."

"And I wouldn't have enjoyed it half as much. Is there any more wine?"

He was surprised again. He had assumed she would go home now. "There's plenty," he said.

"Oh, good. Shall we go upstairs? It would be more comfortable."

Jane was in control, as usual. She had more or less invited herself to supper, and now she was going to make herself at home for the evening. It was not how ladies were supposed to behave. But it was all right with Amos.

"There's a fire in the drawing room," he said.

He carried the bottle and glasses upstairs. He sat on an upholstered sofa and she perched next to him. He continued to feel a mixture of excitement at their sudden intimacy and anxiety about the way they were flouting the rules of respectable behavior.

Jane took off her shoes—low heeled, with pointed toes and a silk bow—and tucked her legs up on the sofa, turning to face him with her arm along the back of the seat, as casually as if she were at home. She asked him about his business, and his trip to Combe, and that poor boy who was waiting to be tried at the assize court and might be hanged for stealing a ribbon. As he answered her questions he watched the play of expressions on her face, her eyes widening with surprise or crinkling with amusement, her mouth opening to laugh, her lips pursing in disapproval; and he wished with all his heart that he could look at her like this every night of his life.

She was closer to him than before, although he had not noticed her moving. Her knees were touching his thigh. He thought of that kiss in the woods at the May Fair and recalled how she had hugged him so hard that he could feel the shape of her body pressing against his.

Her dress was cut low in the front, and when she leaned forward—which she did often, to touch his shoulder or tap his hand, making a point—he could see the roundness of her small breasts inside the bodice of her gown. One time she caught his eye, and she obviously realized what he was looking at.

He blushed hotly.

She said: "Women's clothes are so tantalizing nowadays. I sometimes think I might as well let you see everything."

The thought made his mouth go dry, but the bottle was empty. How had that happened? He vaguely recalled her topping up his glass and her own.

She changed her position. She did it so quickly that he could not have stopped her even if he had wanted to. Suddenly she was lying on her back with her head on his thigh. She continued talking as if nothing had happened. "After all," she said, "there's no commandment against looking. That's why there are so many paintings and sculptures of naked people. God made us beautiful, then we discovered fig leaves. What a shame. Tell me, what do you think is the most attractive part of me?"

"Your eyes," he said immediately. "They're such a lovely shade of gray."

"What a nice compliment." She turned her head to look up at him, and her cheek pressed against his penis, which—he suddenly realized—was standing up shamelessly inside his breeches. She gave a little "Oh!" of surprise, then she pressed her lips against it in a kiss.

He was utterly astonished. He almost thought he might be imagining it. This had never happened even in his most explicit dreams. He was frozen with shock.

Then she sprang up. Standing in front of him, she said: "I think I have nice legs." She lifted her skirts to show him. She was wearing knee-length silk stockings held up with ribbons. "What do you think?" she said. "Aren't they pretty?"

He was too bemused to make any answer.

She said: "But you have to see the whole thing to judge." She reached behind her and began unbuttoning her dress. "I want your honest opinion," she said. He knew this was nonsense, but he could not tear his gaze away. There were many buttons but she undid them quickly, and he wondered whether she had planned this moment and chosen a dress that was easy to take off. In no time the whole thing fell to the floor in a tumble of pale gray silk. Beneath it was a petticoat with a boned bodice. She undid the bodice, then pulled the garment over her head with a swift movement. Wearing nothing but her stockings, she put her hands on her hips and said: "Well, which part do you like best?"

"Everything," he said hoarsely.

She knelt on the sofa, straddling him, and unbuttoned his breeches as rapidly as she had her dress.

He said: "Do you realize I have no experience of this kind of thing?"

"I don't have much experience, despite nine years of marriage," she said, but there was nothing clumsy about the confident way she grasped his penis, lifted her hips, slid it inside her, and sank down with a pleased sigh.

Amos was overwhelmed with love and delight. He knew he was doing wrong but he was no longer able to care. He also knew that Jane did not love him, at least not in the way he loved her, but even that could not diminish his joy. He stared at her breasts as they danced so prettily in front of his face. She said: "You can kiss them if you like," and he did, again and again.

It ended too soon. He was caught by surprise. One spasm after another shook him, and he heard Jane moan and felt her lean forward and press her body against his; and then it was over, and they both slumped, panting.

"We didn't kiss," he said when he had caught his breath.

"We can now," she said, and they did, for long, happy minutes. Then they fell apart and she lay across his knees, face up. He feasted his eyes on her body. He said: "May I touch you?"

"You can do anything you like."

A few minutes later the clock on the mantelpiece struck ten, and she stood up.

Facing him, she stepped into her shoes. She bent and picked up her petticoat, then she hesitated. "You're the second man who's seen me naked, but the first who has looked at me that way," she said.

"What way?"

She thought for a moment. "Like Ali Baba in the cave, gazing at unimaginable treasure."

"That's exactly what I'm doing, gazing at unimaginable treasure."

"You're very sweet." She dropped the garment over her head and straightened it, then put on her dress, reaching behind her back to button it.

When she was dressed she stood looking at him with an expression he could not read. She was in the grip of an emotion he could not identify. After a pause she said: "Oh, goodness, I did it. I really did it."

Her devil-may-care attitude had been an act, he realized. This had been a life-changing moment for her as well as for him—though not in the same way. He was baffled, but happy.

The moment passed and she said: "Would you get my coat and hat?"

He buttoned his breeches and fetched her outdoor clothes. While she put them on he got his own coat and hat. "I'll walk you home."

"Thank you, but let's avoid talking to anyone on the way. I haven't got the energy to dream up a plausible lie about where we've been."

There were not many people on the street, and they were all hurrying through the rain as fast as they could. No one made eye contact with Amos.

She opened the front door of Willard House with a key. "Good night, Mr. Dangerfield," she said. "Thank you for seeing me home."

Mr. Dangerfield, he thought. She had altered his name at the last moment, and the word that had come into her head had been *danger*. It was not surprising.

Walking away, he thought about all the questions he should have asked her. When would they meet again? Had this been a one-off thing or did she intend a relationship? If so, what kind? Would she leave her husband?

He reached home and stepped through the front door into the shop. That made him remember his first sight of her this evening, soaking wet and miserable. He relived their conversation. He went to the kitchen and saw her taking off her coat and hat and throwing them on a chair. He sat on the bench and pictured her opposite, drinking soup with a spoon and tearing a slice of bread, then biting off a morsel of cheese with her white teeth. He went to the drawing room, where the fire was now dying, and sat on the sofa and felt again the weight of her head on his thigh, and the pressure of her lips as she kissed his penis through the wool cloth of his breeches. Then, best of all, he saw her standing in front of him wearing only those knee-length stockings held up by ribbons.

Then, at last, he forced himself to ask the question: What did it mean?

For him it had been an earthquake. For her it had been something less, but still disorienting. But she had planned it. Why? What did she want?

Forcing himself to be realistic, he felt sure she would not leave her husband. Divorce was so difficult as to be virtually impossible. If she lived with Amos in sin his business would be boycotted by all respectable people, which meant all customers, and poverty was something Jane could not tolerate. Did she mean them to run away together, and start a new life under different names somewhere else, perhaps even in another country? That could be done. He might be able to sell his Kingsbridge business for cash and start a new enterprise elsewhere. However, he knew right away that Jane would never agree to something that offered hardship and risk.

So what did she intend? A clandestine affair? Such things certainly happened. Spade and Arabella Latimer had been carrying on for years, if the town gossip was to be believed.

But Amos could not live with the guilt. He had sinned today, a sin he had never committed before. It was adultery, forbidden by the seventh commandment of Moses, a serious offense against God, Northwood, Jane, and himself. He could not entertain the prospect of committing the same sin again and again, much as he wanted to.

Perhaps he would be lucky. Perhaps Northwood would die conveniently.

And then again, perhaps not.

CHAPTER 29

Kit thought a lot about Roger Riddick. As a child he had never appreciated what a remarkable man Roger was. Since Roger's return from his travels Kit had learned more about him, and come to appreciate his qualities. He was very clever, of course, and that made every conversation interesting; but more important than that was his sunny disposition. He was cheerful and optimistic, and his smile could light up a room.

Roger was thirteen years older than Kit, and had had an education that Kit could not even dream of; but despite that they talked as equals about machinery and the techniques of weaving. Roger even seemed quite fond of Kit.

Kit's feelings were so strong that they made him a bit anxious. It was almost as if he was in love with Roger, but that was ridiculous of course. It would mean that Kit was a molly, which was impossible. Admittedly, he had done things with other boys when younger. They used to masturbate together—they called it plunking. They would stand in a circle and see who could be first to spurt. Occasionally they would plunk one another, which always made Kit spurt quicker. But none of them were mollies: it was just youthful experimentation.

All the same he could not get Roger out of his head. Now and again Roger would put an arm around Kit's shoulders and squeeze, briefly, in a manly sort of gesture of affection, and Kit would feel the squeeze for the rest of the day.

He thought about Roger all through the Methodist Communion service. Kit was not a fervent Methodist: he went because his mother did. He had no interest in weeknight prayer meetings and Bible study groups, preferring a book-sharing club that favored scientific texts. So he felt a bit guilty when he came out of the Methodist Hall.

Then he saw Roger leaning up against the wall. "I was hoping to run into you," Roger said, and his smile radiated warmth like a fire. "Can we talk?"

"Of course," said Kit.

"Let's go to Culliver's and have a drink."

Kit had never patronized Culliver's and did not want to start, especially on a Sunday. He said: "How about the Coffee House?"

"Agreed."

The owner of the Bell Inn had opened a new business, the High Street Coffee House, next door to the Guild Hall. Such places were called coffeehouses but in fact they served full meals and wine, with coffee as an afterthought. Kit and Roger walked up Main Street to High Street in winter sunshine. Inside the coffeehouse Roger ordered a tankard of ale and Kit asked for coffee.

Roger said: "You remember me talking about the Jacquard loom?"

"I do," said Kit. "It's very exciting."

"Except that I haven't been able to get hold of one. If I could go to Paris and talk to weavers I feel sure I could find out where to buy one, but even then it would be a struggle to export it to England."

"That's so disappointing."

"Which is why I've come to you."

Kit saw where this was heading. "You're going to make one."

"And I want you to help me."

"But I've never even seen one."

Roger smiled again. "When I was studying in Berlin I had a special friend, a French student." Kit wondered exactly what Roger meant by *a special friend*. "Pierre discovered that Monsieur Jacquard had taken out a patent on his machine, which means there are drawings of it at the patent office in Paris." Roger reached inside his coat. "And here are some copies."

Kit took the papers and unfolded a drawing. He pushed his cup and Roger's tankard aside and spread the drawing on the coffeehouse table.

As he studied it Roger said: "I can't do it on my own. A drawing never tells you everything you need to know. There's always a lot of guesswork and improvisation, and for that you need intimate knowledge of the process. You know everything there is to know about looms. I need your help."

The idea of Roger needing his help thrilled Kit. But he shook his head doubtfully. "This will take a month to make—maybe two."

"That's all right. There's no hurry. We're probably the only people in England who even know about Jacquard looms. We'll still be first."

"But I have a job. I have no spare time."

"Leave your job."

"I haven't had it long!"

"I figure we can sell this machine for a hundred pounds. We'd split the money, half each, so you'd get fifty pounds for a month or so of work, instead of—what do you earn per month now?"

"Thirty shillings a week."

"So a little more than six pounds a month, whereas I'm offering you fifty. And as soon as one such machine is in use, other clothiers will want one just as quickly as they can get it. I propose that you and I go into business together, producing Jacquard looms, and we share the profits equally."

And after the first machine was made, and all the snags ironed out, further machines would be made more quickly, Kit knew. The money to be made was unimaginable, but that was not what tempted him. It was the thought of spending all his working hours with Roger. What a delight that would be.

Seeing his hesitation and misinterpreting it, Roger

said: "Don't decide right now. Think it over. Talk to your mother about it."

"That's what I'll do." Kit stood up. He would have liked to spend the rest of the afternoon here with Roger, but he was expected at home. "They'll be waiting for me to arrive for dinner."

Roger looked awkward. "Before you go . . ."

"Yes?"

"I find myself short of cash. Would you mind paying for the drinks?"

This was Roger's weakness. He gambled his money away, then had to cadge until more money came in. Kit was pleased to have a way of helping him. He called for the bill, paid it, and added payment for a second tankard for Roger.

"Jolly nice of you," said Roger.

"Don't mention it."

Kit left and hurried home.

He still lived in the same house with Sal, Jarge, and Sue, but the place was looking different. They had new curtains at the windows, glasses instead of wooden tumblers, and plenty of coal—all bought with Kit's wages. As he walked in he smelled the joint of beef that Sal was turning on a spit over the fire.

They were all getting older—something that should never have been a surprise but always was. Sal and Jarge were in their thirties now. Sal was fit and strong, having fully recovered from her ordeal in the hard labor prison. Jarge had the red nose and watery eyes of a man who never said no to a tankard. Sue was Kit's age, nineteen. She operated a spinning machine at Amos's mill. She was quite pretty and would probably marry before long, Kit thought. He hoped she would not move too far away. He would miss her.

They all tucked into the beef, still a great luxury. When they sat back, satisfied, Kit told them about Roger's proposition.

Sue said: "What a disappointment for Amos, after he's promoted you so young."

"On the other hand, he's desperate to get his hands on a Jacquard loom. I think he'll be pleased."

"How do you know there'll be more than one?"

"It'll be like the spinning jenny," Kit said confidently. "Once it's arrived, everybody will have to have one. And when everybody's using it, there'll be a new invention."

Jarge said grimly: "It will take work away from weavers."

"Machines always do," said Kit. "But you can't stop them."

Sue was always cautious. "Is Roger reliable, do you think?"

"No," said Kit. "But I am. I'll make sure the machine is built, and that it works as it should."

"It's uncertain," she said. "I think you should stick with Amos."

"Everything's uncertain," Kit shot back. "There's no guarantee that Amos will stay in business. Sometimes mills close."

"You must do what you think right," she said, wanting to close down the argument. "I just think it's a shame, just when we're getting comfortable for the first time in our lives, to put it all at risk again."

Kit turned to Sal. "What do you think, Ma?"

"I knew this would happen," she said. "I could see it, even when you were a little boy. I always said you were headed for great things. You must accept Roger's offer, Kit. It's your destiny."

Spade liked going to the new coffeehouse for his midday dinner. The chairs were comfortable, there were newspapers to read, and the place was clean and quiet. In daytime he preferred it to the noisy conviviality of the Bell—a sign, perhaps, that he was now in his forties.

The clientele was normally all male, but there was no rule, and Cissy Bagshaw had been a leading clothier and was considered an honorary man. She came to sit opposite Spade while he was drinking his coffee and reading the *Morning Chronicle*. She had once wanted to marry Spade, and he had turned her down, but he liked her, and they had worked together to resolve the strike of 1799. He said to her: "What do you think of the new French Civil Code?"

"What is it?"

"Napoleon Bonaparte has issued a new improved legal code for all of France, and abolished all the old customary dues and services given free to landowners."

"But what does the new code say?"

"That all laws must be written and published—no secret rules. Mere customs have no legal force, regardless of how ancient they are, unless they are made part of the code and published—unlike our English 'common law,' which can be vague. No special exemptions or privileges for anyone, no matter who they are—the law considers all men to be equal."

"Just the men."

"I'm afraid so. Bonaparte is not keen on women's rights."

"I'm hardly surprised."

"We should have the same thing here. An agreed code that everyone can read. Simple, but brilliant. Bonaparte is the best thing that ever happened to France."

"Keep your voice down! There are people here who would want you flogged for saying that."

"Sorry."

"You know, Spade, you really should be an alderman. People are already talking about it. You have a big enterprise now, one of the most important in town, and you're well-informed. You'd be an asset on the borough council."

This notion seemed to be in the air, but Spade pretended to be surprised. "You're very kind."

"I've retired from business, and I don't want to serve as an alderman much longer. I'd like to put your name forward as my replacement. I know you're on the side of the hands, but you're always sensible, and I think you would be accepted as a fair-minded person. What do you say?"

Aldermen were elected, in theory, but in practice usually only one person was nominated, so there was no need for a ballot. In that way the council was a self-perpetuating oligarchy, which Spade disapproved of; but if he wanted to change things he needed to belong. "I'd be very pleased to serve," he said.

She got up. "I'll chat to the other aldermen, see if I can drum up support."

"Thank you," he said. "Good luck."

He returned to his newspaper, but he mulled over what she had said. Most aldermen were conservative, but not all: there were some liberals and Methodists. He would strengthen the reform group. It was an exciting prospect.

His thoughts were disturbed again, this time by Roger Riddick, home from his travels. Roger said: "I hope I'm not disturbing your lunch."

"Not at all. I've finished. It's good to see you."

"Great to be back."

"You look like a man with something on his mind."

Roger laughed. "You're right. I'd like to show you something. Will you indulge me?"

"All right."

Spade paid his bill. They left the coffeehouse together and walked down Main Street, then turned into a side street, where Roger stopped in front of a big house. Spade said: "Isn't this your brother Will's place?"

"It is," said Roger, and he opened the front door with a key.

The hall was quiet and dusty. Spade thought the building felt empty. Roger opened a door to a small room that might have been a study or a breakfast room. There was no furniture.

Spade's puzzlement increased as they walked around the house. Most of the furniture had gone, including paintings, whose absence was evident from rectangular patches where the wallpaper had been protected from fading. Less than a palace, it was a family house, but spacious. It needed a good clean.

Spade said: "What happened?"

"When my brother was in charge of purchasing for the Shiring Militia, he took advantage of his position to make money in ways I don't understand."

This was disingenuous. Roger understood quite well what Will had done. However, it would have been unwise to admit knowledge of criminal corruption. Roger was just being cautious. Spade said: "I think I know what you mean."

"After his duties changed he should have reduced his outgoings, but he did not. He spent freely on racehorses, expensive women, lavish hospitality, and gambling. Eventually he ran out of credit. He has already sold all his furniture and pictures, and now he needs to sell this house."

"And you've shown the place to me because . . ."

"You're one of the richest clothiers in town now. I hear you might be made an alderman. Some people think you are about to marry the widow of a bishop. Yet you're living in a couple of rooms in a workshop in the backyard of your sister's shop. It's about time you had a house, Spade."

"Yes," said Spade. "I suppose it is."

Amos loved the theater. He thought it was one of humankind's greatest inventions, on a par with the spinning jenny. He went to ballets, pantomimes, operas, and acrobatic displays; but what he liked most was drama. Contemporary plays were usually comic, but he had been a lover of Shakespeare since seeing *The Merchant of Venice* ten years ago.

He went to the Kingsbridge Theatre for *She Stoops to Conquer*. It was a romantic comedy, and he and everyone else hooted with laughter at the constant misunderstandings. The actress playing Miss Hardcastle was pretty, and very sexy when Miss Hardcastle was pretending to be a barmaid.

In the interval he ran into Jane, who was looking rosily gorgeous. It was two weeks since she had taken off her clothes in the drawing room of his house, and he had not seen her or spoken to her in that time. Perhaps that was because the military exercises had ended and her husband had come home. Or perhaps what happened two weeks ago was a one-off event, never to be repeated.

He hoped the second explanation was the true one. He would be sorry, but relieved. He would escape a titanic struggle between his desire and his conscience. He could accept God's merciful forgiveness and go on to lead a blameless life.

It was impossible to talk to her about that in public, so he asked her about her brothers.

"They're so dull," she said. "They've both become Methodist pastors, one in Manchester and one, believe it or not, in Edinburgh." She spoke as if Scotland were as far away as Australia.

Amos did not see what was so dull about her brothers' choices. They had both studied, then moved to lively cities and taken on challenging work. It struck him as better than marrying for money and a title, as Jane had done. However, he did not say so.

After the show she asked him to walk her home.

"Isn't Viscount Northwood with you?" he said.

"He's attending Parliament in London."

So she was alone again. Amos had not realized that. If he had, he might have avoided her. Or not.

She said: "Anyway, Henry doesn't really like the theater. He doesn't mind Shakespeare's plays about real battles, such as Agincourt, but he sees no point in a story that isn't true."

Amos was not surprised. Northwood was a literal-minded man, intelligent but limited, interested only in horses, guns, and war.

Amos could not politely refuse her request, so he walked down Main Street with her, wondering how this would end. Against his will, his mind filled with images of that January evening: the rustle of silk as her dress fell to the floor, the way her body arched like a bow when she pulled the bodice over her head, the lavender-and-perspiration smell of her skin. He became aroused.

She must have intuited the quality of his silence, for she said: "I know what you're thinking." He blushed, and was grateful for the darkness and the flickering streetlamps; but she guessed anyway and said: "No need to blush—I understand," and his mouth went dry.

When they reached the front door of Willard House he stopped and said: "Good night, then, Viscountess Northwood."

"Come in," she said.

Amos knew that once he was inside he would find temptation impossible to resist. He almost went in anyway, but at the last moment he hardened his heart. "No, thanks," he said. For the benefit of anyone who might hear he added: "I mustn't keep you up."

"I want to talk to you."

He lowered his voice. "No, you don't."

"That's a mean thing to say."

"I don't wish to be mean."

She stepped closer. "Look at my lips," she said. He did so: he could not help it. "In one minute's time we could be kissing," she went on. "And you could kiss me all over. Anywhere. Everywhere."

As he stood there, taut with conflict, he began to understand why he did not simply walk into the house and do everything he longed for. She wanted to have him on a string that she could pull every time she needed him. The thought was humiliating.

He said: "You're offering me half of you—less than half. Am I to have my heart's desire when Northwood goes away, and be starved of love the rest of the time? I can't live like that."

"Isn't half a loaf better than no bread?" she said, quoting a proverb.

He responded with a quote from the book of Deuteronomy. "'Man doth not live by bread only.'"

"Oh, pooh," she said. "You make me sick." And she slammed the door.

He turned away slowly. The cathedral loomed darkly over the empty market square. Although he was a Methodist he still regarded the cathedral as the house of God, and now he walked to its front and sat on the steps, thinking.

He felt strangely liberated. He had stepped away from something that made him ashamed. And he began to see Jane in a different light. Her remark about her brothers came back to him. She thought they were dull for choosing to be pastors. Her values were all wrong.

She used people. She had never loved Northwood, but she had wanted what he could provide. And she had wanted to make use of Amos, exploiting his passion whenever she needed to be loved. It was obvious, but it had taken him a long time to see her plainly and accept the truth bravely. And now that he had done that he was not even sure that he loved her. Was that possible?

He still felt a tug at his heartstrings when he pictured her. Perhaps he always would. But his blind obsession might be over. At any rate he felt optimistic about the future now.

He stood up, turned around, and looked at the cathedral, dimly lit by the streetlamps on the far side of the square. "My mind is clear now," he said aloud. "Thank you."

Hornbeam had a vision for Kingsbridge. He saw it becoming a powerhouse of manufacturing, a place where great fortunes were made, rivaling Manchester for the title of England's second city. But some of the people of Kingsbridge stood in the way, constantly thinking of objections to progress. The worst of them was Spade. Which was why Hornbeam was furious at suggestions that Spade should be made an alderman.

It was no surprise that the proposal had originated with a woman—Cissy Bagshaw.

He was determined to kill this idea.

Fortunately, Spade had a weakness: Arabella Latimer.

Hornbeam spent some time mulling over the best way to use that weakness against Spade, and finally decided to speak to the new bishop, Marcus Reddingcote.

For church the next Sunday he put on a new coat, plain black, the look that was becoming the mark of a serious man of business. After the service he greeted the bishop and his supercilious wife, Una. "You've been with us for half a year, Mrs. Reddingcote," he said. "I do hope you're enjoying Kingsbridge?"

She did not say yes. "We were at a London church before—Mayfair, you know. Quite different. But one serves where one is sent, of course."

So Kingsbridge was a step down, socially, Hornbeam inferred. He forced a smile and said: "If there is anything I can do to assist you, you only have to ask."

"Most kind. We're very well served at the palace."

"I'm glad to hear it." Hornbeam turned to the bishop, a tall man and quite stout, as wealthy clergymen often were. "May I speak to you briefly, my lord bishop?"

"Of course."

Hornbeam glanced at Mrs. Reddingcote and said: "On a matter of some delicacy."

She took the hint and moved away.

Hornbeam stepped closer and spoke quietly. "There is a clothier called David Shoveller—you may have heard people refer to someone called Spade, it's a humorous nickname."

"Ah, yes, I see, Shoveller, Spade. Most amusing."

"He is maneuvering to become an alderman."

"Do you approve?" The bishop looked around, as if he might spot Spade.

"He's not here, sir. He's a Methodist."

"Ah."

"More important, the man is an adulterer, and half the town knows it."

"Good gracious."

"Even more shocking, his mistress is Arabella Latimer, the widow of your predecessor."

"This is extraordinary."

"The affair began long before Bishop Latimer died, and the woman has a five-year-old child which is widely believed to be Spade's. The bishop in his rage christened the child Absalom. The significance of that will be obvious to a learned man such as you."

"Absalom dishonored his father, King David."

"Quite. There is of course no proof of adultery, but I would not like to see Spade become an alderman of this city."

"Nor would I. But, Hornbeam, I have no say in the choice of aldermen—surely that's your field?"

This was the key question, and the most difficult part of Hornbeam's pitch. He said: "I've come to you as you are the moral leader of Kingsbridge."

"Indeed. But I don't see—"

"Might you preach a relevant sermon?"

"I can't condemn a man from the pulpit with no proof."

"Indeed not. But in general terms? A sermon on adultery?"

The bishop nodded slowly. "Perhaps, though it's a bit explicit."

"Then the subject might be not closing our eyes to sin."

"Ah, that's better. The scriptures refer several times to 'winking the eye,' which means exactly what you're talking about."

"If a man does wrong, it should not be overlooked—something like that, you mean?"

"Quite."

Hornbeam was encouraged. "You see, Spade's sin is often talked about, quietly, even furtively, but never openly acknowledged."

"And so he carries on, unrepentant."

"You have hit it exactly, my lord bishop."

"Hmm."

Hornbeam realized he was not quite there. He needed a specific commitment. He said: "You would need only to hint that a known sinner should not be elevated to a position of respect. No accusation need be made. People would take your meaning."

"I must give this some thought. But thank you for alerting me to the problem."

That was all Hornbeam was going to get. He had to accept it and hope for the best.

"You're welcome, my lord bishop," he said.

Spade told Arabella he had something to show her, and asked her to meet him outside no. 15 Fish Lane. He got the key from Roger Riddick.

He arrived early and loitered outside until she arrived, then quickly opened the door and ushered her in. "Let's look around," he said.

She probably guessed what was on his mind, but she did not ask questions. Together they examined the house. It needed work. There were cracked windows and stained floors. The kitchen and the rest of the basement were dark and unhygienic, and there was a dead rat in the pantry.

"The whole place needs to be thoroughly scrubbed," Arabella said.

"Plus a coat of paint."

Upstairs was a spacious drawing room. Farther up was a large bedroom with a lady's boudoir adjacent on one side and a gentleman's dressing room on the other. Above that were rooms for children and servants. The windows were large and the fireplaces generous.

Arabella said: "It could be a very nice house."

"It's for sale. Would you like it?"

She looked at him with a half smile. "What, exactly, are you suggesting?"

He took her hands. "Arabella, you wonderful woman, will you be my wife?"

"David Shoveller, you marvelous man, don't you realize I'm eight years older than you?"

"Is that a yes?"

"It's a yes, please!"

"And would you like us to live in this house? Would you be happy here?"

"Deliriously, my darling."

"We have to wait until the end of your year of mourning."

"September the thirtieth."

"You know the exact date."

"A lady shouldn't be so eager, but I can't help it."

"It's six months."

"If you buy it now that will give us time to clean and paint, and choose furniture and hang curtains, and everything."

They kissed, then Spade pretended to look around furtively. "We seem to be alone . . ."

"How nice! But the floor looks hard—and none too clean."

"That's all right, you can be on top."

"I was talking to some women . . ."

Spade smiled, wondering what was coming. "What did they say?"

Her smile was half playful, half bashful. "They spoke of something they say prostitutes do. I've never heard of it. It might even be made up, but . . ."

"But what?"

"I want to try it."

This kind of talk aroused Spade. "What is it?"

"They do it with their mouth."

He nodded. "I've heard of that."

"Has anyone ever done it to you?"

"No."

"Apparently they do it all the way to the end . . . if you see what I mean."

"I see what you mean." Spade realized he was breathing hard.

"That's what I want to try."

"Then do it. Please."

"Do you really want me to?"

"You have no idea," said Spade.

CHAPTER 30

The assize court judge had a thin, mean face like a vulture, Spade thought. His eyes were close to the bridge of a nose that turned under, like a hooked beak. As he took his seat at the Guild Hall, he ducked his head and raised his arms to spread his gown, like the wings of a vulture coming in to land. Then he looked at the people gathered in front of him as if they were his prey.

Or perhaps this is my imagination, Spade thought. Perhaps he's a kindly old man who shows mercy whenever he can. The face doesn't always mirror the character.

Usually it does, though.

Still, the judge would not be the one to decide whether Tommy was guilty. That was the job of the jury. Spade looked despondently at the twelve well-dressed Kingsbridge worthies being sworn in. As always, they were prosperous tradesmen and merchants—the kind of people least likely to turn a blind eye to theft from a stallholder.

While they were taking the vow, Cissy Bagshaw spoke to Spade in a low voice. "I'm sorry you didn't get made alderman. I did my best."

"I know you did, and I'm grateful."

"It was the bishop's sermon that did the damage, I'm afraid."

Spade nodded. "A sinner should not be elevated to a position of power and responsibility."

"Someone must have prompted him."

"I'm sure it was Hornbeam. He's my only enemy."

"I expect you're right."

Spade had learned an unpleasant lesson from his first

foray into politics. He was annoyed with himself for failing to anticipate the strength and ruthlessness of Hornbeam's opposition. If ever he tried again, his first step would be to figure out how to neutralize his enemies.

The swearing-in was completed and the jury took their seats.

If Tommy was found guilty—which seemed more or less inevitable—the judge would decide the punishment. That was where there was room for mercy. It was unusual for a child to be hanged—unusual, but not unknown. Spade prayed the man was not as mean as he looked.

The courtroom was full, the air already stuffy, the mood somber. Jenn Pidgeon was at the front of the standing crowd, her eyes red with crying, her hands constantly folding and unfolding the end of the sash around her waist. It was hard to imagine anything worse, Spade thought, than waiting to hear whether your child was to be executed.

Spade had expected Hornbeam to stay away. There was already a good deal of muttering in the town about his harsh treatment of Jenn, and this trial would be uncomfortable for him whatever the result. But he looked proud and defiant. He caught Spade's eye, and his lips twisted in a half smile of triumph. Yes, Spade thought, you won that battle.

Spade was disappointed, but not heartbroken. However, he was angry that his relationship with Arabella had been used to defeat him. Of course he and Arabella were sinners, that was bound to attract disapproval, but all the same, he felt she had been demeaned. People had been talking about her and deciding that she brought shame to him. He would never forgive Hornbeam for that.

But he remembered that his woes were trivial when Tommy was brought in.

Assizes were held only twice a year, and Tommy had spent the interim in Kingsbridge Jail. It was no place for a child. He seemed thinner and had a downtrodden look. Spade felt a surge of pity. But perhaps his sad appearance would win the jury's sympathy. Or perhaps not.

The evidence was the same as before. Josiah Blackberry described the theft and the arrest. Elsie Mackintosh corroborated his story, but insisted on pointing out that the child had been starving, because his father had been taken up by the press gang and his mother had been refused Poor Relief. Hornbeam, the overseer of the poor, looked haughtily indignant, but said nothing.

The jury knew the story already. Tommy's committal to the assizes had been reported in the *Kingsbridge Gazette*, and men who had not been at the quarter sessions had heard the details from those who had. The jurymen had probably made up their minds long ago.

In any case, it did not take them many minutes to come to their decision. They found Tommy guilty.

Then the judge spoke.

"Gentlemen of the jury, you have reached a decision which, in my judgment, is the only possible one." His voice had a dry rasp. "You have discharged your duty, and it is now my responsibility to sentence the guilty person to the appropriate punishment."

He paused and coughed into his hand. The room was silent.

"It has been suggested that Thomas Pidgeon is in some way the victim, rather than the perpetrator, in this case. There has been an attempt to blame the press gang, and those responsible for the administration of Poor Relief, and even His Majesty's government, for the crime in question. But the press gang is not on trial here, nor is the system of Poor Relief, still less the government. This is the trial of Thomas Pidgeon and no one else."

He looked at Elsie. "We may feel compassion for those who suffer unfortunate circumstances, but we do not give them permission to steal from the rest of us— such a suggestion is nonsense."

He paused again and did something with his hands, something that was hidden from view. When he raised his arms everyone saw that he was wearing black cotton gloves.

Jenn Pidgeon screamed.

Spade said aloud: "Oh, God save us."

The judge produced a black cap and put it on his head over his wig.

Jenn sobbed uncontrollably, and there were loud hostile comments from the public, but the judge was unperturbed. In the same rasping voice he said: "Thomas Pidgeon, in accordance with the law, you shall return to the place whence you came, and be taken from there to a place of execution, where you shall hang by the neck until your body be dead."

Several people were crying now. But he had not finished.

"Dead," he repeated; and then a third time: "Dead."

Finally he said: "And the Lord have mercy on your soul."

As Jenn Pidgeon was being half-led, half-carried out of the room, Spade stood up and said loudly: "My lord, please be informed that an appeal against this sentence will be made to the king."

There were noises of approval from the crowd.

"Noted," the judge said with little interest. "The sentence will not be carried out before His Majesty's response has been received. Next case."

Spade left.

He went to his manufactory and checked on the work, but he found it hard to concentrate. He had never before been involved in an appeal to the king. He was not sure where to start.

At midday he went to the High Street Coffee House. He drank some coffee and managed to get his brain to focus. He would need help in drafting the appeal, and it would be best to have it signed by several leading citizens. As he was mulling this, men began to come in for their midday dinner. Spade spotted Alderman Drinkwater. He was in his seventies and walking with a cane, but his limping walk was sprightly, and there was nothing wrong with his brain. Spade joined him.

Drinkwater ordered a beefsteak and a tankard of ale. He had been in court, and now he said to Spade: "Hornbeam and that judge are jackals. Sending a child to the gallows!"

Spade said: "Will you put your name to the appeal to the king? It will have a better chance if it comes from a former mayor."

"Certainly."

"Thank you."

"The only Christian thing that judge said was: 'The Lord have mercy on your soul.' I don't know what this world is coming to."

Spade was glad someone else shared his anger. "We should get more people to sign the appeal."

"My son-in-law Charles will, I'm sure. Who else shall we ask?"

Spade considered. "Amos will do it. But we can't have all Methodists. I'll ask Mrs. Bagshaw."

"Good. That will give us two Kingsbridge traders, who would not be expected to go easy on a thief."

"I don't suppose Northwood will help."

Drinkwater looked dubious. "I doubt it, but it's worth a try."

"Maybe your granddaughter could persuade him."

"Jane? I'm not sure she has much influence over her husband, but I'll ask her."

"I need advice on the wording of the appeal. There's probably a protocol."

"That's what lawyers are for. Ask Parkstone."

There were three lawyers in Kingsbridge. Most of their business was in property transactions, wills, and disputes between Shiring farmers over boundaries. Parkstone was the oldest. "I'll go and see him now," said Spade.

"Aren't you going to have some dinner?"

"No," said Spade. "Right now I don't feel I could eat."

Kit resigned from his job as manager of the two Barrowfield mills. Amos was sorry but good-humored about it, and said that if he was offered the chance to buy the first Jacquard loom in England that would be some consolation. He also asked Kit to work for another month to give time for new arrangements. Kit agreed. He was glad the change could be made without bad feeling.

The month was almost up when Kit received a letter.

He had never had a letter before.

It arrived on a Saturday and it was waiting for him when he got home from the mill. The neighbors said it had been delivered to his house by a soldier carrying a canvas bag that appeared to be full of letters.

It informed him that he had been conscripted into the militia.

He felt ill. He had never been a fighter and he was afraid he would be no good at it.

He should have anticipated this possibility, for he had been eligible since he turned eighteen, but he just had not thought about it.

The family discussed it over dinner. "I will hate the army," Kit said. "I know we have to defend our country, but I'll be the worst soldier in the world."

Jarge said: "It will toughen you up." Then he caught a reproving look from Sal and said: "No offense, lad."

Sal said: "The militia is not the army. They can't go abroad. They have to stay home and defend the country in case of invasion."

"Which could happen any day!" Kit said. "Bonaparte has two hundred thousand men waiting to cross the channel."

Even if there was no invasion, this would ruin his plan to build Jacquard looms with Roger. He would lose not just the money but the joy of working with the man he liked best in all the world.

Sal said: "It doesn't have to be you who saves us from Bonaparte. You're allowed to pay someone else to take your place, usually. And it doesn't even cost very much. Hundreds of men have done it. Let the boys down at the Slaughterhouse do the fighting—they enjoy it."

"First we have to find someone willing."

"That won't be hard. There are plenty of men out of work, many of them in debt. With your help, such a man could pay off what he owed and get a job. The wage is low in the militia but you get food and a uniform and a bed. It's not a bad deal for a young man in trouble."

"I'll start asking around tomorrow."

The next day was Sunday. At the Methodist Hall, after the Communion service, Kit was approached by Major Donaldson, who asked him to sit down in a quiet corner. Kit wondered what on earth was coming.

Donaldson said: "I know that your name has been pulled in the lottery."

Kit's spirits lifted. Perhaps Donaldson was going to help him evade recruitment. He said: "I'd be no good as a soldier. I hate violence. I'm looking for someone to take my place."

Donaldson looked solemn. "I'm sorry to disappoint you, but I can tell you now that that won't be possible."

Kit was appalled. He felt as if he was having a nightmare and could not wake up. He stared at Donaldson. The man's face was innocent of deceit. He was completely sincere. "Why on earth not?" said Kit. "Don't hundreds of men do it?"

"Yes, but substitution is always at the discretion of the commanding officer, and in your case Colonel Northwood will not permit it."

"Why? What has he got against me?"

"Nothing. It's the opposite. He knows who you are, he's heard of your talents, and he wants you in his militia.

We have plenty of young ruffians who can brawl. What we're short of is men with brains."

"So I'm doomed?"

"Don't look at it that way. You're an engineer. I can promise you a commission as lieutenant within six months. This offer comes from the colonel himself."

"Engineer? Doing what?"

"For example, we might need to get ten thousand men and twenty heavy cannons quickly across a river with no bridge."

"You'd make a bridge of boats, probably."

Donaldson smiled like a man who has played a trump card. "You see why we need you?"

Kit realized he had just sealed his own fate. "I suppose I do," he said bleakly.

"Conscripted men are in for the duration of the war, which may be many more years. But as an officer you'll be able to resign from the militia within three to five years. And officers' pay is much better."

"I'll never fit in with the military life."

"Our country is at war. I've known you for years: you're mature for your age. Think about your responsibility to England. Bonaparte has overrun half of Europe. Our armed forces constitute the only reason he doesn't rule us . . . yet. If he invades, it will be up to the militia to fight him off."

"Don't say any more. You're making it worse."

Donaldson stood up and clapped him on the shoulder. "You'll learn a lot in the militia. Look on it as an opportunity." He walked away.

Kit buried his head in his hands. Speaking to no one, he said: "It's more like a death sentence."

Spade went to the waterfront to supervise the loading of a consignment onto a barge for Combe. The bargee was a gray-haired man of about fifty with a London accent.

Spade did not know him but he introduced himself as Matt Carver. He struggled with the heavy bales, so Spade helped with the lifting. All the same the bargee had to stop frequently for a breather.

During one such pause the bargee said: "My soul! That man in the black coat. Is his name Joey Hornbeam?"

Spade followed his pointing finger. "He's called Alderman Hornbeam here, but yes, I think his first name is Joseph."

"Well, I'll be damned. An alderman, and wearing a coat that must have cost three months of a workingman's wages. What's he like, these days?"

"Hard as nails."

"Ah, he was always hard."

"You know him?"

"I knew him. I was raised in a district of London called Seven Dials. Me and Joey were the same age."

"Were you poor?"

"Worse than poor. We were thieves, and we had nothing but what we stole."

Spade was intrigued. Hornbeam was a child thief. "What about your parents?"

"I was an abandoned baby. Joey had a mother up until he was about twelve. Lizzie Hornbeam. She was a thief, too. She specialized in elderly men. She'd beg for six pence, and while the old geezer was saying no—or even yes—she'd steal the gold watch right out of his waistcoat pocket. But one day she made a bad choice and picked a man that was quicker than her. He grabbed her wrist and didn't let go."

"What happened to her?"

"She was hanged."

"Dear God," said Spade. "Is that how Hornbeam got to be the way he is, I wonder?"

"No doubt of it. We went to watch." The man's eyes clouded over, and Spade knew he was seeing the execution all over again. "I stood beside Joey when his mother dropped. Some of 'em die easy, broken neck, but she wasn't one of the lucky ones, and it took a few minutes for her to strangle. Horrible sight—mouth open, tongue out, pissed herself. Terrible thing, really, for a son to see at that age."

Spade was chilled with horror. "It almost makes me feel sorry for him."

"Don't bother," said the bargee. "He won't thank you."

CHAPTER 31

The marriage of Spade to Arabella Latimer was the nonconformist wedding of the year in Kingsbridge. The Methodist Hall was packed—a new hall, twice the size, was being built but was not yet finished—and there was a small crowd outside, too. This was despite the air about the marriage, an air of unmentioned sin, of half-hidden shame. Or perhaps, Spade thought, people had flocked to the ceremony because of that air, so scandalous yet so exciting, both wicked and alluring. By now there could not be many people in town who had not heard the rumor that Arabella had been Spade's mistress before her husband died—long before. Perhaps some came to the wedding to frown disapprovingly and tut-tut to their friends; but as Spade looked around the congregation he felt that most people seemed genuinely to wish the couple well.

It was Monday, September 30, 1805.

Arabella wore a new dress of chestnut-brown silk—a color, Spade had noticed, that made her complexion glow. He could not help thinking about the body under that dress, the body he knew so well. He had loved Betsy's slender adolescent figure and perfect skin; and now he loved Arabella's older body, with its soft roundness, its folds and wrinkles, the scattering of silver in her light-brown hair.

Spade himself had had his hair cut, and wore a new coat in a bright shade of navy blue which, Arabella said, gave his blue eyes extra brilliance.

Kenelm Mackintosh was Arabella's son-in-law and only male relative, but he was Dean Mackintosh now and could not be part of a Methodist ceremony, so it was

Elsie who walked Arabella down the aisle. She held the hand of five-year-old Abe, who had a new blue suit, a jacket and trousers that buttoned together, called a skeleton suit because it fitted so closely. It was the favored outfit for small boys.

Pastor Charles Midwinter preached a short sermon on the topic of forgiveness. The text was from Matthew's gospel: "Judge not, that ye be not judged." Forgiveness was essential in marriage, Charles said; it was virtually impossible for two people to live together for any length of time without offending each other occasionally, and sores must not be allowed to fester. He went on to say that the same principle applied to life in general—which Spade took to be a hint that people should forget his and Arabella's sin now that they were getting married.

Spade kept looking at Arabella when he should have been concentrating on the sermon. Years ago they had told each other that they wanted to be a couple forever, that their affair was a lifelong commitment; and the pledge had only strengthened over time. He felt sure of her, and he knew she felt the same about him. Yet he was surprisingly moved to have that promise sealed in church in front of his friends and neighbors. He had no anxieties to be soothed, no doubts to be rebutted; he needed no reassurance of her permanent love. All the same, tears came to his eyes when she agreed to have him as her husband until the moment when death came to part them at last.

They sang Psalm 23, "The Lord is my shepherd, I shall not want." Spade's singing was so bad that he had sometimes been asked to do it quietly so as not to put others off, but today no one minded as he sang loudly and tunelessly.

When they left the hall the congregation followed. Everyone was invited to their new home. Food and drinks were laid out in the hall. Elsie had made the arrangements, and Spade had paid the bills. The house smelled of new paint and was full of furniture he and

Arabella had chosen together. Spade ate nothing: everyone wanted to talk to him, and he had no time for food. Arabella was the same, he saw. He was pleased to receive everyone's congratulations.

After two hours Elsie persuaded the guests to leave. She had put aside some of the food and she laid it out on a table in the drawing room, along with a bottle of wine, then she wished them good night and left. When at last the house was empty Spade and Arabella sat side by side on a sofa, each with a plate and a glass. The windows were open to the mild air of the September evening. When they had eaten they sat holding hands as darkness stole slowly into the room, shadows pooling in the corners.

Spade said: "We're about to do something we've never done before: sleep side by side and wake up together in the morning."

"Isn't that wonderful?" Arabella said.

Spade nodded. "Life doesn't get any better than this," he said.

⁂

Amos came to the deanery carrying a ledger. He kept accounts for the Sunday school, and every three months he went over the numbers with Elsie. The teachers were volunteers and the food was provided by supporters, but the school still needed money for books and writing materials, and donors had the right to know how their gifts were spent.

Elsie was always glad to see Amos. He was thirty-two now, and handsomer than ever. In her dreams she was married to him, not Kenelm. But on this occasion she was nervous. She had something important to tell him. She would have preferred not to, but it was better he heard it from someone who loved him.

She offered him a glass of sherry and he accepted. They sat side by side at the dining room table and looked at the ledger together. Her nostrils picked up a pleasant faint aroma of sandalwood. There was nothing to worry about in the numbers: she could raise the money needed without difficulty.

When he closed the ledger she should have given him the news right away, but she was too tense, and instead she said: "How are you managing without Kit? He was your right-hand man."

"I miss him. Hamish Law is still with me but I'm looking for someone who understands the machines."

"I can't imagine that Kit likes the military life."

"I believe Colonel Northwood is very glad to have Kit."

"I'm sure." This was her chance, and she steeled her nerve. "Speaking of Northwood . . ." With an effort she controlled the trembling in her voice. "Did you know that Jane is expecting a baby?"

There was a long moment of silence.

Then he said: "Good Lord."

He stared at her, and she tried to read his face. He had gone pale. He was feeling some strong emotion, but she could not tell what.

His lips moved as if he was trying to speak. After a few moments he managed to say: "After all this time."

"They've been married nine years." She succeeded in keeping her voice steady.

Belinda Goodnight and the town gossips had said that Jane was unable to conceive—"barren" was the word they used. They also speculated that Northwood could not sire a child, and that another man must be the real father. The truth was that they did not know anything.

Elsie talked to fill the silence. "They'll be hoping for a boy. Northwood and his father must want an heir."

Amos said: "When is the baby due?"

"Soon, I think."

He looked thoughtful. "Perhaps this will bring them closer together."

"Perhaps." Northwood and Jane had always spent a lot of time apart.

Amos said: "Jane has never tried very hard to hide her dissatisfaction."

In the last few months Elsie had sensed that Amos did not care about Jane quite as passionately as he once had. She wondered whether something had changed. But that had been wishful thinking. He was evidently moved by this news.

The other theory of the gossips was that the father of Jane's baby was Amos.

That, Elsie thought, was completely unbelievable.

On a field five miles outside Kingsbridge, Kit was teaching five hundred new recruits how to form a square.

Infantry normally advanced in a line across the battlefield. This was a good formation unless they were attacked by cavalry, when riders could quickly go around the end of the line and attack them from behind. The only way to defeat a cavalry attack was to form a square.

A line of soldiers ordered to form a square without further instruction would mill about confusedly for half an hour, in which time they could all be wiped out by the enemy. So there was a standard procedure.

The men were divided into eight or ten companies, each with two or three sergeants and the same number of lieutenants. Those in the center of the line would stay where they were to form the front of the square. The two wings would wheel back to form the sides of the square, and the elite grenadiers and light companies would run around to form the base. The sergeants had halberds to keep the lines straight.

The men stood a yard apart until there were twenty-five of them in the line. At that point they began to double up. When the lines were four deep, the front two knelt and the back two stood. The officers and medical staff stood in the center of the square.

For three hours Kit made the men form a line, then change to a square, then form a line again, and change again. By the end of the morning they could form a square in five minutes.

In battle, the front line would fire, then run to the back and reload.

They were to fire when the cavalry was thirty yards away. Any sooner, and they would miss their targets and be reloading when the cavalry reached them and mowed them down. Any later, and wounded men and horses would crash into them, breaking the line.

He told the men that they would be able to resist a cavalry charge if they kept their nerve and held formation. He had no experience of battle so he had to fake a tone of conviction. When he imagined himself standing on a side of the square, facing hundreds of men on powerful warhorses charging at him at top speed, brandishing pistols to shoot him with and long, sharp swords to stick into his body, he felt quite sure that he would drop his musket on the ground and run away as fast as his legs could carry him.

※

The christening of Jane's baby was a very grand affair. The cathedral bells rang a long, complicated change that Spade and his ringers had been practicing. Everybody who was anybody in the county came, in their best clothes. The sun shone brightly through the stained glass, and the nave was full of flowers. The earl of Shiring himself attended, tall but now a little stooped, clearly happy that his bloodline had been continued. There were hymns and prayers of thanksgiving, and the choir sang.

Amos looked hard at Viscount Northwood, getting more like his father as he passed through his thirties, his curly hair beginning to recede, giving him a hairline like the letter M. He appeared so pleased with himself that Amos felt sure the man had no suspicion that he might not be the father.

Amos himself did not know the truth of that. He would have liked to ask Jane, but he had not had a chance to speak to her. Anyway she might not tell him the truth. She might not even know the truth. She had told him frankly that she and Northwood made love seldom—but *seldom* was not the same as *never*. With Amos she had done it only once, but once could be enough. And there was yet another possibility: Amos might not have been her only illicit lover.

Whatever the truth of that, he felt sure that when Jane came to his house in the rainstorm she had wanted him to make her pregnant. And she had wanted to make sure of it, which was why she had been so angry when he refused to do it again. She had not been motivated by affection for him, or even lust; she had used him in the hope of conceiving an heir. She wanted to be the mother of an earl.

Jane herself was holding the baby, wrapped in a white shawl of soft wool that looked, to Amos's trained eye, to be cashmere. She was as well-dressed as always, in a fur-trimmed coat, a bonnet tied under her chin, and a double row of pearls around her neck; but she looked drained. No doubt the birth had been an ordeal—birth usually was, Amos understood. She must have been relieved, though. Aristocratic wives who failed to produce children were sometimes treated as if they had shirked their responsibilities. She had escaped that fate. Now no one could call her barren.

Bishop Reddingcote performed the ceremony. He carried himself proudly in his liturgical robes, an ankle-length white cope and a long purple stole. He held a silver aspergillum for sprinkling holy water. He seemed to enjoy being the star of the show. In sonorous tones he said: "In the name of the Father, the Son, and the Holy Spirit I baptize you Henry."

As if to reassure people that the baby really was the son of Henry Northwood, Amos thought sourly.

After the service the congregation walked to the Assembly Rooms, where the earl was giving a reception. A thousand guests had been invited, and for everyone else free beer was poured at trestle tables set up in the road outside. Baby Henry lay in a crib in the ballroom, and Amos was able to get a good look at him for the first time.

The look told him only that the baby had blue eyes, pink skin, and a round face, like every other newborn he had ever seen. Little Henry wore a knitted cap, so Amos could not even tell the color of his hair, if he had any. He did not resemble Henry Northwood or Amos Barrowfield or anyone else. In twenty years' time he might have curly hair and a big nose, like Northwood, or a long face and a long chin, like Amos; but it was equally likely that he would look like Jane's father, the handsome Charles Midwinter, and then no one would ever be able to tell who was the boy's sire.

While Amos thought all that, something else was going on underneath. He felt a powerful urge to take care of this helpless baby. He wanted to soothe him and feed him and keep him warm—even though the child clearly was sleeping contentedly, had plenty of food, and was probably too warm in his cashmere blanket. There was nothing rational about Amos's emotion, but it was no less strong for that.

The baby opened his eyes and let out a cry of mild discontent, and Jane appeared immediately and picked him up. She murmured soothing baby talk into his ear, and he relapsed into serenity.

She caught Amos's eye and said: "Isn't he beautiful?"

"Amazingly beautiful," said Amos politely but dishonestly.

"I'm going to call him Hal," she said. "I can't have two Henries—it's too confusing for them both."

For a moment there was no one nearby. Lowering his

voice, Amos said: "Thinking back to January, I can't help but wonder—"

She interrupted him, her voice almost a whisper, but very intense just the same. "Don't ask me," she said.

"But surely—"

"Never ask me that question," she said fiercely. "Never, ever."

Then she turned to an approaching guest, smiled broadly, and said: "Lady Combe, how very kind of you to come—and such a long way!"

Amos left the building and went home.

King George refused to pardon Tommy Pidgeon.

This was a shock to everyone. A pardon had been expected because the perpetrator was so young and the theft was relatively trivial.

Hornbeam should have been pleased but he was not. A year ago he had been determined that the little thief should die for his crime, but now he was not so sure. Things had changed in the meantime. Opinion in Kingsbridge had turned against Hornbeam. He did not really care whether people liked him or not, but if he continued to be seen as some kind of ogre it might affect his ambitions. It was good for people to be afraid of him, but he wanted one day to be mayor of Kingsbridge, or perhaps its member of Parliament, and for that he would need votes.

An additional irritation was that his wife, Linnie, felt sorry for him. She showed it by ordering his favorite foods for family meals, patting him affectionately at random moments, and telling little Joe to play quietly. He hated to be pitied. He became curt with her, but that only made her more sympathetic.

If the king had pardoned Tommy most of the emotion would have drained out of the drama, and people would have forgotten it. But now it would have to reach its grisly denouement.

Hornbeam still felt he had been right to push for execution. Once you started forgiving thieves because they were hungry, you were on a slippery slope that led to anarchy. But he saw now that he had been too aggressive about it. He should have pretended to feel compassion for Tommy, and to have committed him to the assizes with apparent reluctance. He would try that approach in future. I sympathize with your plight, but I can't change the laws of the country. I'm really sorry. Really.

He was not good at playacting, but he would try.

He put on a black coat and a black neckcloth, signs of respect. He went out before breakfast. There was some danger of trouble from the crowd, so he had told Sheriff Doye to arrange the execution at an early hour, before the worst of the town's ruffians got out of bed.

The scaffold was already in the market square, its rope dangling, the noose tied, a stark outline against the cold stone backdrop of the cathedral. The platform on which the condemned boy would stand was hinged, and propped up by a stout length of oak. Beside the scaffold stood Morgan Ivinson, a sledgehammer in his hand. He would use the sledgehammer to knock aside the prop, and Tommy Pidgeon would die.

A crowd had gathered already. Hornbeam did not mingle with them, but stood some distance away. After a minute Doye approached him. Hornbeam said: "As soon as you like."

"Very good, Alderman," said Doye. "I'll fetch him from the jail right away."

More people entered the square, as if told by invisible heralds that the killing was about to happen, or summoned by funeral bells that only they could hear. In a few minutes Doye returned, accompanied by Gil Gilmore, the jailer. The two men held between them the slight form of Tommy Pidgeon, his hands tied behind his back. He was crying.

Hornbeam looked around the square for Jenn, the thief's mother, but did not see her. A good thing, too: she would have made a fuss.

They guided Tommy to the steps. Going up he stumbled, and they lifted him by his arms and carried him to the platform. They held him firmly while Ivinson put the noose over his head and tightened it with careful professionalism. Then all three men went back down the steps.

A clergyman climbed the steps, and Hornbeam recognized Titus Poole, the vicar of St. John's, who had tried to convince him to give Jenn Pidgeon Poor Relief. Poole spoke clearly, so that his voice carried across the square. "I've come to help you say your prayers, Tommy."

Tommy's voice was panicky, terrified. "Will I go to hell?"

"No, not if you believe in the Lord Jesus Christ and ask him to forgive your sins."

"I do!" Tommy cried. "I believe in him, but will God forgive me?"

"Yes, Tommy, he will," said Poole. "As he forgives the sins of all of us who believe in his mercy."

Poole put his hands on the boy's shoulders and lowered his voice. Hornbeam guessed the two of them were probably saying the Lord's Prayer together. After a minute Poole blessed Tommy, then walked down the steps, leaving Tommy alone on the scaffold.

Doye looked at Hornbeam, and Hornbeam nodded.

Doye said to Ivinson: "Do it."

Ivinson lifted his sledgehammer, swung it back, then accurately struck the oak prop, so that it flew sideways. The platform swung down and hit the base of the scaffold with a bang. Tommy dropped, then the rope went taut and the noose tightened around his neck.

The crowd let out a collective moan of pity.

Tommy opened his mouth, to scream or breathe, but he could do neither. He was still alive: the fall had not broken his neck, perhaps because he was too light in weight, and instead of instant death he now began to suffer slow strangulation. He wriggled desperately, as if his movements might free him, and he began to swing to and fro. His eyes seemed to bulge and his face turned red. The seconds passed with agonizing slowness.

Many people in the crowd were weeping.

Tommy's eyes did not close, but gradually his movements became feeble and stopped. The small body swung through a decreasing arc. At last Ivinson reached up and felt Tommy's wrist. He paused a few moments, then nodded to Doye.

Doye turned to the crowd and said: "The boy is dead."

The crowd were not going to riot, Hornbeam could see. The mood was sorrowful, not furious. Several black looks were directed his way but no one spoke to him. They began to disperse, and Hornbeam turned homeward.

When he arrived his family were having breakfast. Young Joe was at the table. He was a bit young to eat with the grown-ups, but Hornbeam was fond of the boy. He had a napkin under his chin and was eating scrambled eggs.

Hornbeam sipped coffee with cream. He took some toast and buttered it, but ate only one bite.

Deborah said quietly: "I assume the deed has been done."

"Yes."

"And it all went off without trouble?"

"Yes."

They were speaking in generalities, to avoid upsetting Joe, but he was too smart for them. "Tommy Pidgeon has been hanged and now he's dead," the boy said brightly.

His father, Howard, said: "Who told you that?"

"They were talking about it in the kitchen."

Hornbeam muttered: "They should know better—in front of a child."

Joe said: "Grandpa, why did he have to be hanged?"

Howard said: "Don't pester your grandpa when he's drinking his coffee."

"It's all right," said Hornbeam. "The boy might as

well know the facts of life." He turned to Joe. "He was hanged because he was a thief."

That was not enough for Joe. "They say he stole because he was hungry."

"That's probably true."

"Perhaps he couldn't help it."

"Does that make a difference?"

"Well, if he was hungry . . ."

"Suppose he had stolen something else? What would you say if he took your toy soldiers?"

The soldiers were Joe's most treasured possession. He had more than a hundred, and he knew the rank of each by its uniform. He often lay on the carpet for hours, fighting imaginary battles. Now he was disconcerted. After a minute's thought he said: "Why would he steal my soldiers?"

"For the same reason that he stole a pink ribbon—to sell and use the money to buy bread."

"But they're my soldiers."

"But he was hungry."

Joe was so torn by this moral dilemma that he was on the verge of tears. Seeing that his mother, Bel, intervened. "What you'd probably do, Joe, is let him play soldiers with you, and ask the cook to bring him some bread and butter."

Joe's face cleared. "Yes," he said. "And jam. Bread and butter and jam."

Joe's problems were solved, but there was no parallel available for such as Tommy Pidgeon. However, Hornbeam did not say that. There was plenty of time for Joe to learn that not all life's problems could be solved with bread and butter and jam.

Elsie went to see Jenn Pidgeon and make sure she was all right. She crossed the double bridge and followed a track to Morley's farm. Before she got there she saw

Paul Morley in a field and he told her that Jenn lived in a lean-to at the back of his barn. She found the place, but no one was there. It was about the poorest home Elsie had ever seen. There was one mattress and two blankets, plus two cups and two plates, but no table or chairs. Jenn had not been merely short of money, she had been destitute.

Mrs. Morley was in the farmhouse and said Jenn had left late yesterday. "I asked her if she was all right, but she didn't answer."

Elsie's journey had been in vain, and she headed back to the town. Approaching the bridge from the southern side, she saw a man coming along the near bank. He had a fishing rod strapped across his back, and he carried in his arms something that made Elsie's heart stand still.

As he got closer she saw that it was a woman, in a dress so wet it was dripping as he walked.

"No," said Elsie. "No, no."

The woman's head, arms, and legs all dangled helplessly from her body. She was completely unconscious, or worse.

Elsie was shocked to see that the woman's eyes were wide open, staring up at the sky and seeing nothing.

"I found her at the bend in the river, where all the rubbish fetches up," the man said. Judging by Elsie's clothes that she might be a person of some authority, he added: "I hope I done right to bring her."

"Is she dead?"

"Oh, yes, and cold, too. I reckon she went in the water yesterday after dark, and no one seen her till I come along. I don't know who she is, though."

Elsie knew. It was Jenn Pidgeon.

Elsie stifled a sob. "Can you bring her to the hospital on Leper Island?" she said.

"Oh, yes," said the fisherman. "Easily. She don't hardly weigh nothing, poor thing. Nothing at all."

Napoleon never invaded England.

He took the army he had gathered at Boulogne and marched them east, to the German-speaking territories of central Europe. They engaged with the Austrian army, and that autumn the French won battle after battle: Wertingen, Elchingen, Ulm.

However, England's Royal Navy won a major sea battle off the coast of Spain, near Cape Trafalgar, to national rejoicing.

Then in December the French defeated the combined Austrian and Russian armies at Austerlitz.

And so, year after bloody year, the war dragged on.

PART V

The World War

1812–1815

CHAPTER 32

Dear Spade,

Well, I am still alive after 13 years in the army, they should give me a medal just for sticking it out! Now I am in Spain, where they have things they call cigarroes, tobacco wrapped in a leaf, it all burns and no need for pipes, we all smoke them now.

Anyway, we just had a victory although it came at a high price. We besieged a town called Badajoz that had a very strong wall and the French fought back like hell plus the weather was against us, I was digging trenches in the pouring rain.

It took us a week to wheel the guns into position. The wooden roads our engineers built over the mud kept getting washed away. But we managed in the end and I wish I had a pound for every cannonball we fired, they fell on the town like rain. It took nearly another two weeks but we breached their walls in the end and stormed the defenses.

Well, it was the worst battle I seen so far, because they fired down on us with everything they got, shrapnel, grenades, bombs, even bales of burning hay. We lost thousands of men, it was a slaughterhouse, Spade, but we got through in the end, and then I can tell you we gave the citizens hell, I will say no more about that, several men were flogged next day for rape.

It looked worse in the morning, bodies piled high, trenches full of blood. I saw our commander, Wellington, looking at all the corpses of his men, and he was weeping, wiping his tears with a white handkerchief.

Next we march north. In your prayers please ask God to continue to protect me.

Your affectionate brother-in-law Freddie Caines.

The earl of Shiring died in July 1812. Two days later Amos ran into Jane outside Kirkup's Book Shop in the High Street. She was dressed in black but fizzing with excitement. "Don't you dare offer me your sincere condolences," she said. "I'm exhausted from pretending to be bereaved. I hope I don't have to fake it with you. I've lived with that boring old man for sixteen years—who knew he would keep going to the age of seventy-five! I might as well have married him instead of his son."

She was in her fortieth year, and still devastatingly attractive. The little lines at the corners of her eyes and the few silver threads in her dark hair seemed only to add to her allure. And black suited her. However, Amos was no longer in love with her. Ironically, that made their friendship stronger. And she was kind about letting him discreetly spend time with Hal, now approaching seven years old, whom he suspected—without confirmation—to be his son.

He did not regret the change in his relationship with

Jane. He had had a youthful passion for her which had unfortunately lasted long after his adolescence was over. In some ways, he thought, he had been slow to grow up. Now he could fall in love again, theoretically. However, he was less than a year from his fortieth birthday, and he felt too old to go courting. He was lonely only at night. He had many friends, and his days were busy, but there was no one to share his bed.

Jane was focused on herself, as usual. "I'm free from my father-in-law at last," she said jubilantly. "And I'm a countess!"

"Which was what you always wanted," Amos said. "Congratulations."

"Thank you. I have to organize the funeral, because Henry's too busy. He's the earl now, obviously. He'll have to take his seat in the House of Lords. He'll be the new lord lieutenant of Shiring. And little Hal has become Viscount Northwood."

Amos had not thought of that. The boy who might or might not be his son was now an aristocrat. Why, in ten years' time he might go to Oxford and study. Amos had always wished he could have studied, and failing that he had hoped for a son to fulfill his dream. Perhaps it was going to happen after all.

Then it occurred to Amos that Hal might want to be like his father, and become a soldier. The possibility was dismaying. That Hal should be killed by a sword, or a cannonball! For an instant Amos felt ill.

At that moment the boy himself emerged from the shop carrying a book. Amos was suddenly conscious of his own heartbeat. He had to hide the surge of emotion that came over him at the sight of Hal.

As yet the boy's appearance gave no clue to his paternity: he had dark hair and a cute face like his mother. He would change in adolescence. Perhaps Amos would become sure of the truth then.

Hal was followed out of the shop by the proprietor,

Julian Kirkup, a round, bald man who was obsequiously delighted to have an aristocratic customer.

Forcing a casual tone of voice, Amos said: "What book did you get, Hal?"

"It's called *The History of Sandford and Merton*. They're two boys."

Kirkup said: "Very suitable for young Lord Northwood, if I may say so. Good morning to you, Lady Shiring, and Alderman Barrowfield." Amos had been made an alderman some years ago, in a surge of support for liberal tolerance that had also added Spade to the city government at last.

Hal said: "I haven't any money, but Mr. Kirkup said he could put it on your account, Mama."

"Yes, dear, of course," said Jane. "What is the book about?"

Kirkup said: "Tommy Merton is a rather spoiled young man who is befriended by plain, honest Harry Sandford. A most moral tale, my lady, and very popular."

Amos thought it sounded a bit pious, but he said nothing.

Jane said dismissively: "Thank you, Mr. Kirkup."

The bookseller retired, bowing.

Amos said: "I'm sorry that you've lost your grandfather, Hal."

"He was jolly nice," said Hal. "He used to read to me, but I can read for myself now."

Remembering the deaths of his own grandparents Amos did not recall any great emotion. They had seemed so ancient as to be nearly dead anyway, and he had been surprised at the distress of his parents. His reaction had been like Hal's, a matter-of-fact sort of regret that fell short of grief.

He said to Jane: "Funeral at the cathedral, I presume?"

"Yes. He'll be buried at Earlscastle, in the family vault, but the service will be here in Kingsbridge—I do hope you'll come."

"Certainly."

They parted company, and Amos walked on. Almost immediately he met Elsie, in a primrose-yellow dress. They talked about the death of the earl—it was the big news of the moment. Elsie said: "Now that Henry is the earl, Kingsbridge will be looking for a new member of Parliament."

"I had not thought of that," said Amos. "There may be a by-election, though perhaps that will be unnecessary—there's talk of a general election soon." Prime Minister Spencer Perceval had been assassinated, shot dead in the lobby of the House of Commons by an obsessive man with a complicated grievance. The new prime minister was the earl of Liverpool, and he might want to consolidate his position by seeking the endorsement of voters.

Elsie said: "Hal Northwood is obviously too young."

"Hornbeam will want the job," Amos said.

"He always wants everything," she said scornfully. "He's overseer of the poor, chairman of justices, and alderman. If there was a post of inspector of dunghills he'd want it."

"He likes to have power over people."

Elsie pointed a finger at Amos's chest. "You. You should be our member of Parliament."

That surprised Amos. "Why me?"

"Because you're smart and fair-minded, and everyone in town knows that," she said with warm enthusiasm. "You'd be great for the town."

"I don't have time."

"You could appoint a deputy to manage the mills while Parliament is in session."

Amos realized that her suggestion was not a spur-of-the-moment idea, but something she had been mulling. He pulled thoughtfully at the end of his nose. "Hamish Law could do it. He knows the business inside out."

"There you are."

"But could I win?"

"All the Methodists would vote for you."

"But most of the voters are Anglican."

"Nobody likes Hornbeam."

"They're afraid of him, though."

"What a dismal prospect—to get an MP no one wants, just because we're scared of him."

Amos nodded. "It's not the way this is supposed to work."

"Well, please think about running."

She was very persuasive. "All right."

"Perhaps you could make peace."

"I'd certainly be in favor of it." Britain had been at war with Bonaparte's France for twenty years and there was no end in sight. In fact the conflict had spread around the world.

Britain had enraged the new American republic by hijacking American ships and forcing their sailors to join the Royal Navy—a new twist on the press gang idea—so the United States had declared war on Britain and invaded Canada.

Spain had been overrun by the French army, and Bonaparte had made his brother Joseph king. Spanish nationalist insurgents were fighting the French conquerors with the help of a British force that included the 107th (Kingsbridge) Foot Regiment. The commander in chief there, the earl of Wellington, was highly regarded but he had made little progress.

And Bonaparte had now invaded Russia.

Perpetual war caused further decline in world trade and rampant inflation. British people became poorer and hungrier while their sons died in faraway places.

Elsie said angrily: "There must be a way. War isn't inevitable!"

Amos liked how angry she got about such things. What a contrast with Jane, who was angry only on her own behalf.

"Member of Parliament," he said musingly. "I'll have to give this more thought."

Elsie smiled, and as always her smile was radiant. "Keep thinking," she said as she walked away.

Amos crossed the bridge and went to the industrial zone on the south bank of the river. He had three mills now. In one of them, Barrowfield's New Mill, Kit Clitheroe was installing a steam engine Amos had commissioned.

Kit had served five years in the militia, ending up with the rank of major, then he had resigned and set up the joint business he and Roger Riddick had long planned. Roger designed the machines and Kit built them. Despite the wartime slump they were making money.

Amos still thought of Kit as a boy even though he was now twenty-seven, prosperous, and an engineering wizard. Perhaps it was because Kit was still single and seemed to have no interest in finding a girlfriend, let alone marrying one. Amos had wondered whether Kit was a slave to a hopeless passion, as Amos himself had been over Jane.

Kingsbridge was converting to steam power. The river was cheaper, as a driver of machinery, but less reliable. Its force was sometimes strong, sometimes weak. After a dry summer the water level would be low and the current lethargic, and the wheels of the mill would turn lazily while everyone waited for autumn rain. Coal cost money, but it never ran out.

Amos's new steam engine was enclosed in a room of its own, to limit the damage if it exploded, which sometimes happened when a safety valve failed. The room was well-ventilated with a chimney for the exhaust. The boiler was cradled in a sturdy oak plinth. It would use water pumped from the river and filtered. "When will you be ready to connect up to the machinery?" Amos asked.

"Day after tomorrow," said Kit. He was always precise and confident.

Amos checked on the other two mills, his main interest to make sure he would be able to deliver to each customer on the date promised. At the end of the afternoon he returned to his office and wrote letters. The machines slowed to a halt at seven o'clock in the evening, and he went home.

He sat down to the supper his housekeeper had left on the kitchen table. A moment later there was an urgent knocking at the front door, and he got up to answer it.

Jane stood on his doorstep.

"This has happened before," he said.

"But it's not raining and I'm not amorous," she said. "I'm furious. I'm so angry I couldn't stay in the house with my husband." She walked in uninvited.

Amos closed the door. "What's happened?"

"Henry is going to Spain! Just when I thought I could start to live the life of a countess at last!"

Amos guessed why. "He's going to join the Kingsbridge regiment."

"Yes. Apparently it's a family tradition. When the old earl inherited his title, in his twenties, he spent three years on active service with the 107th Foot. Henry says he is expected to do the same—especially now the country is at war."

"It is one of the few sacrifices the English aristocracy make to justify their lives of idle luxury."

"You sound like a revolutionary."

"A Methodist is a revolutionary who doesn't want to chop off anyone's head."

Jane was suddenly deflated. "Oh, don't be smart," she said. "What am I going to do?"

"Come and share my supper."

"I couldn't eat, but I'll sit with you."

They went to the kitchen. Amos poured wine for Jane and she took a sip. He said: "Hal is looking well."

"He's lovely."

"In a few years' time he may start to resemble his father—whoever that may be."

"Oh, Amos, he's yours."

Amos was startled. She had never said that before. He said: "You're in no doubt?"

"You saw him come out of the bookshop! Henry never bought a novel in his life. He only reads military history."

"That doesn't really prove anything."

"I can't prove anything. I just see you in him every day."

Amos thought about that for a while. He was inclined to trust Jane's instinct. He said: "Perhaps when Henry goes to Spain I might see more of Hal? But I suppose you'll be living at Earlscastle."

"On my own? No, thank you. I'll make Henry keep Willard House. I'll have my own apartment, and the militia can use the rest of the building. I'll tell him the nation needs it. He'll do anything if he thinks it's patriotic."

"Are you sure you don't want some of this pie? It's good."

"Perhaps I will."

"I'll cut you a thin slice. You'll feel better with some food inside you."

She took the plate he passed her and put it down, but instead of eating she stared at him.

He said: "What have I done?"

"Nothing," she said. "You've just been your usual thoughtful, loyal self. I should have married you."

"You should have," said Amos. "And now it's too late."

Elsie knew how lucky she was. She was still alive after having five children—the last, George, born in 1806. Many women died in childbirth and few lived to have this many. Even more unusual, all her children were perfectly healthy. But the birth of Georgie had not been like the others: the labor had been long and she had bled a lot. When it was over she had firmly told Kenelm that there were to be no more. He had accepted her ruling. Marital intimacy had never been a high priority for him and he had little regret about giving it up. Now, six years later, she was sensing changes in her body that told her she would soon lose the ability to conceive anyway.

She and Kenelm had never been really close. He was not good with children, so he took little part in raising his own. And he rarely visited her Sunday school. He was not lazy: as dean he carried out his duties energetically. But they shared little. Her real partner was Amos, who was quietly dedicated to the Sunday school and easy with youngsters, despite having none of his own.

All five children came to the dining room of the deanery for breakfast. Kenelm would probably have preferred the younger ones to eat in the nursery, but Elsie said they were old enough—Georgie was six—and anyway this was really the only way to teach them table manners. Stephen, the eldest, was fifteen, and attending Kingsbridge Grammar School.

Kenelm occasionally took the opportunity to test them on religious knowledge, and today he asked who in the Bible had no mother or father. He told them to answer in order of age, starting with the youngest.

Georgie said: "Jesus."

"No," said Kenelm. "Jesus had a mother, Mary, and a father, Joseph." Elsie wondered whether Kenelm would stumble into the question of how Joseph could be the father when the mother was a virgin. The older children might wonder. But he swerved around it by immediately asking: "Martha, do you know?"

Martha was a year older than Georgie and she had a better answer. "God," she said.

"True, God has no parents, but I'm thinking of someone else, a man."

Richie, ten, said: "I know, I know—Adam."

"Very good. And there's one more."

Billy, who was next in line, looked miserable and said: "I don't know."

Kenelm looked at Stephen.

Stephen, who was a grumpy adolescent, said: "It's a trick question."

"Is it?" said Kenelm "Why?"

"The answer is Joshua, because he was the son of Nun. That was his father's name, Nun, but it sounds like a word for nobody."

Billy was outraged. "Not fair!" he said. "You cheated, Daddy."

Elsie laughed. "Billy's right, it wasn't a fair question. I think all the children did very well. They shall each have six pence to buy licorice."

Mason brought in the post and Kenelm turned his attention to his correspondence. The children finished eating and left. Elsie was about to get up when Kenelm looked up from a letter and said: "Oh!"

Elsie said: "What?"

"The bishop of Melchester has died."

"Isn't he quite young?"

"Fifty. It's unexpected."

"Shame."

"So the archbishop will be looking for a replacement."

Kenelm was excited but Elsie felt nothing but dismay. "I know what you're thinking."

He said it anyway. "This is the big chance I've been waiting for. It's not one of the big important bishoprics, so it's suitable for a young man. I'm forty years of age, I've been dean of Kingsbridge for eight years, I have an Oxford degree—I'm the perfect candidate to be bishop of Melchester."

Elsie was grim. "Aren't you happy here?"

"Of course I am, but it's not enough. My destiny is to be a bishop. I've always known that."

That was true, but as young men grew older their

ambitions generally moderated. "I don't want to go to Melchester," she said. "It's a hundred miles away."

"Oh, but you'll have to go," Kenelm said carelessly. "For a bishopric."

He was right, of course. A woman followed her husband. She had less freedom than a servant.

"You're very confident," Elsie said. "You can't know what the archbishop might have in mind."

"But I'll soon find out. Augustus Tattersall is making his triennial tour of the archdiocese and he'll be here in Kingsbridge next week."

Tattersall was the archbishop's right-hand man. "He'll stay at the bishop's palace."

"Of course. But I shall invite him to dine with us one evening."

"Very well."

Looking complacent, Kenelm folded his napkin and said: "I think I shall probably learn everything I need to know."

⁂

Three years ago, while Kit was still in the militia, Roger had come to his house one Monday evening and shared the family supper. Jarge had then gone to ringing practice, Sal had gone to the Bell, and Sue had gone walking out with a boy she liked, Baz Hudson.

Kit and Roger had sat in the kitchen by the fire, Roger puffing at a pipe. Kit felt strange, being alone in the house with Roger, but he did not know why. He should have been happy: he liked Roger.

They sat in silence for a minute or two, then Roger put down his pipe and said: "It's all right, you know."

Kit was puzzled. "What's all right?"

"To feel the way you do."

Kit's face suddenly felt warm. He was blushing. His feelings were secret, because they were shameful. Surely

Roger could not know what was in his heart? It was impossible.

Roger said: "Believe me, I know how you feel."

Kit said: "How can you know how another person feels if he doesn't tell you?"

"I've been through it myself—everything you're going through. And I want you to understand that it's all right."

Kit did not know how to respond to this.

Roger said: "You should say it. Say how you feel. Tell me. I promise you, it will make everything happy again."

Kit was determined not to say anything, but against his will it came out. "I love you," he said.

"I know," said Roger. "I love you, too." Then he kissed Kit.

Soon afterward Kit had been able to resign from the militia and they had set up the business. They rented a house in Kingsbridge with a workshop on the ground floor and living quarters upstairs. From then on they had slept together every night.

Gradually, Kit had become the responsible one, the adult. He handled the money. Roger himself had made this a condition of their partnership, knowing that he would always gamble with everything he had. Kit received the payments, paid the bills, and divided the profits in two. His own money went into his account at the Kingsbridge and Shiring Bank. Roger's half went, sooner or later, to Sport Culliver. Another condition, imposed by Kit, was that Roger would never borrow, but Kit was not sure Roger kept that rule. Roger was a genius—his engineering brain was remarkable—but he was addicted to betting. Kit looked after him and protected him. It was the reverse of the relationship they had had in the old days back in Badford.

On Sundays Roger went to Culliver's to play five-card loo and Kit saw his mother. He met the family at the Methodist Communion service, then walked with them to their home. He had bought them a modest house. Sal was forty-five and Jarge forty-three, and both continued to work, Sal for Amos and Jarge for Hornbeam. Kit gave them a load of coal every winter and sent them a joint of meat on Saturday for the Sunday dinner. They had no desire for luxury. Sal would say: "We don't wish to live like rich folk, because we're not." But Kit made sure they never wanted for anything.

Sue had married Baz Hudson. He was a good carpenter who was rarely short of work. He was not a Methodist, so he and Sue went to St. Luke's, but they joined the family for dinner afterward.

Sal served ale. Kit preferred wine but he never asked Sal for it because he knew Jarge would drink too much. Even sober, Jarge was provocative. Knowing that Baz was a patriotic conservative, he said: "I should think it will do the Russians a lot of good if they're conquered by Bonaparte."

Kit said mildly: "Now there's a surprising point of view. What makes you say that, Jarge?"

"Well, the Russians are slaves, aren't they?"

"Serfs, I believe."

"What's the difference?"

"They work their own land."

"But they're the property of the local count, aren't they?"

"Yes, serfs are like property."

"There you are, then."

Baz spoke. "It was Bonaparte who reinstated slavery in the French empire, wasn't it?"

"No," said Jarge. "The revolution abolished slavery."

"Yes," said Baz, "but Bonaparte brought it back."

Kit said: "Baz is right, Jarge. They were afraid of losing their empire in the West Indies, so Bonaparte made slavery legal again."

Jarge was annoyed. "Well, I still think the Russians would be better off under Bonaparte than under their tsars."

Baz persisted. "I don't think we'll ever know. Apparently it's not going well for the French in Russia. All their soldiers are dying of starvation and disease and they haven't even fought a battle yet, according to the newspapers."

"I don't pay much attention to what the newspapers say," Jarge said grumpily. He did not take correction well.

Sal said: "Well, that was a lovely piece of beef, Kit, thank you, and I've made a nice suet pudding with currants in it."

Baz said: "I love a suet pudding."

The atmosphere cleared as the plates were taken away and the dessert was brought. Baz said: "Business still good for you, Kit?"

"Not bad. That oak mounting you made for Amos's boiler was nicely done, very sturdy, thank you."

"It should last longer than the boiler."

Jarge picked up his spoon but did not eat. He said: "Well, I don't know, the two of you are making machinery to put other men out of work. Where's the sense in it?"

Kit said: "I'm sorry, Jarge, but times change. If we don't keep up with new developments we'll find ourselves left behind."

"Is that what I am, then—left behind?"

Sal put her hand on his arm and said: "Eat some pudding, husband."

Jarge ignored her. "You know what the Luddites are doing up north, don't you?"

Everyone knew about the Luddites. They were said to be captained by a man called Ned Ludd, though that was probably a false name, if he existed at all.

Jarge went on: "They're smashing the machines up!"

Kit said: "They're mostly framework knitters, I believe."

Jarge said: "They're men who won't put up with ill treatment from the masters, that's what they are."

Sal said: "Well, I hope you don't wish for machine smashing here in Kingsbridge."

"I say you can't blame men who get angry about the way they're trodden down."

"We may not blame them, but the government does. You don't want to get transported to Australia."

"I'd rather spend fourteen years in Australia than let myself be exploited by the masters."

Sal got cross. "You've got no idea what it's like in Australia, and anyway, what makes you think it would be only fourteen years?"

"Well that's what my sister got."

"Yes, but she left seventeen years ago and she hasn't come back. Few do."

Kit said: "Anyway, they've changed the law: it's the death penalty now for breaking machinery."

"Since when?" said Jarge.

"Parliament passed the Frame Work Act back in February or March."

"They're trying to break our spirit, that's what it is," said Jarge. "First the Treason Act and the Seditious Meetings Act, then the Combination Act, and now this. Any man who stands up for the rights of working people is liable to be hanged. We're turning into a nation of milksops."

He paused, looking belligerent, then said: "It's no wonder we can't beat the French."

When Augustus Tattersall came to dinner at the deanery he asked Elsie about the Sunday school, questioning her closely with genuine interest, which pleased and flattered her. He ate enthusiastically but drank little wine. Kenelm was clearly irritated by the small talk and soon ran out of patience. When the fruit and nuts arrived he said: "I must ask you, Archdeacon, about the vacant bishopric of Melchester."

"By all means."

"I'm most curious to know what sort of man the archbishop is looking for."

"I'd be glad to satisfy your curiosity," Tattersall said in his soft, precise voice. "I assume you consider yourself a candidate—not unreasonably—therefore I must tell you right away that you have not been chosen."

The quickest way was the kindest way, Elsie thought, but Kenelm could not hide how distraught he was. His face reddened, and for a worrying moment she was afraid he would burst into tears; but anger took over. He clenched his fists on the white tablecloth. "You think I am a good candidate, yet—" He almost choked on the words. "Yet you imply that someone else has got the job."

"Yes."

"Who is he?" Kenelm demanded, then he realized he was being impolite and hastily added: "If you don't mind my asking."

"I don't mind at all. The archbishop has chosen Horace Tomlin."

"Tomlin? I know Tomlin! He was two years behind me at Oxford. I haven't heard that he's had a particularly distinguished career since then. Tell me honestly, Archdeacon—is it because I'm Scottish?"

"Absolutely not. I can assure you of that."

"Then why?"

"I'll tell you. Tomlin has spent the last five years as chaplain to a regiment of dragoons, and has resigned only because of a sickness contracted in Spain."

"A chaplain?"

"I know what you're thinking. The cream of the clergy do not often become army chaplains."

"Exactly."

"In a way that's the point. The archbishop feels strongly about the war. We're fighting against atheistical ideas, he believes, and although Bonaparte has reversed some of the most offensive anti-Christian acts of the French revolutionaries he has not returned the property stolen from the French church. Our clergy should be part of the battle, the argument goes. Soldiers on the front line, knowing they may die at any minute, are most in need of God's comfort. Our best clergymen must not stay at home in comfortable livings, they must go where they're needed. This is the kind of service that the archbishop is most eager to reward."

Kenelm was silent for a long moment. Elsie sensed this was not a time for her to speak. At last Kenelm said: "Let me make sure I understand you."

Tattersall smiled encouragingly. "Please speak freely."

"You think I am deserving of a bishopric."

"I do. You're intelligent, upright, and hardworking. You would be an asset to any diocese."

"But you know that in the present circumstances the archbishop will always favor a man who has served as a chaplain."

"Correct."

"So the only way I can be sure of achieving my hopes is to become a chaplain."

"The only sure way, yes."

Kenelm picked up his wineglass and drained it. He looked like a man facing execution.

Elsie thought: Oh, no.

"In that case," Kenelm said, "I shall offer myself to the 107th Foot Regiment tomorrow morning."

CHAPTER 33

Pastor Midwinter said he would make the announcement on Sunday morning after Communion. Amos was nervous all through the service. He could not foresee how much support he would get. Elsie said that people knew him and liked him, but would they really want him to represent them in Parliament?

They were in the third Methodist Hall to be built in Kingsbridge. This one was the largest—so imposing that some members felt it was too impressive. People should be awestruck by God's work, not by the constructions of men, they felt. But others thought it was time Methodism started to look good as well as feel good.

Amos was neutral in that argument. He had more important matters on his mind.

Midwinter began: "You probably all know that Parliament has been dissolved, and a general election has been called."

He, too, was imposing and impressive. He was sixty-seven, but the years had made him more distinguished. His hair and beard were pure white now, but just as thick as ever. The young girls saw him as a father figure, but middle-aged women often blushed and simpered when he spoke to them in his velvet voice.

"I'm very pleased to tell you that one of our number here is putting his name forward as a candidate," he said. He paused for dramatic effect, then said: "Amos Barrowfield."

People did not clap in church, even in Methodist halls, but they expressed their approval by saying "Amen," or

"Praise the Lord." Several caught Amos's eye and made encouraging signs.

That was good.

Midwinter said: "It's about time our movement made more impact on the way our country is governed. I have agreed to nominate Amos, and I trust this will meet with your approval."

There were more amens.

"Those who would like to help with Amos's election campaign are invited to stay behind for a planning meeting."

Amos wondered how many would stay.

When the service ended, it always took awhile for the congregation to disperse. They greeted one another and chatted, exchanging news. After about thirty minutes half of them had left, and the rest began to sit down again, looking expectant.

Midwinter called them to order and asked Amos to speak.

He had never made a speech before.

Elsie had told him to talk just as he did to a class in Sunday school. "Be natural, be friendly, and just say clearly what you want to say. You'll find it easy." She had always had faith in him.

He stood up and looked around. They were mostly men. "Thank you all," he said, rather stiffly; then he decided to be honest, and added: "I wasn't sure anyone would stay."

They laughed at his modesty, and the ice was broken.

"I will stand as a Whig," he went on. The Whigs were the party of religious tolerance. "But I don't plan to campaign on religious issues. If elected I must work in the interest of all Kingsbridge folk, Methodist and Anglican, rich and poor, voters and nonvoters."

That was too general, he realized. He said ruefully: "I suppose they all say that," and once again his honesty was rewarded with an appreciative laugh.

"Let me be more specific," he went on. "I believe this

country needs two simple things: bread and peace." He took a sip from a glass of water. Some in the audience were nodding agreement.

"It's shameful that we have legislation to keep the price of grain high. That protects the incomes of the richest men in the land, and the ordinary people pay the cost in the increased price of bread. Those laws must be repealed, and people must have bread, which the Bible calls the staff of life."

There was a chorus of amens. He had touched a nerve. The country's landed nobility shamelessly used their power—especially their votes in the House of Lords—to guarantee agricultural profits and therefore high rents for their thousands of acres of farmland. Methodists, who were mostly middle-class craftsmen and small businessmen, were outraged. The poor just went hungry.

"And we need peace almost as much as the poor need bread. The war has done terrible damage to businessmen and working people, yet our prime ministers—William Pitt, the duke of Portland, Spencer Perceval, and now the earl of Liverpool—have not even tried to make peace. That must change." He hesitated. "I could say more, but I see by your faces that you don't need convincing."

They laughed at that, too.

"So let's talk about what we need to do to change things." He sat down and gestured to the pastor.

Midwinter stood up again. "There are about one hundred and fifty men entitled to vote in Kingsbridge," he said. "We need to find out who they are, how they have voted in the past, and how they're inclined this time. Then we can begin the work of changing people's minds."

Amos thought it sounded like a formidable task.

Midwinter said: "The mayor is obliged to publish a list of eligible voters, so we should see that list on town noticeboards in the next few days, and it will also appear in the *Kingsbridge Gazette*. We need to find out how they voted in the last general election, five years ago: this is public information and there will be a record at the Guild Hall, and also in the newspaper files." There was no privacy in voting: men had to call out their choice in front of a room full of people, and every individual vote was reported in the *Gazette*. "And then, once we're informed, we'll begin talking to them." He paused.

"Forgive me if I now say something to you that will seem unnecessary: there will be no bribery, nor any hint of bribery, in our campaign."

In fact Kingsbridge elections had always been fairly free of corruption. In recent years the voters had cheerfully chosen Viscount Northwood. But Midwinter felt that the stance of the Methodists needed to be underlined, and Amos agreed. "We will not buy drinks for voters in public houses," Midwinter went on. "No favors will be offered or promised in return for support. We will ask people to vote for the best candidate, and say we hope they choose ours."

A voice spoke up from the back, and Amos saw that it was Spade. "I think women play an important part in elections," he said. His wife, Arabella, was with him: she had become a Methodist when they married. Between them sat Abe, Spade's thirteen-year-old stepson—or son, if you believed Belinda Goodnight's gossip. Spade went on: "They may not be keen on arguing about the grain laws or Bonaparte, but just about every woman in this congregation can put her hand on her heart and say that she has known Amos Barrowfield for years and he is an honest and hardworking man. A remark like that can do more good than talking about Austria and Russia."

"Very good," said Midwinter. "Now, I suggest we meet again after the Wednesday prayer meeting—by then we should have the list of voters. But before we break up this evening we need to sign the nomination papers. I will propose. Spade, will you second? It would be good to have an alderman on the list."

"Delighted," said Spade.

"And it would help to have an Anglican, too. As Amos said earlier, he doesn't want to be just the Methodist candidate."

Amos said: "What about Cecil Pressman, the builder? He's against the war, I know, but he goes to St. Luke's."

"Good idea."

Spade said: "I know Cecil. I'll talk to him."

And the campaign was on.

Elsie went to see her mother most afternoons. The house was spacious—quite large for two adults and a child, Elsie thought. When it had belonged to Will Riddick it had been all oak paneling and dark velvet, notorious for the number of whores who went in and the quantity of empty bottles that came out. Now it was quite different. Spade liked classical furniture—square-backed chairs, straight table legs—but with elaborately patterned fabrics. Arabella loved curves and cushions, fat upholstery, and curtains that hung in swags and festoons. Elsie had watched, over the years, as their different preferences had melded into a unique style, richly comfortable without being fussy. And in summer there were bowls of roses from the garden.

Arabella was still beautiful at fifty-eight. Spade thought so, too: you only had to see them together to know that. Today she wore an olive-green silk dress with lace on the sleeves and hem. Spade liked her to be well-dressed.

When Elsie visited it was usually just the two of them: Spade was at work and Abe at school. Alone, they talked intimately. Arabella knew that Elsie was still hopelessly in love with Amos, and Elsie knew that Abe was Spade's son, not the bishop's. Abe was a happy boy: the bishop's curse had not worked.

They had tea in the drawing room, which faced west

and was lit now by a pale October sun. Elsie said: "I ran into Belinda Goodnight on the way here."

"You and she were great chums as children," said Arabella.

"I remember she had a toy theater. We used to make up plays about girls who fell in love with Gypsy boys."

"You made me watch one. It was dire."

Elsie laughed. Then she said: "Now Belinda's a terrible gossip."

"I know. They call her the Kingsbridge Gazette."

"She told me something that bothered me. Apparently people are saying openly that Amos is the father of the young Viscount Northwood."

Arabella shrugged. "It might be true, though nobody really knows. There were whispers when he was born, but they died down. I wonder why the rumor has started up again."

"Because of the election, obviously. Hornbeam's supporters are pushing it."

"Do you think the gossip will stop people voting for Amos?"

"It might."

"I'll tell David about this." Arabella liked to call her husband David, not Spade.

There was a minute of silence, unusual between the two women, then Arabella said: "There's something else on your mind."

Elsie nodded. "Kenelm is packing to go to Spain."

"When does he leave?"

"It depends. We're sending reinforcements to Wellington in the New Year, and there will be a ship leaving from Combe to take officers and men who have joined the 107th Foot. Kenelm is waiting for notification."

"You'll have to move out of the deanery. Where will you go?"

"I'm not sure. I may rent a house."

"You look troubled. Tell me what's on your mind."

"Oh, Mother," said Elsie, "I'd love to live here, with you."

Arabella nodded, unsurprised. "And I'd like to have you, you know that."

"But what about Spade?"

"That's what I'm not sure of. He's a kind and generous man, but will he be happy to share his house with another man's children—five of them?"

"It's a lot to ask, I know. But will you speak to him about it?"

"Of course," said Arabella. "But I don't know what he'll say."

Spade was in the hall, getting ready to go to a council meeting, and Arabella was watching him. Breeches were going out of fashion, and he was wearing trousers made of a striped gray cloth. He put on a blue double-breasted tailcoat and a tall-crowned hat with a curly brim, then peered into a mirror that hung by the door.

"I love the way you wear your clothes," she said. "So many men are slovenly and drab. You always look like one of those tailor's advertisements."

"Thank you," he said. "I am an advertisement, though for cloth rather than tailoring."

She said: "I heard some gossip today that I should tell you."

"I hope it's spicy."

"Sort of, but it will trouble you."

"Go on."

"Elsie dropped by this afternoon as usual."

Spade recalled that Arabella's son-in-law had joined the 107th Foot as a chaplain. "When does Kenelm leave for Spain?"

"He's still making the arrangements."

"I interrupted you, sorry. What was the gossip?"

"People are saying that Amos is the father of little Viscount Northwood."

This was bad news, Spade thought. A whiff of immorality could be damaging in an election. Something similar had blighted his first attempt to become an alderman. The second time around he had been married and the scandal had lost its sting.

He said: "What does Elsie mean by 'people'?"

"She got it from Belinda Goodnight, who's a real chatterer."

"Hmm. There were rumors about young Hal, but that was years ago." Spade remembered, because Hal's position was similar to that of Abe. Both boys were thought to have been conceived in adultery. Arabella's first husband, Bishop Latimer, had reacted with fury, but when Jane had presented Henry with a son and heir he had seemed not to question the boy's paternity, and the gossip had faded away.

Arabella said: "The rumors seem to have resurfaced."

Spade gave a disgusted grunt. "And I know why. It's the election."

"Do you think Hornbeam started it?"

"I have absolutely no doubt."

Arabella's face took on an expression of distaste, as if she had eaten something sour. "That man is all knives."

"True. But I think I can get him to shut his mouth. I'll talk to him tonight."

"Good luck."

Spade kissed her lips and went out.

The borough council, consisting of all twelve aldermen, met in the chamber of the Guild Hall. As always, there was a decanter of sherry and a tray of glasses on the table for the aldermen to help themselves. The mayor, Frank Fishwick, chaired the meeting with his usual mixture of amiability and firmness.

Both parliamentary candidates were aldermen and present at the meeting. Spade was struck by the contrast between them. Amos was not yet forty and Hornbeam was pushing sixty, but it was not just age that separated them. Amos seemed comfortable with who he was and what he was, but Hornbeam had the face of a man whose life has been continual conflict. He bent his head and looked out from under his bushy eyebrows as if ready to take on all challengers.

The election was the main topic. Parliament had ordered it to be held between October 5 and November 10—the exact date was up to the local authority. The council decided to have hustings in the market square on St. Adolphus Day and voting the day after in the Guild Hall. Two nominations had been received and both were in perfect order. The count would be supervised by the clerk to the justices, Luke McCullough. The arrangements were not controversial and Spade spent the time planning his conversation with Hornbeam.

As soon as the meeting broke up he went straight to Hornbeam and said: "A word, Alderman, if I may."

Hornbeam looked aloof and said: "I'm pressed for time."

Spade changed his tone. "You've got time for this, Joey, if you know what's good for you."

Hornbeam was too startled to reply.

"Step aside with me for a moment." Spade steered Hornbeam to a corner. "That old rumor about Amos and Hal Northwood has been exhumed."

Hornbeam regained his customary hauteur. "I hope you don't imagine that I go around the town spreading salacious gossip."

"You're responsible for what your friends and supporters say. Don't pretend they're out of your control. They do what you tell them, and when you say stop they stop. Now you have to order them to hold their tongues about Hal Northwood."

Hornbeam raised his voice. "Even if I believed what you're saying, why should I obey you?" One or two men looked over at them.

Spade replied equally loudly. "Because people who live in glass houses shouldn't throw stones."

Hornbeam lowered his voice. "I have no idea what you're talking about," he said, but his manner contradicted his words.

Spade spoke quietly but insistently. "You force me to say it. You're illegitimate yourself."

"Nonsense!" Hornbeam's breath was coming in short gasps and he was struggling to control it.

"You have always said that your mother died during an epidemic of smallpox in London."

"That is perfectly true."

"You can't have forgotten Matt Carver."

Hornbeam grunted as if he had been punched in the belly. His face paled and he struggled to breathe. He seemed unable to speak.

"I met Matt Carver," Spade said. "He remembers you well."

Hornbeam recovered the power of speech. "I don't know anyone of that name."

"Matt stood beside you at the scaffold while you watched your mother die." It was cruel, but he had to make sure Hornbeam understood that he knew everything.

Hornbeam managed to say: "You devil."

Spade shook his head. "I'm not a devil, and I'm not going to destroy your reputation. You don't deserve sympathy, but elections should not be won and lost on malicious gossip. I've known about your past for seven years, and I haven't told anyone—not even Arabella. And I won't— provided the talk about Amos and Hal stops."

Hornbeam gasped: "I'll see to it."

"Good," said Spade, and he walked away. Hornbeam would never forgive him for this, but they had been enemies for years, so Spade had lost nothing.

Back at home, supper was on the dining room table.

Spade took some cabbage soup and cut two slices of cold beef. Arabella sipped wine, and he sensed that she had something to say. When he had finished eating he pushed his plate away and said: "Come on, out with it."

She smiled. "You always know when I'm worried about something."

"Go on."

"We're very happy in this house, you and me and Abe."

"Praise the Lord and thanks to you."

"And thanks to you, David. You like me."

"That's why I married you."

"You think it's commonplace, but it's not. I've never before lived with a man who liked me. My father thought I was ugly and disobedient, and Stephen just wasn't very interested in me."

"It's hard to imagine."

"I don't want anything to change."

"But life changes. And . . ."

"And Elsie and her children have nowhere to live after Kenelm leaves for Spain."

"Oh!" he said. "I assumed they would come here and live with us."

"Really?"

"We've got enough room."

"And you wouldn't mind?"

"I'd be delighted! I love them all."

"Oh, David, thank you," she said, and she burst into tears.

Amos Barrowfield never ceased to infuriate Hornbeam. Amos had frustrated Hornbeam's plan to take over old Obadiah Barrowfield's business, and later he had contrived to get Will Riddick removed from his position in charge of purchasing for the militia. Now Amos was trying to become a member of Parliament. Hornbeam had been waiting to step into Northwood's shoes for so long that he had come to think of it as his right. He had not expected to have to fight for it.

He had hoped to destroy Amos's reputation with the story that he was the father of Hal Northwood, but the cunning Spade had undermined that tactic. Now Hornbeam would have to bring out his big guns.

He set out to visit Wally Watson, a yarn producer. Wally did no weaving, just spun and dyed a product of consistent quality in a manufactory that was the largest yarn mill in town. He ought to be a Tory and vote for Hornbeam, but he was a Methodist, which might incline him to the Whigs and Barrowfield.

Men like Wally formed a substantial part of the electorate. But Hornbeam thought he knew how to deal with them.

As he stepped out of the door his grandson joined him, heading for the grammar school in the square, and they walked down Main Street together. Young Joe Hornbeam was now taller than his grandfather. He was fifteen, but looked grown-up. He even had a fairly respectable mustache. His eyes were still blue but no longer innocent: now they were penetrating and challenging. He was serious, unusually so for his age. He studied hard and planned to go to Edinburgh University to do science and engineering.

Hornbeam had worried for years about who would head the enterprise after him. Deborah had the ability, but it was difficult for a woman to lead men. His son, Howard, was not up to the job. But Joe would be able to do it. He was the only grandchild, and Hornbeam's crown prince.

It was important to Hornbeam that the business should continue. It was his life's work. He had secured for himself a plot in the cathedral graveyard—which had cost him the price of a complete new set of oak choir stalls, elaborately carved—but his real memorial would be the largest cloth-making enterprise in the west of England.

"How is the election campaign, Grandfather?" Joe said. "Getting off to a good start?"

"I wasn't expecting any opposition," Hornbeam said. "There's usually only one nomination."

"I don't see how a Methodist can be a lawmaker. They have already broken the laws of the church."

Young Joe's only shortcoming was a tendency to take a strict moral line. He was not softhearted—far from it—but he would occasionally insist on doing what he thought was the right thing, even when circumstances suggested a compromise. At school he had refused a prize because another boy had helped him write the winning essay. He argued against peace talks because Bonaparte was a tyrant. He admired the military, because the officers gave the orders and the men had to obey. Hornbeam felt sure these attitudes would soften with maturity.

Now he said: "We have to deal with men as they are, not as they ought to be."

Joe looked reluctant to accept that, but before he could think of a reply they arrived at the square and parted company.

Hornbeam crossed the bridge, walked past his own mills, and made his way to Watson's yarn mill. Like most masters, Watson spent much of his time in the factory, watching the machines and the hands who operated them, and that was where Hornbeam found him; but he had a separate office, walled off from the noise, and now he took Hornbeam there.

Wally was young. If people were going to be dissenters they usually converted when young, Hornbeam had noticed. "I trust that red-dyed yarn I made you from silk and merino wool is performing well, Mr. Hornbeam?"

Merino wool was soft, and the silk made it stronger and gave it a slight sheen. It was popular for women's dresses. "Fine, thank you," said Hornbeam. "I'll probably order more soon."

"Splendid. We stand ready to supply you." Wally was nervous because he did not know what was coming. He said: "You and I have done a lot of business over the years, and I believe it has always been to mutual benefit."

"Quite. In the last twelve months I've spent two thousand three hundred and seventy-four pounds with you."

Wally looked startled by the exactness of the sum, but he said: "And very glad I am to have the business, Mr. Hornbeam."

Hornbeam got to the point abruptly. "I hope I can rely on your vote in the coming election."

"Ah," said Wally, and he looked embarrassed and a bit frightened. "Barrowfield is a fellow Methodist, as you know, so I'm in a difficult position."

"Are you?" said Hornbeam. "Really?"

"I wish I could vote for both of you!" Wally gave a stupid laugh.

"But since you can't . . ."

There was a silence.

Hornbeam said: "It's not for me to tell you how to vote, of course."

"Very good of you to say so." Wally seemed to be under the illusion that Hornbeam was backing off.

He would have to be disabused. "You must balance your friendship with Barrowfield against my two thousand three hundred and seventy-four pounds."

"Oh."

"Which is more important to you? That's the decision you face."

Wally looked agonized. "If you put it like that . . ."

"I do put it like that."

"Then please be assured that I will vote for you."

"Thank you." Hornbeam stood up. "I felt confident we would see eye to eye in the end. Good day to you."

"Good day to you, Mr. Hornbeam."

St. Adolphus Day was cold but sunny. The square was packed full, with the hustings an extra attraction. Sal went with Jarge, as always, but she was anxious. He worked at Hornbeam's Upper Mill, which was closed three days a week because Hornbeam was no longer supplying the militia. His income was halved, and he spent his off days in the taverns. The combination of idleness and drink made him bad-tempered. His companions were other struggling weavers, and they fed one another's discontents.

There was always minor trouble at the fair: petty theft, drunkenness, and quarrels that sometimes ended in blows; but today Sal felt a greater menace in the air. Machine smashing had mushroomed earlier in the year, starting in the north and spreading around the country, and it had been organized with a degree of military discipline that terrified the ruling elite. Jarge applauded it.

And something else had unnerved her. Although the murder of Prime Minister Perceval had had nothing to do with the cloth industry—the killer had been obsessed by a personal grudge—the news of the assassination had been greeted by rejoicing in some towns. Class hatred in England had reached a new peak.

Sal was afraid that today there would be a riot when the parliamentary candidates made their speeches. If that happened her main concern would be to keep Jarge out of trouble.

As they were strolling around the stalls, Jarge's friend Jack Camp appeared. "Coming for a tankard, Jarge?" he said.

"Maybe later," Jarge replied.

"I'll be in the Bell." Jack went off.

Jarge said to Sal: "I haven't got any money."

She felt sorry for him, and gave him a shilling. "Enjoy yourself, my love, and just promise me you won't get drunk," she said.

"I promise." He went off.

A recruiting sergeant from the 107th Foot had set up a stall, Sal saw. He was talking to a group of local boys, showing them a musket, and Sal stopped to listen. "This is the latest Land Pattern flintlock musket being issued to infantry regiments," he said. "Three feet and three inches long, without the bayonet. Known as a Brown Bess."

He handed it to a tall lad standing near him, and Sal recognized Hornbeam's grandson, Joe. He was being watched with great interest by a mill girl, and after a moment Sal remembered her name: Reenie Reeve. She was pretty, with a bold expression, and she clearly had designs on Joe. Sal sighed, remembering her own adolescent yearnings.

Joe hefted the gun and held it to his shoulder. Sal watched, amused.

"Notice how the barrel is not shiny but browned," said the sergeant. "Can any of you young men guess why that change has been made?"

Joe said: "To save the trouble of shining it?"

The sergeant laughed. "The army doesn't care to save you trouble," he said, and the other boys laughed with him. "No, the dull brown color is so that the barrel won't reflect light. The sun shining off your weapon could help a Frenchman aim accurately at you."

The boys were agog.

"There's a notched backsight, to improve your aim, and a scrolled trigger guard, to help you keep a steady hand. What do you think is the most important quality for a musketeer to have?"

"Good eyesight." It was Joe again.

"Very important, obviously," said the sergeant. "But for my money what the infantryman needs more than anything else is calmness. That will help you aim carefully and fire smoothly. It's the hardest thing to have, when bullets are flying and men are dying; but it's what will keep you alive when the others are panicking."

He took the musket from Joe and passed it to another boy, Sandy Drummond, son of the wine merchant.

The sergeant said: "We mainly use ready-made cartridges nowadays—the old-fashioned powder horn and bullet bag slow you down. The infantryman of today can reload and fire three times a minute."

Sal moved away.

Near the cathedral steps, two open-sided carts had been parked twenty yards apart, and the rival political groups were putting up bunting and flags, preparing to use them as speaking platforms. Sal noticed Mungo Landsman and his mates from the Slaughterhouse lurking nearby. They were always eager for a fight.

Amos was beside the Whig platform, wearing a bottle-green coat and a white waistcoat, shaking hands and talking to passersby. One of them spotted Sal and said: "Here, Mrs. Box, you work for this man, tell the truth now, what's he like, as a master?"

"Better than most, I'll give him that," said Sal with a smile.

The clerk to the justices and lawyer to the council, Luke McCullough, appeared. Hornbeam was behind him, dressed in sober black, wearing a wig and a hat. McCullough was responsible for making sure the election was run properly. "Mr. Barrowfield, Mr. Hornbeam, I'm going to toss this penny. Mr. Hornbeam, as the senior alderman you have the privilege of calling heads or tails. The winner has the choice of speaking first or second."

He tossed, and Hornbeam said: "Heads."

McCullough caught the penny, closed his fist, and laid the penny on the back of his other hand. "Tails," he said.

Amos said: "I will speak second."

Sal guessed he had made that choice in order to be able to undermine whatever Hornbeam said.

McCullough said: "Mr. Hornbeam, we may begin as soon as you're ready."

Hornbeam returned to the Tory cart and spoke to Humphrey Frogmore, who had nominated him. Frogmore handed Hornbeam a sheaf of papers, and Hornbeam studied them.

Kingsbridge folk still remembered Tommy Pidgeon, and Hornbeam would never be popular, but he did not need to worry about the general public, Sal reflected. Only the voters mattered, and they were businessmen and property owners, unlikely to sympathize with a thief.

Sal saw that Jarge and Jack Camp had come out of the Bell, along with a few more friends, all carrying their tankards. Sal wished they had stayed inside.

McCullough got up on the Tory cart and vigorously rang a handbell. More people gathered around. "Election of a member of Parliament for Kingsbridge," he said. "Joseph Hornbeam will speak first, then Amos Barrowfield. Please listen to the candidates in silence. Rowdiness will not be tolerated."

Good luck with that, Sal thought.

Hornbeam came up onto the stage clutching his papers and stood still for a moment, collecting his thoughts. The crowd was quiet, and in the pause one man shouted: "Rubbish!" There was great hilarity at this witticism, and Hornbeam was disconcerted.

However, he recovered quickly. "Voters of Kingsbridge!" he began.

Of the thousand or so people in the square, about half were listening. However, there were only one hundred and fifty voters in the town. Most of this morning's audience were not enfranchised, and many resented that. In the taverns there was angry talk about the failings of "hereditary government," a euphemism for the king and the House of Lords, who by law could not be criticized.

The most radical men in the taverns spoke approvingly of the French revolution. Sal had talked about France with Kit's partner, Roger Riddick, who had lived there. Roger had nothing but contempt for Englishmen who approved of the revolution. It had replaced one tyranny with another, Roger said, and Englishmen enjoyed much greater liberty than their neighbors. Sal believed him, but said it was not enough just to argue that England was not as bad as other places. There was still enormous injustice and cruelty. Roger did not disagree.

Hornbeam said: "Our king and our church are under threat." Sal respected the church, or some parts of it at least, but she had no time for the king. She guessed that most mill hands felt the same.

Someone near to Jarge yelled: "The king never did nothing for me!" That got cheers from the crowd.

Hornbeam talked about Bonaparte, who was now emperor of the French. Here Hornbeam was on firmer ground. Many Kingsbridge hands had sons in the army and saw Bonaparte as right-hand man to Satan. Hornbeam got a few cheers for denigrating him.

He spoke about the French revolution, implying that Whigs had supported it. Sal wondered how many people would fall for this. Some in the crowd might, perhaps, but most of those entitled to vote were better informed.

Hornbeam's greatest mistake was his manner. He spoke as if giving instructions to his mill managers. He was firm and authoritative, but distant and unfriendly. If speeches changed anything, this was losing him votes.

At the end he returned to the topic of king and church, and spoke about the need of respect for both. This was quite the wrong line to take with mill hands, and the booing and hooting got louder. Sal eased her way through the crowd to stand near Jarge. When she saw Jack Camp bend down and pick up a stone, she grabbed his throwing arm and said: "Now, Jack, think twice before you murder an alderman." It was enough to discourage him.

Hornbeam finished to tepid applause and loud jeers. So far, so good, thought Sal.

Amos was quite different. He came up on the stage and took off his hat, as if to indicate respect for his audience. He spoke without notes. "When I ask Kingsbridge folk what worries them today, most of them say two things: the war, and the price of bread." That drew an immediate burst of applause.

He went on: "Alderman Hornbeam spoke about the king and the church. None of you mentioned those things to me. I think you want peace and a seven-penny loaf." A cheer began, and he had to raise his voice to finish the thought. "Am I right?" The cheer became a roar.

Hostility to the war was not confined to the workers. Among the class of men who could vote, there were plenty who were fed up after twenty years of it. Too many young men had died. Many people wanted to return to normal life, when the European continent was somewhere to visit, to buy clothes in Paris and look at ruins in Rome—not a place where your sons went to be killed. But most MPs were focused on victory, not peace. Some voters might think Parliament needed more men like Amos.

He was a natural speaker, Sal thought, one of those who could win over a crowd without appearing to try. Part of his charm was that he did not know he was charming.

There was little booing, and nobody threw stones.

When it was over she congratulated Amos. "They loved you," she said. "They liked you much better than Hornbeam."

"I believe they did," he said. "But they're more scared of Hornbeam."

The voting took place the next morning. Kingsbridge's 157 voters crammed into the Guild Hall. Luke McCullough and an assistant sat behind a table in the middle of the room, each holding an alphabetical list. The voters crowded around the table, trying to attract McCullough's attention. When he caught someone's eye, or heard their name, he would check his list, to make sure the man was registered, then repeat the name loudly. At that point the voter would shout who he was voting for, and McCullough would write either "H" or "B" next to the voter's name.

Hornbeam got a pleasant feeling of self-esteem every time someone voted for him; each vote for Amos Barrowfield made him wince. The voting was slow and he soon lost count of the exact scores. All the people Hornbeam did business with voted for him—he had made sure of that by his personal visits. But would that be enough? The only thing he felt certain of was that neither candidate was very far ahead.

It took almost two hours, but at last McCullough called out: "Are there any more votes to be cast?" and no one answered.

Then he and his assistant counted. When both had finished, the assistant whispered in McCullough's ear, and McCullough nodded agreement. But then they counted again, just to be sure. It seemed the result was the same, for McCullough stood up.

"The member of Parliament for Kingsbridge has been chosen by a free and fair election," he said; and the room went very quiet. "I hereby declare the winner to be Joseph Hornbeam."

His supporters cheered.

As the applause died down, one of Barrowfield's supporters said loudly: "Next time, Amos."

Alan Drummond, the wine merchant, shook Hornbeam's hand and congratulated him. His son and Hornbeam's grandson were friends. They had played a football match yesterday afternoon, and Joe had asked permission to stay over at the Drummond home last night. Now Hornbeam said: "I imagine our two lads had a good time. They probably stayed up all night talking about girls."

"No doubt," said Drummond, "but I was surprised not to see them at church this morning. Perhaps you should have rousted them out of bed."

Hornbeam was puzzled. "I should have got them up? But they were at your house."

"No, at yours, begging your pardon."

Hornbeam was quite sure the two boys had not spent the night at his house. "But Joe told me he was staying with Sandy."

The two men stared at one another, perplexed.

Drummond added: "And I looked into Sandy's room this morning—his bed had not been slept in."

That seemed to settle it. Hornbeam said: "Then they must be at my house. Obviously I misunderstood." But he did not often misunderstand things and he remained troubled. "I'm going home to check."

"I'll come with you, if I may," said Drummond. "Just to be sure."

They made their way out of the room slowly, for Hornbeam's supporters wanted to congratulate him; but he was brusque with them all, shaking hands and thanking them but keeping moving, ignoring all attempts to engage him in conversation. Out on the cold street he quickened his pace, and Drummond had to hurry to keep up with Hornbeam's long legs.

They reached Hornbeam's place in a couple of minutes. The footman Simpson opened the door and Hornbeam said without preamble: "Have you seen Joe this morning?"

"No, sir, he's at Mr. Drummond's . . ." Simpson spotted Drummond standing behind Hornbeam and tailed off.

"I'm going to check his room." Hornbeam ran up the stairs, and Drummond hurried after him.

Joe's bed had not been slept in.

Drummond said: "Now what the devil are those two up to?"

"I hope it's only mischief," Hornbeam said. "The alternative is that some accident has befallen them, or there has been a fight and they're lying in a ditch somewhere." He frowned, thinking. "Who else was involved in yesterday's football match, do you know?"

"Sandy mentioned Rupe Underwood's boy, Bruno."

"Let's find out if he knows anything."

Rupe's silk ribbon business had prospered and he now had a fine house in Cookshop Street. Hornbeam and Drummond hurried there and knocked at the door. They found the Underwood family just sitting down to their midday dinner. Rupe had once been one of Jane Midwinter's many admirers, Hornbeam recalled, but he had married a woman who looked less pretty and more sensible than Jane, and she had evidently borne him the three healthy adolescents now sitting at the table.

Rupe stood up. "Alderman Hornbeam, Mr. Drummond, this is a surprise. Is something wrong?"

"Yes," Hornbeam said. "We can't find Joe and Sandy. I believe your boy Bruno might have played football with them yesterday, and we'd like to ask him if he has any idea where they might be."

A boy of about sixteen said: "I do know, sir."

Rupe said: "Stand up when Alderman Hornbeam speaks to you, lad."

"Sorry." Bruno scrambled to his feet.

Hornbeam said: "So where are they?"

Bruno said: "They joined the army."

There was a stunned silence.

Then Drummond said: "God in heaven have mercy."

Hornbeam said: "The stupid fools."

Rupe said to his son: "You didn't tell me that, Bruno."

"They asked us not to say anything."

Drummond said: "Why on earth did they do this?"

"Yes," Hornbeam said. "What possessed them?"

Bruno answered the question. "Joe said he had a duty to help defend his country, and Sandy agreed."

"Oh, for God's sake," said Drummond in anxious exasperation.

Bruno said: "The rest of us thought they were mad."

Hornbeam said: "Where have they gone?"

"They left with that recruiting sergeant who was at the fair."

Hornbeam said: "This can't be allowed. They're only fifteen!"

Rupe said: "Fifteen-year-olds are allowed to join up now, as long as they're tall enough. The law was changed back in 1797."

"I'm not going to accept this," Hornbeam said. The idea of his only grandchild risking his life in war was too dreadful to contemplate.

Drummond said: "Who can we go and see about it?"

The 107th Foot was in Spain, and it did not have an office in Kingsbridge. The military was represented by the militia here. Lord Combe was the new ceremonial colonel, but he was not a working officer, unlike Henry, who had been exceptional in that respect. The militia was effectively run by Archie Donaldson, who was now a lieutenant colonel and sat in Henry's old room at Willard House. Hornbeam said: "I'm going to confront Donaldson. He has to bring these boys back."

The two men set off again. Willard House was on the market square. The irritatingly officious Sergeant Beach was on duty in the hall, and after a token display of reluctance he showed them in to Donaldson.

Many militia officers and men had transferred to the 107th Foot for higher pay and the chance to see foreign places, despite the danger; but Donaldson had stayed. He was a Methodist, and might have been squeamish about killing people. Hornbeam remembered him as a fresh-faced ensign, but now he was middle-aged and heavy.

Hornbeam said: "Look here, Donaldson, my grandson and Drummond's son have been tricked into the army by a recruiting sergeant."

Donaldson was unsympathetic. "Nothing to do with me, I'm afraid."

"But you must know where they are."

"No. The recruiters aren't stupid. They don't tell me, or indeed anyone else. The army is quite accustomed to recruits' changing their minds, or relatives trying to get them out. Such cases get little sympathy from an army at war."

Hornbeam was infuriated, but he tried for a persuasive tone. "Come, come, Donaldson, you must have some idea where they go."

"Some idea, yes, of course," Donaldson admitted. "They're on their way to a port where reinforcements are being mustered for Spain. That could be Bristol, Combe, Southampton, Portsmouth, London, or somewhere I've never heard of. And wherever they are, they won't be allowed out of their officers' sight while they're in England. Next time they have a chance to run away they'll be in Portugal."

"I shall go to the War Office in London."

"I wish you well. But I think you'll find the War Office doesn't even have a list of the names of men in the army, let alone details of where individuals may be posted."

"Damnation."

Donaldson got a holier-than-thou light in his eyes. "It's very like what happened to Jim Pidgeon," he said mildly. "His wife couldn't find out where he had gone, you may remember. I expect she felt just the way you do now. And when she realized he had been impressed into the navy she couldn't get him back."

Hornbeam boiled with rage. "How dare you."

"I'm saying no more than the plain truth."

"You're a damned insolent dog, Donaldson."

"It's against my religion to challenge a man to a duel, Hornbeam—luckily for you. But if you can't speak like a gentleman you'd better get out of my office."

Drummond said: "Come on, Hornbeam, let's just go."

The two aldermen walked to the door and Drummond opened it. Hornbeam said: "This isn't over, Donaldson."

Donaldson replied: "You against the army, eh, Hornbeam? Should be an interesting fight. But I know who will win."

Hornbeam went out and Drummond followed. As they passed through the hall Drummond said: "Donaldson is a smug swine, but he's right, Hornbeam. It's a dead end. There's nothing we can do."

"I don't believe in dead ends," Hornbeam said. "Didn't I hear that the cathedral dean has volunteered to be a chaplain in the 107th Foot?"

"Yes, Kenelm Mackintosh, he's married to the daughter of the old bishop."

"Has he left for Spain yet?"

"I don't think so. I believe he's still living in the deanery."

"Let's find out if he can help us."

The dean's house was a few steps away. A maid answered the door and showed them into Mackintosh's study. They found him packing books into a trunk. His handsome face was creased with anxiety. Drummond said: "You're taking books to a war zone?"

"Of course," said Mackintosh. "A Bible, a prayer book, and a few devotional volumes. My mission is to give the troops spiritual nourishment. What else would I pack—pistols?"

Hornbeam did not want to discuss the role of army chaplain. "Joe Hornbeam and Sandy Drummond joined the 107th Foot yesterday and we can't find out where they are."

"My word!" said Mackintosh, startled. "I hope my boy Stephen isn't tempted."

"They're almost certainly on their way to Spain, where the 107th is fighting under Wellington."

"What do you want me to do?"

"Have them sent home!"

"Well, I sympathize, but I can't do that. I'm not going there to undermine the army by having its best young men sent home. If I tried it I'd probably be sent home myself—they'd undoubtedly feel that chaplains aren't as useful as healthy lads. If it's any consolation, I will give them a Christian burial if the need arises."

Suddenly Hornbeam felt his strength drain away. It was the mention of burial that floored him. For decades he had been sustained by the idea that pain and loss were over, that he was master of his fate now, and that life owed him no more tragedy. But that conviction crumbled inside him and left him with a trembling fear that he had not known since he was a child thief. "Mackintosh, please, I beg you," he said miserably, "when you get there, seek Joe out, and discover how he is, whether he is in good health, and well enough fed and clothed, and write to me if you can. He's closer to my heart than any other human being, and now, suddenly, he's out of reach, on his way to war, and I can't take care of him anymore. I'm a helpless man, on my knees to you, pleading with you: keep an eye on my boy—will you?"

Drummond and Mackintosh were staring at him in astonishment. He knew why: they had never seen him like this, never even imagined him like this, and they could hardly believe what they were seeing and hearing. But Hornbeam no longer cared what they thought of him. "Will you, Mackintosh, please?" he said.

Looking bemused, Mackintosh said: "I'll do what I can."

CHAPTER 34

Jarge came home in a foul mood, smelling of ale and tobacco smoke. He had clearly spent most of the day in a tavern with his friends. Sal was dismayed. "I thought you were going to see Moses Crocket today."

Crocket was a clothier. For a year or two his mill had struggled, but now he had won an army contract with a Devon regiment and his business was looking up. Jarge was still working only three days a week for Hornbeam, and Sal had suggested that Crocket might now be looking for weavers to work a full six days.

"Yes," said Jarge. "I saw Mose this morning."

"What went wrong?"

"He's changing to steam looms, that's what. He can't employ all the weavers he used to, let alone take on more. One man can monitor three or four steam looms at a time."

"What a shame."

"He's got to move with the times, he says."

"Can't argue with that."

"I can. The times may have to move back, I say."

Sal felt sorry for the mild-mannered Mose Crocket confronted by an angry Jarge. "I hope you didn't quarrel." She put a steaming bowl in front of him. "It's your favorite, potato soup, and there's fresh butter for your bread." She hoped the food would soak up some of the drink inside him.

"No, I didn't quarrel with Mose," said Jarge. "But Ned Ludd may quarrel with him, one of these days." He slurped some soup.

Ned Ludd had first appeared as the mythical leader

of machine breakers in the Midlands and the north, then Luddism had spread to the West Country, too.

Sal sat down opposite Jarge and began to eat. Soup and bread was good and filling. It was just the two of them at table since Sue had got married and Kit had set up home with Roger.

Sal said: "You know what's happening up in York, don't you?"

"They've arrested people."

"There will be a trial. And do you suppose it will be a fair trial?"

"Fat chance. They've probably arrested all the wrong men. They won't care. They'll hang some and transport others to Australia. They just want workers to be too scared to protest."

"And if there's machine breaking here in Kingsbridge, who do you think would be the first man to be arrested?" She buttered a slice of bread and handed it to him.

Jarge did not answer her question. Instead he said: "You know who sold Mose his damned steam looms, don't you? Your son, that's who."

"Kit is yours, too, and has been for seventeen years."

"My stepson."

"Aye, and for a stepfather you've done bloody well out of him, haven't you? A decent place to live and a good dinner every Sunday, all at his expense."

"I don't want charity. I want a good dinner at my own expense. A man wants to work and earn and pay for things himself."

"I know," said Sal, softening her tone. She did know. Money was no longer her number one problem, with Kit doing so well and being so generous. It was Jarge's pride. All men were proud, but he was more so than most. "Idleness is hard on a good man. The wastrels love it, but someone like you chafes. Just don't let that be your downfall."

They ate in silence for a while, then Sal washed up. It was ringing practice tonight. Sal had got into the habit of accompanying Jarge. In the old days she had gone to the Bell with Joanie to wait for the ringers, but since Joanie had been transported she had not liked to go to the tavern on her own.

They walked down the lamplit Main Street to the cathedral. As they crossed the square they passed Jarge's friend Jack Camp, dressed in an old coat with holes in it. He said: "All right, Jarge?"

"All is well," said Jarge. "Ringing practice, now."

"Maybe see you later, then."

"Aye."

As they approached the cathedral Sal said: "Jack seems very fond of you."

"What makes you say that?"

"He's spent all day in the tavern with you and now he wants to see you this evening."

Jarge grinned. "I can't help it if I'm lovable."

That made Sal laugh.

The north door to the church was unlocked, indicating that Spade was already inside. They climbed the spiral stairs to the rope room, where the ringers were taking off their coats and rolling up their sleeves. Sal sat up against the wall, out of the way. She enjoyed the music of the bells but more than that she liked the back-and-forth banter of the men, which was sometimes clever and always funny.

Spade called them to order and they began to warm up with a familiar change. Then they moved on to special-occasion changes, for weddings and christenings. Sal's mind wandered as she listened.

As always, she worried about her loved ones. Keeping Jarge out of trouble had been her life's work. It was good to stand up for your rights, but you had to do it the right way, more in sorrow than in anger. Jarge leaped straight into a quarrel.

Kit was twenty-seven and still single. As far as she

knew he had never had a girlfriend—he had certainly never brought one home. She was pretty sure she knew why. People would say he was "not the marrying kind," which was a polite expression. She did not mind, but she would be disappointed not to have grandchildren.

Kit had always been good with machines, and the business was prospering, but Roger was not the ideal type to have as a partner. A gambler was never really reliable.

Her niece, Sue, caused her the least concern. She was married and seemed happy. She had two daughters, so at least Sal had two grandnieces.

Her reverie was interrupted by Jarge. "I've got to step outside—call of nature. You know this next piece, Sal, can you take my place?"

"Glad to." She had done this often over the years, usually when a ringer canceled at the last minute. She was plenty strong enough, and her timing was good.

She stood by Jarge's dangling rope as he went down the stone staircase. She was a bit surprised at his exit—he was not usually subject to sudden calls of nature. Maybe he had eaten something bad—not her potato soup, she felt sure, but perhaps a dish he had got at the Bell.

She put the thought out of her mind and concentrated on Spade's instructions. Time passed quickly and she was surprised when the rehearsal came to an end. Jarge had not returned. She hoped he was not ill. Spade gave her Jarge's shilling payment, and she said she would pass it on.

They all went across the square to the Bell and met Jarge at the door. "Are you sick?" Sal asked him anxiously.

"No."

She gave him the shilling. "You can buy me a tankard out of that," she said. "I've earned it."

They settled down for an hour of relaxation before going home to bed. People who had to be at work at five in the morning did not stay up late.

However, the relaxation did not last an hour. After only a few minutes Sheriff Doye came in, wearing his cheap wig and carrying his heavy cane, looking both aggressive and frightened. He was accompanied by two constables, Reg Davidson and Ben Crocket. Sal stared at them, wondering what had got them agitated. She caught a worried glance from Spade that suggested he could guess what was on the sheriff's mind. Sal could not.

The drinkers in the tavern soon picked up the change in atmosphere. The room gradually went quiet and everyone looked at Doye. No one liked him.

"There has been a fire at Mose Crocket's mill," Doye announced.

There was a buzz of surprise around the room.

"It's clear from the debris that many of the machines had been smashed before the fire started."

There was a shocked reaction from the crowd.

"Also, the lock on the door had been broken."

Sal heard Spade say: "Oh, hell."

"On the wall outside, someone has written 'NED LUDD' in red paint."

That settled it, Sal thought; the mill had been attacked by Luddites.

"The men who did this will hang for it, you may be sure of that," Doye went on. Then he pointed directly at Jarge. "Box, you're the worst troublemaker in town. What have you got to say?"

Jarge smiled, and Sal wondered how he could look so confident when he was being threatened by the death penalty. He said: "Are you deaf, Sheriff?"

Doye looked angry. "What are you talking about?"

Jarge seemed to be enjoying himself. "We'll have to start calling you Deffo Doye."

"I'm not deaf, you oaf."

"Well, if you're not deaf, you must have heard what everyone else in Kingsbridge has been hearing this evening—me ringing the number seven cathedral bell for the last hour."

The crowd in the tavern laughed, pleased to see the unpopular Doye made a fool of. But Sal was not smiling. She understood what Jarge had done and she was angry. He had embroiled her in a plot—without telling her. She had no doubt that he had been one of the men who had broken into Crocket's Mill. But he had an alibi: he had been at ringing practice. Only Sal and the other ringers knew that he had slipped away—and he was relying on them to keep his secret. Either I lie about it, Sal thought, or I betray my husband and see him hanged. This was completely unfair.

For the second time that evening she met Spade's intelligent gaze. He had surely followed the same reasoning process and come up with the same conclusion: Jarge had compromised them all.

For the moment, however, Doye was flummoxed. He was not a quick thinker. His prime suspect had an alibi, and he did not know what to do next. After a long pause he said emphatically: "We shall see about that!" It was so weak that the crowd laughed again.

Doye made a hasty exit.

Conversation resumed, and the noise filled the room. Spade leaned forward and spoke to Jarge in a low, clear voice that could be heard by the other ringers. "You shouldn't have done this, Jarge," he said. "You've put us all in a position where we have to lie for you. Well, all right, I'll do it. But perjury is a serious crime, and I'm not willing to commit a crime for you."

The others nodded agreement.

Jarge pretended to be scornful. "It'll never get to court."

"I hope not," said Spade. "But if it does, and I can't avoid giving evidence, I'm telling you now, I shall speak the truth. And if you hang, it will be your own damn fault."

Early in February, when Elsie was living with her mother and Spade, she received a letter from Spain, addressed in Kenelm's familiar neat handwriting. She took it to the drawing room and opened it eagerly.

> *Ciudad Rodrigo, Spain*
> *Christmas Day, 1812*
>
> *My dear wife,*
> *Here I am in Rodrigo City in Spain. It's a small town perched on a cliff above a river. It has a cathedral—sadly Roman Catholic, of course. I live in a tiny room in a house occupied by officers of the 107th Foot Regiment.*

Well, he had got there safely, which relieved her. A sea journey was always worrying.

She was not in love with Kenelm—she never had been—but over the years she had come to appreciate his strengths and tolerate his weaknesses. And he was the father of her five children. His safety was important to her.

She read on:

> *I thought Spain was a hot country, but the weather is bitter cold, and the house has no glass in its windows—like most houses here. To the east, we can see snow on the mountains, which they call sierras.*

She would have to send him some warm wool clothes: underwear, perhaps, and hose. Poor thing. And people talked of Spain's intolerable heat.

> *The army is recovering from something of a setback.*
> *The siege of Burgos was a failure and our forces*
> *retreated in some disarray, losing men to cold and hunger*
> *on the long march back to winter quarters. This was*
> *before I arrived.*

She had read about the retreat in the newspapers. The marquis of Wellington had enjoyed some victories in the past year, but at the end of it he seemed to be back where he had started. She wondered whether he was as good a general as he was made out to be.

> *The men here are in dire need of spiritual*
> *guidance. One would imagine that battle would remind*
> *them of the nearness of heaven and hell, and make them*
> *take stock of their situation and turn to God, but it*
> *doesn't seem to work that way. Few of them wish to*
> *attend services. Many spend their time drinking*
> *strong liquor, gambling their wages away, and—forgive me,*
> *my dear—whoring. There is a great deal for me to*
> *do! But mainly I tell them that I am their chaplain*
> *and I am always ready to pray with them if they*
> *need me.*

That was something of a change, Elsie felt. Kenelm had always been attached to the ceremonial aspect of Christianity. He attributed great importance to robes and jeweled vessels and processions. Praying with men in distress had not been a priority until now. The army was broadening his mind already.

> Now that I have settled in I thought I should pay a call on Wellington. His headquarters is in a village called Freineda, a bit of a walk from here, but I would not demand the use of an army horse. The village is frightfully dilapidated and dirty. I was sorry to notice the presence of several young women of a certain type—you will skip over that sentence when you read this letter to the children.
>
> Our commander in chief occupies the house next to the church. It's the best house in the place, which is not saying much; just a few rooms over a stable. His father was the earl of Mornington, and he was raised in Dangan Castle, so this must be a change for him!
>
> When I arrived I spoke to an aide-de-camp and learned that Wellington was hunting. I suppose he must do something with his time when there are no battles to be fought. The aide was rather supercilious, and said he was not sure whether the general would have time to see me. Of course I had no choice but to wait.
>
> While doing so, guess who I met: Henry, earl of Shiring! He's thin but he looks cheerful, in fact I would say he's in his element. He has been seconded to headquarters staff, so works closely with Wellington. They are exactly the same age and met back in 1786 as students at the Ecole Royale d'Equitation in Angers.

And the two men had something else in common, Elsie reflected: Henry was more interested in the army than in his wife, and if the rumors were true Wellington was the same.

I remembered the distress of Alderman Hornbeam and mentioned that Joe Hornbeam and Sandy Drummond had volunteered for the army out of patriotism, and Henry was interested. I told him that they were two bright young men from Kingsbridge Grammar School, and might be officer potential, and Henry said he would look out for them; so please tell Hornbeam that I have done what I can to pave the way for his grandson to become an officer.

Elsie certainly would pass that on to Hornbeam. It was not particularly reassuring, but at least he would know that two Kingsbridge men were looking out for his grandson in Spain.

At last Wellington showed up, wearing a sky-blue coat and a black cape, which I later learned was the uniform of the Salisbury Hunt. I saw immediately why they call him Old Nosey: he has a magnificent beak, with a high bridge and a long end. Otherwise he is a handsome man, a little taller than the average, with curly hair brushed forward to hide the slight extent to which it is receding.

Henry introduced me, and Wellington spoke to me for several minutes, standing by his horse. He asked me about my career at Oxford and Kingsbridge, and said he was glad to see me. He did not invite me into his house, but I was quite pleased that so many people had seen him taking an interest in me. He was amiable and informal, though something gave me the feeling that I should not like to be in the position of having displeased him. The iron fist in the velvet glove, was my instinctive thought.

Elsie was glad for Kenelm. She knew how much he valued that sort of thing. A conversation with the commander in chief in front of numerous people would make him happy for months. This was a harmless weakness, and she had learned to be tolerant of it.

> *I will finish now and make sure this gets on the weekly packet from Lisbon to England. My letter will travel alongside Wellington's dispatches and many more letters home to loved ones. I think often of the children—please express my love to them. And I need hardly say that I convey the fondest sentiments of esteem and love for you, my dear wife.*
>
> *Your devoted husband,*
> *Kenelm Mackintosh.*

She put the letter down and thought about it for a while, then she read it again. In the last paragraph he had mentioned love three times, she noticed. That was about as many times as he had said the word in the seventeen years they had been married.

After a minute or two she asked all her children to come to the drawing room. "We have a letter from your father," she said, and they all said ooh and aah. "Sit quietly," she said, "and I'll read it to you."

Mayor Fishwick called an emergency meeting of the town council to discuss the outbreak of Luddism. Spade knew more about what had happened than anyone else, but he had to conceal his knowledge. He decided to attend but say little or nothing. He could have stayed away, but that would have looked suspicious.

Meetings of the council—which consisted of all the aldermen—were usually ebullient affairs, as well-dressed and self-assured men confidently made decisions about the management of the town's affairs, while helping themselves from the decanter of sherry in the middle of the ancient table. They believed it was their right to run Kingsbridge, and they felt they made a pretty good job of it.

They were not so smug today, Spade thought. The mood was pessimistic. They looked scared.

Fishwick outlined why. "Since the assault on Moses Crocket's mill, three more establishments have been targeted by these evildoers," he said. "Alderman Hornbeam's Piggery Mill, Alderman Barrowfield's Old Mill, and my own mill. In all cases machines were damaged, fires were started, and the name Ned Ludd was written in large capital letters with red paint on the wall. And there have been similar incidents in nearby towns."

Hornbeam said: "Do we think this man has moved here from the north?"

"I don't think he even exists," said Fishwick. "Ned Ludd is probably a mythical character, like Robin Hood. These atrocities aren't organized by any central figure, in my opinion. It's just a case of discontented men imitating other discontented men."

Rupe Underwood said: "I've been lucky enough to escape this kind of trouble so far." Rupe was in his forties, like Amos. His blond forelock was graying, but he still had the habit of tossing his head to get his hair out of his eyes. He probably would continue to escape vandalism, Spade thought. The processes involved in making silk ribbons were the same as for wool cloth—spinning, dyeing, and weaving—but it was a specialist enterprise employing a small number of people. "I have to ask," Rupe went on, "whether the mills that suffered these assaults were guarded."

"All of them," said Fishwick.

"So why were the guards ineffective?"

"My men were overcome and tied up."

Hornbeam said disgustedly: "Mine threw aside their cudgels and ran away. I've hired new men and given them pistols, but I'm closing the stable door after the horse has bolted."

Amos Barrowfield frowned. "I'm worried about firearms. If our guards have them, perhaps the Luddites will get them, and then there will be deaths. I've increased the number of my guards, but kept the same weapons, just cudgels."

That irritated Hornbeam. "If we're squeamish about countermeasures we'll never get rid of the damn Luddites."

Fishwick bristled. "I realize emotions are running high, but we generally try to avoid indecorous language at council meetings, Alderman Hornbeam, if you'll forgive me."

"I beg your pardon," Hornbeam said sullenly. "But surely most of us have read about the trial of Luddites in York. Sixty-four men were brought before a special assize court. Seventeen were hanged and twenty-four transported. And the machine breaking has stopped."

Fishwick said: "But we've never caught the perpetrators in the act. They always attack at night. They wear hoods with eye holes, so we don't even know the color of their hair. They obviously know their way around the mills, because they work so fast. They get in, do the damage, and get out again before the alarm can be raised. Then they vanish."

Rupe said: "They probably run a short distance away, take off their hoods, then return in the guise of helpful neighbors and start pouring water on the fire."

Spade thought that was exactly what they would do.

"Just a minute," said Hornbeam. "These problems did not defeat the authorities at York. They knew who the troublemakers were and found them guilty, not worrying about lawyer-like hairsplitting over proof."

That was true, Spade knew. He had read about the

trial in the newspapers. It was very controversial. Some of those accused were nothing to do with the Luddites, and some had alibis, but they were found guilty just the same. Hornbeam clearly wanted the same kind of justice in Kingsbridge.

Hornbeam went on: "We know which Kingsbridge hand workers have lost their living because of new machinery. We simply need to make a list."

Amos said: "What, and hang them all?"

"We could start by arresting them all. At least we could be sure we had the Luddites in the net."

"And a couple hundred law-abiding men."

"It's not that many."

"When did you count them, Mr. Hornbeam?"

Hornbeam did not like to be questioned. "All right, Barrowfield, tell me what your plan is."

"Do more for unemployed hand workers."

"Such as?"

"Make sure they get Poor Relief—and no quibbling."

That was a direct reproof to Hornbeam as overseer of the poor. He said indignantly: "They get what they're entitled to."

"And so they smash machines," said Amos. "And perhaps they will continue so to do unless we help them—regardless of what they might be entitled to according to a strict interpretation of the rules."

Spade silently cheered Amos.

Hornbeam said: "Rules are rules!"

"And men are men," said Amos.

Hornbeam was getting angry. "We need to teach them a lesson! A few hangings will put an end to Luddism."

"If we knowingly hang innocent men we may stop the vandalism but we will be guilty of murder."

Hornbeam was red in the face. "None of them are innocent!"

Amos sighed. "Look, if we treat the hands as our enemies they will behave like enemies."

"You make excuses for criminals."

"We'll be the criminals if we do as the court did in York."

Fishwick intervened. "Gentlemen, allow me. We are not going to make excuses for criminals and we are not going to hang innocent men. We are going to assemble witnesses and make a case against people who are genuinely guilty. Then if we hang them we will do so with God's blessing."

Amos said: "Amen."

Hornbeam stood in the weaving room of his number 2 mill, which was still operating. It had not been attacked yet, but it was vulnerable because it used steam looms, which seemed to inflame the Luddites.

Hornbeam had never been in a battle but he imagined it must sound much like a room full of steam looms. All day long the machines clattered and banged so loudly that it was impossible to hold a conversation. Hands who worked the looms for a period of years often ended up deaf.

The main job of the hands was to look for faults in the cloth: stitching, picking over, and picking under were the main ones. They mended breaks in threads using the small, flat weaver's knot, and they had to do it quickly to minimize the loss of product. The other important task was to change each shuttle every few minutes, because the thread ran out so quickly due to the fast pace of the machine. One person could manage two or three looms at a time.

Accidents were frequent—because the hands were careless, in Hornbeam's opinion. He had seen a man's loose shirtsleeve get caught in a driving belt that tore the man's arm off his shoulder.

The flying shuttle was the cause of most accidents. It moved very fast, passing through the shed two or three times a second. It was made of wood but had to have metal ends to protect it from damage as it hit the buffer. If the operator worked the loom too fast the shuttle would hit the buffer too fast and fly out of the loom at high speed, injuring anyone in the way.

When Phil Doye arrived, Hornbeam left the weaving room and saw the sheriff in an office away from the noise.

"We must find at least one of the Luddites and prosecute him," he said. "I'm going to give you half a dozen names of men I think might give us information." They were all people who owed Hornbeam money and could not pay, but Doye did not need to know that.

Doye said: "Very good, Mr. Hornbeam. What sort of information am I seeking?"

"Obviously the names of Luddites, but we need more than that. Try to find someone who has seen them approaching one of the vandalized mills after dark. They might have been spotted putting their hoods on or off."

"Well, I can try," said Doye dubiously.

"Anyone who can help us this way may be offered a discreet reward. They will be putting themselves at risk by informing against violent men, so they need an incentive. We could pay a pound to anyone who gives evidence at the trial. However, these payments must be kept secret, otherwise the hands will insinuate that our witnesses have been bribed and their evidence is therefore untrustworthy."

"I see, sir."

In a more musing tone Hornbeam said: "I still suspect Jarge Box."

"But he was ringing the bells."

"Find out whether anyone saw him walking through town while the bells were sounding."

"How could that happen?"

"He might have been replaced by another man. How would we know?"

"It's a skill, sir. You have to learn it."

"The replacement could be a former ringer who has

now retired. Or a ringer from another town. Speak to people who know the ringers and might have heard something."

"Yes, sir."

"All right," Hornbeam said dismissively. "You'd better get started. I want someone found guilty. And I want him to hang."

CHAPTER 35

Kit Clitheroe visited Spade's mill and asked how he was getting on with his Jacquard loom. "It's quite remarkable," Spade said. "Sime Jackson operates it, but the machine doesn't really require a weaver. Once it's been set up it could be run by a youngster. The skill now is in designing the pattern and making the punch cards."

"You should order another one," Kit said. "Double your output." This was the reason for his visit.

"If I still had my French customers I would," Spade said. "Paris has lots of little shops called *marchands de modes*. They sell dresses and hats and all kinds of accessories—lace, scarves, buckles, and so on. Those establishments used to buy almost half my output."

"But you've replaced them with buyers in the Baltic and America."

"I have, thank God. But they want plain hard-wearing cloth. I'll buy another of your Jacquard looms as soon as this damned war is over."

"I'll come knocking on your door." Kit put on a brave face but he was downhearted.

Spade, who was sensitive to people's moods, said: "I'm sorry to disappoint you. Is business slow for you right now?"

"It is, a bit. It's the Luddites."

"I would have thought a lot of clothiers would be replacing their smashed machines."

"Not soon. They can't afford it. Wally Watson won't buy another scribbling machine—he's gone back to hand scribblers."

"I suppose someone who splashed out on new machines might attract a second visit from the Luddites."

"That's exactly the problem." Kit stood up. Even with Spade he did not want to appear weak. "But we live to fight another day."

"Good luck."

Kit left.

He had tried to hide his feelings but he was demoralized. For the first time since he and Roger had started the business he had no work in hand and none in prospect. He was not sure what he could do. He was reluctant to spend his savings.

It was the end of a gray February day, and he could not lift his spirits enough to make another desperate sales call, so he went home. He let himself into the ground-floor workshop. It smelled of sawn wood and machine oil, an aroma that always gave him a sense of well-being. All was perfectly clean and tidy: the floor swept, the tools neatly racked, the timber stacked at the back. This was his doing: Roger was less meticulous about such things.

He climbed the stairs to the living area on the upper floor. He found Roger slumped on the sofa, gazing into a coal fire. He kissed Roger's lips and sat beside him.

"Can I have some money?" Roger said. "I know it's not due yet, but I'm broke."

This happened often. Each month Kit calculated the profits, put some aside for contingencies, then divided the rest in two and gave half to Roger; but more often than not Roger ran out before the end of the month. Normally Kit gave him an advance, but times had changed. "I can't," Kit said. "I don't think there will be any profit this month."

"Why not?" Roger said petulantly.

"Nobody's buying machines because of the Luddites." Kit stroked Roger's blond hair. He was surprised to see a little strand of gray over Roger's ear. Roger was almost forty: perhaps it was not so surprising. Kit decided not to mention it. "You'll have to stop playing cards for a while," he said. "Stay home with me in the evenings." He put his mouth close to Roger's ear and said in a low voice: "I'll think of something for you to do."

Roger smiled at last. "Danke schoen," he said. He was teaching Kit German. "Perhaps poverty will be fun."

But Kit felt he was holding something back.

"Let's have a glass of wine," Kit said. "That might cheer us up." He got up and went to the sideboard. They always had a bottle of Madeira handy. Kit poured two glasses and sat down again.

He had loved Roger for a long time. As a boy he had been possessed of a childish adoration for his grown-up protector. Then Roger had gone to Germany and Kit had grown out of his hero worship. But when Roger came back into his life he had been overwhelmed by feelings that surprised and frightened him. He had suppressed those thoughts and tried to hide them.

But Roger had known, and he had told Kit the facts of life. "It's not unusual for men to love each other," he had said. Kit could hardly believe this. "Take no notice of what people say. It happens all the time—especially at Oxford." Roger had giggled, then become serious again. "I love you, and I want to lie down with you and kiss you and touch your body all over, and you want the same—I know! Don't even try to pretend otherwise."

When Kit got over the shock he had been blissfully happy, and he still was. Roger had moments of unhappiness, like now. Kit was thinking about how to ask him what the matter was when there was a loud knocking at the front door.

"I'll go," said Kit. They had a housekeeper but she had finished for the day. He ran down the stairs and opened the door.

The caller was Sport Culliver, wearing a red top hat. He said abruptly: "I need to talk to Roger."

"And good evening to you, too, Sport," said Kit sarcastically.

"Never mind the courtesies."

Kit turned and shouted: "Are you in to Sport Culliver?"

Roger replied: "You'd better let him in."

Kit said: "He will be delighted to see you." He closed the door and led Sport up the stairs.

Keeping his hat on, Sport sat down without being asked, choosing a chair opposite Roger. "Time's up, Roger," he said.

"I haven't got any money," Roger said. "Why are you wearing that stupid hat?"

Kit said: "Oh, Lord save us. Have you been gambling with borrowed money?"

Roger looked shamefaced and did not answer.

Sport said: "Yes, he has, and he was supposed to pay me yesterday."

Kit had long suspected that Roger might be breaking his promise, so the revelation was not as much of a shock as it might have been. He refrained from saying anything about the promise now: Roger was already miserable enough. "Oh, Rodge," he said. "How much do you owe?"

Sport answered the question. "Ninety-four pounds, six shillings, and eight pence."

Now Kit was shocked. "We haven't got that much!" he said.

Sport said: "How much have you got?"

Kit was about to tell him, but Roger spoke first. "Never mind that," he said. "You'll get your money, Sport. I'll pay you tomorrow."

Kit was sure he was bluffing.

Sport suspected the same. "I'll give you until tomorrow," he said. "But if you fail again, you'll have to have a meeting with Frogeye and Bull."

Kit said: "Who are they?"

Roger answered the question. "They work for him, throwing drunks out and beating up men who owe him money."

"What's the point of that?" said Kit. "If someone

hasn't got the money, he still won't have it after he's been beaten."

Sport said: "But other people will be scared of trying to cheat me." He stood up. "See me tomorrow, or see Frogeye and Bull the day after."

He left the room. Kit followed him down the stairs. Sport opened the door himself and walked away without speaking. Kit closed it and went back up the stairs.

Roger did not meet his eye but said: "I'm sorry. I'm so sorry. I've let you down."

Kit put his arm around Roger and said: "Never mind that. What are we going to do?"

"It's not your problem. You're not involved, you've never gambled."

"What do you think I'm going to do, wait for the men with funny names to come here and beat you?"

"I'll be gone before they get here. I'll have to leave tomorrow."

Kit was hurt. How could Roger talk about leaving him? He said: "But where would you go? What would you do?"

"I've thought about it," Roger said. "I'm going to join the Royal Artillery. They always need people who are good at mending things, especially cannons."

Kit was silent, letting that sink in. Roger in the army! They would probably send him to Spain. He might never come back. Kit could hardly bear to think about it.

But what could Kit do? He could not pay the debt, he could not defend Roger—or himself—against Sport's paid ruffians, and he could not live without Roger.

Eventually he realized what the solution was.

"Do you mean it?" he said to Roger. "You'll really join up?"

"Yes," said Roger. "It's the only answer."

"When?"

"I'll get the stagecoach to Bristol tomorrow. I hear there's a ship there waiting to take reinforcements to Spain."

"So soon!"

"It has to be tomorrow."

"In that case," said Kit, "I'll go with you."

Sal and Jarge closed up Kit's house. Jarge greased the tools and wrapped them in oilcloth. Sal put the clothing and bed linen into sacking and sewed it up with lavender inside to repel moths. She put the other household effects into borrowed tea chests.

She had Kit's note tucked into her sleeve:

My beloved Mother,

We have to run away. Roger owes money and can't pay, and our business has collapsed because of the Luddites. By the time you read this I will be far from Kingsbridge. We're going to join the Royal Artillery.

I'm sorry to give you this shock.

Please send all our stuff to Roger's workshop in Badford. The key is with this note.

Your loving son,
Kit.

Sal was horrified and tearful. He was her only child. She knew, in her head, that a man of twenty-eight did not have to live close to his mother, but in her heart she felt deserted. And she was terrified about what might happen to him in war. Kit had many lovely qualities and one remarkable talent, but he had never been a fighter. "Artillery" meant cannons, so both Kit and Roger would be at the heart of any battlefield, with enemy soldiers trying their hardest to kill them. If Kit died it would break Sal's heart. And to make matters even worse, she would always feel it was Jarge's fault, because he had caused the crisis by smashing machines.

While they were working two men appeared. One was short and thick necked, the other had bulging eyes. Each carried in his hand a roughly hewn heavy oak club.

The one with the bulging eyes said: "Where's Roger Riddick?"

Jarge turned slowly to face the man. "And why are you looking for him with a cudgel in your hand, Frogeye?"

Sal was ready to join in a fight but she did not want it. She murmured a proverb: "'A soft answer turneth away wrath,' Jarge, remember."

Frogeye said: "Riddick owes money, if you must know."

"Does he?" said Jarge. "Well, he's not here, and I've got half a mind to break that cudgel over your ugly head, so I advise you to piss off away from here while I'm still in a sunny mood." He turned to the other man. "And the same goes for you, Bull."

Frogeye said: "And what about Mr. Culliver's money? Riddick owes him ninety-four pounds, six shillings, and eight pence."

Sal was shocked by the amount. It was more than all Kit's savings. She said indignantly: "If Sport Culliver let Roger Riddick run up that much of a debt, he's even more of a fool than I took him for."

"We're supposed to fetch Mr. Culliver's money."

Jarge said: "Well, I've got about six pence in my pocket. You could try to take that from me, if you fancy your chances."

"Where's Riddick gone?"

"He went to talk to the archbishop of Canterbury about the evils of gambling."

Frogeye looked puzzled, then his face cleared and he said: "Quite the joker, aren't you?" He turned away, and Bull followed him.

When they were at a safe distance Frogeye called back: "I'll see you again, Jarge Box. I wonder how funny you'll be when you're swinging from a hangman's rope."

Jarge appeared at the March quarter sessions, with Hornbeam presiding as chairman of justices. A grand jury was empaneled to decide whether Jarge should be committed to the assize court for trial on the capital charge of machine breaking.

Sheriff Doye was the prosecutor. This did not always happen. Usually the prosecution was brought by the injured party—which in this case would be Moses Crocket—but there was no strict rule.

The first witness was Maisie Roberts, a mill hand who lived in one of the Hornbeam-owned streets on the south side of the river near the mills. She was young and raggedly dressed. Sal knew her by sight but had never spoken to her.

Maisie looked pleased to be the center of attention. Sal thought she would probably commit perjury for six pence.

She testified that she had seen Jarge walking toward Crocket's Mill and had noticed that the bells were ringing at the same time. She remembered it because she had been surprised. "I knew he was a ringer, see," she said.

Sal had discussed with Jarge the questions he should ask witnesses. He did not have them written down because he could not read, but he was used to remembering important things. He said to Maisie: "Do you recall that it was dark that evening when we were ringing?"

"Yes, it was dark," said Maisie.

"So how did you recognize me?"

"You were carrying a lamp."

The response came quickly, and Sal guessed that someone had prepared Maisie for that question.

Jarge said: "And the light from the lamp was enough for you to know me."

"That and your size," Maisie said. With a grin she added: "There's not many that big." She was quick-witted.

There was a little laugh in the courtroom, and Maisie looked pleased.

Jarge said: "The man you saw, who you thought was me, did he speak to you?"

"No."

Jarge looked as if he had forgotten what to say next. Sal whispered: "Ask who her landlord is."

Jarge followed her instruction.

"Mr. Hornbeam is my landlord," said Maisie.

"And how much rent do you owe?"

"I'm fully paid up." She looked even more pleased with herself.

Sal felt sure Maisie had been bribed somehow. But it was hard to feel indignant: Jarge was, after all, guilty.

The second witness was Marie Dodds, widow of Benny Dodds, who had been a bell ringer. Years ago Benny had fallen for Sal, and although Sal had never encouraged him, Marie had taken against Sal. She still bore a grudge.

Marie testified that Benny had told her Sal occasionally stood in for Jarge. This was very damning: it invalidated Jarge's alibi.

Jarge said to Marie: "But women can't ring those bells—they're not strong enough."

"*She* can," said Marie. "Just look at her," she added cattily, and the spectators laughed.

Sheriff Doye then surprised Sal by calling her as a witness.

She had a decision to make, and just a few seconds in which to make it. She was angry with Jarge—furious—for putting her in this position, but there was no point in seething over that. Would she perjure herself for him? It was a sin as well as a crime. She might suffer for it in the afterlife as well as on this earth.

But if she told the truth Jarge would probably hang.

She took the oath, then Doye said: "Mrs. Box, were you in the rope room with the ringers during their rehearsal on the night we're talking about?"

There was no harm in admitting that. "Yes," she said.

"For the whole time?"

Someone had told Doye what to say, Sal thought. On his own he was not this smart. "Yes," she said.

"And during that time, did your husband, Jarge Box, leave the room?"

The moment had come, and Sal did not hesitate. "No," she lied. "He did not."

"Have you ever rung a church bell?"

"No." The lies came easily now.

"Do you think you could?"

"No idea."

"Mrs. Box, would you commit the crime of perjury to save your husband from hanging?"

That question took her by surprise. She had just committed the crime, of course, but she could not answer yes to the question—that would undermine her testimony. On the other hand, she was not sure that no was a good answer: it would make her seem callous. Men disliked a callous woman. And all the jury were men.

She hesitated, but that was all right: it was, after all, a hypothetical question, so why shouldn't she be uncertain?

In the end she decided to say that. "I don't know," she said. "I've never been asked to do that."

Looking at the faces of the jurymen she felt it had been the right answer.

At the end Sal and Jarge conferred briefly, then he got up to say what they had agreed. "Maisie Roberts probably did see a biggish chap walking along the dark street while the bells were ringing. She didn't exchange words with him, so she can't say the voice sounded like mine. She's mistaken, that's all."

That was true, and the jury ought to see it.

Jarge went on: "My old friend Benny Dodds was

prone to exaggerate a bit, and he may have told his wife that Sal Box looked strong enough to ring a church bell. Benny has been dead for six years, rest his soul, so Mrs. Dodds could be forgiven for not remembering it quite right. And that's all the jury has heard! You can't hang a man on that sort of evidence." He stepped back.

Hornbeam spoke last. "Gentlemen of the jury, Jarge Box is a weaver who has lost work due to steam looms, so he has a motive for Luddism. He claims to have been bell ringing, but Mrs. Roberts is sure she saw him in the street while the bells were ringing. He says his wife is not strong enough to ring the bells for him, but Benny Dodds, another ringer, said that she was and she did.

"Remember, jurymen, that today you are not asked to say whether Jarge Box is guilty. You are here to decide whether there is enough of a case against him for you to send him to the assize court. There is evidence, but doubt has been thrown upon it, and you may well feel that the issue must be decided by the higher court.

"Kindly make your decision."

The twelve men conferred, and to Sal's dismay the heads quickly began to nod in agreement. A few moments later one of them stood up and said: "We commit the accused man to the assize court."

CHAPTER 36

Kit Clitheroe had never seen a desert before, but he was pretty sure this was one. The ground was hard and dusty, and the sun was relentless all day. He had always imagined a desert to be flat, but in the last few weeks he had crossed mountains higher than any he had ever seen.

He and Roger sat on the ground, eating mutton stewed with beans, as the sun went down over the river Zadorra in the north of Spain. Everyone said the big battle would be tomorrow. It would be Kit's first, and it might be his last. He was so tense with fear that he had to force himself to swallow.

It was June, and they had been in Spain for two months. When they arrived in Rodrigo City they had immediately been put to work servicing cannons. The guns had been stored away for the winter and now had to be got ready for action. The commander of the Royal Artillery there was Lieutenant Colonel Alexander Dickson, a man Kit had quickly come to respect for his energy and intelligence. Kit had been a manager himself and understood the paramount need for clear orders that made sense to the men.

The cannons were bronze and rested on two-wheeled carriages that were timber reinforced with iron. Spain's climate was not damp, but iron rusted there as it did everywhere. Kit and Roger supervised the men as they cleaned and oiled and tested the wheeled artillery ready for a march. British guns weighed three-fifths of a ton: moving them from place to place on unpaved roads was never less than a challenge and often a nightmare. Each gun was attached to a two-wheeled limber, and the ensemble required six horses to pull it.

Most days Kit had been so busy that he forgot to worry about fighting.

The army moved with hundreds of vehicles, mostly supply wagons, and they, too, had to be serviced, checked, and often mended at the end of the winter. The oxen and horses that pulled them were, fortunately, someone else's responsibility. Kit had never had a horse of his own and had hated them ever since Will Riddick's wild-eyed stallion had cracked his skull when he was six years old.

New recruits were drilled, taught to shoot, and sent on long marches in full gear to harden their feet and teach them resilience. Shiploads of supplies arrived from England: new boots, fresh uniforms, muskets and ammunition, and tents. This was how the government spent the money raised by all the new taxes back home.

Promotion was fast. Last year's battles had deprived Wellington's army of many officers. Kit and Roger were quickly elevated, to give them authority as they supervised the work. Roger was made a lieutenant. Kit, because of his years of service in the militia, became a captain.

In Rodrigo City they had often recognized men of the 107th Foot. Joe Hornbeam and Sandy Drummond had both been made ensigns, the lowest rank of officer.

Kit had been surprised to see hundreds of Englishwomen in the city. He had not realized how many wives traveled with their soldier husbands. The army tolerated this, he learned, because the women were useful. On the battlefield they brought their men food, drink, and sometimes ammunition. Away from the fighting they did all the things wives always did: laundry, cooking, and love in the night. Officers believed that the presence of wives made the men less likely to drink to excess, quarrel and brawl, and catch nasty diseases from prostitutes.

They had met Kenelm Mackintosh in his role as chaplain to the 107th, and found him changed—his clerical robes covered with dust, his face unshaven, his hands grubby. His attitude was different, too. He had always been arrogantly remote, talking down to uneducated mill hands, but now he had lost that haughty air. He asked whether they were getting enough to eat and had decent blankets for the cold nights. He had in fact turned into a more or less likable fellow.

Halfway through May, Wellington's army had left Rodrigo City heading north. Some of the men were eager, having been bored all winter. Kit just thought it was better to be bored than dead.

The allied army was approximately 120,000 strong, Roger learned by chatting to the headquarters staff. The 50,000 British formed the largest contingent, reinforced by 40,000 Spanish and 30,000 Portuguese troops. The guerrilla fighters of the Spanish resistance were an unknown quantity.

The French army in the north of Spain was thought to be about 130,000 men. They would get no reinforcements. It was said that more than half the entire French national army had been lost in Bonaparte's catastrophic march on Moscow. So far from augmenting his army in Spain, Bonaparte had withdrawn the best men for his ongoing battles in northeast Europe—whereas Wellington's force had received a stream of men and supplies over the winter.

Bonaparte always surprised his enemy—but Bonaparte was not in Spain. His brother Joseph was in command here.

The march had been hard. Kit's neck was scorched by the sun and his feet got blisters. Although small in stature he was not a weakling, but every day he found himself dead tired by the time the sun went down and he could rest. It came as a relief when an axle snapped or a wagon wheel buckled, and they could stop for an hour and mend it. Even better was a patch of soft or sandy ground where wheels sank too deep to roll, and an afternoon had to be spent making a temporary road of planks across the obstacle.

Kit consoled himself with the thought that no matter how hard the march, it was better than fighting.

Roger kept in touch with friends in the headquarters staff and learned of the intelligence coming in, much of it from the Spanish guerrillas. King Joseph of Spain—Bonaparte's brother—had moved his capital from Madrid north to Valladolid, a city with a commanding position in the center of northern Spain. Wellington's army was marching northeast, toward Valladolid, but he had also sent a flanking force on a northerly curve to approach the French from an unexpected angle.

Rather than resist this maneuver, the French unexpectedly retreated. British headquarters staff wondered why. Intelligence estimated that the enemy were fewer than expected: only about sixty thousand men. Perhaps many of them were up in the mountains fighting the guerrillas. Their retreat northeast took them nearer to the French border. Was it possible they would flee across the mountains to their home country? The thought crossed Kit's mind that the British might win without fighting. Then he told himself that that was wishful thinking.

It was. King Joseph made a stand in the Zadorra River valley west of the Basque city of Vitoria, and now, at last, Kit would have to fight.

They were on a broad plain with mountains north and south, narrow canyons east and west, and the river snaking across from northeast to southwest. The French were camped on the far side of that diagonal river. Wellington's army would have to cross the water to attack.

Kit was terrified. "How will it start?" he asked Roger anxiously.

"They will form a line across our route, to stop our onward march."

"And then what?"

"We'll attack in columns, probably, trying to make holes in their line."

That made sense to Kit.

Roger said: "The river is our problem. An army crossing a river, by bridge or ford, is packed close and slow moving—an easy target. If King Joseph has any sense he will place strong forces at every crossing point and hope to mow us down just when we're most vulnerable."

"We can build makeshift bridges."

"That's what the Royal Engineers are for. But if the enemy are nimble they will attack while we're trying to do that."

Kit began to think there was no way for a soldier to stay alive. Men did survive, he told himself. He just could not imagine how.

He slept fitfully that night and got up with the sun to oversee putting the oxen in harness.

Each gun carriage came with two auxiliary vehicles, called caissons, carrying ammunition. For speed of loading, a round came as a preformed charge: a canvas bag containing the cannonball and the correct amount of gunpowder. The British Army used mostly six-pound iron balls measuring three and a half inches across. The caissons were heavy, drawn by a team of six horses.

The British, Spanish, and Portuguese armies moved forward at eight o'clock. Walking to our graves, Kit thought.

To everyone's surprise, most of the existing bridges and fords were not defended by the enemy. The officers could hardly believe their luck. Roger said: "Joseph is not Napoleon."

The gunners, including Kit and Roger, moved the cannons across the river without meeting resistance, and approached a village called Ariñez that was occupied by the enemy. They remained well out of range of musket fire, but soon the French artillery began to harry them from the village, which was up a slope. The British soldiers got behind the carriages and pushed the guns faster. Kit had to survey the ground and guide the guns to relatively level places where the recoil would not send them rolling back downhill. He was dangerously exposed but he was able to make himself do it.

It took five men to fire a cannon. Aiming was the job of the gun commander, usually a sergeant, equipped with a quadrant and a plumb line. The spongeman had the simple task of cleaning the inside of the brass barrel with a wet cloth on a long stick, to quench any leftbehind embers and prevent premature ignition when the gun was reloaded. The loader then inserted the round into the barrel. The spongeman reversed his stick and used the dry end to ram the shot hard down the barrel, while the fourth soldier, the ventsman, blocked the touchhole with his thumb to prevent accidental detonation by a stray spark. When the charge was firmly in place, the ventsman pushed a sharpened stick through the touchhole to pierce the bag, then filled the vent with more gunpowder. Finally, when the commander was satisfied that the gun was well aimed, he would shout "Fire!" and the fifth man would put the smoldering tip of his long slow match to the touchhole and the gun would fire.

The gun recoiled about six feet. Anyone foolish enough to get in the way was killed or maimed.

The crew immediately pulled and pushed the gun back into position and the process began all over again.

The team had to pause every ten or twelve shots to cool the gun with water. If it got too hot the gunpowder in the bag would explode as soon as it was pushed into the barrel, causing a misfire.

Kit had been told that an efficient team could fire about a hundred shots in a daylong battle.

Soon the guns were firing as fast as the crews could reload. They worked in a fog of dense smoke from the black powder used in the ammunition.

Kit went up and down behind the line of guns, troubleshooting. One crew managed to set fire to an insufficiently wetted sponge; another spilled water on the gunpowder; a third lost half its men to a French cannonball. Kit's task was to get the guns firing again with minimum delay. He realized he was no longer frightened. This struck him as most peculiar, but he had no time to think about it.

The noise and the heat were overwhelming. Men cursed as they burned themselves by accidentally touching the gun barrels. All were deafened. Kit had noticed that long-serving artillery veterans became permanently deaf: now he knew why.

As soon as they had emptied an ammunition caisson it was sent back to the artillery park to be refilled. Meanwhile the crew used the second caisson.

It was hard to see what effect they were having, for the enemy positions were shrouded in smoke from their own guns. It was said that a cannonball aimed at a line of infantry would kill three men. If a red-hot shard from an exploding shell hit a box of gunpowder it would kill many more.

The enemy fire was certainly hurting the British gunners. Men fell, often screaming. Guns and their carriages were wrecked. Female camp followers dragged away the wounded and the dead. In a distant corner of Kit's mind, barely conscious, a terrible memory came alight: his father, crushed by Will Riddick's cart, screaming every time they tried to move him. He could not quite thrust the picture out of his mind, but he was able to ignore it.

The allied infantry attacked Ariñez from the far side, and the British guns were ordered to cease fire, for fear of hitting their own people.

At last the French guns fell silent, and Kit guessed that meant the allies had won the battle for the village. He did not know how or why. Mostly he was astonished at the way he had lost himself in the job he had to do and had forgotten about the danger he was in. He had not been brave, he thought; just too busy to think about it.

The smoke had not completely cleared when the order came to move again. The horses and oxen were brought forward. As they were being put into harness, a group of officers rode by, their leader a tall, lean figure in a dusty general's uniform. Someone said: "That's Old Nosey!"

It must be Wellington, Kit thought. The man did, indeed, have a big nose, with a slight hook at the end.

"Move on!" Wellington shouted urgently.

A nearby colonel said: "In column or in line, sir?"

Wellington said impatiently: "Anyhow, but for God's sake get moving!" Then he rode on.

They moved the guns forward a mile then, not far from a village that someone said was called Gomecha, they came up against a massive French battery. As they took position, more guns were brought to join them. Kit estimated there were at least seventy cannons on each side. There was so much smoke that the sergeants could not see their target, and had to aim by guesswork. Now the allied guns were grouped too close together, and French cannonballs found their targets despite the smoke.

A wagon bringing fresh supplies of ammunition crashed into a gun and damaged the carriage. Kit saw that the wheels and axle of the carriage were intact, and he was mending the shafts with wood when a shell landed on a neighboring gun, striking the ammunition. Kit was knocked over by the blast, and the world went silent. He lay dazed, he did not know for how long, then struggled to his feet. His neck felt sore. He touched something sticky and his hand came away red with blood.

He resumed fixing the shafts. His hearing returned slowly.

The allied infantry advanced. The guns fired over their heads, hoping to disable the French guns, but despite their efforts Kit saw many infantrymen fall. Their surviving comrades just ran on, straight into the mouths of the enemy cannons. Yesterday Kit would have marveled at their courage. Today he understood: they were past caring, as he was.

Then the French guns went quiet.

The allied artillery moved forward again, but this time they could not catch up with their own infantry. As the smoke cleared Kit saw that the allied forces were spread across the width of the plain in a line that must have been two miles long. The line was advancing, and resistance seemed to be melting away. The gunners were told to halt and await fresh orders.

Kit suddenly realized he felt completely exhausted, and he lay on the ground. Stillness was the greatest luxury he had ever felt. He rolled on his back and closed his eyes against the sun.

After a while a voice said: "Oh, my God, Kit, are you dead?"

It was Roger. Kit opened his eyes. "Not dead, not yet."

He sprang to his feet and they hugged. They held the embrace for a few moments, then slapped each other on the back in a manly way, just for show.

Roger stood back, looked at Kit, and laughed.

Kit said: "What is it?"

"You don't know what you look like. Your face is black with smoke, there's blood on your uniform, and one leg of your trousers seems to have gone."

Kit looked down. "I wonder how that happened."

Roger laughed again. "You must have had quite a day."

"Yes, I did," said Kit. "Did we win?"

"Oh, yes," said Roger. "We won."

Jarge Box's case came up at the summer assize court. Sal stood beside him in the council chamber of the Guild Hall. When the judge came in she was dismayed to see that it was the beak-nosed vulture who had hanged young Tommy Pidgeon eight years ago. She almost gave up hope there and then.

If Tommy had lived he would be a young man now,

she thought sadly. He might have turned out a decent citizen, given a chance. But he had not been given a chance.

She prayed that Jarge might be given a chance today.

As the jury was sworn in she looked at the men's faces—well fed, confident, self-righteous—and realized they were all masters in the cloth business. No doubt Hornbeam had bullied Sheriff Doye into making sure of this. These were the people who had the most to fear from Luddism, those who would be most eager to make an example of someone—anyone—in the hope of scaring the Luddites into giving up.

Then she saw that Doye had made a mistake. One of the jurors was Isaac Marsh. His daughter was married to Howard Hornbeam, and Doye had probably presumed that Marsh would be a hard-liner. However, he was a dyer, in a branch of the cloth industry that had not been mechanized, so he had less of a motive for convicting. On top of that he was a Methodist, and might hesitate to condemn a man to death.

It was a faint ray of hope.

The evidence from the quarter sessions was repeated. Maisie Roberts claimed she had seen Jarge in the street while bells were ringing, and Marie Dodds said that Sal could have rung the bells, but Sal swore that Jarge had not left the rope room while the bells were ringing—thereby perjuring herself a second time.

The judge, summing up, did not pretend to be evenhanded. He told the jury they had to weigh the evidence of two people, Mrs. Roberts and Mrs. Dodds, who had no reason to lie, against that of one person, Mrs. Box, who might be lying to save her husband's life.

The jury, the only people sitting down except for the judge, began to confer, but they did not reach a quick conclusion. It was soon obvious that eleven of them were in agreement and there was one holdout: Isaac Marsh. He was not saying much, but as the others talked he sometimes shook his head solemnly.

Her hopes rose. The jury had to return a unanimous verdict. If they could not, there would be a retrial, in theory. In practice, she had heard, the jury sometimes tried for a compromise, such as finding the accused guilty of a lesser crime.

After a while they all started to nod and sit back, as if they had arrived at a resolution.

Then one of them stood up and announced that they had reached a unanimous verdict. "Guilty, my lord, with the strongest possible recommendation for mercy."

The judge thanked him, then reached for something below the table. Sal knew instantly that he was about to put on his black cap and sentence Jarge to death despite the jury's recommendation. "No," she murmured, "please, Lord, no."

His hands, holding the cap, appeared above the level of the table in front of him; and then Amos Barrowfield stepped forward and said in a loud, clear voice: "My lord, the 107th Foot Regiment is fighting the French in Spain."

The judge looked irritated. Such an intervention at the sentencing stage was unusual, though not unknown. He said: "What has that to do with this trial?"

"Many Kingsbridge men have died in the cause, and the regiment needs recruits. I believe you have the power to send a man into the army as an alternative to the death penalty. Then it is up to God whether he lives or dies. I urge you to take this course with Jarge Box, not out of compassion, but because he is a strong man who would be a formidable soldier. I thank you for letting me speak." He stepped back.

Amos had spoken unemotionally, as if he had no care for Jarge personally, but just wanted to help the army. Sal knew this was a pose: Amos had taken the line most likely to persuade the judge, who was evidently not much troubled by compassion.

But would it work? The judge hesitated, sitting there

with his black cap held between his two hands. Sal's breath came in gasps. The room was silent.

Finally the judge said: "I sentence you to join the 107th Foot Regiment."

Sal felt weak with relief.

The judge said: "If you fight bravely for your country you may go some way toward atoning for your crimes."

Sal murmured to Jarge: "Don't say anything."

Jarge remained silent.

The judge said: "Next case."

CHAPTER 37

After the Battle of Vitoria, everything went wrong for Napoleon Bonaparte.

The Battle of Leipzig was the largest ever fought in Europe up until then. It took place in October and involved more than half a million men, and Bonaparte lost. Meanwhile Wellington's army crossed the Pyrenees mountains and invaded France from the south.

Bonaparte returned to Paris, but the armies that had defeated him at Leipzig chased him. In March 1814 the allies, led by the tsar of Russia and the king of Prussia, entered Paris in triumph.

A few days later Amos read a headline in the *Kingsbridge Gazette* that said:

BONAPARTE ABDICATES!

Could it be true?
The text went on:

> *This event is officially confirmed by dispatches from General Sir Charles Stewart. The fallen tyrant has resigned the cares of royalty and accepted a retreat in the Isle of Elba, an insignificant spot off the coast of Tuscany.*

"Thank God," said Amos. The war was over.

That evening there was rejoicing in the streets of Kingsbridge. Men who had never served in any army raised their tankards and shared in the glory. Women asked when their husbands and sons would be home, but no one had answers for them. Small boys made wooden swords and vowed to fight the next war. Little girls dreamed of marrying a brave soldier in a red coat.

Wellington was made a duke.

Amos called at Jane's house with a gift for their son, a globe on a stand. He spent an hour explaining it to Hal, who had a lively curiosity about such things. Amos showed him the places where the armies of Britain and its allies had done battle with Bonaparte's forces.

Then he sat in the upstairs drawing room of Willard House, looking out at the cathedral, while Jane read him a letter from her husband.

My dear wife,

I am in Paris and it is peace at last. The 107th Foot distinguished itself right up to the end—we won a smashing victory at Toulouse. (That was actually a few days after Bonaparte admitted defeat, but that news did not reach us until after the battle.)

The regiment has had a good war. We lost relatively few men in the last battles. Among the officers, only Ensign Sandy Drummond, the son of the wine merchant, was killed. The chaplain, Kenelm Mackintosh, took a bullet in his posterior—terribly embarrassing for a clergyman! The surgeon took out the ball, washed the wound with gin, and tied on a bandage, and the chaplain seems all right, though he limps a bit. Ensign Joe Hornbeam turned out to be a rather good soldier despite his youth. You may tell the bullying alderman that his grandson is still alive.

> *The two Kingsbridge men who joined the gunners proved useful at Vitoria, particularly Kit Clitheroe, who I already knew to be a good officer from his service in the militia. I have poached him to be my aide-de-camp.*
>
> *Now the regiment is moving to Brussels.*

"Brussels?" said Amos. "Why Brussels?"
"Listen," said Jane, and she read on.

> *The great men of the winning nations are gathering in Vienna, where they will divide Europe up for the future, and try to ensure that we never again have such a long and terrible war as this. Among the issues confronting them is what to do about the Netherlands. Bonaparte has surrendered the territory he conquered there—but to whom does it belong now? While the answer to that question is thrashed out in Vienna, someone has to rule in Brussels, and the rumor is that a British army and a Prussian army will have joint control of the Netherlands until a decision is handed down.*
>
> *And the 107th Foot will be part of the British force.*

"Which means that none of the Kingsbridge men will be coming home," said Amos. "There will be a lot of disappointed people here."

"Well, I shan't be among them. It makes little difference to me whether Henry is here or a thousand miles away."

Amos wished she would not harp on about how unhappy she was with her husband. There was nothing anyone could do about it. But he did not complain. He wanted to stay on the right side of her in order to be able to see Hal.

"Read me the rest," he said.

By August 1814 the regiment was encamped in a field outside Brussels. Kit's transfer from the Royal Artillery to the 107th Foot to be aide-de-camp to the earl of Shiring was an honor, but Kit would have refused had he been given a choice because it separated him from Roger, who remained with the gunners. Kit had no idea where Roger was now, which distressed him.

In other respects he was happy. He earned ten shillings a day, before deductions. A regular soldier got eight pence a day. His work was carrying messages and running errands for the earl, but in peacetime there was not much to do, and he spent his spare time working on his German.

He had befriended a junior officer of the King's German Legion, a British Army unit fourteen thousand strong, based in Bexhill-on-Sea. The main reason for this peculiarity was that King George III of England was also the ruler of the German state of Hanover. A battalion of Germans was camped in the next field, and Kit and his friend gave each other language lessons.

Kit had made the men of the 107th Foot pitch their tents in neat lines and dig latrines at the edges of the field. There was a fine for pissing in the wrong place. He had learned in Barrowfield's Mill that even rules that benefited everyone had to be enforced.

Chaplain Mackintosh had a small tent of his own, like the officers. Kit went to see him and found him lying on a thin mattress, wrapped in blankets. His fair hair was damp. Kit knelt beside him and felt his forehead: he was hot. "You're not well, Mr. Mackintosh," he said.

"I think I've got a cold. I'll get over it."

"Let me see your arse." Without waiting for consent Kit drew the blankets away and pulled down the waist of Mackintosh's breeches. His wound was seeping and the skin around it was reddened. "This doesn't look good," Kit said, and he straightened the chaplain's clothing and tucked the blankets around him.

"I'll be all right," Mackintosh said.

A water jug and a cup stood on an empty ammunition box. Kit poured some water and gave it to Mackintosh, who drank thirstily. There was not much left, so Kit picked up the jug and said: "I'll fetch you more water."

"Thanks."

There was a clear stream running across one corner of the field—part of the reason this site had been chosen for the camp. Kit filled the jug and returned. When he reentered the tent he had made up his mind what to do. "I don't think you should be sleeping on the ground," he said. "I'm going to see about putting you somewhere more comfortable until you recover."

"My place is here with the men."

"We'll let the colonel decide that."

It was part of Kit's job to make sure the colonel knew about everything important that happened in the regiment, and he reported the chaplain's illness. "His wound hasn't healed up properly," he said. "He's feverish."

"What do you think we should do?" The earl knew that when Kit brought him a problem he usually had a solution to suggest.

"We should put him in a decent boardinghouse in Brussels. Warmth, a soft bed, and rest may be all he needs."

"Can he afford it?"

"I doubt it." Chaplains were paid less than officers. "I'll write home to his wife for money."

"Very well."

"I have to go into the town tomorrow to pick up some new recruits from England. I'll see if I can find a good boardinghouse while I'm there."

"Good plan. I'll pay the bill until the money comes from England."

Kit had expected the earl to offer this. "Thank you, sir."

Early the next morning Kit went to the stable where a few horses were kept for the officers' use. He picked out an elderly mare. He had got used to horses in the army and now he rode without thinking about it, but he still preferred a slow, lazy mount.

He took with him a young ensign who spoke some French. The lad chose a broad-chested pony.

They rode into Brussels. Ignoring the grand, expensive town center, they looked around the busy narrow side streets for boardinghouses. Some were so dirty that Kit rejected them in seconds. Eventually he found a clean place owned by an Italian widow called Anna Bianco. She looked like a kindly person who might take an invalid under her wing, and there was a mouthwatering aroma coming from the kitchen. She had a spacious upstairs front room with large windows. Kit paid for two weeks in advance and said the tenant would move in tomorrow.

Mackintosh would have to be driven there in a cart. With that wound he could not sit on a horse.

Next, Kit and the ensign rode to a tavern called Hôtel des Halles, on the east bank of the canal from Antwerp. He saw a large horse-drawn barge moored beside the place and guessed that the recruits had already arrived. There were about a hundred men and a handful of women in the courtyard, with an English sergeant in charge. "One hundred and three men, sir," he said to Kit, "plus six female camp followers, all quite respectable."

The canal barge must have been crowded, Kit thought. Probably the sergeant had been given money for two boats, then had crammed the recruits into one and pocketed the difference. "Thank you, Sergeant. When did they last eat?"

"They had a good breakfast at first light, sir. Bread and cheese and small beer."

"That should keep them going awhile longer."

"Easily, sir."

"All right. Form them up five abreast and I'll march them off."

"Yes, sir."

He looked them over appraisingly as the sergeant marshaled them. Their uniforms were grubby from the trip. Apart from a few eager youths they were a sullen lot, probably regretting the impulse that had made them volunteer. Mostly they looked healthy, though. They would be drilled and marched to keep them on their toes, but they would not have to fight. The war was over.

His eye was caught by the back of a tall man with broad shoulders, and he thought how useful that man would have been when maneuvering cannons in battle. The man had long, straggly fair hair, and seemed vaguely familiar. He turned, and Kit was astonished to recognize Jarge Box.

Why was he here? Perhaps he had lost hope of finding work, and had joined the army in desperation. Or, more likely, he had been convicted of a serious crime—of which he might well have been guilty—and had been sentenced to the army.

Kit's relationship with his stepfather had been rocky, but now he felt glad to see him. As he approached, Jarge's face—which had borne the look of one who is staunchly bearing the trials of a long, uncomfortable journey—broke into a smile. "Well, I'll be damned," he said. "I wondered if I might run into you."

Kit shook his hand energetically. "You've come at the right time," he said. "The fighting's over." Then he glanced over Jarge's shoulder and saw his mother.

He burst into tears.

He went to her and they embraced. Kit could not find words. He was overwhelmed by happiness and love.

Eventually she stood back and looked him up and down. "My, my," she said. "So brown-faced, so thin, and yet so much a man." She touched his neck just below his ear. "With a scar, too."

"A souvenir of Spain. Mother, you look well." She was in her middle forties but seemed as healthy and strong as ever. "How was the journey?"

"That barge was overcrowded. But we're out of it now."

"Have you eaten?"

"A scanty breakfast."

"There'll be dinner at the camp."

"I can hardly wait."

"In that case we'll get going." He stepped back and let the sergeant get on with forming them into a marching body.

When they were ready he got on his horse to address them. Raising his voice in the way he had learned to make it carry, he said: "Being in the army is very easy. If you do what I tell you, when I tell you, and do it right you will have a happy time." There was a rumble of quiet assent to that: it was fair. "If you piss me off I will make you so miserable you will wish you were dead." They laughed at that, though with an undercurrent of nervousness.

The truth was that Kit never made anyone's life miserable. However, the threat was effective.

Finally he said: "On my word . . . march."

He turned his horse and nudged it into a walk, and the recruits followed.

<hr />

It was midmorning when Elsie received the letter from Kit Clitheroe. She remembered him as a bright little boy in Sunday school. So little Kit was now a captain in the 107th Foot and based in Brussels.

If Kit and his mother had stayed in their village they would both still have been poor agricultural laborers who never traveled farther than Kingsbridge. How their lives had been transformed by industry and war.

She read Kit's letter several times. It seemed to her that Kenelm was seriously ill. She brooded all morning, then took the letter with her at dinnertime and showed it to her mother and Spade.

Arabella agreed with her that it looked bad. "The infection has persisted too long," she said. "I wish he was here, so that we could look after him, but the journey would make him worse."

Elsie said: "It's kind of the earl to pay for the boardinghouse, and I'll send money right away. I still have most of my inheritance from Father."

Arabella still looked worried. "I can't think what more we can do for poor Kenelm."

This was the question that had troubled Elsie all morning, but she had found a solution. "I must go to Brussels and look after him," she said.

"Oh, Elsie, no!" said Arabella. "Such a dangerous journey."

"No, it's not," Elsie said. "Stagecoach to Folkestone, a short sea crossing, then a canal boat to Brussels."

"Any sea voyage is dangerous."

"But this less so than most."

"How long would you stay in Brussels?"

"Until Kenelm gets well."

"We can look after the children, of course—can't we, David?"

"We'd be delighted."

Elsie's five children were between eight and seventeen years old. "That won't be necessary," she said. "They can come with me. I'll rent a house there. It will be good for the children. They'll learn French."

"It will broaden their minds," said Spade. "I approve."

Arabella still did not like Elsie's plan. "What about the Sunday school?"

"Lydia Mallet will run it in my absence. Amos will help her."

"Still . . ."

"I have to help Kenelm. I married him and I owe him that."

Arabella was thoughtful for a long moment, and then she gave in. "Yes," she said reluctantly. "I suppose you do."

Jane read a long report in *The Lady's Magazine* that caught her imagination, and she showed it to Amos. Brussels was the newly popular destination for the fashionable set, the article said. People who for years had flocked to Bath, ostensibly to take the waters, actually to dance, gossip, and show off their most beautiful clothes, were now doing all the same things in Brussels. Dinner parties, picnics, hunting, and theater were the favorite occupations of the expatriates. The town was full of gallant officers in splendid uniforms. The risqué waltz, with its scandalously intimate touching, was danced there at every opportunity. Rewarding friendships could spring up between people who would not normally meet in London—a comment that struck Amos as hinting at adultery. There were many aristocratic English visitors, and the leader of Brussels society was the duchess of Richmond.

Amos was mildly disgusted. "Empty-headed socialites doing an obscene dance," he said grumpily. Then he had another thought. "But they'll all want to be buying new clothes."

"Oho!" said Jane triumphantly. "Now you've changed your tune."

There would be growing demand for luxury cloth, Amos was thinking. This would be useful, as the demand for army uniforms—the bread-and-butter of his business—would now plummet. He needed to get in touch with buyers in the Netherlands.

Jane said: "I might go to Brussels."

"You, too!" said Amos.

"What do you mean?"

"Elsie is going there to look after Kenelm. He's been wounded. Lydia will take charge of the Sunday school, and I'll help her."

"You'll do anything for Elsie."

Amos was puzzled by that. "What do you mean?"

"You're a peculiar man, Amos Barrowfield."

"I have no idea what you're talking about."

"No, you don't."

Amos had no patience for enigmatic conversation. "Anyway, who will look after Hal while you're away?"

"I'll take him with me."

"Oh." That would mean Amos would not see him. "For how long?"

"I don't know. As long as Henry is there—at least."

"I see."

"I can't wait. It sounds like just the kind of life I've always wanted but Henry would never give me—all parties and dances and new gowns."

She would never change, Amos thought. What a good thing she had refused him. If he ever married it would be to someone serious.

He had had a lucky escape.

CHAPTER 38

Elsie had never traveled on a ship, never been to a foreign country, and never stayed in a lodging house. She had only a smattering of French, she struggled with foreign currency, and she was astonished by the alien appearance of the houses, the shops, and the people's clothes. She was not a timid person, but she had never imagined the difficulties she would face on her own.

She knew now that it had been a terrible mistake to journey to Brussels with the five children, and when finally she sat on a lumpy bed in a dusty hotel room with her trunks and her children scattered all around her, she cried.

With considerable effort she was able to get a message to the earl of Shiring at the encampment of the 107th Foot Regiment, and after that things improved. Her messenger returned with a friendly note from the earl and a separate letter, not sealed, for her to take to the duchess of Richmond. The letter asked the duchess to extend the hand of friendship to Mrs. Kenelm Mackintosh, and mentioned that Elsie was the daughter of the late bishop of Kingsbridge and the wife of a British army chaplain who had been wounded at Toulouse.

The next day Elsie went to the Richmond residence in the rue de la Blanchisserie. The house was three stories high and had room enough for the fourteen children the duchess had borne. The location was not the most expensive neighborhood in Brussels, and there were rumors that the duke and duchess had come here to save money. It was cheaper to live here than in London. Champagne was only four shillings a bottle, which made little difference to Elsie's budget, but probably saved a fortune for the party-loving Richmonds.

The recommendation of an earl, combined with the mention of a bishop and a wounded army chaplain, were together enough to overcome the duchess's famous snobbery, and she welcomed Elsie graciously. She was handsome rather than pretty, with a strong nose and chin that sandwiched a rosebud mouth. She gave Elsie a note to a Brussels merchant who spoke good English and would help her find a good house to rent.

Elsie settled on a town house near the cathedral of St. Michael and St. Gudula and moved in with the five children. She went to the lodging house to fetch Kenelm, and was amused to note that he seemed almost sorry to say goodbye to Signora Bianco, who had evidently won his gratitude.

The house Elsie rented was not grand, but it was comfortable. Best of all, it was not far from the jewel of Brussels, its park, which was thirty or forty delightful acres of lawns, gravel walks, statues, and fountains. No horses were allowed, which meant that people could let the children race around without fear of being run down by carriages.

Whenever the weather was good Elsie took Kenelm to the park. At first she had to push him in a wheelchair, but soon he recovered enough to walk, albeit slowly. They were always accompanied by two or three of the children, who usually brought a ball to play with.

She occasionally ran into Jane, countess of Shiring, who was living in Brussels now. They chatted amiably. Jane had become a close friend of the duchess of Richmond.

Jane asked Elsie why she turned down so many invitations to parties from the duchess and others. Elsie said she hardly had time for such things, with five children and a convalescent husband to take care of. That was true, but she also found balls and picnics and horse races trivial and boring. She hated the constant meaningless small talk. She did not say that to Jane.

On one occasion Elsie saw Jane with a handsome officer, Captain Percival Dwight; and that time Jane did not stop to chat. She was being particularly gay and charming, flirting with the captain, and Elsie wondered whether they were having an affair. She could imagine that adultery would happen more easily in a foreign town—she was not sure why.

On a December afternoon, cold but sunny, Elsie and Kenelm rested on a bench, watching the play of water in a fountain, keeping an eye on Martha and Georgie, the two youngest. Elsie was amazed by the transformation in her husband. His wound was only part of the reason. He had seen suffering and death, and it showed in his gaunt face. His eyes looked inward, and he saw remembered carnage. Little trace was left of the cockily ambitious young clergyman she had married. She liked him better this way.

He said: "I'm almost ready to return to the regiment."

He was not ready, in Elsie's opinion. His body was healing faster than his mind. A sudden noise in the street outside—a heavy crate dropped on the flatbed of a cart, or a workman's hammer demolishing a wall—would make him duck his head and drop to his knees on the drawing room carpet.

"Don't be in a rush," she said. "Let's make sure you're fully recovered. I believe it was returning to duty too early that made you ill."

He did not accept that. "God sent me here to care for the spiritual welfare of the men of the 107th Foot. It's a holy mission." He seemed to have forgotten that the only reason he became a chaplain was to improve his prospects of being made a bishop.

"The war is over," she said. "Surely the need is less."

"Soldiers find it difficult to return to normality. They've got used to the idea that life is cheap. They've killed men, and seen their friends die. Such experiences blunt the edge of compassion. The only way they can get through is to become callous. They can't simply go back to being ordinary chaps. They need help."

"And you can give them that help."

"I most certainly cannot," he said with a flash of the old assertiveness. "But God can help them, if they will only turn to him."

She looked at him in silence for several moments, then said: "Are you aware of how much you've changed?"

He nodded thoughtfully. "It goes back to Spain," he said. He was staring at the fountain but she knew he was seeing a sun-parched battlefield. "I saw a young soldier dying on the ground, his blood soaking into the dry earth."

He paused, but Elsie said nothing, giving him time.

"The enemy was almost on us. The wounded man's comrades had no time to console him—they were firing their muskets and reloading and firing again as fast as they could. I knelt beside him and told him he was going to heaven. He spoke, and I had to put my ear to his mouth to hear his words, because of the crash of the muskets and the boom of cannons. 'Heaven?' he said. 'Am I, really?' and I answered: 'Yes, if you believe in the Lord Jesus.' Then I suggested we should say the Lord's Prayer together. 'Don't worry about the noise,' I said. 'God can hear us.' That was when he told me he did not know the words." Tears came to Kenelm's eyes as he remembered. "Can you imagine?" he said. "He couldn't say the Lord's Prayer."

Elsie could imagine it. New children coming to Sunday school sometimes did not know who Jesus was. It was unusual, but not unknown.

"I held his hand and said the prayer for him, and by the time I got to 'Thine is the kingdom, the power, and the glory,' the boy had left this world behind, and gone to a place where there is no war."

"May his soul rest in peace," said Elsie.

Spade was bowled over by the Passage des Panoramas in Paris. There was nothing like it in London. It was a walkway, paved and glass roofed, lined on both sides with shops selling jewelry, lingerie, bonbons, hats, writing paper, and more. It ran from the boulevard Montmartre to the rue St.-Marc. At each end stood a burly man in uniform—in England he might have been called a beadle—to keep out ragamuffins and pickpockets. Elegant Parisian women, and many from other countries, too, could shop without getting their hair wet in the rain or their shoes muddy from the tons of muck on the streets. An added attraction was a rotunda featuring panoramic paintings of famous cities including Rome and Jerusalem.

Arabella was enchanted. She bought a straw hat, a scarf, and a box of sugared almonds. Spade led her into a shop selling luxury fabrics: silk, cashmere, fine linen, and mixtures, in many colors and patterns. He took from his pocket a stiff card that said, in French, that he was a manufacturer of exceptional cloth for high-end gowns and he would be glad to show the manageress some samples at a time of her convenience.

She replied in rapid French. Abe, who was fifteen and learning French at Kingsbridge Grammar School, asked her to repeat what she had said but slower, and then he translated: "She would be pleased to see you tomorrow morning at ten."

Spade bowed and thanked her in French. His accent was terrible but he gave his most charming rueful grin and she laughed.

When they stepped outside the arcade Spade sensed a change in the atmosphere on the street. Some people strolled idly along, but others were deep in excited conversation. Not for the first time he wished he understood the language.

They passed a woman sitting at the roadside by a table loaded with newspapers for sale. Spade's eye was caught by a headline that said:

NAPOLÉON A FUI!

He asked Abe: "What does that say?"

"I don't know. Bonaparte did something, obviously, but I don't know what."

"Ask the vendor."

Abe pointed at the headline and said: "Madame, qu'est-ce que ça veut dire?"

"Il a échappé," she said. Seeing that they did not comprehend, she tried several times more. "Il est parti! Il s'est sauvé! Il a quitté son prison!"

Abe said to Spade: "I think he's escaped."

Spade was astonished. "From Elba?"

The news vendor nodded frantically. "Oui, oui, oui!" Waving a goodbye hand she said: "Au revoir, Elba! Au revoir!" Then she cackled.

They knew what that meant.

Spade said: "Ask her where he's going."

Abe said: "Où va-t-il?"

"Il est déjà arrivé en France! Au Midi!"

Spade bought the paper.

Arabella looked distraught. "How could this happen? I thought he was guarded!"

Spade shook his head, baffled and worried. Surely the man could not make a comeback? "Let's return to our lodgings," he said. "Someone there may have more news."

They were staying at a boardinghouse run by a Frenchman with an English wife, and therefore popular with English tourists. When they arrived, everyone was in the sitting room, talking animatedly. Spade showed them the paper, saying: "Can anyone read this?"

The landlady, Eleanor Delacroix, picked it up and scanned the story. "This is extraordinary!" she said. "Somehow he managed to assemble a small fleet of ships and an army of a thousand men!"

Spade said: "There was an Englishman who was supposed to guard him."

"Neil Campbell," said Madame Delacroix. "It seems he had departed from Elba on HMS *Partridge* carrying a dispatch for Lord Castlereagh."

Spade laughed humorlessly. "What was in the dispatch—a warning that Bonaparte was planning to escape?"

"I wouldn't be surprised, but it doesn't say here."

"Where is he now?"

"Golfe-Juan, on the south coast."

"So he's not coming here. That's a relief."

"If it's true," the landlady said. "These newspapers don't know everything."

"But what could he do in France, with only a thousand men?"

She shrugged like a Frenchwoman. "All I know," she said, "is that one should never underestimate Napoleon."

Amos Barrowfield was about to take a large consignment of dark blue merino wool cloth on a barge downstream to Combe and then by sea to Antwerp. It was his first big order from the newly liberated Netherlands, and he was concerned that the cloth should be delivered swiftly and securely, because he hoped to win more business from the same customer and others there; so he was taking it across the channel personally.

The day before he was due to depart he had dinner at the High Street Coffee House—roast lamb with potatoes—and read the latest news.

The headline in the *Gazette* was:

BONAPARTE IN FRANCE

"Hell," he said.

"My sentiments exactly," said a voice, and Amos looked up to see Rupe Underwood at the next table, eating the same lamb and reading the same newspaper.

Amos and Rupe were friendly enough now, though they had once been rivals for the affections of Jane

Midwinter. They were both in their forties and Amos was struck by how Rupe had aged, then realized that he had aged, too, in the same way: a little gray in the hair, a softness around the waist, an aversion to running.

Rupe said: "Bonaparte has landed on the south coast of France at a place called Cannes, it says here. Then he went to Mass at a local church."

Amos said: "Worst of all, it seems local men are flocking to join his army."

"Everyone thought he would run to someplace where his empire hasn't yet collapsed."

"Probably Naples."

"But we misjudged him—again."

Amos nodded agreement. "There's only one reason for him to return to France with an army, even a small one. He wants to be emperor again."

"Is that possible?"

"I believe a lot of French people would welcome him back. The new king, Louis XVIII, seems to have done all he can to remind them why they had a revolution in the first place."

"Such as?"

"I understand he's revived the ancient royal custom of forgetting to pay the soldiers."

"Will Bonaparte reach Paris?"

"That's what I'm wondering. I'm due to leave tomorrow for Antwerp."

"Which is what, seven or eight hundred miles from the south coast of France?"

"Something like that."

"It's a long way."

"All the same, I'm wondering whether to cancel my trip."

"The road to Paris is not exactly open to all comers. There are units of the French army who could bar the way."

Amos nodded. The French army was now at the service of the new king, in theory at least, and would be ordered to defend the country against Bonaparte. "Yes," said Amos. "From Paris to Antwerp is another couple of hundred miles. And the Netherlands is now defended by British and Prussian armies. So . . ."

"The danger of Napoleon getting as far as Antwerp seems small."

"And my consignment is big, so I'm reluctant to let it go unsupervised. Plus I want to shake the hands of my customers there. Business is so much easier when you've seen one another's faces."

"So what will you do?"

"I still haven't decided. I mean, how much blue merino cloth is my life worth?"

Rupe sighed. "This bloody war," he said. "Twenty-two years now and it's still not really over. For most of our adult lives it's plagued our business. Plus we've had bread riots and machine breaking and laws that make it a crime to criticize the government. And what have we gained?"

"I suppose the government would say we've prevented Europe being turned into a French empire."

"Except that we haven't," said Rupe. "Not yet."

The residents of Madame Delacroix's boardinghouse studied the newspapers anxiously, translating with her help. Provence and the southwest of France were royalist, against the revolution and hostile to Napoleon. Spade presumed that was why he clung to the eastern border, marching north from Cannes on icy mountain roads. Nonetheless, many commentators said he would be stopped as soon as he encountered the French national army.

The newspapers reported that in six days he had reached Grenoble, which was about twelve days from Paris. But news took four days to reach the capital, so Napoleon must now have been eight days away.

And the news from Grenoble was bad.

Napoleon and his growing army had been confronted outside the town of Laffrey, not far from Grenoble, by a battalion of the Fifth Regiment of the Line. Napoleon's force was outnumbered by that of the government. This should have been the end of his comeback.

Apparently he had stepped away from his men and walked, alone and fearless, toward the armed ranks of the regiment that was there to stop him.

According to the newspaper report—which might have been somewhat dramatized—Napoleon threw open his famous gray coat, pointed to his heart, and said: "Well, men, do you want to kill your emperor?"

No one fired.

One of the soldiers of the Fifth shouted: "*Vive l'empereur!*" Long live the emperor!

The cheer was repeated, and the men threw away their white Bourbon cockades—representing King Louis XVIII—and embraced Napoleon's men.

Then the regiment changed sides and marched with Napoleon.

Spade said to Arabella: "Until now it's just been peasants and the National Guard, but this is the first time soldiers of the regular army have gone over to him. It's a big change."

The same thing happened at the next town, Vizille, where the Seventh Regiment of the Line defected to Napoleon. Then at the city of Grenoble he was welcomed like a conquering hero.

"Oh, shit," said Spade, as these details became incontrovertibly clear; and he went out and booked three seats on a stagecoach to Brussels.

He was asked to pay ten times the usual price, and he did so without hesitation. They left the following morning at daybreak.

On March 20, in the early hours of the morning, Louis XVIII fled Paris.

A few hours later Napoleon entered the capital unopposed.

CHAPTER 39

After Amos had visited his customers in Antwerp he went to Brussels. Hal should not be in a potential war zone, and Amos wanted Jane to take the boy back to England and safety. He no longer had any doubt that Hal was his son. Jane loved their child—surely she would see that Brussels was no place for a nine-year-old?

Jane had rented a grand house near the park. A family of three hardly needed so much space, Amos thought as he studied the place from the street. When he stepped into the hall he noticed there was little evidence of a male resident: no riding boots on the floor, no sword hanging from a hook, no bicorn hat on the hat stand. It would not be surprising, Amos reflected, if Henry spent more nights with the regiment than with his family.

Amos was shown into the drawing room, where Jane sat reading a fashion magazine. She was beautifully dressed, as always, and the air around her had a faint aroma of flowers.

Her face was flushed with excitement. She seemed happy, and he wondered why. It was not his presence that energized her: those days were over for both of them. The thought crossed his mind that she might have a lover. It was a mean suspicion, he told himself, but he could not quite manage to dismiss the possibility.

She rang for tea, and they made small talk for a few minutes. He brought her up to date on events in Kingsbridge, and she spoke enthusiastically about social life in Brussels. "The duchess of Richmond is giving a ball," she said. "You must come. I'll get you an invitation." Once upon a time she had complained that she never got to attend parties. Amos guessed she went to plenty now.

The duchess was a famous snob. "Are you sure she won't object to a lowly clothier?" he asked.

"Quite sure. She has already invited more than two hundred people. She won't mind another one."

The tea came, and Hal appeared. Amos felt a familiar tug on his heartstrings. Although manhood was some years away his son was changing. Hal shook hands solemnly with Amos, who cherished the touch of his soft skin. With the appetite of a growing boy he ate three slices of cake in rapid succession.

Watching him, Amos was struck by something about his face, and realized that it reminded him of the face he saw in his shaving mirror. If others saw the resemblance it could cause trouble. He resolved to grow a beard.

Hal left, and Amos turned the conversation toward the purpose of his visit. "The allies meeting in Vienna have declared war," he said. "Not on France, but on Napoleon personally. I don't think that's ever been done before."

Jane said: "That's because we have no quarrel with France as a peaceable monarchy. We're going to invade France only to depose Bonaparte. And this time the Corsican upstart won't escape."

It was the kind of thing the English might repeat parrot fashion. Jane had no sense of how difficult it was to defeat Bonaparte. Amos said: "You know that he's massing his army only fifty miles from here, just on the other side of the border."

"Yes, of course I know," she said. "But the duke of Wellington is here now, and he has proved himself more than a match for Bonaparte."

That was not true. The two generals had never yet met in battle. But Amos did not want to quibble. "I just feel you and Hal would be so much safer back in England."

"In Earlscastle, I suppose," she said with disdain. "Where nothing ever happens. I think we're safe enough here."

"Really, you're not," he insisted. "It's reckless to underestimate Bonaparte."

"My husband is on Wellington's headquarters staff, you know," Jane said with a touch of hauteur. "I might know more about the military situation than you do."

"I'm no expert," Amos conceded. "But I believe the outcome of a battle is utterly impossible to predict."

Jane shifted her ground. "I do hope you haven't come here to lecture me."

"I want you and Hal to be safe, that's all."

"It's Hal you're worried about. You don't care about me."

"Of course I care about you!" he protested. "You're the mother of my only child!"

"Keep your voice down, for God's sake."

"Sorry."

There was a pause, then Amos said: "Just think about what I've said, please."

She was clearly annoyed and embarrassed. "I'll think about it, I'll think about it," she said in a dismissive tone that told him she would not.

Disappointed, he took his leave.

Northwest Europe was having a rainy spring, but today was a rare fine day, and he walked through the sunlit streets to the less expensive neighborhood where Elsie had taken up residence with her husband and children. Elsie met him in the hall with her familiar wide smile. As they walked up the stairs she said: "Please don't tell Kenelm how well he looks. I'm trying to stop him returning to the regiment before he's ready."

Amos suppressed a smile. Typical Elsie, determined to keep control, he thought fondly. "I'll bear that in mind," he said.

Kenelm was in the drawing room. His face, once cherubically handsome, was now gaunt. However, in other respects he did not look like an invalid. He was fully dressed in clerical robes, wearing outdoor shoes as if he was about to go for a walk. Amos said tactfully: "It's good to see you. I gather you're recovering fairly well."

"I'm perfectly fit," Kenelm said as if disagreeing. "It took longer than expected, but now I'm ready to return to my duties."

Amos said: "What's the hurry?"

"The men need me."

Do they? Amos wondered. They would probably say they needed good boots and plenty of ammunition and intelligent leaders.

Kenelm read his mind. "You don't know what life is like in an army camp," he said. "Drink, gambling, and wicked women. Elsie will forgive me for speaking coarsely, but I don't want to understate the situation. Do you know what a British soldier's daily rations are?"

"I'm afraid I don't."

"A pound of beef, a pound of bread, and half a pint of gin. Half a pint! And when they have any money, and don't lose it at cards, they spend it on more gin."

"And you're able to rescue them from this life?"

Kenelm smiled ruefully. "Ah, Amos, I could almost think you were making fun of me. No, I can't rescue them, but sometimes God can."

"But you tell them not to indulge in such vices."

"One of the many things I've learned in the army is that telling men to be good is not effective. Instead of forbidding vice, I try to encourage other things. I hold services in the fields. I tell them Bible stories. When they're wounded, or homesick, or terrified out of their wits before a battle I pray with them. They like singing, and occasionally I get a whole platoon singing a familiar hymn together. When that happens I feel I have justified my existence here on earth."

Amos had to hide his surprise. He had heard that army life had altered Kenelm, but the man was utterly transformed.

Elsie said: "That's all very well, Kenelm, but you shouldn't return until you're completely fit."

"There are plenty of men in the camp who aren't completely fit."

The argument was ended by a burst of excited chatter from the hall. "That's the children coming back," Elsie explained. "They've been to the park with my mother and Spade."

Amos had not expected to see Spade and Arabella. He knew they had gone to Paris but had heard no more since then. He was glad to see that they had escaped from Bonaparte. He hoped they would all be safe here in Brussels, but he knew they might not.

The children burst in. They knew Amos well and felt no need to be on their best behavior. The younger ones were overflowing with accounts of what they had seen and done in the park. The older ones were more restrained—Elsie's Stephen was eighteen and Arabella's Abe was fifteen—but they had clearly enjoyed the park just as much.

Spade had taken a lot of orders in Paris, he told Amos; business had picked up quickly. He hoped he would be able to deliver the goods. That depended on what happened to Bonaparte.

Arabella had bought clothes in Paris, Amos guessed. She was sixty-one now, slim and gracious in a green silk gown.

Amos was offered tea for the second time that afternoon, and accepted to be polite. The children fell on the sandwiches. Then they went elsewhere.

Kenelm said: "Now that the tide has gone out, Amos, I have a favor to ask of you."

"Anything I can do, of course."

"Would you escort Elsie to the duchess of Richmond's ball? She has been invited, and I want her to go—she deserves an evening of relaxation and pleasure—but I can't go. For me to be seen drinking champagne at an aristocratic shindig would give quite the wrong impression."

Elsie was embarrassed. "Kenelm, please! What an imposition that would be on Amos. Besides, I don't suppose he's been invited."

"As a matter of fact, Jane, the countess of Shiring, has promised to get me an invitation."

"Has she," said Elsie, in a disapproving tone of voice.

"I wasn't planning to accept, but I'd be very happy—indeed, honored—to escort you, Mrs. Mackintosh."

"There," said Kenelm with satisfaction. "That's settled, then."

The duke of Wellington had been away from the army, performing other tasks such as being British ambassador in Paris, but now he had returned to military duties and taken charge of the British and Dutch armies. The allied Prussian army was under separate command.

On his return Wellington had asked Henry, earl of Shiring, to join his headquarters staff, as he had in Spain. Henry had agreed—it was more of an order than a request—and had asked to have Kit as his aide. "He's a very capable young man," Henry had told the duke. "He started work in a mill at the age of seven, and by the time he was eighteen he was its manager."

Henry told Kit that the duke had said: "That's the kind of man I want."

Today Kit had to take a message to the new commanding officer of the 107th Foot. He rode there in a rainstorm. While at the camp he took the opportunity to seek out his mother.

Sal was wearing men's clothing. This was not a disguise, Kit knew. She was not trying to pass as a man. But trousers and waistcoats were more practical than dresses in an army camp. Many of the female camp followers dressed the same. Another advantage was that it distinguished them from prostitutes, so they did not have to deal with unwelcome advances.

She naturally asked him how soon the allies would

invade France. "Wellington hasn't made up his mind," Kit said, which was the truth. "But I don't think it's many days away."

Kit wished his mother would go home to England and safety, but he did not try to persuade her. She had decided to stand beside her man when he risked his life in battle, and Kit had to respect her choice. After all, he had done the same thing by joining up with Roger. Both couples would march into France with the army and be part of the attack on Bonaparte's forces. He hoped they would all come back.

That was a depressing thought and he pushed it aside.

They were sitting in a tent, for shelter. A soldier came in and bought a pipeful of tobacco from Sal. When the man had gone, Kit said: "So you're a tobacconist now?"

"More than that," said Sal. "The men are confined to camp. Some of them break the rules, but not many—the punishment is flogging. So I walk into Brussels once a week. It takes me two hours to get there. I buy stuff the men can't get in camp: not just tobacco, but writing materials, playing cards, oranges, English newspapers, that sort of thing. I sell it at double what I pay."

"They don't mind the price?"

"I tell them the truth: half of that is what it cost me, and the other half is my payment for walking six miles there and six miles back."

Kit nodded. In any case, men were not quick to quarrel with his broad-shouldered mother.

The rain eased, and he said goodbye. He retrieved his horse and set off but he did not go straight back to headquarters. Roger's artillery battery was only a mile away, and he rode there in the hope of seeing the man he loved. Officers were not confined to camp, so Roger might not be there.

However, Kit was in luck, and he found Roger in a tent playing cards with some fellow officers—not surprisingly. He would probably ask Kit to lend him some money, as usual, and Kit would refuse, as usual.

Kit watched the game for a few hands, then Roger excused himself, put his money in his pocket, and left the table. They strolled away in a light drizzle. Kit told Roger about Sal's enterprising business. "Remarkable woman, your mother," Roger said.

Kit agreed.

After a few minutes walking on soggy ground he got the feeling Roger was steering him in a particular direction. Sure enough, they passed through a patch of rough woodland and came to a derelict hut. Roger led the way inside.

There was only one door and no windows. The door was hanging off its hinges. Roger closed it and wedged it with a large stone. "In the unlikely event that anyone should try to come in, we'll hear him shoving at the door in plenty of time to make ourselves respectable and pretend that we came in here to get out of the rain."

"Good thinking," said Kit, and then they kissed.

Wellington called a meeting of headquarters staff to review the latest intelligence. They gathered at Wellington's rented house in the rue Royale and stood around a large map on the dining room table. Outside the windows it was raining hard, as it had been for much of June. Kit was at the back of the group, struggling to see the map past the shoulders of taller men. The mood was tense. They were soon to clash with the most successful general of their time, perhaps of all time. By Kit's count, Bonaparte had fought sixty battles and won fifty. He was a man to fear.

The French national army was divided into four and placed strategically to defend the country against invasions from north, east, and southeast, and against a potential royalist insurrection in the southwest. For the British the important group was the Army of the North, defending a sixty-mile stretch of the border from

Beaumont to Lille. "We estimate Bonaparte has one hundred and thirty thousand men," the head of intelligence said. "The nearest are roughly fifty miles from where we stand."

The British and Dutch were spread over a huge area: they had to be, for the countryside to supply them with food for the men and forage for the horses. "Our strength is one hundred and seven thousand," the officer went on. "But our allies the Prussians, stationed southeast of us, are one hundred and twenty-three thousand strong."

So, Kit thought, Bonaparte is outnumbered almost two to one. Kit had been a part of Wellington's army for more than two years, and he knew that "Old Nosey" always tried to fight with an advantage, and would rather retreat than risk a battle against the odds. This went a long way toward explaining his success.

Someone said: "What will Bonaparte's strategy be?"

Wellington smiled. "While I was in Vienna I discussed that with a Bavarian field marshal, Prince Karl Philipp Wrede, who fought on Napoleon's side until a couple of years ago, when he defected. Wrede said that Bonaparte had told him: 'I have no strategy. I never have a plan of campaign.' Bonaparte is an opportunist. The only thing you can predict is that he is unpredictable."

That was no help, Kit thought. Of course he said nothing.

"The Prussians would like to invade immediately," Wellington went on. "Blücher says he left his old pipe in Paris and he wants it back." The men around the duke chuckled. The seventy-two-year-old Prussian commander was likably roguish. "The truth is that his government is short of money and wants to get the war over with, and his men are desperate to go home for the harvest. I would prefer to wait, but I don't want to delay so long that Blücher's men start to melt away. I have fobbed him off by promising we would attack in July."

Kit welcomed the delay. He was in no hurry to fight

another battle. He wanted to survive and return home and resume his old life making machines for the cloth industry and sharing a bed with Roger. Anything could happen in a two-week postponement. Bonaparte could die. The French could surrender. There might be no more battles.

"One more thing," said the intelligence officer. "Yesterday a patrol of the British Ninety-Fifth Rifles regiment encountered a group of French lancers southwest of here, which suggests they may cross the border and attack through Mons."

"Very likely," said Wellington. "He might hope to encircle us and cut us off from the coast, so that we could not receive supplies. But we can't be sure until we know more. Meanwhile, we must exude an air of unruffled calm. We have a superior force, we have the power to choose the moment of battle, we have little to fear." He smiled. "And to prove it, tomorrow I shall attend the duchess of Richmond's ball."

CHAPTER 40

The rue Royale was a street of magnificent mansions bordering the park. Wellington's house there was his headquarters as well as his home. On the day of the ball, Thursday, June 15, his senior staff assembled for dinner at three o'clock in the afternoon. It was not a social occasion: his wife was in England and there were no women around the table. The food was not fancy. Wellington liked beef and very good wine, and not much else.

Henry, earl of Shiring, was at the dinner. Kit waited in the large hall with the other aides-de-camp. The earl was worried. There were persistent rumors that the French were on the point of invading. However, Wellington had trusted spies in Paris and they had seen no sign of imminent action. He suspected that Bonaparte started such rumors to deceive him.

One of the rumors said that Bonaparte would send a small diversionary force to attack the Prussians southeast of Brussels, tempting Wellington to deploy the Anglo-Dutch armies there; then the main attack would come in the west, cutting Wellington's lines of communication with the coast. To Kit that sounded like a typical Bonaparte deception. Wellington was not so sure.

Minutes after the senior staff had sat down William, Prince of Orange, arrived. He was commander of Wellington's First Corps, which included the Dutch troops. A slight figure, he was nicknamed Slender Billy. The dining room door was left open so that the aides could hear what he reported.

The prince announced that outlying Prussian troops had skirmished with a French force that had crossed the border due south of Brussels.

This had been anticipated by a rumor that Wellington had mistrusted.

The duke was momentarily taken aback. His spies had given no warning of this. "It may have been a minor attack," Wellington said. "A scouting party, perhaps."

"But it may not!" said the prince.

Feint or attack? There was no way to know for certain. The commander in chief had to choose. All he had was his instinct.

Wellington said: "We must get more information."

The prince's tone of voice showed that he was deflated. Clearly he felt Wellington should send troops south to support the Prussians. Kit did not know what to think. Bonaparte was famous for moving fast: any delay in responding could be fatal. But if Wellington moved troops based on scant information he could be wrong-footed.

Move or wait?

The dinner resumed, though not for long. The next breathless arrival was the duke and duchess of Richmond's son, who had galloped twenty-two miles—changing horses several times—with the news that French soldiers had captured the tiny medieval city of Thuin, just inside the border, driving Prussian troops into retreat.

How serious was this? The young nobleman, his clothes covered with mud from his pell-mell journey, did not have an estimate of the strength of the attacking force. That was unfortunate. Wellington now badly needed to know how many French troops had crossed the border. His judgment was on the line.

Heads or tails?

Minutes later the Prussian liaison officer, Major General von Müffling, arrived to say that the French had now advanced ten miles farther northward and were attacking the larger town of Charleroi.

Wellington still thought it unlikely that the entire French army was involved in this infiltration. It was more probable, he judged, that this was the rumored feint, to draw defensive forces away from the real invasion somewhere else. Others around the table thought differently.

However, as a precaution Wellington summoned the quartermaster general, Colonel Sir William De Lancey, and ordered all allied forces to be ready to march. He also briefed De Lancey on what marching orders to issue.

Kit was worried. From the start he had agreed with Wellington that the appearance of French lancers near Mons, southwest of Brussels, indicated a main attack farther west—but contrary evidence was mounting. Nevertheless Wellington was holding to his original judgment, and interpreting new reports as further signs of a feint.

What if Wellington was wrong? Right now the allied forces were spread over hundreds of miles of countryside—they had to be, to find enough food for the men and forage for the horses. Before they could fight they had to be rounded up and marched to the war zone, which took time; whereas Bonaparte's army might already be assembled for the fight.

And daylight was running out.

Kit feared that a giant menace was looming and Wellington was refusing to see it.

When the much-interrupted dinner was at last over, Wellington walked in the park, as was his custom. This was not as insouciant as it seemed: his subordinates knew to find him there at that hour, and as he walked he gave out a stream of orders.

Then he returned to his house. Carriages were waiting to take everyone to the ball, but Wellington and his staff lingered. At dusk von Müffling reappeared with a further report from the Prussian army, and this was deeply shocking. The French had taken the fortress of Charleroi, only forty miles from Brussels, and the Prussians had been forced to retreat.

Worse, it was confirmed that the Imperial Guard was part of the attacking French force. This was an elite corps that always traveled with Bonaparte.

Kit felt the chill of fear. Wellington had guessed wrong. This was no feint. While the allies had been getting ready to invade France, Bonaparte had turned the tables on them and invaded the Netherlands. The invaders had been invaded.

Wellington's face turned slightly pale.

Kit recalled Wellington's own words: "Bonaparte is an opportunist. The only thing you can predict is that he is unpredictable."

We're in trouble now, Kit thought.

Wellington recovered fast. He looked at a map. Two roads leading from Charleroi were like the hands of a clock at two o'clock. "Which way did the Prussians retreat, exactly?"

"Northeast." Müffling ran his finger along the hour hand to where the number two would be and stopped at the town of Ligny. "Blücher will make a stand here."

Wellington put a finger on the minute hand, a long, straight road that ran due north to Brussels. There were coal mines near Charleroi, and Kit knew that a constant stream of heavy carts drawn by ox teams trundled up this road to bring coal to the manufactories and fireplaces of Brussels. Wellington said: "Is the coal road now left unguarded? Or has Blücher got it covered?"

"I'm not sure."

Kit felt panicked. The coal road was on the border between Prussian and British forces, and he now realized that there had been no discussion in the general staff about who should defend it.

Wellington held his nerve. "So we must guard against any French attack along that road."

He then ordered General Picton's division to march from Brussels twelve miles south to block the coal road at the village of Mont St.-Jean.

Then, to Kit's amazement, Wellington went to the ball.

Elsie looked lovely.

She was not generally thought of as a beautiful woman. For conventional beauty, her mouth was too wide and her nose too big. Now Amos wondered if convention had got it all wrong. Her wide-smiling mouth suited her generous spirit, and her soft hazel eyes fitted with her warm heart. Or perhaps she was one of those women who became more alluring in middle age. And then again, maybe what she was wearing suited her particularly well. Her dress was a gift from Spade, and made by his sister, Kate, from silk in two colors, flame red and bright yellow. It hardly needed to be enhanced by jewelry, but most of the women at the ball would be glittering with diamonds, so she had borrowed a necklace from Arabella.

Whatever the reason, Amos's heart fluttered as he looked at her. This reaction confused him. They were just friends, partners in running a Sunday school. He knew her better than any other woman, even Jane. This was an odd feeling to have about a friend. They sat opposite one another in the carriage, both smiling for no reason Amos could think of.

The Richmond residence was in the rue de la Blanchisserie. A *blanchisserie* was a laundry, and the duke of Richmond sometimes referred to his home jokingly as "the washhouse."

There was a queue of carriages in the street, and a crowd of spectators gathered to stare at the rich and noble guests as they arrived, the women in elaborately draped silk and flamboyant jewelry, most of the men in uniform.

The ballroom was not in the house but in a very large separate building which, Amos had been told, had formerly been a showroom for a carriage maker. Stepping inside, Amos was astonished by the blaze of light: there were hundreds of candles, perhaps thousands, and more flowers than he had ever seen in one place. It made him feel a little light-headed, as if he had just downed a glass of champagne.

Elsie said: "This is more lavish than anything we've seen in the Kingsbridge Assembly Rooms."

"It's amazing."

They were welcomed by the duchess of Richmond, an attractive woman in her forties. Elsie said: "Your Grace, may I present Mr. Amos Barrowfield, a dear friend of mine."

Amos bowed. The duchess looked coquettish and said: "The countess of Shiring told me that Mr. Barrowfield was the handsomest man in the west of England, and I see what she meant."

Amos was taken aback by her flirting and said the first thing that came into his head. "It was kind of you to invite me, Your Grace."

"Keep him close, Mrs. Mackintosh, or someone will steal him from you."

Now she was implying that Amos and Elsie were a romantic couple, which was not true.

Elsie nudged him and they left the duchess and walked farther into the room. A waiter appeared with champagne on a tray, and they each took a glass.

Amos said: "I'm sorry, I don't know how to respond to that sort of nonsense. It's so embarrassing."

"She was being playful. Your being bashful is part of the game. Don't worry, you did fine."

"I suppose most men at these affairs are used to it, and know what to say."

"Yes, and I'm glad you don't. I like you the way you are."

"I feel the same about you. Let's not change."

She smiled, seeming pleased.

The band struck up a jolly tune in three-four time, and Elsie said: "I know you like dancing, but how do you feel about the waltz?"

"I think I can manage it."

Elsie put her glass down on a table and said: "Then let's give it a try."

Amos drained his glass and got rid of it, then took her in his arms. They waltzed onto the dance floor.

Elsie's waist was warm under his right hand. How pleasant it was, he thought, to dance with a woman he liked so much.

He gently eased her a little closer.

When the Wellington party arrived there was a traffic jam outside the Richmond residence. Wellington was impatient and jumped out of the carriage fifty yards from the gate. Walking along with the group, Kit was startled to see, among the crowd, the square body and round face of Sal, his mother.

He was with the duke, and for one shameful moment he pretended he had not seen her. Then the duke happened to glance at him, and he thought how pleased Sal would be if he acknowledged her, so he stepped away from the party, went up to her, and threw his arms around her.

"Well, well," she said, beaming with pleasure. "My little Kit, with the duke of Wellington. I never thought I'd see the like."

"How are you, Ma? And Jarge?"

"We're all right. He's at the camp. I've come here to buy a few things. You'd better go back to your duke."

Remembering that he was in uniform, he bowed formally, and they returned to the party.

Wellington did not miss much, and he had seen what happened. "Who was that?"

"My mother, sir," said Kit.

"Good Lord," said Wellington.

Kit was offended. He said: "The only person in the world I admire more than you, sir."

For a moment the duke was not sure how to take that

remark. It might have been seen as insolent. But then he smiled and nodded. "Good man," he said, and they all walked on.

The ball was in full swing, and the younger guests were waltzing enthusiastically. Kit felt bewildered. How could people dance when Bonaparte was on his way?

The duke's arrival caused a stir. He was the most important person in Brussels and a hero for his victories at Vitoria and Toulouse. Everyone wanted to greet him and shake his hand.

Kit was hungry as well as scared. He looked longingly through the door to the supper room, but he had to stay close to the earl of Shiring in case he was needed. He would have to wait until the earl was hungry.

Wellington did not dance, but he walked around arm in arm with the pregnant Lady Frances Webster, rumored to be his mistress. Although the revels continued, a constant stream of uniformed officers came in, marched across the ballroom, and murmured in the duke's ear. He engaged each one in brief discussion and then sent them away with fresh orders.

He revisited the problem of the coal road and decided it was not enough to send Picton's division to Mont St.-Jean. He now directed the Dutch under Slender Billy to move to a crossroads called Quatre Bras, farther south on the coal road, to provide an earlier block to any French advance.

Between dances, when the band stopped playing, everyone could hear the sounds of marching feet and jingling harness from the street outside as more and more troops assembled.

Men from the quartermaster general's staff appeared and interrupted the dancing to give movement orders to the officers. The shocking news of the Prussian retreat from Charleroi spread anxiety around the ballroom. During a display of Scottish dancing by the Gordon Highlanders, men began to melt away, some obeying orders, others just guessing they must be needed.

Some of the farewells between young officers and girls were startlingly passionate, as couples realized they might never meet again.

The duke left at three o'clock in the morning and his aides could at last go to bed.

Kit and the earl were part of Wellington's entourage when he set off at eight o'clock that morning, Friday, June 16.

They rode out of Brussels by the Porte de Namur and headed south on the coal road. The surface was cobbled for the benefit of wheeled vehicles, and on each side was a wide dirt track for riders. Coal dust from the wagons had blackened the mud. The road passed through woods on both sides.

The rain held off, for a change, though the ground was puddled and muddy. The sun was already hot: the day would be sultry.

Wellington was tense. The duke's face did not reveal his heart, but those who knew him could read the signs. The invasion had caught him by surprise. Worse, he had made an error of judgment in letting Bonaparte get as far as Charleroi: he should have concentrated his troops sooner, he knew with hindsight. But Bonaparte had assembled his forces quickly and quietly, and managed to keep his invasion secret until it was well under way. Kit had twice heard Wellington say: "Bonaparte has humbugged me."

Everyone knew that the main objective now was to join forces with the Prussians to form an army overwhelmingly larger than Bonaparte's. And the crafty Bonaparte would do all he could to prevent that.

The headquarters party, all on horseback, overtook the regular troops heading south. Kit was thrilled to see Roger with his artillery, the heavy horse-drawn guns making steady progress on the cobblestones. For a minute Kit rode beside Roger, who looked well and energetic even though he must have started out in the early hours. "Take care of yourself," Kit said, and he had never uttered that trite phrase with so much emotion. Then he touched his horse with his heels and rode on.

A little farther on they passed the 107th Foot. Kenelm Mackintosh was leading some of the soldiers in a hymn called "Awake Our Drowsy Souls," a good choice for men who had got up in the middle of the night. The Baptists had all the best tunes, and Kit had a feeling that this was one of theirs, but Mackintosh was long past sectarian pettiness.

He scanned the faces as he rode past and soon picked out his mother and stepfather. Jarge had a standard soldier's pack, called the Trotter pack. Sal had a similar one that she must have scrounged from the supply wagon. Jarge was in uniform, a short red jacket and gray trousers; Sal in men's clothing, trousers and a waistcoat. They marched cheerfully in the sunshine. Both were strong enough to walk all day without distress. As Kit watched, Sal took from inside her waistcoat a length of the spicy local sausage called boudin, drew an unnecessarily long knife from a sheath at her belt, cut an inch of sausage, and gave it to Jarge, who put it in his mouth and chewed happily.

Kit was tempted to stop, but he had talked to his mother only a few hours ago, so he contented himself with attracting her attention and waving, then he rode on.

While he was still alongside the Kingsbridge contingent he saw Joe Hornbeam ride up, apparently having gone ahead and returned. Joe shouted to the marching men: "Up ahead there's a clear stream just inside the woods on your left—stop and quickly fill your canteens with fresh water." He went up the line repeating the message.

He was hardly more than a boy, but he had become a good officer, Kit reflected, taking care of the men's needs. He did not get that quality from his grandfather.

The road passed through a farmstead which someone said was Mont St.-Jean, where there was a fork in the road. Wellington pulled up to speak to his staff. "I picked this spot a year ago," he said. "The left fork leads ultimately to Charleroi, the right to Nivelles; so here we can block two main approaches to Brussels."

They were near the summit of a long ridge, looking across fields of wheat and rye, still green but summer-high. The coal road went down a gentle slope into a dip with two large farmhouses spaced a mile or two apart. It crossed an east-west track and rose again to the opposite ridge, where there was a tavern.

Wellington said: "If the worst comes to the worst this is where we would make our last stand. If we fail here, we will have lost Brussels, and perhaps all of Europe."

It was a sobering thought, and the group went quiet.

Someone said: "What was that last village we passed through?"

"The place is called Waterloo," said the duke.

PART VI

The Battle of Waterloo

JUNE 16–18, 1815

It was a damned close-run thing.

–Field Marshal Sir Arthur Wellesley,
duke of Wellington

CHAPTER 41

Wellington's face was grave, thoughtful. He did not speak much as they rode. He had suffered a setback, but he was not a man to brood over his mistakes. He surveyed the country constantly, and Kit knew from past experience that he was appraising every hill, field, and wood for its military potential. The entourage respected his silence and took care not to disturb his thoughts. Kit had faith that Wellington would come up with the right solution to the problem.

At ten o'clock he drew the party to a halt at a crossroads. A small force of Dutch troops was there already, and to the right more were arriving from the west, bringing artillery. Kit guessed this must be Quatre Bras. There was a farmhouse on one corner and an inn diagonally opposite. The eastward road, also cobbled, presumably led into the territory occupied by Britain's Prussian allies.

When the sound of horses' hooves was quieted Kit could hear sporadic musket fire to the south, indicating that a French force of some description had come up from Charleroi on the coal road and had been halted, before reaching the crossroads, by the Dutch. The enemy was close. Looking that way, across a field of wheat, he could see puffs of smoke. It was probably a small advance party, but that might herald a larger force. However, the troops already here were relaxed, cooking dinner.

Wellington surveyed the view, and Kit did the same. He saw a mostly flat landscape with ripening crops. On his right the fields gave way to a dense wood of beech and oak trees; straight ahead the road was straddled by a farmstead; and a mile or so away on the left was a village that someone said was called Piraumont. The group rode around the area, noting terrain features that would become important if the skirmish they were hearing should turn into a more serious battle.

As the sun rose higher in the sky, the day became hot.

Finally Wellington drew the group together and made a simple announcement. "Before the end of today we must achieve two objectives: the first, to join forces with the Prussians; the second, to stop Bonaparte's advance."

He paused to let that sink in.

Then he said: "And we have two problems. First, where is Blücher?" He was referring to Field Marshal Gerhard von Blücher, prince of Wahlstatt and commander in chief of the Prussian army in the Netherlands. "And second," Wellington continued, "where is Bonaparte?"

The Prussian liaison officer, Müffling, who was with the party, pointed east. "My latest information, Your Grace, places Field Marshal Blücher seven miles away at the village of Sombreffe, near Ligny."

"Then let us go there."

The party turned onto the eastbound road and rode at a brisk pace. When they were close to Sombreffe they met a British liaison officer who offered to guide them to Blücher. He took them to a windmill that had wooden stairs leading up to a viewing platform—probably constructed by the Prussian engineers, Kit guessed, since windmills did not normally have viewing platforms.

There was not enough room on the platform for all of Wellington's entourage but he told Kit to follow him because he knew Kit spoke a little German.

Blücher was in his early seventies, with receding white hair and an enormous brown mustache. He was said to be a rough diamond, having little education but a shrewd military brain. He had the flushed cheeks of a heavy drinker, and a large curved pipe was clenched between his teeth. Wellington greeted him amiably, and seemed to like him, which surprised Kit: the duke could be fastidious about his acquaintances.

Blücher was using a telescope to look southwest. Wellington took out his own spyglass and pointed it in the same direction. The two men spoke French with a few English words mixed in, occasionally asking for a translation. Kit felt his German was really not good enough, and feared he would be useless, but in the end he managed well enough.

Without taking his telescope from his eye Blücher said: "French troops."

"About five miles away," Wellington said.

"I see two columns."

"On a country road."

"Approaching Ligny."

They agreed that Bonaparte had split his army in two at Charleroi. The part they were seeing was chasing the Prussians; the rest was almost certainly on the coal road. There was no way to know the different strengths of the two parts, but Blücher felt most of the French were here, and Wellington agreed. After some discussion—not all of which Kit followed—it was decided that Wellington would bring the greater part of his army from Quatre Bras to Ligny to reinforce the Prussians.

Kit felt relieved. At least they had a plan.

But the plan fell apart almost immediately.

While they were riding back the way they had come, they began to hear the boom of distant artillery. The sound came from the west, the direction in which they were heading, which meant there was a battle at Quatre Bras.

Wellington spurred his horse—a magnificent beast called Copenhagen—and the rest of the party struggled to keep up with him.

Nearing Quatre Bras they ran into musket fire that came from their left, south of the road. Kit ducked his head and the party veered right, off the road and into the woods to the north. As far as he could tell no one was hit, but they were forced to slow down.

The presence of French troops so close to the road was bad news. Clearly the enemy had gained ground since this morning.

Wellington's sangfroid was severely tested as they struggled to hurry the horses through the undergrowth while listening helplessly to the sounds of heavy fighting ahead.

At last they reached the Quatre Bras crossroads and gained a clear view of the battlefield. Only a thousand yards to the south, the combat looked fierce on both sides of the coal road. The French line extended northeast all the way to the village of Piraumont, bordering the Ligny road, which explained the musket fire.

It occurred to Kit that if the French could hold that village they would control the eastbound road and could prevent Wellington and the Anglo-Dutch army from joining forces with the Prussians; whereupon Wellington's objectives for the day would become impossible.

Kit was dismayed. He was used to Wellington being always master of the situation. But Wellington had not changed: the difference was that he was now up against an enemy general of his own caliber. Bonaparte was a military genius to match Wellington. It's a battle of giants, Kit thought; I wonder whether I'll live to see who wins.

Wellington quickly resumed command and said: "Our task now is to wipe out the French force here so that we can march to Ligny and reinforce the Prussians."

He ordered the Ninety-Fifth (Rifle) Regiment to liberate Piraumont, then turned his attention to the main battle.

It was going badly. The French had taken the farmstead on the coal road and seemed on the point of overwhelming the Anglo-Dutch force. Kit felt despair: everything was going wrong so quickly.

But more troops seemed to be arriving. The Ninety-Fifth Rifles were the vanguard of General Picton's division, and now the rest were appearing. Wellington disliked Picton, a bad-tempered Welshman who failed to show the deference owed to an English duke. However, everyone was glad to see him now, and Wellington ordered him to throw his forces into the fray immediately.

But French reinforcements arrived, too, and the attackers edged closer, yard by yard, to the strategically vital crossroads.

When yet more British troops arrived at five o'clock, Wellington counterattacked, and drove the French back—but too slowly. And the French retained control of Piraumont. Wellington was pinned down, unable to join the Prussians.

Kit ran with messages from Wellington to the frontline commanders and back. As always in battle, he forgot that he might be killed at any moment.

He kept an eye open for the 107th Foot, saw Joe Hornbeam running into the trees to the west, and concluded that the Kingsbridge troops were engaged in the woods; but he did not see his mother.

The battle surged to and fro. Men were maimed and died screaming, and the wheat was trampled to ruin. The women brought ammunition and gin to the front line, and went back dragging the wounded to the surgeons' tent. In doing so several women were mutilated by indiscriminate cannonballs and random musket fire, but Kit did not see Sal among them.

There was no clear ending. The fighting petered out as darkness fell. The two sides were left not far from the positions in which they had begun the day.

The last message Wellington received came from Blücher. The Prussians had taken heavy casualties, he said, but they could hold their positions until nightfall.

Kit fell asleep on a bench and did not wake until dawn.

Sal and Jarge erected a makeshift shelter in the woods using leafy branches. It was far from waterproof but it kept some of the rain off. They wrapped themselves in blankets and went to sleep on the wet ground.

Sal woke at first light. The rain had stopped. She heard faint cries for help. Leaving Jarge asleep, she walked west to the edge of the wood and looked across the battlefield.

It was a sight she would never forget. The dead and wounded lay in the trampled wheat, thousands of them, dismembered and disfigured, heads without bodies, bowels spilling on the ground, severed legs and arms, faces covered with blood. There was a vile smell of entrails and crushed crops.

Sal was not a stranger to bloodshed. She had seen men and women maimed in mill accidents, and her own Harry had been horribly killed by Will Riddick's cart, but she had never imagined suffering on this scale. She was filled with despair. Why did people do this to one another? Spade said the war was to stop the French dominating Europe, but would that be such a bad thing? In any case this was surely worse.

Her gaze fell on a man with shattered legs, and he caught her eye and said in a croak: "Help me." She saw that a dead man lay across him and he could not move the body or himself. She pulled the corpse away.

"Water," said the wounded man. "For the love of the Lord."

"Where's your canteen?"

"Backpack."

She managed to open his pack and extract the flask. It was empty. "I'll bring you water," she said.

She had noticed a ditch in the woods. Now she returned to it and followed it to a pond. To her horror there was a dead man in the water. She considered looking for another source but decided against. The man with the shattered legs would not care about the taste of blood. She filled his canteen, returned to him, and helped him to drink. He slurped the tainted water greedily.

Gradually others roused themselves and began to move around. The walking wounded set off on the long road back to Brussels. Others were picked up by their comrades and carried to the crossroads, where carts were waiting to take them away. Kenelm Mackintosh continued conducting nonstop burial services.

Sal learned that the 107th Foot had lost several senior officers yesterday. The lieutenant colonel, one of the two majors, and several captains were dead or seriously wounded. The surviving major was in command.

The living looted the dead. Any equipment lost or damaged could be replaced from the corpses of men who would never again need knives, cups, belts, cartridges—or money. Sal took the riding boots of a small-boned officer to replace her own worn-out footwear. In the backpack of a dead Frenchman she found a cheese and a bottle of wine, and she took them both to Jarge for breakfast.

Before dawn on Saturday, June 17, Wellington had again asked the question: "Where is Blücher?" This time Müffling had no new information, so Wellington sent an aide to look for the Prussian commander. The man returned at nine to say Blücher was missing, presumed dead.

And there was worse news. The Prussians had fled north in the night and planned to regroup at Wavre.

"Wavre?" said Wellington. "Where the devil is Wavre?"

An aide produced a map. "Good God, that's miles away!" said Wellington furiously. Kit looked hard at the map and calculated that Wavre was fifteen miles from Ligny. So far from joining up, the British and the Prussians were now even farther apart.

This was a catastrophe. Bonaparte had succeeded in splitting the allies into two smaller armies, each easier to defeat than the joint force would have been. Meanwhile the road was open for him to march from Ligny to Quatre Bras, join the French force already here, and with that enlarged army attack the smaller Anglo-Dutch force.

Indeed, Kit reckoned, Bonaparte was probably on his way here already. The solution was obvious, and Wellington announced it: they had to retreat, and immediately.

The army would fall back to Mont St.-Jean and camp there tonight, Wellington said. It was twelve miles from Wavre. If the Prussians could make it to Mont St.-Jean to reinforce the British, together they could still beat Bonaparte.

Kit's spirits lifted a little.

Wellington wrote to Blücher saying he would stand and fight at Mont St.-Jean tomorrow if the Prussians could get there.

The message was sent, the orders went out, and the retreat began.

"I don't understand why we're retreating," said Jarge. "I thought we won yesterday."

"We succeeded in stopping the French advance, if you call that winning," said Kit. "But the Prussians didn't do quite as well, and they've marched away. That freed Bonaparte to come at us sideways."

"Yeah, but what's the point of running? He'll only chase us."

"True. But we'll turn and fight, eventually. It's just that Wellington wants to choose the battleground."

"Hmm." Jarge thought about that for a minute, then nodded. "Makes sense."

They were marching north up the coal road, but the retreat was threatening to turn into a stampede. In Genappe, a village with narrow streets, the ambulances going back to Brussels had collided with artillery and food wagons heading for Quatre Bras. To add to the confusion, panicked local residents were fleeing toward Brussels, driving their cattle before them.

A lieutenant and thirteen grenadiers cleared the traffic jam by emptying the food wagons, throwing the supplies away, and sending the wagons back to Brussels loaded with wounded men.

Sal wondered what they were going to eat when they got to Mont St.-Jean. As a precaution, she retrieved a discarded fifty-pound sack of potatoes from a ditch and tied it to her back.

Soon after midday the rain started again.

In Brussels the rain came down in torrents. Amos pulled his hat down low to keep the water out of his eyes, and still he had to wipe his face with his handkerchief constantly, otherwise he could hardly see. The roads were jammed with carts, some bringing wounded men to already-overcrowded hospitals, others loaded with ammunition and other supplies and trying to leave the city to reach the army. Ambulance drivers unable to get through the traffic around the hospitals just dumped the wounded on the elegant streets and squares, and Amos had to pick his way around the bodies, some still alive, some dead, as rain washed their blood into the gutters. Residents of the city panicked, and as he passed the Hôtel des Halles he saw well-dressed men fighting for tickets on barges and coaches leaving the city.

He went to Jane's house, intent on renewing his plea to her to take Hal back to England. His visit was unnecessary: she was packing her trunks, wearing an old dress, her hair tied up in a scarf. "I have a carriage and horses in the stable here," she said. "I'll leave as soon as Henry gives me the word—if not sooner." She did not seem frightened so much as cross, and Amos guessed she was sorry to be leaving her young beau. Trust Jane to see the war principally as an irritating interruption to her romance. Amos remembered how much he had adored her, and for how long, and it now seemed to him incomprehensible.

He went from Jane's house to Elsie's. He hoped to find Elsie doing the same as Jane, packing to leave. He could hardly bear to think about the danger she was in. He wanted her to leave this nightmare city today.

But she was not packing. A council of war was in session in the drawing room. Elsie, Spade, and Arabella looked solemn, anxious. Amos said immediately: "You must go, Elsie. Your life is in danger."

Elsie shook her head: "I can't leave. My place is with Kenelm, and he's risking his life a few miles from here."

Amos despaired. Elsie did not love her husband, he knew; but he also knew that she had a very strong sense of duty. He admired that in her, but now it might cause her to risk her life. He feared she was determined to stay. "Please, Elsie, reconsider," he said.

She looked at Spade, her stepfather.

Amos wanted Spade to exert his authority as head of the family and insist that Elsie leave. But he knew that was not Spade's way.

He was right. Spade said to Elsie: "You must follow your heart."

"Thank you."

Arabella was on Amos's side. She said: "But what about the children—my grandchildren?" There was fear in her voice.

Elsie said: "They must stay with me. I'm their mother."

"I could take them back to Kingsbridge." Now Arabella was pleading. "They'd be safe with me and David."

"No," Elsie said decisively. "We're a family, we're better off together. I can't let them out of my sight."

Arabella turned to Spade. "What do you think, David?"

"I'm sorry to repeat myself, but I think Elsie must follow her heart."

"In that case, I'm staying here, too. But you could leave, David."

He smiled. "I'm not leaving you," he said in a voice that did not invite argument. "I must follow my heart, too."

There was a long moment of silence. Amos knew he had lost the argument.

Then Elsie spoke. "So that's that," she said. "We all stay here."

―――

That evening Sal stood with Kit outside the farmstead of Mont St.-Jean, at the summit of the ridge, looking out over the landscape to the south. The storm seemed to be breaking up: the sun came through in a few patches even while rain continued. Swags and ribbons of vapor floated up as the sun heated the sodden wheat. The woods at the eastern end of the ridge, to their left, were dark.

The coal road bisecting the valley was one long mass of men, horses, and wheeled artillery, as the survivors of Quatre Bras arrived. Officers holding written orders directed them to sections of the up slope according to a plan worked out at Quatre Bras by Wellington and De Lancey.

Sal wondered how far behind them Bonaparte was.

She and Kit stood near a tree that had already been stripped of its leafy branches, which were being used by Kingsbridge men to construct makeshift shelters. Jarge and some others were making a shelter in a different way, by standing several muskets upright with their bayonets stuck in the ground and draping blankets over them to form a tent. Neither type of construction would be waterproof, but both were better than nothing.

She noticed that men were being deployed in each of two farmsteads in the valley and pointed it out to Kit. "The one on the right is called Hougoumont," he said, "and the other is La Haye Sainte."

"Why do we care about defending farmhouses?"

"They'll create an obstacle in Bonaparte's way when he wants to attack us."

"They won't be able to stop his whole army."

"Perhaps not."

"So those men will be sacrificed."

"It's not certain, but quite likely."

Sal was profoundly grateful that the 107th Foot had not been chosen for that duty. Not that her own prospects were very good. She said: "I wonder how many of us will die here tomorrow. Ten thousand? Twenty thousand?"

"More, probably."

"Is this Wellington's last stand?"

Kit nodded. "If we're defeated here, there's nothing to keep Bonaparte from Brussels—and victory. And then the French will dominate Europe for many years ahead."

It was what Spade had said, Sal recalled. She said: "The French can have Europe, as far as I'm concerned. I just want my family back home and alive and well."

"It's make-or-break for Bonaparte as well," said Kit. "If we can destroy his army here we'll go all the way to Paris. It will be the end for him."

"And I suppose then we'll give the French back their fat king."

The corpulent Louis XVIII was neither competent nor popular, but the allies were determined to restore the French monarchy and prove that the republican revolution had been a failure.

Sal said: "And twenty thousand men are going to die tomorrow for that. I don't understand it. Tell me, my clever son, am I stupid? Or is it the government that's stupid?"

Jarge emerged from the improvised tent, his trousers

soggy with mud, and stood up. "There's no food," he said to Kit. His tone suggested he blamed officers in general and Kit in particular.

Kit said: "Most of the supplies were thrown away in the panic at Genappe."

Sal remembered seeing the food wagons emptied. "Our dinner is in a ditch," she said.

"We could cook them taters," said Jarge.

Sal still had the sack of potatoes on her back. She had got so used to the ache that she had not troubled to put the burden down. She said: "What are we going to cook the taters on? Everything's too wet to burn. Even if you could light a fire you'd get smoke, not flame."

"Are we going to eat them raw?"

Kit said: "You could take them to the village of Waterloo, Ma. It's about three miles north of here. There's bound to be someone there with an oven."

"You just want me away from the battlefield."

"I plead guilty," said Kit. "But what have you got to lose?"

Sal thought for a minute. There was nothing she could do here for Jarge and the other Kingsbridge men. She might as well do her best to get the potatoes cooked. "All right," she said. "I'll give it a try."

CHAPTER 42

Rain clouds hid the moon. Sal could hardly see anything. She knew she was on the road only by the feel of the cobblestones under the soles of the boots she had taken from the dead French soldier. When a foot slipped on mud she knew she had wandered off to left or right. Occasionally there was a glimmer showing through the shutters of a cottage, coming from a late candle, perhaps, or a dying fire: country people did not stay up long after dark. Little though it was, it gave her encouragement that somewhere there was light and warmth.

She trudged through the pouring rain, counting her blessings. Kit was still alive, and so was Jarge. She, too, was unhurt, despite the savagery of Quatre Bras. And tomorrow's battle might be the last, one way or another. If they survived it, she and her family might not be called on to risk their lives in war again.

Or perhaps that was too hopeful.

Anyway, she was carrying fifty pounds of potatoes, and even though they were making her back ache she was glad to have them. She had not eaten since this morning's breakfast of cheese without bread.

Seeing several gleams of light together, she deduced that she was in a village. She guessed the time was approaching midnight. There was one person sure to be awake and working: the baker. But how to find him?

She continued on the road until the lights became fewer and she guessed she had gone too far, then she turned around and walked back. She would have to knock on a door, wake someone up, and ask for directions.

Then she smelled smoke. It was not the ashy smell of a dying kitchen fire, but the sharp aroma of a blaze, perhaps from an oven. She spun around, sniffing the air from different directions, and went where the smell was strongest. It took her down a swampy lane to a house where there was a lot of light. Her nose seemed to pick up the aroma of new bread, but perhaps that was her imagination. She banged hard on the door.

A fat middle-aged man opened it. There were white smears on his clothes and white dust in his beard: the white was undoubtedly flour and he was the baker. He spoke irritably, in French, and she did not understand.

She put out a hand and held the door open. The baker seemed surprised by her strength. She said: "I don't want bread." Using a few French words she had picked up in Brussels, she said: "Cherche pas de pain."

The baker said something that probably meant that in that case she had come to the wrong shop.

She stepped inside uninvited. It was warm. She untied the strings that held the sack and lowered her burden. Her back hurt more when the weight was lifted. She put the sack down on a table where the baker had been kneading dough.

She pointed at the potatoes and then to the large oven in the corner of the room. "Cuire," she said, which she thought meant "cook." Then she used a phrase she had learned. "Je vous paie." I pay you.

"Combien?"

It was the first French word she had learned when she began to go shopping in Brussels, and meant: "How much?" She reached inside her waistcoat. She had plenty of money: she had made good profits on her trips from the camp to Brussels. She guessed the baker would ask for five francs, knowing she was desperate, but would accept three. Before leaving Mont St.-Jean she had put three francs in a pocket. Now she took them out. Holding them close so that he could not see, she counted out two francs and put them on the table.

He said something negative, shaking his head.

She added another coin.

When he shook his head again she showed him her empty hand.

He shrugged and said: "Bien."

He opened the oven door and pulled out a rack of small loaves that looked just about cooked. He tipped the bread into a big basket and put down the rack.

Sal opened her sack and spread the potatoes on the rack, then pricked the skins with her knife so that they would not burst. Then the baker shoved the rack back into the oven.

He took a swig from a bottle that stood next to his kneading board. Sal smelled gin. Then he resumed kneading. Sal watched him for a minute, wondering whether to ask for some of his gin. She decided she did not need it.

She lay on the floor next to the oven, relishing the heat. Her sodden clothes began to steam. Soon they would be dry.

She closed her eyes and fell asleep.

Every night since he joined the army had been the same for Kit: he fell asleep as soon as he lay down and slept until someone woke him. This time, however, he felt as if he had only just closed his eyes when he was shaken vigorously. He wanted to sleep on, then he heard the voice of Henry, earl of Shiring, and he sat upright, saying: "What time is it?"

"Half past two in the morning, and Wellington is about to brief us. Put your boots on quickly."

He remembered that he was in a barn at the village of Waterloo, and today there would be a big battle. He felt a tremor of the old fear, but it was not as bad as it used to be, and he was able to put it out of his mind. He threw off his blanket and found his boots. A minute later he followed the earl out of the barn.

It was raining hard.

They went to the farmhouse that Wellington had made his headquarters. The farmer and his family were probably sleeping in the cowshed: armies in wartime took what they needed and paid little heed to civilian protests.

Wellington stood at the head of the long kitchen table. His senior officers sat around the table and the aides stood against the walls. Wellington nodded to Henry and said: "Morning, Shiring. I think that completes the roster. Let's have the latest news."

Henry bowed and took a seat. Kit remained standing.

The head of intelligence stood up. "I sent our French-speaking spies, men and women, into Bonaparte's camp yesterday evening, selling the usual stuff that soldiers want: tobacco, gin, pencils, soap. They had a difficult task, in this teeming rain, with the French spread over several square miles. But based on our previous knowledge plus their reports I estimate that Bonaparte has about seventy-two thousand men."

"Almost the same as us," said Wellington. "We estimate our own strength as about sixty-eight thousand. What about French morale?"

"They're cold and wet, as we are, and they've been marching all day, just like us. But our spies note a difference. They're nearly all French, and they want to fight. They worship Bonaparte like a god."

Kit knew what was being left unsaid. Most of the French—officers and men—were of low-class origin, and owed their rise to the revolution and Bonaparte. In Wellington's army the officers mainly came from the aristocracy and the gentry, and the other ranks were all from the lower levels of society. Furthermore, two out of three allied soldiers were Dutch or Hanoverian; only a third were actually British. And many of those British served unwillingly, having been sentenced by justices to join the army, or tricked by recruiting sergeants. The most loyal of Wellington's soldiers belonged to the King's German Legion.

"As for artillery," said the intelligence officer, "Bonaparte seems to have about two hundred and fifty big guns."

"And that's a hundred more than we have," said Wellington.

Kit was dismayed. It looked as if the allies were at a disadvantage. Bonaparte had maneuvered brilliantly and had outsmarted Wellington. And so I might die, Kit thought.

There was a silence for a few moments. The commander in chief had all the available information. Now he alone could decide what to do.

At last Wellington spoke. "An even contest means losing lives to no purpose," he said. "And we are somewhat less than even." Kit was not surprised. Wellington aimed to join battle only when he had the advantage. "At these numbers I will not fight," he said decisively, and he paused to let that sink in.

"Two possibilities," he went on. "One: the Prussians join forces with us. With something like seventy-five thousand men they would tip the balance. If they can get here, we will fight."

No one dared to comment, but there were nods of agreement around the table.

"If they cannot, we will retreat again, through the forest of Soignes. There is a road the Prussians could take from Wavre through the forest to meet the main road just south of Ixelles. That will be our last stand."

This time no one nodded.

Kit knew that this was a plan of desperation. The road the Prussians would have to use was a woodland trail: it was impossible to move thousands of men quickly through such terrain. In any event, with only a few hours left until dawn, time was now running out for a retreat.

Wellington echoed his thoughts. "My strong preference is for Plan A," he said. "Fortunately, Field Marshal Blücher has reappeared. It seems he was wounded and unconscious for a time, but he is now back in command at Wavre, his army camped east of the town. Late yesterday I got a message saying that he will join us this morning."

Kit was deeply relieved. There would be no battle today unless the British side was likely to win.

"However, the situation can change fast in war, and I must have confirmation that Blücher's intentions this morning are the same as they were last night. And if they are, I need to know what time of day he will get here." Wellington looked at the earl. "Shiring, I want you to ride to Wavre and put a letter into Blücher's hands. Take young Clitheroe with you—he speaks a little German."

"Yes, sir," said Henry.

Kit was thrilled to be chosen for such an important mission, even though it meant riding twelve miles in darkness and pouring rain.

Wellington said: "Get your horses ready while I'm writing."

Kit and the earl left the room and found their way to the stables. The earl woke a couple of grooms. Kit watched the bleary-eyed men carefully as they saddled two horses: he did not want to have to stop and readjust the straps on the road.

The grooms fixed a storm lantern to each saddle in front of the rider's thigh. It would light the road for only a few yards ahead, but it was better than nothing.

When the horses were ready the two men returned to the farmhouse kitchen. Wellington and a small group of generals were poring over a hand-drawn map of the battlefield, trying to guess what Bonaparte would do. Wellington looked up and said: "Shiring, be so kind as to return with Blücher's answer posthaste. Clitheroe, assuming the answer is yes, I want you to stay with the Prussians a bit longer. As soon as they're well on the way, ride ahead of them and bring me an update on their estimated time of arrival."

"Yes, sir."

"Lose no time. Depart instantly."

They returned to the stables and mounted up.

They walked their horses on the mud track alongside the cobbled road, down the slope to the crossroads near La Haye Sainte. There they turned left and took the unpaved road toward Wavre.

It was too dark even to trot. They rode side by side, to benefit each from the other's lantern. The rain got in Kit's eyes and made his vision even worse. The country lane meandered through hilly territory deep in mud. Every valley bottom was flooded, and Kit feared that moving the Prussian guns along this road would be maddeningly difficult and very slow.

The monotony of riding allowed him to feel the wearying effect of sleep cut short. The earl took sips from a brandy flask, but Kit drank nothing, fearing that strong liquor would make him nod off in the saddle. I hope we get the answer we want, he kept thinking. I hope Blücher says that he still intends to join us this morning.

At last a feeble dawn light struggled through the clouds. As soon as they could see the road ahead they nudged the horses into a canter.

They still had a long way to go.

On her way back, Sal got lost.

She felt mud underfoot and turned toward where she imagined the road to be, but felt no cobblestones. She must have lost her concentration, she thought.

She tried going around in ever-increasing circles, figuring that she had to come across the road sooner or later; but being blind she could never be sure she was really walking in a circle. Holding her hands out in front of her, she came up against a tree. Shortly afterward she felt another. She had wandered into the woods, she realized. She turned through a half circle and went, she hoped, back the way she had come; but she came up against another tree.

She stopped, despairing. There was no point in moving when she had no idea where she was going. She wanted to cry, but stopped herself. So, my back hurts and I'm lost and exhausted and soaking wet, she thought; worse things will happen a few hours from now, when the battle begins.

She found a large tree trunk and sat with her back to it. The leaves gave her some protection from the rain. Her sack was wet but the potatoes inside were still hot, and she hugged the bundle to her chest to keep her warm.

She had suffered a nasty moment in the bakery. She had dreamed she was in bed with Jarge, and he was caressing her; and she woke up to find the baker kneeling beside her. He had unbuttoned her trousers and his hand was inside.

She was instantly transported back to the hard labor prison, where the women had to put up with this sort of thing or be flogged for disobedience. But she was not a prisoner now, and rage filled her in a flash. She knocked the man's hand aside with a strong blow and jumped to her feet. He stepped back quickly. She drew the long knife from the sheath at her belt and stepped toward him, ready to plunge the blade into his fat belly; then reason returned.

The man was terrified.

She sheathed the knife and buttoned her trousers.

Without speaking she opened the oven door. Using the baker's wooden hook she pulled out the rack of potatoes. She could see immediately that they were cooked: the skins were darkened and slightly wrinkled. She quickly put them back into the sack, then tied the sack to her back.

She picked up a newly baked loaf and put it under her arm, staring hard at the baker, daring him to protest. He said nothing.

She left the bakery in silence. She ate the loaf as she walked along the road, and finished it in minutes.

Now, sitting under the tree, she felt her eyes closing. But she must not go to sleep here: she needed to get the potatoes back to the regiment. She stood up to keep herself awake.

Then, almost without her noticing, the sky lightened. It was dawn. Only a minute later she began to perceive the wood around her. Then she looked through the trees and saw, only a hundred yards away, the cobbled surface of the road. She had never been far from it.

She retied the sack, made her way to the road, and began to walk south.

It stopped raining, and she sent a silent prayer of thanks up to heaven.

The sun was edging up in the east, giving light but no warmth, when she arrived at Mont St.-Jean. She picked her way through the camp. Most of the men were lying on the boggy ground, wrapped in sopping blankets. Wet horses disconsolately tried to graze the ruined wheat. She saw Kenelm Mackintosh, standing bareheaded, saying morning prayers with a few of the men. Among them she noticed Spade's brother-in-law, Freddie Caines, a sergeant now.

Sal moved as quickly as she could, fearing that if anyone realized what she had in the sack she could be murdered for it.

She found Jarge's makeshift tent and crawled gratefully inside. Jarge and several Kingsbridge men were lying on the wet ground, crowded together like fish in a box. "Wake up, you lucky soldiers," she said. She opened the sack, and the aroma of baked potatoes filled the small space.

Jarge sat upright and she handed him a potato. He bit into it. "Oh, my goodness," he said.

The others grabbed potatoes and ate. Jarge finished his and took another. "This is heaven," he said. "Sal Box, you are an angel."

"Well," she said, "I've never been called that before."

Now that it was daylight, Kit and the earl could go faster. However, no horse could gallop twelve miles. They alternately trotted and walked their horses, which Kit found frustratingly slow, but the earl said was the proven fastest way to cover a long distance without killing your horse. They began to see early rising farmers, and the earl frequently spoke to them, checking—Kit gathered—that this was the road to Wavre. Kit felt tense and impatient: Wellington had ordered them to hurry.

He noticed that the earl was splattered with mud, not just his boots and trousers but all the way up to his face. He guessed that he himself must look just as bad.

They were stopped at a cavalry outpost manned by men in Prussian uniforms. The guards confirmed that they were near Wavre and told them that Blücher had made his headquarters at the large inn on the town square.

A church clock struck five as they rode into the town. The road was a dirt track, puddled and marshy after the rain. As they neared the center the streets became narrow and winding, the mud a foot or more deep. "Wellington said the Prussians are camped east of the town," the earl said anxiously. "It's going to take hours to move Blücher's army through this warren."

The main road took them directly to the town center, and they entered the largest tavern on the square. A Prussian soldier stopped them in the lobby, eyeing their filthy uniforms. The earl spoke to him in halting French and he made negative noises.

The problem was that they did not look authoritative. Simple-minded people sometimes thought that foreigners who spoke their language badly must be stupid. Kit shouted at the man: "Achtung! Der Graf sucht Blücher! Geh holen!" The count is looking for Blücher—go and get him!

It worked. The soldier made an apologetic noise and disappeared through a door.

The earl murmured: "Well done, Clitheroe."

When the soldier reappeared he told Kit that the field marshal would emerge very soon. Kit found this maddening. Why did the man not come out immediately, even if he was in his nightshirt? Where was his sense of urgency? Earl Henry looked frustrated but did not complain.

Kit ordered the soldier to fetch coffee and bread for the count of Shiring, and the man hurried off obediently and returned a few minutes later with breakfast.

Blücher appeared, freshly shaved, in uniform, and smoking a pipe. His bloodshot eyes suggested heavy drinking the night before, perhaps many nights before, but he was energetic and decisive. The earl bowed and immediately handed over Wellington's letter, which was written in French. While Blücher was reading it, the Prussian soldier poured him a cup of coffee, and the field marshal emptied the cup without taking his eyes off the page.

The subsequent conversation was in French, but Blücher kept using the word "Oui," which Kit knew meant "yes." That seemed a good sign.

While the two men were talking in a language foreign to both of them, senior Prussian officers began to appear. The conversation ended with the earl and Blücher both nodding, then Blücher gave orders to the aides.

The earl clarified the situation for Kit. A part of Bonaparte's army had chased the Prussians here, and Blücher had to leave a section of his force behind to hold them. However, he was ready and willing to lead the larger part to Mont St.-Jean this morning, and in fact the vanguard had already crossed the river.

Kit said: "When will they get there?"

"Too soon to say. I'll ride back now and tell Wellington they're on their way. You'll stay with the Prussians, as Wellington ordered, until you can make a reliable estimate of their arrival time. Your job has now become crucial. Wellington will be desperate to know when he's going to get reinforcements that will double the size of his army."

Kit was thrilled to be trusted with such an important task, and at the same time, he felt the weight of a heavy responsibility.

"Stay with them at least until they've cleared the town," the earl said. "Then use your judgment."

"Yes, sir."

The earl bowed to Blücher and took his leave.

I'm on my own now, Kit thought.

The town of Wavre lay on the west bank of the river Dyle. Kit retrieved his horse and rode the short distance from the market square to the bridge. Blücher's men were already marching across. It struck him immediately that it would take hours to move thousands of men over this narrow span. The river was in flood after the recent heavy rain, and clearly could not be forded. On the far side he scouted upstream and downstream and found two more bridges, one at the south end of town and one a mile north, both narrow.

When he returned to the main bridge the marching soldiers were interspersed with guns in batteries of eight, and a tailback had developed. A growing crowd of soldiers waited to cross. Soldiers were used to waiting, and they cheerfully sat on the ground and rested. Kit asked a captain how many guns they were taking to Mont St.-Jean. "Einhundertvierundvierzig" was the reply. After some thought Kit worked out that that meant a hundred and forty-four.

Kit followed the army's route into the town. Here it was not so calm. The marching boots churned up the mud underfoot, turning it into a slurry that was almost liquid. He soon found the cause of the holdup: one of the heavier cannons had a broken axle and was blocking the road. It had to be dragged out of the way but the street was narrow. A red-faced officer was flogging the horses and cursing furiously while a dozen soldiers, straining for a footing in the swampy street, heaved at the carriage, desperately trying to get it to move.

He forced his way through and went to the far side of the town, where he made sure that the troops who had made it through were taking the country road that led to Mont St.-Jean.

Back at the bridge there were now several thousand men immobilized on the east bank. Kit was beginning to fear that it would take all day to get them across.

The line started to move again—the broken-down gun carriage must have been removed at last. The soldiers had to stand aside while the heavy horse-drawn cannons crossed one by one, then entered the town. At eight o'clock they still had not moved all their guns through the town.

Then fire broke out.

Kit smelled it before he saw it: the odor of burning thatch. It should have been too wet to burn. Many of the buildings were of wood, and the smoke rising from the center of the town grew from a column to a cloud and then to a fog that filled the streets, causing the soldiers to cough and their eyes to water.

The army came to a complete halt. Some of the men abandoned cannons and horses and retreated to get away from the flames. Those near ammunition wagons panicked and fled for fear of a huge explosion. Officers ordered those remaining to march back the way they had come. In the narrow streets, trying to turn the entire procession around—including the gun carriages with their six-horse teams—caused a great deal more cursing and confusion.

Kit returned to the bridge, intending to suggest to the Prussians that they make use of other bridges, but the officers were ahead of him and were already sending battalions on the more roundabout routes.

Kit crossed the nearer, southerly bridge and skirted around to the west of the town. He found the road to

Mont St.-Jean and confirmed that the Prussians were taking that route.

He returned to the main bridge and saw that troops were now moving smoothly along alternative routes. The guns were being pulled back from the town center. Ammunition wagons were joining the exodus.

It was now ten thirty, the time when Wellington was expecting the Prussians to arrive at the battlefield.

Kit tried to estimate their new arrival time. Once they got onto a clear road they might march at two to three miles an hour, he thought. So he could tell Wellington that the main body might begin arriving at Mont St.-Jean in about five hours, at three thirty in the afternoon—if nothing else went wrong.

He set off to ride ahead and give Wellington the news.

CHAPTER 43

ellington ordered all women off the battlefield. Some obeyed the order. Sal was among those who ignored it.

And now she was bored. She would never have imagined this could happen. She lay on the ground near the summit of the ridge, with Jarge and others of the 107th Foot, looking down over the landscape, waiting for the battle to begin. They were not supposed to be this far forward, but they were in a spot where a slight dip hid them from view.

She found herself impatiently wishing it would get going. What a fool I am, she thought.

Then, at half past eleven, it started.

As expected, the French first attacked the chateau and farm buildings of Hougoumont, the allied outpost that was half a mile from where she lay and dangerously close to the French front line.

She could make out a compound with houses, barns, and a chapel, all surrounded by trees. A walled garden and an orchard were on the west, the right-hand side as Sal looked. On the far side, to the south, but still visible to Sal, a small wood—just a couple of acres—stood between the farmstead and the French front line. Sal had been told that Hougoumont was defended by two hundred British guardsmen and a thousand Germans. The troops were stationed in the wood and the orchard as well as within the compound.

The French attack opened with a heavy cannonade from the artillery, which Sal thought must have been devastating at such short range.

Next, French infantrymen marched from their front line across an open field toward Hougoumont. Then the allied guns replied, firing shrapnel at the infantry.

The allies in the wood began to shoot at the French from behind the trees. The Germans had rifles, which had greater range and accuracy.

The shrapnel and the rifles were lethally efficient, and blue-coated French troops fell in their hundreds; but they held their line and kept coming.

"They're such an easy target," Sal said. "Why don't they run forward, instead of walking?"

The question was not addressed to anyone in particular, but it was answered by a veteran of the war in Spain. "Discipline," he said. "In a minute they'll stop and all fire together."

I would run anyway, Sal thought.

Kit arrived back at Mont St.-Jean soon after midday.

He found Wellington on horseback near the Guards, on the ridge above Hougoumont, watching the intense fighting at the farmstead.

Wellington saw him and said irately: "Where the devil are those Prussians? I expected them hours ago!"

Wellington's anger could be vitriolic, and it was not always targeted at the right people.

Kit steeled his nerve to give his commander the bad news. "Sir, I confirm that most of the Prussians had left Wavre by ten thirty, and I estimate they will get here not earlier than half past two this afternoon."

"Then what the blazes have they been doing? It's been light since before five o'clock!"

Kit gave him an edited version. "Wavre is a bottleneck, with a narrow bridge over the river and winding little streets in the town—where, to make matters worse, there was a serious fire this morning. And once past the town, their road from there to here is waterlogged—"

"Fire? How could that happen, after all the rain?"

It was a stupid question, and Kit said: "No information, sir."

Wellington said: "Go and find Shiring. He'll have a lot for you to do this afternoon."

Kit rode away.

He found the 107th Foot at the western end of the allied line. Some of the men had crawled forward, out of position, to sneak a look at the battlefield, and Lieutenant Joe Hornbeam was ordering them back so that they could not be seen by the French. "We don't want old Bonaparte to know where we are, or how many," he said. "Let's keep the bugger guessing, eh?"

Kit saw Jarge, pulled up his horse, and dismounted. Jarge said: "Young Joe isn't a bad officer, you know, 'specially when you remember he's only eighteen."

"You wouldn't expect it," said Kit. "With a grandfather as nasty as Alderman Hornbeam . . ." Kit was distracted by seeing his mother. He was dismayed. "What are you doing here?" he said to her. "Women have been ordered off the battlefield."

"That order never reached me," said Sal.

"Well, it's reached you now."

"I'm here to be with my husband and I'm not going to run away."

Kit opened his mouth to argue, then changed his mind. It was futile to disagree with Sal when her mind was made up.

He approached Joe Hornbeam and said: "Lieutenant, have you seen the earl of Shiring?"

"Yes, sir." He pointed north, down the back of the ridge. "A few minutes ago he was about three hundred yards in that direction, speaking to General Clinton."

"Thank you."

"Yes, sir."

Kit mounted up and rode down the slope to where Earl Henry and General Clinton were, both on horseback. Before he could speak to the earl there was a booming cacophony like ten thunderstorms at once, a noise that could only mean the end of the world; but Kit had served in an artillery battery and he knew it was the sound of cannons—just more of them at one time than he had ever heard before.

He turned his horse and hurried back up the slope, with the earl of Shiring and General Clinton close behind him. At the top they stopped and stared.

They were on the west side of the coal road, and Kit saw immediately that the French cannons were on the east side, shooting at the center and left of the allied line. There were at least seventy big guns lined up and firing as fast as they could.

However, they were finding few targets. The allied troops on the southern downslope suffered badly, but most of Wellington's army was behind the ridge, and many of Bonaparte's cannonballs plunged uselessly into mud.

So what was the point of the barrage?

Some minutes later Kit saw it.

Blue-coated French soldiers began to advance, passing through the line of guns and marching across the valley. The French cannonballs went over their heads and discouraged allied troops from coming over the ridge to meet them.

It soon became clear that this advance was a major assault. Kit estimated the number of approaching infantry at five thousand, then ten thousand, then more, maybe twenty thousand.

The allied guns opened up against them, and Kit could tell they were firing canisters, thin tins packed with iron balls and sawdust, which exploded and spread out into a lethal cone thirty yards wide that mowed down the enemy troops like a gigantic scythe. But the French stepped over the bodies of their comrades and marched on.

The battle had begun.

The aim of an attack was normally to destroy the integrity of the enemy line by getting behind it. This could be achieved either by going around one end of the line—sometimes called turning the flank—or by punching a hole in the middle. The men in the line could then be surrounded, trapped, and attacked from all sides.

Kit used his spyglass—taken from the corpse of a dead French officer at Vitoria—to study the far eastern end of the battlefield. The advancing French troops there were first to reach the allied positions, and they attacked energetically, driving the defenders back. The allied front followed the course of a narrow sunken lane with hedges, and the French quickly reached this refuge. Then the British counterattacked. The fighting was fierce and bloody, and Kit was glad he was not there.

The French advance lost momentum, but did not stop. Kit saw with dismay that the story was the same all along the line on the far side of the coal road: a vigorous French attack, a counterattack, and a slow French advance.

It was two o'clock, and the allies were losing.

The allied troops around Kit and the earl were restless, eager to go to the aid of their comrades; but Wellington had not ordered it, and the earl barked: "Stay where you are, you men! Anyone who runs forward without orders will be shot in the back."

Kit was not sure he meant it, but the threat was effective and the men settled down.

French casualties were high but more men kept arriving, including the cavalry they called cuirassiers. Kit looked back to the downslope behind the ridge and saw that Wellington had few reserves of infantry to throw into the melee. However, the British cavalry were waiting. Kit could see at least a thousand of the Household Cavalry brigade standing by their horses, waiting impatiently for the order to attack. The Life Guards and the Horse Guards all had jet-black steeds. They were led by the earl of Uxbridge, one of that considerable number of men Wellington disliked.

Kit had heard headquarters officers say that the British cavalry had the best horses but the French had the best men. It was at least true that the French cavalry had more battle experience.

A bugle sounded and a thousand men mounted; then a different bugle call caused them all to draw their swords simultaneously. It was a formidable sight, and Kit was grateful he was not among those who would have to resist their attack.

Responding to further bugle calls they formed an east-west line a mile long, then walked their horses forward, up the slope, still out of sight of the enemy. They broke into a trot, breasted the ridge, and then, with shouts and cries, charged downhill into the melee.

The allied infantry scampered out of the way. The French tried to flee back to their lines but they could not outrun the horses, and the cavalry chopped and sliced them mercilessly with their sabers, amputating arms and legs and heads. Running men tripped and fell and were trampled by the mighty horses. The cavalry rode on and the slaughter was terrible.

Earl Henry was cock-a-hoop. "Bonaparte's assault has been turned back!" he crowed. "God bless the cavalry!"

When the horses came within range of the French front line Uxbridge commanded the trumpeters to sound the order to turn back. Kit heard it clearly, but to his astonishment, the cavalry seemed deaf. They ignored the repeated signal and rode on, cheering and waving their swords. Beside Kit, Earl Henry gave a disgusted grunt. The riders were consumed with bloodlust and all discipline had broken down. Their lack of battle experience was showing.

Their elation was suicidal. As they charged the French line they began to be mown down by cannon and musket fire. Their momentum slowed as the ground beneath them turned uphill and the horses tired.

The cavalry went from triumph to annihilation in minutes. Suddenly they were the ones being slaughtered. As they split into small groups the French surrounded them and methodically dispatched them. Kit gazed in despair as the cream of the British Army were wiped out. A few lucky survivors flogged their horses into an exhausted gallop back toward the allied line.

Bonaparte's assault had indeed been turned back—but at what a cost.

The French had more men, and could launch another infantry attack; but the British could not mount another such cavalry charge.

Kit was overwhelmed by despair.

There was a lull. The battle did not pause, but went on at a lower level. The French artillery fired intermittently across the valley, occasionally killing an officer on horseback or smashing a cannon; and the skirmishing around Hougoumont and La Haye Sainte continued, sharpshooters on both sides sniping and sometimes hitting a target.

A messenger spoke to Wellington, who summoned Earl Henry and said: "There is a report that some Prussians have appeared. Go to the eastern end of our line and check it out. If it's true, tell their commander that I want them to reinforce my left flank. Go!"

The instruction made sense to Kit. Wellington's left wing had been the focus of Bonaparte's artillery and infantry attacks, whereas the right flank—where Sal and Jarge were—had hardly been involved so far. It was the left that needed the Prussians.

They set off at a gallop.

A mile or two beyond the easternmost end of the allied front line were two small patches of woodland, Ohain Wood to the north and Paris Wood to the south, and as they rode Kit thought he saw activity in both areas. Coming closer he saw, emerging from Ohain Wood, hundreds of troops in dark blue uniforms.

It was true. The Prussians were arriving at last.

Kit and Earl Henry reached Ohain Wood unhurt. Two or three thousand Prussians had now arrived, and more at the southerly wood. A few thousand would make little difference, but when the rest arrived the allies would have an overwhelming advantage.

But was there time to wait for that?

The troops at Ohain belonged to I Corps, commanded by the much-decorated von Zieten, a balding forty-five-year-old who was about to fight his third battle in four days. Blücher himself had not yet arrived, so Earl Henry and Kit delivered Wellington's message to Zieten in the usual mixture of languages.

Zieten said only that he would pass Wellington's request to Blücher as soon as possible. Kit got the impression that the Prussians would make up their own minds about where best to join the battle.

Zieten would not estimate how soon the rest of the Prussians would arrive.

Earl Henry and Kit rode back to Wellington and reported.

Kit looked at his watch—another prize stolen from a corpse—and was astonished to see that it was five o'clock in the afternoon. It seemed like only minutes since the first French infantry attack.

Throughout the intense fighting of the last three days Bonaparte's aim had been to prevent the Prussians' joining up with the Anglo-Dutch. In the next few hours it would at last happen.

Bonaparte had undoubtedly seen the Prussians, and must have realized that time had suddenly become crucial. His only hope now was to destroy the allied army before the Prussians could join the fighting in sufficient numbers to turn the tide.

Kit saw intense activity behind the French lines. For several minutes he could not figure out what was going on, until the earl said: "The cuirassiers are assembling. There's going to be a cavalry assault."

The British and Dutch gunners were bringing forward reserve cannons to replace those damaged. Kit looked for Roger but could not spot him.

The French artillery were still firing intermittently while their cavalry assembled, and at that moment a shell landed twenty yards from Kit, striking a replacement cannon that was being maneuvered into place. There was a bang and a flash, shouts from the men, and the horrible scream of a wounded horse, then a second, bigger explosion as the gunpowder reserve behind the cannon exploded, smashing the cannon to bits. Kit was thrown to the ground and deafened, but a second later he knew he had not been burned or hit by flying debris. Feeling dazed, he struggled to his feet. All the cannon crew were dead or wounded and the gun itself was a ruin of twisted metal and burned wood. Kit's gaze fell on Earl Henry, lying on the ground, not moving. There was blood around his head. The wound had probably been caused by a piece of the destroyed gun flying through the air. Kit knelt beside him and saw that he was still breathing.

He saw a group of infantry staring at the smashed gun. He pointed at two of them and said: "You and you! This is the earl of Shiring. Pick him up and carry him to the surgeon. Double quick!"

They obeyed.

Kit wondered whether the earl would survive. There was nothing much surgeons could do for head wounds except bandage them. Everything depended on how much damage had been done to the brain.

There was no time to ponder. Kit turned back to the battlefield. A new French assault was beginning.

What emerged from the French lines looked like a tidal wave of horsemen. The sun came out from behind a cloud and glittered off swords and armor. Kit felt the ground beneath his feet tremble with the impact of tens of thousands of hooves.

The allies had little cavalry left to oppose them.

Wellington shouted: "Prepare to receive cavalry!"

The shout was repeated up and down the line, and the infantry battalions quickly shuffled into squares, as they had been trained. Looking along the line Kit saw that the 107th Foot were forming up with brisk efficiency.

As the enemy cavalry drew near, Wellington rode

around the squares, shouting encouragement. Kit and other aides followed him. Then the French were on them.

At first the defenders had the best of it. The French cavalry charged around the outsides of the squares, shouting: "Vive l'empereur!" Many of them were felled by intense fire from the edges of the squares where the musketeers stood four deep. Each British soldier knelt and fired, then stepped to the back of the four to reload so that the next man could fire, in a lethally efficient dance.

After several terrifying minutes the cavalry retreated, but reinforcements on fresh horses took their place, some armed with nine-foot-long lances that they hurled at the squares in an attempt to create gaps. The dead and wounded were dragged into the center of the square and the gaps were closed up.

Kit could not help admiring the courage of the French riders as they charged again and again, riding over the bodies of their comrades, jumping over dead and wounded horses. The remains of the British cavalry counterattacked but there were not enough of them to make a difference.

During a lull, Kit wondered where Bonaparte's infantry were. They should have been supporting the cavalry—that was the way it was usually done. Then he looked across the valley, peering through the clouds of gunpowder smoke, and saw the reason: the Prussians had at last joined in.

Ignoring Wellington's request, most of the newcomers had swung behind the eastern end of the French line and attacked at the village of Plancenoit, high on the opposite ridge and close to enemy headquarters. Bonaparte had been blindsided.

The fighting there seemed fierce, and Kit figured that Bonaparte could not spare infantry from that zone to support his cavalry attack. As Kit watched he thought he saw additional troops from the reserve higher up on the slope deploying into Plancenoit. But he could also see more dark blue uniforms coming from the east and charging into battle.

The French infantry were tied down there and could not support the cavalry attack. That might save Wellington's army.

Bonaparte must be desperate, Kit reasoned. He had to win today, for tomorrow the combined forces of the Anglo-Dutch and the Prussians would be unbeatable.

There was a murmur of anguish among Wellington's aides, and someone said in a low voice: "La Haye Sainte has fallen." Looking across Kit could see, escaping from the farmstead, a pitiful remnant of the German defenders, a tiny fraction of the initial deployment; and the French at last took possession. That was a boost for Bonaparte, for it badly weakened the allied line.

The allied artillery immediately began firing at La Haye Sainte, and Kit thought: That's Roger shooting. But the French held the outpost.

The French cavalry attack petered out around half past six. However, the allies had been seriously damaged, especially in the center of the line. This was the moment for Bonaparte to strike a killing blow. Wellington clearly understood how dangerously vulnerable the allies were, and he rode furiously along the line, careless of his own safety, giving orders that Kit and the other aides ferried to the officers: calling reserves forward to reinforce the line, summoning ammunition wagons, replacing destroyed cannons from spares that were now perilously low. Meanwhile Zieten's I Corps had at last done what Wellington wanted and reinforced the allied left wing, permitting Wellington to draw men from there to strengthen the enfeebled center. And all the while Bonaparte was prevented from attacking the allies' vulnerable spot by the Prussian attack at Plancenoit.

A French colonel deserted and rode to the allied line shouting: "*Vive le roi!*" Long live the king! When interrogated by intelligence officers he revealed that Bonaparte had decided to use his elite troops, the Imperial Guard—held in reserve until now—to attack the allied right wing.

The Imperial Guard were normally brought in at the end, to deliver the coup de grace. Had the battle reached that stage?

Aides were dispatched to take this news to the forces on the far side of the coal road, who had so far seen little action. Kit rode to the 107th Foot and warned Major Denison, who was in command. The men around Denison seemed glad to be going into action at last, even if only to have an answer to the question: What did you do at Waterloo?

Just after seven o'clock, with the sun sinking over the western end of the valley, the Imperial Guard appeared, six thousand men by Kit's rough estimate, wearing uniform blue tailcoats, marching to a drumbeat across fields littered with dead and wounded men and horses, in a stink of blood and entrails. Kit sat on his horse and watched through his spyglass as they approached. They skirted Hougoumont—still occupied by the allies—and passed La Haye Sainte, which was now in French hands.

The allied troops waited behind the ridge, out of the enemy's sight. Joe Hornbeam went up and down the line saying: "Stay where you are. Wait for the word. Nobody jump the gun. Stay where you are."

Kit saw that the French were now attacking all along the allied line, no doubt to tie troops down and prevent them coming to reinforce the defense against the Imperial Guard. Looking at the sinking sun he realized that this was going to be the final drama of the battle—one way or another. He decided to stay with the 107th.

When the Guards were two hundred yards away the allied guns opened fire. Kit saw that they were again firing canisters, and as the Imperial Guard started to fall he murmured: "Good shooting, Roger." But the French discipline held: without breaking step they marched around the dead and wounded, closed the gaps in the ranks, and kept coming forward.

When the Guards were only thirty yards away the troops behind the ridge suddenly stood up and fired a musket volley. At that range many bullets found targets. The French fired back, and some of the Kingsbridge men fell, including the commanding officer, Major Denison. Kit saw the chaplain, Kenelm Mackintosh, take a bullet to the chest that looked fatal, and he thought of Elsie's five children, who had just lost their father.

With the enemy only thirty yards away there was no time to reload and the allies followed up with a bayonet charge. The Guards faltered, but did not retreat, and the conflict became a bloody hand-to-hand fight.

The 107th was among the forces far to the right of the battlefield, shooting into the advancing enemy at an angle. Now one battalion charged downhill and swung left to attack the vulnerable flank of the Imperial Guard. There had been no order from Wellington: the officers were taking the initiative. Immediately afterward another group joined the assault. Suddenly Joe Hornbeam yelled: "Charge!" A lieutenant had no right to give such an order, but Denison was dead and Joe was the only officer in sight; and the eager men followed young Hornbeam without hesitation.

Kit saw that this could be the turning point of the battle, and therefore of the twenty-three-year war, and he acted instinctively. He snatched up a bayoneted musket from a fallen soldier, jumped back on his horse, and joined the charge. As he rode away he heard Sal behind him shouting: "Kit, don't go!" He rode on.

The Imperial Guard were now being attacked on two sides, and they began to waver. The allies pressed their advantage. The 107th charged with their bayonets. A French bullet hit Kit's horse and the poor beast stumbled. Kit was able to jump off before the horse hit the ground. He ran on, brandishing his weapon. He found himself side by side with his stepfather, Jarge.

Some of the French were fleeing now but most stayed

and fought. Kit stood shoulder to shoulder with Jarge, both stabbing furiously with bayoneted muskets. Kit had killed many men, but always with cannonballs, and now he felt the horribly strange sensation of penetrating human flesh with a blade. It made no difference to his fighting spirit: his entire being was taken up with the need to kill enemy soldiers, and he did it as fast and efficiently as he could.

In front of him Joe Hornbeam's horse fell, and Joe hit the ground. An Imperial Guardsman stood over him with sword raised, and for a helpless second Joe looked up at his killer. Then Jarge stepped forward and lunged with his bayonet. The Guard pivoted and brought his upraised sword down on Jarge, a mighty blow that chopped deep into Jarge's neck at the same time that Jarge's bayonet sliced through the man's uniform, entered deep into his belly, and disemboweled him. Both men fell. Jarge's neck pumped bright red blood, and the Guard's guts spilled on the ground.

Joe jumped up. "Dear God, that was close," he said to Kit. Glancing down he said: "Jarge saved my life." Then he picked up his sword and returned to the fray.

The Imperial Guard began to fall apart. Men at the rear no longer pushed forward but turned and ran back. Seeing their numbers diminish, the men at the front retreated; and the retreat turned into a rout. The allies chased them, yelling triumphantly.

Looking over the battlefield Kit saw that all along the line the French were demoralized. Some retreated; others saw that and did the same; some began to run, and others copied them; and in seconds panic took hold. Then the allies chased the defeated French downhill and up the other side.

Kit immediately thought of Roger.

Leaving his comrades to complete the rout, he turned and ran back up the slope, jumping over the twisted dead and the crying wounded, to the artillery on the ridge. Some of the gunners had abandoned their cannons and were joining in the final slaughter, but he felt sure Roger would not be among them.

He hurried along the line, staring hard at the gunners sitting or lying down by the guns, some exhausted, some dead. He searched for Roger's face, praying to spot it among the living. He was more afraid now than he had been all day. The worst outcome would be him alive and Roger dead: he would rather they were both dead.

When at last he caught sight of Roger he was slumped on the ground with his back against a cannon wheel, and his eyes were closed. Was he breathing? Kit thought the worst. He knelt beside him and touched his shoulder.

Roger opened his eyes and smiled.

"Oh, thank God," said Kit, and he kissed him.

Sal had seen Kit heading up the slope, walking upright and evidently unhurt, and she had felt a moment of pure relief; then she began to look for Jarge.

The 107th Foot were running across the valley, chasing the retreating French. She hoped Jarge was among them, but she checked those left on the battlefield, lying in the ruined wheat. Among them, the corpses were the lucky ones, she thought: for them, pain was over. The others cried for water, or a surgeon, or their mothers. She hardened her heart and ignored them all.

When her eyes at last lit on Jarge she did not at first recognize him, and her gaze moved on; then something made her glance back, and she gasped with horror. He lay on his back, his neck cut half through, and his blind eyes were directed up at the darkening sky.

Sal was possessed by grief. She wept so much that she could hardly see. She knelt by the body and put her hand on his chest, as if she might feel a heartbeat, though she knew that was impossible. She touched his cheek, still warm. She smoothed his hair.

She had to bury him.

She stood up and wiped her eyes and looked around. The farmstead of Hougoumont was a couple of hundred yards away, and something was on fire in the compound. But one of the buildings looked like a small church or chapel.

Two men who looked familiar, and were probably part of the 107th, were returning across the valley, one limping slightly, the other carrying a sack that undoubtedly contained loot. She asked them to help her by hoisting Jarge's body onto her shoulder, and they did.

Jarge was heavy, but she was strong, and she thought she could manage. She thanked the two looters and set off, crying as she went.

She picked her way across the battlefield, skirting the bodies, and passed through the gate into the compound. The chateau was burning but the chapel was intact. By the south wall of the little building was a small clear patch of grass. It might or might not have been consecrated ground, but it looked to her like the right place to bury her man.

She put the body down as gently as she could. She straightened his legs and folded his arms across his chest. Then, tenderly, she put her hands to both sides of his head and moved it so that the neck wound closed and he looked more normal.

She stood up again and looked around the compound. There were bodies everywhere, hundreds of them. But this was a farm so there had to be a spade somewhere. She went into a barn. The debris of battle was everywhere: ammunition boxes, broken swords, empty bottles, random body parts—an arm, a booted foot, half a hand.

Hanging on a wall, suspended from wooden pegs, were a few peacetime tools. She seized a spade and returned to Jarge.

She began to dig. It was hard work. The earth was sodden with rain, which made it hard to lift. She wondered why her back hurt so much, then remembered that she had spent last night—was it only last night?—carrying fifty pounds of taters three miles to Waterloo and three miles back.

When she had dug down about four feet she felt as if she would die of exhaustion if she carried on, so she decided it would have to be enough.

She grabbed Jarge under his shoulders and dragged him slowly into the grave. When she had him in position she again arranged his body: legs straight, arms folded, head set properly on his neck.

She stood by the grave, looking at him, as the evening faded into night. She said the Lord's Prayer. Then she looked up to heaven and said: "Go easy on him, Lord. There was—"

She choked up, and waited until she could speak again, and then she said: "There was more good in him than bad."

She picked up the spade and began replacing the earth in the hole. She had done this once before, when she buried Harry twenty-three years ago. Then she had hesitated to drop earth on the man she loved, and it was the same now; but now as then she forced herself, for it was part of acknowledging that he had gone, and what remained was a shell. Earth to earth, she thought.

The worst part was when his body was covered but she could still see his face. Again she hesitated, and again she forced herself to do it.

When the grave was filled in she dropped the spade on the ground and wept until she had no more tears to shed. Then she said: "That's it, then, Jarge."

She stood by the grave a little longer, until it was too dark to see.

She spoke to him for the last time. "Goodbye, Jarge," she said. "I'm glad I got you them taters."

Then she walked away.

PART VII

The Peace

1815–1824

CHAPTER 44

After the allies entered Paris, Napoleon Bonaparte abdicated for the second time and was imprisoned, this time on the remote mid-Atlantic island of St. Helena, two thousand miles west of Cape Town and two thousand and five hundred miles east of Rio de Janeiro.

The 107th Foot returned to Kingsbridge, as did the earl of Shiring; his wife, Jane; and their boy, Hal. Two days later Amos, who had arrived home a little earlier, got a note from Jane asking him to call at Willard House for tea.

He found her unpacking, her travel-stained trunks around her on the drawing room carpet. With the help of a laundrymaid she was picking up her magnificent gowns one at a time and deciding whether they should be sponged and pressed, or washed, or given away. "Peace at last!" she said to Amos. "Isn't it wonderful?"

"Now we can get back to normal life," said Amos. "If any of us can remember what that was like."

"I can remember," she said firmly. "I'm going to enjoy it."

Amos studied her. She was forty-two, he calculated, and she had remained slim and attractive. For many years he had adored her, but now he could be objective. He still liked her joie de vivre, which was what made her sexy; but now he often noticed her calculating look and the selfish pout as she schemed to manipulate people.

He said: "How is the earl? He's lucky to have survived a head wound."

"You'll see," she said. "He'll join us in a minute or two." The reference to the battle led her thoughts to another casualty, and she said: "Poor Elsie Mackintosh, with five children and no husband."

"I'm sorry Mackintosh died. He turned into a brave man, you know, after he became an army chaplain."

"Still, you can marry Elsie now."

Amos frowned. "Whatever makes you think I would marry Elsie Mackintosh?" he said crossly.

"The way you danced with her at the duchess of Richmond's ball. I've never seen you so happy."

"Really." Amos was more irritated because she was right. He had had a wonderful time. "That doesn't mean I want to marry her," he said.

"No, of course not," Jane said, with a dismissive gesture of her hand. "It was just a thought."

A butler brought in a tea tray, and Jane cleared space on a sofa and two armchairs. Amos thought about what she had said. He had been happy with Elsie in his arms, it was true, but that did not mean he loved her. He was fond of her. He admired her for her courage in defying everyone to feed the children of striking mill hands. He was never bored when he was with her. All that, but not love.

Recalling the ball, he remembered how much he had liked the intimacy of the waltz, touching Elsie's body, warm through the silk of her gown, and he realized he would like to do that again.

But dancing was not marriage.

Jane said to the maid: "Take away the clothes I've looked at, and the empty trunks, then come back in half an hour and we'll do the rest." She sat down and poured tea.

The earl appeared in uniform. His head was bandaged and he walked rather unsteadily. Amos stood to shake his hand, then looked at him hard as he sat down and accepted a cup of tea from Jane. "How are you feeling, my lord?" Amos asked.

"Never better!" said Henry, but he said it too quickly and too assertively, as if he needed to deny the opposite.

"Congratulations on the part you played in winning the greatest battle ever."

"Wellington was absolutely astonishing. Brilliant."

"From what I hear, it was a close-fought contest."

Henry shook his head. "At moments, perhaps, but in my mind there was never any doubt about the final result."

This was not what Amos had heard. "Blücher seems to have arrived in the nick of time."

For a moment Henry was nonplussed. "Blücher?" he said. "Who's Blücher?"

"The commander of the Prussian army in the Netherlands."

"Oh! Yes, yes, of course, Blücher. But it was Wellington who won it, you know."

Amos was puzzled. Warfare had always been the one thing that interested the earl, and he knew a lot about it. But he was conducting this conversation in platitudes, like an ignoramus in a tavern. Amos changed the subject. "For myself, I'm glad to be back in England and Kingsbridge. How is Hal?"

Henry answered: "He'll start at the local grammar school next year."

Jane made a face. "I don't see why he can't just have a tutor, as you did, Henry, when you were a boy."

Henry disagreed. "A lad needs to spend time with other boys, learn how to rub along with all sorts, as you do in the army. We don't want to raise the kind of officer who doesn't know how to talk to the men."

Amos was momentarily taken aback by the assumption that Hal—his son—would become a soldier; then he remembered that one day Hal would have all the duties of the earl, including becoming colonel of the 107th (Kingsbridge) Foot Regiment.

Jane sighed. "Whatever you think best, of course, Henry." Amos was sure she did not mean that. The argument would resurface.

Hal came in. He was now ten, so it was almost time for him to go to school.

Henry glanced at Hal, frowned, then looked away, almost as if he had not recognized the boy. Then Jane said brightly: "Here's Hal to have tea with us, Henry. Isn't our son growing fast?"

Henry looked momentarily startled, then said: "Hal, yes, come in, my lad, and have some cake."

That was a strange interaction. It seemed to Amos that Henry had not known who Hal was until Jane had spoken. And he had forgotten Blücher, the third-most important man at Waterloo after Wellington and Bonaparte. Perhaps that fragment of a gun carriage flying through the air had done more than scratch Henry's scalp. He was behaving like a man with brain damage.

Hal ate three slices of cake—just as he had in Brussels—then drank his tea and left. The earl followed soon after. Amos looked at Jane, and she said: "So now you know."

Amos nodded. "How bad is it?"

"He's a different man. Much of the time he gets along all right." She lowered her voice. "Then he'll say something, and you think: Oh, Lord, he has no idea what is going on."

"That's very sad."

"He's completely incapable of organizing the regiment, and he leaves all the decisions to Joe Hornbeam, who's supposed to be his aide but is a major now."

Amos did not care about Henry, but was concerned for his son. "Does Hal understand that the earl is . . . ?"

"Of unsound mind? Not really."

"What have you told him?"

"That his father is still confused on account of the wound, and we're sure he'll get better soon. The truth is I don't think he will ever recover. But it's better for Hal to realize that gradually."

"I'm very sorry to hear this—for the earl's sake, and yours, but most of all for Hal's."

"Well, there's something you could do to help."

Amos guessed this was why he had been asked to tea. "Gladly," he said.

"Be a kind of mentor to Hal."

Amos perked up. He would love an excuse to spend more time with Hal.

"Nothing formal," Jane went on. "Just talk to him about life in general. About school, and business, and girls—"

"You know I have very little experience in that last topic."

She gave him a flirtatious grin. "You may not have had many lessons, but your teacher was very good."

He blushed. "Seriously . . ."

"It's more about how to talk to girls, how to treat them, things not to joke about. Women like you, Amos, and it's because of the way you treat them."

This was news to Amos. "You should be his adviser, not me."

"He won't listen to me, I'm his mother. He's approaching that age when children think their parents are foolish and senile and don't understand anything."

Amos remembered feeling that way about his father. "Of course I'll do it. I'll be delighted to."

"Thank you. You could let him spend a day at one of your mills, and perhaps take him to a borough council meeting, that sort of thing. He'll be the earl one day, and he'll need to know about everything that goes on in the county."

"I'm not sure I'll be any good at it, but I'll give it a try."

"That's all I want." She stood up, came over to him, and kissed his lips warmly. "Thank you," she said.

Alderman Hornbeam left the mill at twelve noon, heading for the town center. He was sixty-two, and walking was not as effortless as it had once been. The doctor told him to smoke fewer cigars and drink less wine, but what pleasure was there in such a life?

He passed the long rows of back-to-back houses where many of the hands lived. Business would grow again, now that the war was over, and more housing would be needed for the extra employees.

He crossed the first bridge, passed the hospital on Leper Island, and crossed the second bridge, then began the climb up Main Street. This was the part that always puffed him out.

He went through the market square, passing the cathedral, and continued to the High Street Coffee House, where his son, Howard, was waiting to have dinner with him. He sat down with relief. He felt a slight pain in his chest. It would go away in a minute or two. He looked around the room, nodding to several acquaintances, then he and Howard ordered dinner.

As he expected, the pain did not last, and he ate with relish, then lit a cigar. "We're going to have to build another street or two before long," he said to Howard. "I expect a postwar boom."

"I hope you're right," said Howard. "Anyway, we own several acres of land there and we can throw up the houses in no time."

Hornbeam nodded. "I want to bring your son into the business."

"Joe's still in the army."

"That won't last. Now that the war is over, he'll get bored with it."

"And he's only eighteen."

"He's growing up fast. And I'm not going to live forever. One day the business will need a new master."

Howard looked hurt. "So that won't be me, then."

Hornbeam sighed impatiently. "Come on, Howard, you know yourself better than that. You manage the housing well enough, but you're not the type to run the whole enterprise. You don't even want the job, in your heart of hearts. You'd hate it."

"My sister could do it."

"Don't be daft. Debbie's smart but the hands won't

take orders from a woman. She can advise her nephew, though, and Joe will listen to her if he's got any sense, which he has."

"I can see that your mind's made up."

"It is." Hornbeam put his cigar between his teeth and stood up, and Howard got up, too. Father and son left together, but Howard headed for the house—he still lived with his parents—and Hornbeam turned into Main Street, smoking contentedly, grateful for the downhill slope.

In the market square, near Willard House, he saw Joe—a sight that always pleased him. The lad was tall and broad shouldered, and looked handsome in a new uniform he had acquired—from Hornbeam's tailor—since coming back from Brussels. However, Hornbeam could not help noticing that Joe no longer looked young. There was absolutely nothing boyish about him.

The war had done that. It had grown the boy up fast. Hornbeam likened it to his own experience of being orphaned at the age of twelve, having to steal food and find a warm place for the night with no help from adults. You did what you had to, and it changed your view of the world. One cold night, he remembered, he had knifed a drunk man for his purse, and had slept contented afterward.

Then he noticed that Joe was not alone. He was with a girl of about his own age, and in fact had his arm around her waist, his hand resting lightly on her hip, suggesting a pleasant familiarity that fell slightly short of possession. She was a well-dressed working girl with a pretty face and a saucy smile. Anyone seeing the two of them like this would assume they were walking out.

Hornbeam was horrified. The girl was not good enough for his grandson, not by a long way. He wanted to ignore them and walk on by, but it was too late to pretend that he had not seen them. He had to say something. He could not think of any words appropriate to this excruciating encounter, so he just said: "Joe!"

Joe was not embarrassed. "Good afternoon, Grandfather," he said. "This is my friend Margery Reeve."

She said: "Pleased to meet you, Mr. Hornbeam."

Hornbeam did not offer his hand.

She seemed not to notice the snub. "Call me Miss Margie, everybody does."

Hornbeam had no intention of calling her anything.

She was oblivious to his cold silence. "I used to work for you at the Piggery." She added proudly: "But I'm a shopgirl now." She clearly thought she was going up in the world.

Joe had noticed Hornbeam's disapproval—which surely could not have surprised him—and now he said: "My grandfather is very busy, Margie—we mustn't keep him talking."

Hornbeam said: "I'll speak to you later, Joe." And he walked on.

A shopgirl: that explained why her clothes were quite good—they had been supplied by her employer. But she had been a mill hand originally, with dirty fingernails and homemade clothes. Joe should not be courting such a girl! She was a pretty little thing, there was no doubt about that, but it was not enough, not nearly.

Hornbeam returned to the mill for the afternoon, but had difficulty concentrating and kept thinking about Joe's girlfriend. An unsuitable liaison in youth could ruin a man's life. He had to protect Joe.

He asked the manager of Piggery Mill if he knew the Reeve family. "Oh, yes," the man said. "Young Margie was here until she got a better job, and both her parents work at our Old Mill. The mother operates a spinning engine and the father a fulling machine."

Hornbeam's mind was still full of the problem as he walked home in the evening. As soon as he entered the hall he said to Simpson, the melancholy footman: "Is Mr. Joe in the house?"

"He is, Alderman," Simpson said as if it were a tragedy.

"Ask him to come to my study. I want to speak to him before supper."

"Very good, sir."

Waiting for Joe to appear, Hornbeam had the chest pain again; not severe, but sharp for a moment or two. He wondered if it was caused by worry.

Joe came in talking. "Sorry to spring Margie on you like that, Grandfather—I meant to mention her name before you met her, but I didn't get a chance."

Hornbeam got straight to the point. "She won't do, you know," he said firmly. "I don't want you to be seen walking out with a woman of that type."

Joe paused thoughtfully, then frowned. "What type do you mean, exactly?"

Joe knew perfectly well what type his grandfather meant. However, if the boy wanted it said out loud, so be it. "I mean she's a low-class girl, only a little above a mill hand, and you must set your sights higher."

"She's very bright, she can read and write perfectly well, she's got a kind heart, and she's fun to be with."

"But she's a worker. So are her parents, who both work at my Old Mill."

Joe replied calmly and rationally, as if this was something he had thought about. "In the army I became close to a lot of working people, and I found them pretty much like the rest of us. Some are dishonest and unreliable, and some are the stoutest friends you could wish to have. I won't hold it against a person that he's a worker. Or she."

"That's not the same thing, and you know it. Don't pretend to be more foolish than you are, boy." Hornbeam immediately regretted saying *boy*.

But Joe did not seem to take offense. Perhaps he had learned that words were not worth fighting over. He was thoughtful for a few moments, then he said: "I don't think I told you the full story of how I nearly died at Waterloo."

"Yes, you did. You said someone else got in the way of a sword meant for you."

"There was a bit more to it than that. I'll tell you now, if you've got time."

Hornbeam did not want to hear it. He found it too painful to think that his only grandchild had nearly died. But he could not refuse. "All right."

"It was the end of the afternoon, and what turned out to be the last phase of the battle. The 107th Foot were on the far western end of Wellington's front line, waiting for orders. Major Denison had been killed and I was the most senior officer left standing, so I took command."

Hornbeam could not help thinking that this was just the spirit he wanted in the man who would one day take over his business.

"Bonaparte sent in the Imperial Guard, his best troops, presumably hoping they would finish off our army. I ordered a charge and we—and others—attacked the Guards from the side, going for the soft underbelly. In the middle of the melee my horse was shot from under me and I fell on my back. I looked up to see a Guard with his sword raised high ready to dispatch me. I was quite sure it was the end for me."

Heaven forbid, Hornbeam thought. He could hardly bear to think about this. But he had to let Joe carry on.

"One of my men stepped forward with his bayonet thrust out. The Guard saw it coming, pivoted, and swung the sword at my man. Sword and bayonet struck at the same time. The Guard was disemboweled, and my man's neck was sliced halfway through. And I got up, completely unharmed, and fought on."

"Thank God."

"That man saved my life by giving his own."

"Who was he? I don't think you said."

"I believe you knew him. His name was Jarge Box."

Hornbeam was floored. "Knew him?" He could not think what to say. "I certainly knew him. And his wife."

"Sal. She was at Waterloo, too. A camp follower. One of the good ones. As useful as a man."

Hornbeam searched for words to express his feelings.

"For years past they've been the worst troublemakers in Kingsbridge!"

"And yet he saved me."

Hornbeam was bewildered. He did not know what to feel. How could he be grateful to a man who had been his enemy for decades? On the other hand, how could he hate the man who had saved the life of his grandson?

"So," Joe said, "I hope you can understand why I don't accept that Margie Reeve isn't good enough for me. I hope I might be good enough for her."

Hornbeam was silenced.

After a minute Joe stood up. "I'll go and see if supper's ready."

"Very well," said Hornbeam.

Kit still did not like horses. He would never take pleasure in them, never admire their strength and beauty, never enjoy the challenge of a spirited mount. But nowadays he rode as thoughtlessly as he walked.

He rode to Badford side by side with Roger. Kit had not been back to Badford since the day he left, twenty-two years ago. The village might be different from how he remembered it. Would he feel affection for the place of his birth? Or would he hate it for throwing him and his mother out?

Roger had gone back many times over the years, and now Kit asked him: "How do you feel about Badford these days?"

"A tedious backwater," said Roger. "The people are ignorant, uneducated farmers. They're ruled badly by my brother Will, but they're too stupid to resent it. I've hated Badford ever since I left and went to Oxford and realized there was a better world."

"Oh, dear," said Kit. "Perhaps we shouldn't go back after all."

"But we have to."

They were restarting their old business. They had given up their Kingsbridge house when they joined the army, and all their tools had been taken by Sal and Jarge to Roger's old workshop in Badford. They planned to work there and live at the manor house rent free.

Kit was nervous about this, though Roger said it would be all right. Will had hated Kit and his mother. Would he remember that and feel the same now? Kit was afraid he might.

The problem was that they had very little money. Some men had come back from the war with their purses full, mostly from stealing the possessions of dead soldiers. Kit had never been very good at that. Roger was better, but he always lost the money gambling. Roger still had the debts that had forced him to flee—although creditors would hesitate to dun a man who had fought at Waterloo. The upshot was that they lacked ready cash to buy materials.

Amos had rescued them. He had ordered another Jacquard loom and paid half the price in advance. Kit had been grateful, but Amos would accept no thanks. "When I was up against the wall people helped me," he had said. "Now I do the same." So they were able to buy timber and iron, nails and glue, but they had nothing to spare.

As they entered the village Kit spotted the house where he had used to live. It looked the same but smaller. Seeing it gave him a warm feeling, and he guessed that was because he had been happy there, until his father died and everything began to go wrong.

As he looked a small boy came out of the house with a little wooden bowl of seeds and threw them to a few scrawny hens. The birds rushed to him and pecked at the seeds eagerly. The boy watched them. That could be me, Kit thought, and he tried to bring to mind what it had been like to be a child and have no worries; but he could not. He smiled and shook his head. Some phases of the past were just impossible to retrieve.

They passed the church. My father lies there, Kit thought. He was tempted to stop but decided against. His father's grave had been marked only with a wooden cross that must surely have rotted away by now, and Kit would not be able to locate the exact spot. On Sunday he would spend a few minutes in the churchyard just remembering.

They came to the manor house and Kit was shocked to see that it was in poor repair. The paint was peeling from the front door, and a broken window had been mended with a board. They rode around to the stable, but no one came to unsaddle their horses, so they did it themselves.

They went in by the front door. There were several big dogs in the hall, but they recognized Roger and wagged their tails. The room smelled foul. No woman would have tolerated this much dirt and dereliction, but Will and his wife were separated, George had died without marrying, and of course Roger was single.

Roger had told Kit that Will had spent all he had plus all he could borrow. They found him in the drawing room, playing cards with a man Kit recognized as Platts, the butler. Will's hair was down to his shoulders. Platts wore a shirt but no jacket or tie. An empty port bottle stood on the table, and two dirty glasses showed where the contents had gone. This room, too, smelled of dogs.

Kit remembered how Will had been all those years ago: a big, strong young gentleman, arrogant, well-dressed, his pockets full of money, his heart full of pride.

Will looked up at his brother and said: "Roger. What are you doing here?"

What an unfriendly way to welcome your brother, Kit thought.

"I knew you would want to congratulate me on my part in winning the Battle of Waterloo," Roger said sarcastically.

Will had played no part in the war except to make money from it.

Will did not smile. "I hope you're not planning to stay long. I can't afford to feed you." He noticed Kit and said: "What the devil is that little shrimp doing here?"

"Kit and I are business partners, Will. We'll be using my workshop."

"Just tell him to stay out of my sight."

"You might be wise to stay out of his," Roger said. "He's not the little boy you used to torment. He's been in a war, and learned how to kill men. If you cross him, he'll slit your throat quicker than you can say *knife*."

This was an exaggeration, but Will looked uncertain. He stared at Kit, then turned his head away, almost as if he was frightened.

Kit was no longer afraid of Will. But he was horrified at having to live in this dirty, run-down house owned by a drunk. Oh, well, he thought, I slept in worse places in the war. This will be better than a sodden blanket in a muddy field.

Roger said: "We'll take a look upstairs. I hope my bedroom has been kept clean and tidy while I've been away protecting you from Bonaparte."

Platts spoke for the first time. "We're short-staffed," he whined. "Can't get servants—too many men gone to soldiers. What can we do?"

"You could clean the place yourself, you useless idler. Come on, Kit, let's go and see my room."

Roger went out and Kit followed. They climbed the staircase, Kit remembering how vast it had seemed to him as a child. Roger opened a door to a bedroom and they went in. The room was bare. There was a bed, but no mattress, let alone pillows or sheets.

Roger opened drawers and found them empty. "I left clothes here," he said. "And a silver hairbrush and a shaving mirror and a pair of boots."

A maid came in, a skinny woman in her thirties with dark hair and a bad complexion. She wore a plain home-made dress and had a bunch of keys attached to a belt around her narrow waist. She smiled warmly at Kit, and after a moment he recognized her. "Fan!" he said, and he hugged her.

He turned to Roger. "Fan took care of me when my skull was cracked. We became great friends."

"I remember it well," said Roger. "And every time I've seen Fanny since then she's asked me how you are."

Kit had not realized that. He said to her: "I'm surprised you're still here."

Roger said: "She's the housekeeper now."

"And still unpaid," said Fanny.

Kit said: "Why did you never leave?"

"I've got nowhere to go," she said. "I'm an orphan, you know that. This is the only family I've got, God help me."

"But the place is so run-down."

"Most of the staff have gone. There's only me and Platts, and Platts hardly does any work. And there's not much money for soap, and polish, and blacklead for the fireplaces, and so on."

Roger pointed to the empty drawers. "What happened to all my things?"

"I'm sorry, Mr. Roger," she said. "The servants took everything in lieu of unpaid wages. I told them it was stealing, and they said you'd probably get killed in the war and no one would ever know what they'd taken."

Kit hated this. He was feeling unwelcome in a horrible house. He said: "Let's have a look at the workshop."

"That's not too bad," Fanny said quickly. "It's locked up, and I'm the only person with a key, except for you, Mr. Roger. I've looked after the place, and all your tools and whatnot."

"I don't know what happened to my key," said Roger. "I haven't got it."

"Then take mine." Fanny removed a key from her bunch and handed it over. Roger thanked her.

Kit and Roger left the manor house and walked half a mile through the village. It took awhile because Kit kept stopping to speak to people he remembered. Brian

Pikestaff, the Methodist leader, had got fat. Alec Pollock, the threadbare surgeon who had bandaged Kit's skull, had a new coat at last. Jimmy Mann was still wearing that three-cornered hat. Kit had to tell everyone about Waterloo.

At last they reached the workshop. It was a sturdily built stable that Roger had altered, putting in large windows for better light. Kit saw the tools ranged neatly on hooks along the wall. A cupboard held crockery and glassware, all clean.

At one end was a former hayloft that could easily be converted into a bedroom. A love nest, Kit thought.

He said: "We could live here, couldn't we?"

"I'm so glad you said that," said Roger.

Hornbeam could not stop thinking about Jarge Box saving Joe at the Battle of Waterloo. He wanted to forget about the whole thing but it kept coming back. He brooded over it as he sat in his office at Piggery Mill, staring at letters from customers without reading them. He could not get used to the idea that he owed a huge debt of gratitude to one of the worthless cattle he employed in his mills. It was an indigestible fact, as if someone had told him that the king of England was in fact an ostrich.

What could bring him peace of mind? If he could have given Box some kind of reward, perhaps that would have restored the balance, but Box was dead. However, it occurred to him that he might do something for the widow. But what? A gift of money? Knowing Sal Box, she might spurn it, and humiliate Hornbeam further.

He decided to give the problem to Joe.

Once he had worked this out he wanted to implement it right away: that was his style. He left the mill at midmorning and went to Willard House.

He was shown into the room at the front with the view

of the cathedral. This was still the earl's office, he gathered, but Henry was somewhere else. Joe's red coat was hanging on a hook behind the door, and he sat at the big desk with a small pile of paperwork in front of him, a vase of sharpened quills and an inkwell by his right hand.

Hornbeam sat down and accepted a cup of coffee. Joe knew how he liked it: strong with cream.

"I'm proud of you," he said to Joe. "You're a major, and you're only eighteen."

"The army believes I'm twenty-two," Joe said.

"Or they pretend to."

"And this is temporary. A new lieutenant colonel is on his way here to take charge."

"Good. I don't want you to spend your life in the army."

"I haven't actually made any plans for the rest of my life, Grandfather."

"Well, I have." This was not what Hornbeam had come to talk about, but he was finding it difficult to get to the point. His debt of gratitude to Jarge Box was humiliating. He continued to avoid the issue. "I want you to leave the army and start work in the family business."

"Thank you. That's certainly an option."

"Don't be a fool, it's the best option. What else would you do? Don't answer that, I don't want a list. I have three mills and a couple of hundred rented houses, and it's all yours, as my only grandchild."

"Thank you, Grandfather. I'm truly honored."

That was polite, but it was not consent, Hornbeam noted. However, it would probably have to do for now. This was not the moment to insist. An acrimonious row might tip Joe in the wrong direction. Joe could not easily be bullied: in that way he was different from his father and similar to his grandfather.

Hornbeam stood up. "I want you to think about this hard. You're very able, but you have a lot to learn. The sooner you begin, the more capable you'll be when I retire." He still had not said what he had come to say. This is so unlike me, he thought.

"I promise to think about it very hard," Joe said.

Hornbeam went to the door. Pretending he had just remembered something, he said: "Oh, and go and see Jarge Box's widow. I should probably do something for her by way of reward. Find out what she wants."

"I'll do my best."

"You should always do your best, Joe," said Hornbeam, and he went out.

Kenelm Mackintosh was buried in a Protestant churchyard in Brussels. Elsie had been one of hundreds of women searching the valley for the bodies of loved ones after the Battle of Waterloo. It had been the worst day of her life, looking at the dead faces of thousands of men, mostly young, as they lay sprawled in fields of mud and flattened wheat, their bodies horribly mangled, their unseeing eyes open to the sky. The weight of grief she felt was almost unbearable. Most of them would be buried where they lay, the officers in single graves, the men in communal pits; but chaplains were privileged, and she was able to take Kenelm's corpse away and arrange a proper funeral for him.

The children were distraught. She told them to be proud of him, for risking his life to bring spiritual comfort to soldiers, and she reminded them that he was in heaven now, and they would see him again there someday. She only half believed it, but it gave the children consolation.

She herself was more grief-stricken than she would have expected. She had never been in love with Kenelm, and he had been a self-centered person until the army changed him; but they had been together a long time and had brought five wonderful children into the world, and his death left a hole in her life. She cried when they lowered his coffin into the grave.

And now she was back in Kingsbridge, living with her mother and Spade and running the Sunday school with Amos. Her eldest child, Stephen, had been readily accepted to study at Oxford, being the grandson of a bishop, so he had left, but otherwise they were the same as before, except that she was a widow now, and there would be no more letters from Kenelm.

She did not think she would marry again. Many years ago she had longed to marry Amos, but he had wanted Jane. He still spent a lot of time with Jane. He had looked quite grumpy during the visit of a certain Major Percival Dwight, from the office of the army commander in chief in London. Dwight had come to inspect the 107th Foot Regiment, he said, but he had found time to escort Jane to the racecourse, the theater, and the Assembly Rooms, standing in for her convalescent husband. Amos had said he did not like to see Jane flirting while her husband was recovering from a war wound. Admittedly this was the kind of stern moral attitude Amos would typically take, but Elsie suspected jealousy, too.

She had enjoyed dancing with Amos at the duchess of Richmond's ball. The waltz was a kind of symbolic adultery, she felt; an exciting and very physical encounter with a man who was not her husband. Amos may have felt something similar. But that was all.

One Sunday in October, after the Sunday school was over and they had cleared up, Amos casually asked her how she felt about the Anglican church.

"It's the only religion I'm familiar with," she said. "I believe most of it, and I'm happy to go to church and pray and sing hymns, but I'm perfectly sure that clergymen don't know as much as they pretend to. My father was a bishop, remember, and I didn't trust half of what he said."

"Goodness me." She could see that he was shocked. "I had no idea you were so agnostic."

"I tell the children that their daddy is waiting for them in heaven. But we now know too much about the planets and stars to believe that heaven is up there in the sky—so where is it?"

He did not answer the question, but instead asked her one. "Do you think you'll marry again?"

She said: "I haven't thought about it," which was not true.

"What do you think about Methodism?"

"You and Spade are good advertisements for it. You're not dogmatic, you respect other people's opinions, and you don't want to persecute Catholics. You don't know any more than the Anglicans, but the difference is that you admit your ignorance."

"Have you ever been to a Methodist service?"

"No, as it happens, but I might go one day, to see what it's like. Why are you asking me these questions?"

"Oh, just idle curiosity."

They went on to talk about finding a new mathematics teacher, but Elsie mulled over the religious conversation afterward. When she got home she told her mother about it. "Don't you think it's a bit odd?"

Arabella laughed. "Odd?" she said. "Not a bit. I've been wondering when he would raise that subject."

Elsie did not understand. "Really? Why? Why has it become important?"

"Because he wants to marry you."

"Oh, Mother," said Elsie. "Don't be ridiculous."

Sal was living in a room of a house owned by a woman who took in lodgers, Patience Creighton, known as Pat. At one stage Kit had suggested she live with him and Roger, but she had declined. She was not convinced they really wanted her. She had long ago guessed that they were a married couple in every sense but the official, and she felt sure they needed privacy. And then they had moved to Badford.

Pat was a pleasant person and a decent landlord, but Sal was unhappy and she missed Jarge. She was not working: she had made money in the Netherlands, mainly by selling the soldiers things the army did not provide, and it would be several months before she needed to go back to a mill. But she felt that life was purposeless. There were times when she wondered whether there was any point in getting up in the morning. Pat believed this was not unusual in bereavement; she had felt the same, she said, after Mr. Creighton died. Sal believed her but it did not help.

She was astonished to be visited by Joe Hornbeam, elegant in a new uniform. "Hello, Mrs. Box," he said. "I haven't seen you since Waterloo."

She was not sure whether she could trust him. He had been a good officer, but the foul blood of Alderman Hornbeam ran in his veins. She decided to keep an open mind. "What can I do for you, Major?" she said neutrally.

"You know that your husband saved my life."

Sal nodded. "Several people who were nearby described the event to me."

"More than that, he *died* saving my life."

"He was a man with a big heart."

"And yet you and he were my grandfather's great enemies."

"This is true."

"Grandfather Hornbeam finds it difficult to deal with this paradox."

"I hope you're not going to ask for my sympathy."

Joe smiled ruefully and shook his head. "It's more complicated than that."

Sal was intrigued. "You'd better sit down." She pointed to the one chair in the room, and she sat on the edge of the bed.

"Thanks. Look, my grandfather will probably never change."

"People generally don't, especially when they're old."

"All the same, he wants to make some acknowledgment of your husband's heroic sacrifice. He would like to do something by way of thanks, and since he can't give anything to Jarge, he would like to give something to you."

Sal was not sure she would welcome a gift from Hornbeam. She did not want a reminder of him in her life. She said guardedly: "What does he have in mind?"

"He doesn't know, so he asked me to talk to you. Is there anything you need or want that he could provide?"

I just want my Jarge back, Sal thought; but there was no point in saying that. "Anything at all?" she said.

"He didn't set any limits. I'm here to find out what you would like. He didn't give me a hint of price. But whatever you ask for, I'm going to do everything I can to make sure you get it."

"This is like a fairy tale, where someone rubs a magic lamp, and a genie appears."

"In the uniform of the 107th Foot."

She laughed. Joe really wasn't a bad kid.

But should she accept a gift? And if so, what should she ask for?

She thought for several minutes, while Joe waited patiently. The truth was that she had thought of something, and had been contemplating the idea for some months now, imagining how it would be, trying to figure out ways of making it happen.

Finally she said it. "I want a shop."

"You want to open a shop? Or take one over?"

"To open one."

"In the High Street?"

"No. I don't want to sell fancy gowns to rich women. I'd be no good at it."

"What, then?"

"I want to have a shop on the other side of the river, near the mills, in one of the streets built by your father.

The people there are always complaining that they have to walk a long way to the town shops."

Joe nodded. "I remember, in the Netherlands, you always used to have little things the soldiers wanted to buy: pencils, tobacco, peppermint drops, needles and thread to sew their torn clothes."

"Having a shop is a matter of knowing what people need and putting those things on the shelves."

"And how do you know what they need?"

"You ask them."

"Very logical." Joe nodded. "How should we proceed?"

"Well, if your grandfather agrees, he'll give me one of the houses, on a corner. I'll use the downstairs as the shop and live upstairs. In time I may do some alterations to the place, if I make enough profit; but at first all I need is some stock, and I've got enough money to make a start."

"All right. I'll ask him. I think he'll say yes."

"Thank you," she said.

He shook her hand. "I'm glad to know you, Mrs. Box."

Shortly before Christmas, during the interval at the theater, Jane took Amos aside and spoke to him in serious tones. "I really don't like the way you're treating Elsie," she said.

Amos was astonished. "What on earth do you mean? I'm not ill-treating her."

"Everyone thinks you're going to marry her, but you don't propose!"

"Why do people think I'm going to marry her?"

"For heaven's sake, Amos! You see her nearly every day. At the Assize Ball you danced with her all evening. Neither of you shows the least interest in anyone else. Elsie is forty-three, attractive, and single, and she has five children who need a stepfather. Of course people think you're going to marry her—it's the only thing that makes sense! They just can't understand why you still haven't asked her."

"It's none of their business."

"But it is. There must be half a dozen men who'd propose if they thought they stood a chance. You're ruining her prospects. It's not fair! You've got to either marry her or get out of the way."

An usher rang a handbell, and they returned to their seats. Amos looked at the stage but did not see the play, he was so absorbed in his thoughts. Was Jane right? Probably, he decided. She would not make up something like this—there was no reason to.

He would have to cool his friendship with Elsie and let it be known that they were not romantically involved. But when he thought of that he felt sad. Life without her seemed a dismal prospect.

And his feelings had changed since the duchess of Richmond's ball. He always told himself that he wanted only to be Elsie's friend, but the truth was that he was no longer content with that. Another feeling was surging up inside him, something to do with how warm and soft her body under the silk dress had felt when he touched her in the waltz. He felt a bit like a volcano that seems extinct, but has boiling lava hidden in its depths. Deep down he wanted to be more than her friend.

This was a big change. But he had no doubt about it. He loved her. Why had it taken him so long to realize it? I've never been very smart about such things, he thought.

He began to think about how life would be if they were married. He felt so eager about it that he wanted to marry her tomorrow.

But there was a problem. Amos was the father of an illegitimate child. Did Elsie know or guess that? And if so, how did she feel about it? Her brother, Abe, was illegitimate, and she was always kind and loving to him. On the other hand, she was the daughter of a bishop. Would she marry an adulterer?

He did not know. But he could ask her.

Spade was surprised to be visited by Joe Hornbeam. He was intrigued, too. The lad had gained a good reputation with the men of the 107th Foot—which was unexpected, as everyone said, given who his grandfather was.

Joe shook his hand and said: "I'm glad your brother-in-law, Freddie, survived Waterloo."

Spade nodded. "He's decided to stay in the army."

"I'm not surprised. He's a good sergeant. They'll be glad to have him."

Spade happened to be with Sime Jackson, who was sitting at the Jacquard loom. Joe looked with interest at the machine and said: "I don't think my grandfather has anything like that."

"He'll have one before long, I guarantee you," said Spade.

Sime explained: "The holes punched in the card tell the loom how to weave the pattern. Makes the whole process faster."

"Amazing."

"I'll show you," said Sime, and he worked the loom for a few minutes. Joe was fascinated. "Then when the pattern needs to change, you just put a different card in," Sime said. "It was invented by a Frenchman. I know we're supposed to hate the French, on account of Bonaparte, but the Froggy who devised this was bloody clever."

"Did you buy it in France?"

"No, Kit Clitheroe and Roger Riddick make them."

Spade said: "But you didn't come here to learn about the Jacquard loom, Joe."

"No. I'd like a quiet word with you, if I may."

"Of course." The word *quiet* suggested that Joe did not want to be overheard, so Spade said: "Come to my little office."

They made their way there and Joe looked around the room. "Not as magnificent as my grandfather's office, but more comfortable," he commented.

They sat down, and Spade said: "What's on your mind?"

"My grandfather wants me to leave the army and start work in his business."

"And how do you feel about that?"

"I want to know more about the business before I decide."

How sensible, Spade thought.

Joe's next remark surprised him. "You run the friendly society."

"Yes . . ."

"My grandfather says it's a trade union in disguise, merely a way of getting around the Combination Act."

Spade wondered whether this was some kind of trap. "I've heard him say that," he said noncommittally. "If he's right, the society is against the law."

"I don't really care whether it is or not, I just guessed you would be a good person to give me advice."

Spade thought: Now where the hell is this going? He said nothing.

Joe went on: "You see, I don't want to run the business my grandfather's way. He's turned his workers into his enemies. To be frank, they hate him. I don't want to be hated."

Spade nodded. Joe was right, though not everyone saw it that way.

Joe said: "I think he'd do better to try to make them—not his friends, that's unrealistic—but perhaps his allies. After all, they want to produce good cloth and get paid well for it, and he wants the same."

This was what all reasonable people felt, but it was remarkable to hear it from someone whose surname was Hornbeam. "So what do you want to do?"

"I've come to ask you that. How can I make things different?"

Spade sat back. This was all highly surprising. But he was being given an opportunity to educate a young man who was going to be a power in Kingsbridge. This could be a key moment.

He thought for a minute about what to tell Joe, but really the question was not difficult. "Talk to the hands," he said. "Whenever you decide to make a change—bring in a new machine, for example, or alter the hours of work—talk to them first. Half the squabbles in our industry happen because something has been sprung on the hands without warning, and their instant reaction is to oppose it. Tell them why you want to make the change, discuss with them the problems that might arise, see what suggestions they have."

Joe objected: "You can talk to your people, you've only got a dozen or so. My grandfather has more than a hundred at the Piggery alone."

"I know," said Spade. "That's where a trade union is so useful."

"Except that they're illegal, as you said."

"A lot of masters, in the cotton industry as well as the wool, want to get that Combination Act repealed. What with that and the Treason Act and the Seditious Meetings Act, the hands can hardly speak without risking their necks—and men are quick to resort to violence when violence is all they've got."

"That makes sense," said Joe. "Thank you."

"Anytime. I mean that. I'll be glad to help you if I can."

Joe got up to leave, and Spade walked him to the door.

Joe said: "Is there one thing I could do right away, maybe a small thing, that would signal that things are going to be different?"

Spade thought for a moment and said: "Abolish the rule prohibiting people from going to the privy except at certain scheduled times."

Joe stared at him. "Good Lord, does my grandfather do that?"

"He certainly does. So do other masters in the town—though not all. I don't have such a rule. Nor does Amos Barrowfield."

"I should think not. It's barbaric!"

"The women in particular hate it. The men, if they're desperate, just piss on the floor."

"Disgusting!"

"So change it."

Joe shook Spade's hand. "I will," he said, and he left.

Amos waited until he was alone with Elsie. This happened once a week, after Sunday school. They sat at a table in a room that still smelled of unwashed children. Amos said without preamble: "Has it ever crossed your mind that Earl Henry might not be the father of young Hal?"

She raised her eyebrows. The question had startled her, he saw. But her response was low-key. "It's crossed everybody's mind," she said. "At least, all those interested in gossip, which is most of the population of Kingsbridge."

"But what makes them suspect?"

"The simple fact that it took Jane nine years to conceive. So when she did people naturally wondered how that had come about. Of course there are several possibilities, but gossips will always prefer the most sordid one."

So she thought adultery was sordid. Well, she was right. He almost gave up there and then.

He knew what he had to say, but, now that the moment had come, he felt mortified. All the same he forced it out. "I think I'm the real father of Hal," he said, and he felt his cheeks warm with a flush of shame. "I'm sorry to shock you."

"I'm not very shocked," she said.

"Really?"

"I've always suspected it. So have other people."

He felt even more embarrassed. "You mean people in this town guessed I was responsible?"

"Well, everyone thought you were having an affair with Jane."

"It wasn't an affair."

"All right, but you seemed quite put out by the visit of Major Dwight."

"I was, because I hate to see Jane behaving disgracefully. I did love her once, and I don't now, and that's the truth."

"So how could you be Hal's father?"

"Because of one time. I mean, it wasn't a long-term sin. Oh, Lord, I don't know what I'm saying."

"Amos, one of the lovable things about you is your innocence. But you don't need to be ashamed, or even embarrassed, at least not on my account."

"But I'm an adulterer."

"No, you're not. You sinned once. And it was long ago." She reached across the table and put her hand over his. "I know you well, probably better than anyone else in the world knows you, and you're not a bad man. Most definitely not."

"Well, I'm glad you think so, at least."

There was a pause. She opened her mouth to say something, changed her mind, then changed it back again and said: "Why have you raised this issue with me now, more than a decade after the event?"

"Oh, I don't know," he said, then he realized how stupid that was, and he said: "Yes, of course, I do know."

"So . . . why?"

"I was afraid you wouldn't want to marry an adulterer."

She froze. "Marry?"

"Yes. I was afraid you would refuse me."

"Are you asking me?"

"Yes. I'm not doing this very well, am I?"

"You're not being very clear."

"True. All right. Elsie, I love you. I think I must have loved you for an awfully long time without realizing it. I'm happy when I'm with you, and when I'm not with you I miss you. I want you to marry me and come and live in my house and sleep in my bed, and I want to have breakfast with you and your children every morning. But I'm afraid my sordid past makes it impossible."

"I didn't say that."

"You don't mind what I did with Jane?"

"I don't mind. Well, not a lot, anyway. Well, I do mind, really, but I love you anyway."

Had she really said that?

I love you anyway.

She had said it.

Amos said: "Then . . . will you marry me?"

"Yes. Yes, I will. It's what I've always wanted. Of course I'll marry you."

"Oh," said Amos. "Oh. Oh, thank you."

On his way home from the mill on Monday, Hornbeam went into the cathedral on impulse. He thought he might be able to think straight in the church, and he was right. The pillars and the arches all seemed to make a kind of sense, and looking at them in the light of a few candles he found that his thoughts became more ordered. Outside, his mind was just confusion and anger. All the things he had ever believed had turned out to be wrong and he had nothing to take their place. In here he felt calm.

He walked along the nave to the crossing, then skirted the altar and carried on to the east end of the church, the holiest part. He stopped there, turned, and looked back.

He thought about Jarge Box. He had always judged Box worthless, or worse. Box caused trouble, he got into fights, he went on strike, he smashed machines. And yet, in the end, he had given Hornbeam a gift more precious than anything: the life of Joe.

Box had been subjected to the ultimate test. He had been asked to save a comrade at the risk of his own life. It had been a double challenge: his courage had passed the test, and so had his selflessness.

Today was Monday. Yesterday's sermon had been on the verse "Greater love hath no man than this, that a man lay down his life for his friends." The bishop had spoken of all those who had given their lives at Waterloo, but Hornbeam had thought only of Box. He had asked: What is my life compared to his? Jesus had given the answer: no man had greater love than that which Jarge Box had shown.

Hornbeam's life now seemed valueless. As a boy he had lived by violence and theft. As a man he had done the same things less openly: he had paid bribes to win business, and he had sentenced people to flogging and hard labor, or sent them to the assizes to be condemned to death.

His excuse had always been the cruel death of his mother. But many children suffered cruelty and lived good adult lives: Kit Clitheroe was an example.

His reverie was interrupted by loud chatter and laughter: at the other end of the cathedral, the bell ringers were coming in for their rehearsal. Hornbeam really could not spend his time in melancholic reflection. He retraced his steps.

When he came to the crossing he noticed a small door in the corner of the north transept. It was open. He recollected that there had been workmen on the roof today, probably repairing the lead. They must have left without locking up. On impulse he went through the door and climbed the spiral stairs.

He had to stop several times on the way because of the pain in his chest, but he just rested awhile, then carried on to the roof.

It was a clear night with a moon. He walked along a narrow footway and found himself near the top of the bell tower. Looking up at the spire, he could see the statue of the angel that was said to represent Caris, the nun who had built the hospital during the terrible plague of the Black Death. She was another person who had done something good with her life.

Hornbeam was on the north side of the roof, and when he looked down he could see the graveyard in the moonlight. The people lying there had peace of mind.

He knew there was a solution to his problem, a cure for his illness. It was mentioned regularly in every Christian church in the world: confession and repentance. A man could be forgiven for doing wrong. But the price was humiliating. When Hornbeam imagined himself admitting that he had done wrong—to his family, to his customers, to other clothiers, to the aldermen—he shuddered with horror. Repentance? What did that mean? Should he apologize to those he had wronged? He had not apologized for anything in the last half century. Could he give back the money he had made from corrupt army contracts? He would be prosecuted. He might go to jail. What would happen to his family?

But he could not live like this. He slept so little at night because of his tormented thoughts. He knew he was not running the business as he should. He hardly spoke to anyone. He smoked all the time. And his chest pain was getting worse.

He went to the very edge of the roof and looked down at the tombstones. The ringers began their practice, and right next to him the booming notes of the huge bells began to sound, a noise that he seemed to feel in his very bones, possessing him. His whole being vibrated. Peace of mind, he thought; peace of mind.

He stepped over the edge.

As soon as he had done it he felt terrified. He wanted to change his mind, to turn back. He heard himself scream like a tortured animal. His eyes were open and he could see the ground racing up at him. Fear possessed him and grew and grew, but he could not scream any louder. Then the worst happened, and the ground hit him with a mighty blow that filled his whole body with excruciating, unbearable agony.

And then nothing.

CHAPTER 45

Arabella looked up from the newspaper and said: "Parliament has been dissolved."

Her son, Abe, who was eighteen, swallowed his bacon and said: "What does that mean?" Abe's knowledge of life was patchy. In some areas he was well-informed; in others ignorant. Perhaps that was normal at his age. Spade tried to remember whether he had been the same, but he could not be sure. Anyway, Abe would go to the University of Edinburgh in the autumn, and from then on his understanding would grow fast.

Arabella answered his question. "It means there will be a general election."

Spade said: "And a chance to get rid of Humphrey Frogmore." That was an attractive prospect. Humphrey Frogmore had won the by-election held after the death of Hornbeam. He had been a lazy and ineffective MP.

"How come?" said Abe.

Arabella said: "Mr. Frogmore will have to stand for reelection if he wants to continue as our member of Parliament."

Spade said: "What's the timetable?"

Arabella looked down at the paper again, then said: "The new Parliament will be summoned on the fourth of August."

"That gives us almost two months," Spade said, calculating. It was now mid-June 1818. "We must get someone to stand against Frogmore."

Abe said: "Why?"

"Mr. Frogmore supports the Combination Act," Spade explained. There was a movement to repeal that hated law, but Frogmore wanted it to remain. It was the only issue about which he had spoken in Parliament. He represented the hard-liners in Kingsbridge who had formerly been led by Hornbeam.

Arabella said: "One way or another, we need a new candidate. I think it should be our son-in-law."

Spade nodded agreement. "Amos is popular." Amos Barrowfield had been elected mayor after Hornbeam died. Spade looked at his pocket watch. "I might go and talk to him now. I could catch him before he leaves for the mill."

"I'll come with you," said Arabella.

They put on their hats and left the house. It was a fine June day, cool but sunny, and the town wore its fresh morning coat, bright with dew. They found Amos and family still at breakfast. Elsie's children were growing up fast. Stephen was away at Oxford, Billy and Richie looked like young men, and Martha had the beginnings of a woman's figure. Only Georgie was still a child.

Extra places were laid for the grandparents, and coffee was poured. Spade waited until the youngsters had finished and left, then said: "Did you read that Parliament has been dissolved?"

Amos said: "Yes. We need someone to run against the useless Frogmore."

Spade smiled. "We do indeed. And I think it should be you."

"I was afraid of that."

"You're a popular mayor. You can beat Frogmore."

"I hate to disappoint you." Amos looked at Elsie for support.

Elsie said: "We're not going to London. I'm not willing to leave my Sunday school."

"You don't have to," Spade said. "Amos could go to London on his own when he needed to be there." But he felt he was losing the argument. Amos was just too comfortable as he was. He even looked contented. He had put on some weight.

Amos shook his head. "I wasted half my life not being

married to Elsie," he said. "Now that we're together, I'm not going to spend months up in London without her."

"But surely—"

Arabella interrupted Spade. "Drop it, my love," she said. "They mean it."

Spade dropped it. Arabella was usually right about such things.

Amos said: "But we need a candidate. And I think the best prospect is the other man at this table." He looked at Spade.

"I'm not educated," Spade said.

"You can read and write, and you're smarter than most."

"But I can't make speeches with quotations in Latin and Greek."

"Nor can I. That kind of thing is unnecessary. The Oxford men love to show off in debates, of course, but most of them are quite ignorant about the industries that make our country prosperous. You'd be a very effective advocate for repeal of the Combination Act."

Spade became thoughtful. The act had been a determined attempt by the ruling elite to crush all efforts by working people to better their lot. He was being offered the chance to help abolish that wicked law. How could he refuse?

Arabella said: "Would they really repeal the act? Don't they all just want to keep the workers under their thumbs?"

"Some do, but members of Parliament aren't all the same," Amos said. "Joseph Hume is the leader of the Radicals, and he's against the act. The editor of the *Scotsman* newspaper agrees with Hume. And there's a retired tailor called Francis Place who briefs Hume and all the more enlightened members about the bad effects of the act. Place also supports a political newspaper called *The Gorgon*."

Spade turned to Arabella. "How would you feel about going to London?"

"I'd miss Elsie and the grandchildren, of course," she said. "But we could still spend much of the year here. And living in London could be quite lively."

Spade could see by the gleam in her eye that she meant it. She was sixty-three, but she had more fizz than most women half her age.

"Let me think about it," he said.

The next day he agreed to stand.

And he won.

The Irish who had come to Kingsbridge twenty years ago, brought by Hornbeam to break the strike, had melted into the town's population and were no longer called scabs. They still had charming Irish accents, but their children did not. They went to the town's small Catholic church, but otherwise made no show of their religion. In most respects they were mill hands like the rest. Colin Hennessy, their leader, came into Sal's shop often.

The ground floor of Sal's house was divided in two by a counter. Behind the counter, where she stood most of the day, were shelves and cupboards crammed with goods. She stocked everything people needed except gin. She could have made a lot of money selling gin by the glass, but she hated to see drunkenness—perhaps on account of Jarge's weakness—and she preferred to have nothing to do with strong drink.

They often chatted. She had always liked Colin. They were the same age and both were community leaders. They had gone together to confront Hornbeam. And Sal had dreamed about being in bed with him.

One day in 1819 she said to him: "I don't know if I ever told you, but my son was the first person to speak to you when you came here."

"Is that so?"

"And your wife, rest her soul. I was sorry to hear that she had passed away."

"It's half a year ago now."

"And the children all grown up and married."

"Yes."

"I remember the day you arrived. My son, Kit, came running home with news of four wagons full of foreigners."

"I think I remember a little fellow."

"You asked his name, and told him yours. He said he had spoken to a tall man with black hair who talked very strangely."

Colin laughed. "Well, that's me all right."

Sal looked out of the window and saw that night was falling. "It's time for me to close," she said.

"Right. I'll be off."

She looked at him speculatively. He was still a handsome devil. "Would you like a cup of tea?"

"Well, now, I won't say no to that."

She locked the shop door and led him upstairs. A small fire burned in the grate for cooking, and she put the kettle on to boil.

She had had the shop for nearly four years, and it was a great success. She had made so much money that she had been obliged to open a bank account for the first time in her life. But what she liked most was the people. All day long they came in and went out, each one having a life full of joys and sorrows, and they shared their stories with her. She felt lonely only at night.

She said to Colin: "People thought you Irish would all go back home, but most of you stayed."

"I love Ireland, but it's hard to make a living there. The government in London is not kind to the Irish."

"Nor to the English, unless they're noblemen or rich businessmen. Prime ministers run things for the benefit of people of their own ilk."

"That's God's own truth."

She made the tea, gave him a cup, and offered sugar. He drank some and said: "This is very good. Funny how tea tastes better when someone else has made it."

"You miss your wife."

"I certainly do. And you?"

"The same. My Jarge had his faults, but I loved him."

There was silence for a minute or two, then he put down his cup and said: "I'd better be going."

Sal hesitated. I'm fifty years old, she thought; I can't do this. But she said: "You don't have to go." Then she held her breath.

"I don't?"

"You can stay if you want."

He said nothing.

"You can stay the night," she said, making it perfectly clear. "If you'd like to," she added nervously.

He smiled. "Yes, dear Sal," he said. "Oh, yes, I'd like to."

Henry, earl of Shiring, died in December 1821. In the end his death had nothing to do with his head wound: he was killed by a fall from a horse.

Jane looked good in black but Amos knew she was not really mourning. Henry had been a good soldier but a poor husband.

The funeral was held in Kingsbridge Cathedral, with old Bishop Reddingcote in charge. Just about all the gentry in the county came, plus every man of importance in Kingsbridge, and all the officers of the regiment. Amos reckoned there were more than a thousand people in the nave.

Major Percival Dwight came from London. He told everyone he was representing the duke of York, who was commander in chief of the army, and no doubt it was true, but those in the know believed he had come to woo the widow.

After the service the coffin was carried outside and loaded into a carriage drawn by four black horses. There was a light fall of snow, and flakes caught in their manes and melted on their warm backs. When the coffin was secured the carriage drew away, heading for Earlscastle, where Henry would be laid to rest in the family tomb.

The wake was held in the Assembly Rooms. Amos was invited into a side room for special guests. Jane lifted her veil to talk to people, showing no evidence of tears.

After the first rush of people expressing their condolences to her, Amos got her alone for a few minutes and asked what her plans were.

"I shall go to London," she said. "We have a house there, which Henry hardly ever used. It's Hal's now, of course, but I've talked to him and he's happy for me to live there."

"Well, you'll have at least one friend."

"Who are you referring to?"

"Major Dwight."

"I'll have more friends than him, Amos. The duchess of Richmond, for one. And several others I knew in Brussels."

"Will you have enough money?"

"Hal has agreed to continue my dress allowance, which was always rather generous."

"I know. You made Spade's sister quite rich."

"That's not all I did. I took out insurance on Henry's life, and paid the installments out of the money he gave me, without telling him. So I'll have money of my own."

"I'm very glad." I might have guessed, Amos thought, that Jane would have taken care of her financial future. "Will you marry again?"

"A very inappropriate question to ask me at my husband's funeral."

"I know, but you hate people to be mealymouthed about such matters."

She chuckled. "You know me too well, you dog. But I'm not going to answer you."

"Fair enough."

Someone else came to offer condolences, and Amos moved to the buffet. His stepson Stephen was talking to

Hal, the new earl at the age of sixteen. Amos heard Hal say: "So how many lectures do you have to attend every week?"

"You don't have to attend any of them," Stephen said. "But most people do about one a day."

They were talking about Oxford, obviously. Amos recalled how jealous he had used to feel of young men who went to universities, and how he had wondered whether a son of his would ever have that privilege. Now his unacknowledged illegitimate son was about to fulfill the dream. How strange, Amos mused. I got my wish in a way I never imagined.

But that was life, he had learned. Things never turned out quite how you expected.

Shortly before Christmas 1823 Spade, now a member of Parliament, went to a secret meeting at the London home of Francis Place.

The campaign against the Combination Act was approaching its climax. In the coming year there would be a parliamentary Waterloo. If the government represented Bonaparte, and the opposition was Wellington, then the little group meeting in Charing Cross were the Prussians, hoping to tip the balance.

Several Radical members of Parliament were there, including Joseph Hume. All had campaigned for years against the Combination Act, with no result. Most members disagreed with them, acting as if any meeting of working people was likely to lead to revolution and the guillotine.

But now there would be a showdown.

Hume announced that he had persuaded the government to appoint a select committee on artisans and machinery. "The committee will investigate emigration of artisans and export of machinery," Hume said. "Both subjects are important to the government and to manufacturers. And, almost as an afterthought, we are commanded to study the operation of the Combination Act. As it was my idea, the government has agreed that I will be chairman. This is our big chance."

Spade said: "We'll have to be clever. We don't want to stir up our enemies too early in the game."

"How will we manage that?" asked a cautious northern member called Michael Slater. "We can't keep the committee secret."

Spade said: "No, but we can keep it low-key. Speak about it as if it's a tedious chore and won't achieve anything very much." Spade had learned a lot about Parliament in the last five years. As in chess, an attack must not look like an attack until it was impossible to resist.

"Good thinking," said Hume.

Spade said: "But everything will depend upon the members of the committee."

"That's taken care of," said Hume. "In theory, the members will be chosen by the president of the Board of Trade. But I will present him with a list of recommendations, and—unknown to him—it will consist only of men who sympathize with our cause."

Spade thought that might work. Both Hume and Place were experienced in managing parliamentary business. They would not easily be outmaneuvered.

Hume went on: "What is crucial—and the reason for convening this meeting—is that we must bring convincing witnesses to give evidence to the committee, witnesses who have personal experience of the injustice and disruption caused by this act. First, we need hands who have been savagely punished by the justices for breaking the act."

Spade thought of Sal, who was now Sal Hennessy, having married Colin. Spade said: "There's a woman in Kingsbridge who served two months' hard labor for telling a master that he was breaking an agreement that the clothiers themselves had agreed to."

"That's exactly what we need. Stupid, malicious court decisions based on the act."

Slater said skeptically: "Uneducated workers make poor witnesses. They come out with ridiculous complaints. They say the masters are using witchcraft, and that kind of thing."

Slater was a useful pessimist, Spade thought. He was always gloomy but he pointed to real problems.

Hume said: "Our people will be interviewed beforehand by Mr. Place here, who will brief me on each witness's personal experience so that I can be sure to ask the right questions."

"Good," said Slater, satisfied.

Hume resumed: "And we also need mill owners to testify that it's easier to manage your hands if there's a union to negotiate with."

Spade said: "I know some of those as well."

Francis Place spoke up. "There are places where wages are so low that employed people are receiving Poor Relief. The ratepayers get angry because they're subsidizing the profits of the mill owners."

"Good point," said Hume. "We must get men to testify to that. It's very important."

Slater said: "Our enemies will bring witnesses, too."

"Undoubtedly," said Hume. "But if we handle things carefully they won't think about it until the last minute, and their briefings will be done in a rush."

This was how politics was carried on, Spade mused as the meeting broke up. It was never enough to have right on your side. You had to be more cunning than the opposition.

He returned to Kingsbridge for Christmas. MPs received no salary, so those who were not independently rich had to have another job. Spade continued to run his business.

While he was in Kingsbridge he persuaded Sal and Amos to testify before Hume's committee.

The committee sat in Westminster Hall from February

to May 1824 and questioned more than a hundred witnesses.

Amos testified to the advantages of dealing with trade unions, and his wife, Elsie, looked on proudly.

The high point of the proceedings came when mill hands gave evidence. It became shockingly clear that the Combination Act had been used to bully and punish workers in ways which Parliament had never intended, and many MPs were outraged.

A master bootmaker in London had halved the pay of his men and, when they refused to work, had summoned them before the lord mayor, who had sentenced them all to hard labor. A similar story was told by a cotton weaver from Stockport, who had been beaten up by a constable and jailed for two months, along with ten other men and twelve women.

Sal said: "A strike in Kingsbridge was settled by negotiation between a group representing the masters and a group representing the hands. Part of the agreement was that when a master planned to introduce new machinery he would discuss it with the hands."

Hume said: "Was the master obliged to do as the hands wanted?"

"No. He was obliged to discuss, that's all."

"Carry on."

"One of the masters, Mr. Hornbeam, surprised his hands by introducing a new scribbling engine without discussion. I went to his house with another member of the hands' delegation, Colin Hennessy, and one of the masters, David Shoveller, and the three of us spoke to him about it."

"Did you threaten him?"

"No, we merely reminded him that the best way to avoid a strike would be to stick to the agreement."

"What happened next?"

"The following day I was awakened early and taken to the home of Mr. Will Riddick, a justice. The same happened to Mr. Hennessy."

"What about Mr. Shoveller?"

"No action was taken against him. But Mr. Hennessy and I were accused of combination and sentenced to hard labor."

"Was there any relationship between Mr. Hornbeam and the justice?"

"Yes. Hornbeam was Riddick's father-in-law."

There was a murmur of shock and disapproval among the committee members.

Hume said: "So, to sum up: you told Mr. Hornbeam that he was breaking an agreement; he then had you arrested and accused you of combination; whereupon his son-in-law sentenced you to hard labor."

"Yes."

"Thank you, Mrs. Hennessy."

The committee produced a report that condemned the Combination Act without reservation.

The act was repealed a few days later.

Will Riddick died the same year, and Roger became the squire.

Sal and Colin moved to Badford and took over the village general store.

Sal never saw Joanie again, but a man with a strange accent came to Badford with a letter from her. When Joanie had served her sentence she had married a settler and they had started a sheep farm in New South Wales. It was hard work, and she thought often about her daughter, Sue, but she loved her new husband and she was not planning to return to England.

Kit, Roger, Sal, and Colin all moved into the manor house.

The first thing they did was to put Will's dogs out of the house to live in the yard next to the stables, permanently.

Then they scrubbed the hall clean, with help from Fanny.

A week later they put on ragged old clothes and painted all the paneling in the house a creamy shade of white.

Sal said: "Well, at least now the house has a new smell."

Kit said: "There's a lot more to do."

Fan said: "I can hardly wait to get on with it. But the squire and his family shouldn't be doing the work. I could manage it, with a bit of help." Platts had gone—not that he was ever much use—and Fan was the only servant.

Kit said: "We'll get you some help, eventually, but we have to live frugally for a while. Our machinery business makes money, but we have to pay off all the debts Will left." He decided not to mention Roger's debts. "I have to investigate the finances of the manor and start repaying the mortgages out of income from rents."

Kit continued to control all the money. Roger got a monthly allowance, and when it was gone he had to stop gambling until the next month. He had got used to it, and now he said he preferred it that way.

They went to the kitchen and Fanny prepared a supper of bacon and potatoes. Kit saw a rat wriggle through a crack in the skirting board and said: "We need cats to keep down the rats and mice."

"I'll get you some cats," said Fan. "There's always someone in the village trying to sell a litter of kittens for a few pennies."

When it got dark they all went to bed. Kit and Roger had bedrooms with a shared dressing room in between, but that was for show: they always slept together. Fanny had guessed their secret, but when they had more servants they would have to rumple one of the beds every morning to keep up the appearance of respectability.

Kit undressed and got into bed but sat upright, looking around by candlelight.

"Aren't you sleepy?" said Roger. "I'm exhausted after all that painting."

"I'm just remembering the time I slept here as a boy," Kit said. "I thought it must be the biggest house in the world, and the people who lived here were like gods."

"And now you're one of the gods."

Kit laughed.

Roger got into bed. "Greek gods, probably," said Roger. "And you know about the Greeks, don't you?"

"No. I never had your education, you know that. What did the Greeks do?"

Roger put his arms around Kit. "Let me show you," he said.

Acknowledgments

My historical consultants for *The Armor of Light* were Tim Clayton, Penelope Corfield, James Cowan, Emma Griffin, Roger Knight, and Margarette Lincoln.

I'm also grateful for the help of the following: David Birks and Hannah Liddy at Trowbridge Museum; Ian Birtles, Clare Brown, Anna Chrystal, Jim Heaton, Ally Tsilika, and Julie Whitehouse at Quarry Bank Mill; and Katherine Belshaw at the Science and Industry Museum, Manchester.

I made much use of *William Pitt the Younger: A Biography* by William Hague, who was so kind as to enlarge on his book in a personal interview.

The staff and volunteers of Waterloo Uncovered were always willing to look up from their trowels and answer questions.

My editors were Brian Tart at Viking and Vicki Mellor, Susan Opie, and Jeremy Trevathan at Macmillan.

Friends and family who gave helpful advice included: Lucy Blythe, Tim Blythe, Barbara Follett, Maria Gilders, Chris Manners, Alexandra Overy, Charlotte Quelch, Jann Turner, and Kim Turner.

ALSO AVAILABLE

THE KINGSBRIDGE NOVELS
(in historical order)

The Evening and the Morning
The Pillars of the Earth
World Without End
A Column of Fire
The Armor of Light

THE CENTURY TRILOGY
(in historical order)

Fall of Giants
Winter of the World
Edge of Eternity

WORLD WAR TWO THRILLERS

Eye of the Needle
The Key to Rebecca
Night over Water
Jackdaws
Hornet Flight

OTHER NOVELS

Triple
Never
The Man from St. Petersburg
Lie Down with Lions
A Dangerous Fortune
A Place Called Freedom
The Third Twin
The Hammer of Eden
Code to Zero
Whiteout

EARLY NOVELS

The Modigliani Scandal
Paper Money

NON-FICTION

On Wings of Eagles
Notre-Dame

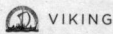

Ready to find your next great read? Let us help. Visit prh.com/nextread